Will  Irma  Taranee  Cornelia  Hay Lin

Part VII.
New Power
Volume 2

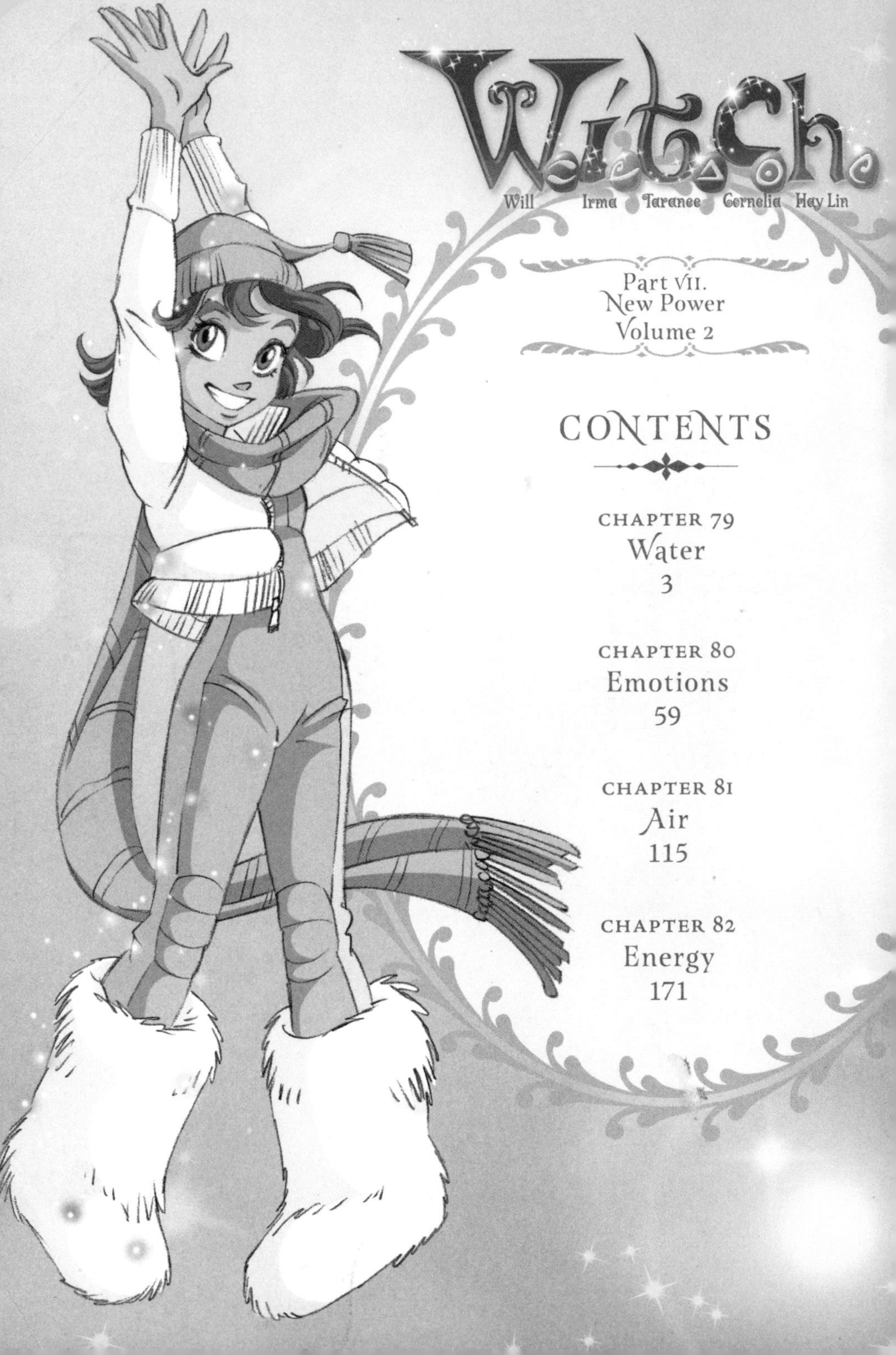

# W.i.t.c.h

Will Irma Taranee Cornelia Hay Lin

Part VII.
New Power
Volume 2

## CONTENTS

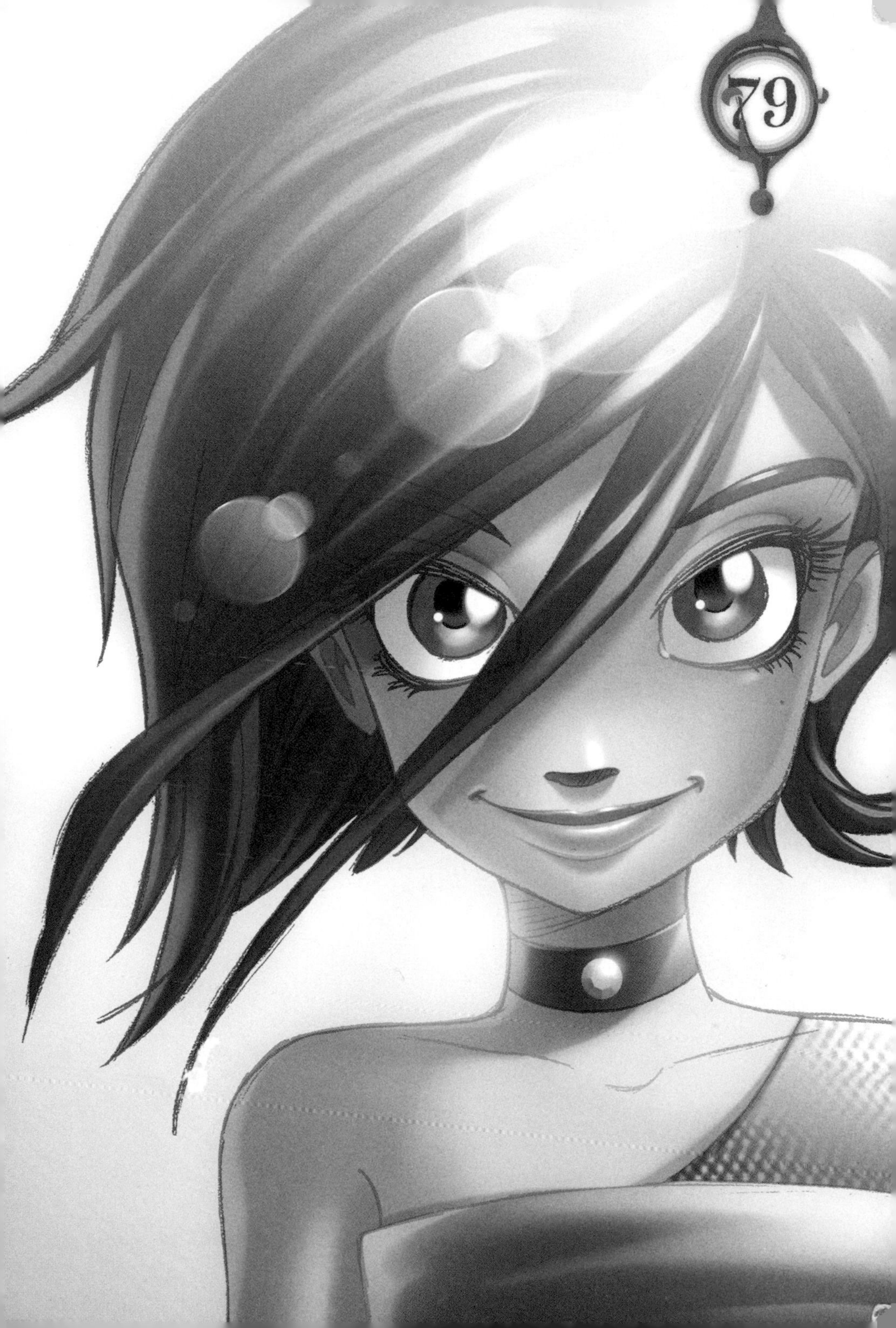
79

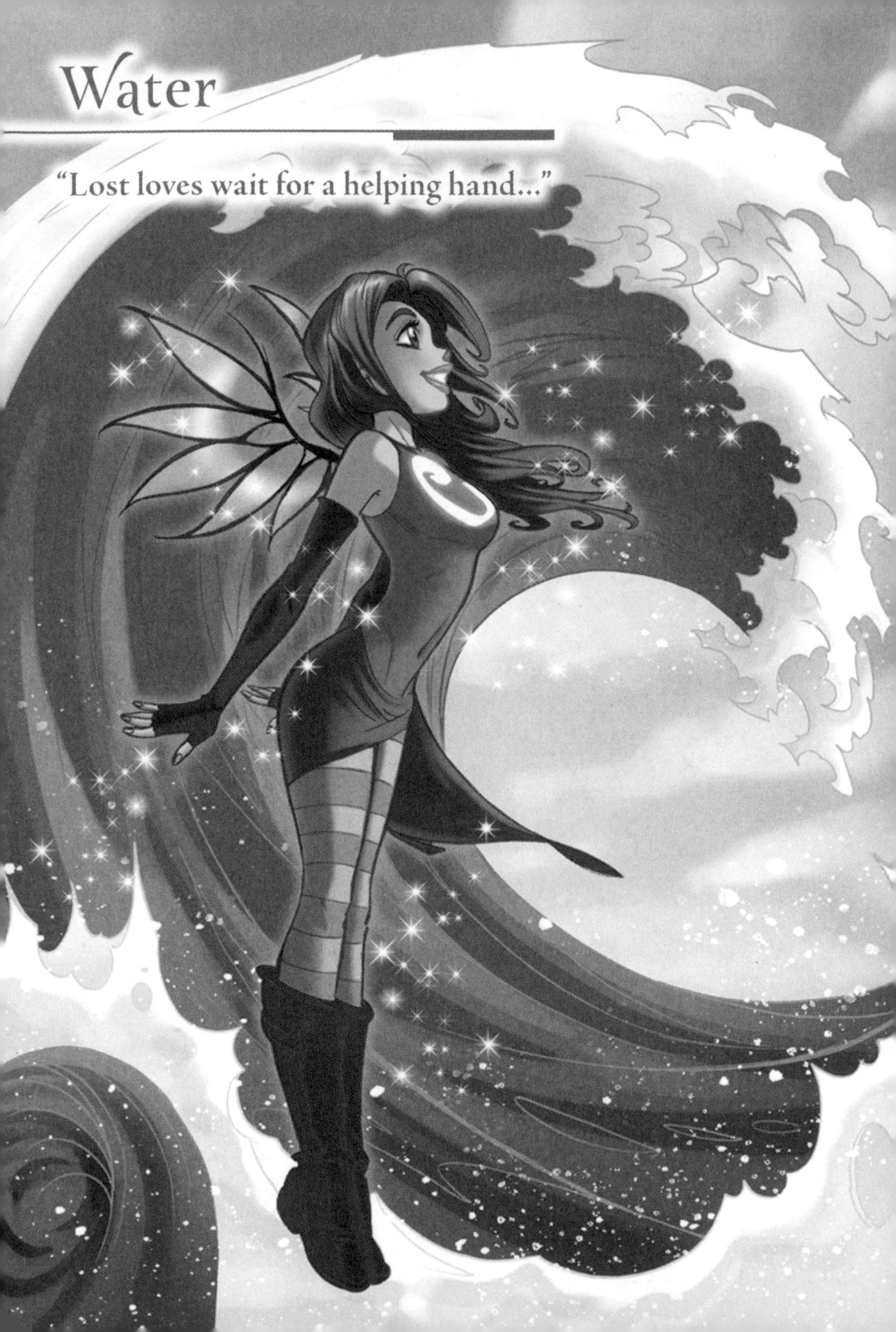
Water
"Lost loves wait for a helping hand..."

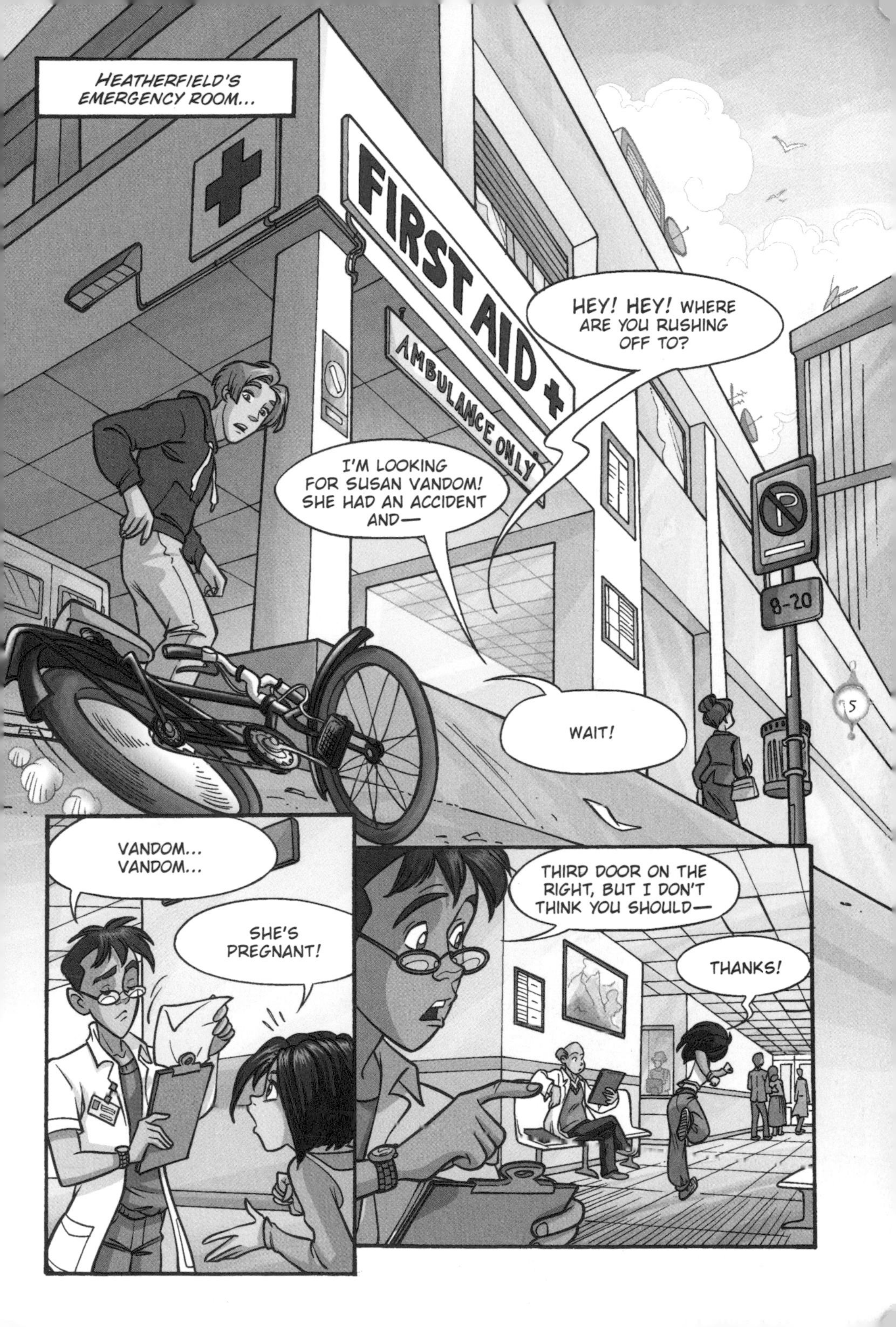
HEATHERFIELD'S EMERGENCY ROOM...
FIRST AID
AMBULANCE ONLY
HEY! HEY! WHERE ARE YOU RUSHING OFF TO?
I'M LOOKING FOR SUSAN VANDOM! SHE HAD AN ACCIDENT AND—
8-20
WAIT!
VANDOM... VANDOM...
SHE'S PREGNANT!
THIRD DOOR ON THE RIGHT, BUT I DON'T THINK YOU SHOULD—
THANKS!

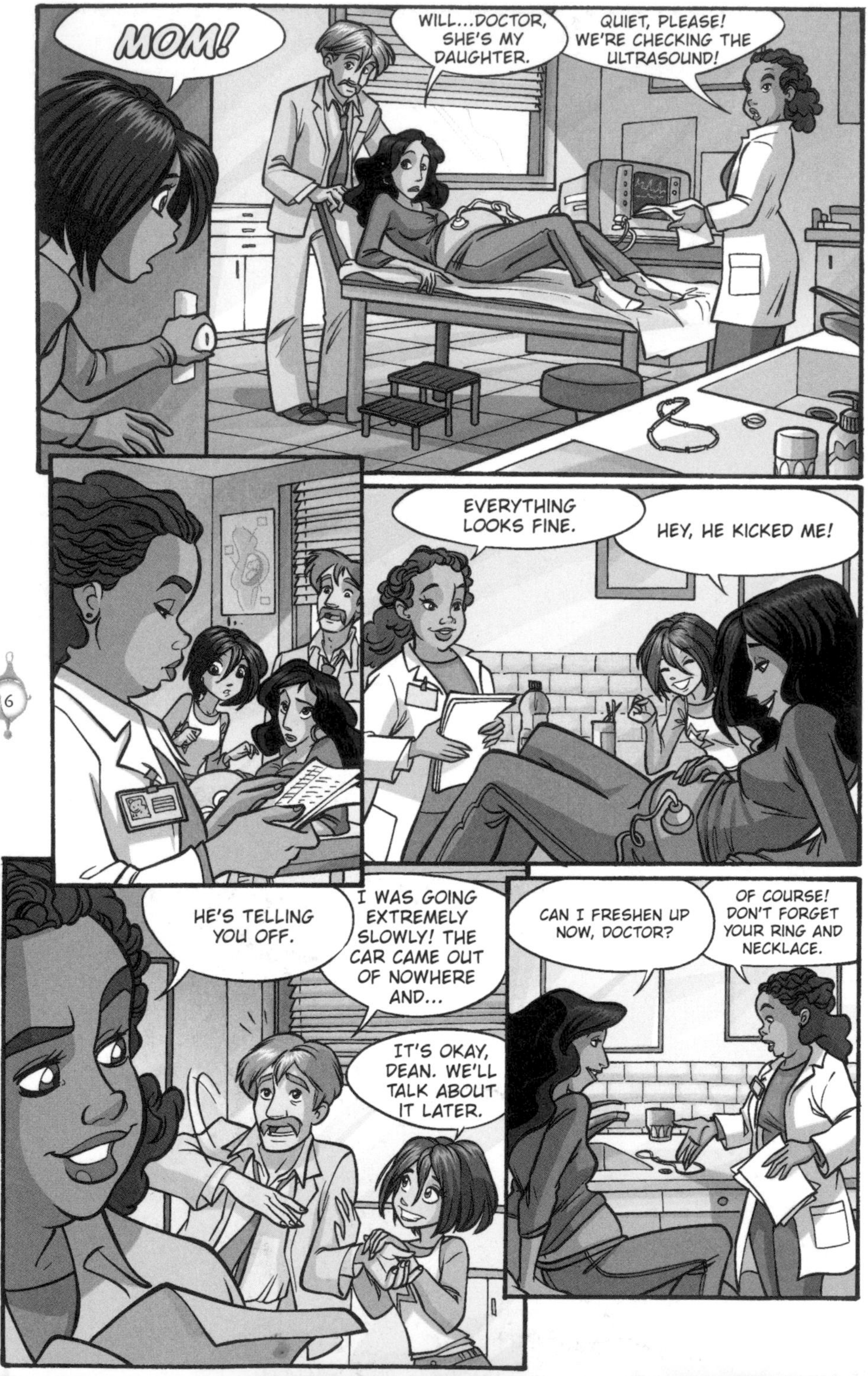

MOM!
WILL...DOCTOR, SHE'S MY DAUGHTER.
QUIET, PLEASE! WE'RE CHECKING THE ULTRASOUND!
EVERYTHING LOOKS FINE.
HEY, HE KICKED ME!
HE'S TELLING YOU OFF.
I WAS GOING EXTREMELY SLOWLY! THE CAR CAME OUT OF NOWHERE AND...
IT'S OKAY, DEAN. WE'LL TALK ABOUT IT LATER.
CAN I FRESHEN UP NOW, DOCTOR?
OF COURSE! DON'T FORGET YOUR RING AND NECKLACE.

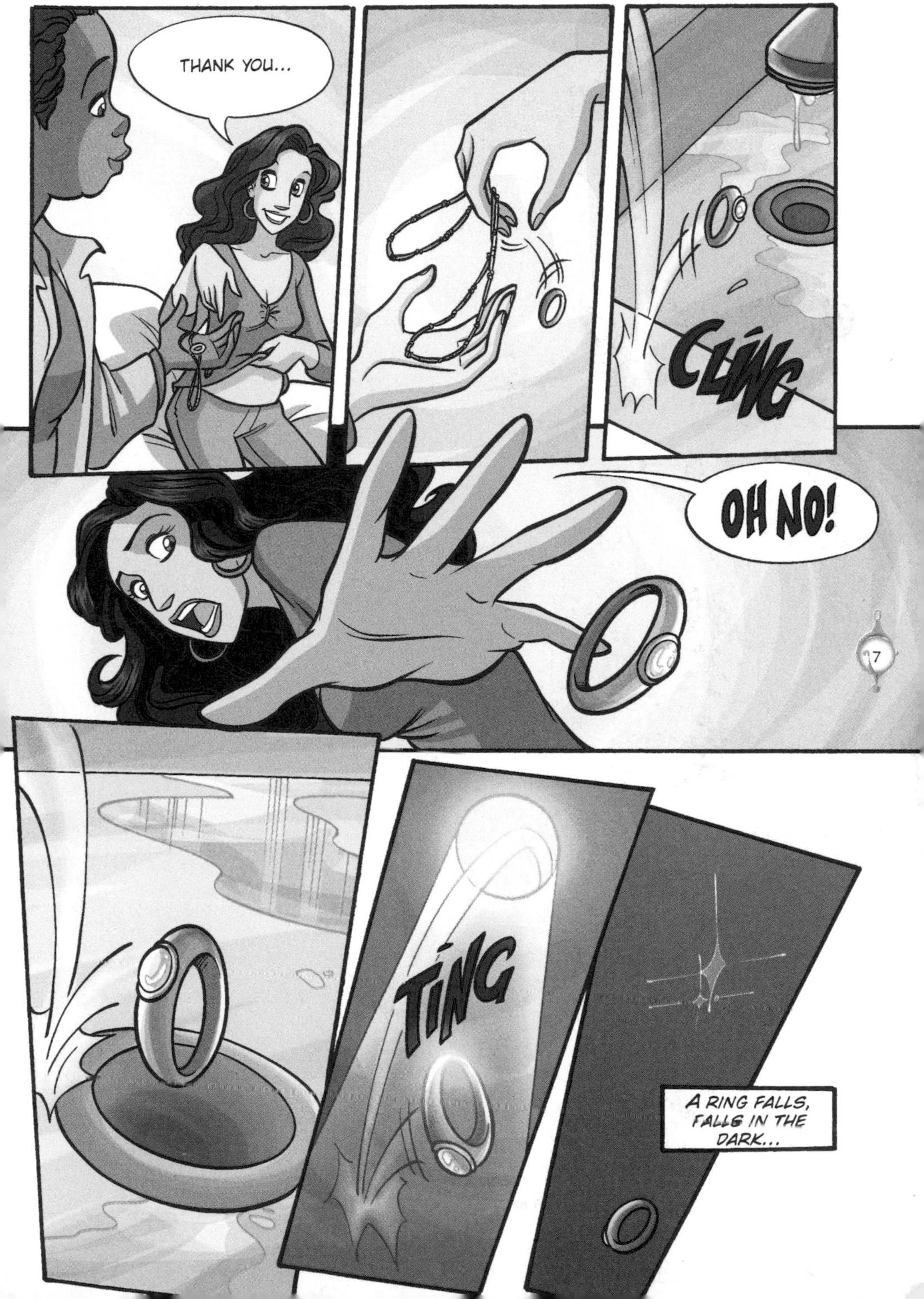
THANK YOU...
CLING
OH NO!
TING
A RING FALLS, FALLS IN THE DARK...

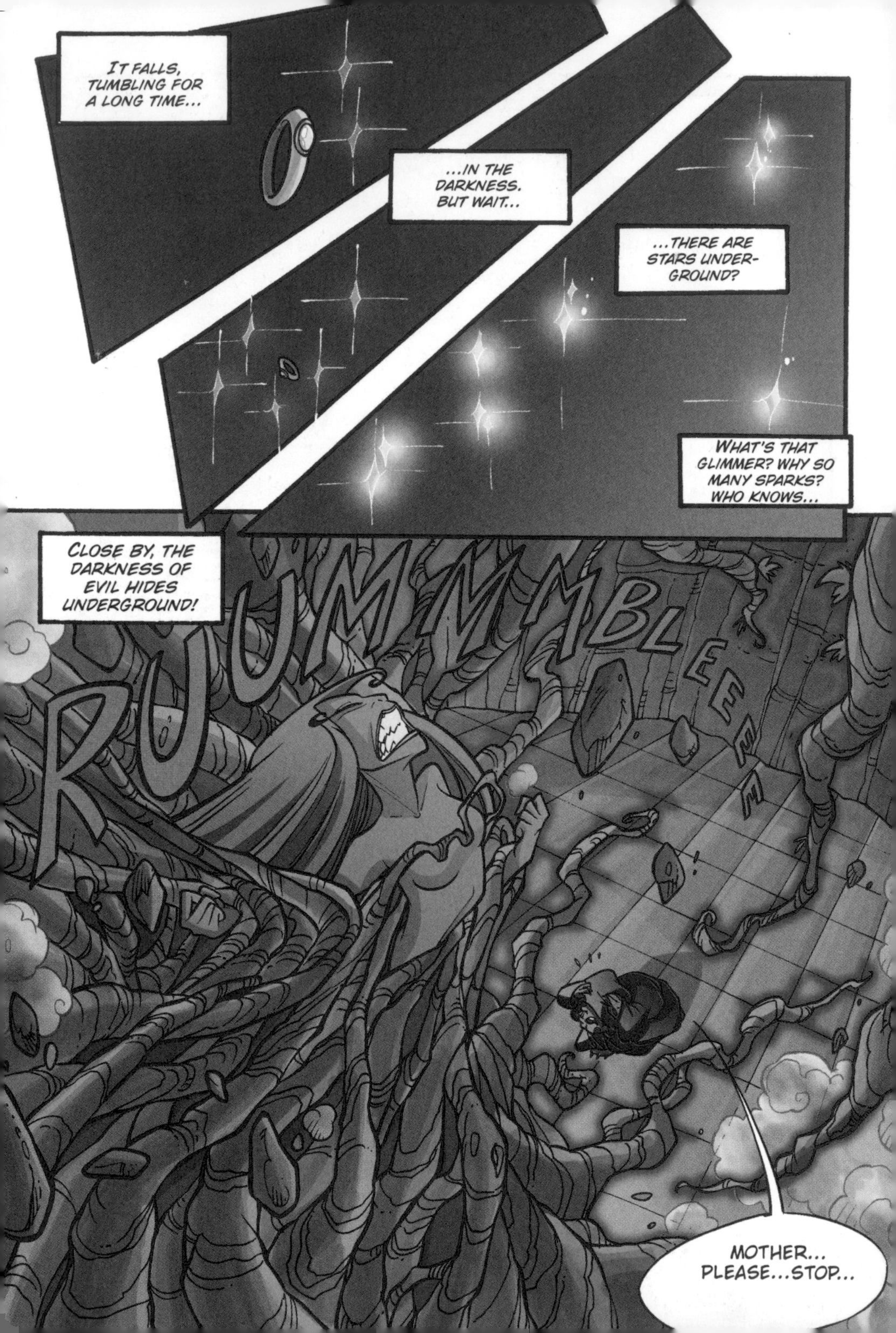
IT FALLS, TUMBLING FOR A LONG TIME...
...IN THE DARKNESS. BUT WAIT...
...THERE ARE STARS UNDER-GROUND?
WHAT'S THAT GLIMMER? WHY SO MANY SPARKS? WHO KNOWS...
CLOSE BY, THE DARKNESS OF EVIL HIDES UNDERGROUND!
RUUMMMBLEEEE
MOTHER... PLEASE...STOP...

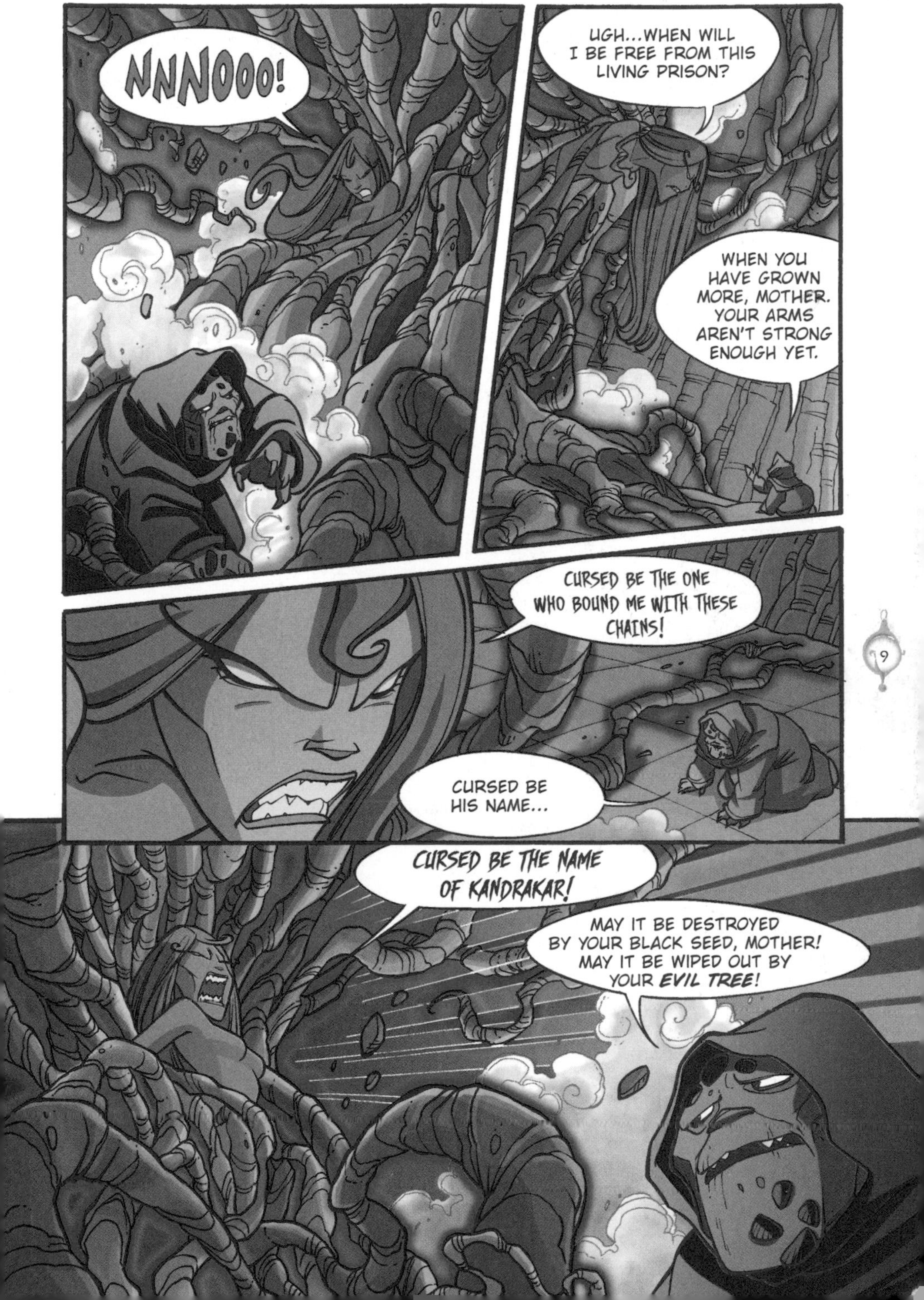
NNNOOO!
UGH...WHEN WILL I BE FREE FROM THIS LIVING PRISON?
WHEN YOU HAVE GROWN MORE, MOTHER. YOUR ARMS AREN'T STRONG ENOUGH YET.
CURSED BE THE ONE WHO BOUND ME WITH THESE CHAINS!
CURSED BE HIS NAME...
CURSED BE THE NAME OF KANDRAKAR!
MAY IT BE DESTROYED BY YOUR BLACK SEED, MOTHER! MAY IT BE WIPED OUT BY YOUR *EVIL TREE*!

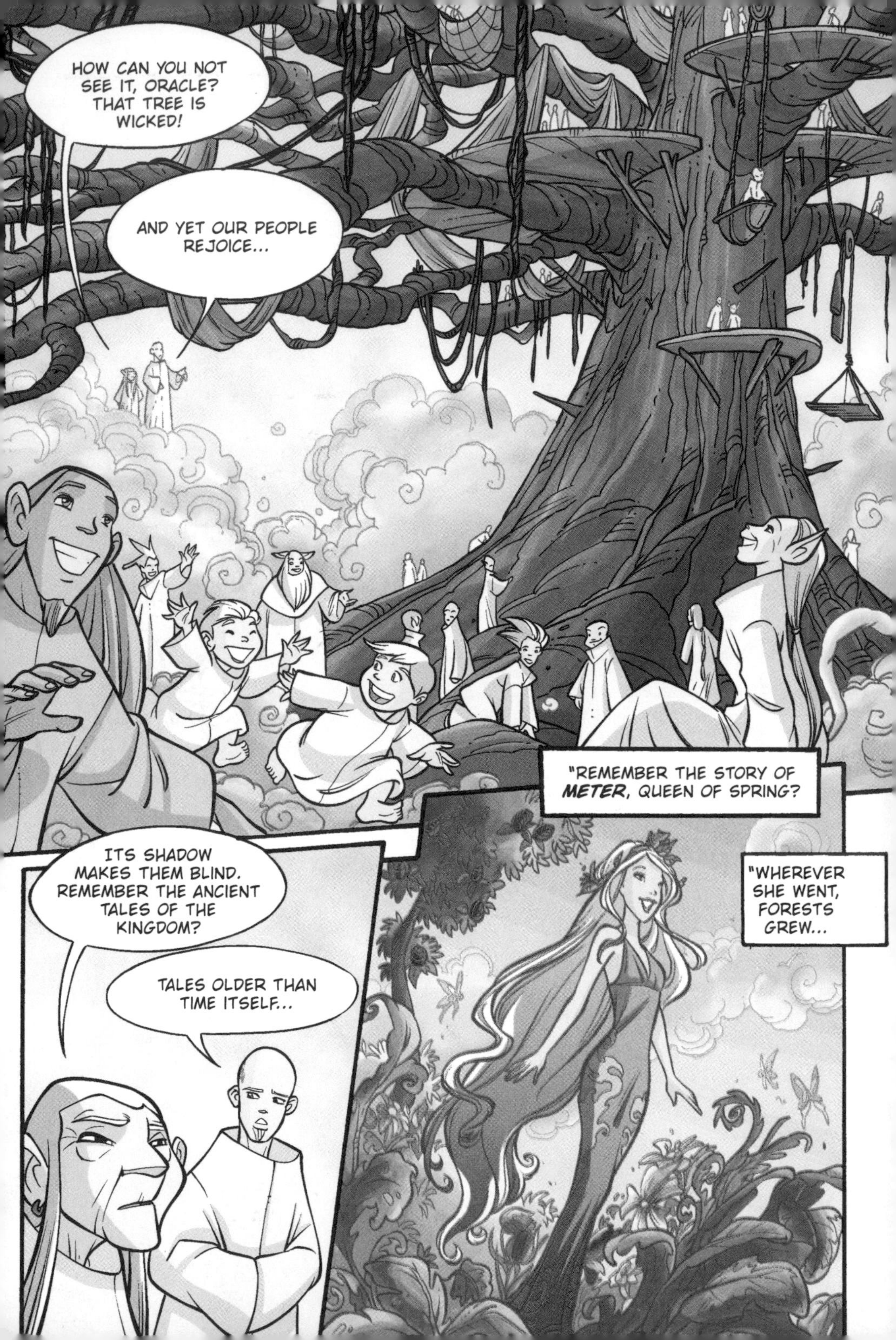
HOW CAN YOU NOT SEE IT, ORACLE? THAT TREE IS WICKED!
AND YET OUR PEOPLE REJOICE...
"REMEMBER THE STORY OF **METER**, QUEEN OF SPRING?
ITS SHADOW MAKES THEM BLIND. REMEMBER THE ANCIENT TALES OF THE KINGDOM?
TALES OLDER THAN TIME ITSELF...
"WHEREVER SHE WENT, FORESTS GREW...

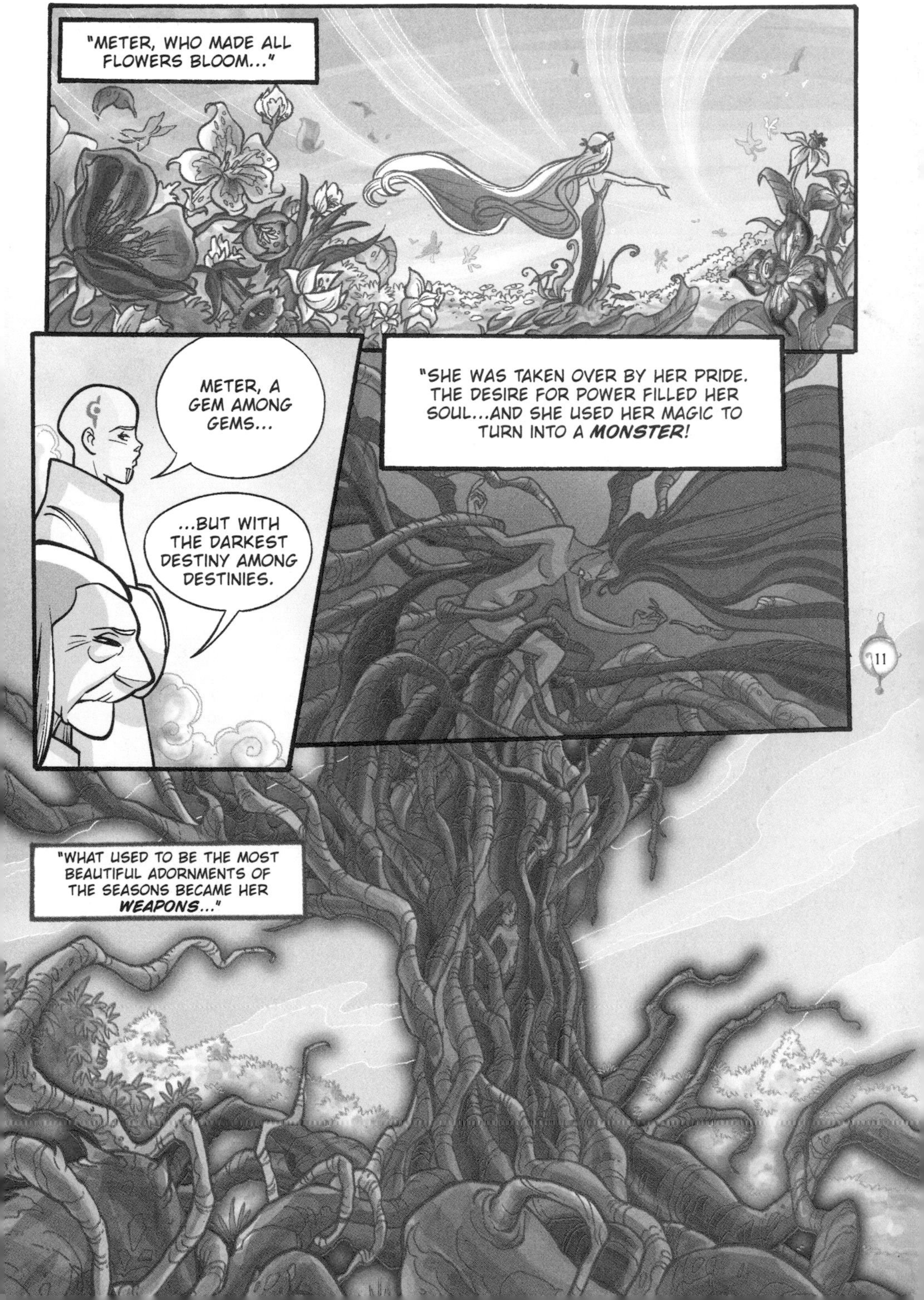
"METER, WHO MADE ALL FLOWERS BLOOM..."
METER, A GEM AMONG GEMS...
...BUT WITH THE DARKEST DESTINY AMONG DESTINIES.
"SHE WAS TAKEN OVER BY HER PRIDE. THE DESIRE FOR POWER FILLED HER SOUL...AND SHE USED HER MAGIC TO TURN INTO A ***MONSTER!***
"WHAT USED TO BE THE MOST BEAUTIFUL ADORNMENTS OF THE SEASONS BECAME HER ***WEAPONS...***"

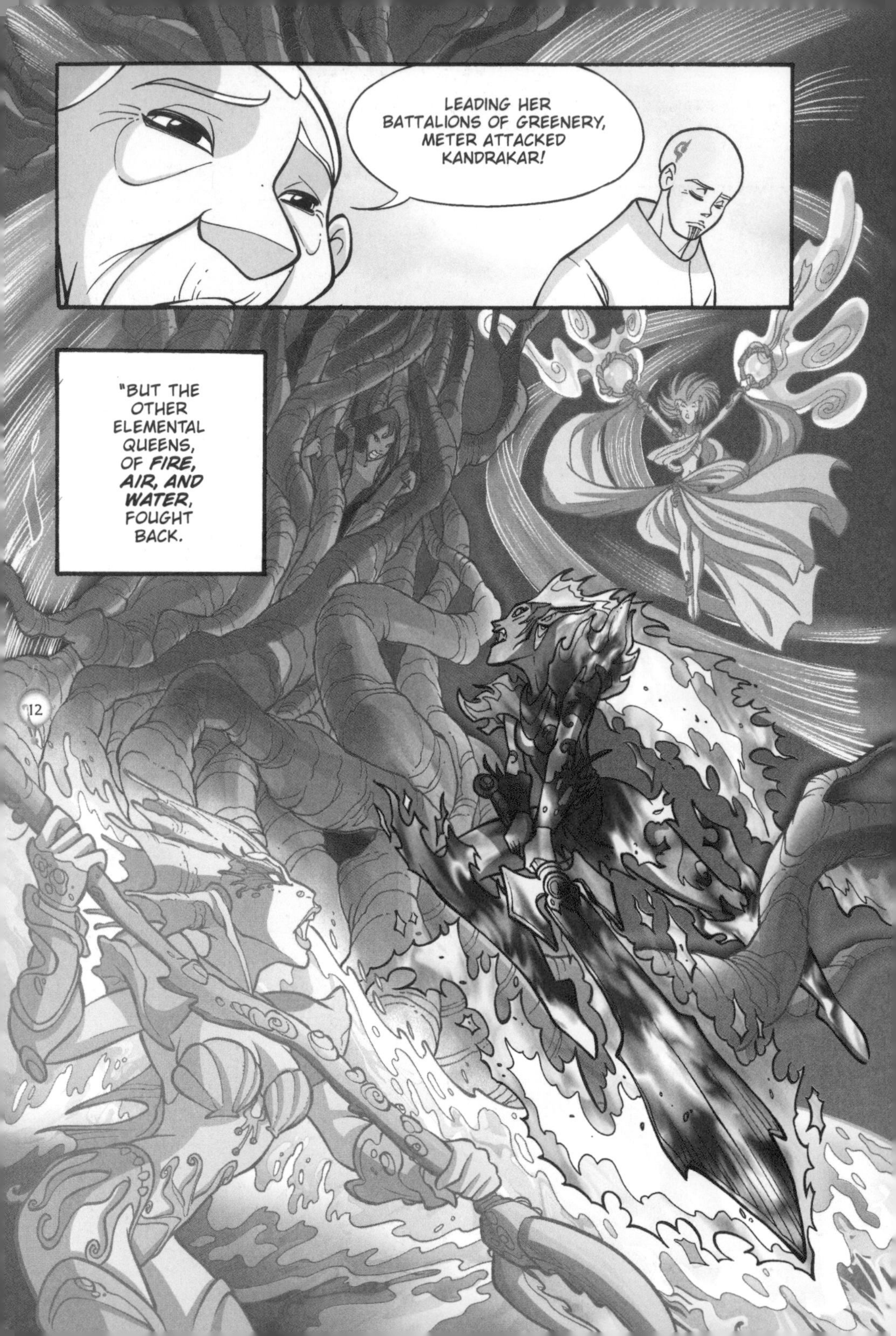

LEADING HER BATTALIONS OF GREENERY, METER ATTACKED KANDRAKAR!
"BUT THE OTHER ELEMENTAL QUEENS, OF ***FIRE, AIR, AND WATER***, FOUGHT BACK.

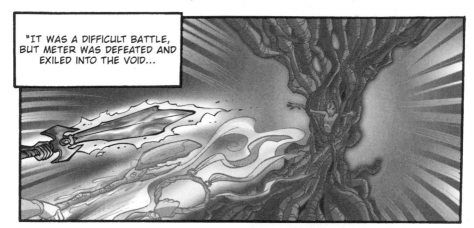

"IT WAS A DIFFICULT BATTLE, BUT METER WAS DEFEATED AND EXILED INTO THE VOID..."

"...BANISHED FOREVER FROM ALL THE WORLDS!"

BUT WHAT IF SHE FOUND A PLACE TO SINK HER ROOTS INTO AGAIN?

THAT STORY IS JUST A LEGEND...

WHAT IF THAT TREE HAS GROWN FROM ONE OF METER'S BLACK SEEDS?

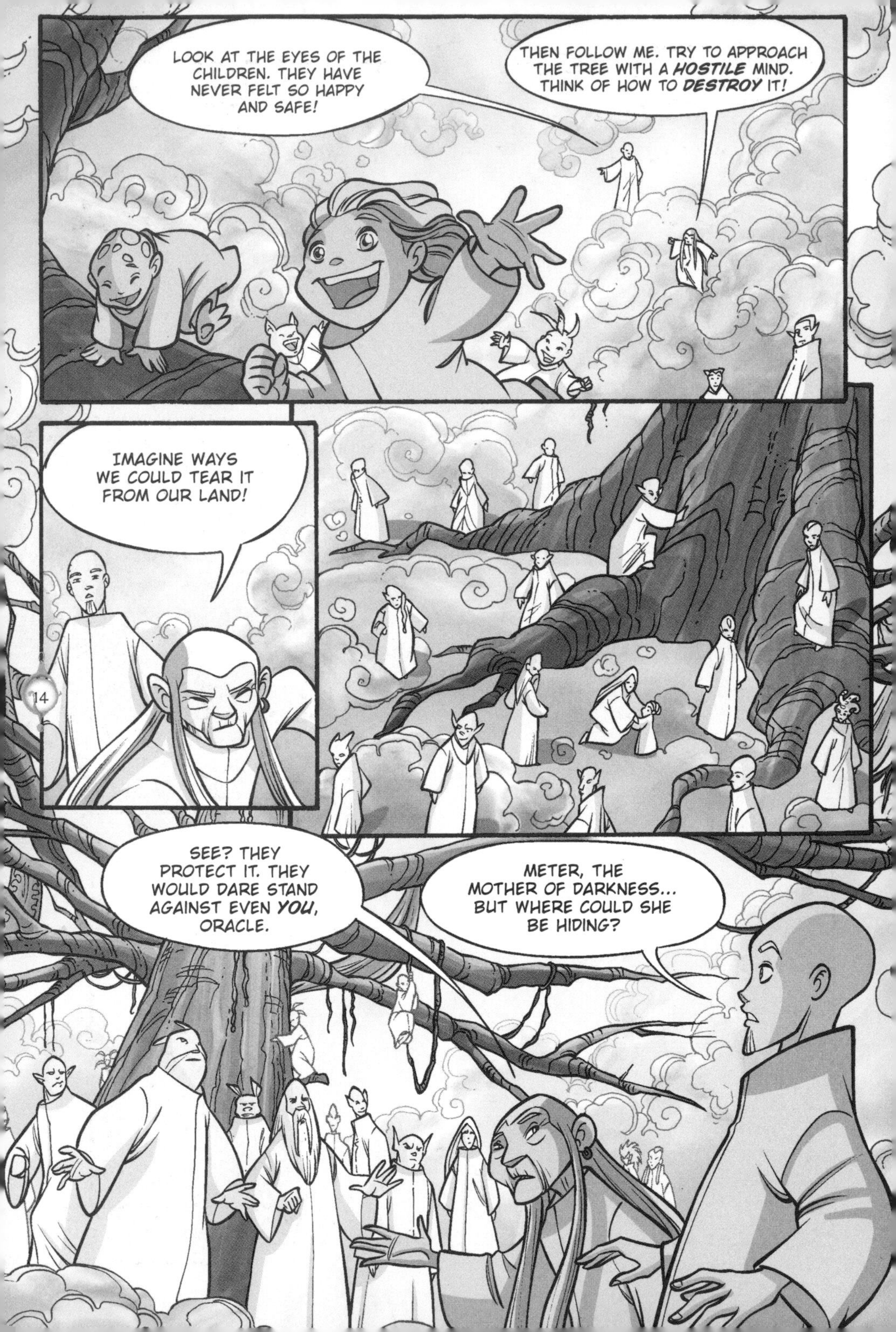
LOOK AT THE EYES OF THE CHILDREN. THEY HAVE NEVER FELT SO HAPPY AND SAFE!
THEN FOLLOW ME. TRY TO APPROACH THE TREE WITH A HOSTILE MIND. THINK OF HOW TO DESTROY IT!
IMAGINE WAYS WE COULD TEAR IT FROM OUR LAND!
SEE? THEY PROTECT IT. THEY WOULD DARE STAND AGAINST EVEN YOU, ORACLE.
METER, THE MOTHER OF DARKNESS... BUT WHERE COULD SHE BE HIDING?

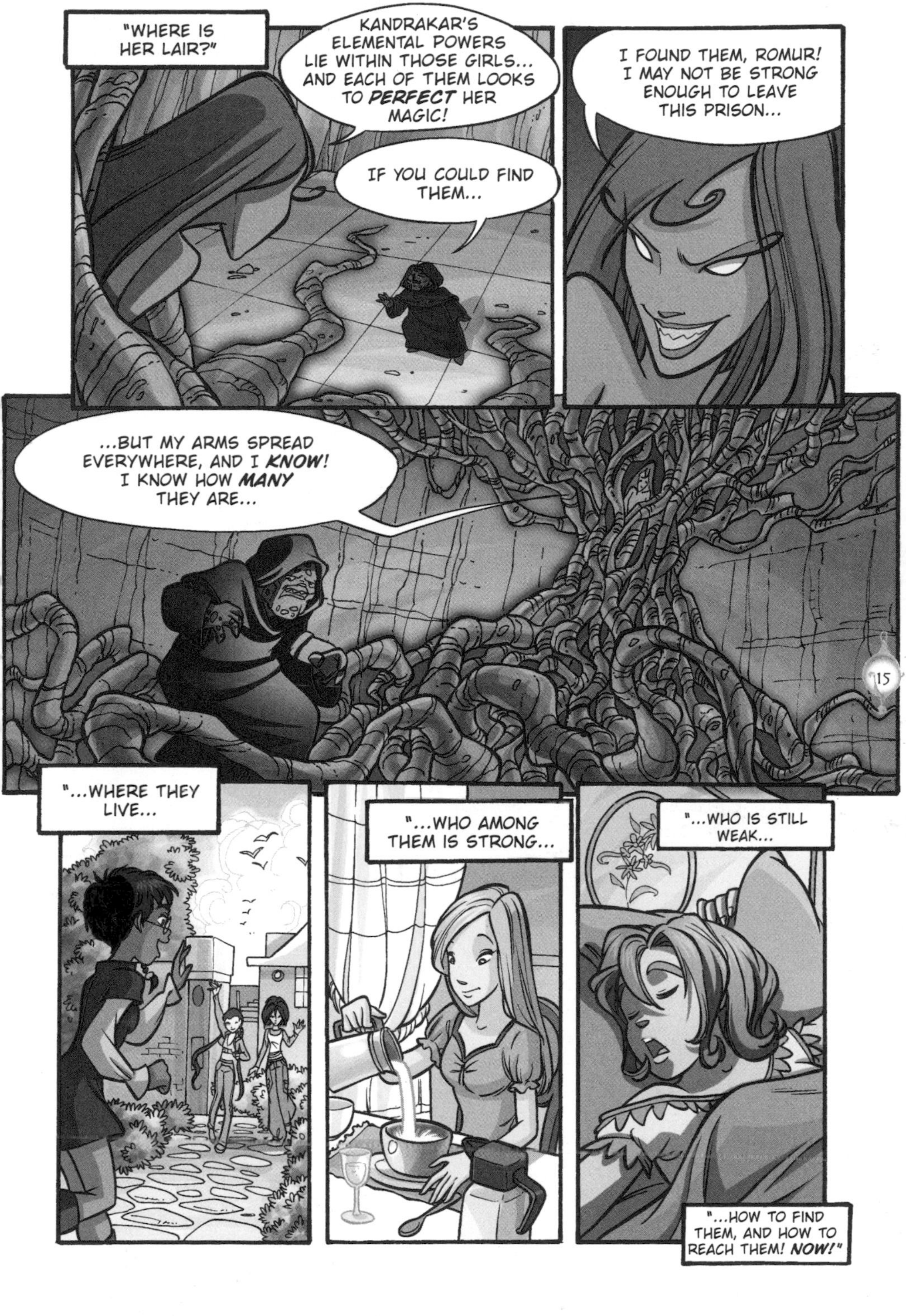
"WHERE IS HER LAIR?"
KANDRAKAR'S ELEMENTAL POWERS LIE WITHIN THOSE GIRLS... AND EACH OF THEM LOOKS TO PERFECT HER MAGIC!
IF YOU COULD FIND THEM...
I FOUND THEM, ROMUR! I MAY NOT BE STRONG ENOUGH TO LEAVE THIS PRISON...
...BUT MY ARMS SPREAD EVERYWHERE, AND I KNOW! I KNOW HOW MANY THEY ARE...
"...WHERE THEY LIVE...
"...WHO AMONG THEM IS STRONG...
"...WHO IS STILL WEAK...
"...HOW TO FIND THEM, AND HOW TO REACH THEM! NOW!"

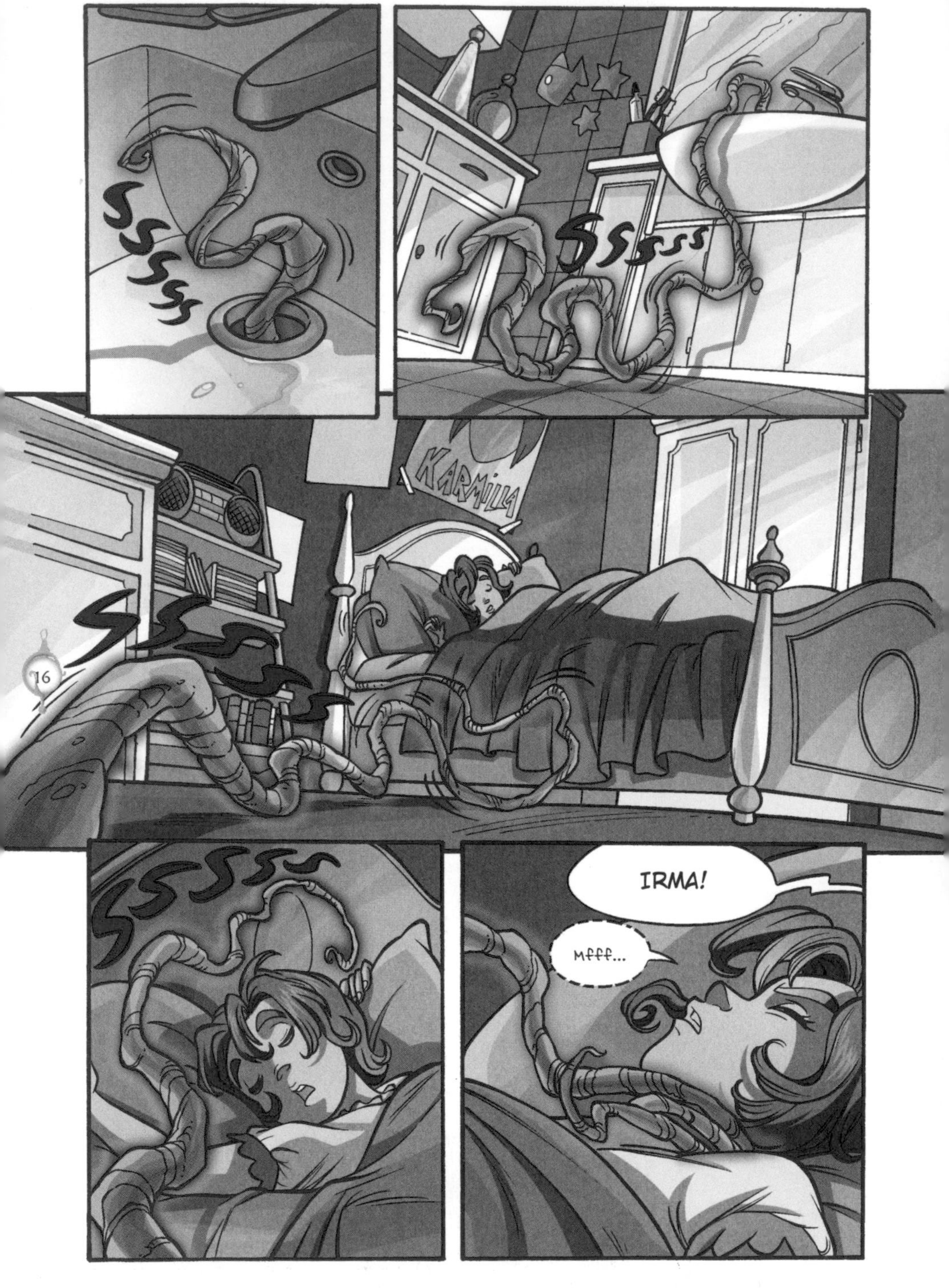
SSSSSS
SSSSSS
SSSSS
SSSSSS
IRMA!
Mfff...

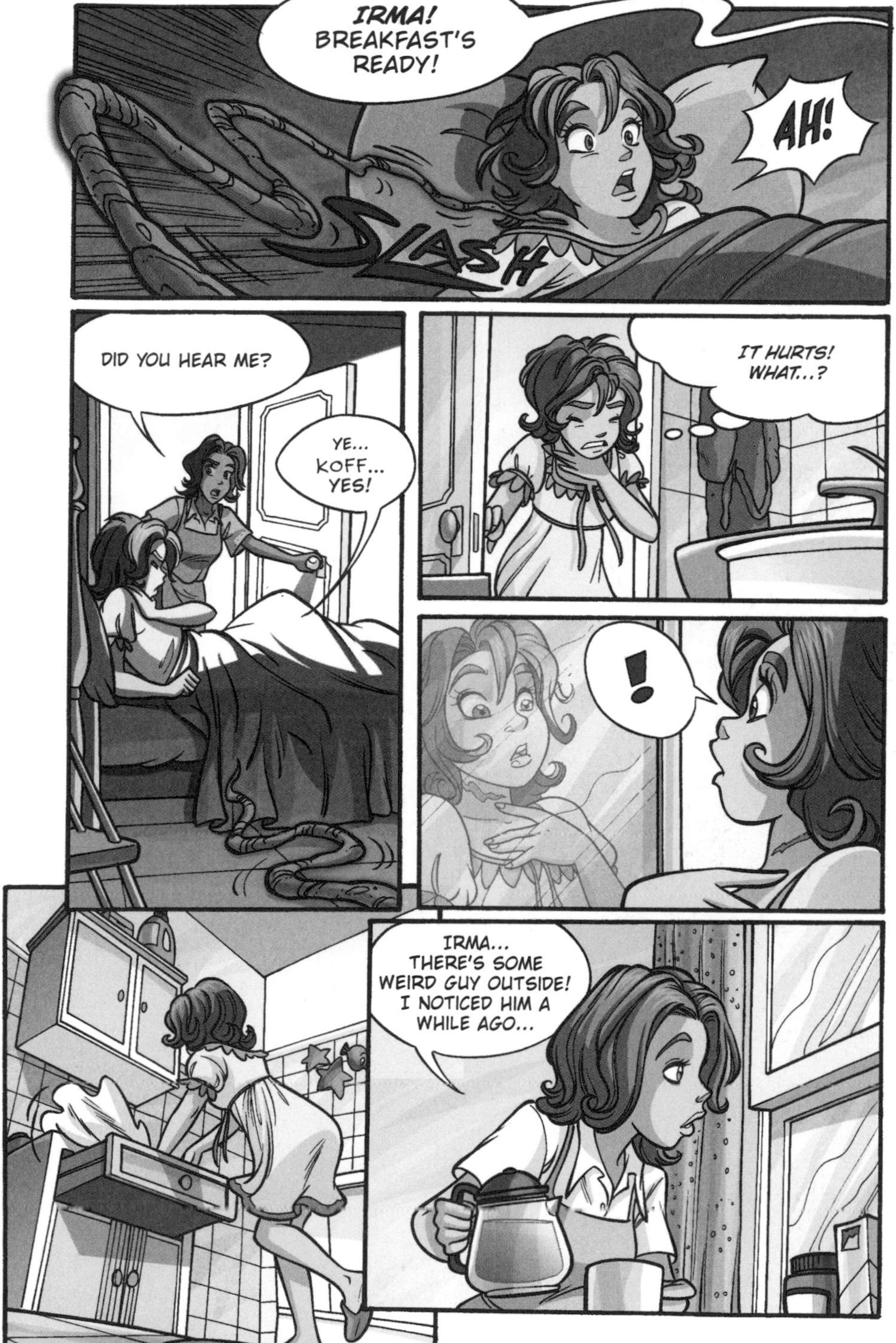
IRMA! BREAKFAST'S READY!
AH!
SLASH
DID YOU HEAR ME?
YE... KOFF... YES!
IT HURTS! WHAT...?
!
IRMA... THERE'S SOME WEIRD GUY OUTSIDE! I NOTICED HIM A WHILE AGO...

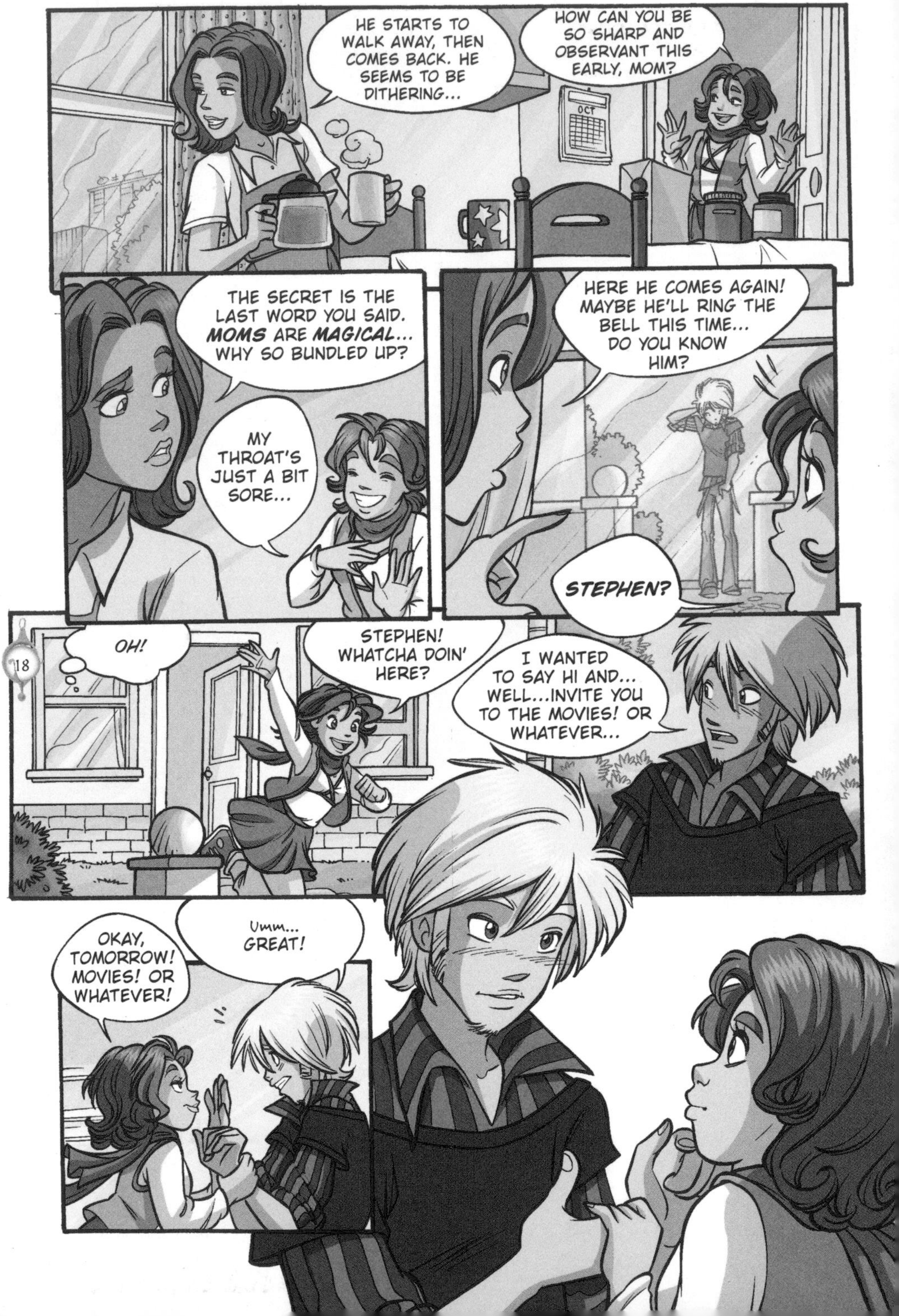
HE STARTS TO WALK AWAY, THEN COMES BACK. HE SEEMS TO BE DITHERING...
HOW CAN YOU BE SO SHARP AND OBSERVANT THIS EARLY, MOM?
OCT
THE SECRET IS THE LAST WORD YOU SAID. MOMS ARE MAGICAL... WHY SO BUNDLED UP?
MY THROAT'S JUST A BIT SORE...
HERE HE COMES AGAIN! MAYBE HE'LL RING THE BELL THIS TIME... DO YOU KNOW HIM?
STEPHEN?
OH!
STEPHEN! WHATCHA DOIN' HERE?
I WANTED TO SAY HI AND... WELL...INVITE YOU TO THE MOVIES! OR WHATEVER...
OKAY, TOMORROW! MOVIES! OR WHATEVER!
Umm... GREAT!

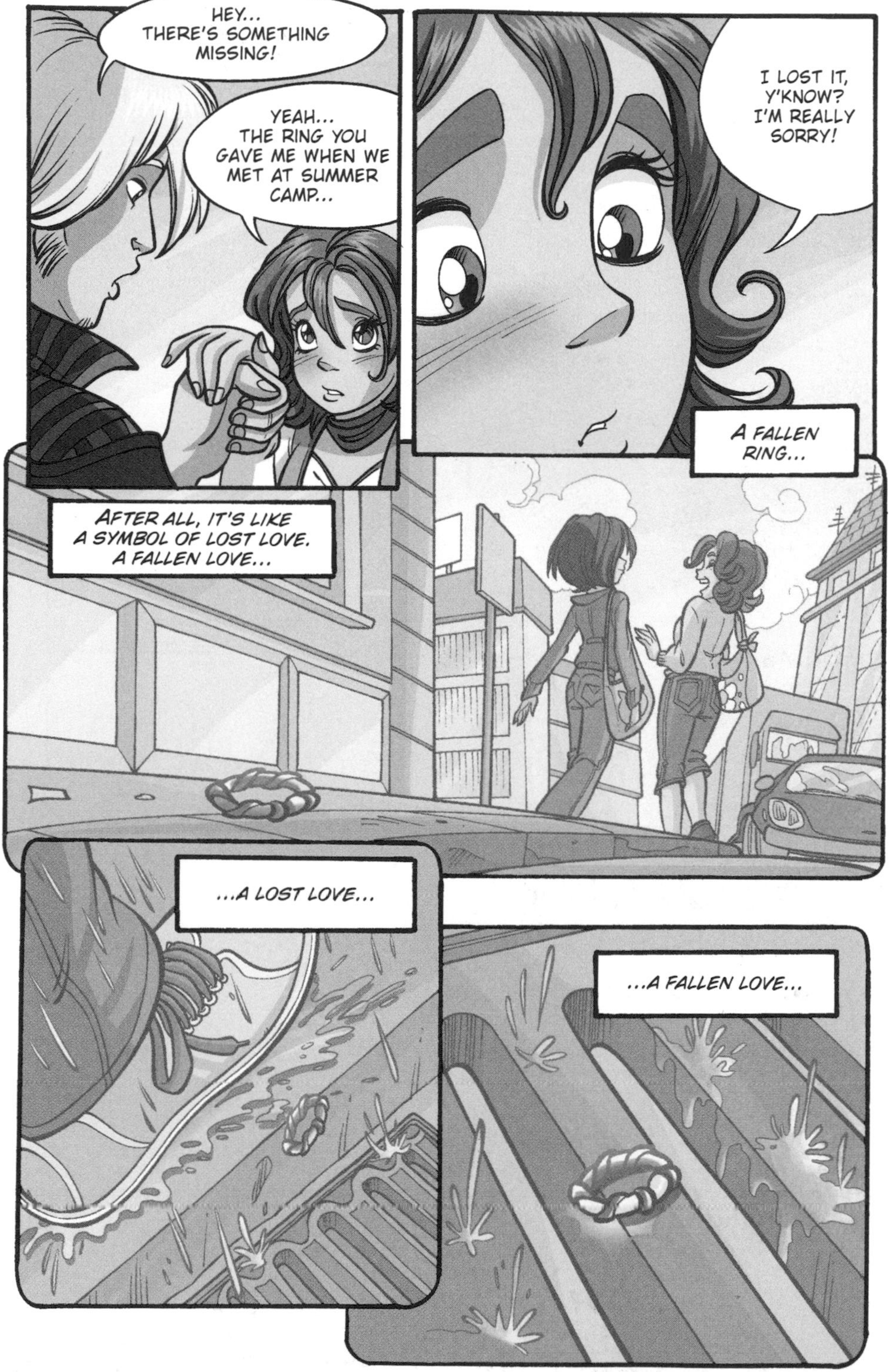
HEY... THERE'S SOMETHING MISSING!
YEAH... THE RING YOU GAVE ME WHEN WE MET AT SUMMER CAMP...
I LOST IT, Y'KNOW? I'M REALLY SORRY!
A FALLEN RING...
AFTER ALL, IT'S LIKE A SYMBOL OF LOST LOVE. A FALLEN LOVE...
...A LOST LOVE...
...A FALLEN LOVE...

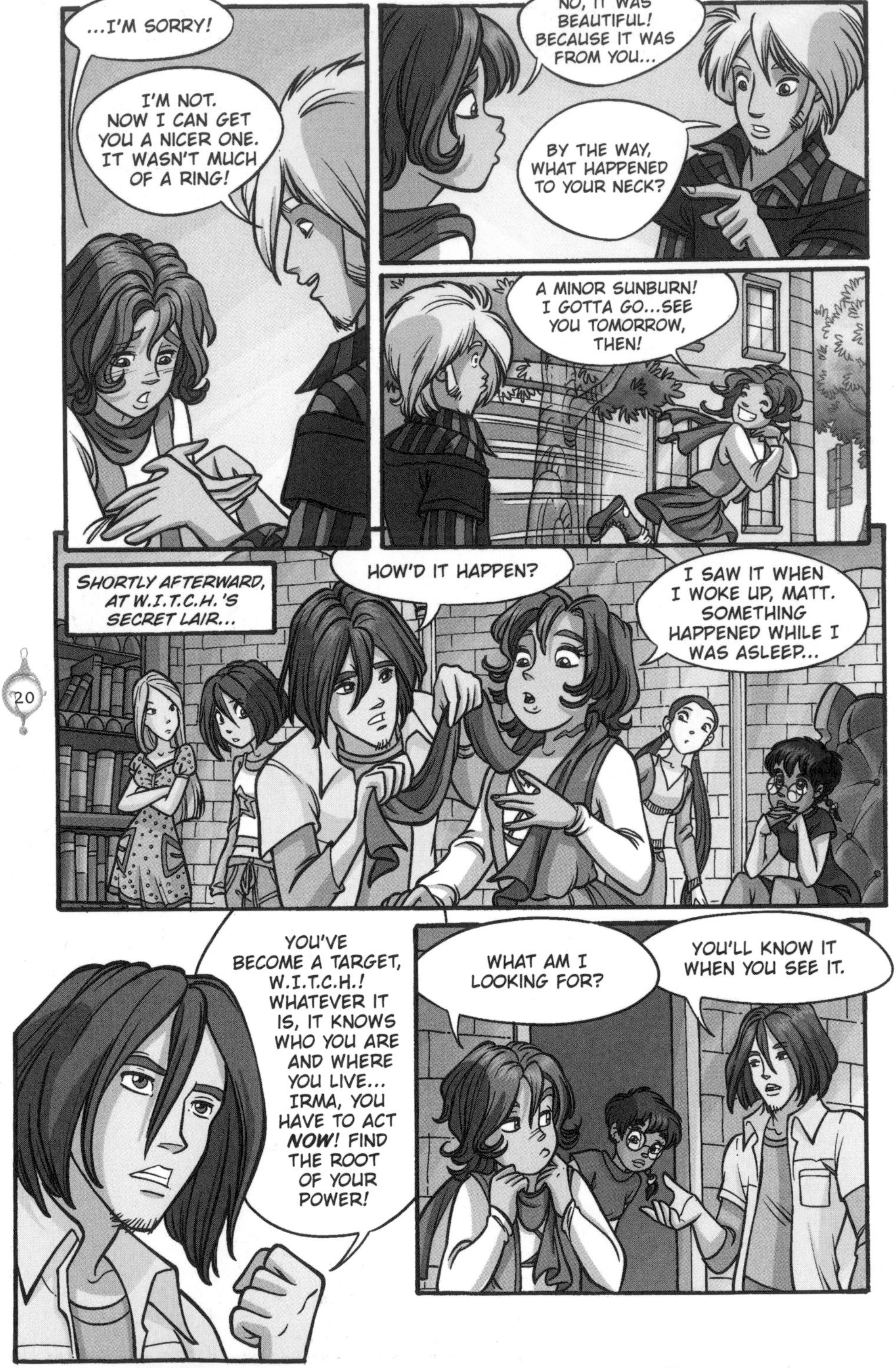
...I'M SORRY!
I'M NOT. NOW I CAN GET YOU A NICER ONE. IT WASN'T MUCH OF A RING!
NO, IT WAS BEAUTIFUL! BECAUSE IT WAS FROM YOU...
BY THE WAY, WHAT HAPPENED TO YOUR NECK?
A MINOR SUNBURN! I GOTTA GO...SEE YOU TOMORROW, THEN!
SHORTLY AFTERWARD, AT W.I.T.C.H.'S SECRET LAIR...
HOW'D IT HAPPEN?
I SAW IT WHEN I WOKE UP, MATT. SOMETHING HAPPENED WHILE I WAS ASLEEP...
YOU'VE BECOME A TARGET, W.I.T.C.H.! WHATEVER IT IS, IT KNOWS WHO YOU ARE AND WHERE YOU LIVE... IRMA, YOU HAVE TO ACT NOW! FIND THE ROOT OF YOUR POWER!
WHAT AM I LOOKING FOR?
YOU'LL KNOW IT WHEN YOU SEE IT.

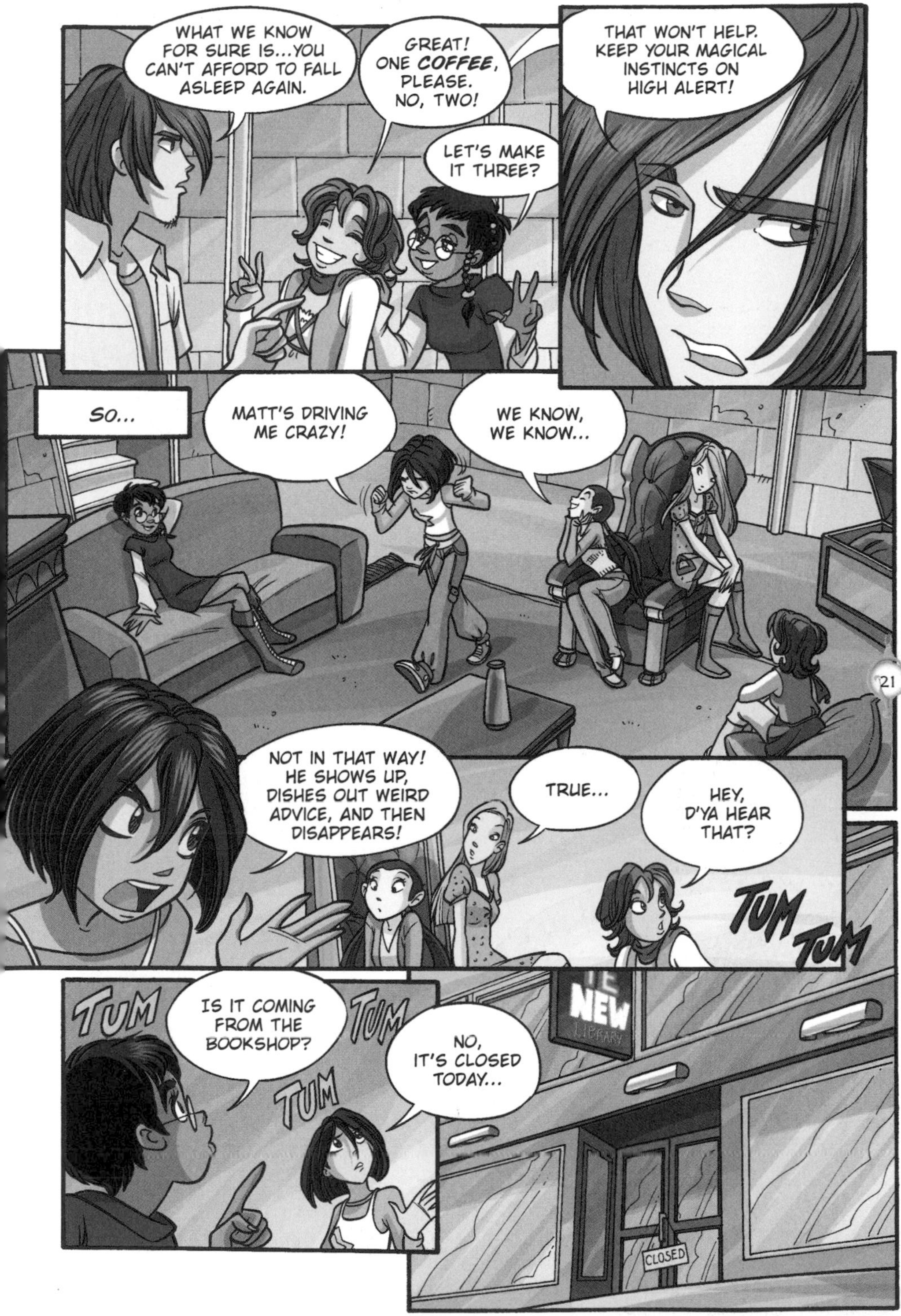
WHAT WE KNOW FOR SURE IS...YOU CAN'T AFFORD TO FALL ASLEEP AGAIN.
GREAT! ONE COFFEE, PLEASE. NO, TWO!
LET'S MAKE IT THREE?
THAT WON'T HELP. KEEP YOUR MAGICAL INSTINCTS ON HIGH ALERT!
SO...
MATT'S DRIVING ME CRAZY!
WE KNOW, WE KNOW...
NOT IN THAT WAY! HE SHOWS UP, DISHES OUT WEIRD ADVICE, AND THEN DISAPPEARS!
TRUE...
HEY, D'YA HEAR THAT?
TUM TUM
TUM
IS IT COMING FROM THE BOOKSHOP?
TUM
TUM
NO, IT'S CLOSED TODAY...
NEW
CLOSED

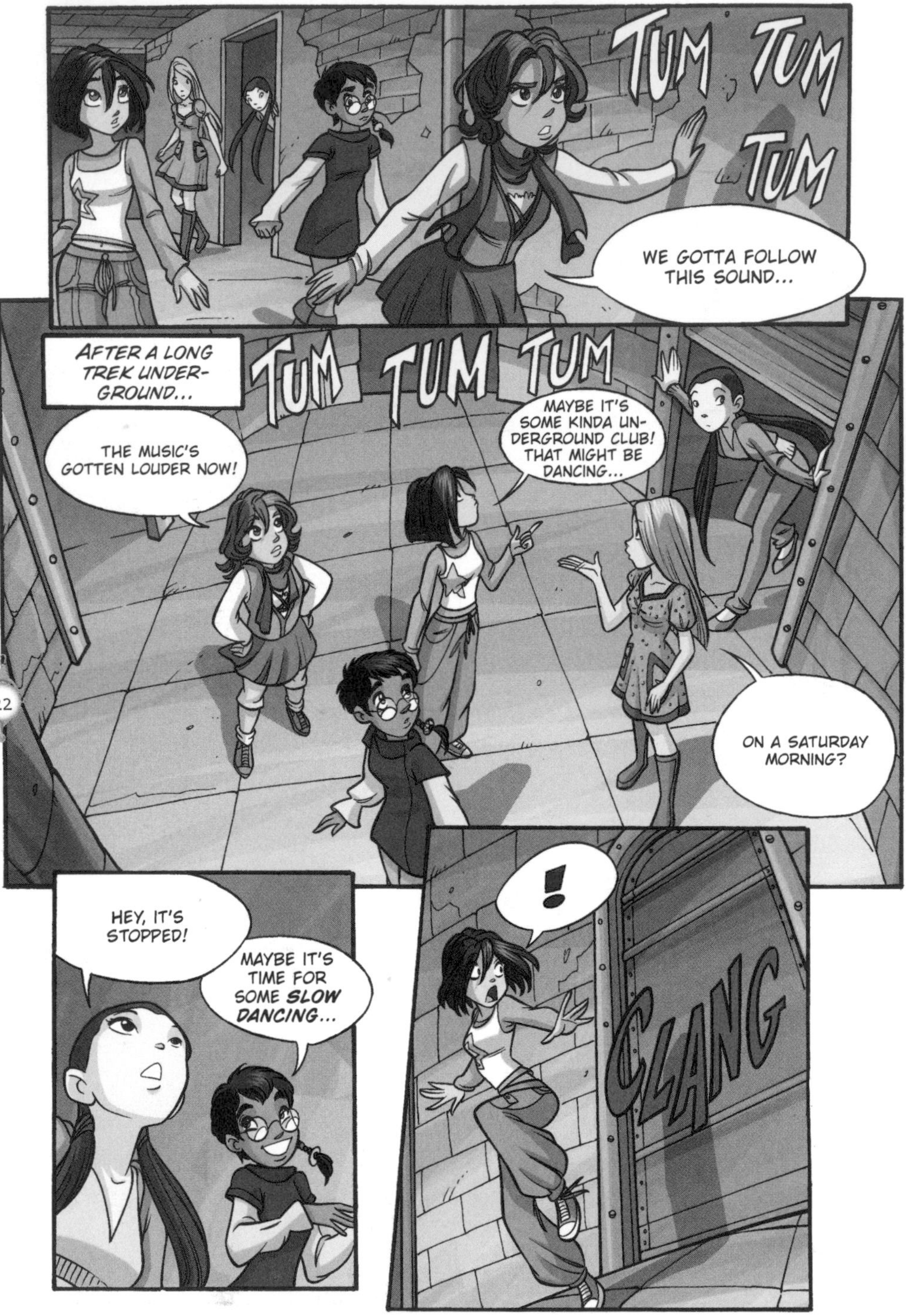
TUM TUM TUM
WE GOTTA FOLLOW THIS SOUND...
AFTER A LONG TREK UNDERGROUND...
TUM TUM TUM
THE MUSIC'S GOTTEN LOUDER NOW!
MAYBE IT'S SOME KINDA UNDERGROUND CLUB! THAT MIGHT BE DANCING...
ON A SATURDAY MORNING?
HEY, IT'S STOPPED!
MAYBE IT'S TIME FOR SOME **SLOW DANCING**...
!
CLANG

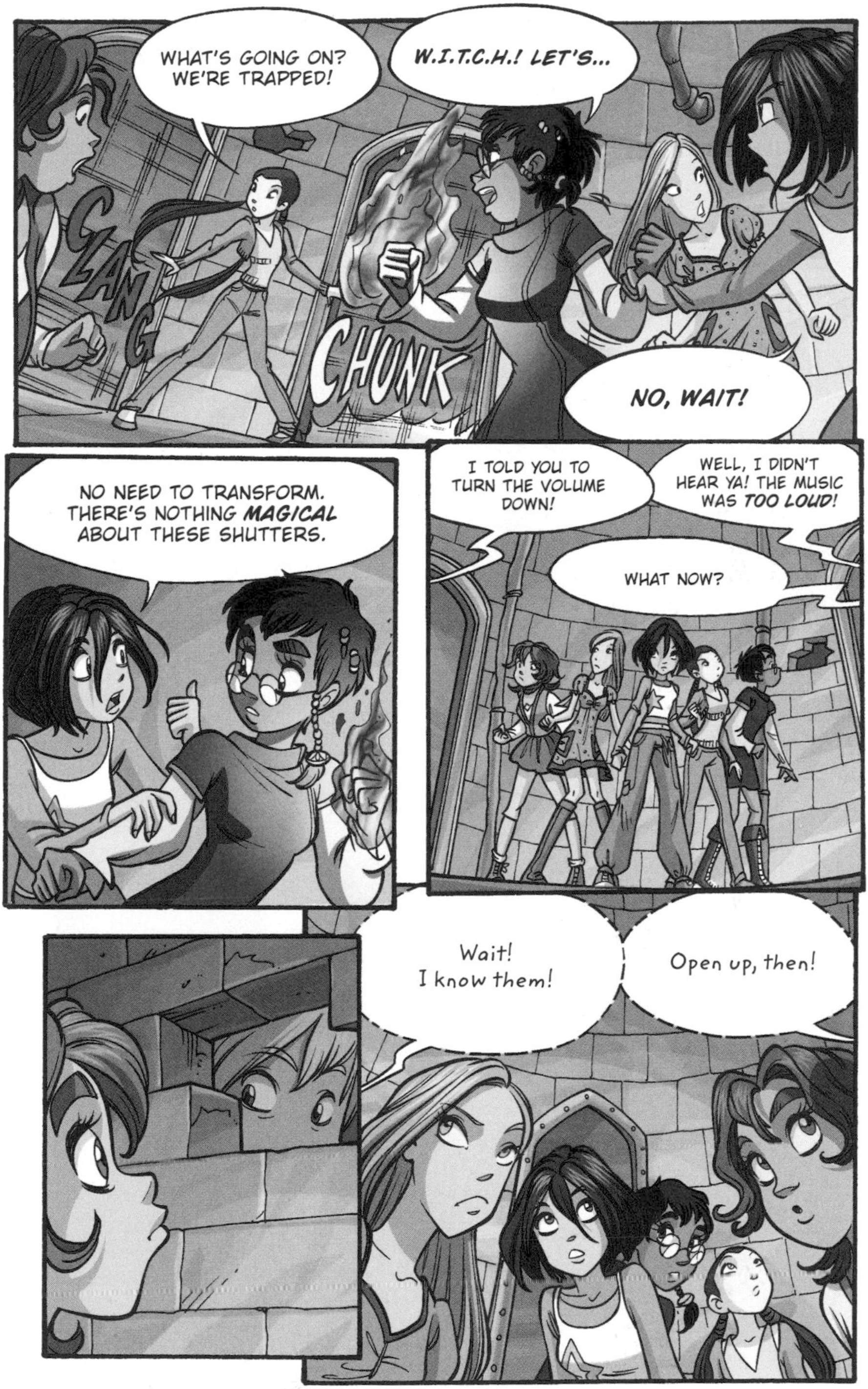
WHAT'S GOING ON? WE'RE TRAPPED!
W.I.T.C.H.! LET'S...
CLANG
CHUNK
NO, WAIT!
NO NEED TO TRANSFORM. THERE'S NOTHING MAGICAL ABOUT THESE SHUTTERS.
I TOLD YOU TO TURN THE VOLUME DOWN!
WELL, I DIDN'T HEAR YA! THE MUSIC WAS TOO LOUD!
WHAT NOW?
Wait! I know them!
Open up, then!

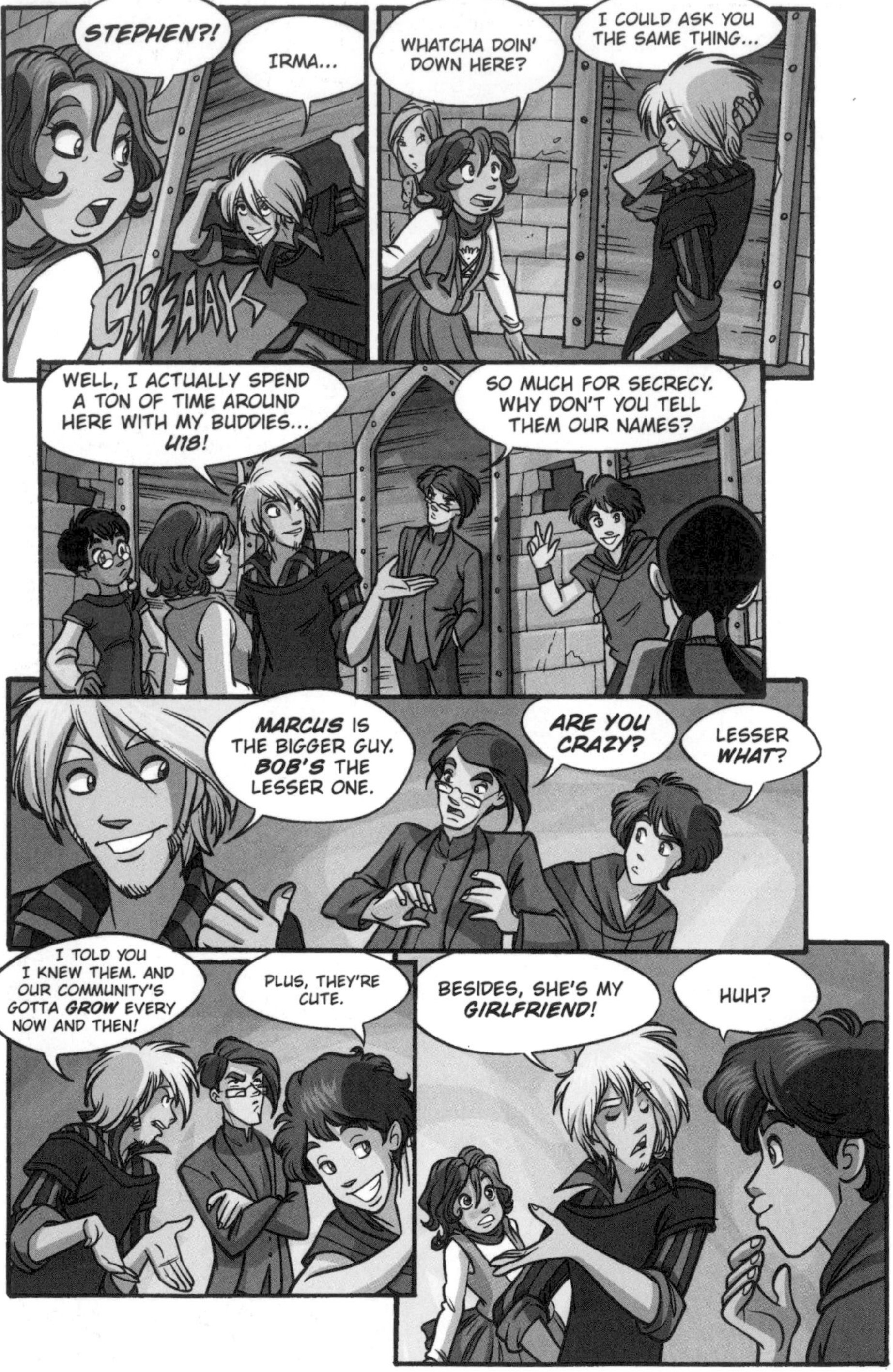
STEPHEN?!
IRMA...
CREAAK
WHATCHA DOIN' DOWN HERE?
I COULD ASK YOU THE SAME THING...
WELL, I ACTUALLY SPEND A TON OF TIME AROUND HERE WITH MY BUDDIES... U18!
SO MUCH FOR SECRECY. WHY DON'T YOU TELL THEM OUR NAMES?
MARCUS IS THE BIGGER GUY. BOB'S THE LESSER ONE.
ARE YOU CRAZY?
LESSER WHAT?
I TOLD YOU I KNEW THEM. AND OUR COMMUNITY'S GOTTA GROW EVERY NOW AND THEN!
PLUS, THEY'RE CUTE.
BESIDES, SHE'S MY GIRLFRIEND!
HUH?

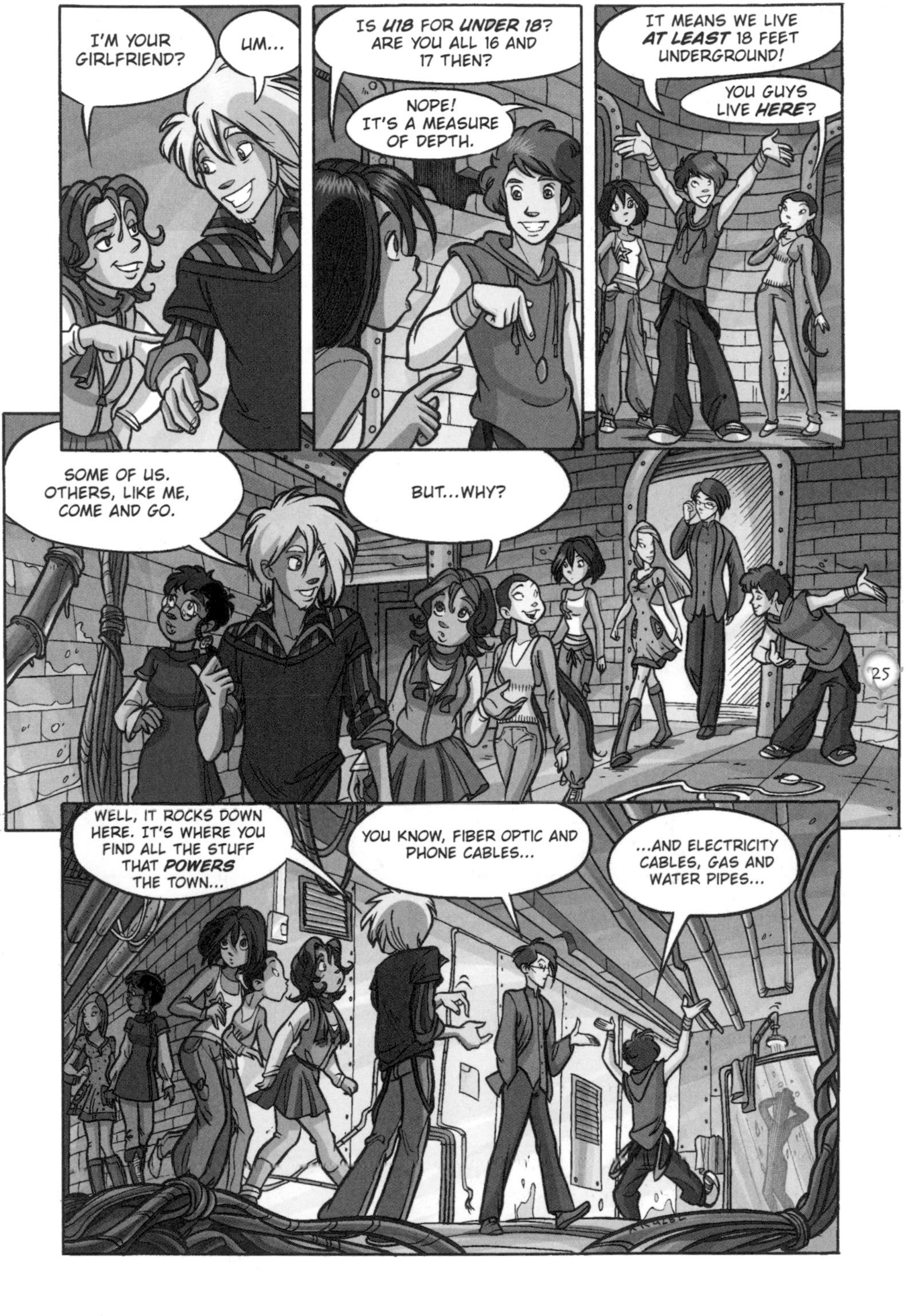
I'M YOUR GIRLFRIEND?
UM...
IS U18 FOR UNDER 18? ARE YOU ALL 16 AND 17 THEN?
NOPE! IT'S A MEASURE OF DEPTH.
IT MEANS WE LIVE AT LEAST 18 FEET UNDERGROUND!
YOU GUYS LIVE HERE?
SOME OF US. OTHERS, LIKE ME, COME AND GO.
BUT...WHY?
WELL, IT ROCKS DOWN HERE. IT'S WHERE YOU FIND ALL THE STUFF THAT POWERS THE TOWN...
YOU KNOW, FIBER OPTIC AND PHONE CABLES...
...AND ELECTRICITY CABLES, GAS AND WATER PIPES...

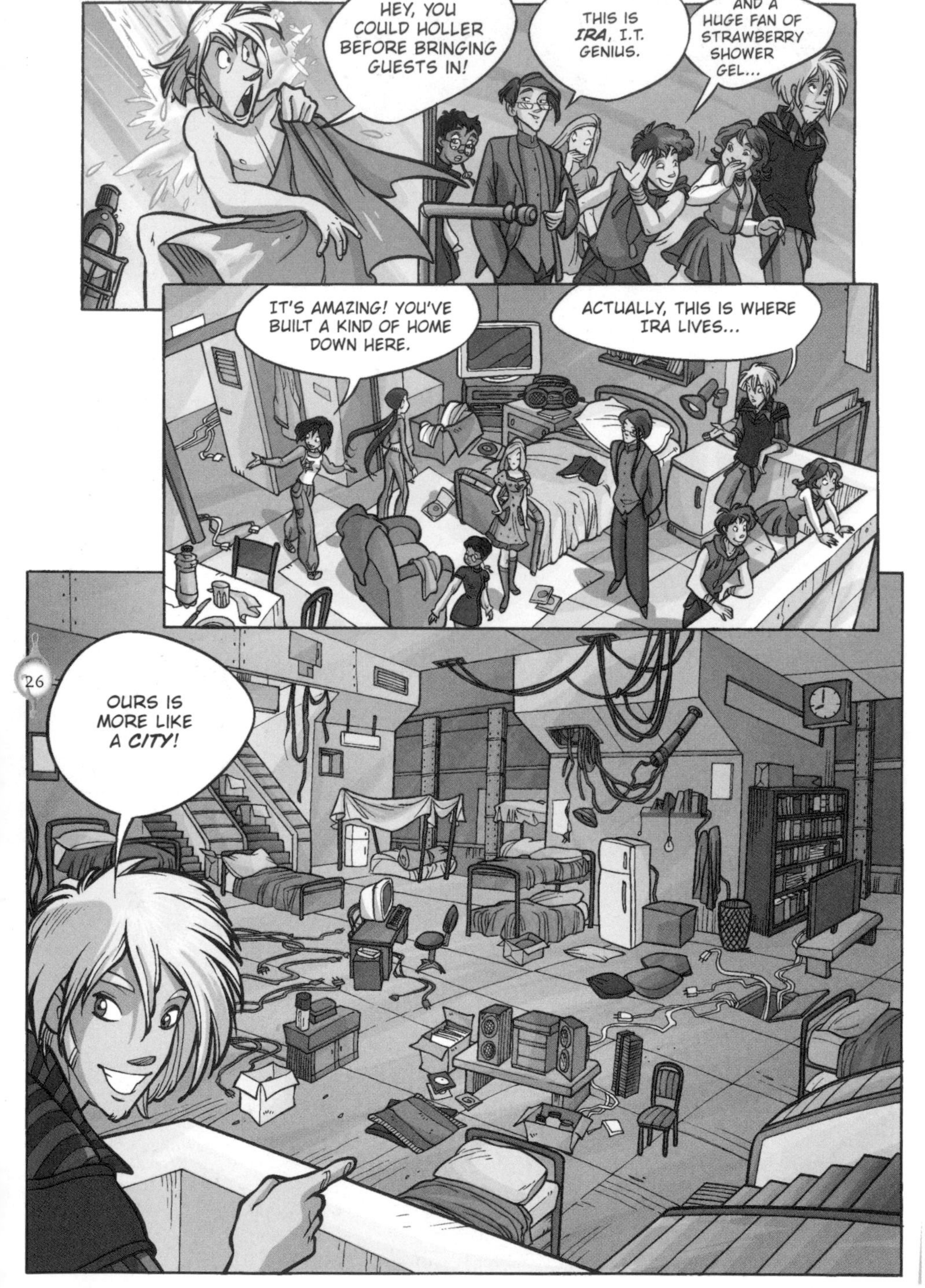
HEY, YOU COULD HOLLER BEFORE BRINGING GUESTS IN!
THIS IS IRA, I.T. GENIUS.
AND A HUGE FAN OF STRAWBERRY SHOWER GEL...
IT'S AMAZING! YOU'VE BUILT A KIND OF HOME DOWN HERE.
ACTUALLY, THIS IS WHERE IRA LIVES...
OURS IS MORE LIKE A CITY!

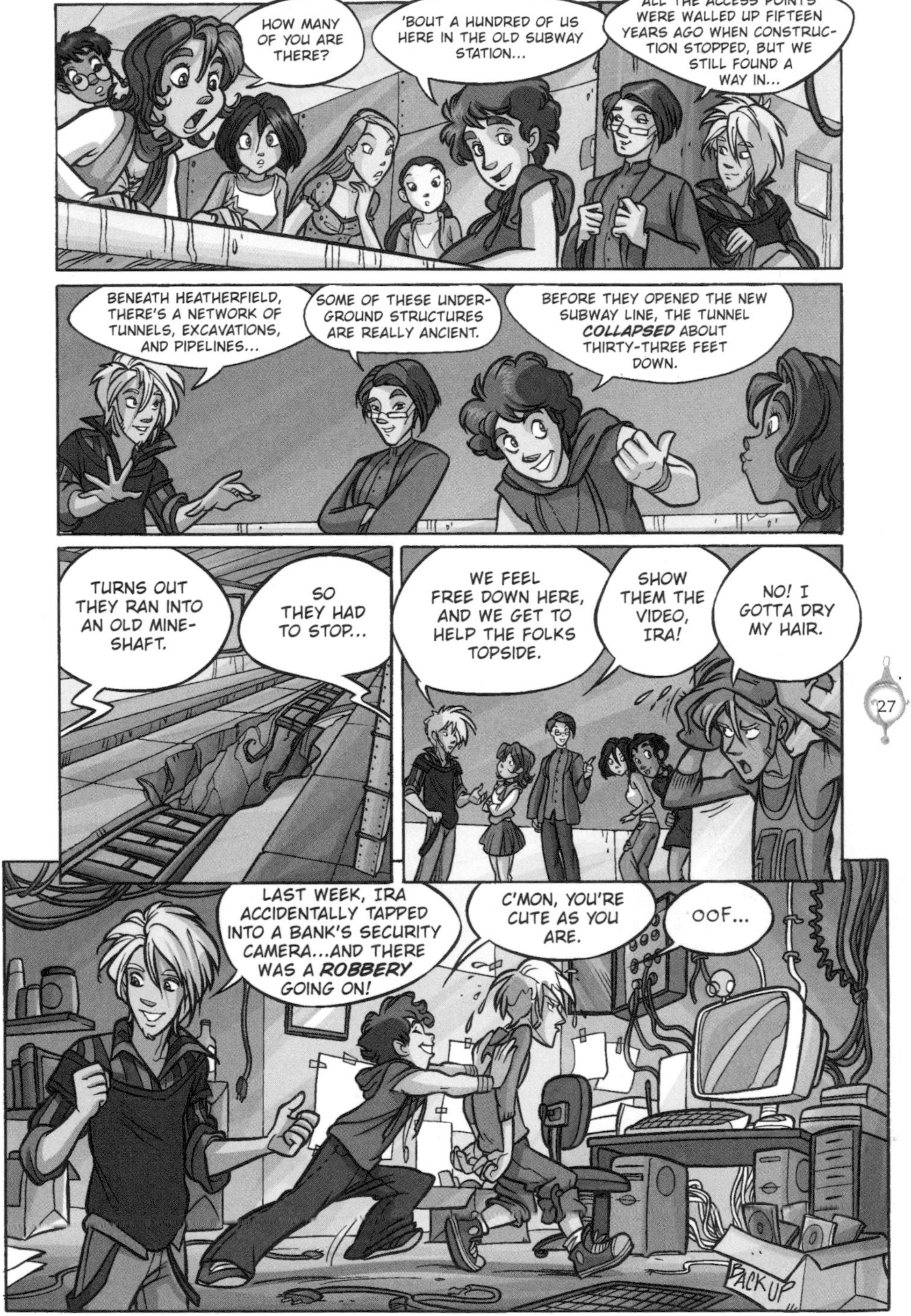
HOW MANY OF YOU ARE THERE?
'BOUT A HUNDRED OF US HERE IN THE OLD SUBWAY STATION...
ALL THE ACCESS POINTS WERE WALLED UP FIFTEEN YEARS AGO WHEN CONSTRUCTION STOPPED, BUT WE STILL FOUND A WAY IN...
BENEATH HEATHERFIELD, THERE'S A NETWORK OF TUNNELS, EXCAVATIONS, AND PIPELINES...
SOME OF THESE UNDERGROUND STRUCTURES ARE REALLY ANCIENT.
BEFORE THEY OPENED THE NEW SUBWAY LINE, THE TUNNEL ***COLLAPSED*** ABOUT THIRTY-THREE FEET DOWN.
TURNS OUT THEY RAN INTO AN OLD MINESHAFT.
SO THEY HAD TO STOP...
WE FEEL FREE DOWN HERE, AND WE GET TO HELP THE FOLKS TOPSIDE.
SHOW THEM THE VIDEO, IRA!
NO! I GOTTA DRY MY HAIR.
LAST WEEK, IRA ACCIDENTALLY TAPPED INTO A BANK'S SECURITY CAMERA...AND THERE WAS A ***ROBBERY*** GOING ON!
C'MON, YOU'RE CUTE AS YOU ARE.
OOF...
BACK UP

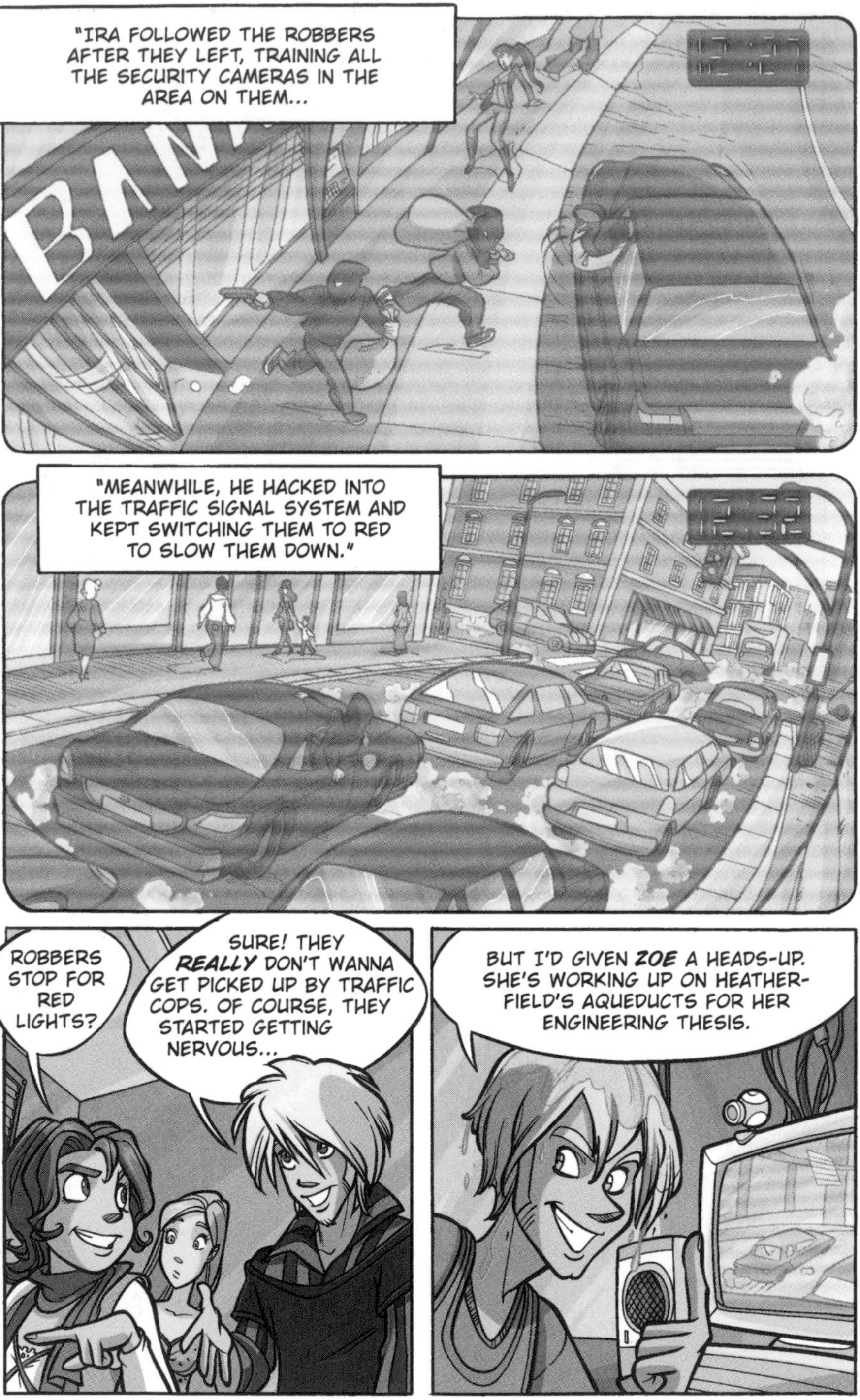
"IRA FOLLOWED THE ROBBERS AFTER THEY LEFT, TRAINING ALL THE SECURITY CAMERAS IN THE AREA ON THEM...
"MEANWHILE, HE HACKED INTO THE TRAFFIC SIGNAL SYSTEM AND KEPT SWITCHING THEM TO RED TO SLOW THEM DOWN."
ROBBERS STOP FOR RED LIGHTS?
SURE! THEY *REALLY* DON'T WANNA GET PICKED UP BY TRAFFIC COPS. OF COURSE, THEY STARTED GETTING NERVOUS...
BUT I'D GIVEN *ZOE* A HEADS-UP. SHE'S WORKING UP ON HEATHER-FIELD'S AQUEDUCTS FOR HER ENGINEERING THESIS.

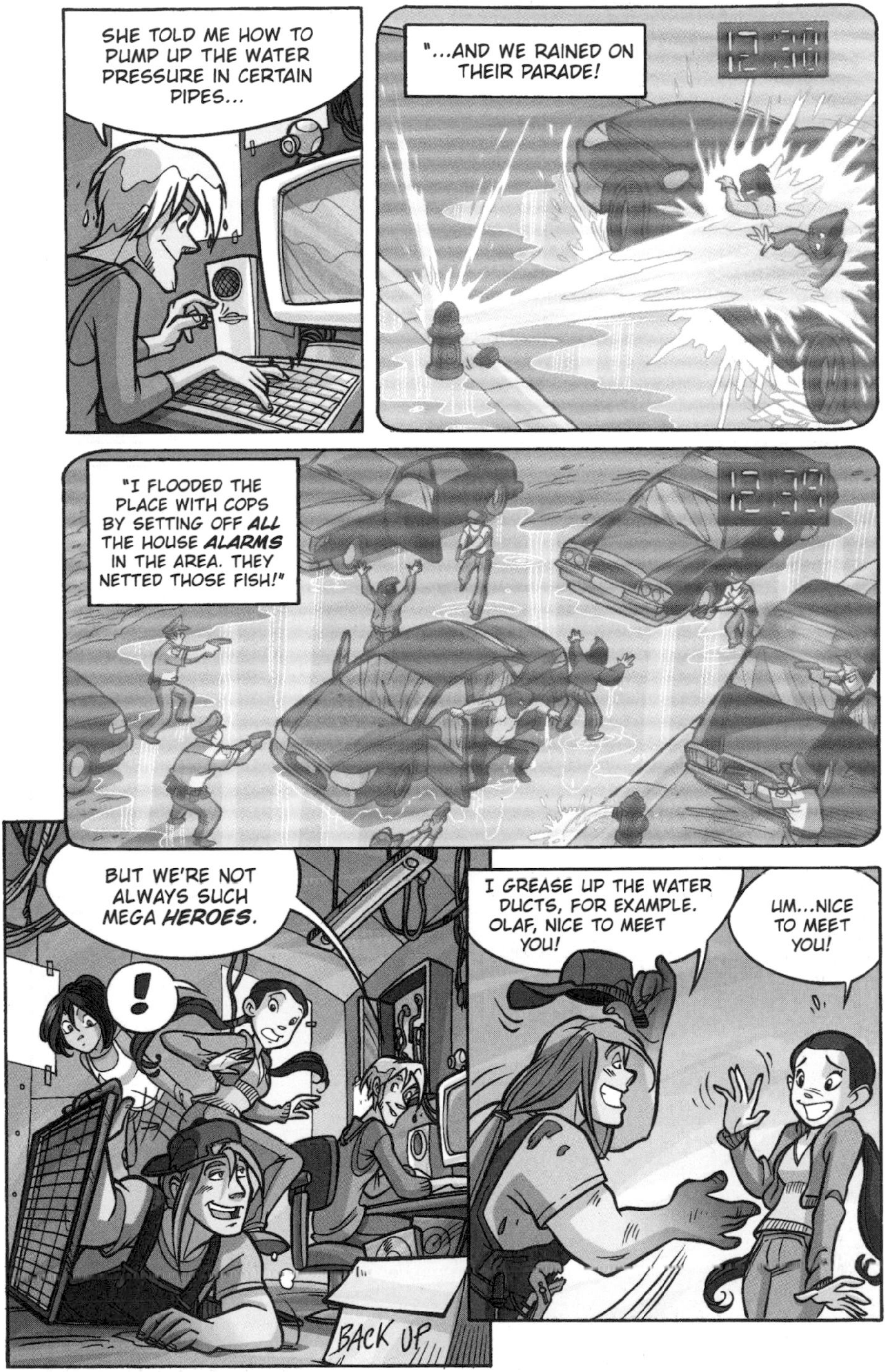
SHE TOLD ME HOW TO PUMP UP THE WATER PRESSURE IN CERTAIN PIPES...
"...AND WE RAINED ON THEIR PARADE!
"I FLOODED THE PLACE WITH COPS BY SETTING OFF ALL THE HOUSE ALARMS IN THE AREA. THEY NETTED THOSE FISH!"
BUT WE'RE NOT ALWAYS SUCH MEGA HEROES.
!
BACK UP
I GREASE UP THE WATER DUCTS, FOR EXAMPLE. OLAF, NICE TO MEET YOU!
UM...NICE TO MEET YOU!

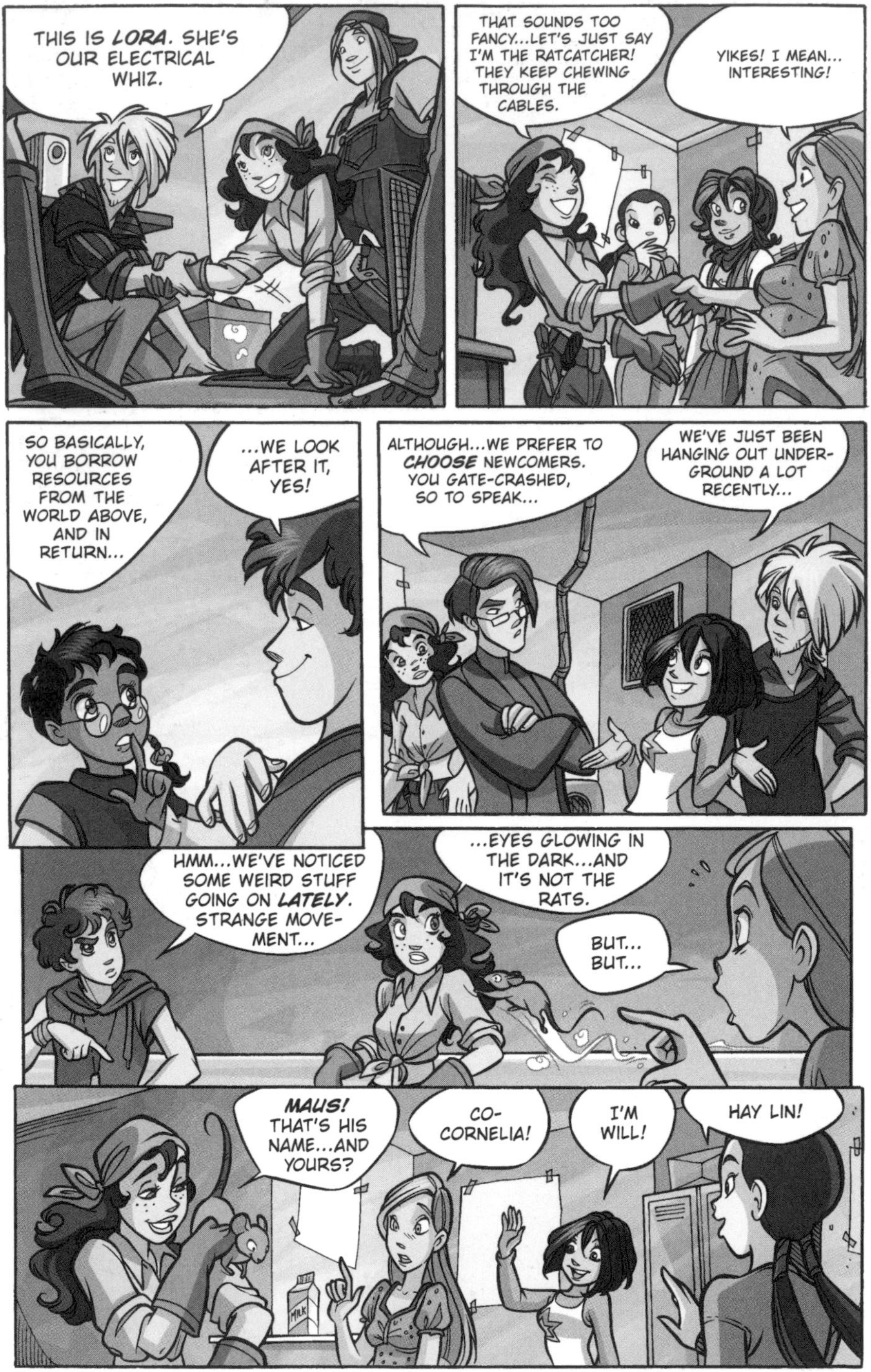
THIS IS LORA. SHE'S OUR ELECTRICAL WHIZ.
THAT SOUNDS TOO FANCY...LET'S JUST SAY I'M THE RATCATCHER! THEY KEEP CHEWING THROUGH THE CABLES.
YIKES! I MEAN... INTERESTING!
SO BASICALLY, YOU BORROW RESOURCES FROM THE WORLD ABOVE, AND IN RETURN...
...WE LOOK AFTER IT, YES!
ALTHOUGH...WE PREFER TO CHOOSE NEWCOMERS. YOU GATE-CRASHED, SO TO SPEAK...
WE'VE JUST BEEN HANGING OUT UNDER-GROUND A LOT RECENTLY...
HMM...WE'VE NOTICED SOME WEIRD STUFF GOING ON LATELY. STRANGE MOVE-MENT...
...EYES GLOWING IN THE DARK...AND IT'S NOT THE RATS.
BUT... BUT...
MAUS! THAT'S HIS NAME...AND YOURS?
CO-CORNELIA!
I'M WILL!
HAY LIN!

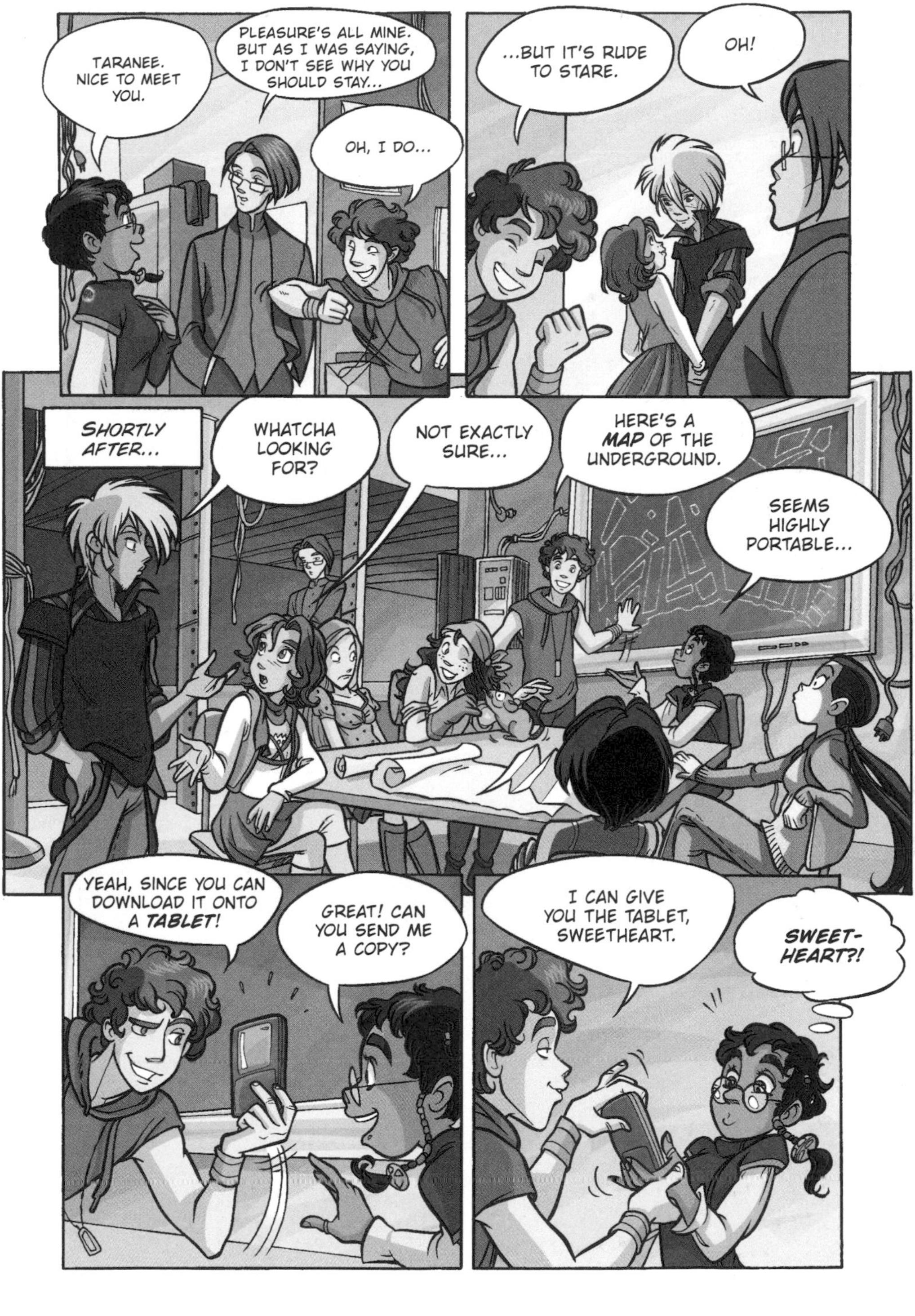
TARANEE. NICE TO MEET YOU.
PLEASURE'S ALL MINE. BUT AS I WAS SAYING, I DON'T SEE WHY YOU SHOULD STAY...
OH, I DO...
...BUT IT'S RUDE TO STARE.
OH!
SHORTLY AFTER...
WHATCHA LOOKING FOR?
NOT EXACTLY SURE...
HERE'S A MAP OF THE UNDERGROUND.
SEEMS HIGHLY PORTABLE...
YEAH, SINCE YOU CAN DOWNLOAD IT ONTO A TABLET!
GREAT! CAN YOU SEND ME A COPY?
I CAN GIVE YOU THE TABLET, SWEETHEART.
SWEET-HEART?!

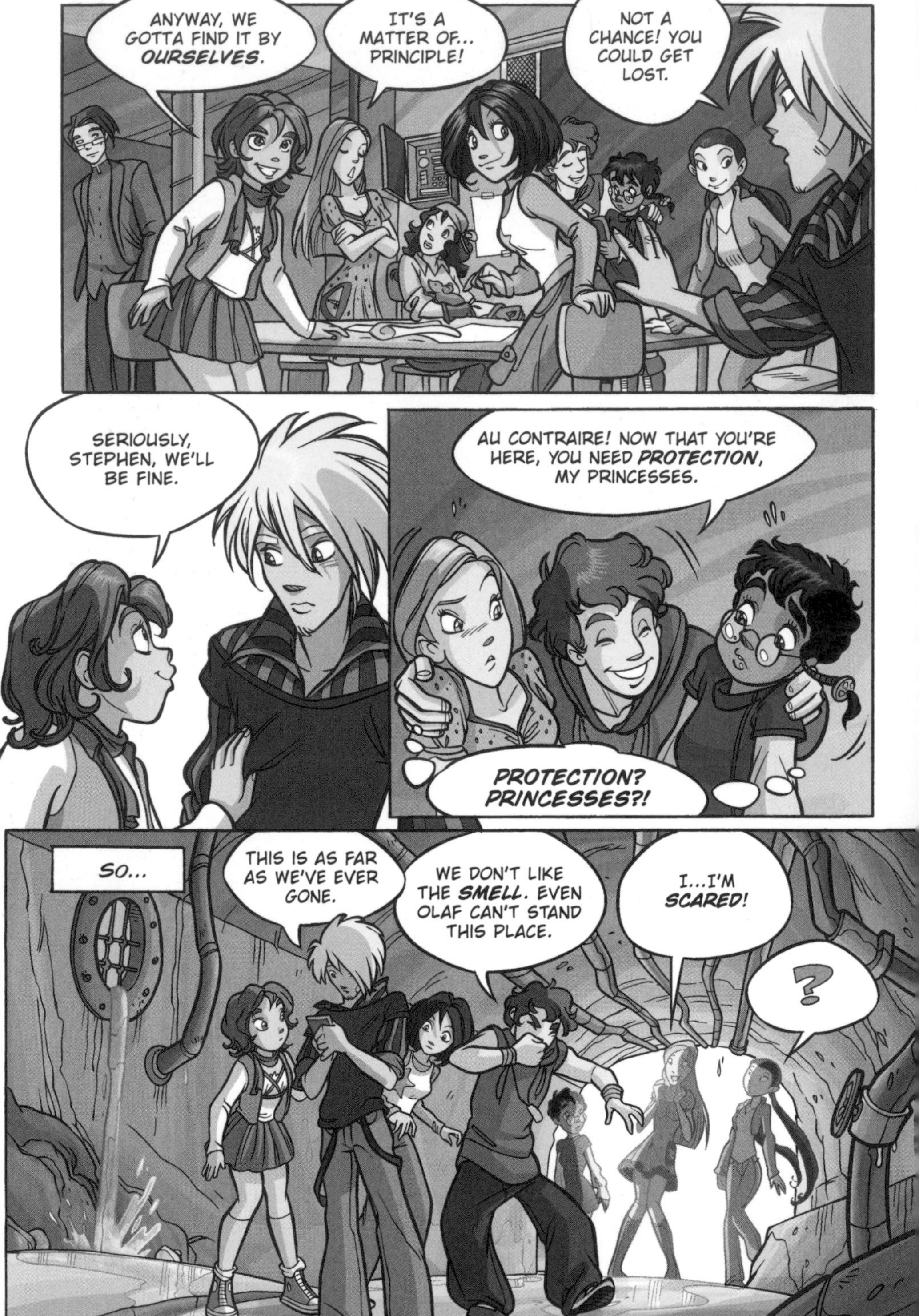
ANYWAY, WE GOTTA FIND IT BY OURSELVES.
IT'S A MATTER OF... PRINCIPLE!
NOT A CHANCE! YOU COULD GET LOST.
SERIOUSLY, STEPHEN, WE'LL BE FINE.
AU CONTRAIRE! NOW THAT YOU'RE HERE, YOU NEED PROTECTION, MY PRINCESSES.
PROTECTION? PRINCESSES?!
SO...
THIS IS AS FAR AS WE'VE EVER GONE.
WE DON'T LIKE THE SMELL. EVEN OLAF CAN'T STAND THIS PLACE.
I...I'M SCARED!
?

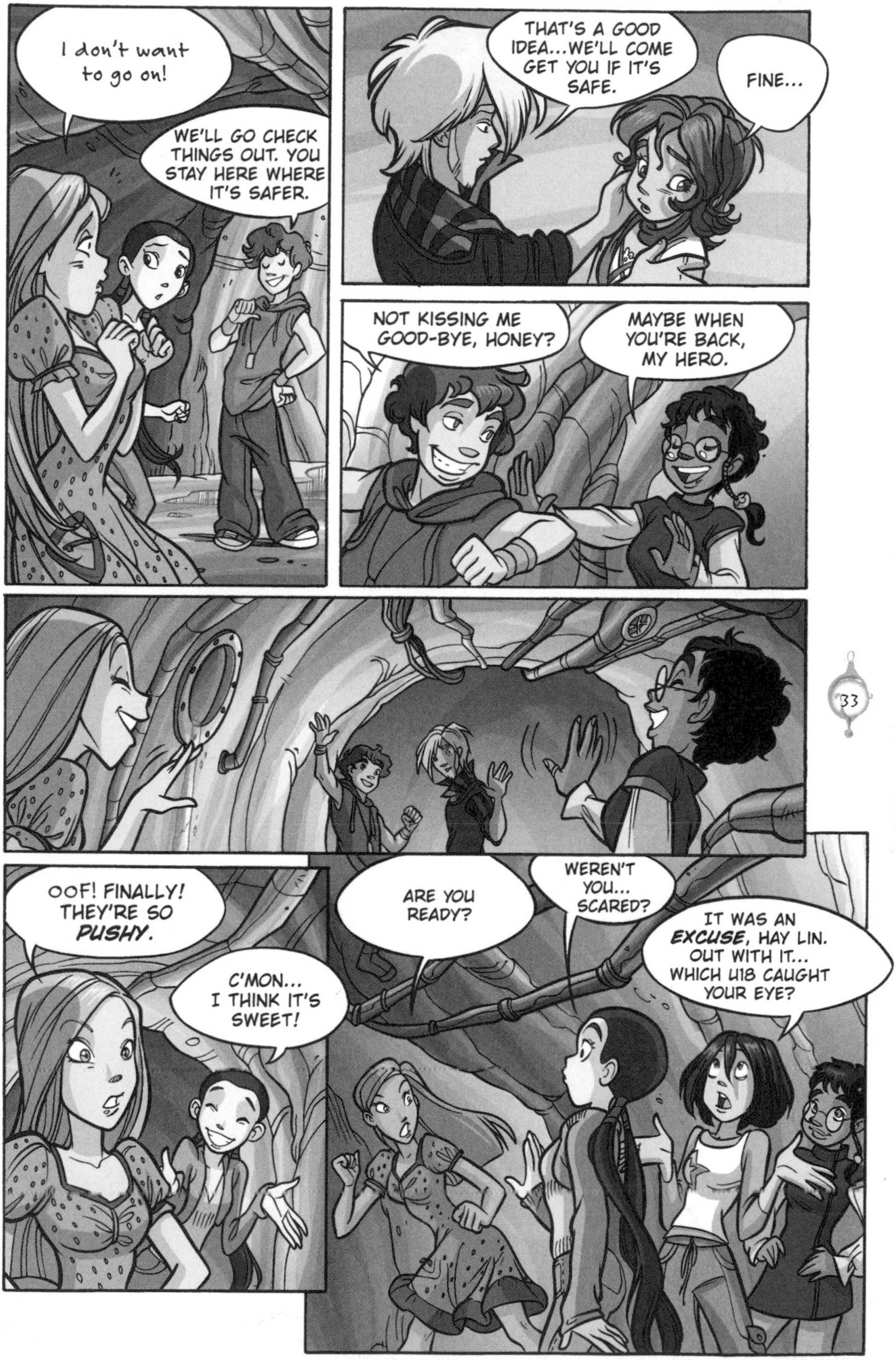
I don't want to go on!
WE'LL GO CHECK THINGS OUT. YOU STAY HERE WHERE IT'S SAFER.
THAT'S A GOOD IDEA...WE'LL COME GET YOU IF IT'S SAFE.
FINE...
NOT KISSING ME GOOD-BYE, HONEY?
MAYBE WHEN YOU'RE BACK, MY HERO.
OOF! FINALLY! THEY'RE SO *PUSHY*.
C'MON... I THINK IT'S SWEET!
ARE YOU READY?
WEREN'T YOU... SCARED?
IT WAS AN *EXCUSE*, HAY LIN. OUT WITH IT... WHICH U18 CAUGHT YOUR EYE?

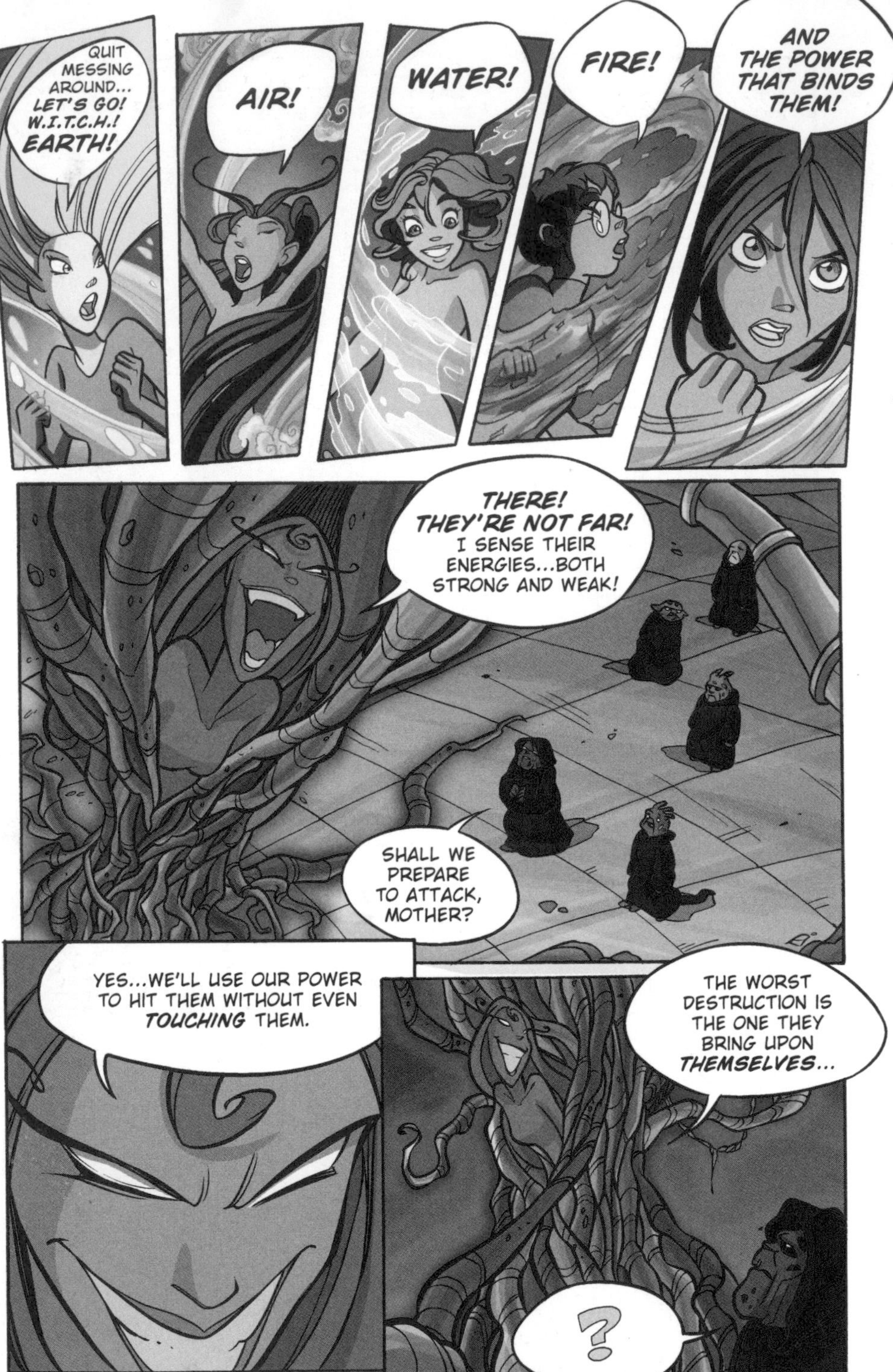
QUIT MESSING AROUND... LET'S GO! W.I.T.C.H.! EARTH!
AIR!
WATER!
FIRE!
AND THE POWER THAT BINDS THEM!
THERE! THEY'RE NOT FAR! I SENSE THEIR ENERGIES...BOTH STRONG AND WEAK!
SHALL WE PREPARE TO ATTACK, MOTHER?
YES...WE'LL USE OUR POWER TO HIT THEM WITHOUT EVEN TOUCHING THEM.
THE WORST DESTRUCTION IS THE ONE THEY BRING UPON THEMSELVES...
?

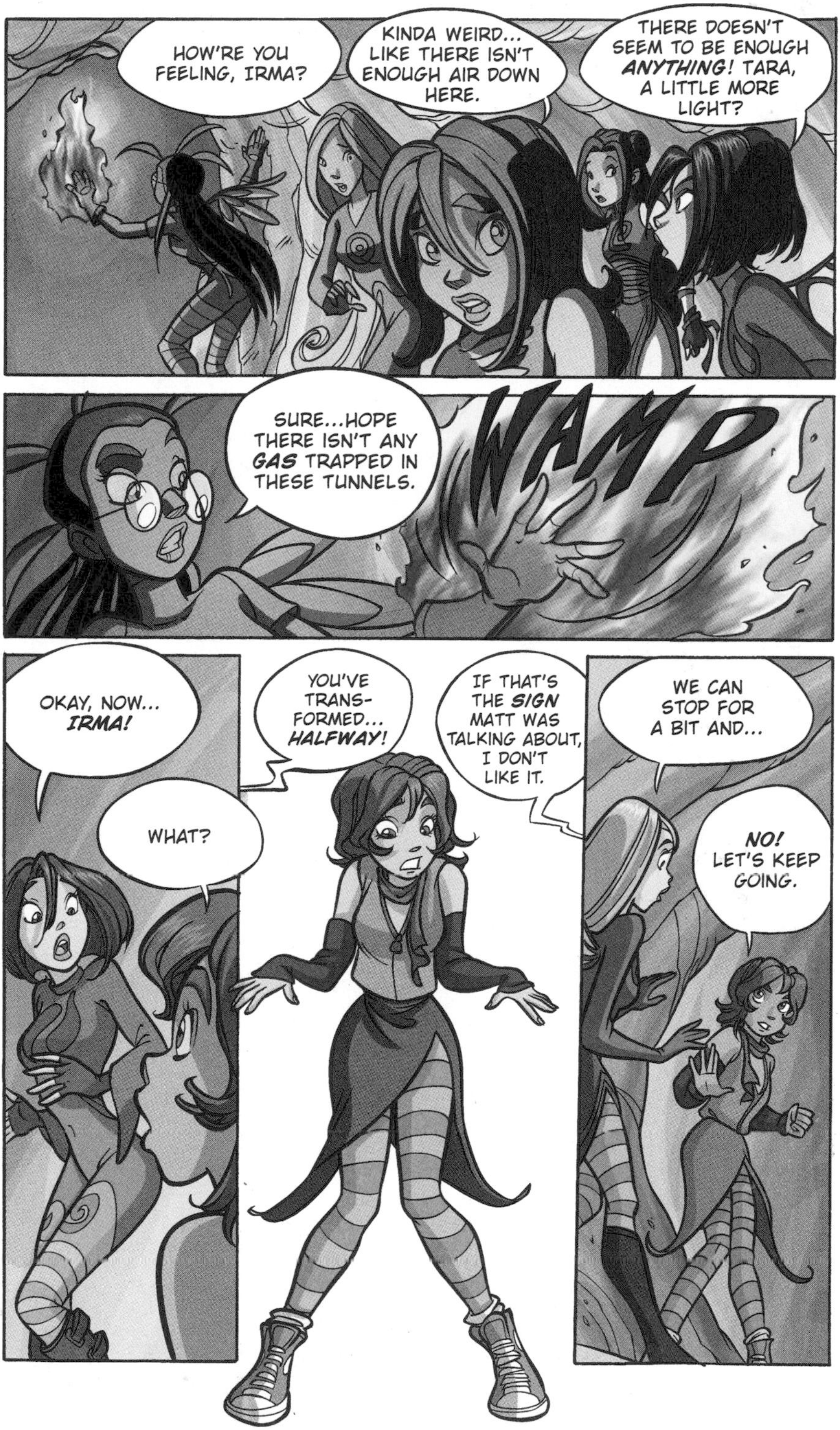
HOW'RE YOU FEELING, IRMA?
KINDA WEIRD... LIKE THERE ISN'T ENOUGH AIR DOWN HERE.
THERE DOESN'T SEEM TO BE ENOUGH ANYTHING! TARA, A LITTLE MORE LIGHT?
SURE...HOPE THERE ISN'T ANY GAS TRAPPED IN THESE TUNNELS.
WAMP
OKAY, NOW... IRMA!
WHAT?
YOU'VE TRANS-FORMED... HALFWAY!
IF THAT'S THE SIGN MATT WAS TALKING ABOUT, I DON'T LIKE IT.
WE CAN STOP FOR A BIT AND...
NO! LET'S KEEP GOING.

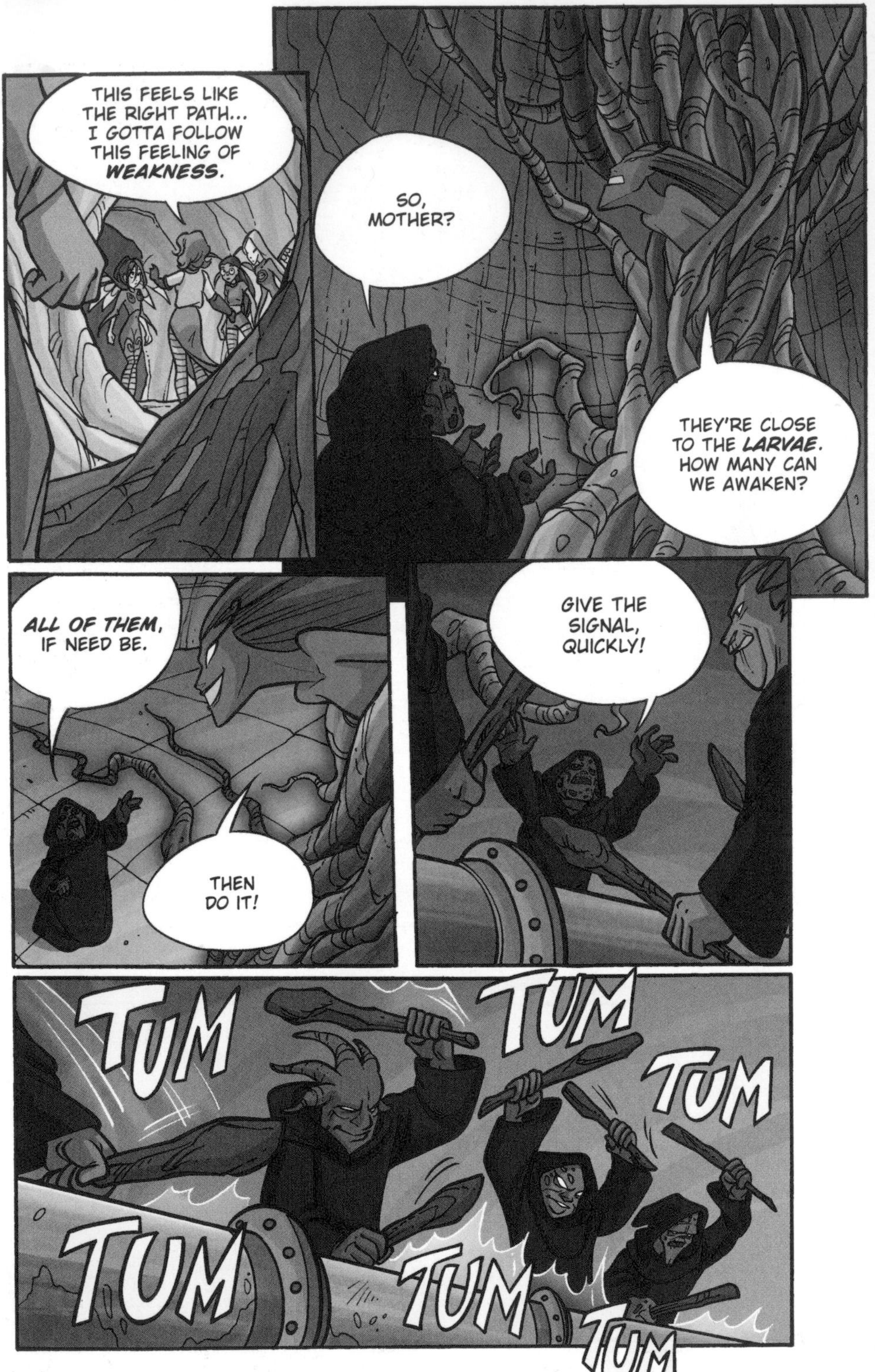
THIS FEELS LIKE THE RIGHT PATH... I GOTTA FOLLOW THIS FEELING OF **WEAKNESS**.
SO, MOTHER?
THEY'RE CLOSE TO THE **LARVAE**. HOW MANY CAN WE AWAKEN?
**ALL OF THEM**, IF NEED BE.
THEN DO IT!
GIVE THE SIGNAL, QUICKLY!
TUM
TUM
TUM
TUM
TUM
TUM

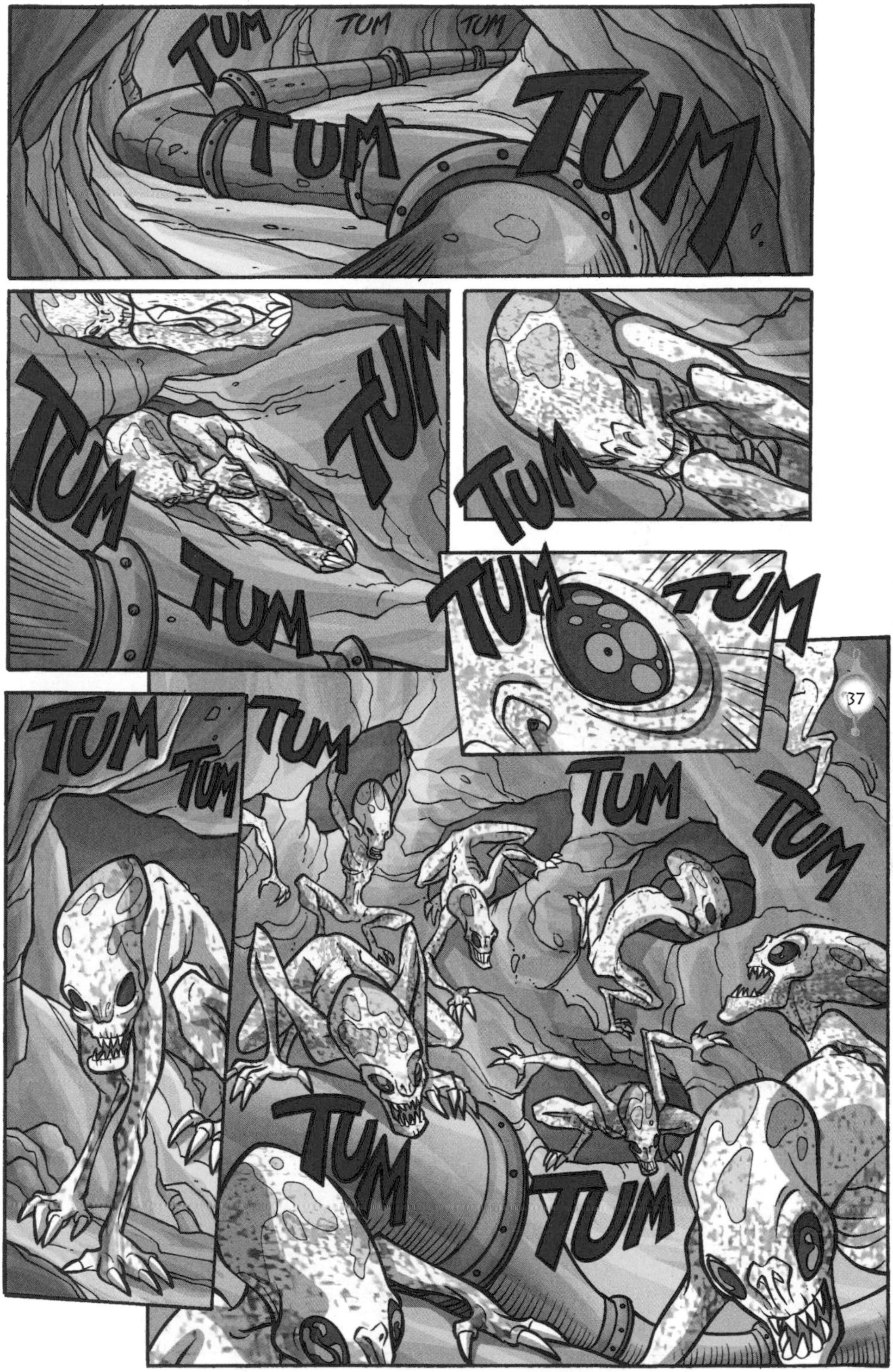
TUM TUM TUM
TUM TUM
TUM TUM
TUM
TUM TUM
TUM TUM
TUM TUM
TUM TUM
TUM TUM
TUM TUM

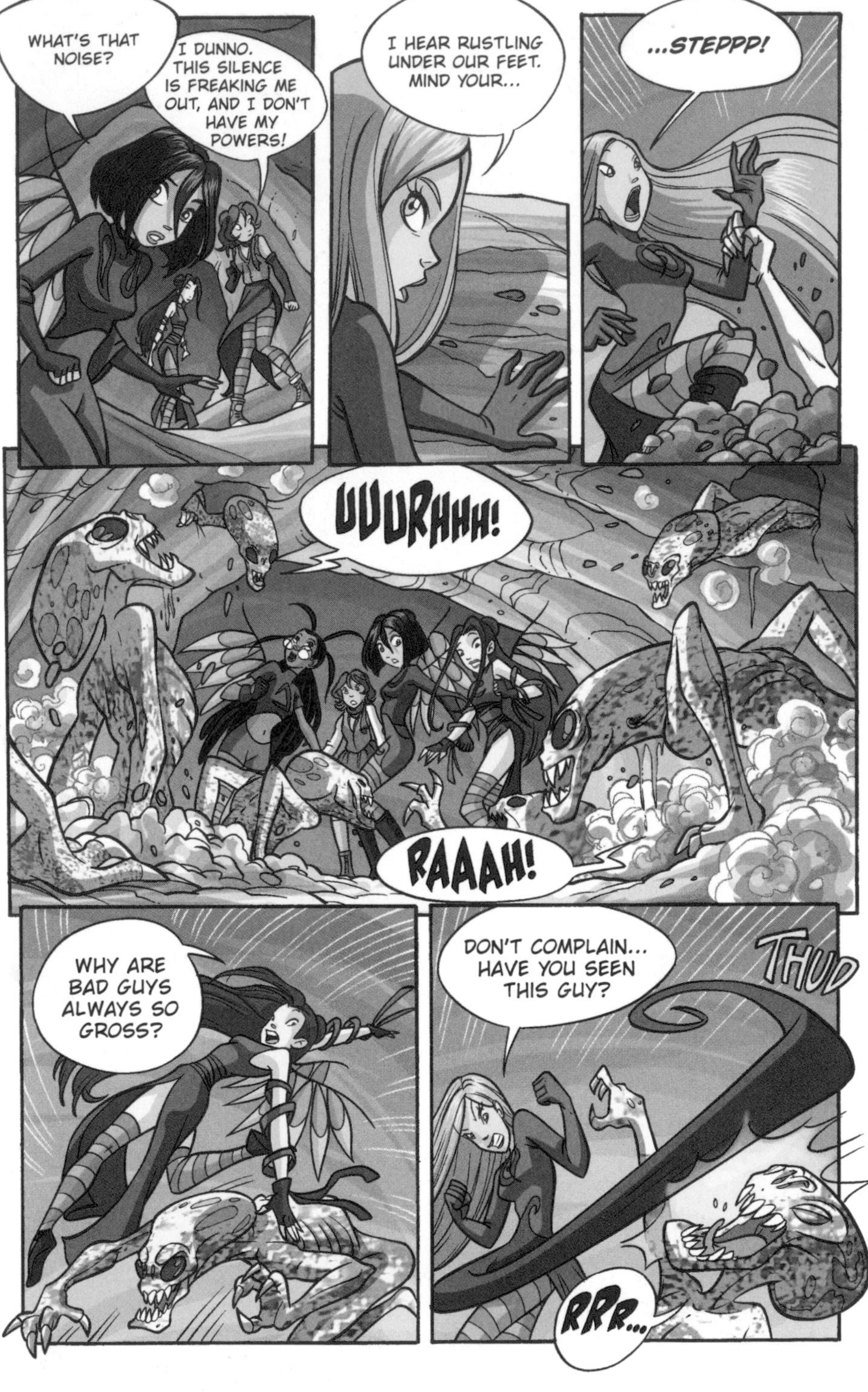
WHAT'S THAT NOISE?
I DUNNO. THIS SILENCE IS FREAKING ME OUT, AND I DON'T HAVE MY POWERS!
I HEAR RUSTLING UNDER OUR FEET. MIND YOUR...
...STEPPP!
UUURHHH!
RAAAH!
WHY ARE BAD GUYS ALWAYS SO GROSS?
DON'T COMPLAIN... HAVE YOU SEEN THIS GUY?
THUD
RRR...

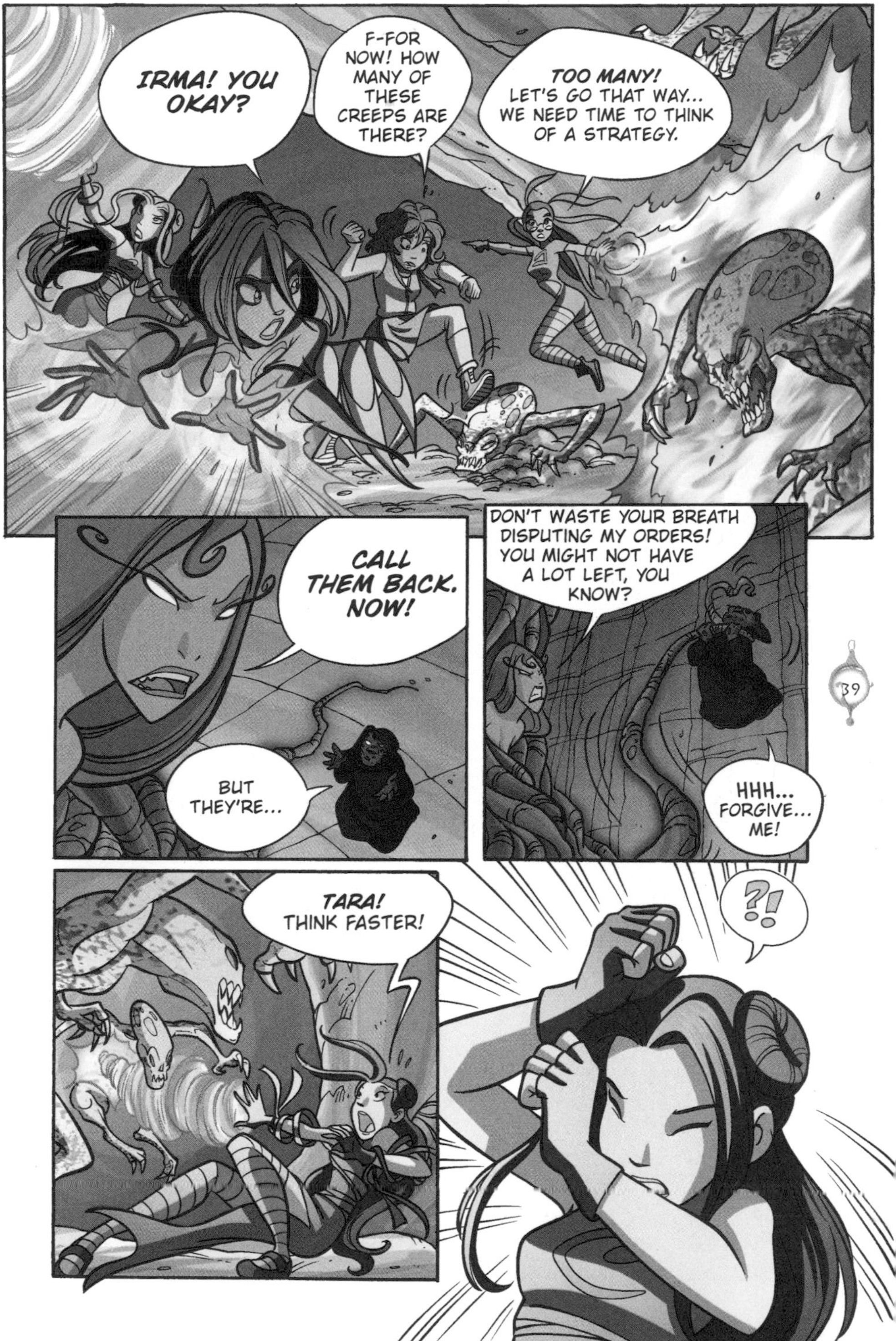
IRMA! YOU OKAY?
F-FOR NOW! HOW MANY OF THESE CREEPS ARE THERE?
TOO MANY! LET'S GO THAT WAY... WE NEED TIME TO THINK OF A STRATEGY.
CALL THEM BACK. NOW!
BUT THEY'RE...
DON'T WASTE YOUR BREATH DISPUTING MY ORDERS! YOU MIGHT NOT HAVE A LOT LEFT, YOU KNOW?
HHH... FORGIVE... ME!
TARA! THINK FASTER!
?!

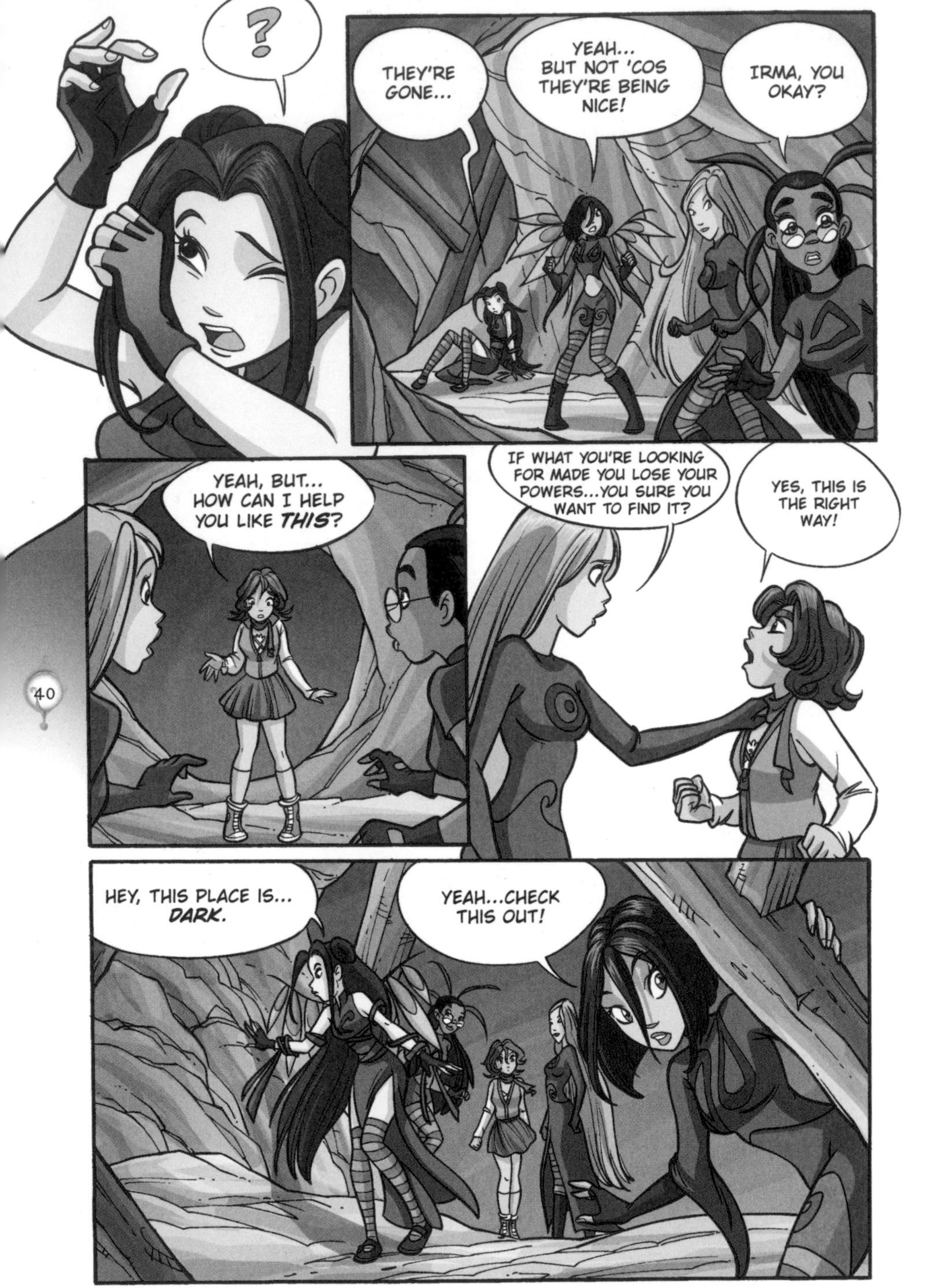
?
THEY'RE GONE...
YEAH... BUT NOT 'COS THEY'RE BEING NICE!
IRMA, YOU OKAY?
YEAH, BUT... HOW CAN I HELP YOU LIKE THIS?
IF WHAT YOU'RE LOOKING FOR MADE YOU LOSE YOUR POWERS...YOU SURE YOU WANT TO FIND IT?
YES, THIS IS THE RIGHT WAY!
HEY, THIS PLACE IS... DARK.
YEAH...CHECK THIS OUT!

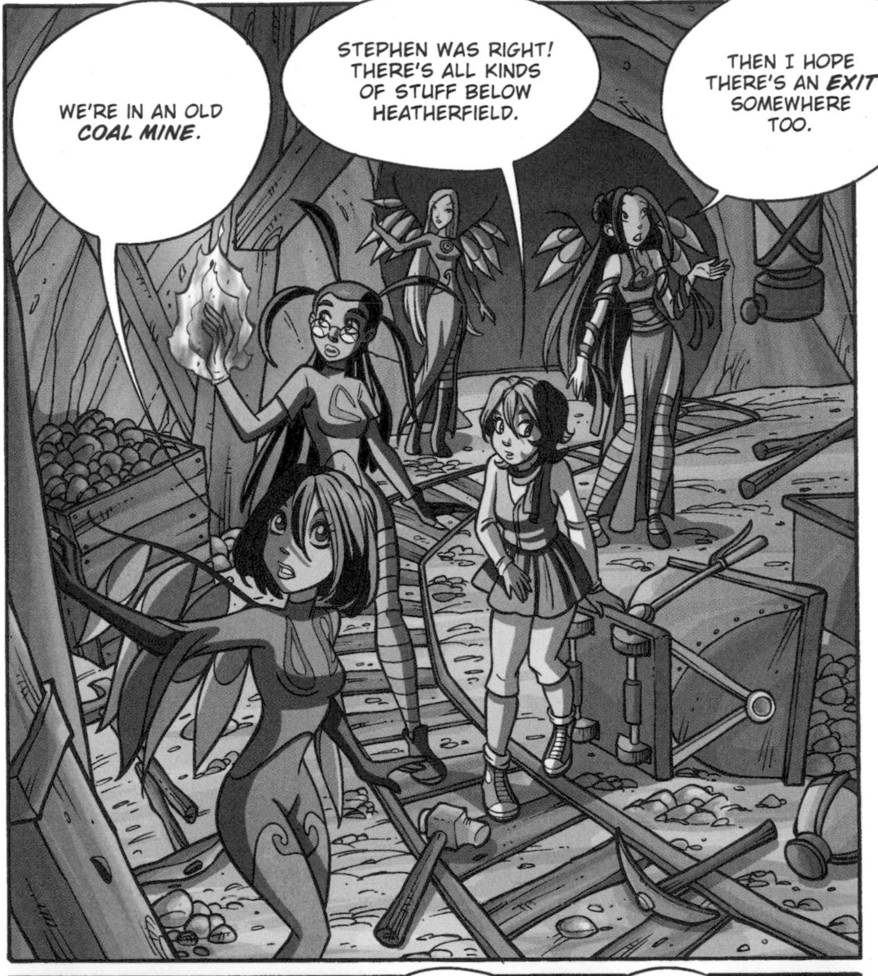
WE'RE IN AN OLD COAL MINE.
STEPHEN WAS RIGHT! THERE'S ALL KINDS OF STUFF BELOW HEATHERFIELD.
THEN I HOPE THERE'S AN EXIT SOMEWHERE TOO.

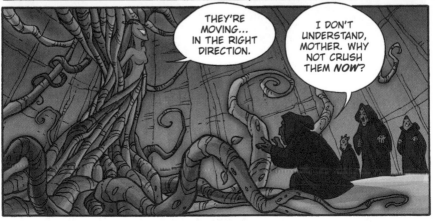

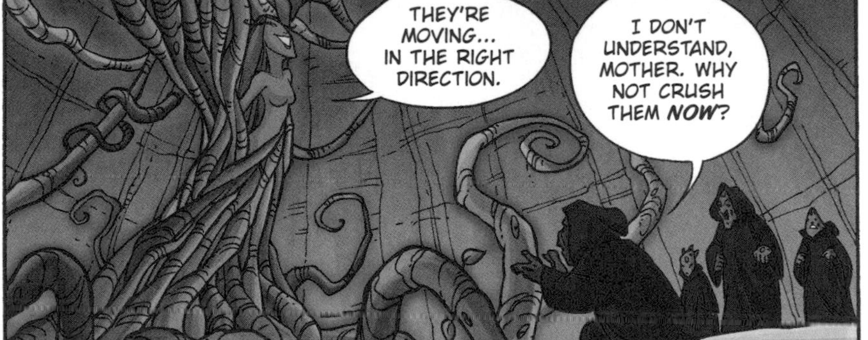
THEY'RE MOVING... IN THE RIGHT DIRECTION.
I DON'T UNDERSTAND, MOTHER. WHY NOT CRUSH THEM NOW?

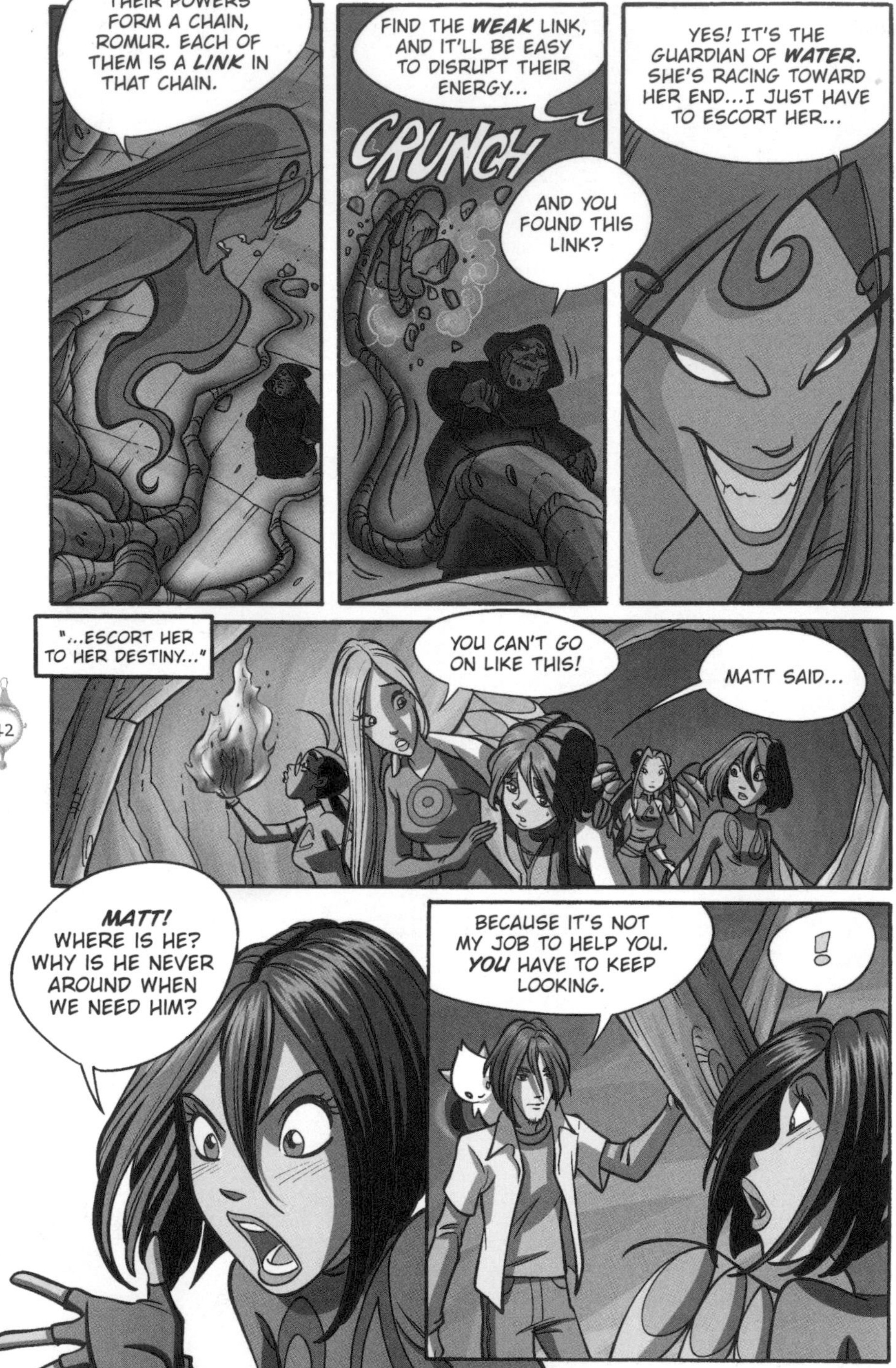
THEIR POWERS FORM A CHAIN, ROMUR. EACH OF THEM IS A *LINK* IN THAT CHAIN.
FIND THE *WEAK* LINK, AND IT'LL BE EASY TO DISRUPT THEIR ENERGY...
CRUNCH
AND YOU FOUND THIS LINK?
YES! IT'S THE GUARDIAN OF *WATER*. SHE'S RACING TOWARD HER END...I JUST HAVE TO ESCORT HER...
"...ESCORT HER TO HER DESTINY..."
YOU CAN'T GO ON LIKE THIS!
MATT SAID...
*MATT!* WHERE IS HE? WHY IS HE NEVER AROUND WHEN WE NEED HIM?
BECAUSE IT'S NOT MY JOB TO HELP YOU. *YOU* HAVE TO KEEP LOOKING.
!

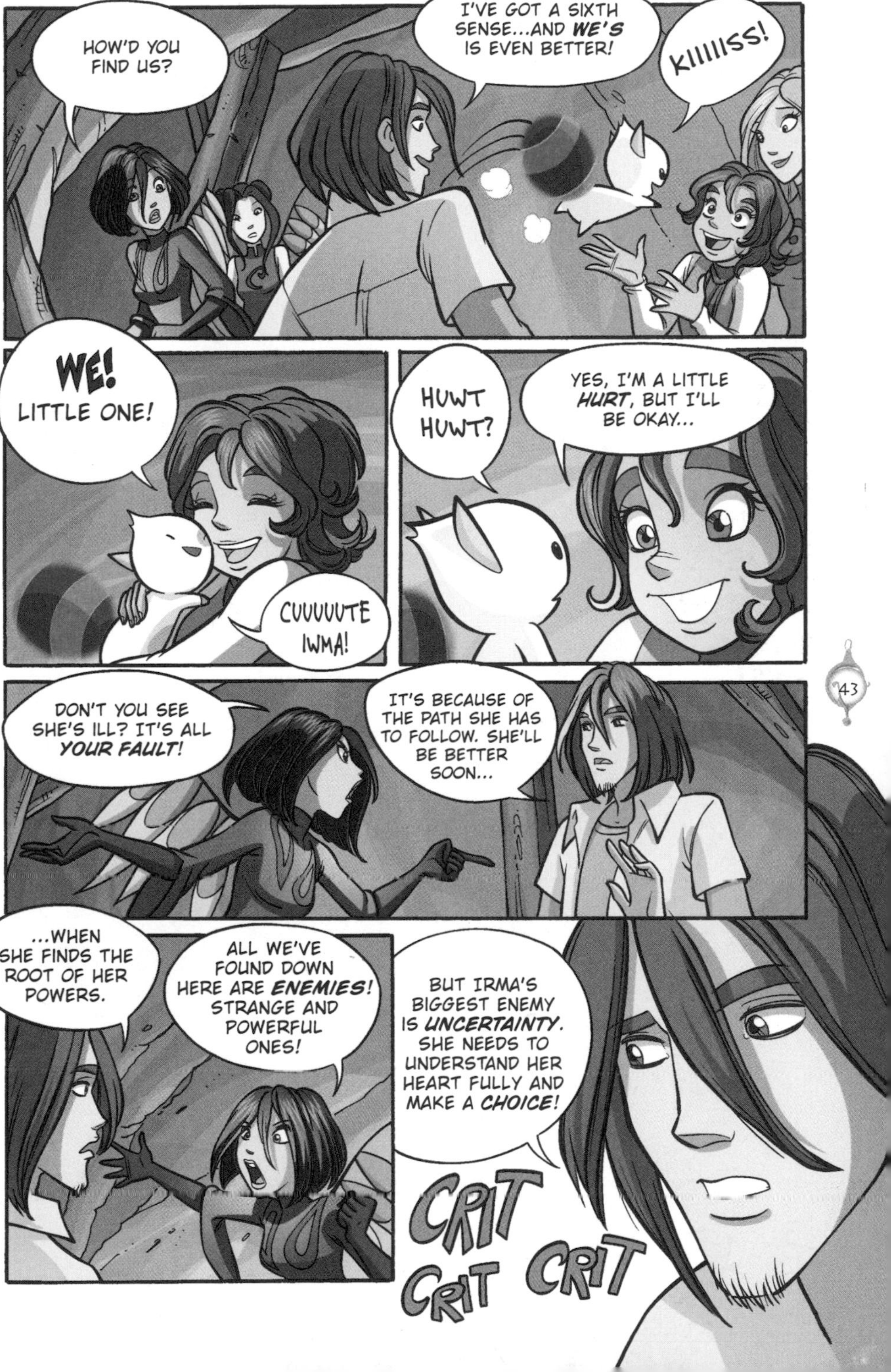
HOW'D YOU FIND US?
I'VE GOT A SIXTH SENSE...AND WE'S IS EVEN BETTER!
KIIIIISS!
WE! LITTLE ONE!
CUUUUUTE IWMA!
HUWT HUWT?
YES, I'M A LITTLE HURT, BUT I'LL BE OKAY...
DON'T YOU SEE SHE'S ILL? IT'S ALL YOUR FAULT!
IT'S BECAUSE OF THE PATH SHE HAS TO FOLLOW. SHE'LL BE BETTER SOON...
...WHEN SHE FINDS THE ROOT OF HER POWERS.
ALL WE'VE FOUND DOWN HERE ARE ENEMIES! STRANGE AND POWERFUL ONES!
BUT IRMA'S BIGGEST ENEMY IS UNCERTAINTY. SHE NEEDS TO UNDERSTAND HER HEART FULLY AND MAKE A CHOICE!
CRIT
CRIT CRIT

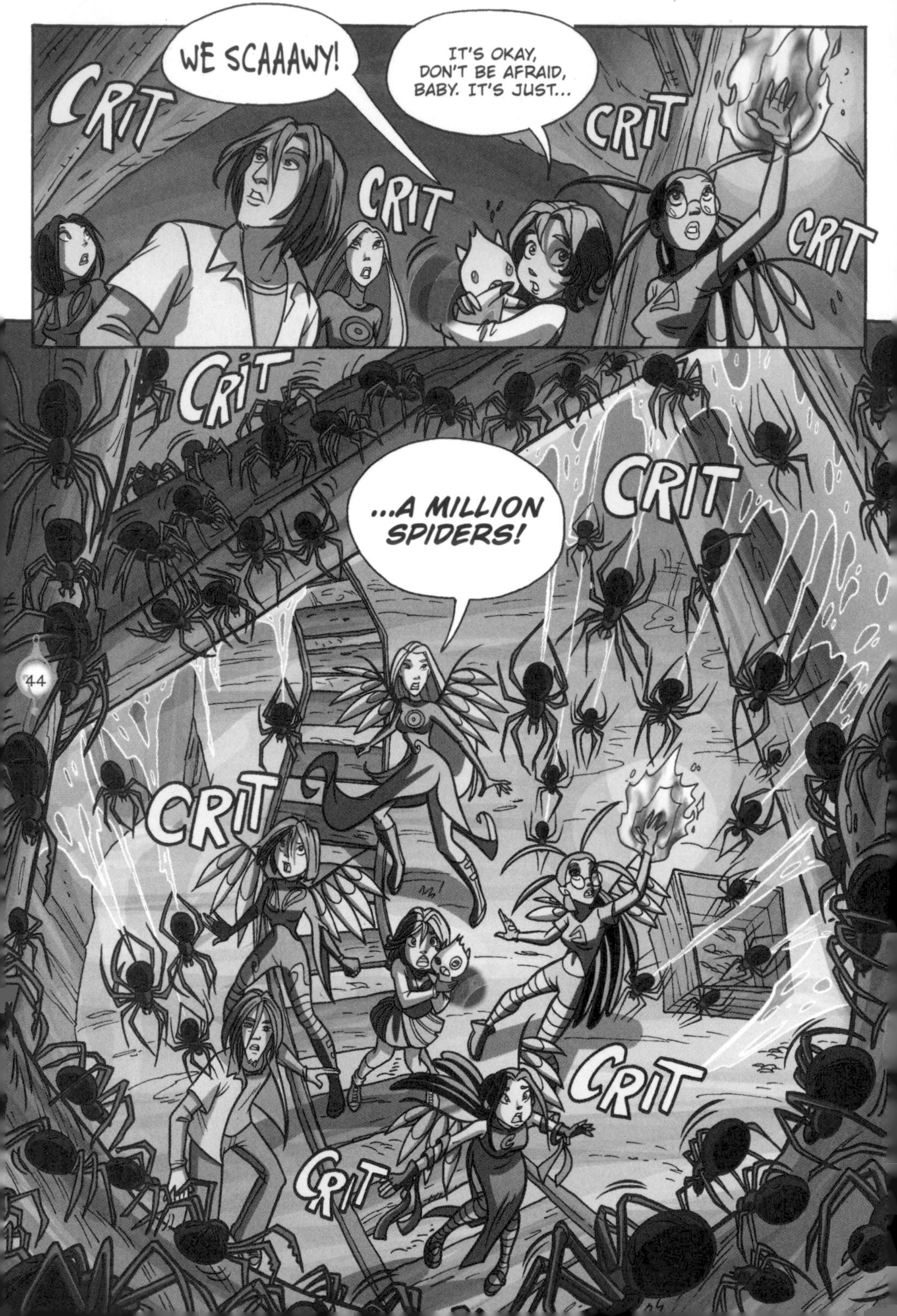
CRIT
WE SCAAAWY!
CRIT
IT'S OKAY, DON'T BE AFRAID, BABY. IT'S JUST...
CRIT
CRIT
CRIT
CRIT
...A MILLION SPIDERS!
CRIT
CRIT
CRIT

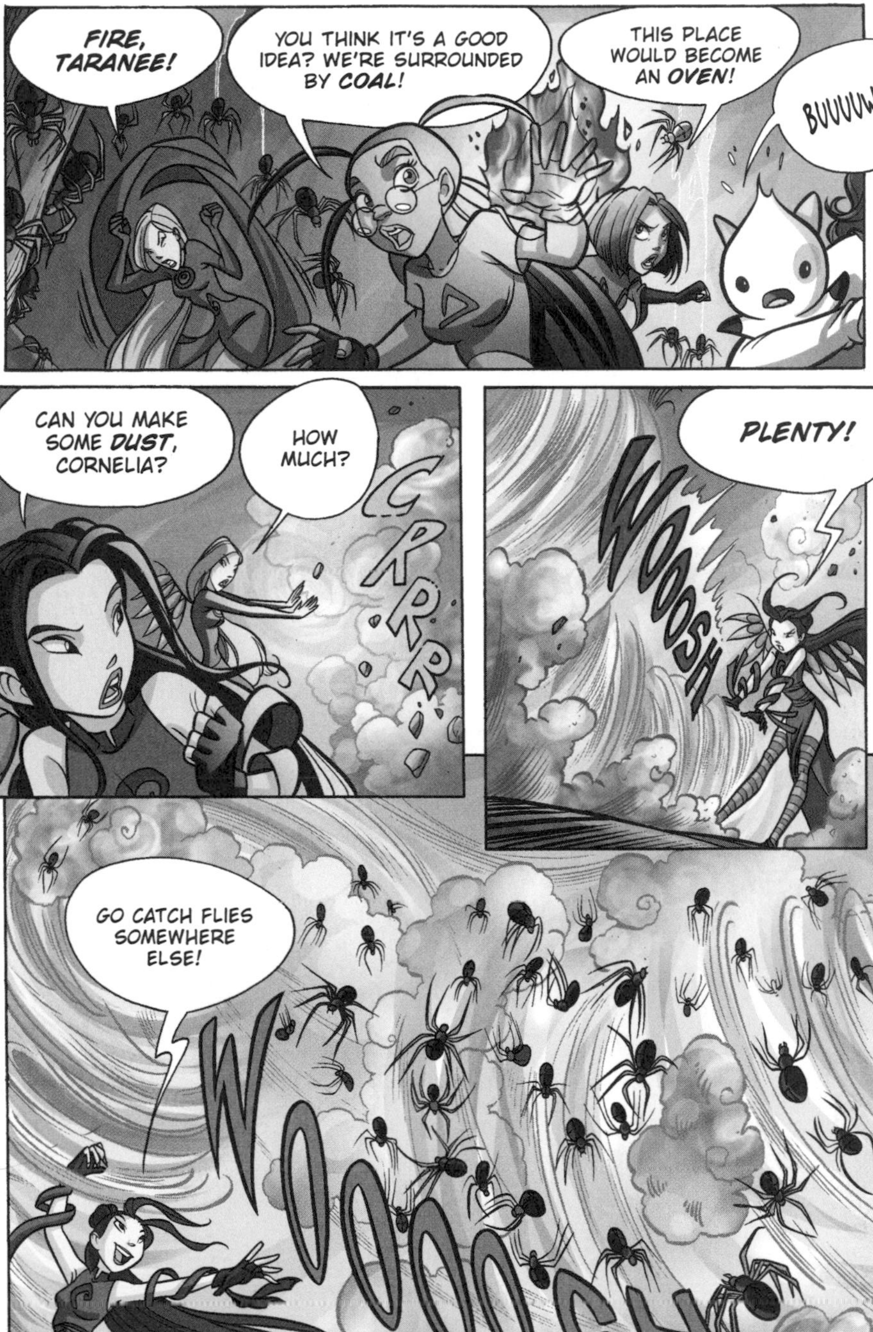
FIRE, TARANEE!
YOU THINK IT'S A GOOD IDEA? WE'RE SURROUNDED BY COAL!
THIS PLACE WOULD BECOME AN OVEN!
BUUUUWN!
CAN YOU MAKE SOME DUST, CORNELIA?
HOW MUCH?
CRRR
PLENTY!
WOOOSH
GO CATCH FLIES SOMEWHERE ELSE!
WOOOOOSH

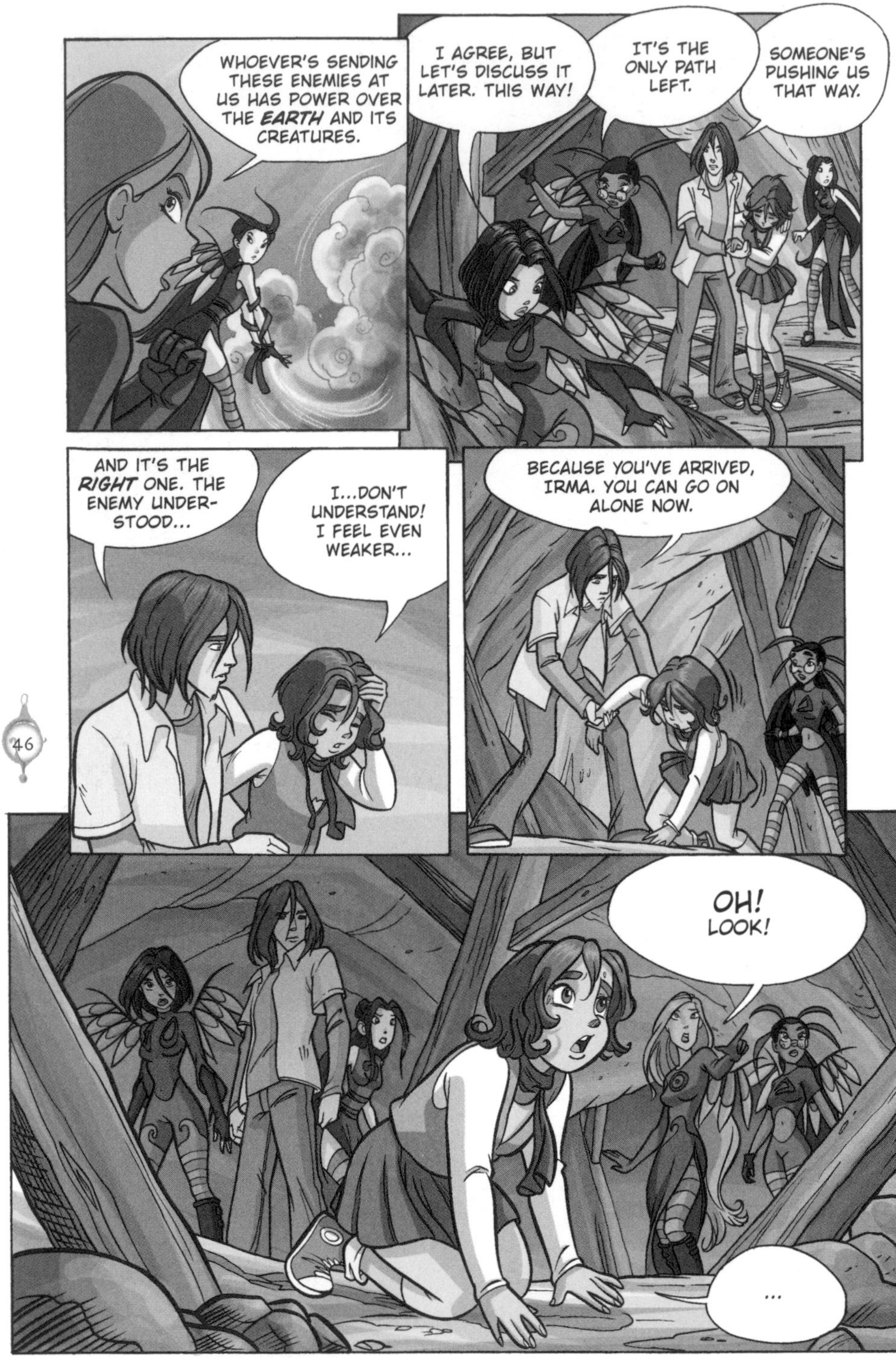
WHOEVER'S SENDING THESE ENEMIES AT US HAS POWER OVER THE *EARTH* AND ITS CREATURES.
I AGREE, BUT LET'S DISCUSS IT LATER. THIS WAY!
IT'S THE ONLY PATH LEFT.
SOMEONE'S PUSHING US THAT WAY.
AND IT'S THE *RIGHT* ONE. THE ENEMY UNDERSTOOD...
I...DON'T UNDERSTAND! I FEEL EVEN WEAKER...
BECAUSE YOU'VE ARRIVED, IRMA. YOU CAN GO ON ALONE NOW.
OH! LOOK!
...

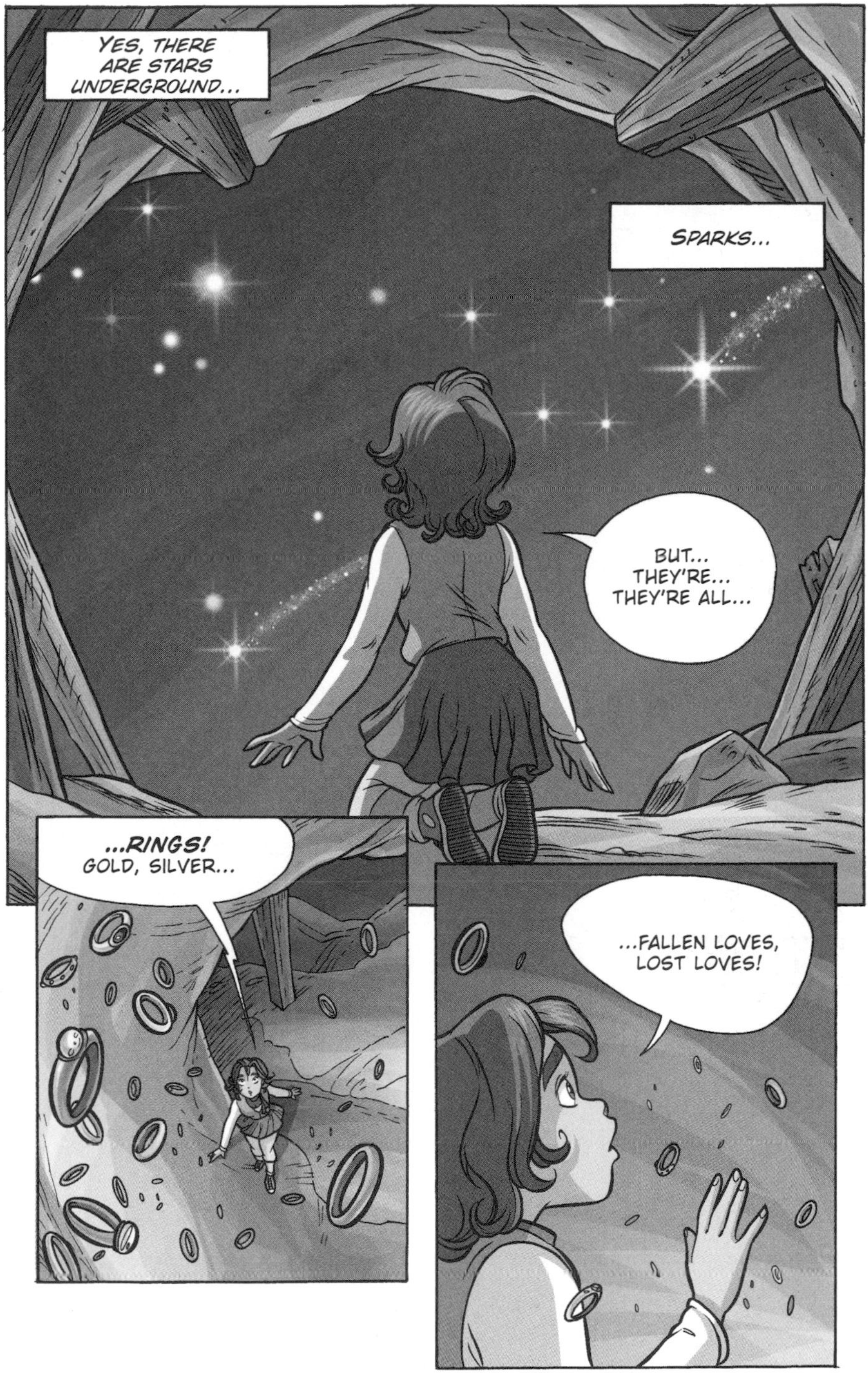
YES, THERE ARE STARS UNDERGROUND...
SPARKS...
BUT... THEY'RE... THEY'RE ALL...
...RINGS! GOLD, SILVER...
...FALLEN LOVES, LOST LOVES!

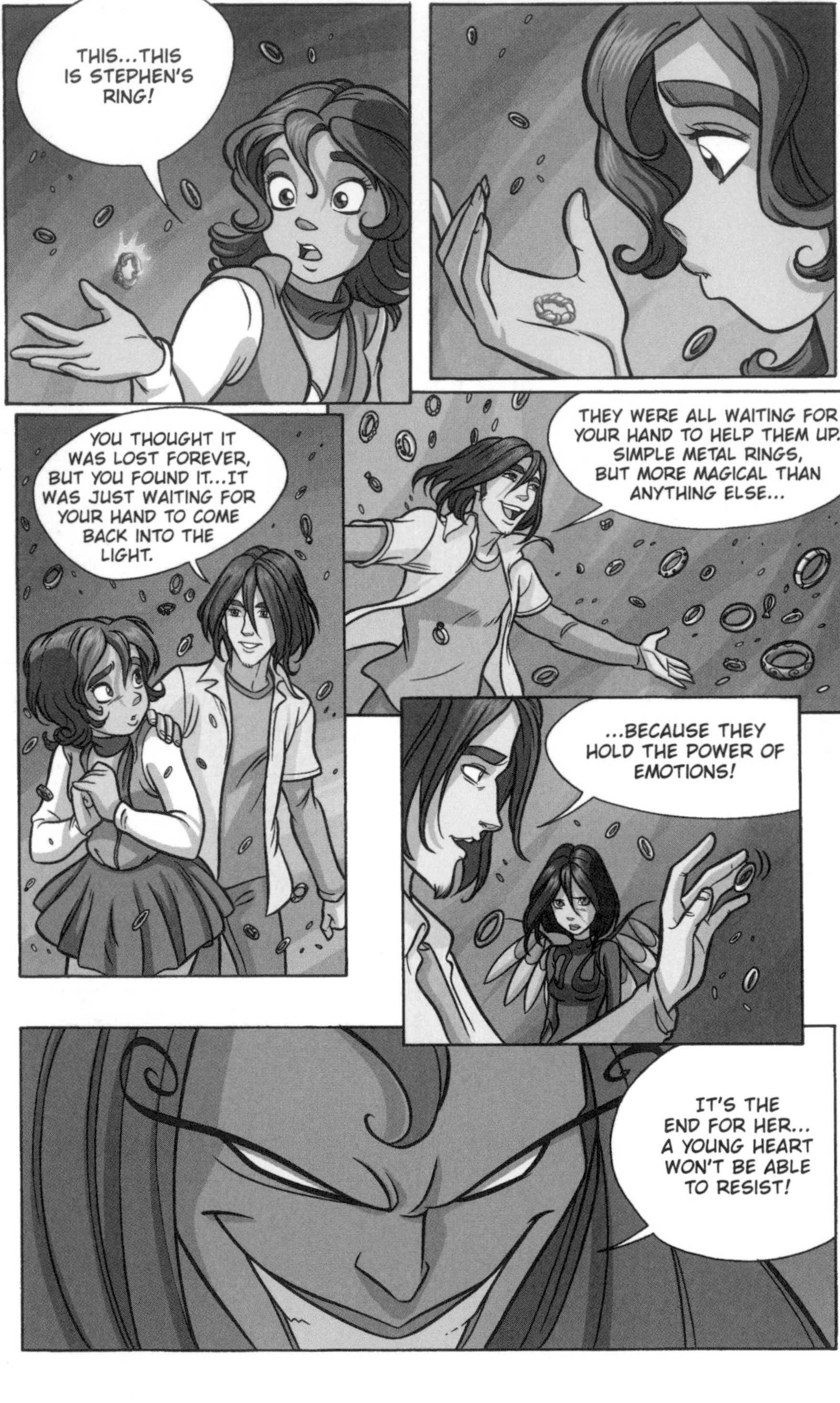
THIS...THIS IS STEPHEN'S RING!
YOU THOUGHT IT WAS LOST FOREVER, BUT YOU FOUND IT...IT WAS JUST WAITING FOR YOUR HAND TO COME BACK INTO THE LIGHT.
THEY WERE ALL WAITING FOR YOUR HAND TO HELP THEM UP. SIMPLE METAL RINGS, BUT MORE MAGICAL THAN ANYTHING ELSE...
...BECAUSE THEY HOLD THE POWER OF EMOTIONS!
IT'S THE END FOR HER... A YOUNG HEART WON'T BE ABLE TO RESIST!

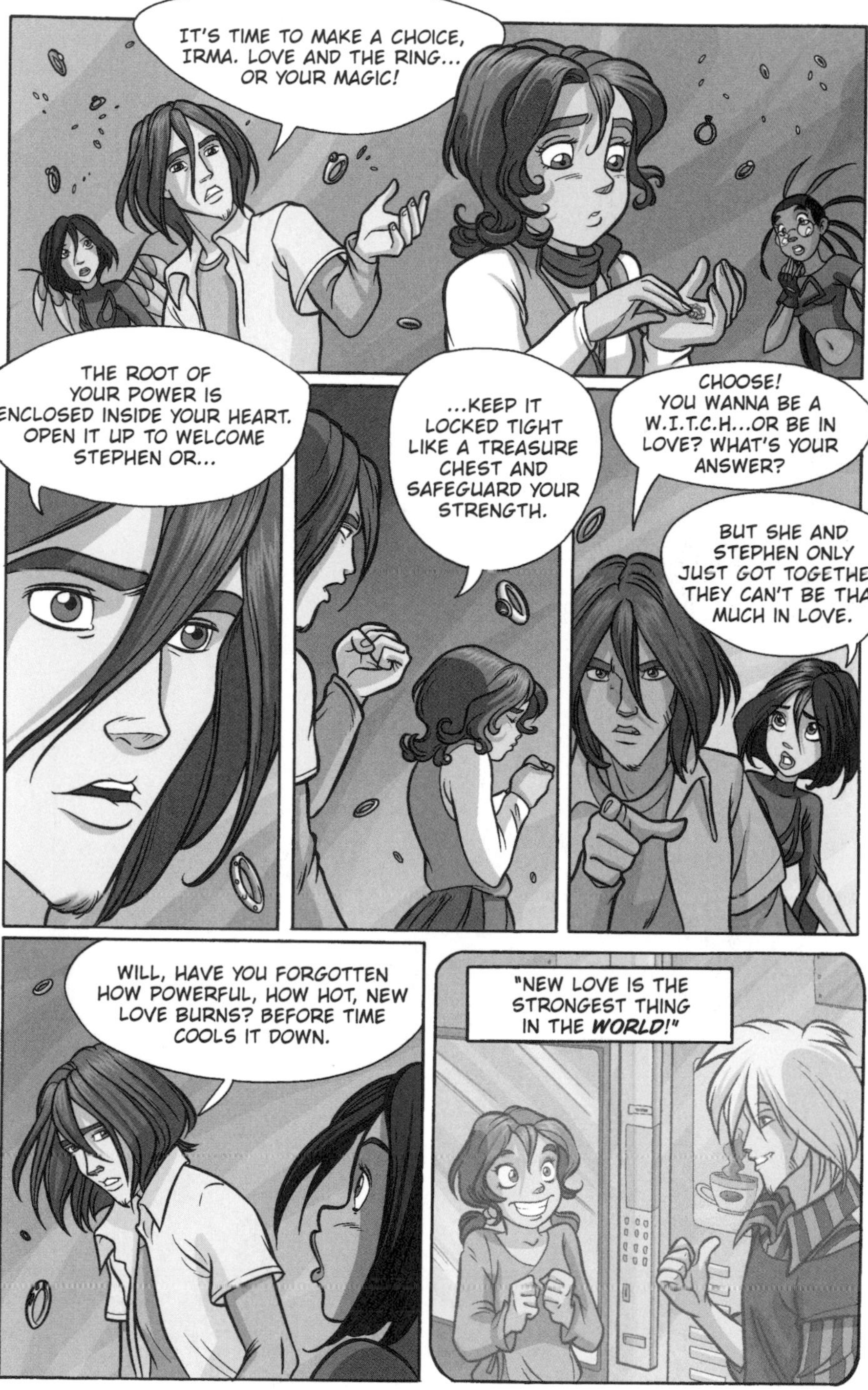
IT'S TIME TO MAKE A CHOICE, IRMA. LOVE AND THE RING... OR YOUR MAGIC!
THE ROOT OF YOUR POWER IS ENCLOSED INSIDE YOUR HEART. OPEN IT UP TO WELCOME STEPHEN OR...
...KEEP IT LOCKED TIGHT LIKE A TREASURE CHEST AND SAFEGUARD YOUR STRENGTH.
CHOOSE! YOU WANNA BE A W.I.T.C.H...OR BE IN LOVE? WHAT'S YOUR ANSWER?
BUT SHE AND STEPHEN ONLY JUST GOT TOGETHER. THEY CAN'T BE THAT MUCH IN LOVE.
WILL, HAVE YOU FORGOTTEN HOW POWERFUL, HOW HOT, NEW LOVE BURNS? BEFORE TIME COOLS IT DOWN.
"NEW LOVE IS THE STRONGEST THING IN THE WORLD!"

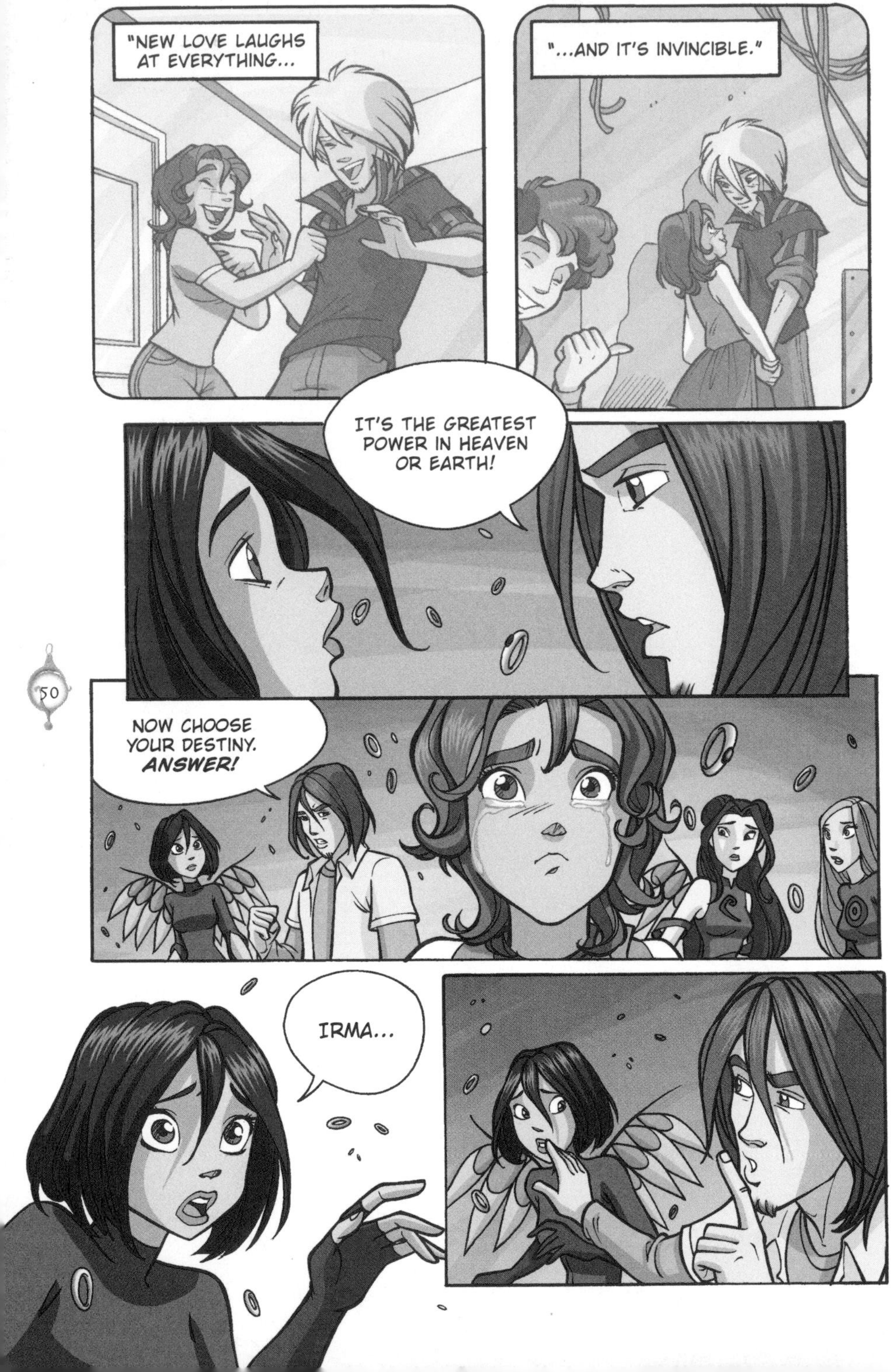
"NEW LOVE LAUGHS AT EVERYTHING...
"...AND IT'S INVINCIBLE."
IT'S THE GREATEST POWER IN HEAVEN OR EARTH!
NOW CHOOSE YOUR DESTINY. ANSWER!
IRMA...

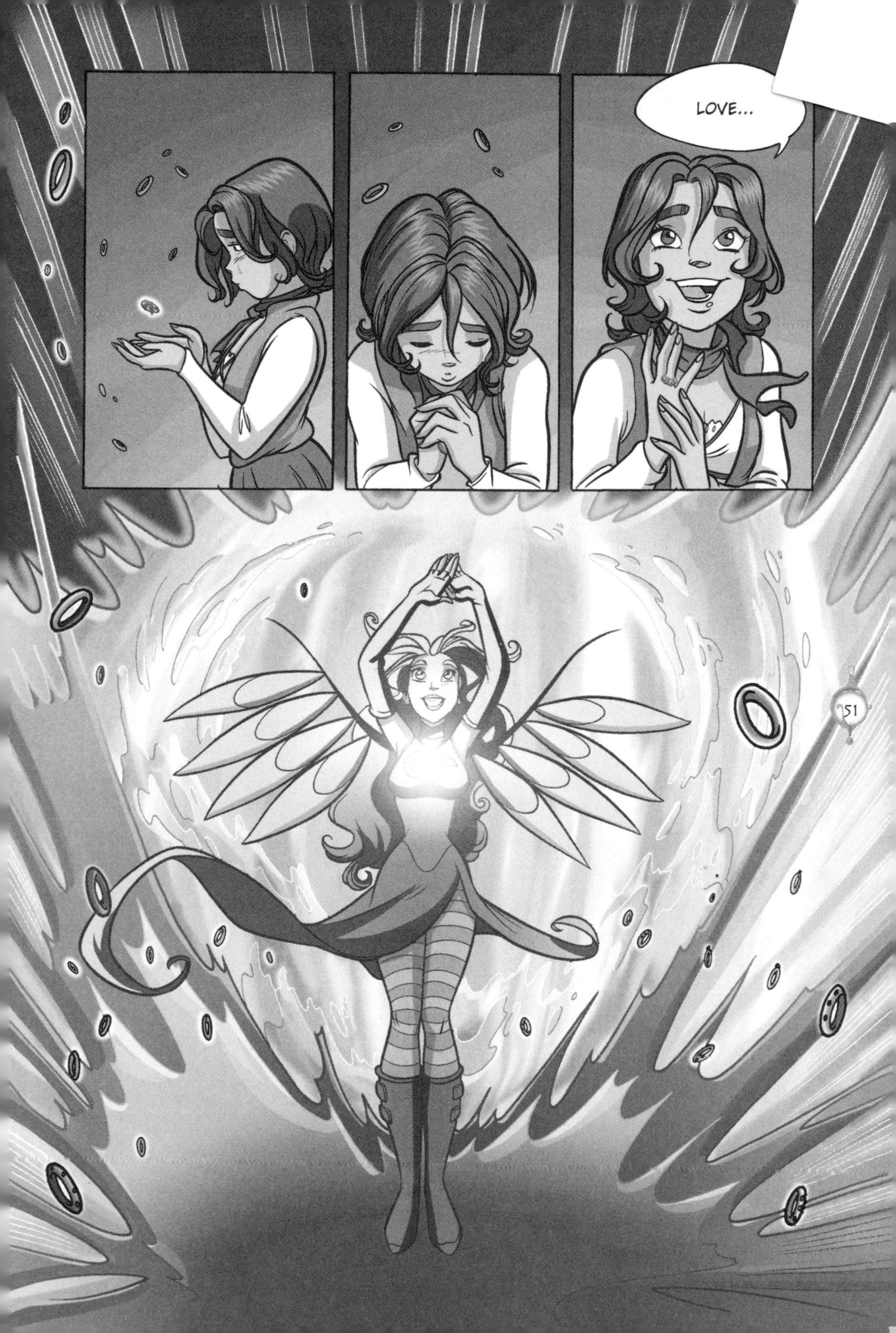
LOVE...

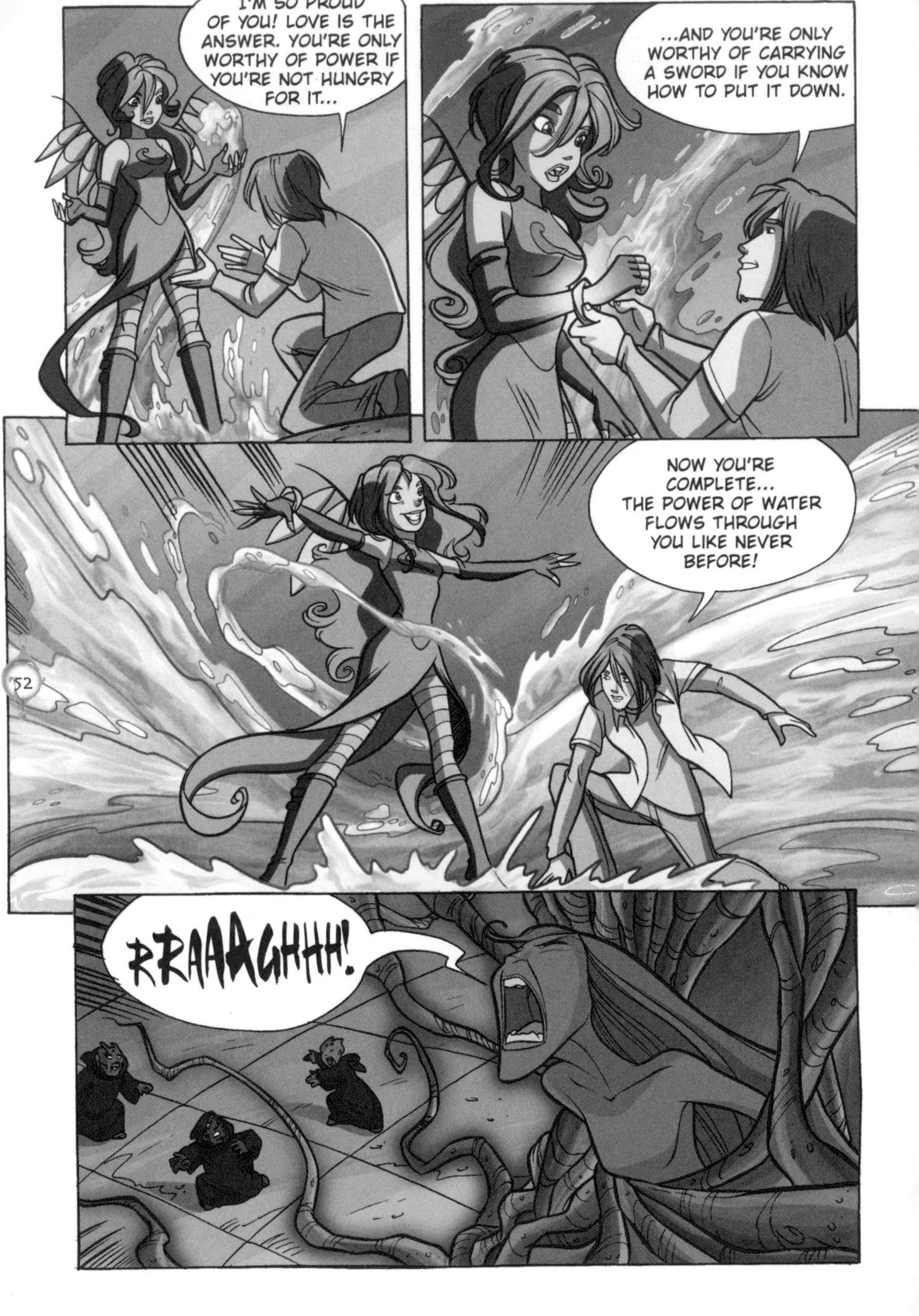
I'M SO PROUD OF YOU! LOVE IS THE ANSWER. YOU'RE ONLY WORTHY OF POWER IF YOU'RE NOT HUNGRY FOR IT...
...AND YOU'RE ONLY WORTHY OF CARRYING A SWORD IF YOU KNOW HOW TO PUT IT DOWN.
NOW YOU'RE COMPLETE... THE POWER OF WATER FLOWS THROUGH YOU LIKE NEVER BEFORE!
RRAAAGHHH!

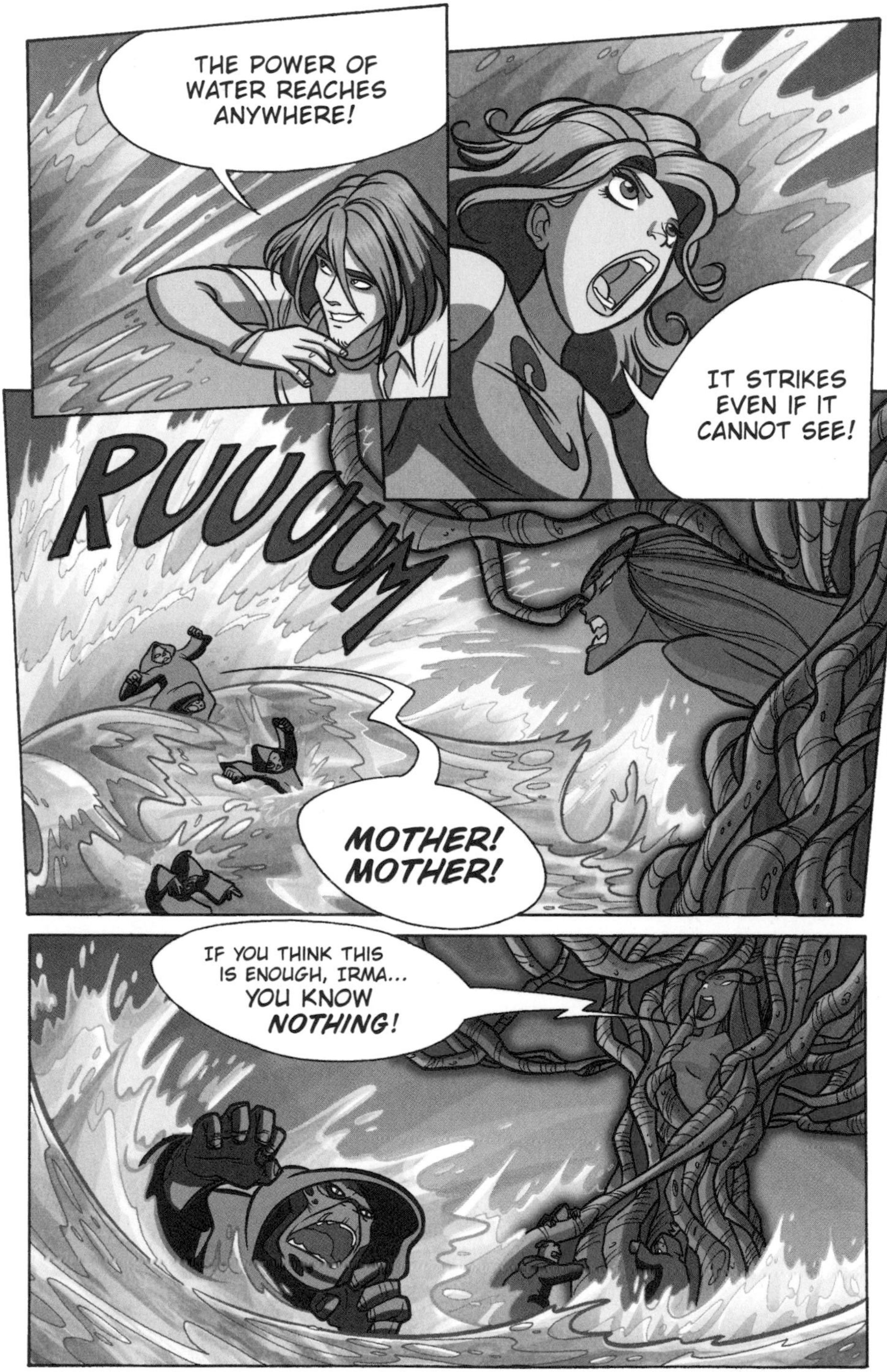
THE POWER OF WATER REACHES ANYWHERE!
IT STRIKES EVEN IF IT CANNOT SEE!
RUUUUM
MOTHER! MOTHER!
IF YOU THINK THIS IS ENOUGH, IRMA... YOU KNOW NOTHING!

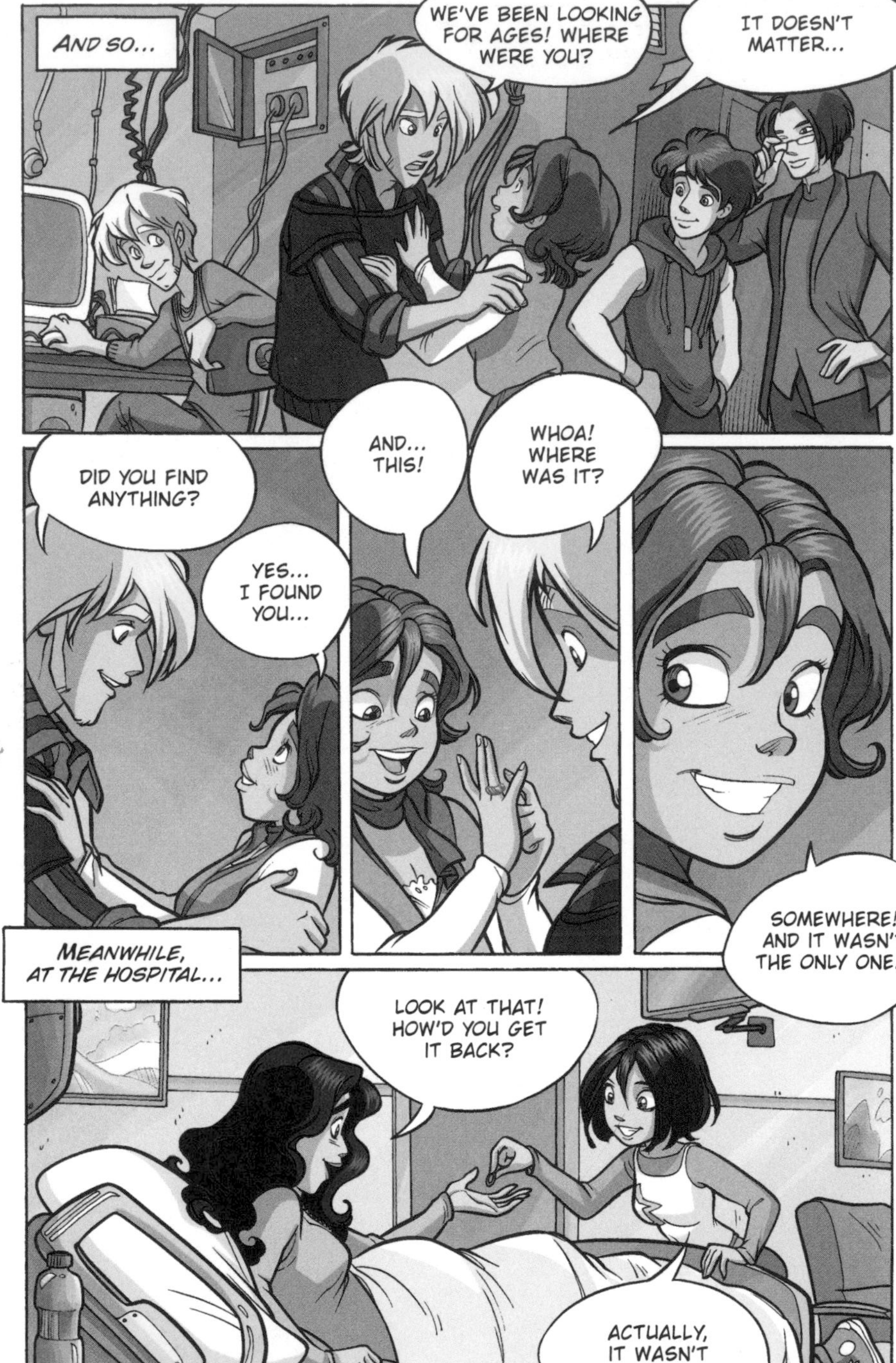
AND SO...
WE'VE BEEN LOOKING FOR AGES! WHERE WERE YOU?
IT DOESN'T MATTER...
DID YOU FIND ANYTHING?
YES... I FOUND YOU...
AND... THIS!
WHOA! WHERE WAS IT?
SOMEWHERE! AND IT WASN'T THE ONLY ONE...
MEANWHILE, AT THE HOSPITAL...
LOOK AT THAT! HOW'D YOU GET IT BACK?
ACTUALLY, IT WASN'T ME...

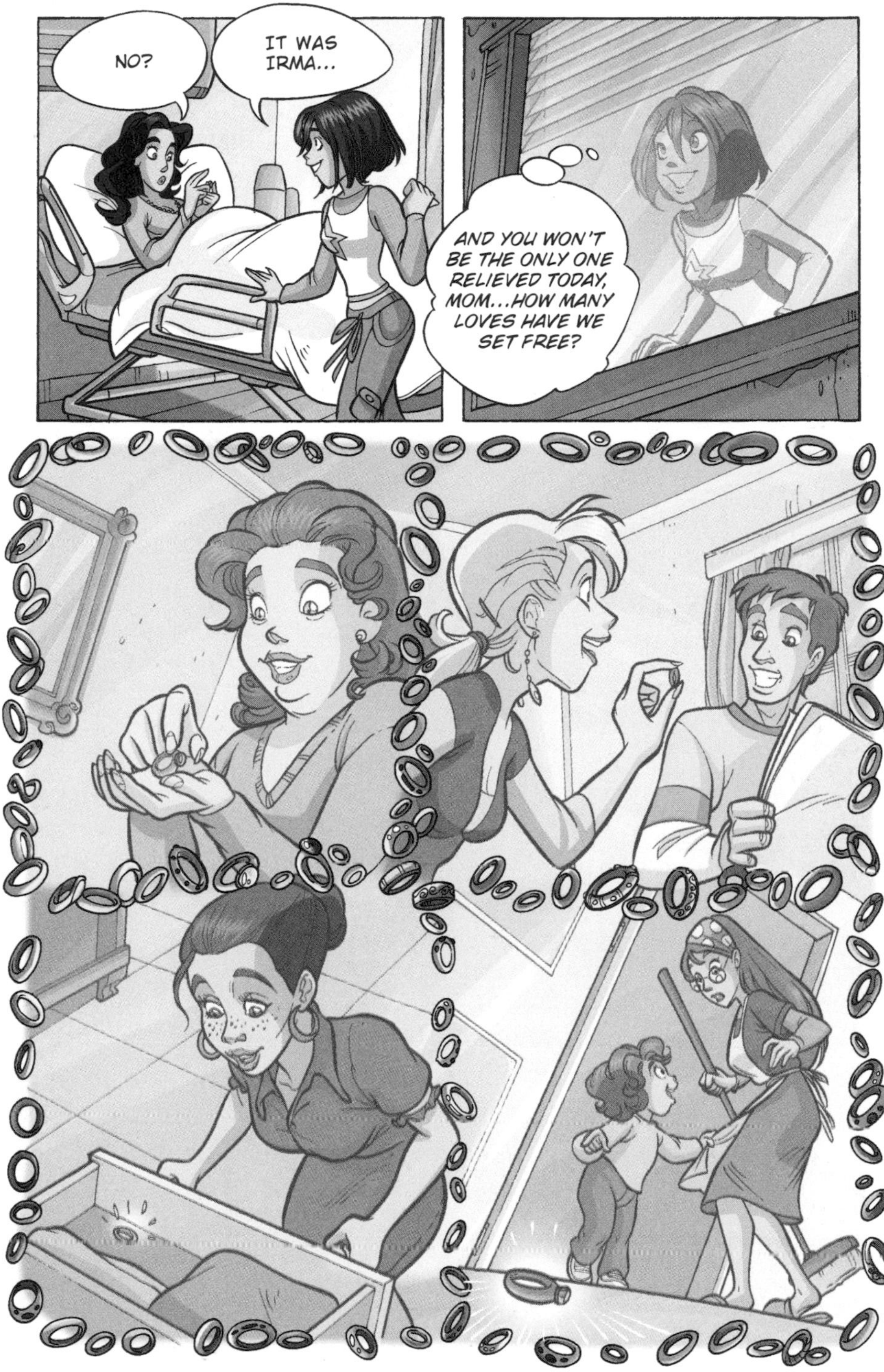
NO?
IT WAS IRMA...
AND YOU WON'T BE THE ONLY ONE RELIEVED TODAY, MOM...HOW MANY LOVES HAVE WE SET FREE?

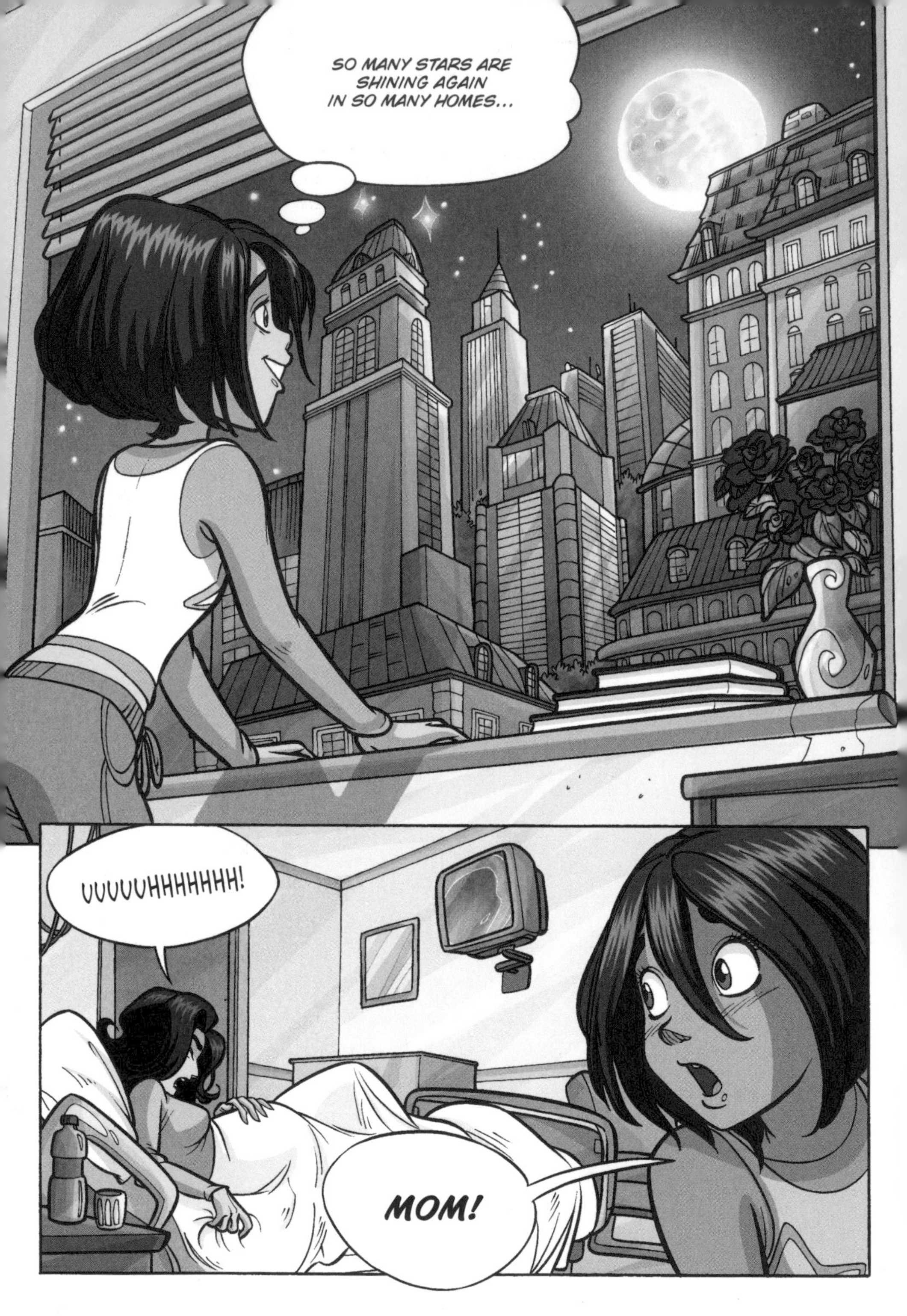
SO MANY STARS ARE SHINING AGAIN IN SO MANY HOMES...
UUUUUHHHHHHH!
MOM!

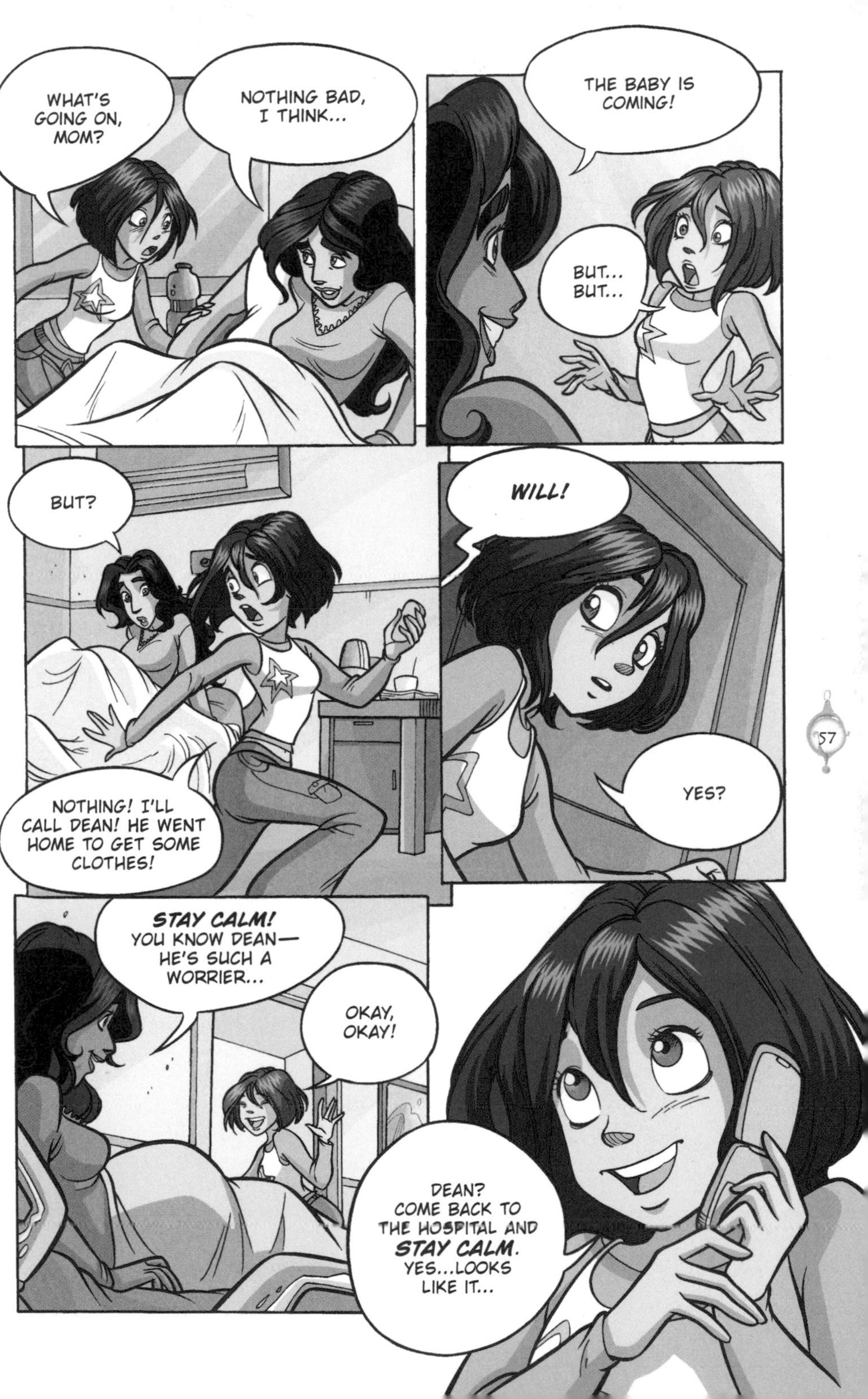
WHAT'S GOING ON, MOM?
NOTHING BAD, I THINK...
THE BABY IS COMING!
BUT... BUT...
BUT?
NOTHING! I'LL CALL DEAN! HE WENT HOME TO GET SOME CLOTHES!
WILL!
YES?
STAY CALM! YOU KNOW DEAN— HE'S SUCH A WORRIER...
OKAY, OKAY!
DEAN? COME BACK TO THE HOSPITAL AND STAY CALM. YES...LOOKS LIKE IT...

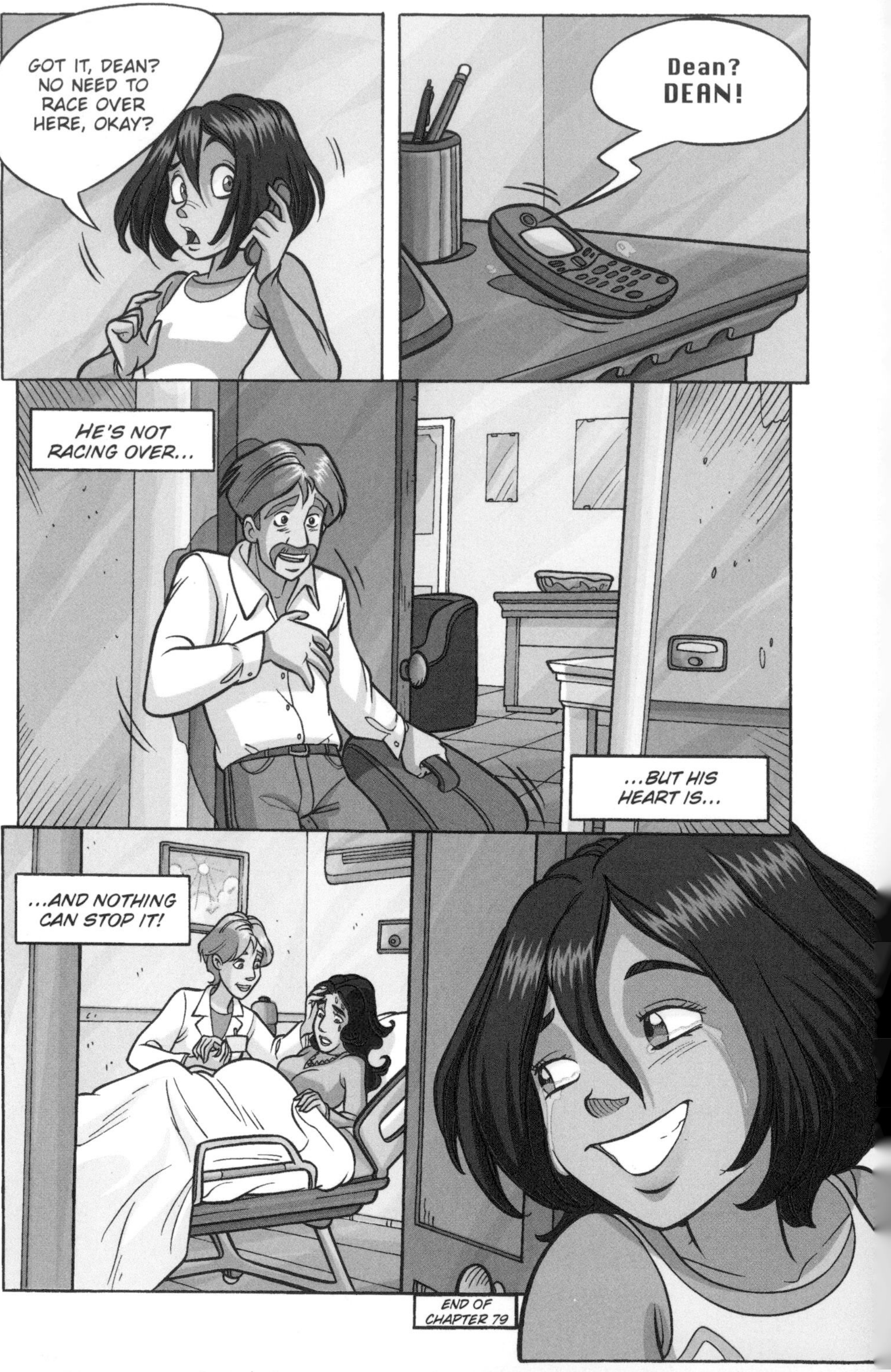
GOT IT, DEAN? NO NEED TO RACE OVER HERE, OKAY?
Dean? DEAN!
HE'S NOT RACING OVER...
...BUT HIS HEART IS...
...AND NOTHING CAN STOP IT!
END OF CHAPTER 79

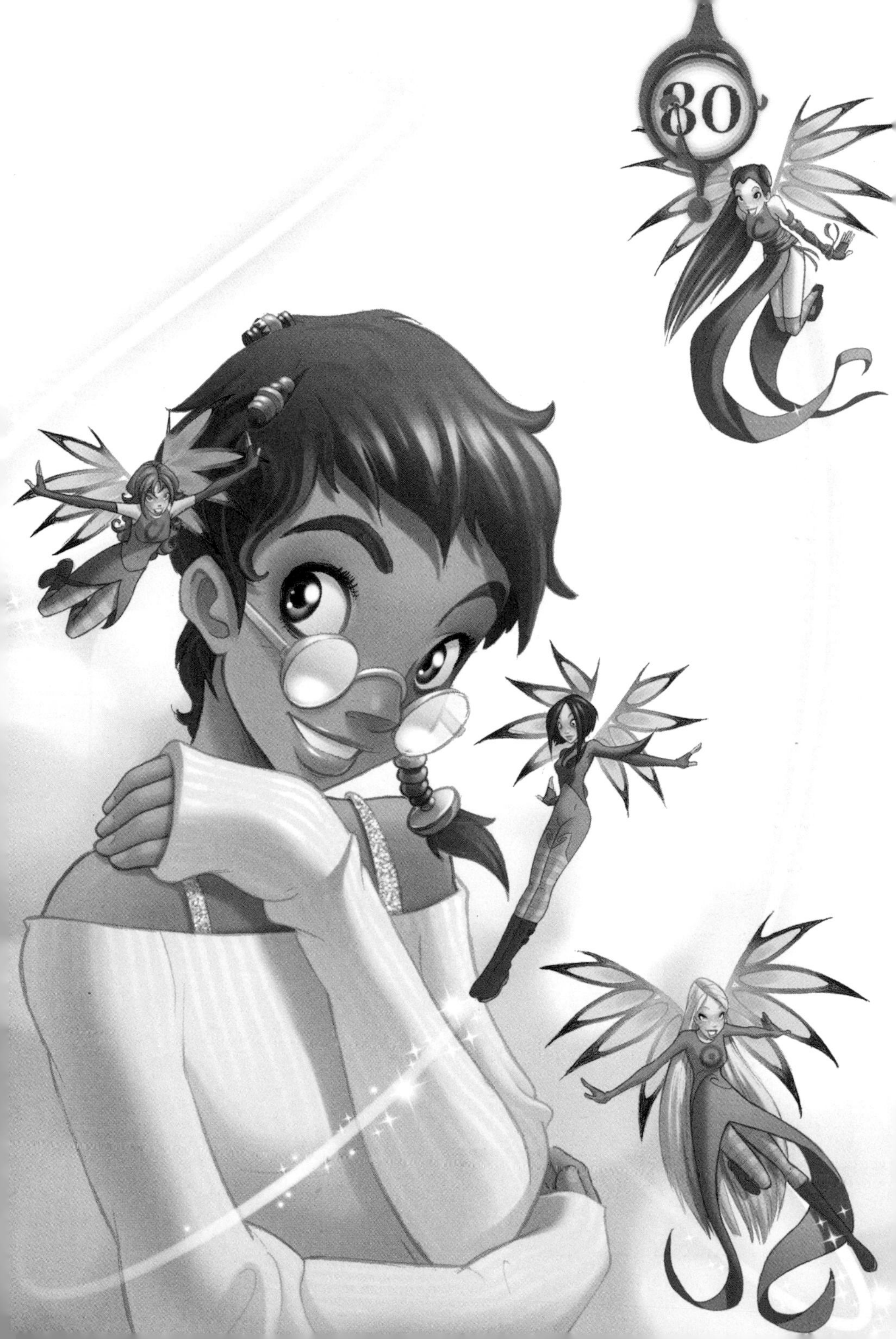
30

# Emotions

"I have a brother! I still can't believe it!"

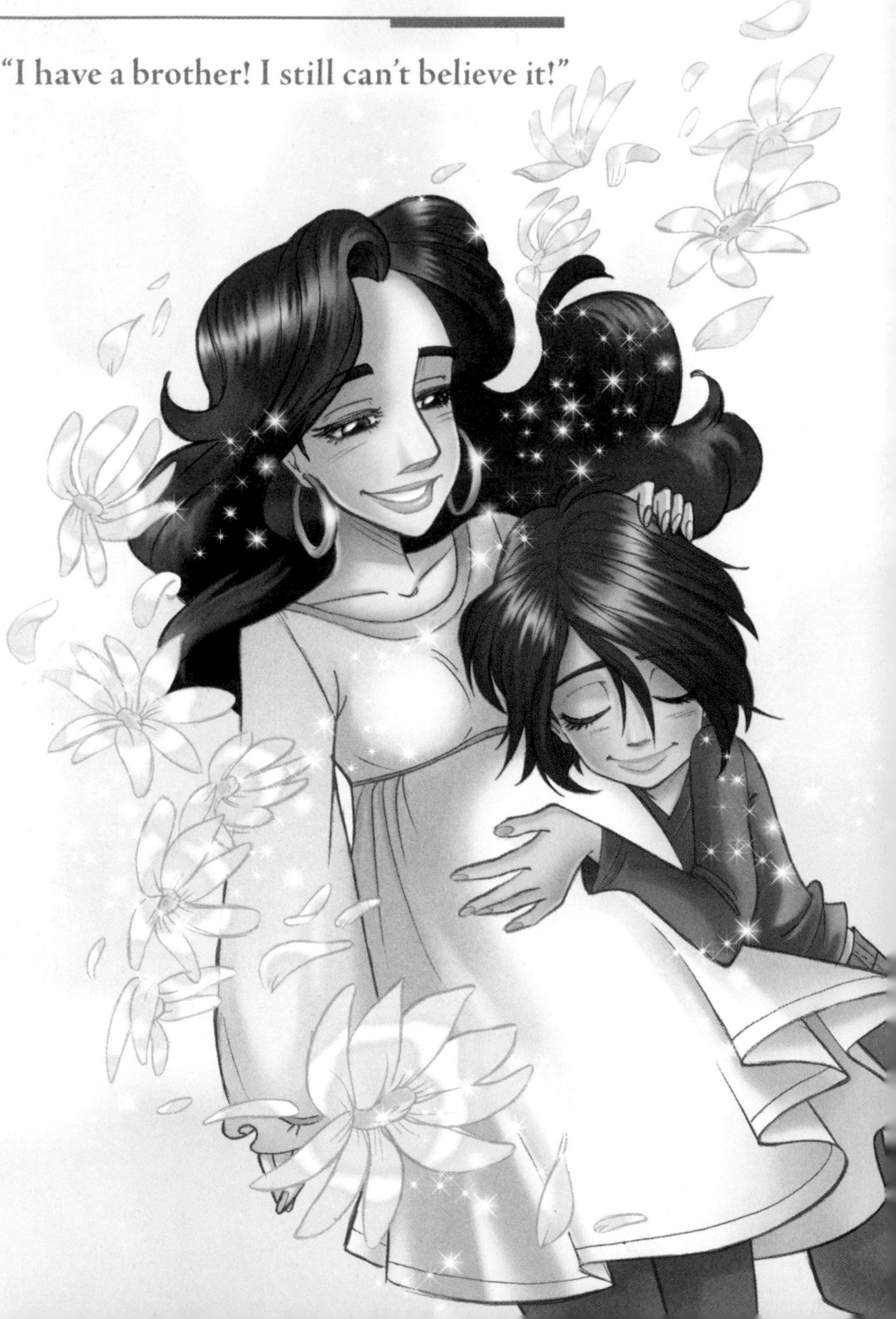

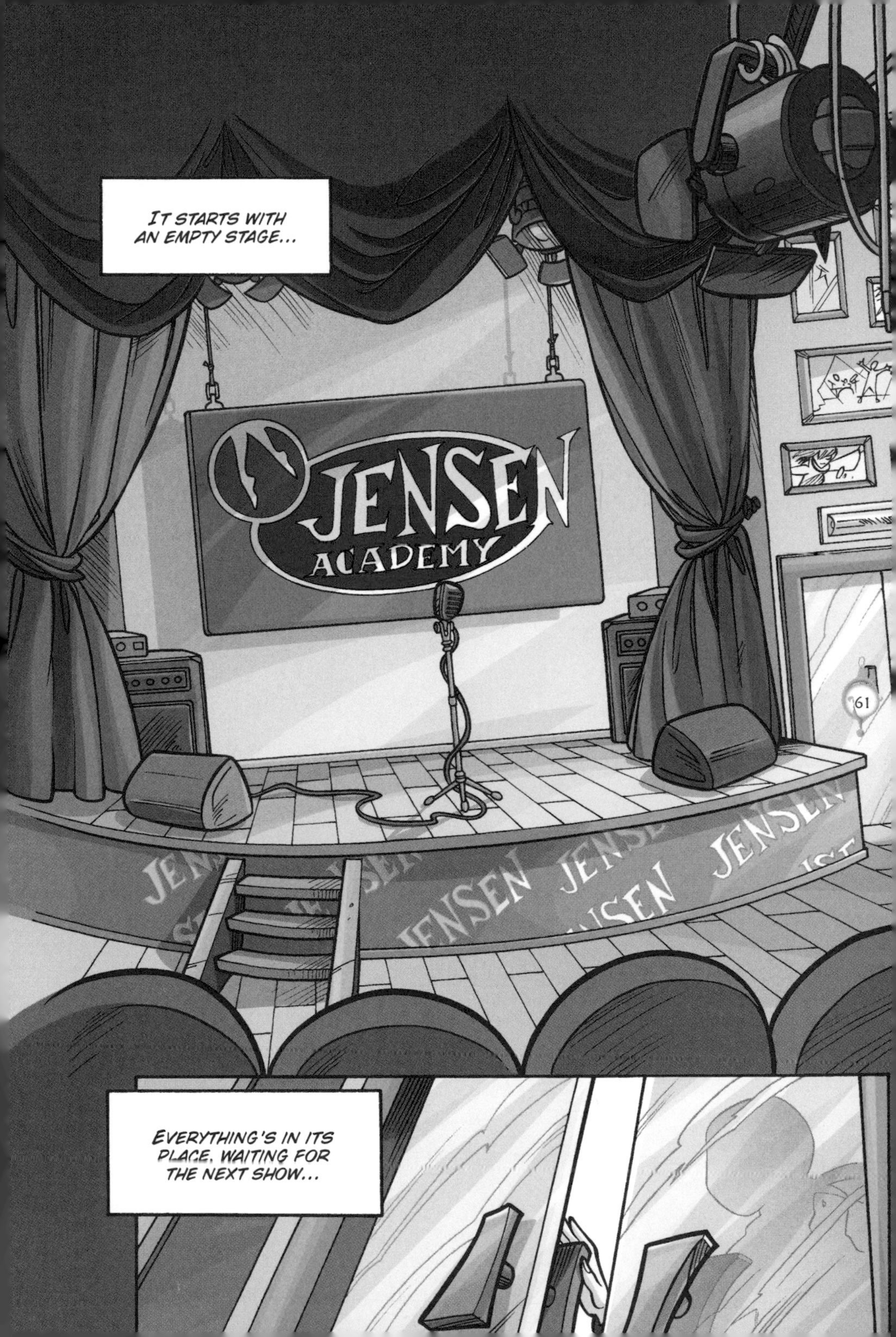
IT STARTS WITH AN EMPTY STAGE...
JENSEN
ACADEMY
EVERYTHING'S IN ITS PLACE, WAITING FOR THE NEXT SHOW...

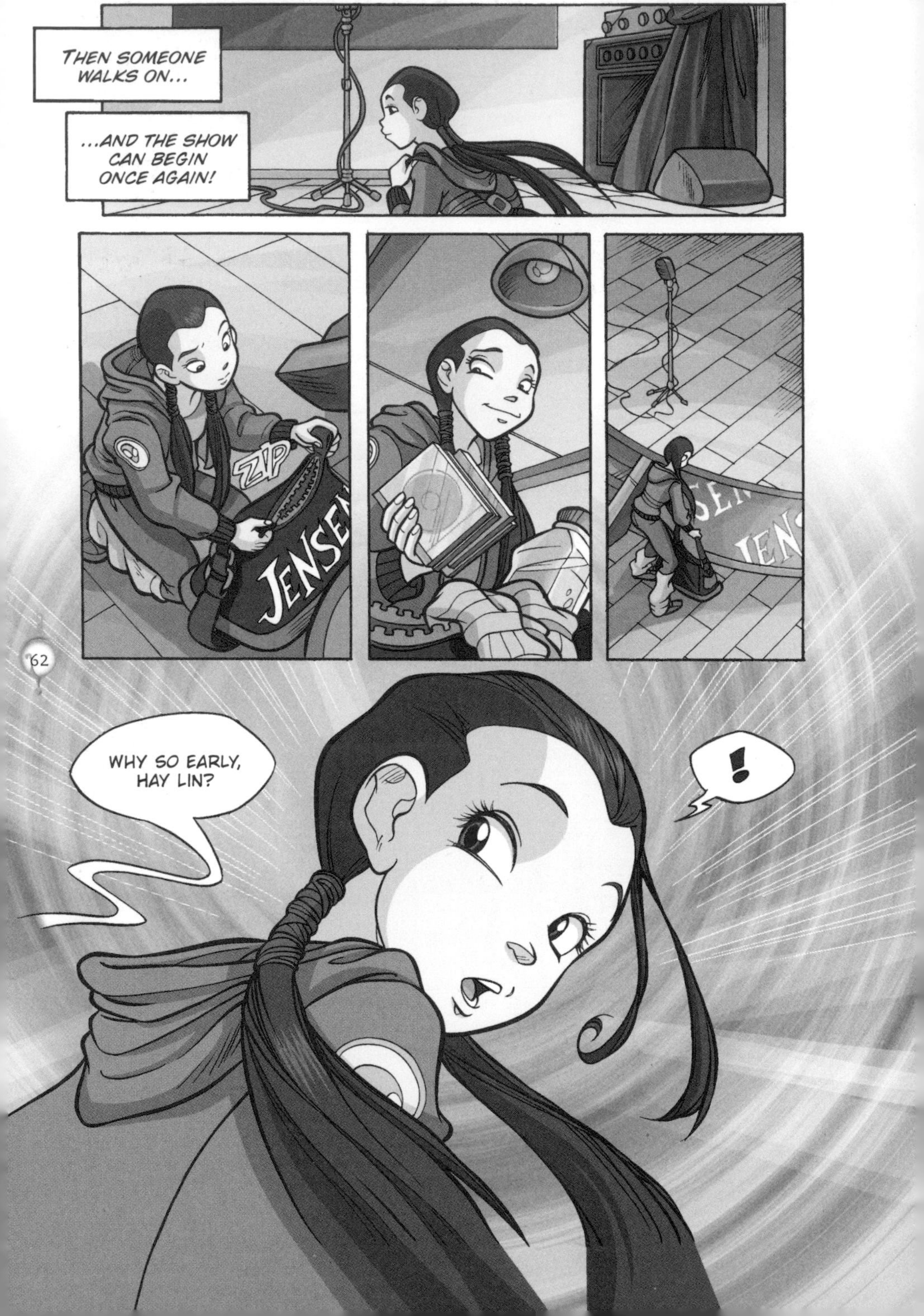
THEN SOMEONE WALKS ON...
...AND THE SHOW CAN BEGIN ONCE AGAIN!
ZIP
JENSEN
JENSEN
WHY SO EARLY, HAY LIN?
!

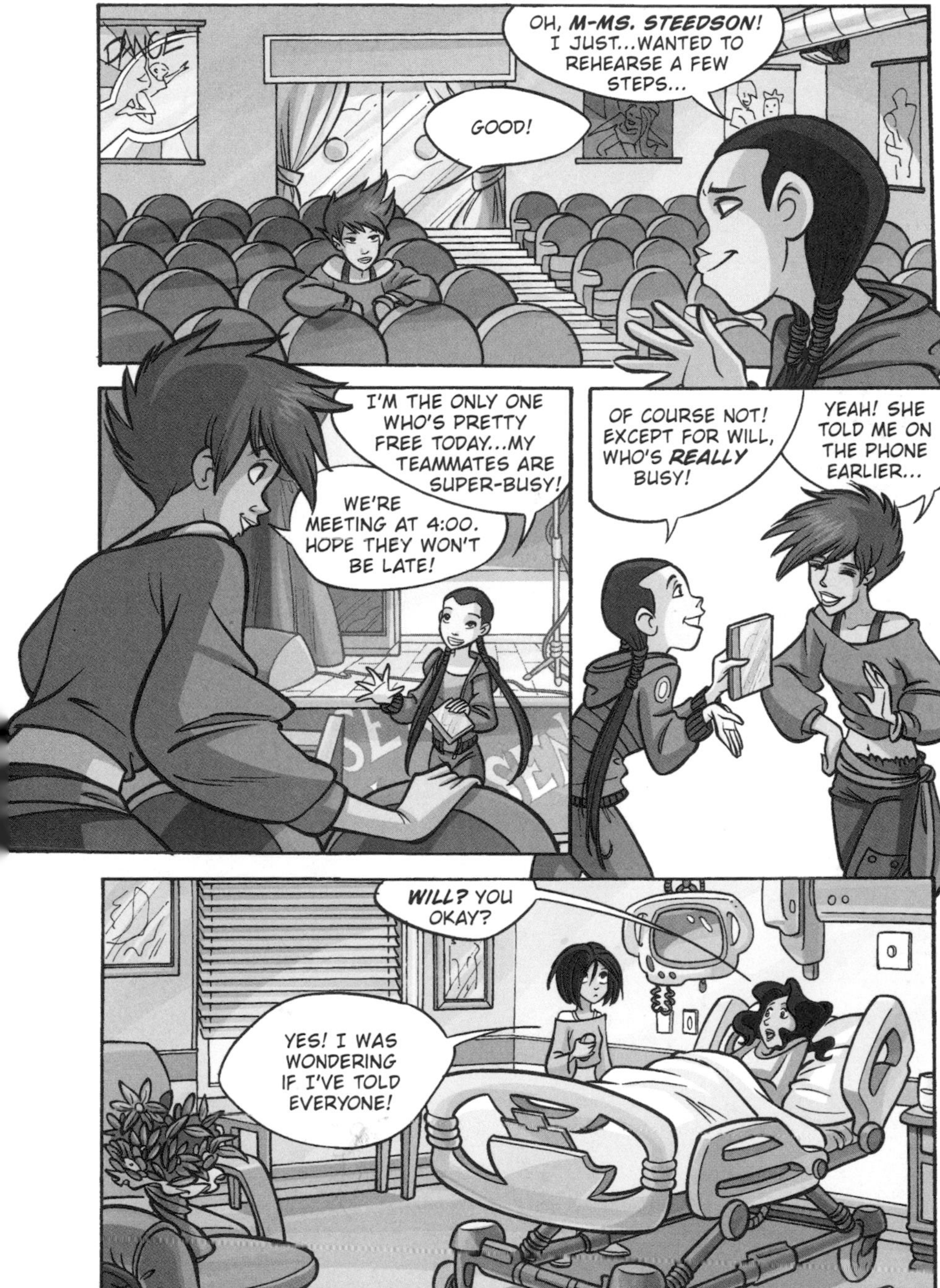
OH, M-MS. STEEDSON! I JUST...WANTED TO REHEARSE A FEW STEPS...
GOOD!
I'M THE ONLY ONE WHO'S PRETTY FREE TODAY...MY TEAMMATES ARE SUPER-BUSY!
WE'RE MEETING AT 4:00. HOPE THEY WON'T BE LATE!
OF COURSE NOT! EXCEPT FOR WILL, WHO'S REALLY BUSY!
YEAH! SHE TOLD ME ON THE PHONE EARLIER...
WILL? YOU OKAY?
YES! I WAS WONDERING IF I'VE TOLD EVERYONE!

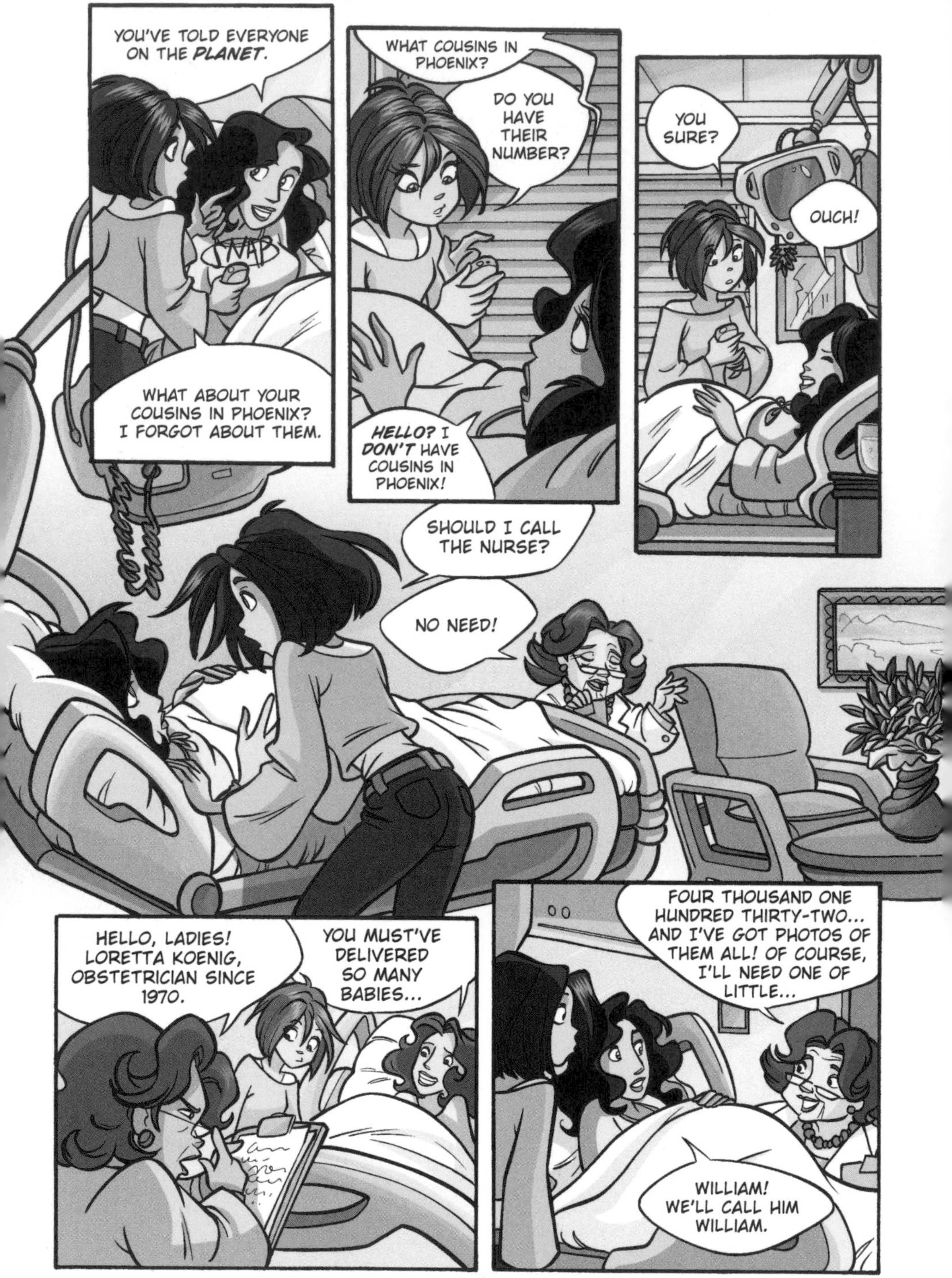
YOU'VE TOLD EVERYONE ON THE *PLANET*.
SNAP
WHAT ABOUT YOUR COUSINS IN PHOENIX? I FORGOT ABOUT THEM.
WHAT COUSINS IN PHOENIX?
DO YOU HAVE THEIR NUMBER?
*HELLO?* I *DON'T* HAVE COUSINS IN PHOENIX!
YOU SURE?
OUCH!
SHOULD I CALL THE NURSE?
NO NEED!
HELLO, LADIES! LORETTA KOENIG, OBSTETRICIAN SINCE 1970.
YOU MUST'VE DELIVERED SO MANY BABIES...
FOUR THOUSAND ONE HUNDRED THIRTY-TWO... AND I'VE GOT PHOTOS OF THEM ALL! OF COURSE, I'LL NEED ONE OF LITTLE...
WILLIAM! WE'LL CALL HIM WILLIAM.

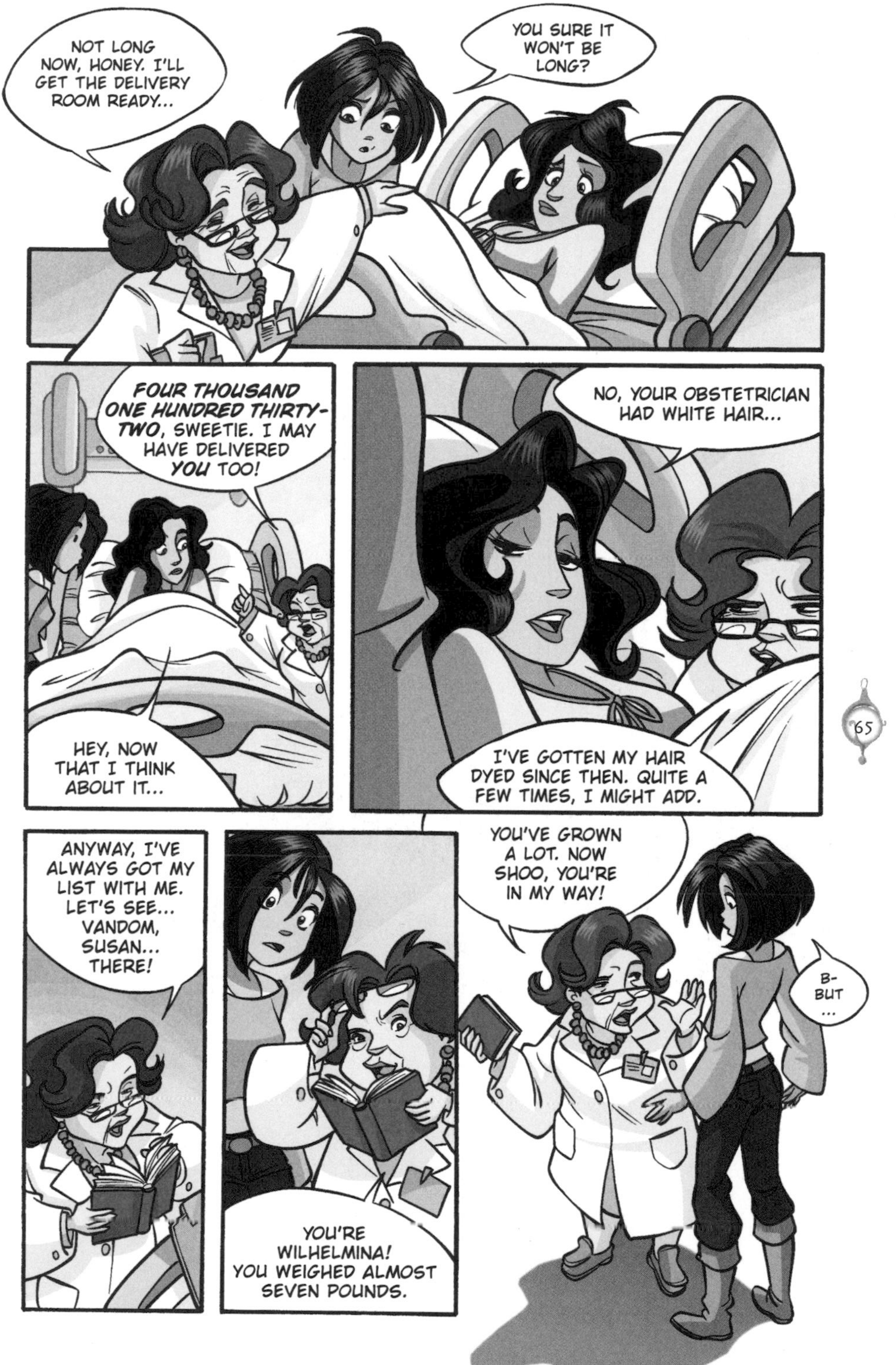
NOT LONG NOW, HONEY. I'LL GET THE DELIVERY ROOM READY...
YOU SURE IT WON'T BE LONG?
FOUR THOUSAND ONE HUNDRED THIRTY-TWO, SWEETIE. I MAY HAVE DELIVERED YOU TOO!
HEY, NOW THAT I THINK ABOUT IT...
NO, YOUR OBSTETRICIAN HAD WHITE HAIR...
I'VE GOTTEN MY HAIR DYED SINCE THEN. QUITE A FEW TIMES, I MIGHT ADD.
ANYWAY, I'VE ALWAYS GOT MY LIST WITH ME. LET'S SEE... VANDOM, SUSAN... THERE!
YOU'RE WILHELMINA! YOU WEIGHED ALMOST SEVEN POUNDS.
YOU'VE GROWN A LOT. NOW SHOO, YOU'RE IN MY WAY!
B-BUT ...

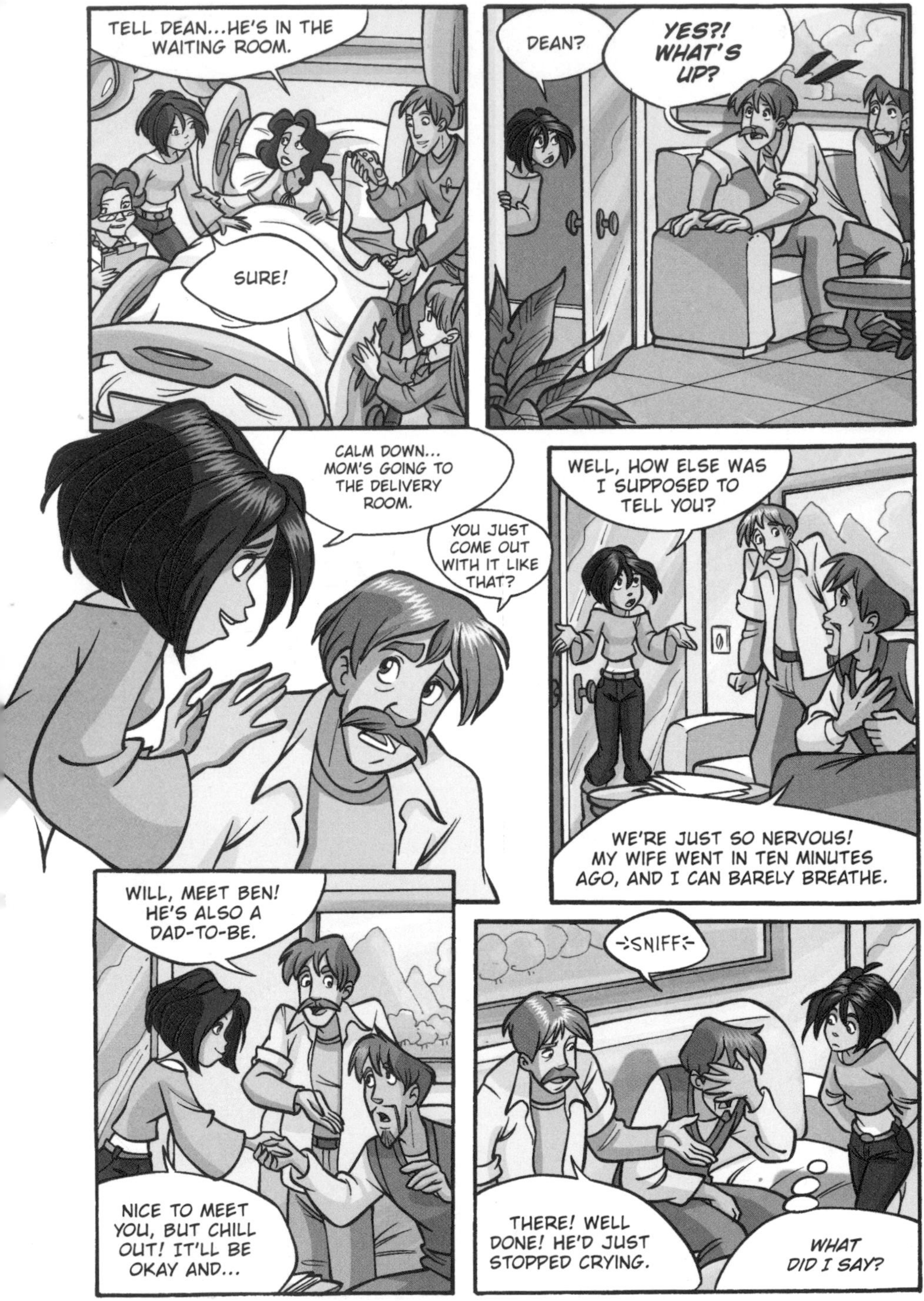
TELL DEAN...HE'S IN THE WAITING ROOM.
SURE!
DEAN?
YES?! WHAT'S UP?
CALM DOWN... MOM'S GOING TO THE DELIVERY ROOM.
YOU JUST COME OUT WITH IT LIKE THAT?
WELL, HOW ELSE WAS I SUPPOSED TO TELL YOU?
WE'RE JUST SO NERVOUS! MY WIFE WENT IN TEN MINUTES AGO, AND I CAN BARELY BREATHE.
WILL, MEET BEN! HE'S ALSO A DAD-TO-BE.
NICE TO MEET YOU, BUT CHILL OUT! IT'LL BE OKAY AND...
SNIFF
THERE! WELL DONE! HE'D JUST STOPPED CRYING.
WHAT DID I SAY?

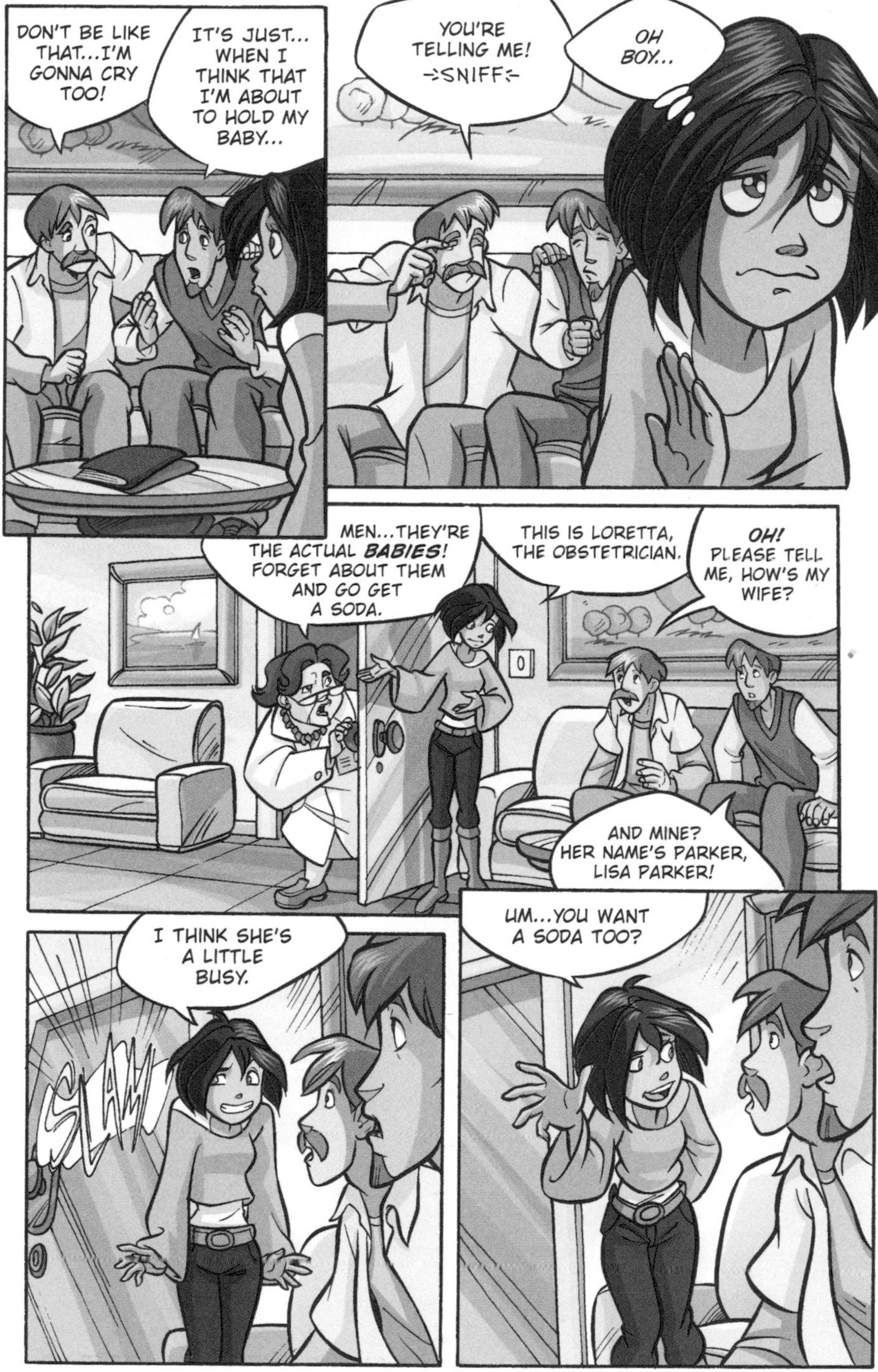
DON'T BE LIKE THAT...I'M GONNA CRY TOO!
IT'S JUST... WHEN I THINK THAT I'M ABOUT TO HOLD MY BABY...
YOU'RE TELLING ME! -SNIFF-
OH BOY...
MEN...THEY'RE THE ACTUAL BABIES! FORGET ABOUT THEM AND GO GET A SODA.
THIS IS LORETTA, THE OBSTETRICIAN.
OH! PLEASE TELL ME, HOW'S MY WIFE?
AND MINE? HER NAME'S PARKER, LISA PARKER!
I THINK SHE'S A LITTLE BUSY.
SLAM
UM...YOU WANT A SODA TOO?

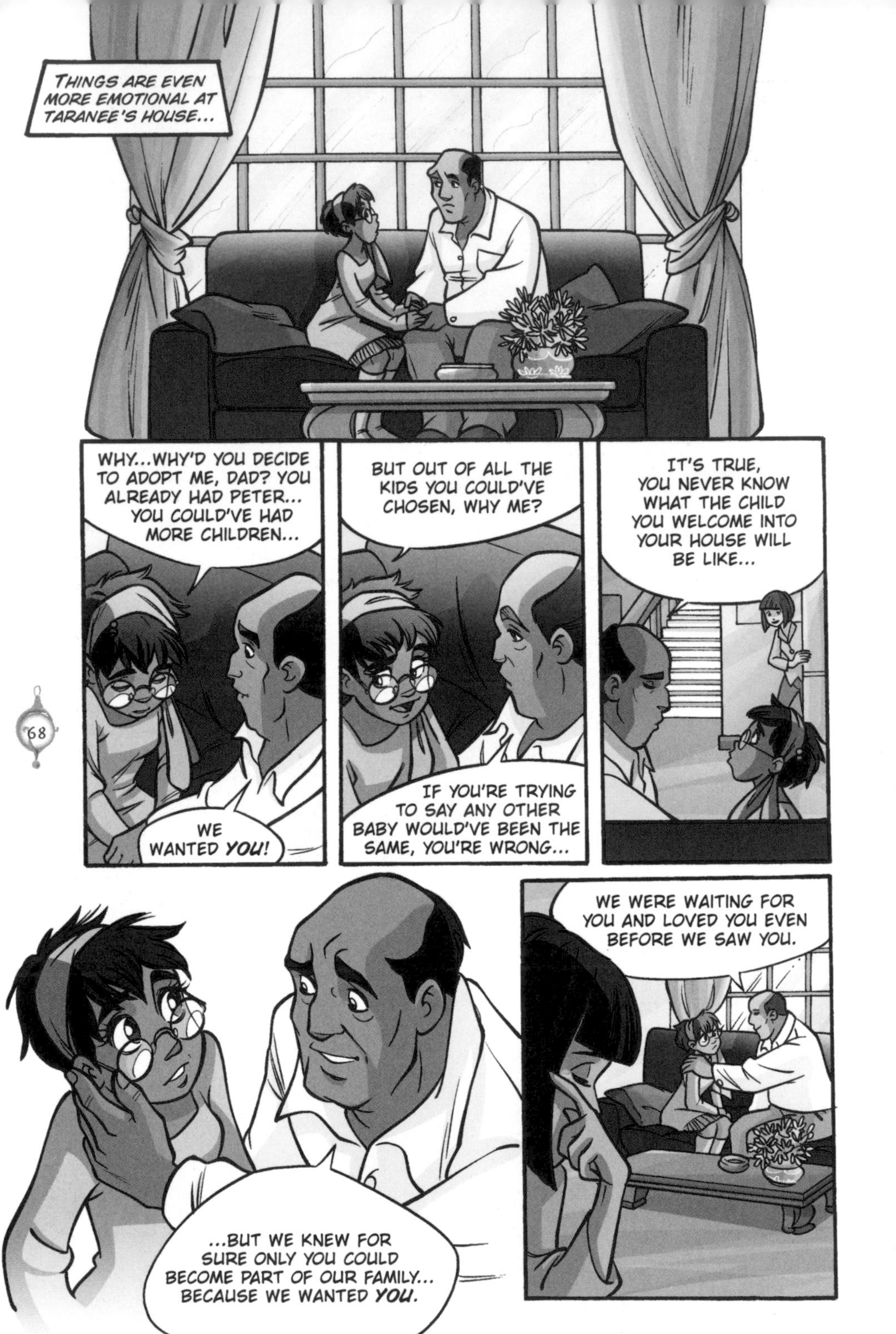
THINGS ARE EVEN MORE EMOTIONAL AT TARANEE'S HOUSE...
WHY...WHY'D YOU DECIDE TO ADOPT ME, DAD? YOU ALREADY HAD PETER... YOU COULD'VE HAD MORE CHILDREN...
WE WANTED YOU!
BUT OUT OF ALL THE KIDS YOU COULD'VE CHOSEN, WHY ME?
IF YOU'RE TRYING TO SAY ANY OTHER BABY WOULD'VE BEEN THE SAME, YOU'RE WRONG...
IT'S TRUE, YOU NEVER KNOW WHAT THE CHILD YOU WELCOME INTO YOUR HOUSE WILL BE LIKE...
WE WERE WAITING FOR YOU AND LOVED YOU EVEN BEFORE WE SAW YOU.
...BUT WE KNEW FOR SURE ONLY YOU COULD BECOME PART OF OUR FAMILY... BECAUSE WE WANTED YOU.

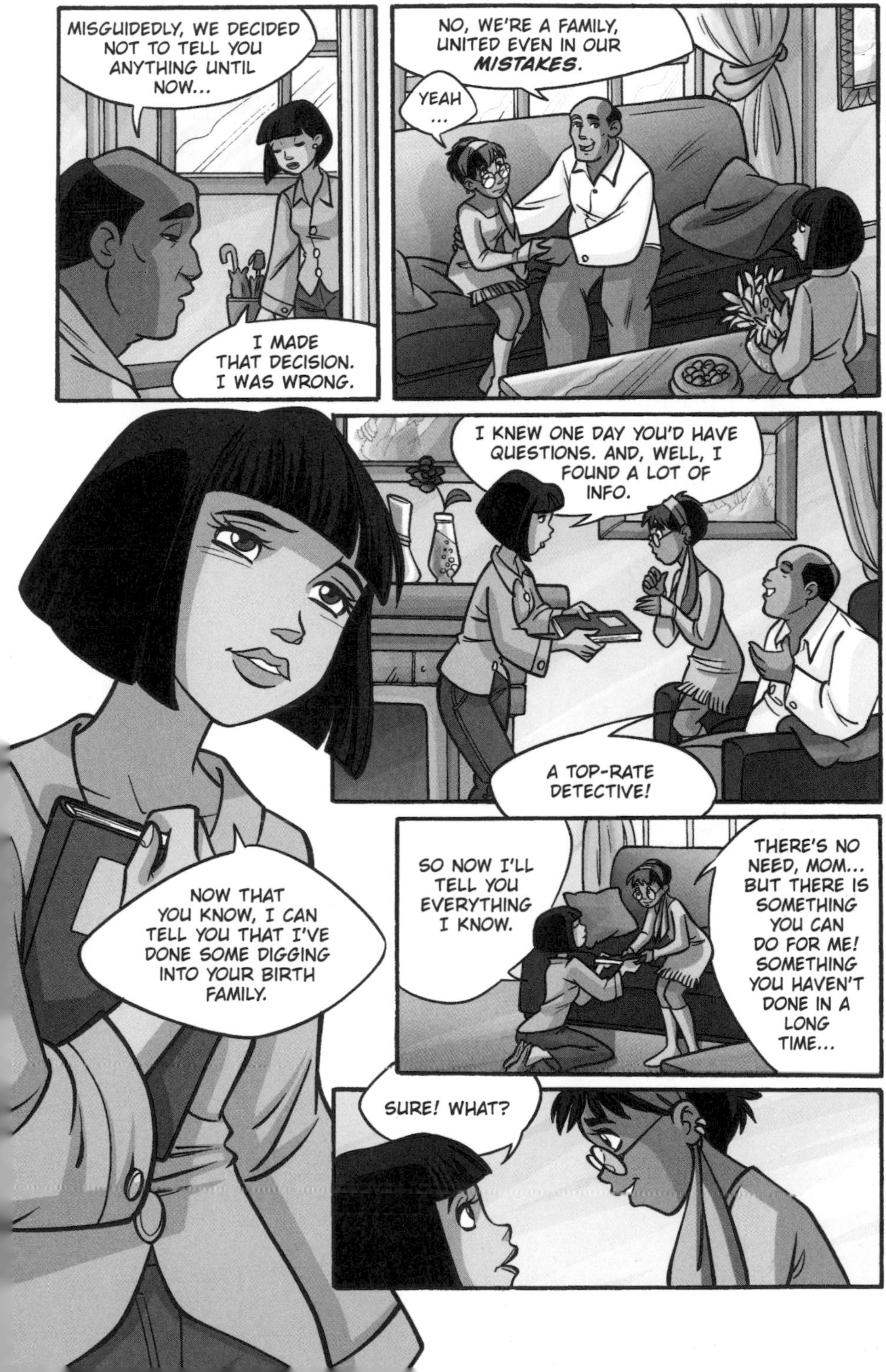
MISGUIDEDLY, WE DECIDED NOT TO TELL YOU ANYTHING UNTIL NOW...
I MADE THAT DECISION. I WAS WRONG.
NO, WE'RE A FAMILY, UNITED EVEN IN OUR *MISTAKES*.
YEAH ...
I KNEW ONE DAY YOU'D HAVE QUESTIONS. AND, WELL, I FOUND A LOT OF INFO.
A TOP-RATE DETECTIVE!
NOW THAT YOU KNOW, I CAN TELL YOU THAT I'VE DONE SOME DIGGING INTO YOUR BIRTH FAMILY.
SO NOW I'LL TELL YOU EVERYTHING I KNOW.
THERE'S NO NEED, MOM... BUT THERE IS SOMETHING YOU CAN DO FOR ME! SOMETHING YOU HAVEN'T DONE IN A LONG TIME...
SURE! WHAT?

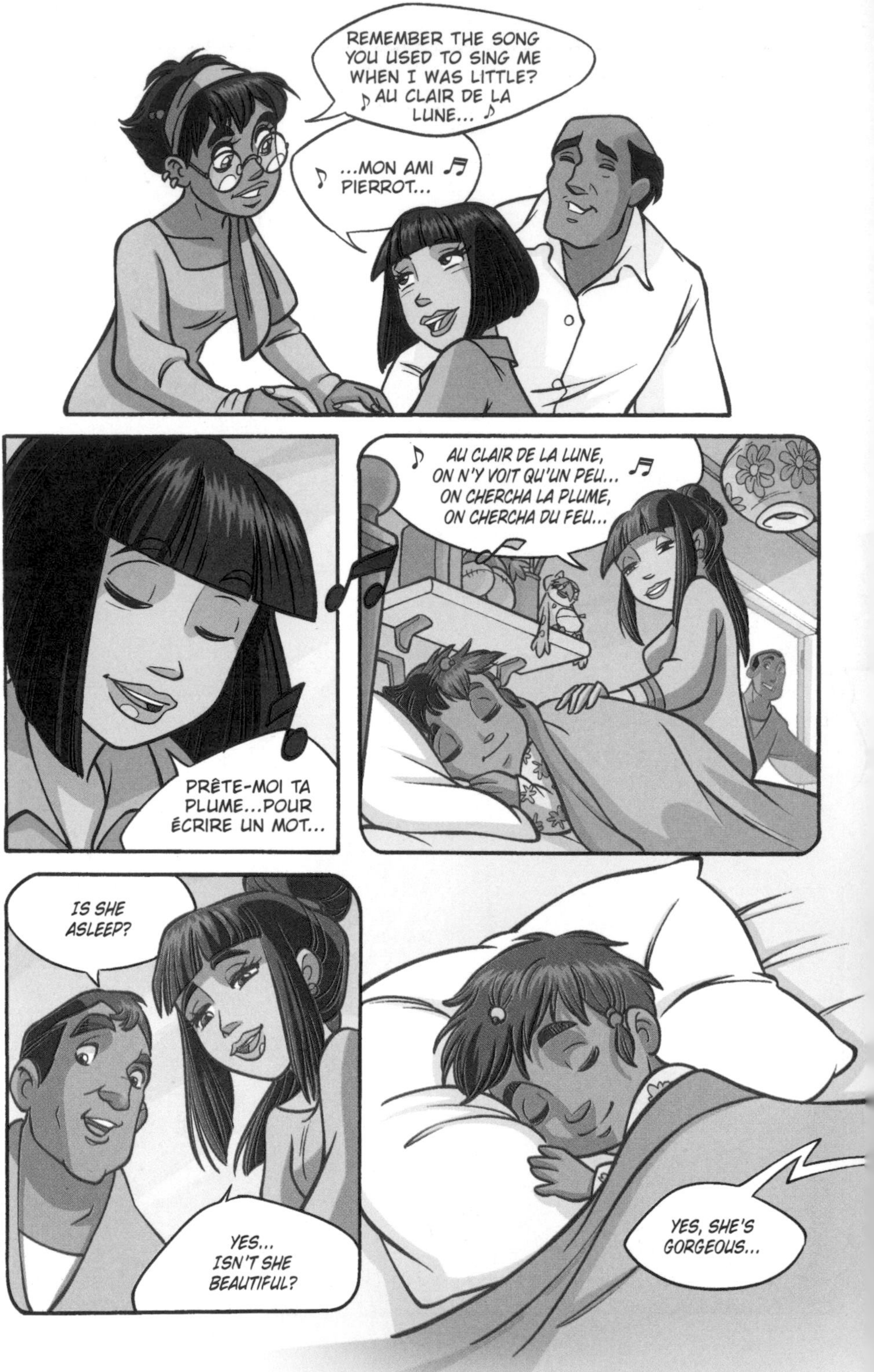
REMEMBER THE SONG YOU USED TO SING ME WHEN I WAS LITTLE? AU CLAIR DE LA LUNE...
...MON AMI PIERROT...
PRÊTE-MOI TA PLUME...POUR ÉCRIRE UN MOT...
AU CLAIR DE LA LUNE, ON N'Y VOIT QU'UN PEU... ON CHERCHA LA PLUME, ON CHERCHA DU FEU...
IS SHE ASLEEP?
YES... ISN'T SHE BEAUTIFUL?
YES, SHE'S GORGEOUS...

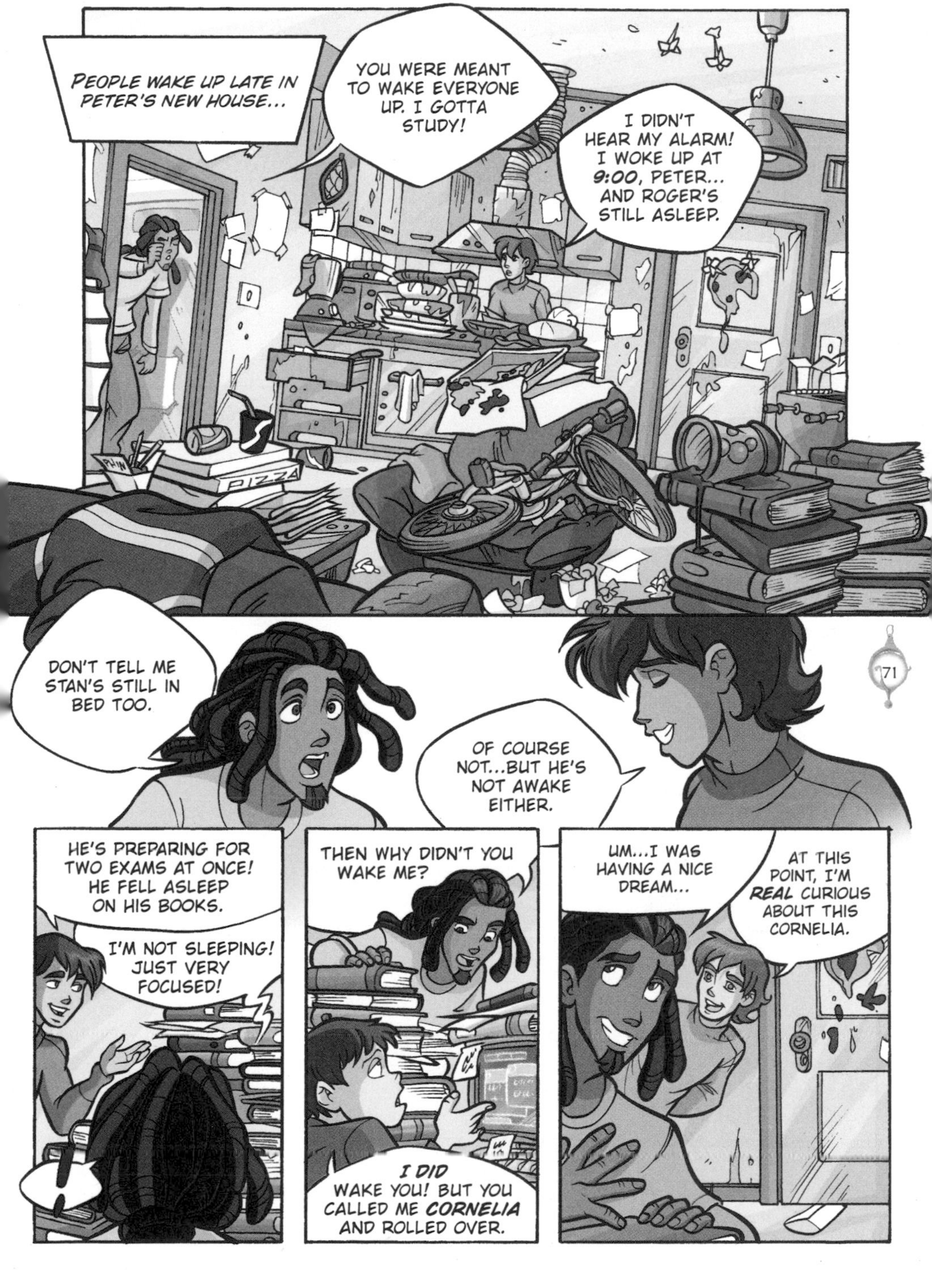
PEOPLE WAKE UP LATE IN PETER'S NEW HOUSE...
YOU WERE MEANT TO WAKE EVERYONE UP. I GOTTA STUDY!
I DIDN'T HEAR MY ALARM! I WOKE UP AT 9:00, PETER... AND ROGER'S STILL ASLEEP.
DON'T TELL ME STAN'S STILL IN BED TOO.
OF COURSE NOT...BUT HE'S NOT AWAKE EITHER.
HE'S PREPARING FOR TWO EXAMS AT ONCE! HE FELL ASLEEP ON HIS BOOKS.
I'M NOT SLEEPING! JUST VERY FOCUSED!
!
THEN WHY DIDN'T YOU WAKE ME?
I DID WAKE YOU! BUT YOU CALLED ME CORNELIA AND ROLLED OVER.
UM...I WAS HAVING A NICE DREAM...
AT THIS POINT, I'M REAL CURIOUS ABOUT THIS CORNELIA.

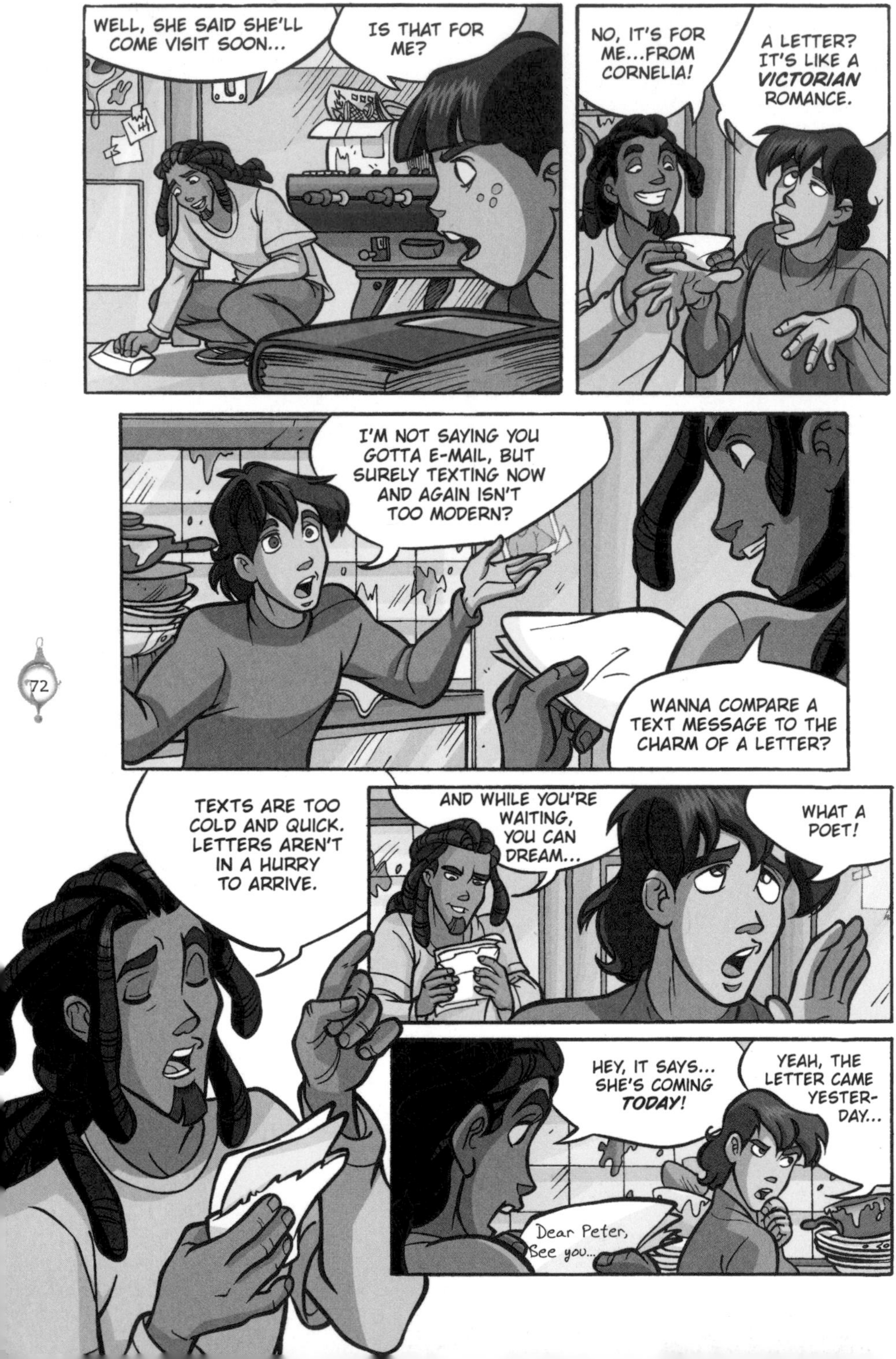
WELL, SHE SAID SHE'LL COME VISIT SOON...
IS THAT FOR ME?
NO, IT'S FOR ME...FROM CORNELIA!
A LETTER? IT'S LIKE A *VICTORIAN* ROMANCE.
I'M NOT SAYING YOU GOTTA E-MAIL, BUT SURELY TEXTING NOW AND AGAIN ISN'T TOO MODERN?
WANNA COMPARE A TEXT MESSAGE TO THE CHARM OF A LETTER?
TEXTS ARE TOO COLD AND QUICK. LETTERS AREN'T IN A HURRY TO ARRIVE.
AND WHILE YOU'RE WAITING, YOU CAN DREAM...
WHAT A POET!
HEY, IT SAYS... SHE'S COMING *TODAY*!
YEAH, THE LETTER CAME YESTER-DAY...
Dear Peter,
See you...

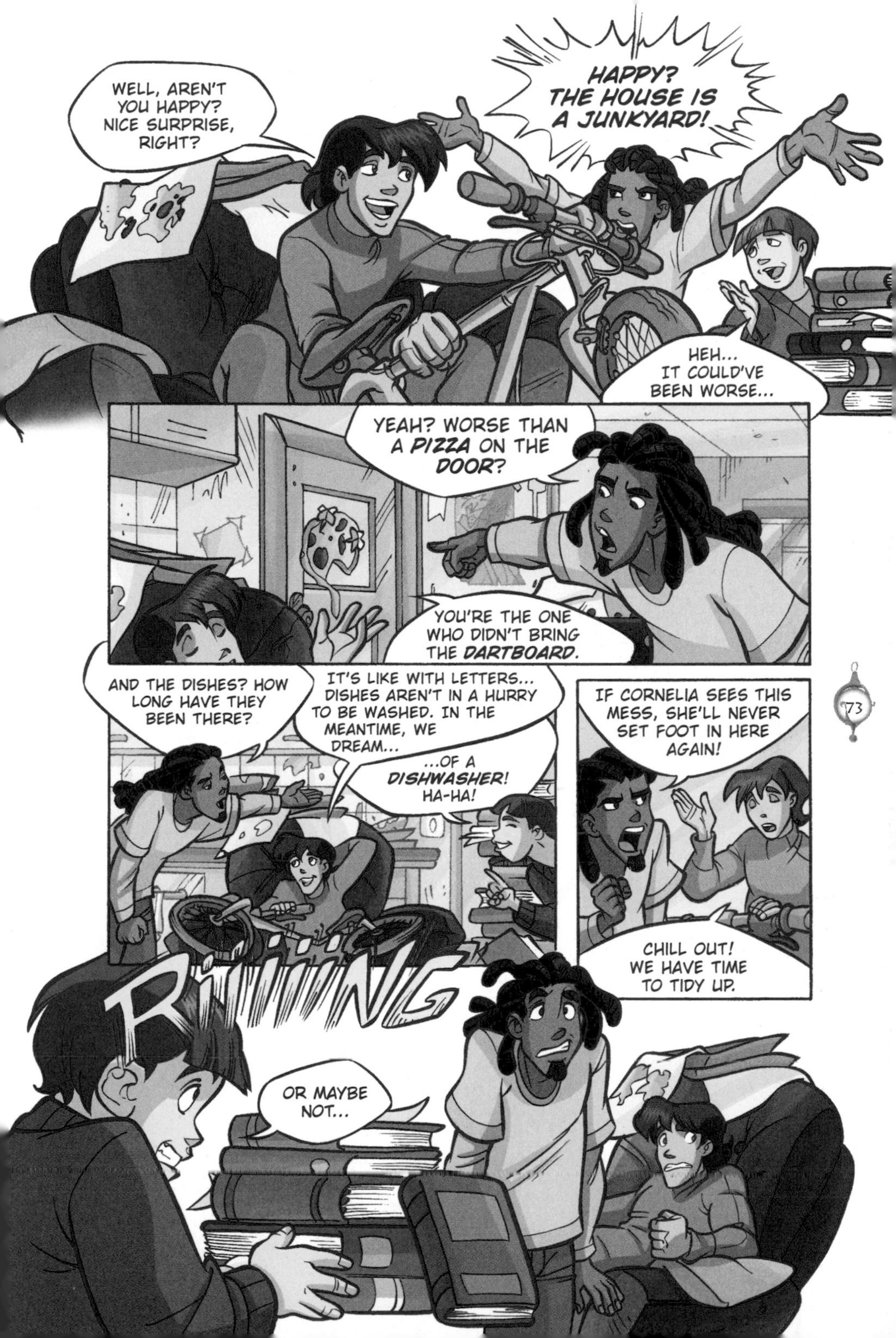

WELL, AREN'T YOU HAPPY? NICE SURPRISE, RIGHT?
HAPPY? THE HOUSE IS A JUNKYARD!
HEH... IT COULD'VE BEEN WORSE...
YEAH? WORSE THAN A PIZZA ON THE DOOR?
YOU'RE THE ONE WHO DIDN'T BRING THE DARTBOARD.
AND THE DISHES? HOW LONG HAVE THEY BEEN THERE?
IT'S LIKE WITH LETTERS... DISHES AREN'T IN A HURRY TO BE WASHED. IN THE MEANTIME, WE DREAM...
...OF A DISHWASHER! HA-HA!
IF CORNELIA SEES THIS MESS, SHE'LL NEVER SET FOOT IN HERE AGAIN!
CHILL OUT! WE HAVE TIME TO TIDY UP.
RIIIING
OR MAYBE NOT...

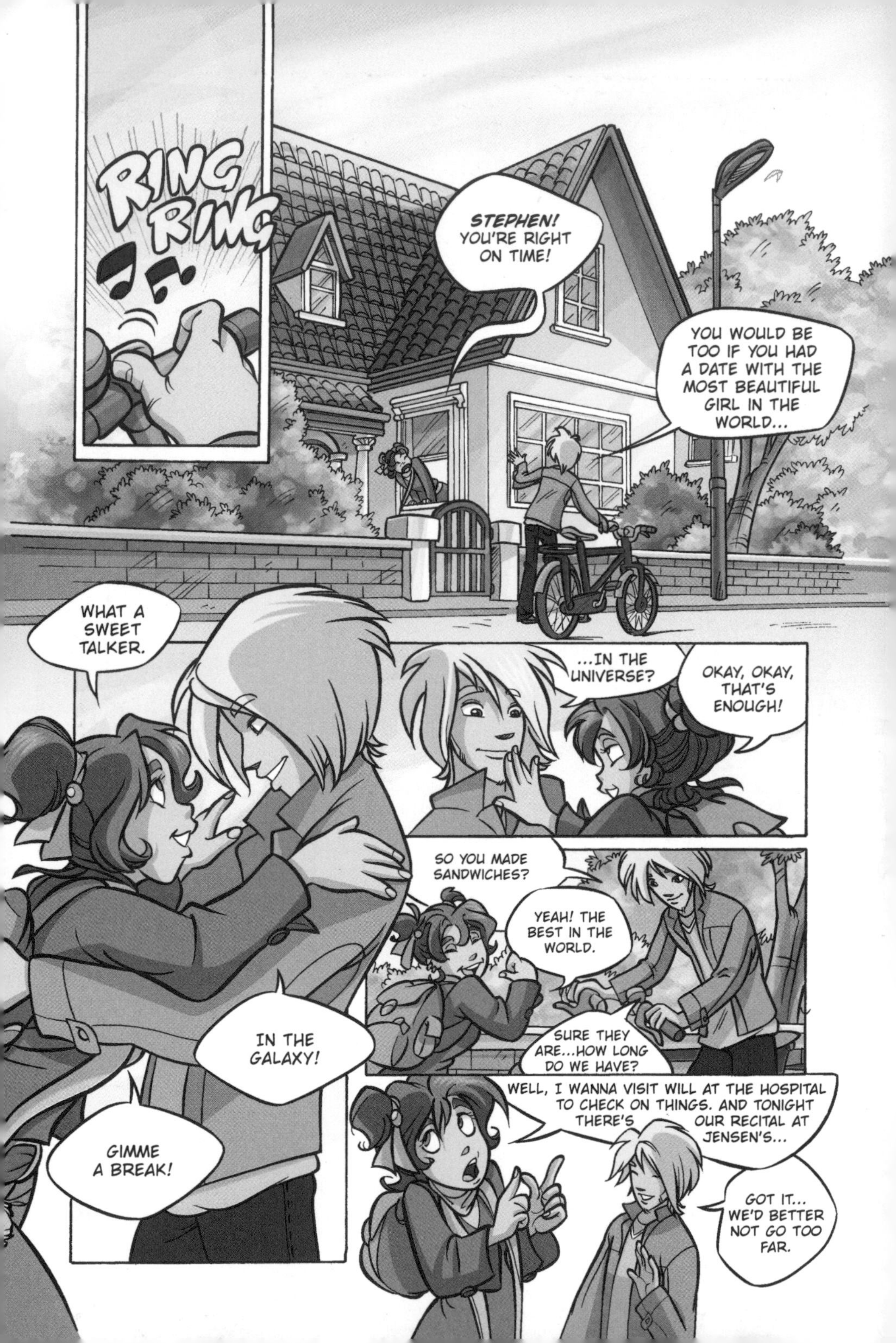
RING RING
STEPHEN! YOU'RE RIGHT ON TIME!
YOU WOULD BE TOO IF YOU HAD A DATE WITH THE MOST BEAUTIFUL GIRL IN THE WORLD...
WHAT A SWEET TALKER.
...IN THE UNIVERSE?
OKAY, OKAY, THAT'S ENOUGH!
IN THE GALAXY!
GIMME A BREAK!
SO YOU MADE SANDWICHES?
YEAH! THE BEST IN THE WORLD.
SURE THEY ARE...HOW LONG DO WE HAVE?
WELL, I WANNA VISIT WILL AT THE HOSPITAL TO CHECK ON THINGS. AND TONIGHT THERE'S OUR RECITAL AT JENSEN'S...
GOT IT... WE'D BETTER NOT GO TOO FAR.

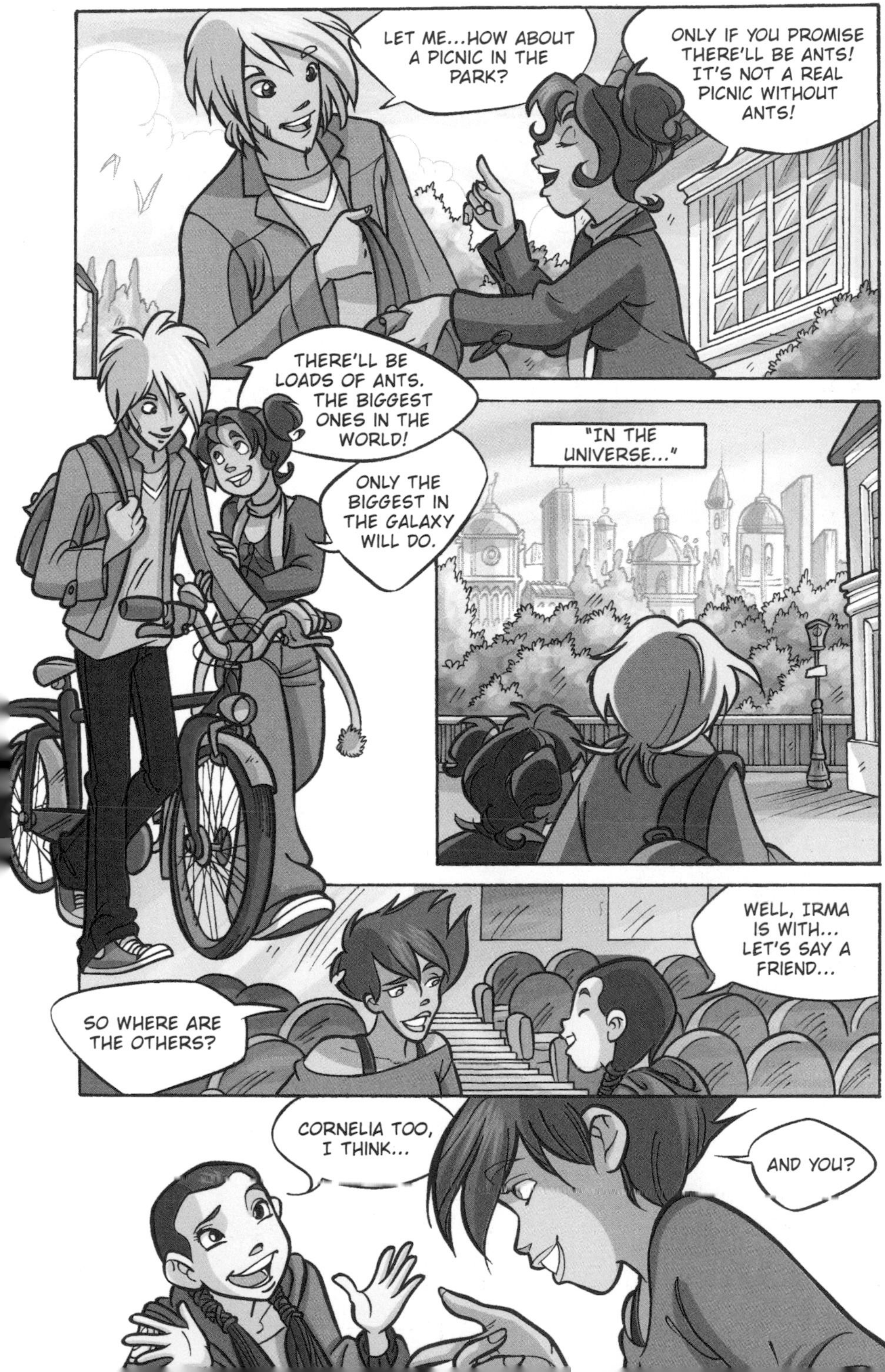
LET ME...HOW ABOUT A PICNIC IN THE PARK?
ONLY IF YOU PROMISE THERE'LL BE ANTS! IT'S NOT A REAL PICNIC WITHOUT ANTS!
THERE'LL BE LOADS OF ANTS. THE BIGGEST ONES IN THE WORLD!
ONLY THE BIGGEST IN THE GALAXY WILL DO.
"IN THE UNIVERSE..."
SO WHERE ARE THE OTHERS?
WELL, IRMA IS WITH... LET'S SAY A FRIEND...
CORNELIA TOO, I THINK...
AND YOU?

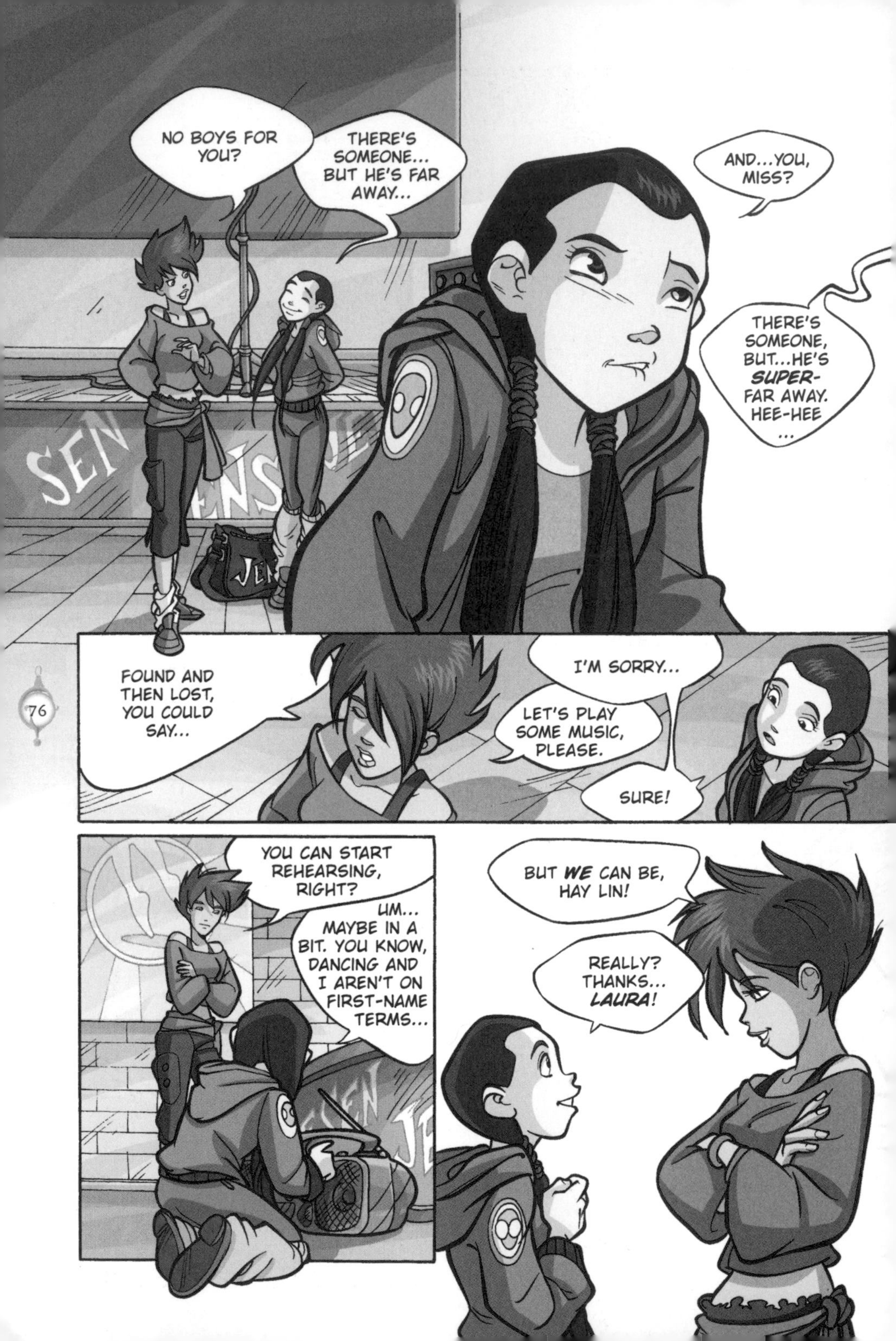
NO BOYS FOR YOU?
THERE'S SOMEONE... BUT HE'S FAR AWAY...
AND...YOU, MISS?
THERE'S SOMEONE, BUT...HE'S ***SUPER***-FAR AWAY. HEE-HEE ...
FOUND AND THEN LOST, YOU COULD SAY...
I'M SORRY...
LET'S PLAY SOME MUSIC, PLEASE.
SURE!
YOU CAN START REHEARSING, RIGHT?
UM... MAYBE IN A BIT. YOU KNOW, DANCING AND I AREN'T ON FIRST-NAME TERMS...
BUT ***WE*** CAN BE, HAY LIN!
REALLY? THANKS... ***LAURA***!

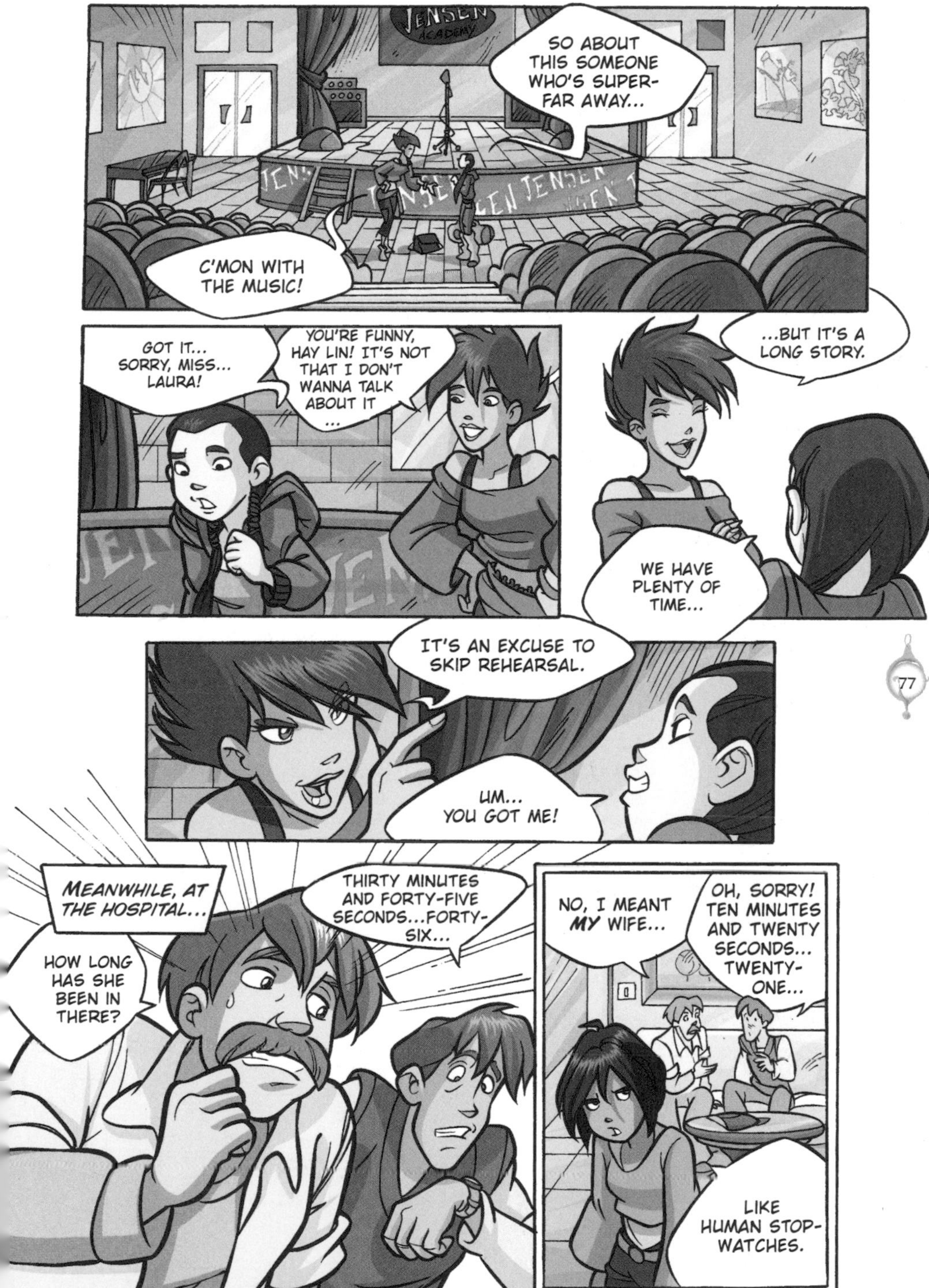

JENSEN ACADEMY
SO ABOUT THIS SOMEONE WHO'S SUPER-FAR AWAY...
C'MON WITH THE MUSIC!
GOT IT... SORRY, MISS... LAURA!
YOU'RE FUNNY, HAY LIN! IT'S NOT THAT I DON'T WANNA TALK ABOUT IT ...
...BUT IT'S A LONG STORY.
WE HAVE PLENTY OF TIME...
IT'S AN EXCUSE TO SKIP REHEARSAL.
UM... YOU GOT ME!
MEANWHILE, AT THE HOSPITAL...
HOW LONG HAS SHE BEEN IN THERE?
THIRTY MINUTES AND FORTY-FIVE SECONDS...FORTY-SIX...
NO, I MEANT MY WIFE...
OH, SORRY! TEN MINUTES AND TWENTY SECONDS... TWENTY-ONE...
LIKE HUMAN STOP-WATCHES.

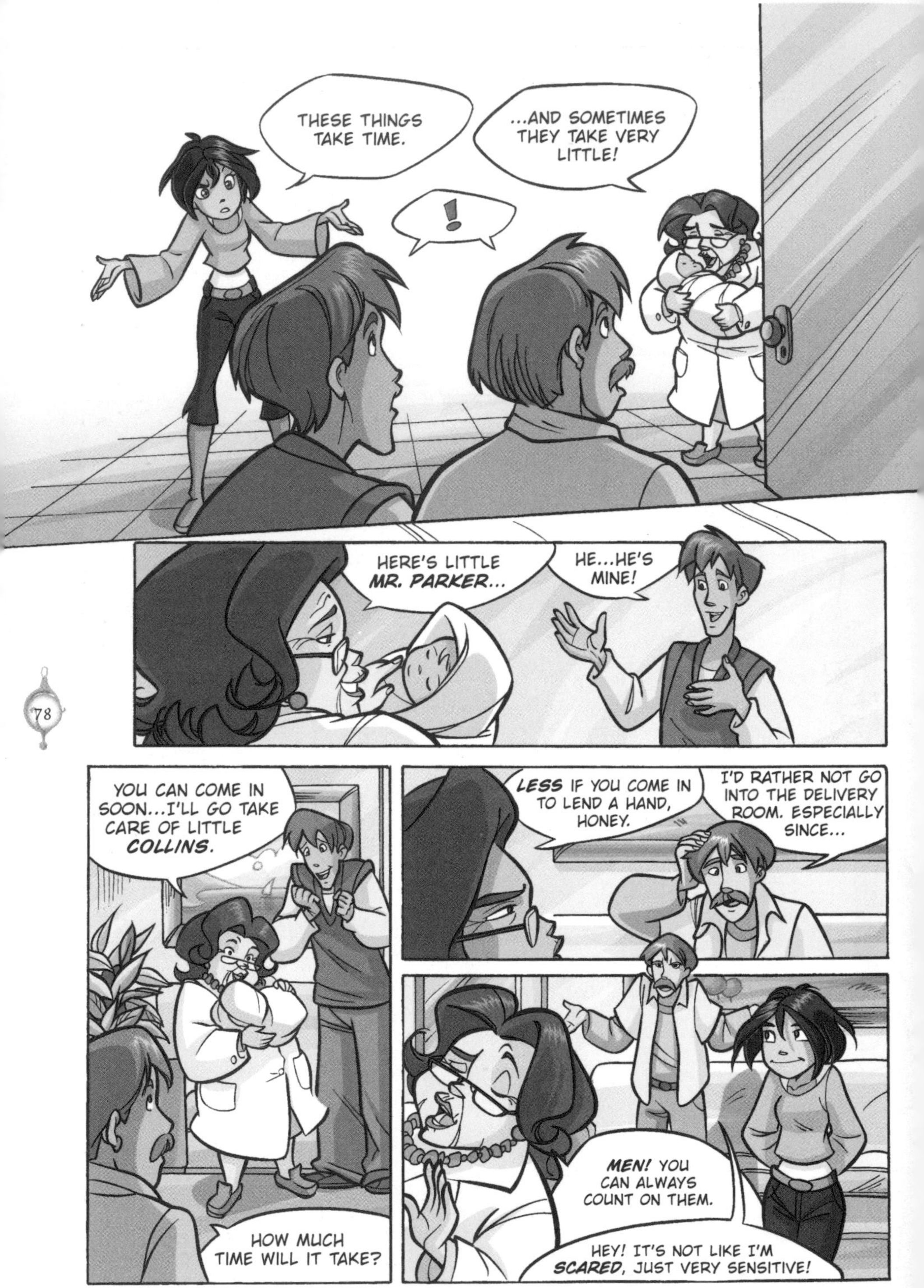
THESE THINGS TAKE TIME.
...AND SOMETIMES THEY TAKE VERY LITTLE!
!
HERE'S LITTLE **MR. PARKER**...
HE...HE'S MINE!
YOU CAN COME IN SOON...I'LL GO TAKE CARE OF LITTLE **COLLINS**.
HOW MUCH TIME WILL IT TAKE?
**LESS** IF YOU COME IN TO LEND A HAND, HONEY.
I'D RATHER NOT GO INTO THE DELIVERY ROOM. ESPECIALLY SINCE...
**MEN!** YOU CAN ALWAYS COUNT ON THEM.
HEY! IT'S NOT LIKE I'M **SCARED**, JUST VERY SENSITIVE!

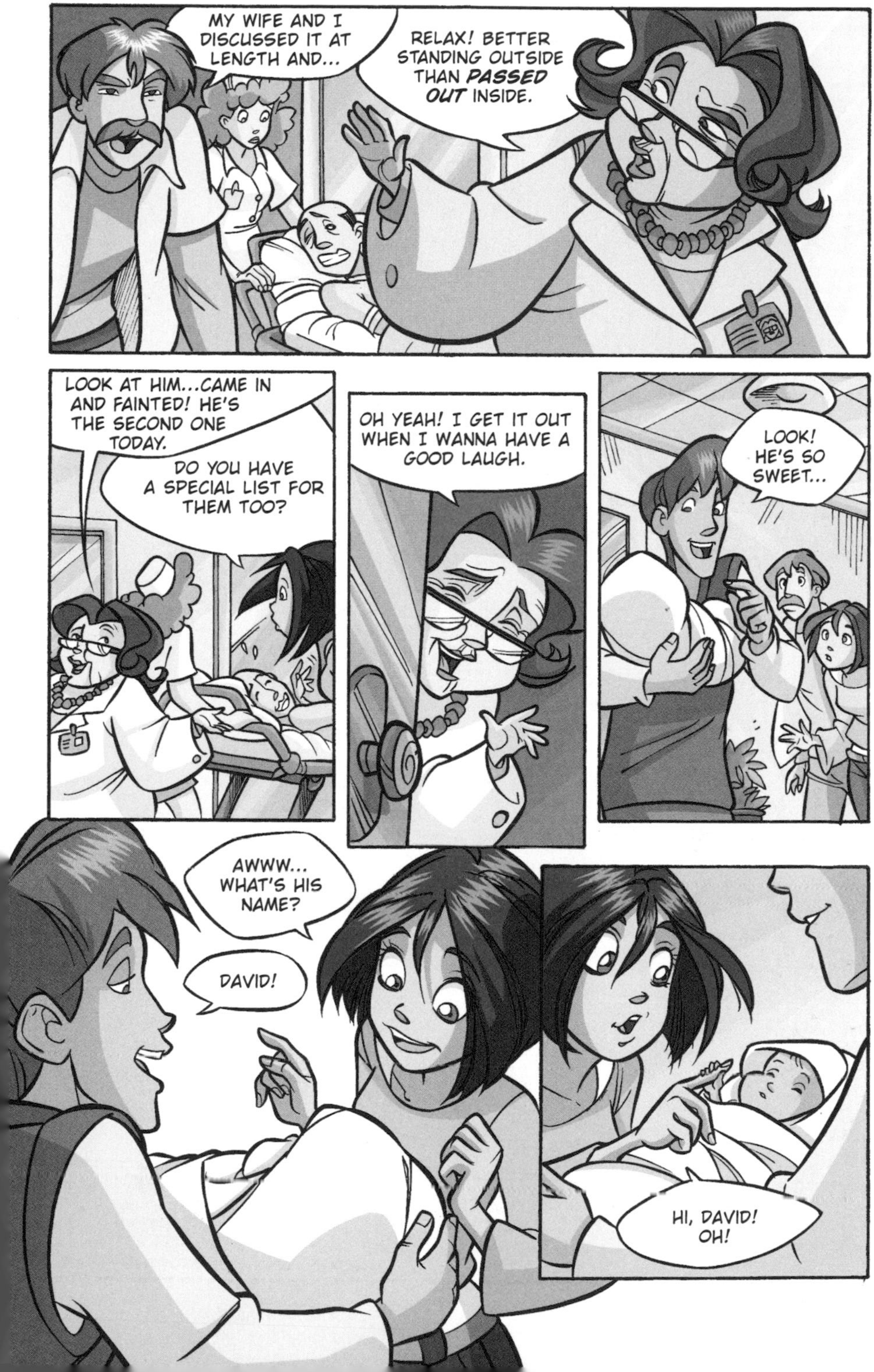
MY WIFE AND I DISCUSSED IT AT LENGTH AND...
RELAX! BETTER STANDING OUTSIDE THAN PASSED OUT INSIDE.
LOOK AT HIM...CAME IN AND FAINTED! HE'S THE SECOND ONE TODAY.
DO YOU HAVE A SPECIAL LIST FOR THEM TOO?
OH YEAH! I GET IT OUT WHEN I WANNA HAVE A GOOD LAUGH.
LOOK! HE'S SO SWEET...
AWWW... WHAT'S HIS NAME?
DAVID!
HI, DAVID! OH!

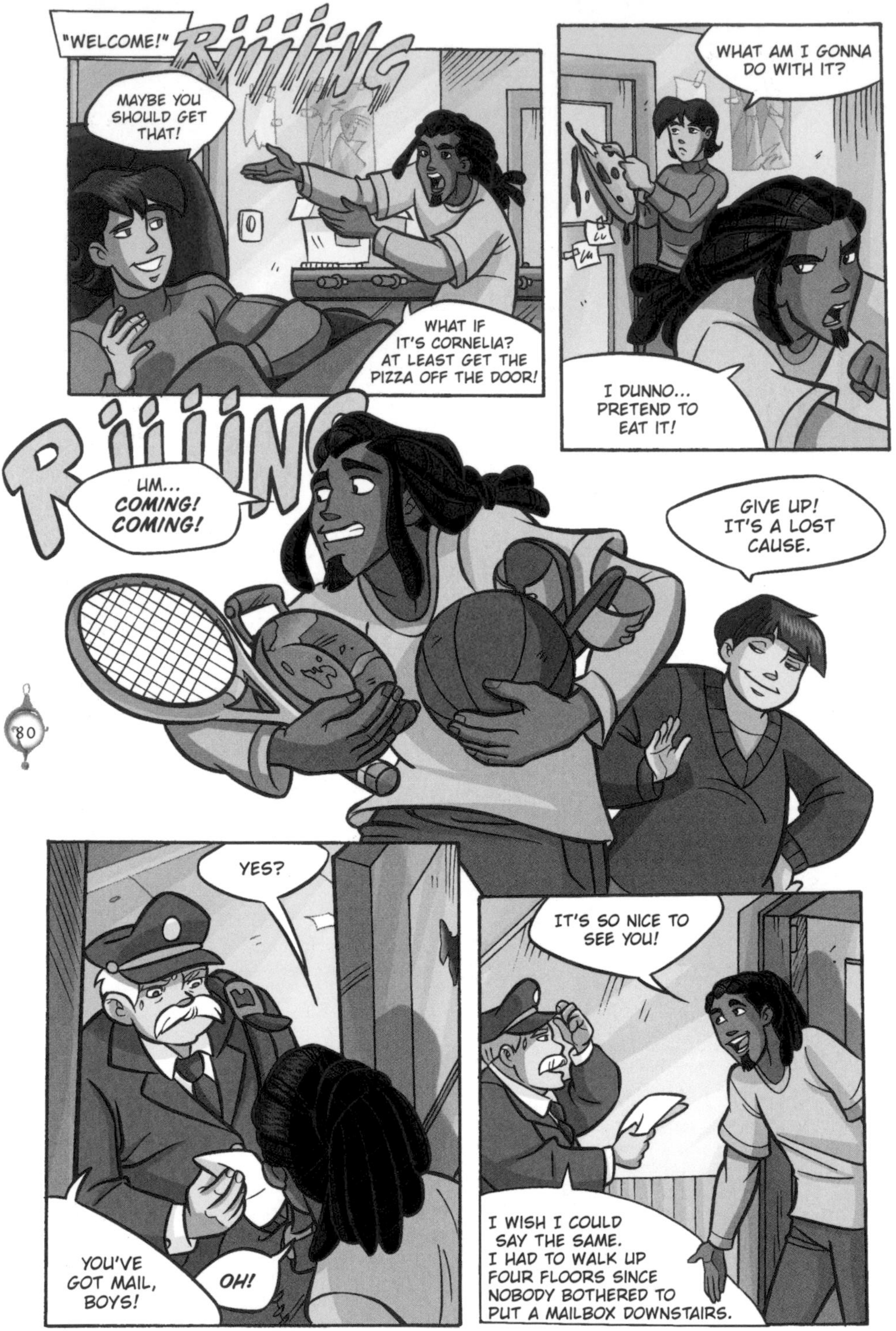

"WELCOME!"
RIIIIING
MAYBE YOU SHOULD GET THAT!
WHAT IF IT'S CORNELIA? AT LEAST GET THE PIZZA OFF THE DOOR!
WHAT AM I GONNA DO WITH IT?
I DUNNO... PRETEND TO EAT IT!
RIIIING
UM... *COMING! COMING!*
GIVE UP! IT'S A LOST CAUSE.
YES?
YOU'VE GOT MAIL, BOYS!
*OH!*
IT'S SO NICE TO SEE YOU!
I WISH I COULD SAY THE SAME. I HAD TO WALK UP FOUR FLOORS SINCE NOBODY BOTHERED TO PUT A MAILBOX DOWNSTAIRS.

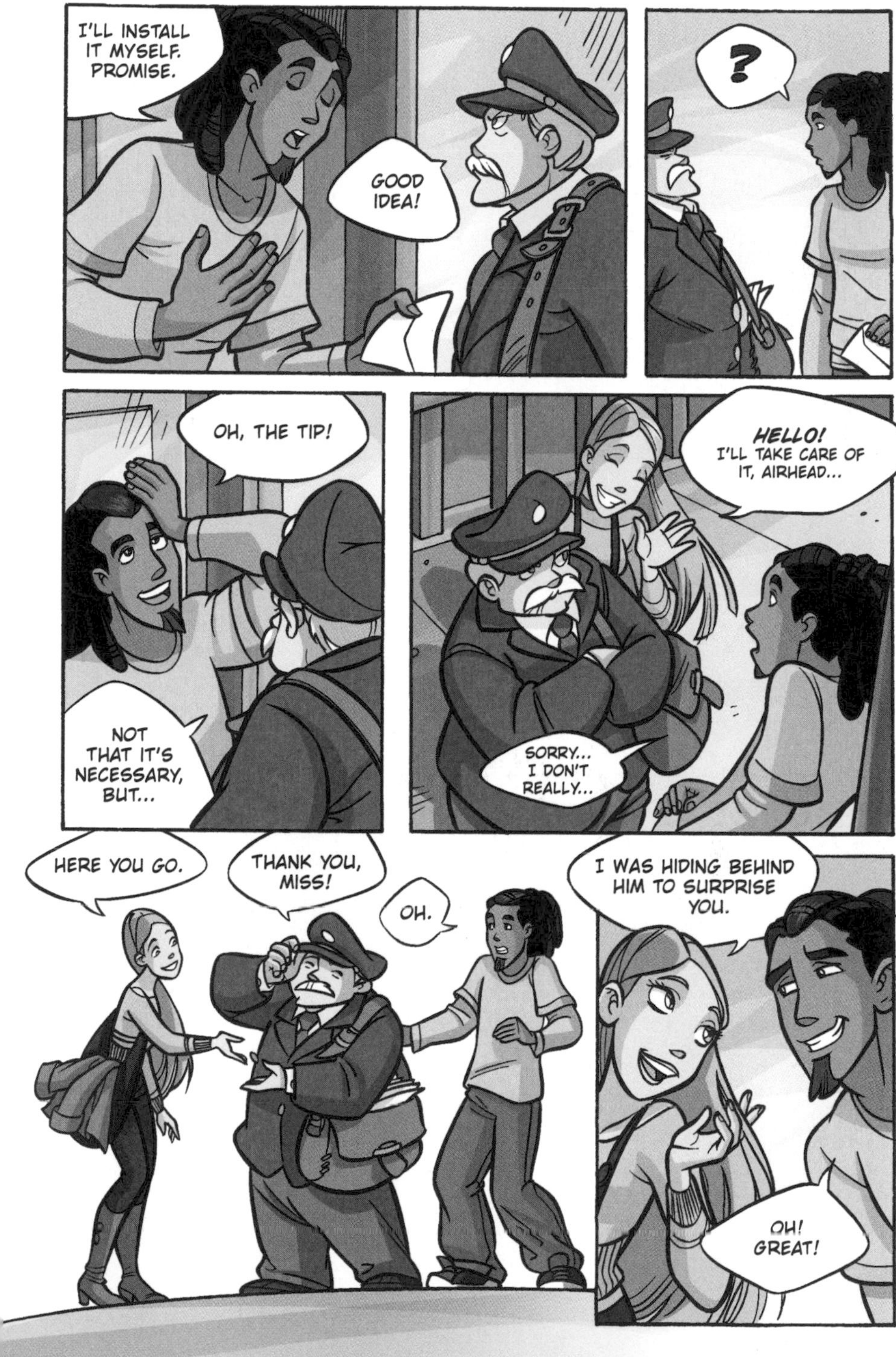
I'LL INSTALL IT MYSELF. PROMISE.
GOOD IDEA!
?
OH, THE TIP!
NOT THAT IT'S NECESSARY, BUT...
HELLO! I'LL TAKE CARE OF IT, AIRHEAD...
SORRY... I DON'T REALLY...
HERE YOU GO.
THANK YOU, MISS!
OH.
I WAS HIDING BEHIND HIM TO SURPRISE YOU.
OH! GREAT!

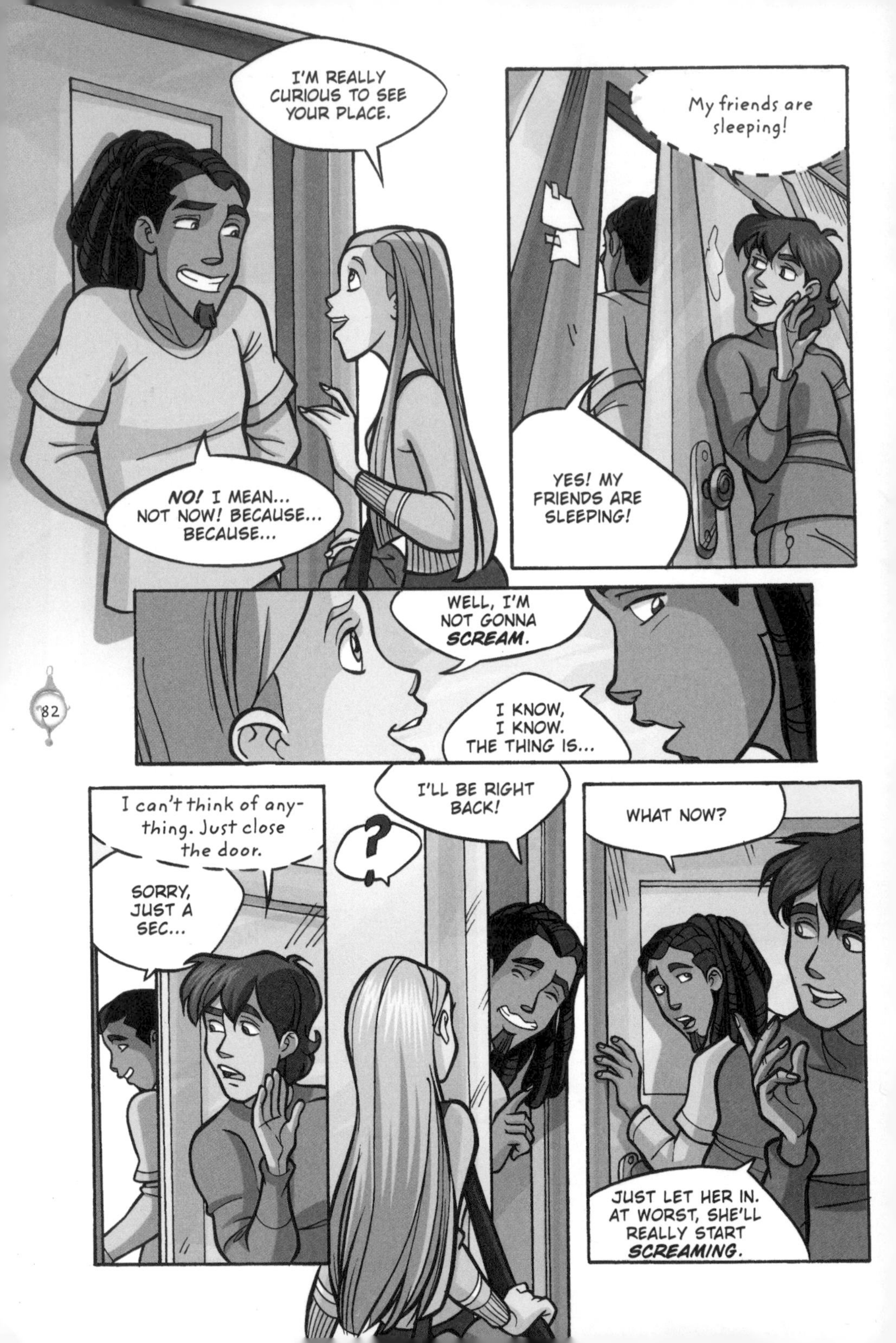
I'M REALLY CURIOUS TO SEE YOUR PLACE.
NO! I MEAN... NOT NOW! BECAUSE... BECAUSE...
My friends are sleeping!
YES! MY FRIENDS ARE SLEEPING!
WELL, I'M NOT GONNA SCREAM.
I KNOW, I KNOW. THE THING IS...
I can't think of anything. Just close the door.
SORRY, JUST A SEC...
?
I'LL BE RIGHT BACK!
WHAT NOW?
JUST LET HER IN. AT WORST, SHE'LL REALLY START SCREAMING.

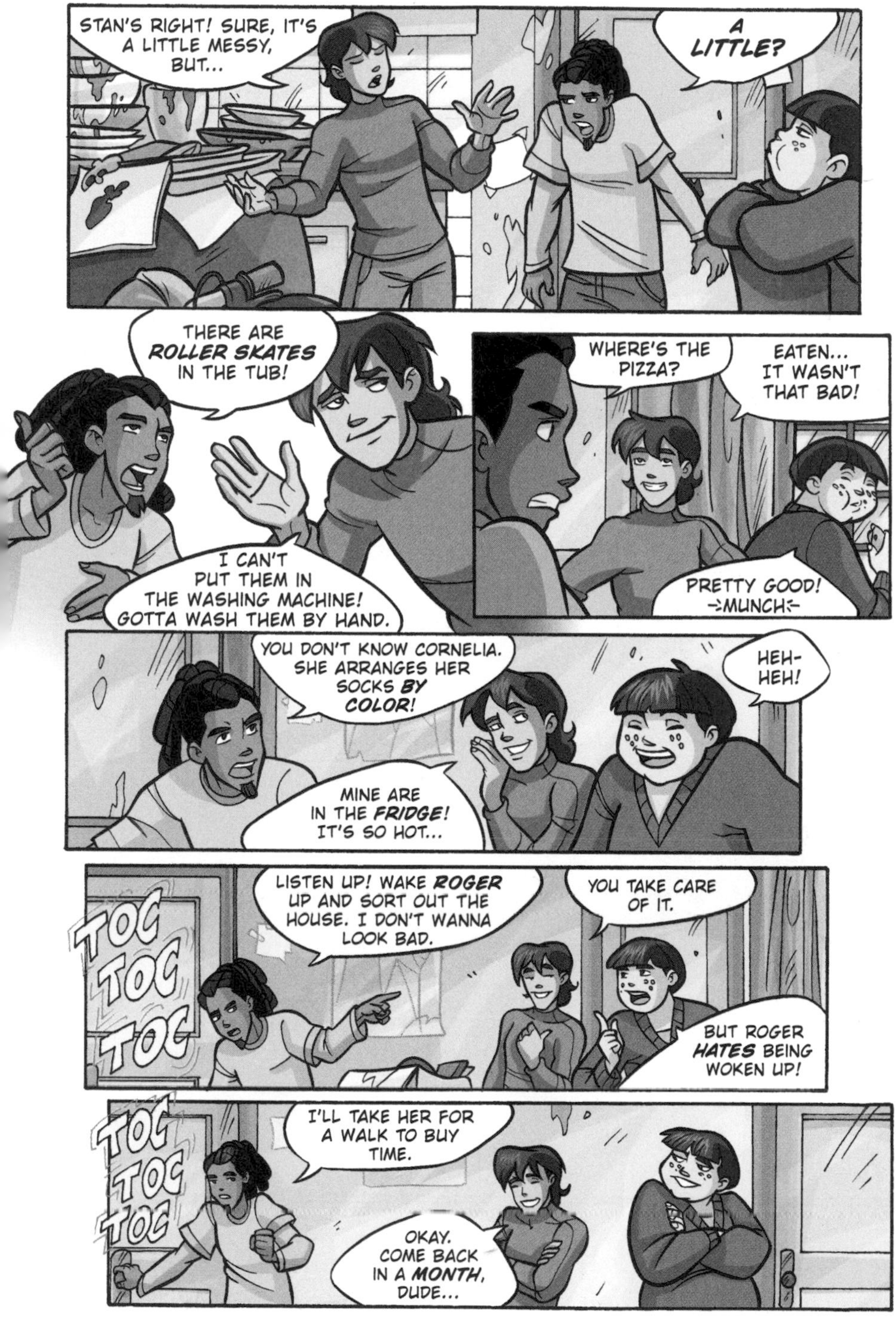
STAN'S RIGHT! SURE, IT'S A LITTLE MESSY, BUT...
A LITTLE?
THERE ARE ROLLER SKATES IN THE TUB!
I CAN'T PUT THEM IN THE WASHING MACHINE! GOTTA WASH THEM BY HAND.
WHERE'S THE PIZZA?
EATEN... IT WASN'T THAT BAD!
PRETTY GOOD! -MUNCH-
YOU DON'T KNOW CORNELIA. SHE ARRANGES HER SOCKS BY COLOR!
HEH-HEH!
MINE ARE IN THE FRIDGE! IT'S SO HOT...
TOC TOC TOC
LISTEN UP! WAKE ROGER UP AND SORT OUT THE HOUSE. I DON'T WANNA LOOK BAD.
YOU TAKE CARE OF IT.
BUT ROGER HATES BEING WOKEN UP!
TOC TOC TOC
I'LL TAKE HER FOR A WALK TO BUY TIME.
OKAY. COME BACK IN A MONTH, DUDE...

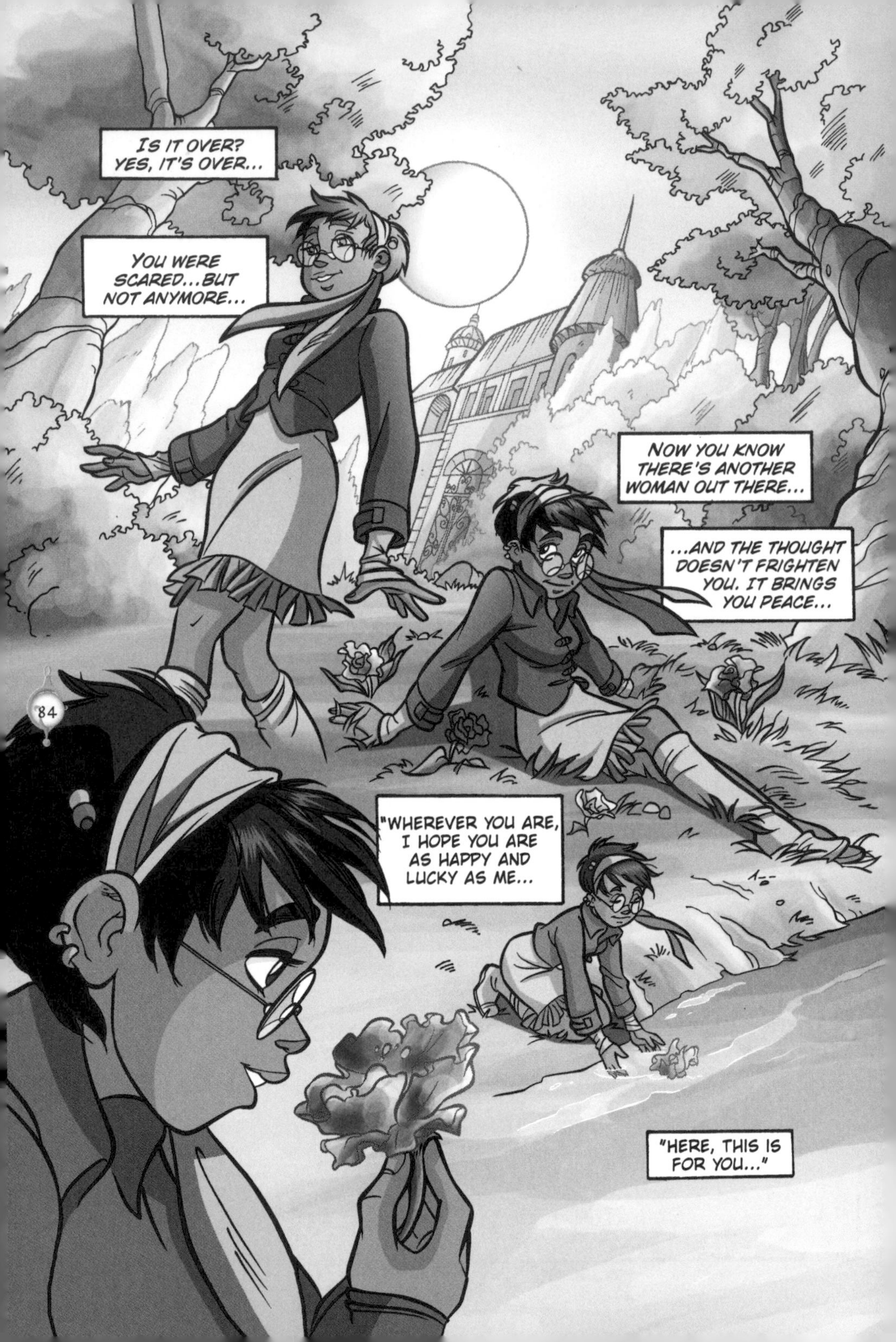

IS IT OVER? YES, IT'S OVER...
YOU WERE SCARED...BUT NOT ANYMORE...
NOW YOU KNOW THERE'S ANOTHER WOMAN OUT THERE...
...AND THE THOUGHT DOESN'T FRIGHTEN YOU. IT BRINGS YOU PEACE...
"WHEREVER YOU ARE, I HOPE YOU ARE AS HAPPY AND LUCKY AS ME...
"HERE, THIS IS FOR YOU..."

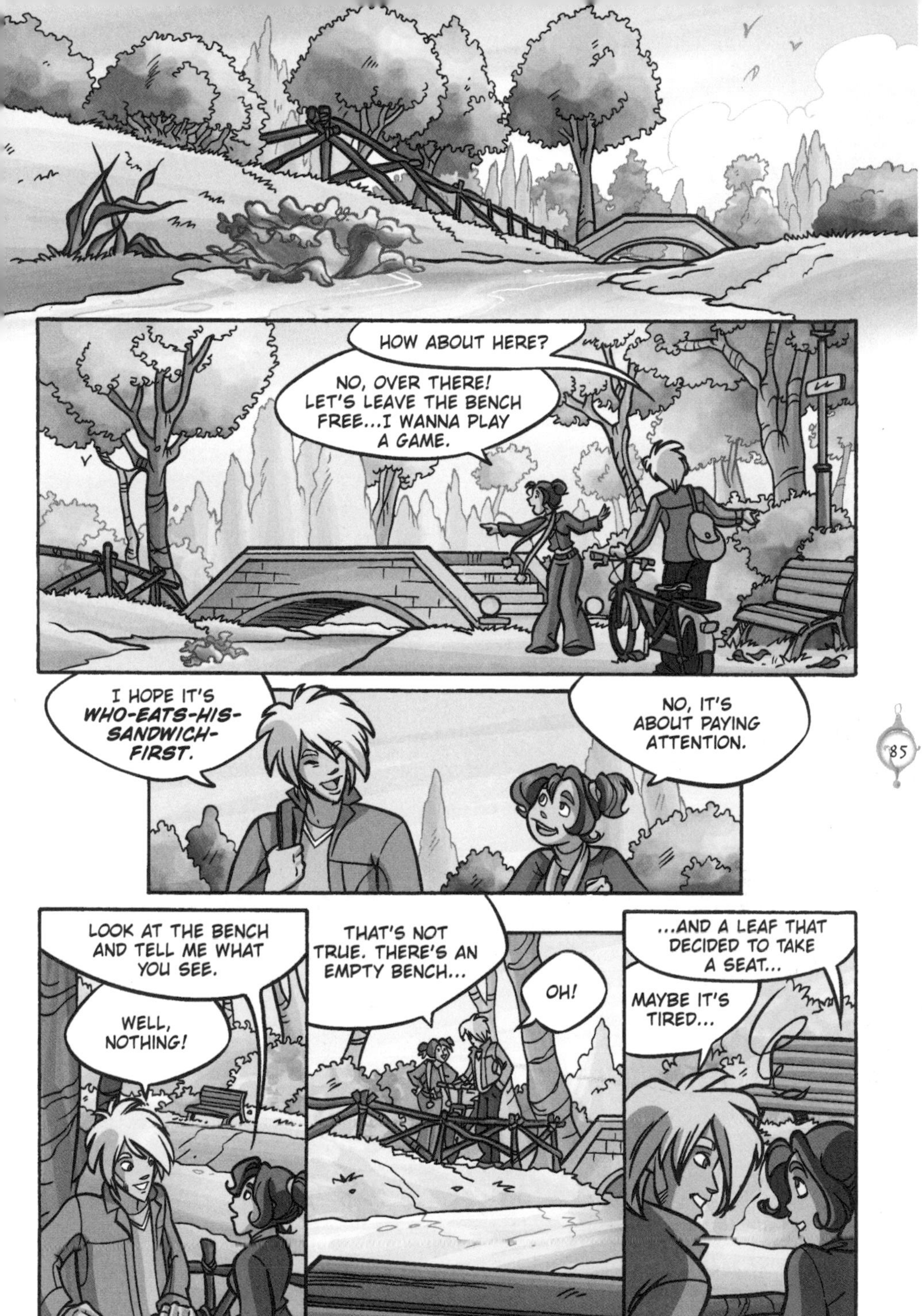
HOW ABOUT HERE?
NO, OVER THERE! LET'S LEAVE THE BENCH FREE...I WANNA PLAY A GAME.
I HOPE IT'S *WHO-EATS-HIS-SANDWICH-FIRST*.
NO, IT'S ABOUT PAYING ATTENTION.
LOOK AT THE BENCH AND TELL ME WHAT YOU SEE.
WELL, NOTHING!
THAT'S NOT TRUE. THERE'S AN EMPTY BENCH...
OH!
...AND A LEAF THAT DECIDED TO TAKE A SEAT...
MAYBE IT'S TIRED...

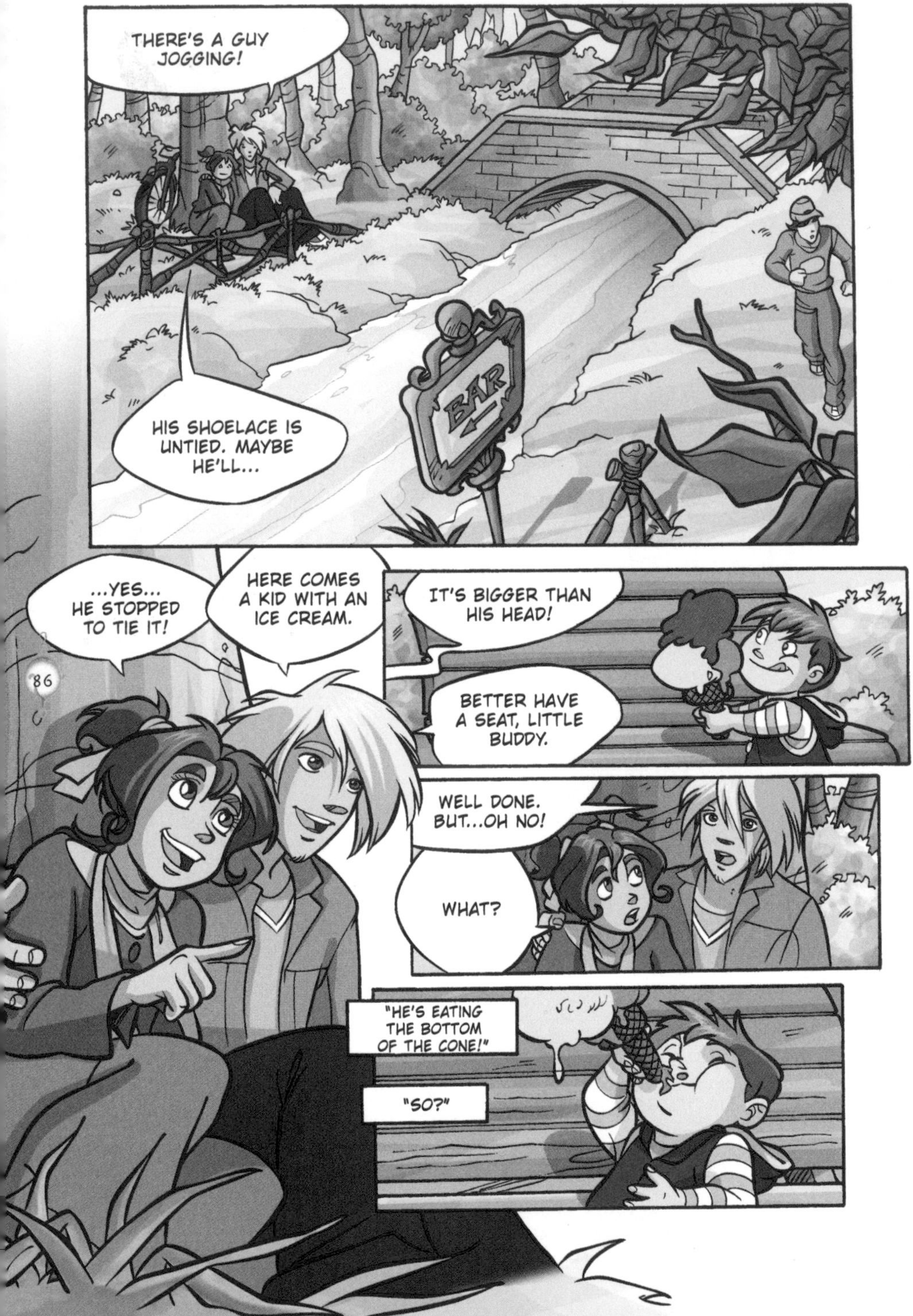
THERE'S A GUY JOGGING!
HIS SHOELACE IS UNTIED. MAYBE HE'LL...
BAR
...YES... HE STOPPED TO TIE IT!
HERE COMES A KID WITH AN ICE CREAM.
IT'S BIGGER THAN HIS HEAD!
BETTER HAVE A SEAT, LITTLE BUDDY.
WELL DONE. BUT...OH NO!
WHAT?
"HE'S EATING THE BOTTOM OF THE CONE!"
"SO?"

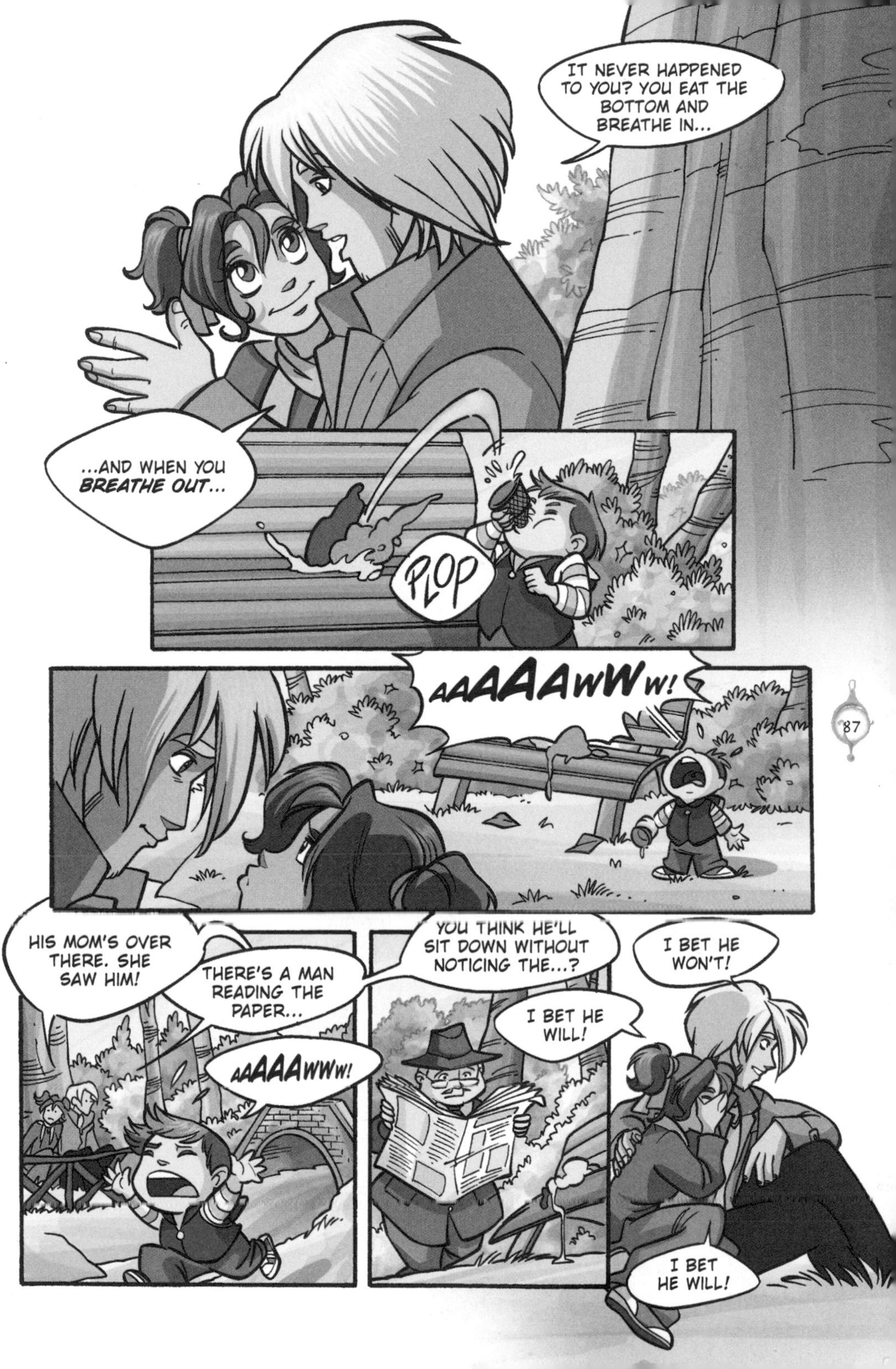

IT NEVER HAPPENED TO YOU? YOU EAT THE BOTTOM AND BREATHE IN...
...AND WHEN YOU *BREATHE OUT*...
PLOP
AAAAAWWW!
HIS MOM'S OVER THERE. SHE SAW HIM!
THERE'S A MAN READING THE PAPER...
AAAAAWWW!
YOU THINK HE'LL SIT DOWN WITHOUT NOTICING THE...?
I BET HE WILL!
I BET HE WON'T!
I BET HE WILL!

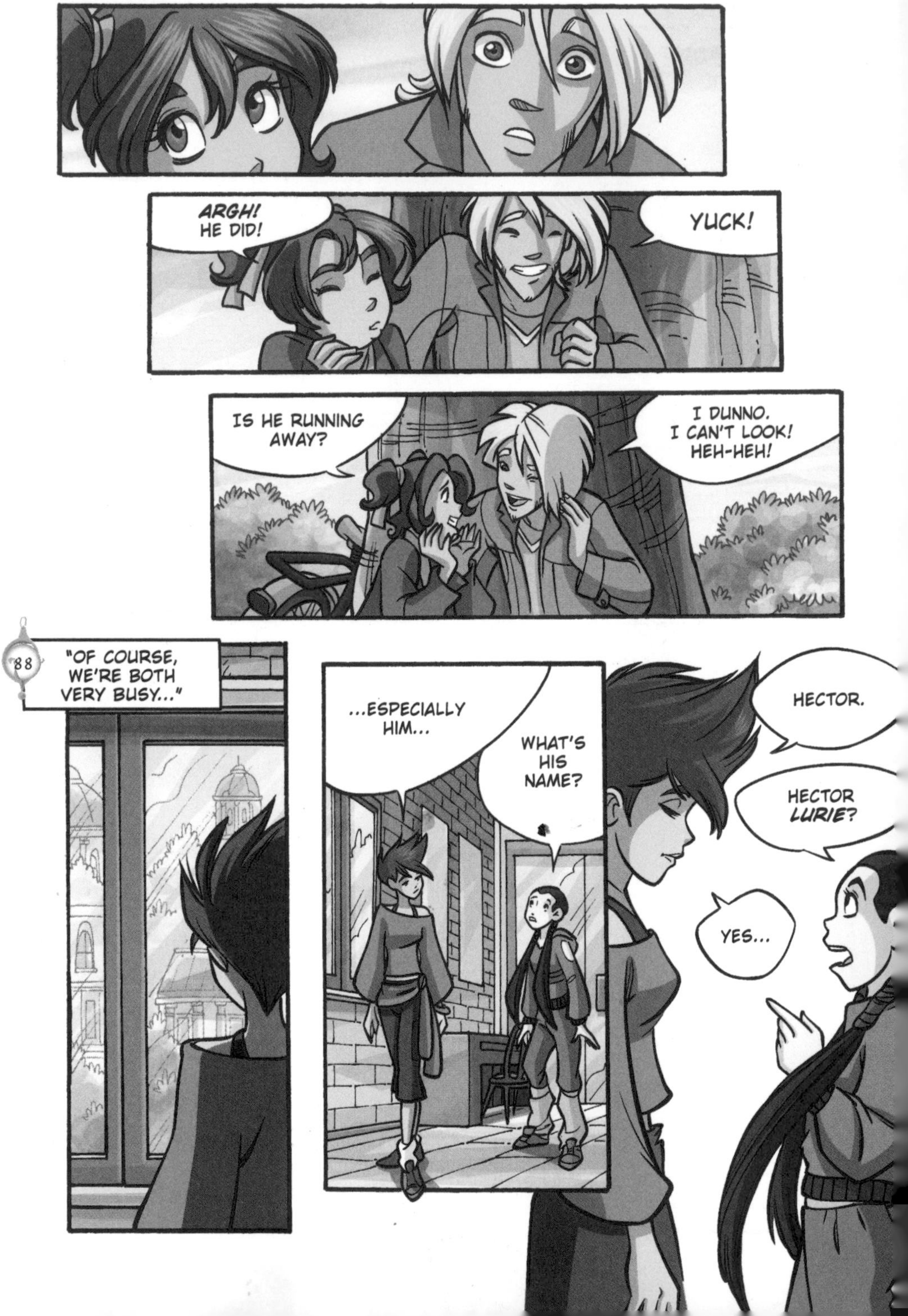
ARGH!
HE DID!
YUCK!
IS HE RUNNING AWAY?
I DUNNO. I CAN'T LOOK! HEH-HEH!
"OF COURSE, WE'RE BOTH VERY BUSY..."
...ESPECIALLY HIM...
WHAT'S HIS NAME?
HECTOR.
HECTOR LURIE?
YES...

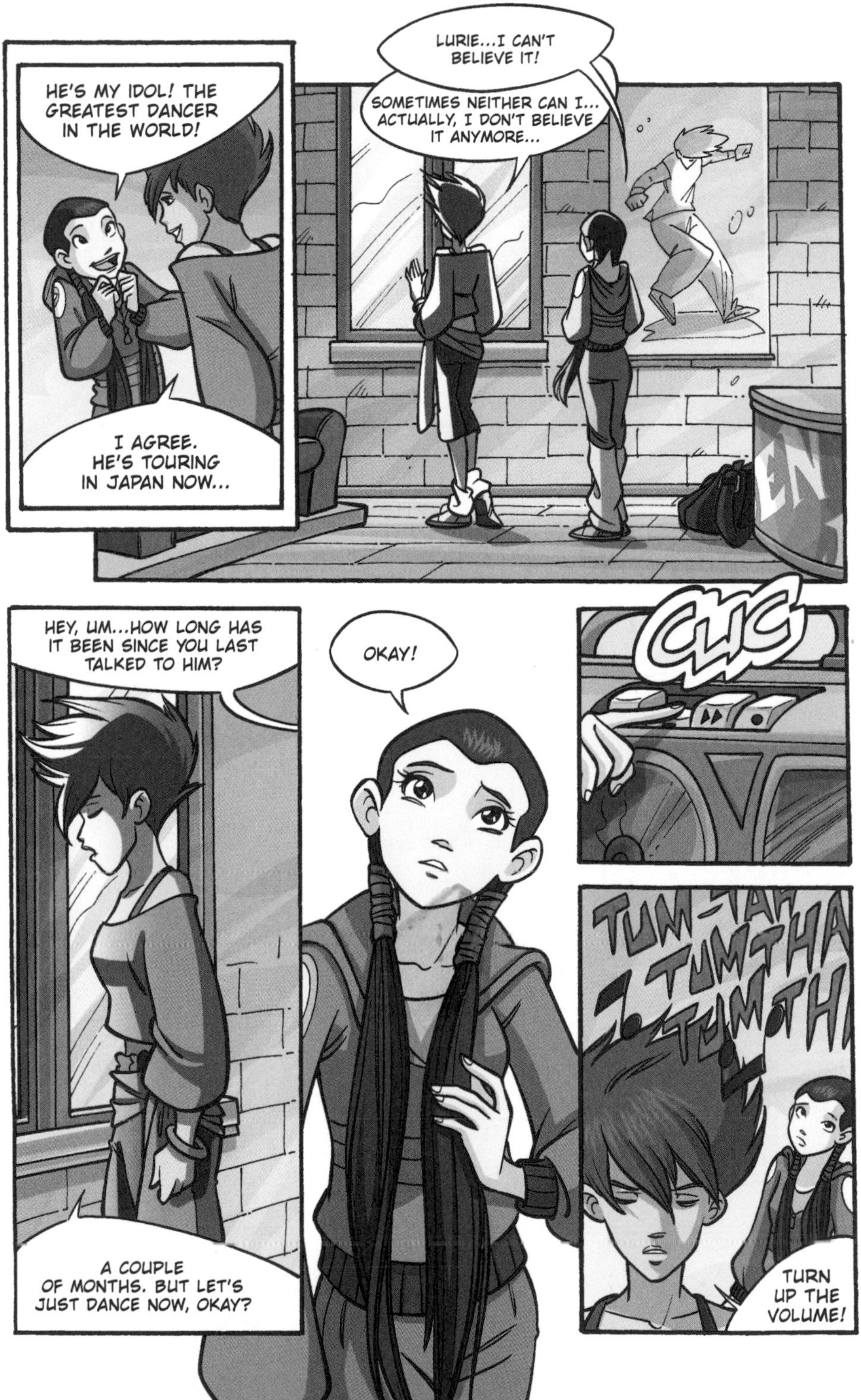
HE'S MY IDOL! THE GREATEST DANCER IN THE WORLD!
I AGREE. HE'S TOURING IN JAPAN NOW...
LURIE...I CAN'T BELIEVE IT!
SOMETIMES NEITHER CAN I... ACTUALLY, I DON'T BELIEVE IT ANYMORE...
HEY, UM...HOW LONG HAS IT BEEN SINCE YOU LAST TALKED TO HIM?
A COUPLE OF MONTHS. BUT LET'S JUST DANCE NOW, OKAY?
OKAY!
CLIC
TUM-TAH TUMTHA TUMTH
TURN UP THE VOLUME!

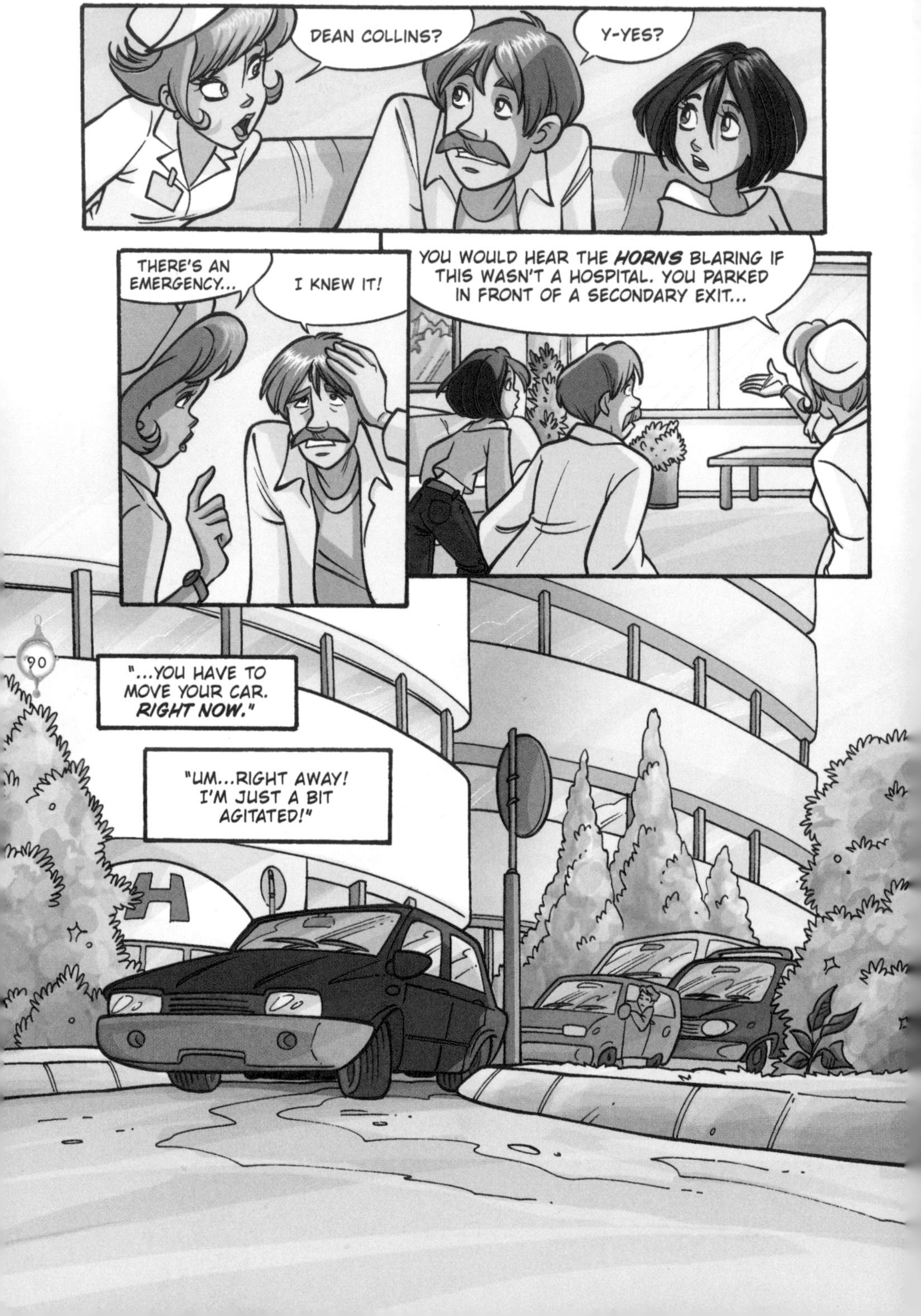
DEAN COLLINS?
Y-YES?
THERE'S AN EMERGENCY...
I KNEW IT!
YOU WOULD HEAR THE *HORNS* BLARING IF THIS WASN'T A HOSPITAL. YOU PARKED IN FRONT OF A SECONDARY EXIT...
"...YOU HAVE TO MOVE YOUR CAR. *RIGHT NOW.*"
"UM...RIGHT AWAY! I'M JUST A BIT AGITATED!"

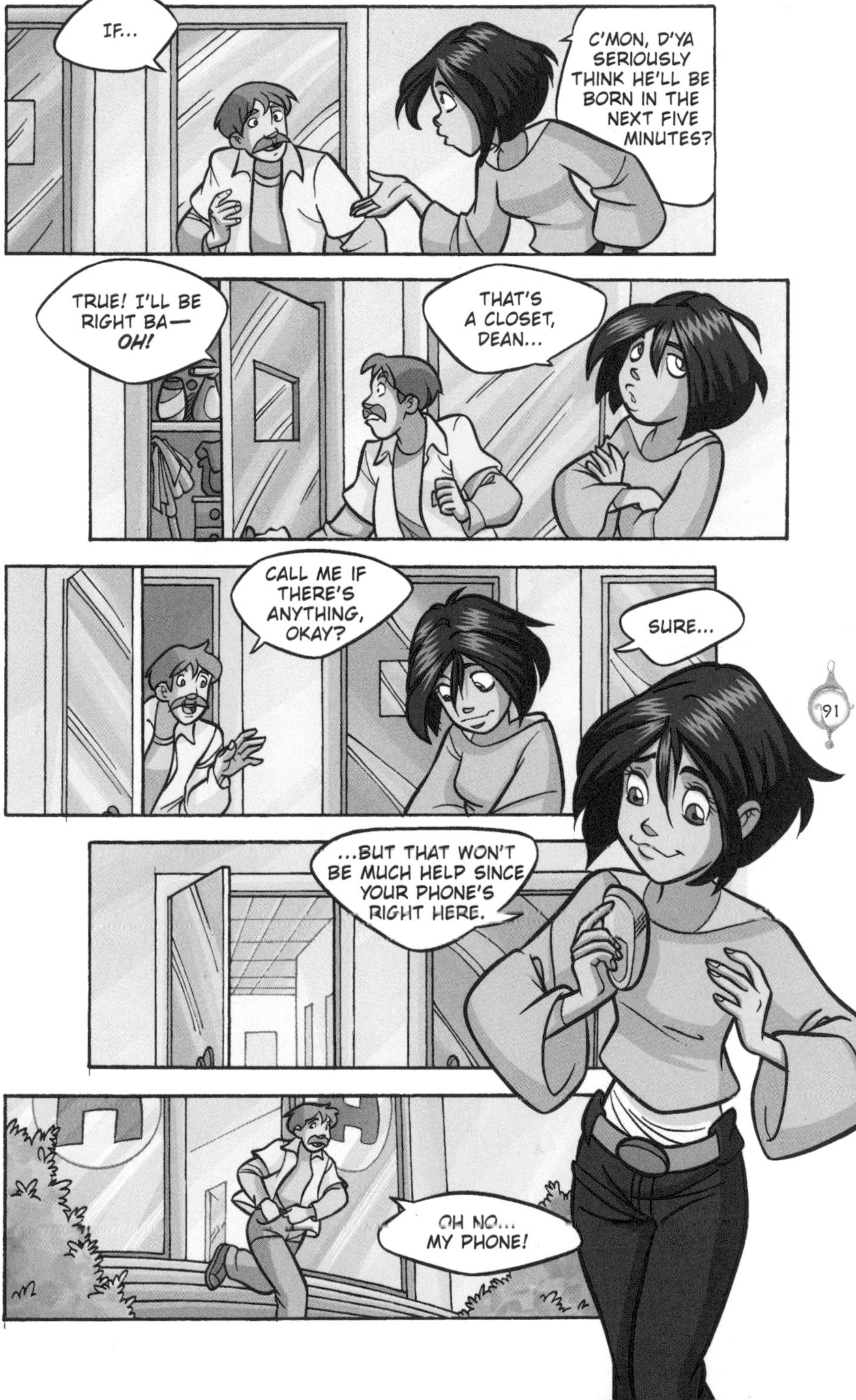
IF...
C'MON, D'YA SERIOUSLY THINK HE'LL BE BORN IN THE NEXT FIVE MINUTES?
TRUE! I'LL BE RIGHT BA— OH!
THAT'S A CLOSET, DEAN...
CALL ME IF THERE'S ANYTHING, OKAY?
SURE...
...BUT THAT WON'T BE MUCH HELP SINCE YOUR PHONE'S RIGHT HERE.
OH NO... MY PHONE!

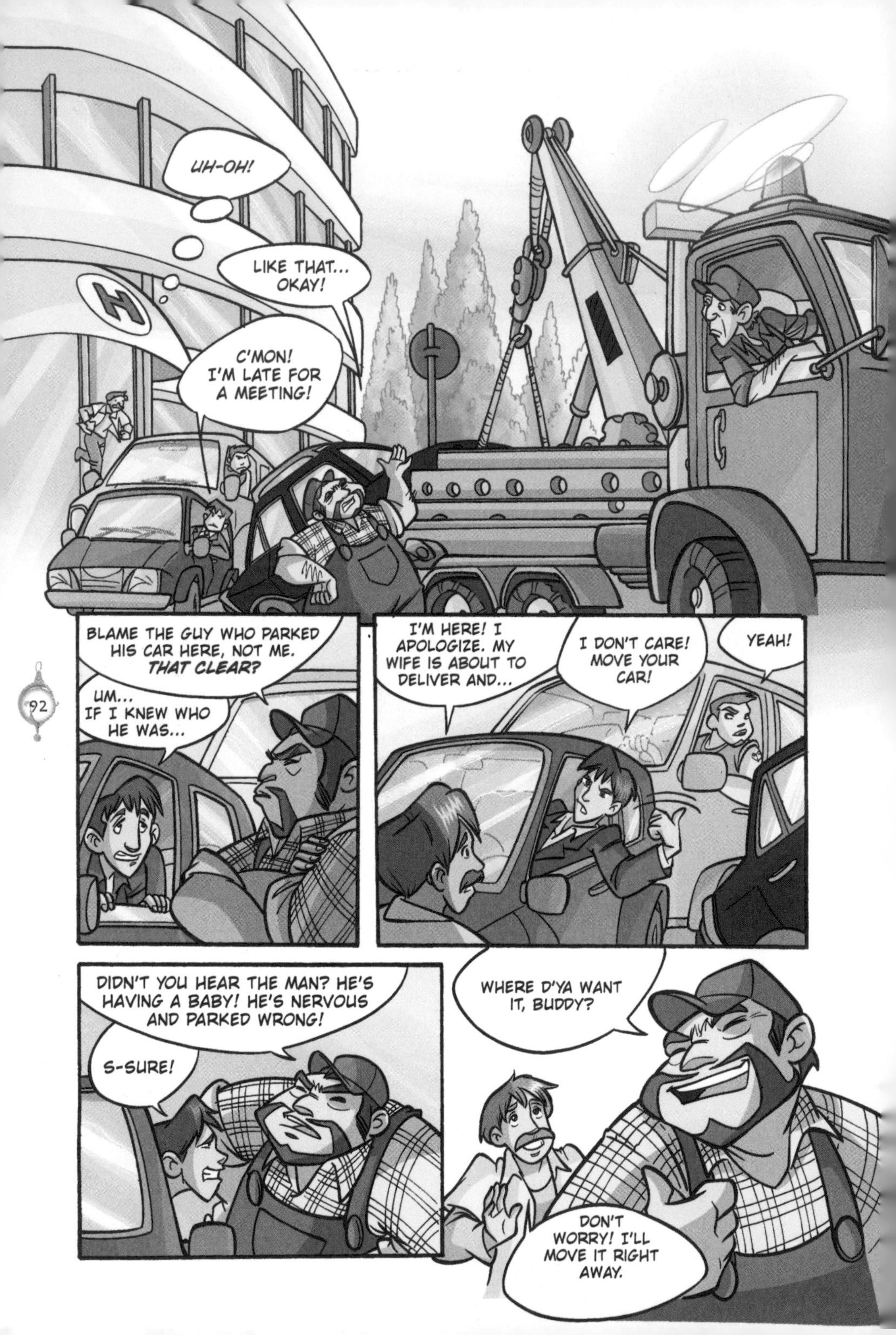
UH-OH!
LIKE THAT... OKAY!
C'MON! I'M LATE FOR A MEETING!
BLAME THE GUY WHO PARKED HIS CAR HERE, NOT ME. *THAT CLEAR?*
UM... IF I KNEW WHO HE WAS...
I'M HERE! I APOLOGIZE. MY WIFE IS ABOUT TO DELIVER AND...
I DON'T CARE! MOVE YOUR CAR!
YEAH!
DIDN'T YOU HEAR THE MAN? HE'S HAVING A BABY! HE'S NERVOUS AND PARKED WRONG!
S-SURE!
WHERE D'YA WANT IT, BUDDY?
DON'T WORRY! I'LL MOVE IT RIGHT AWAY.

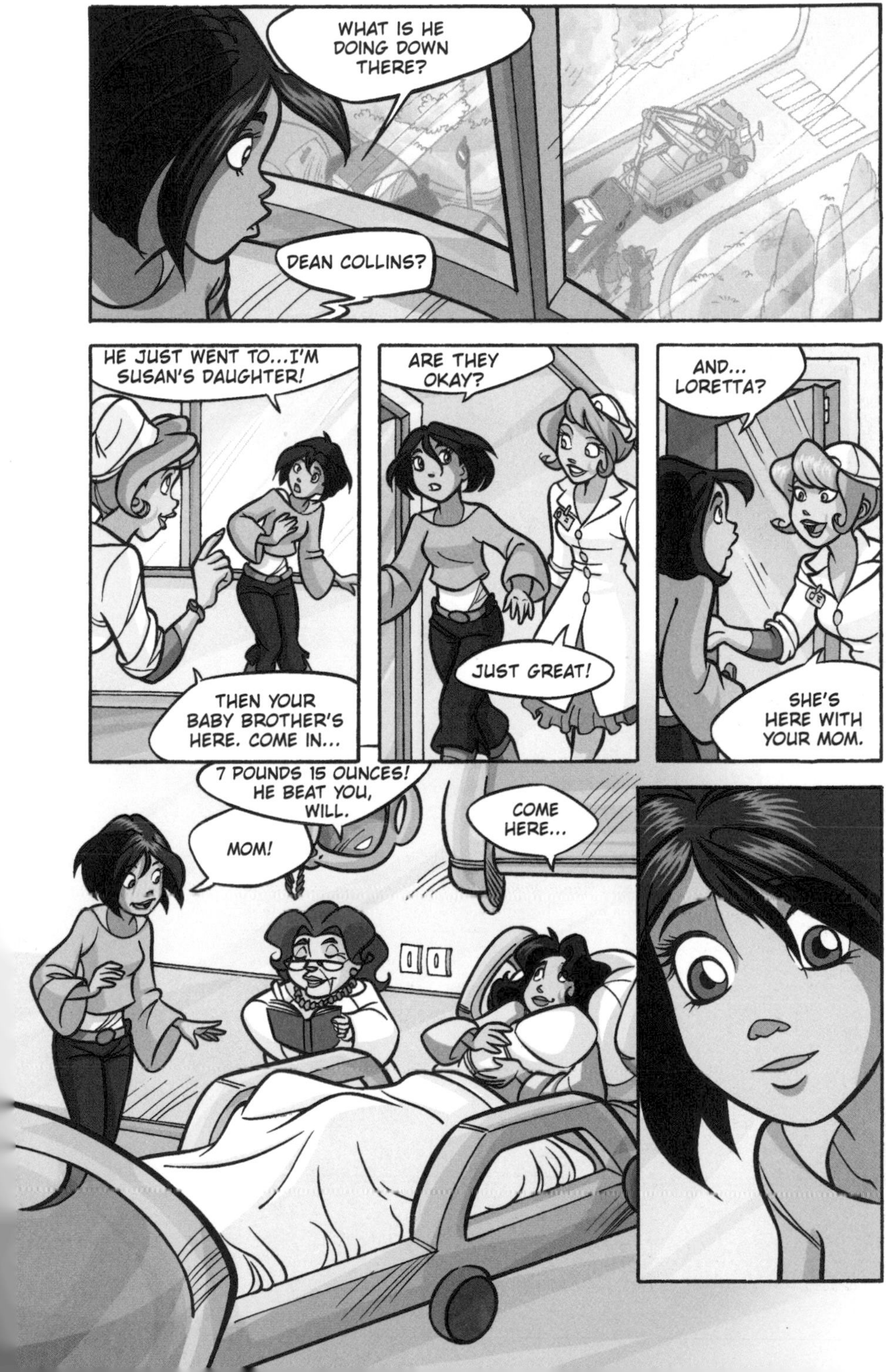
WHAT IS HE DOING DOWN THERE?
DEAN COLLINS?
HE JUST WENT TO...I'M SUSAN'S DAUGHTER!
THEN YOUR BABY BROTHER'S HERE. COME IN...
ARE THEY OKAY?
JUST GREAT!
AND... LORETTA?
SHE'S HERE WITH YOUR MOM.
MOM!
7 POUNDS 15 OUNCES! HE BEAT YOU, WILL.
COME HERE...

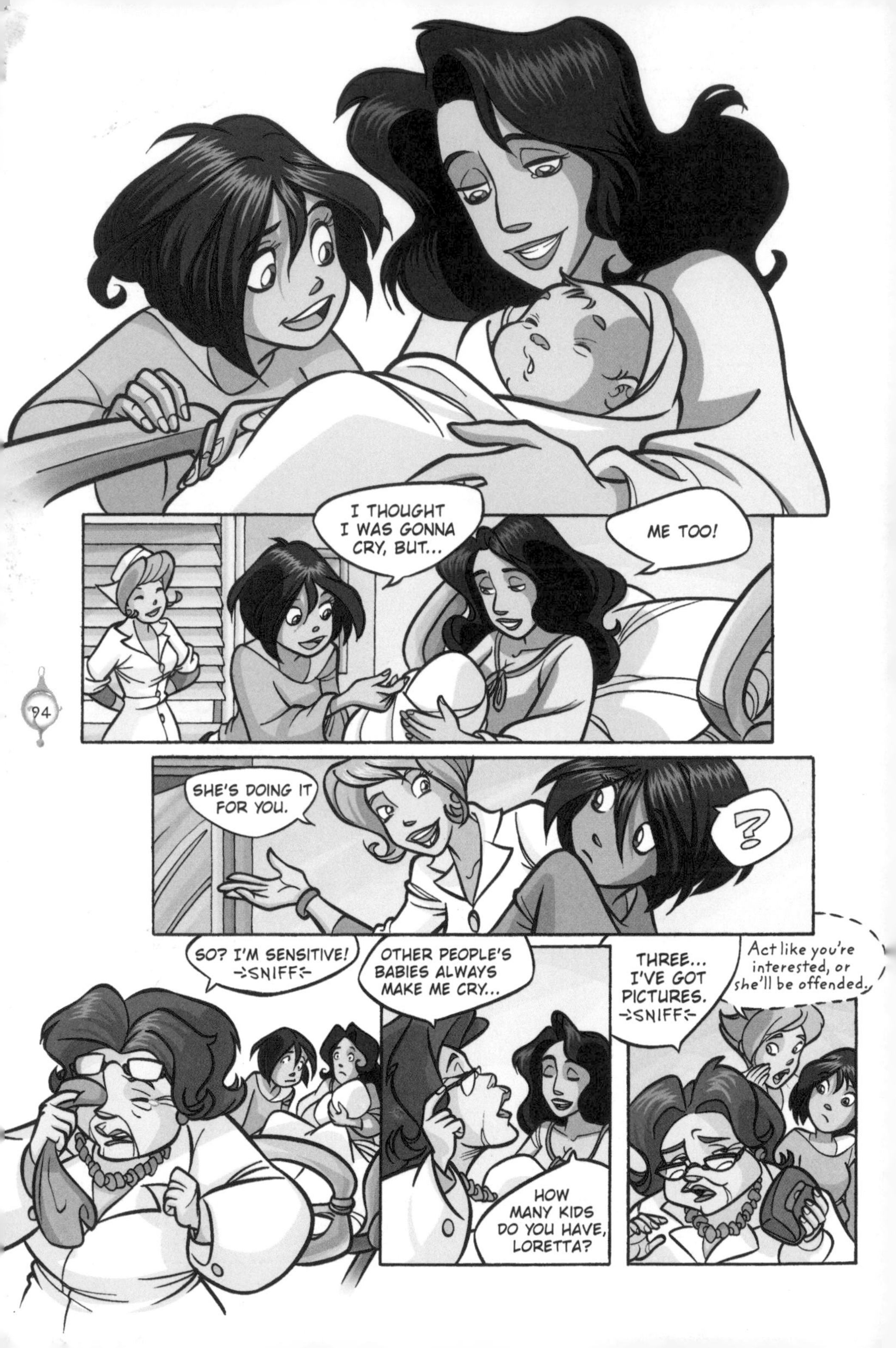

I THOUGHT I WAS GONNA CRY, BUT...
ME TOO!
SHE'S DOING IT FOR YOU.
?
SO? I'M SENSITIVE! -SNIFF-
OTHER PEOPLE'S BABIES ALWAYS MAKE ME CRY...
HOW MANY KIDS DO YOU HAVE, LORETTA?
THREE... I'VE GOT PICTURES. -SNIFF-
Act like you're interested, or she'll be offended.

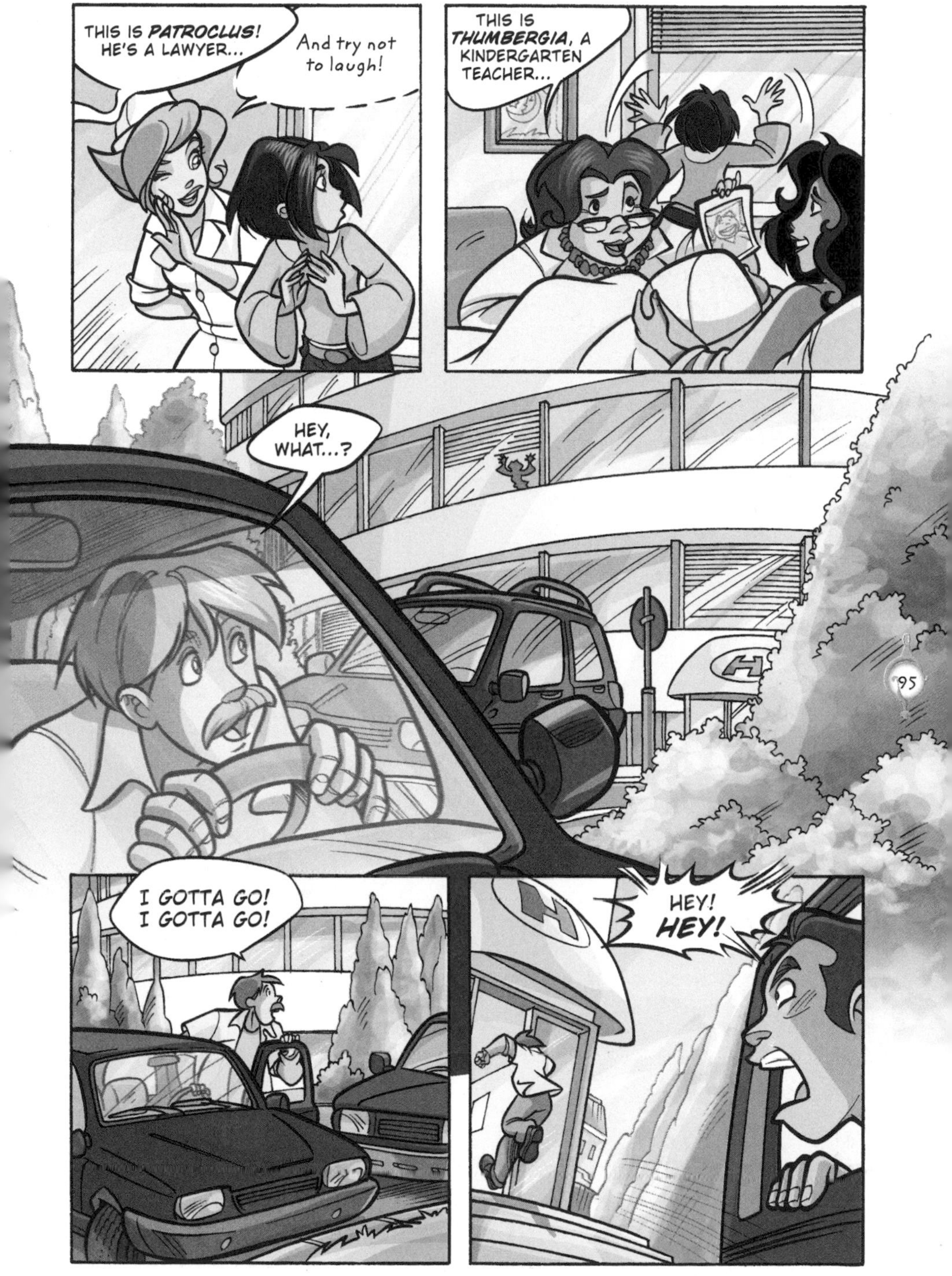
THIS IS **PATROCLUS**! HE'S A LAWYER...
And try not to laugh!
THIS IS **THUMBERGIA**, A KINDERGARTEN TEACHER...
HEY, WHAT...?
I GOTTA GO! I GOTTA GO!
HEY! **HEY!**

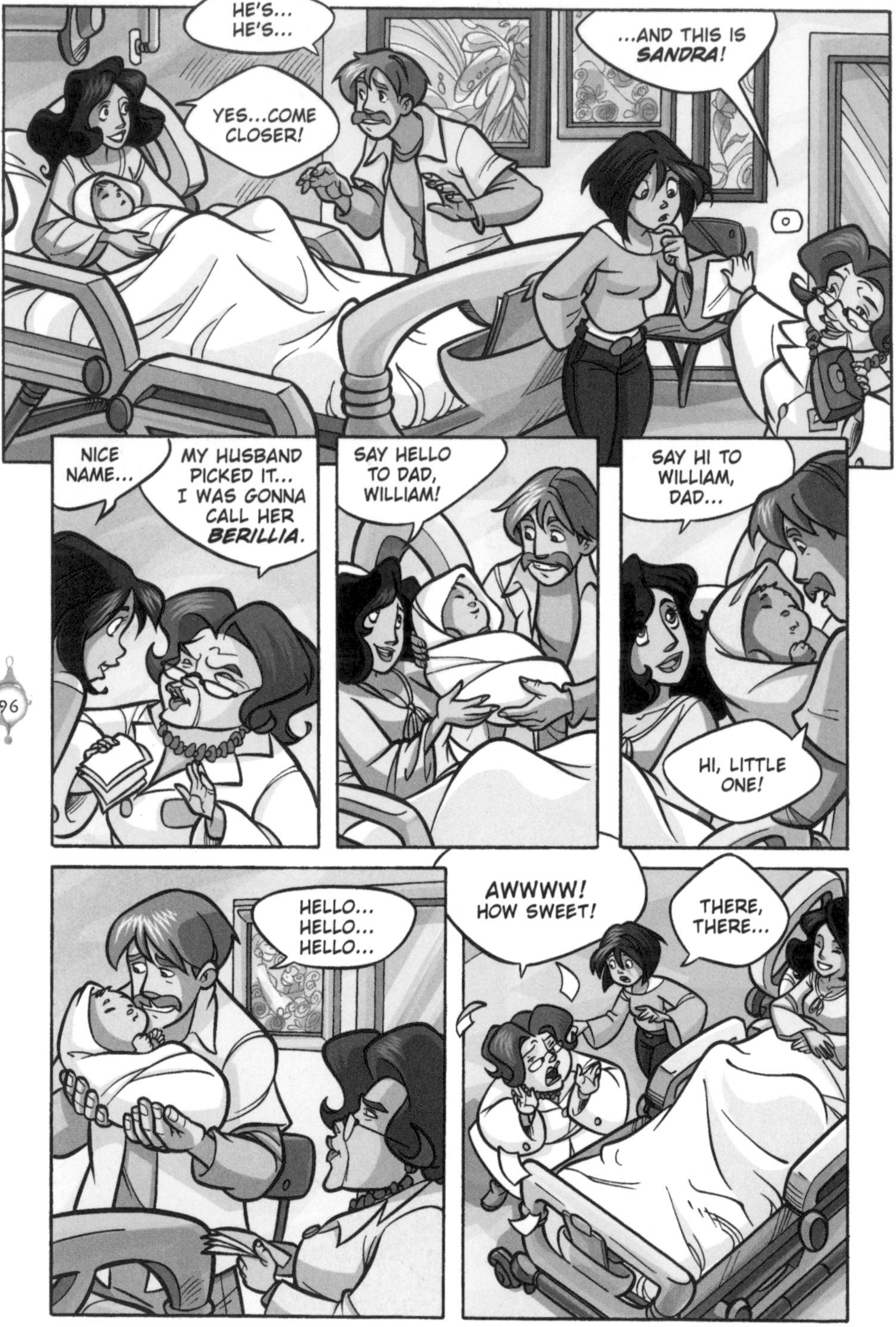
HE'S...
HE'S...
YES...COME CLOSER!
...AND THIS IS *SANDRA*!
NICE NAME...
MY HUSBAND PICKED IT... I WAS GONNA CALL HER *BERILLIA*.
SAY HELLO TO DAD, WILLIAM!
SAY HI TO WILLIAM, DAD...
HI, LITTLE ONE!
HELLO... HELLO... HELLO...
AWWWW! HOW SWEET!
THERE, THERE...

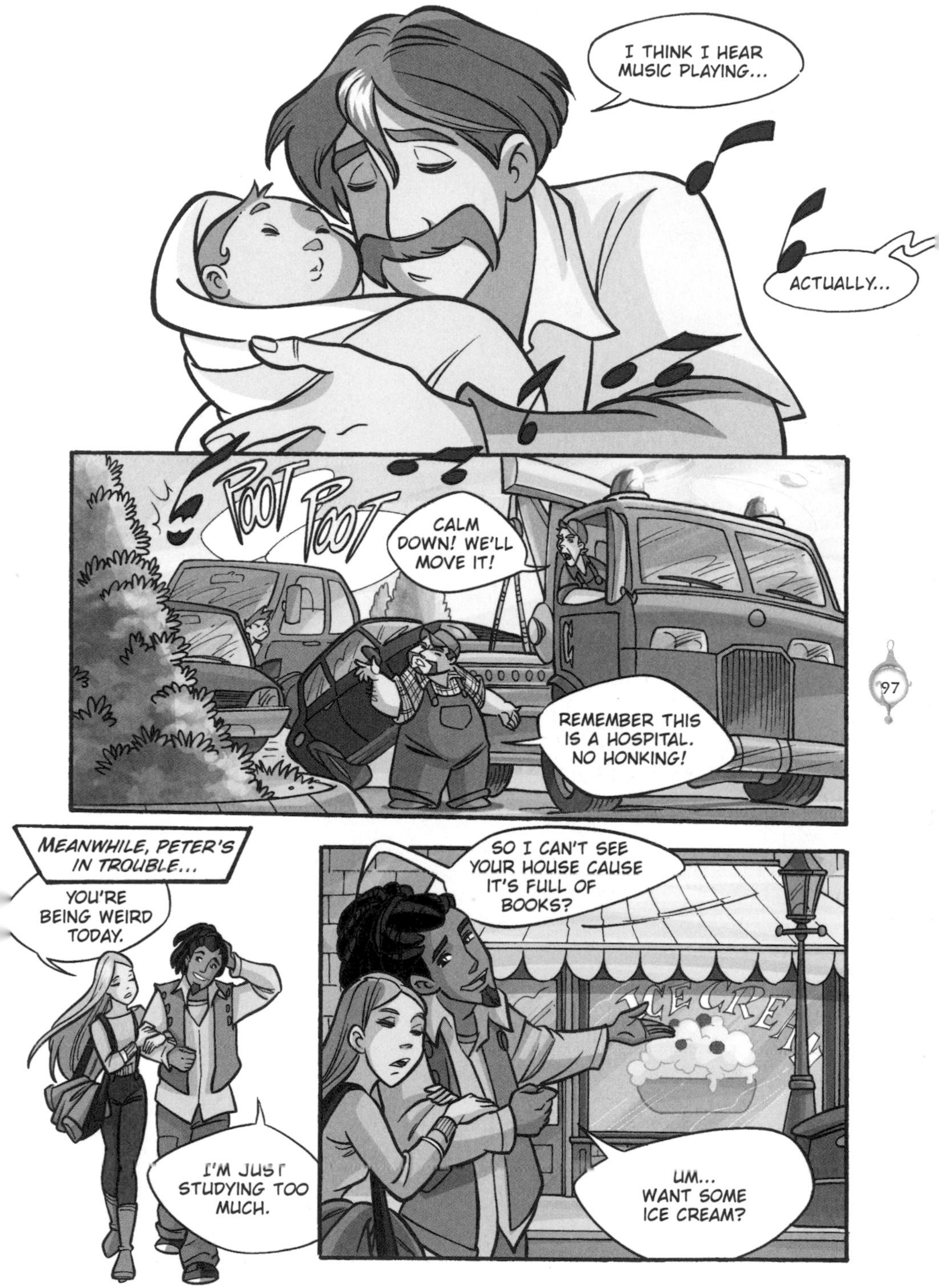
I THINK I HEAR MUSIC PLAYING...
ACTUALLY...
POOT POOT
CALM DOWN! WE'LL MOVE IT!
REMEMBER THIS IS A HOSPITAL. NO HONKING!
MEANWHILE, PETER'S IN TROUBLE...
YOU'RE BEING WEIRD TODAY.
I'M JUST STUDYING TOO MUCH.
SO I CAN'T SEE YOUR HOUSE CAUSE IT'S FULL OF BOOKS?
ICE CREA
UM... WANT SOME ICE CREAM?

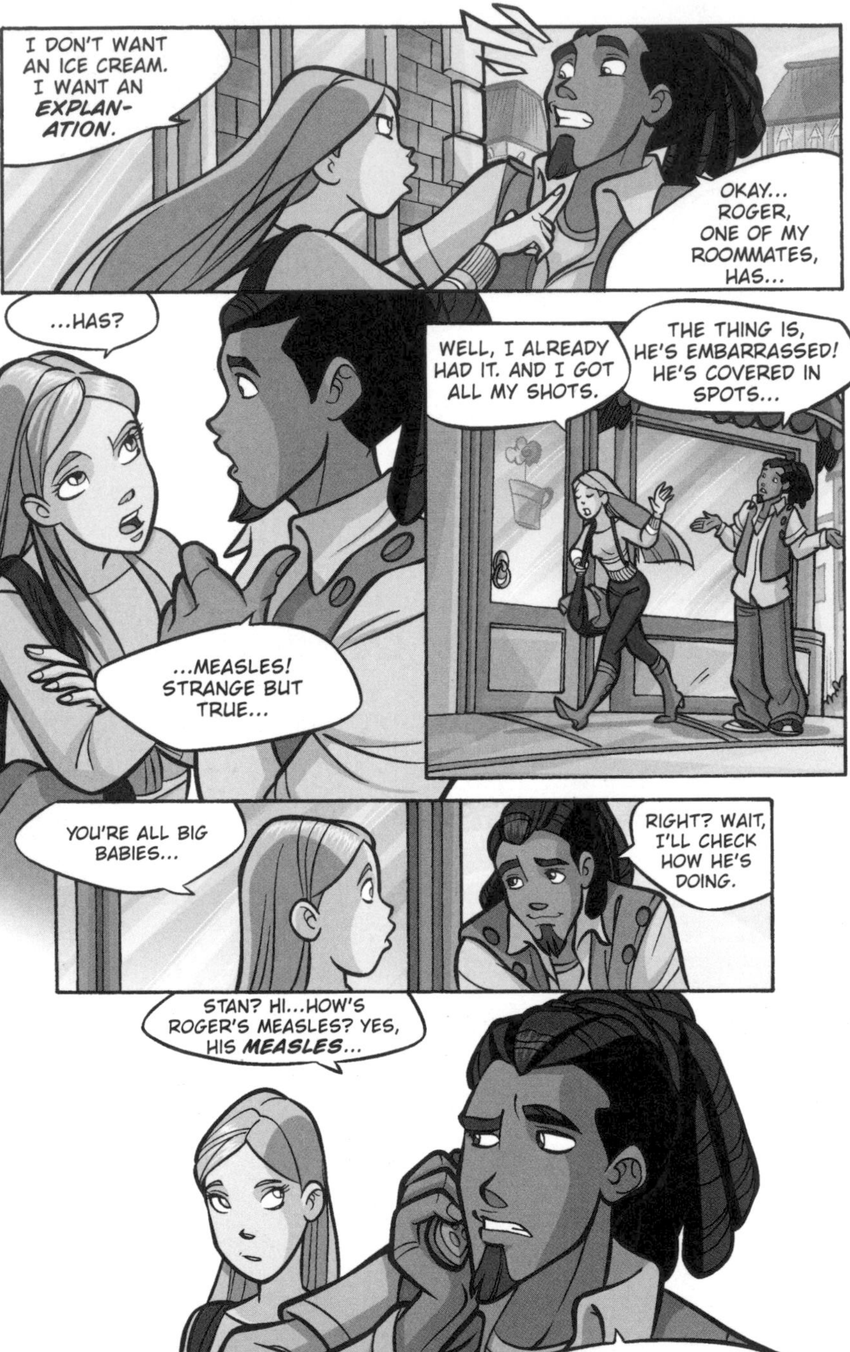
I DON'T WANT AN ICE CREAM. I WANT AN EXPLAN-ATION.
OKAY... ROGER, ONE OF MY ROOMMATES, HAS...
...HAS?
...MEASLES! STRANGE BUT TRUE...
WELL, I ALREADY HAD IT. AND I GOT ALL MY SHOTS.
THE THING IS, HE'S EMBARRASSED! HE'S COVERED IN SPOTS...
YOU'RE ALL BIG BABIES...
RIGHT? WAIT, I'LL CHECK HOW HE'S DOING.
STAN? HI...HOW'S ROGER'S MEASLES? YES, HIS MEASLES...
A BIT BETTER? HE'S STILL ALL SPOTTY, RIGHT?

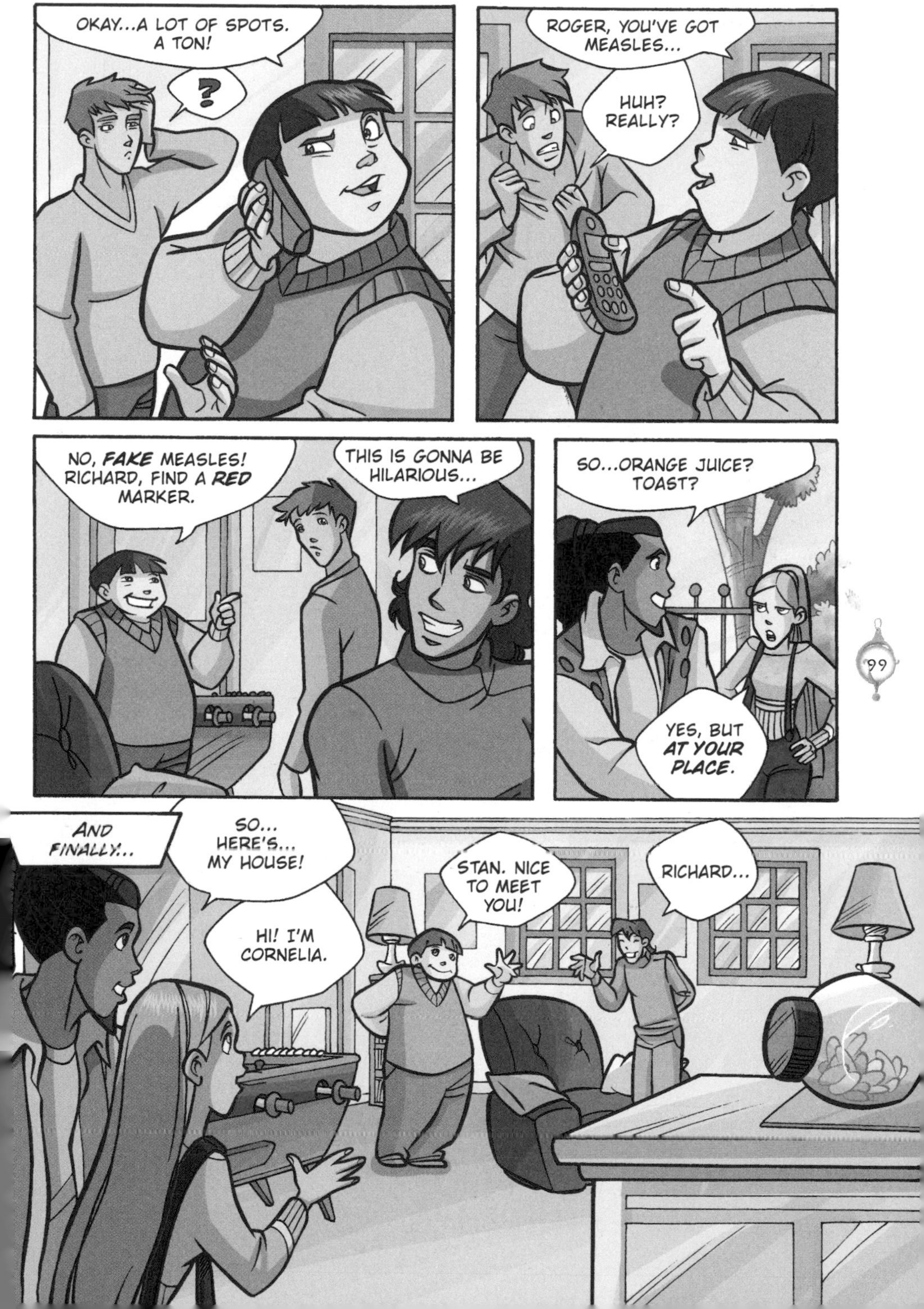
OKAY...A LOT OF SPOTS. A TON!
?
ROGER, YOU'VE GOT MEASLES...
HUH? REALLY?
NO, FAKE MEASLES! RICHARD, FIND A RED MARKER.
THIS IS GONNA BE HILARIOUS...
SO...ORANGE JUICE? TOAST?
YES, BUT AT YOUR PLACE.
AND FINALLY...
SO... HERE'S... MY HOUSE!
HI! I'M CORNELIA.
STAN. NICE TO MEET YOU!
RICHARD...

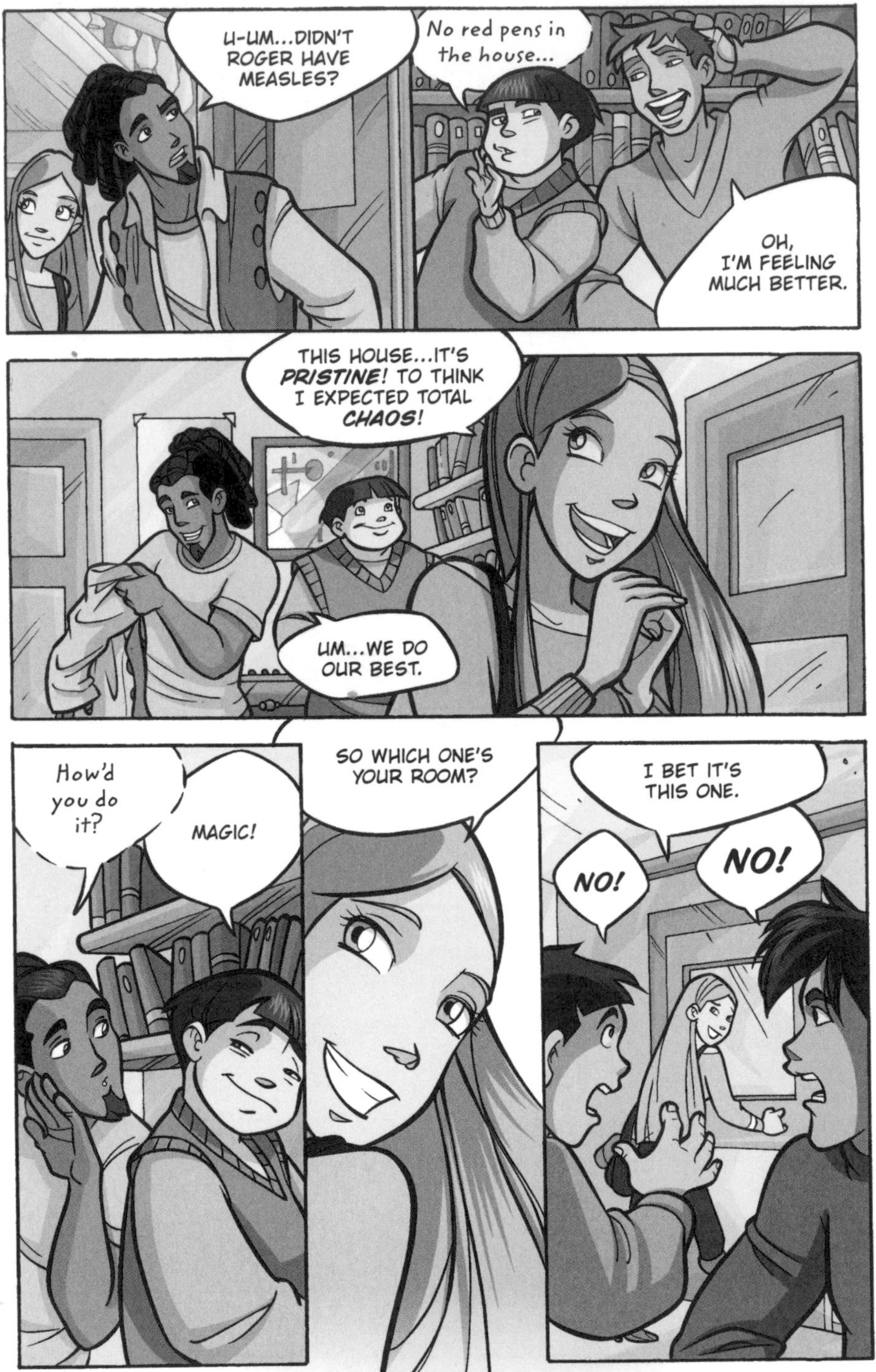
U-UM...DIDN'T ROGER HAVE MEASLES?
No red pens in the house...
OH, I'M FEELING MUCH BETTER.
THIS HOUSE...IT'S *PRISTINE!* TO THINK I EXPECTED TOTAL *CHAOS!*
UM...WE DO OUR BEST.
How'd you do it?
MAGIC!
SO WHICH ONE'S YOUR ROOM?
I BET IT'S THIS ONE.
NO!
NO!

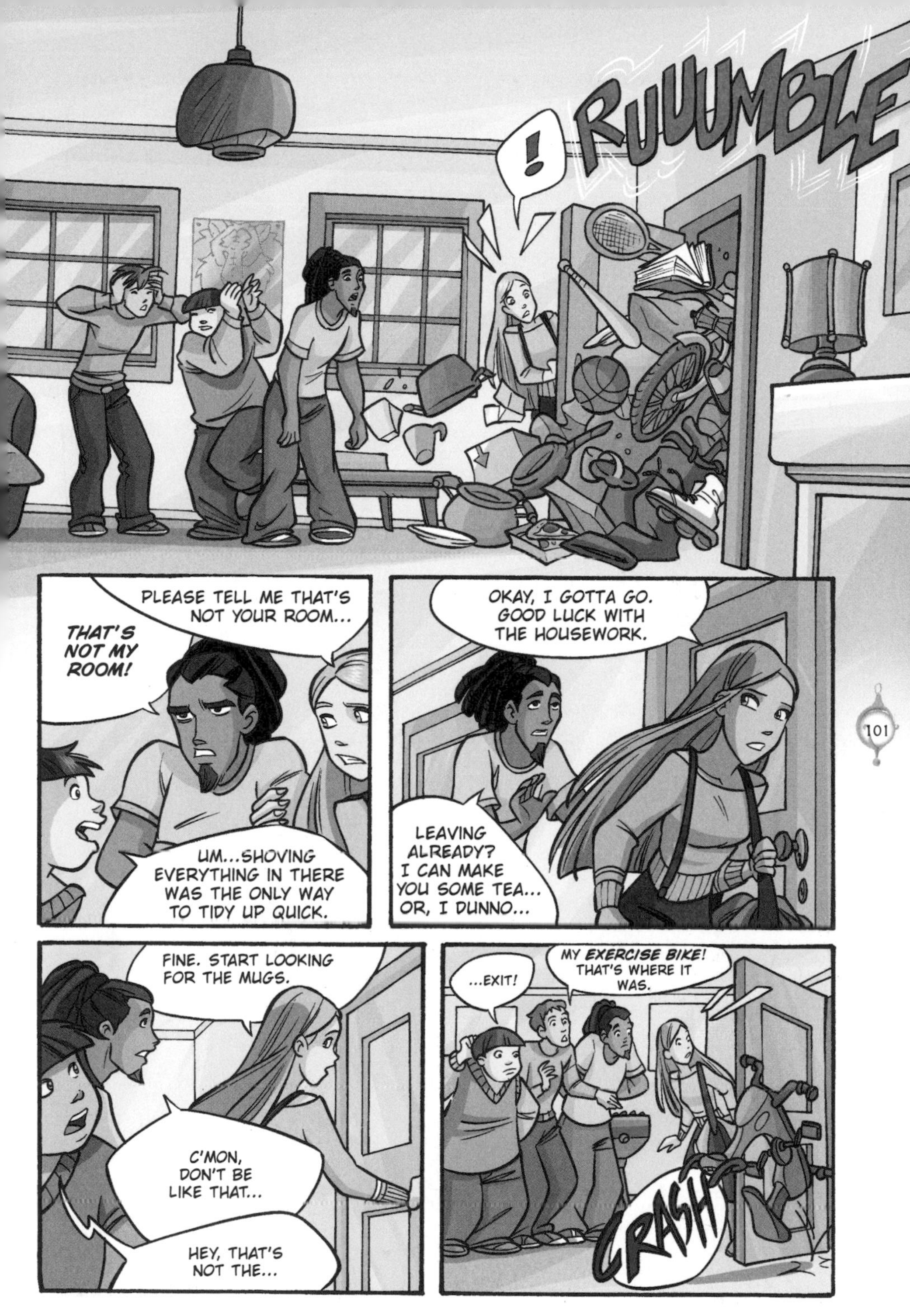
!
RUUUMBLE
PLEASE TELL ME THAT'S NOT YOUR ROOM...
THAT'S NOT MY ROOM!
UM...SHOVING EVERYTHING IN THERE WAS THE ONLY WAY TO TIDY UP QUICK.
OKAY, I GOTTA GO. GOOD LUCK WITH THE HOUSEWORK.
LEAVING ALREADY? I CAN MAKE YOU SOME TEA... OR, I DUNNO...
FINE. START LOOKING FOR THE MUGS.
C'MON, DON'T BE LIKE THAT...
HEY, THAT'S NOT THE...
...EXIT!
MY EXERCISE BIKE! THAT'S WHERE IT WAS.
CRASH

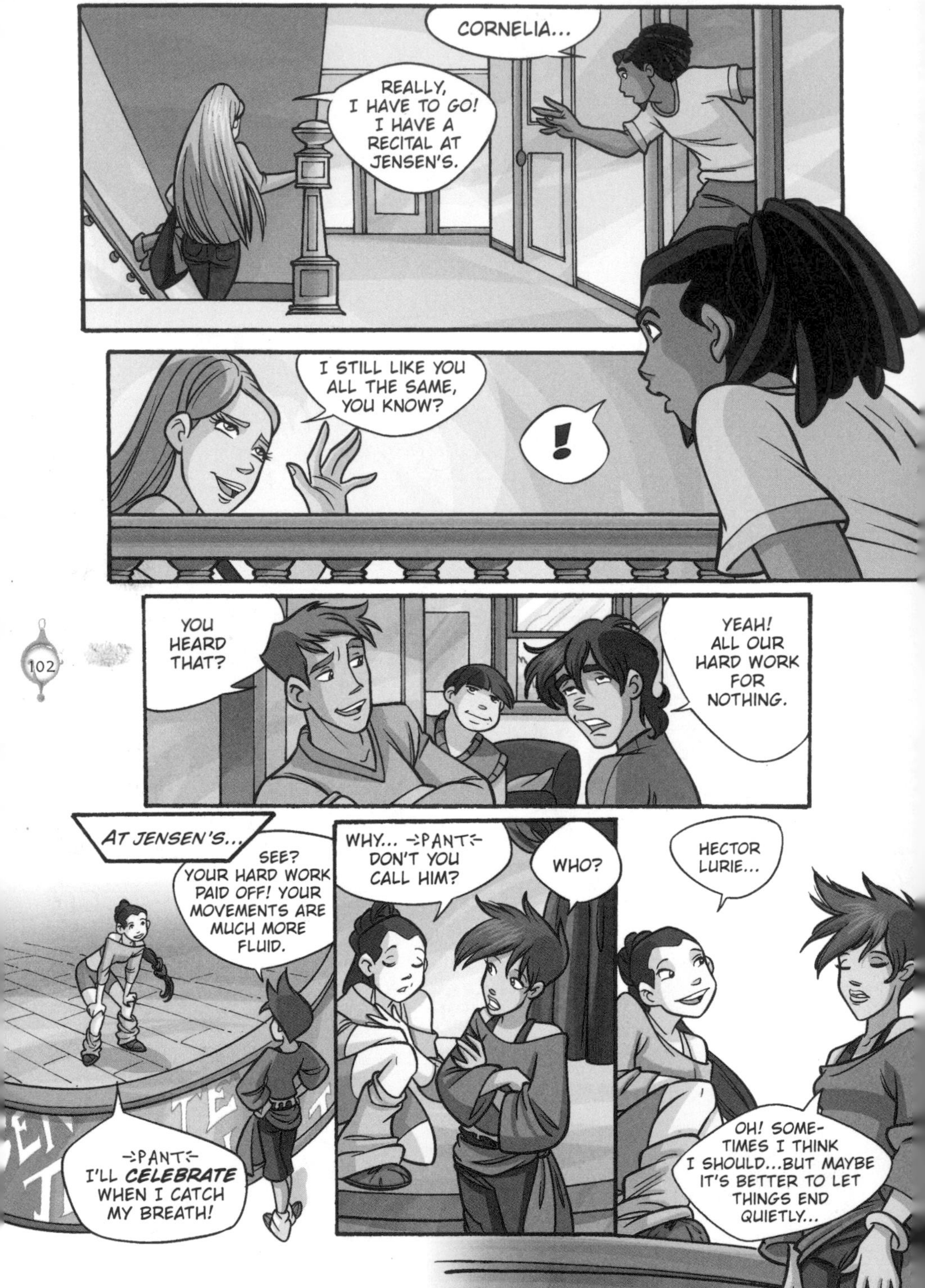
CORNELIA...
REALLY, I HAVE TO GO! I HAVE A RECITAL AT JENSEN'S.
I STILL LIKE YOU ALL THE SAME, YOU KNOW?
!
YOU HEARD THAT?
YEAH! ALL OUR HARD WORK FOR NOTHING.
AT JENSEN'S...
SEE? YOUR HARD WORK PAID OFF! YOUR MOVEMENTS ARE MUCH MORE FLUID.
⇒PANT⇐ I'LL ***CELEBRATE*** WHEN I CATCH MY BREATH!
WHY... ⇒PANT⇐ DON'T YOU CALL HIM?
WHO?
HECTOR LURIE...
OH! SOMETIMES I THINK I SHOULD...BUT MAYBE IT'S BETTER TO LET THINGS END QUIETLY...

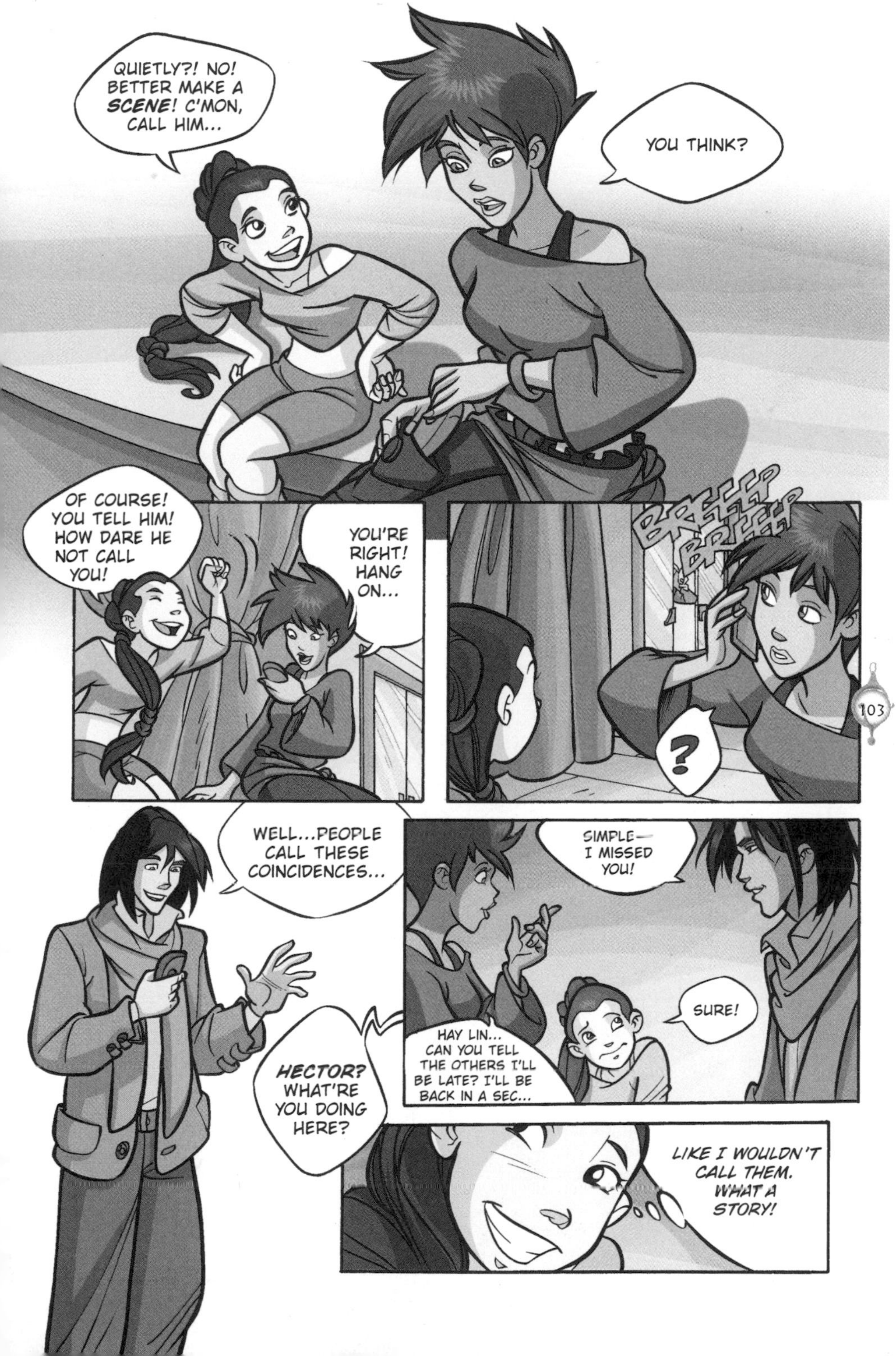
QUIETLY?! NO! BETTER MAKE A **SCENE**! C'MON, CALL HIM...
YOU THINK?
OF COURSE! YOU TELL HIM! HOW DARE HE NOT CALL YOU!
YOU'RE RIGHT! HANG ON...
BREEEP BREEEP
?
WELL...PEOPLE CALL THESE COINCIDENCES...
**HECTOR?** WHAT'RE YOU DOING HERE?
SIMPLE— I MISSED YOU!
SURE!
HAY LIN... CAN YOU TELL THE OTHERS I'LL BE LATE? I'LL BE BACK IN A SEC...
*LIKE I WOULDN'T CALL THEM. WHAT A STORY!*

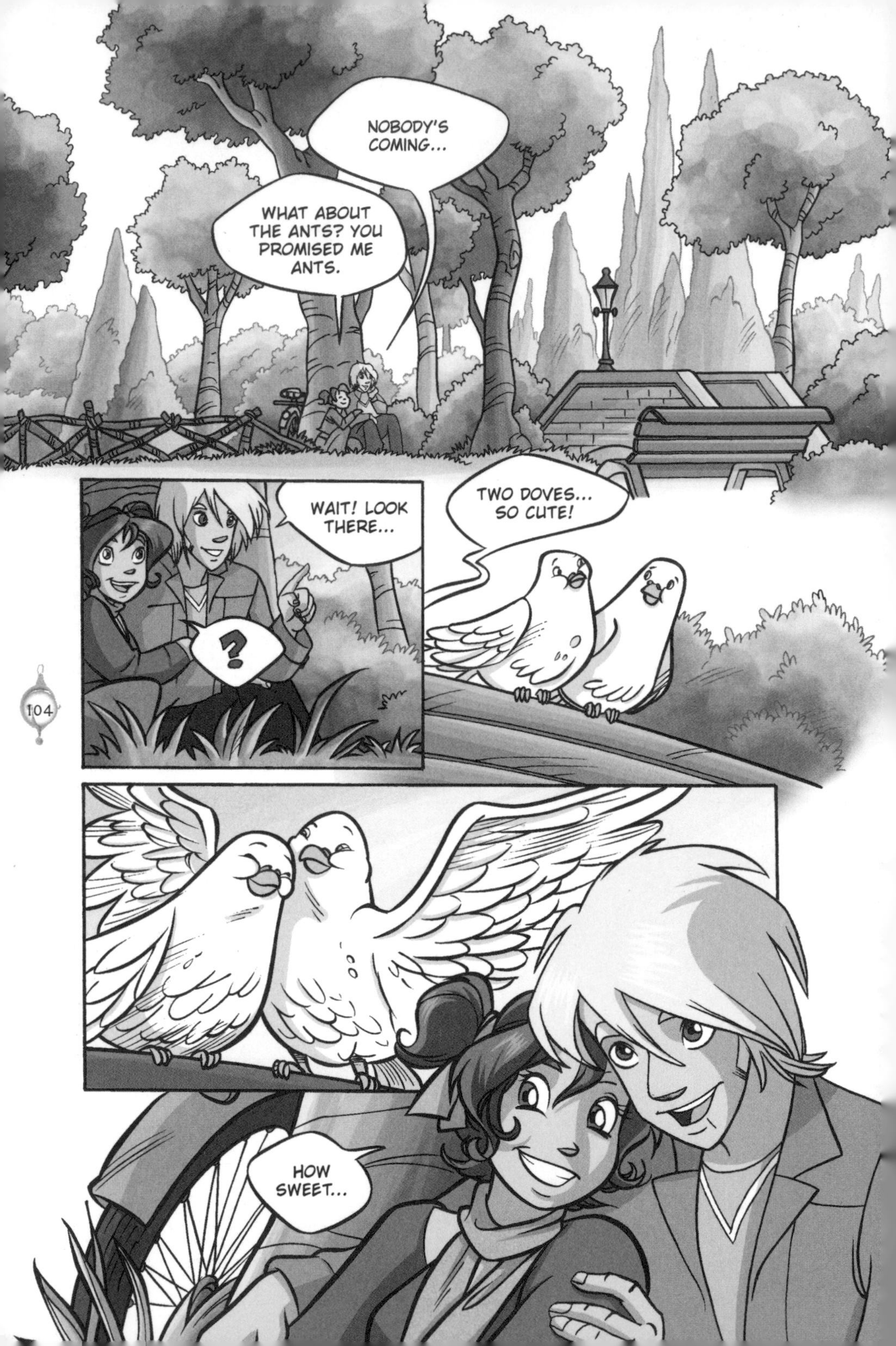
NOBODY'S COMING...
WHAT ABOUT THE ANTS? YOU PROMISED ME ANTS.
WAIT! LOOK THERE...
?
TWO DOVES... SO CUTE!
HOW SWEET...

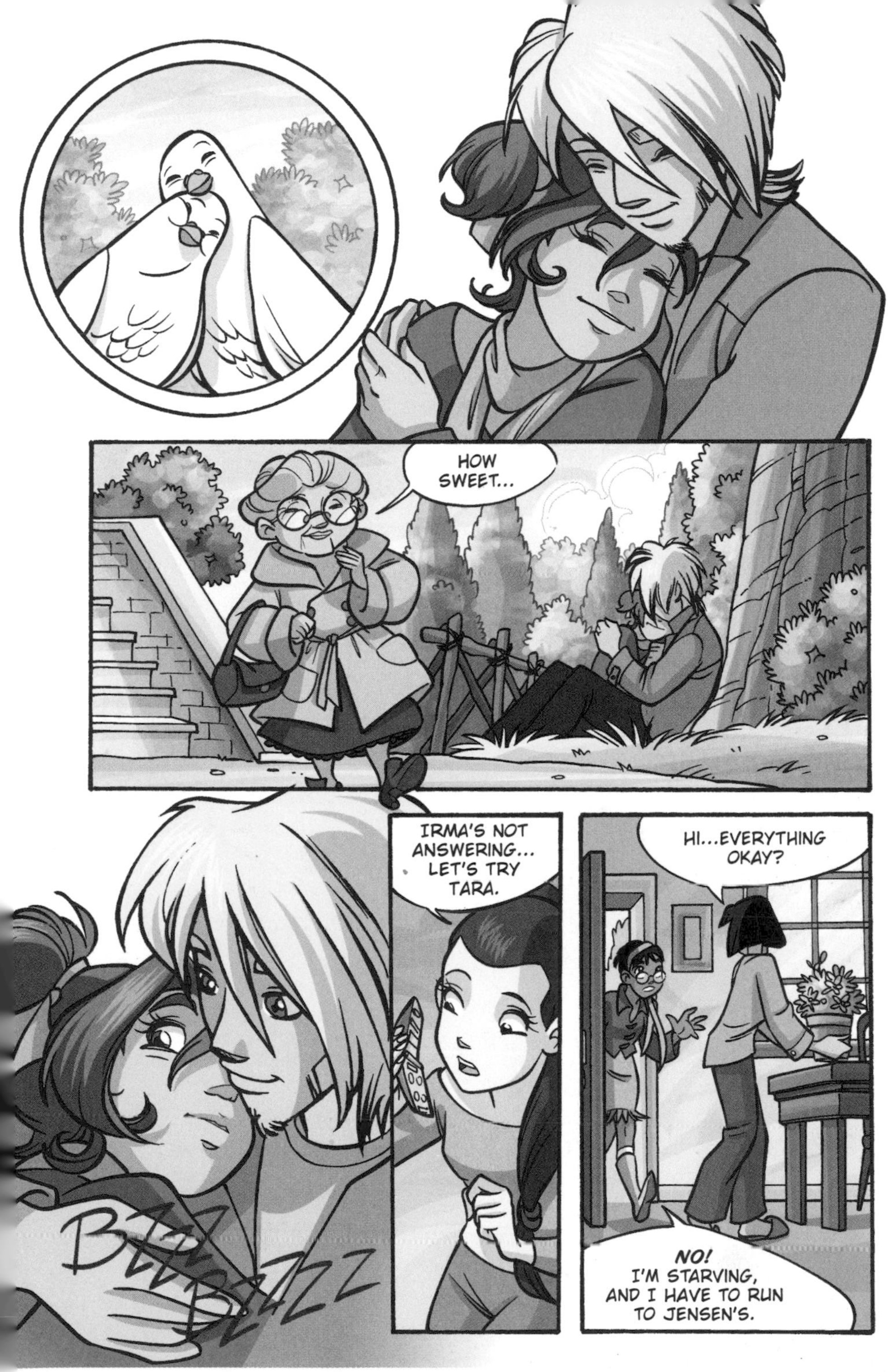
HOW SWEET...
IRMA'S NOT ANSWERING... LET'S TRY TARA.
BZZZ BZZZ
HI...EVERYTHING OKAY?
NO! I'M STARVING, AND I HAVE TO RUN TO JENSEN'S.

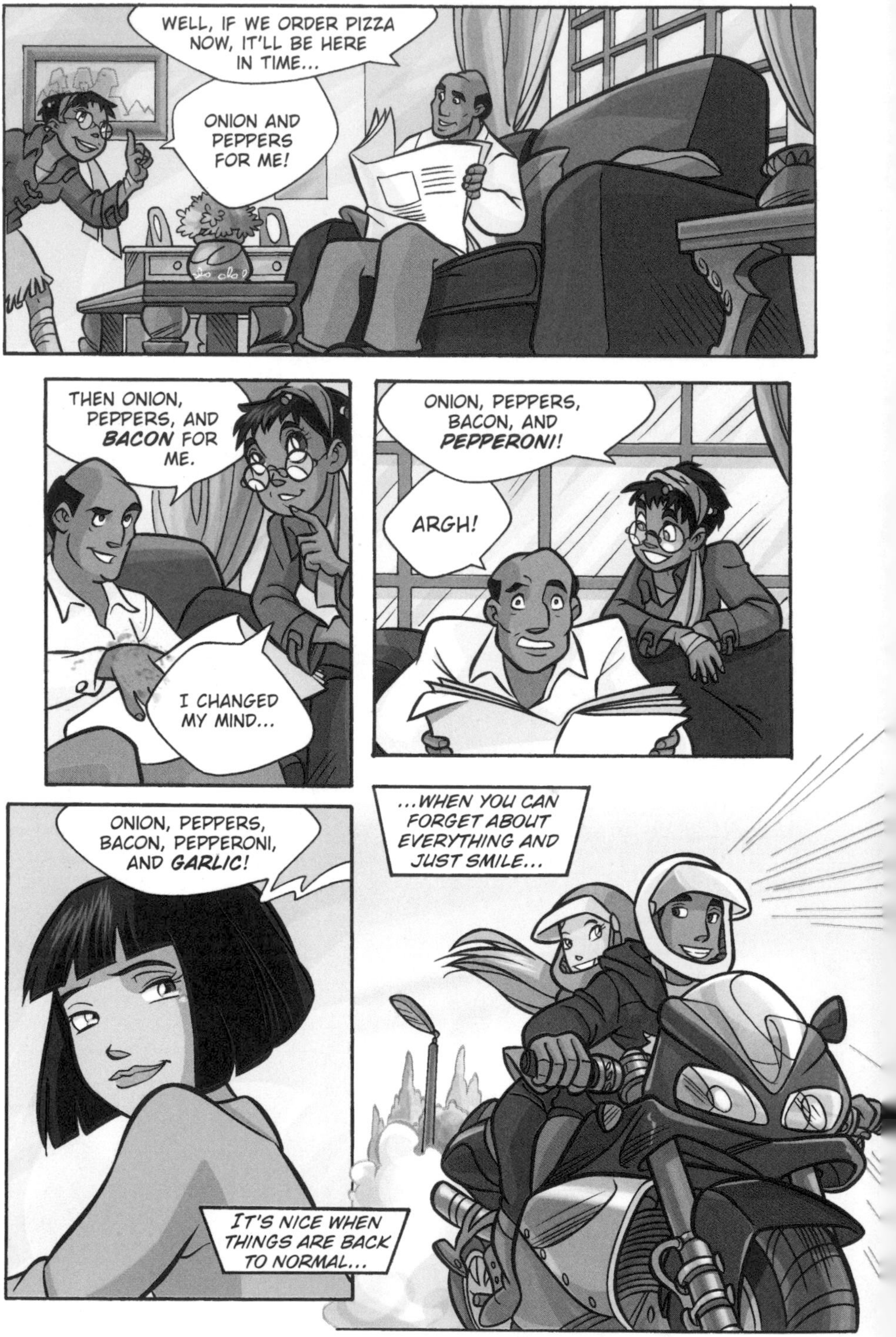
WELL, IF WE ORDER PIZZA NOW, IT'LL BE HERE IN TIME...
ONION AND PEPPERS FOR ME!
THEN ONION, PEPPERS, AND BACON FOR ME.
I CHANGED MY MIND...
ONION, PEPPERS, BACON, AND PEPPERONI!
ARGH!
ONION, PEPPERS, BACON, PEPPERONI, AND GARLIC!
IT'S NICE WHEN THINGS ARE BACK TO NORMAL...
...WHEN YOU CAN FORGET ABOUT EVERYTHING AND JUST SMILE...

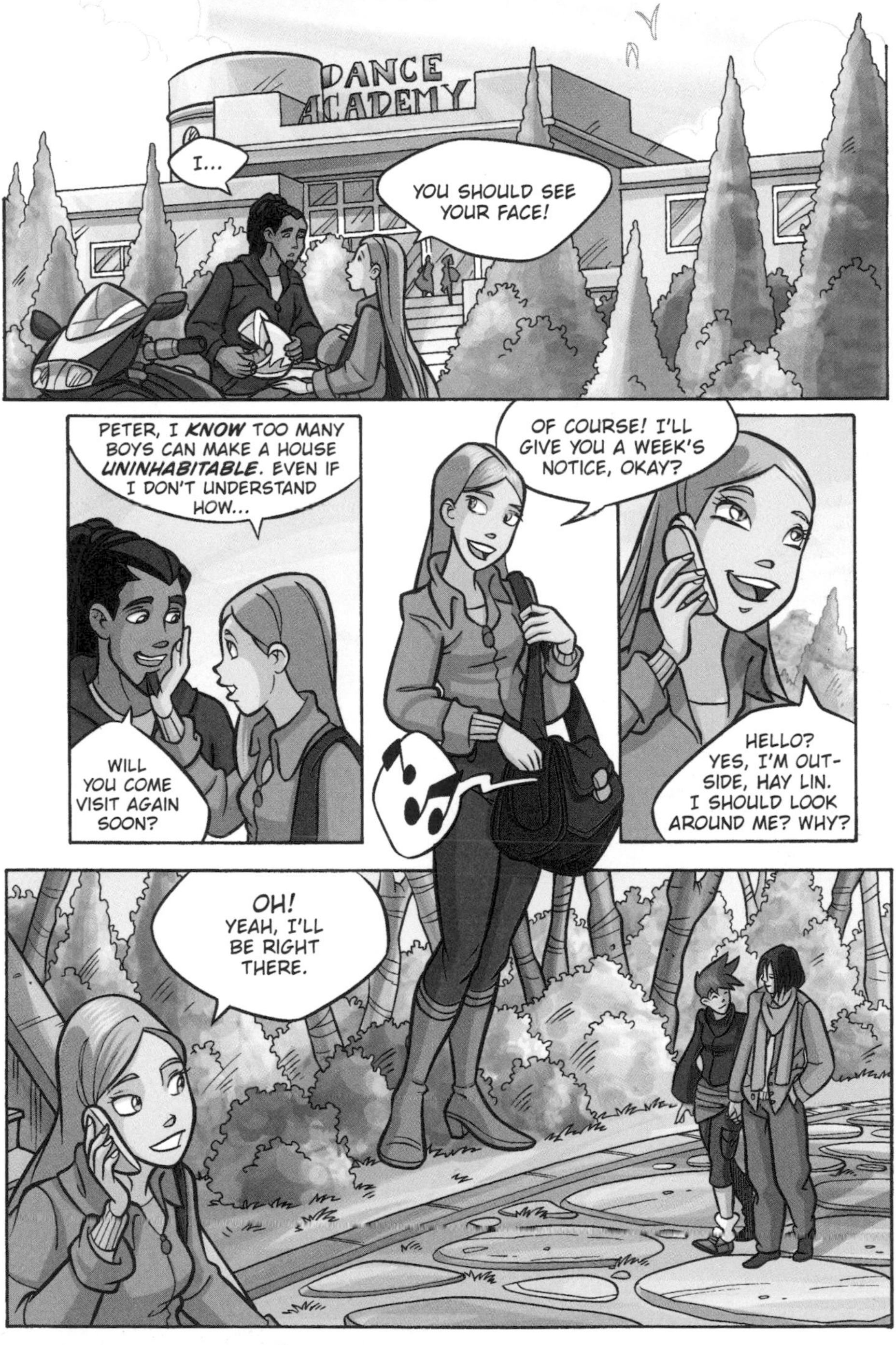
I...
YOU SHOULD SEE YOUR FACE!
PETER, I KNOW TOO MANY BOYS CAN MAKE A HOUSE UNINHABITABLE. EVEN IF I DON'T UNDERSTAND HOW...
WILL YOU COME VISIT AGAIN SOON?
OF COURSE! I'LL GIVE YOU A WEEK'S NOTICE, OKAY?
HELLO? YES, I'M OUT-SIDE, HAY LIN. I SHOULD LOOK AROUND ME? WHY?
OH! YEAH, I'LL BE RIGHT THERE.

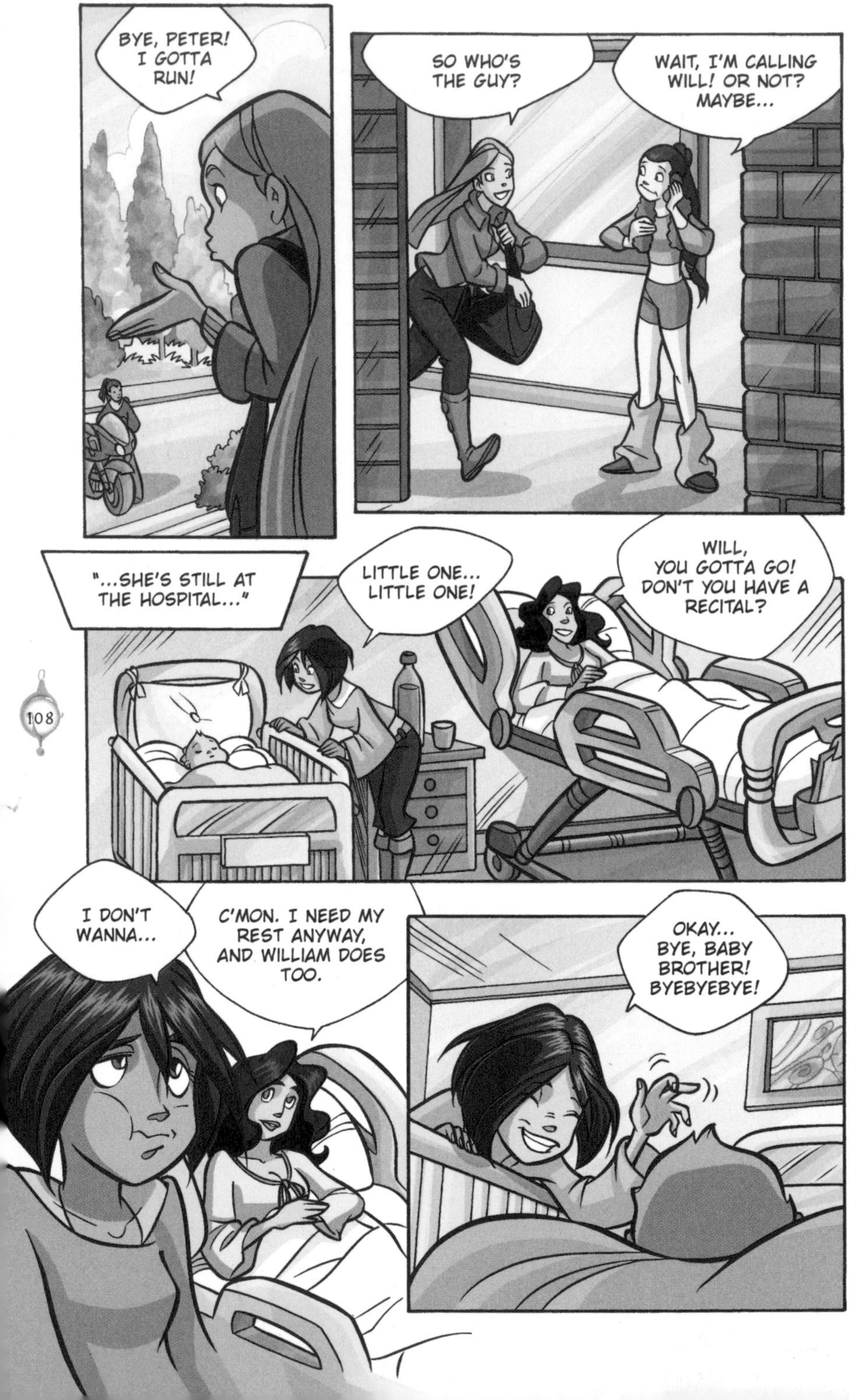
BYE, PETER! I GOTTA RUN!
SO WHO'S THE GUY?
WAIT, I'M CALLING WILL! OR NOT? MAYBE...
"...SHE'S STILL AT THE HOSPITAL..."
LITTLE ONE... LITTLE ONE!
WILL, YOU GOTTA GO! DON'T YOU HAVE A RECITAL?
I DON'T WANNA...
C'MON. I NEED MY REST ANYWAY, AND WILLIAM DOES TOO.
OKAY... BYE, BABY BROTHER! BYEBYEBYE!

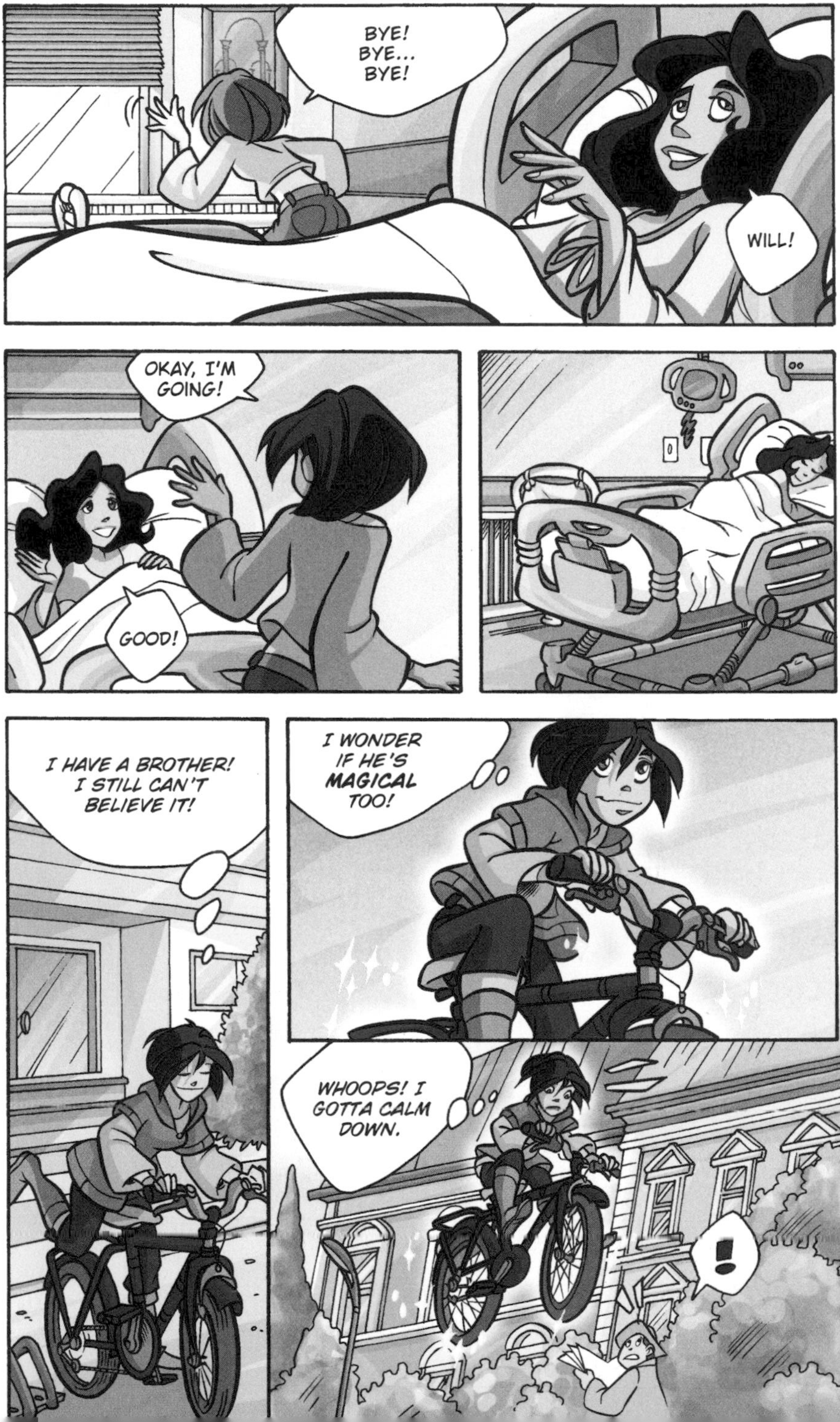
BYE!
BYE...
BYE!
WILL!
OKAY, I'M GOING!
GOOD!
I HAVE A BROTHER! I STILL CAN'T BELIEVE IT!
I WONDER IF HE'S **MAGICAL** TOO!
WHOOPS! I GOTTA CALM DOWN.
!

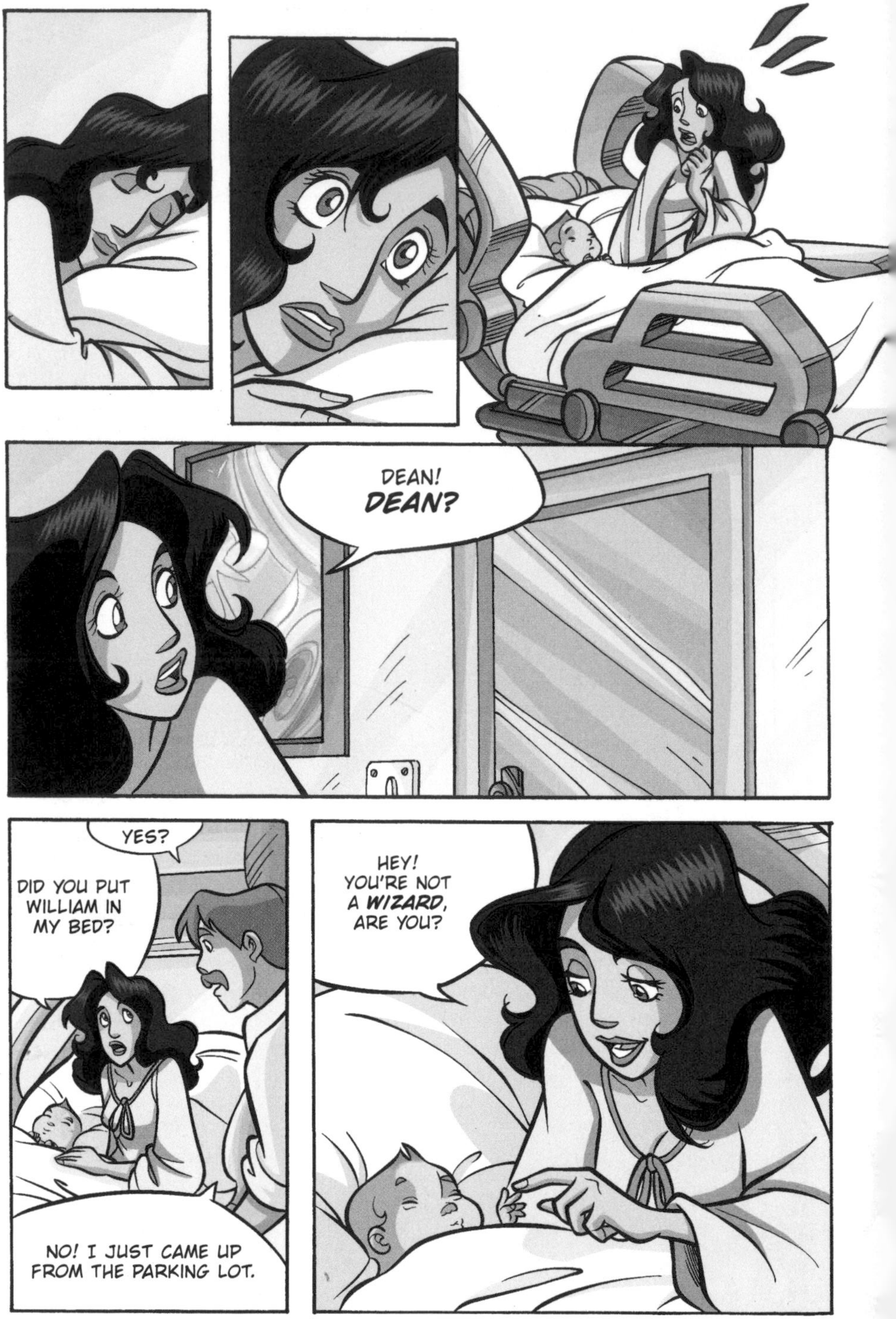
DEAN!
DEAN?
YES?
DID YOU PUT WILLIAM IN MY BED?
NO! I JUST CAME UP FROM THE PARKING LOT.
HEY! YOU'RE NOT A WIZARD, ARE YOU?

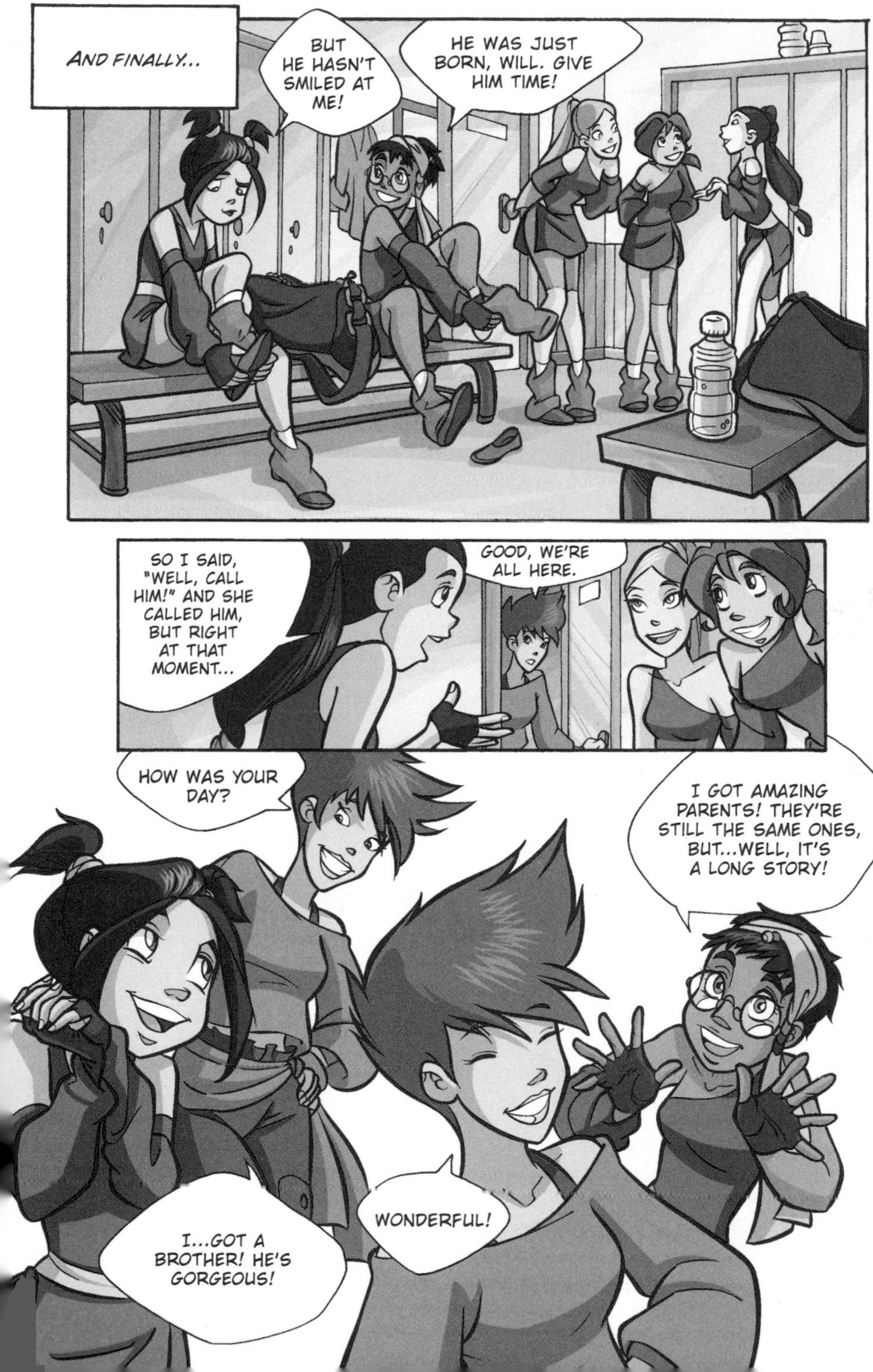
AND FINALLY...
BUT HE HASN'T SMILED AT ME!
HE WAS JUST BORN, WILL. GIVE HIM TIME!
SO I SAID, "WELL, CALL HIM!" AND SHE CALLED HIM, BUT RIGHT AT THAT MOMENT...
GOOD, WE'RE ALL HERE.
HOW WAS YOUR DAY?
I GOT AMAZING PARENTS! THEY'RE STILL THE SAME ONES, BUT...WELL, IT'S A LONG STORY!
WONDERFUL!
I...GOT A BROTHER! HE'S GORGEOUS!

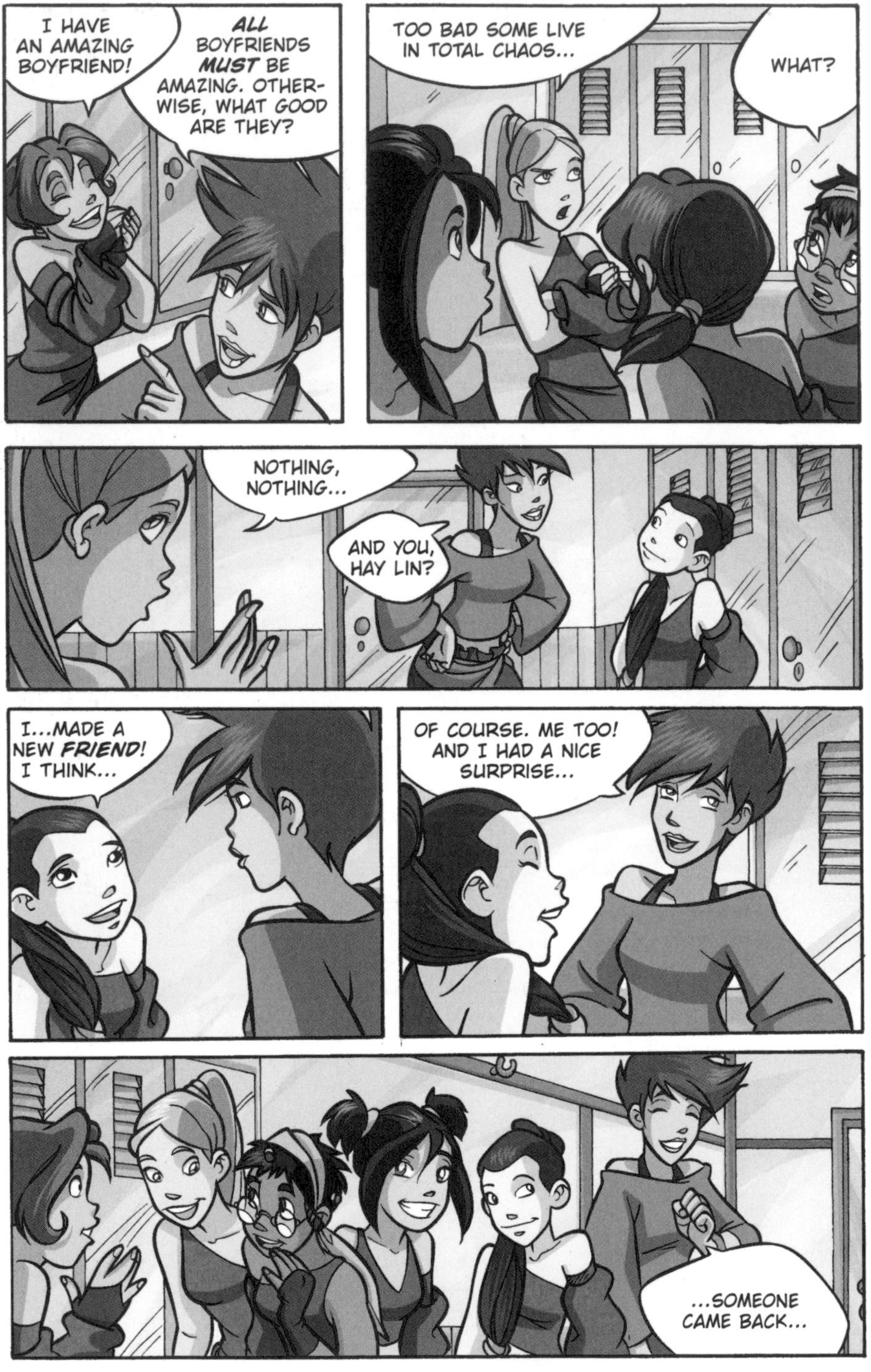

I HAVE AN AMAZING BOYFRIEND!
ALL BOYFRIENDS MUST BE AMAZING. OTHERWISE, WHAT GOOD ARE THEY?
TOO BAD SOME LIVE IN TOTAL CHAOS...
WHAT?
NOTHING, NOTHING...
AND YOU, HAY LIN?
I...MADE A NEW FRIEND! I THINK...
OF COURSE. ME TOO! AND I HAD A NICE SURPRISE...
...SOMEONE CAME BACK...

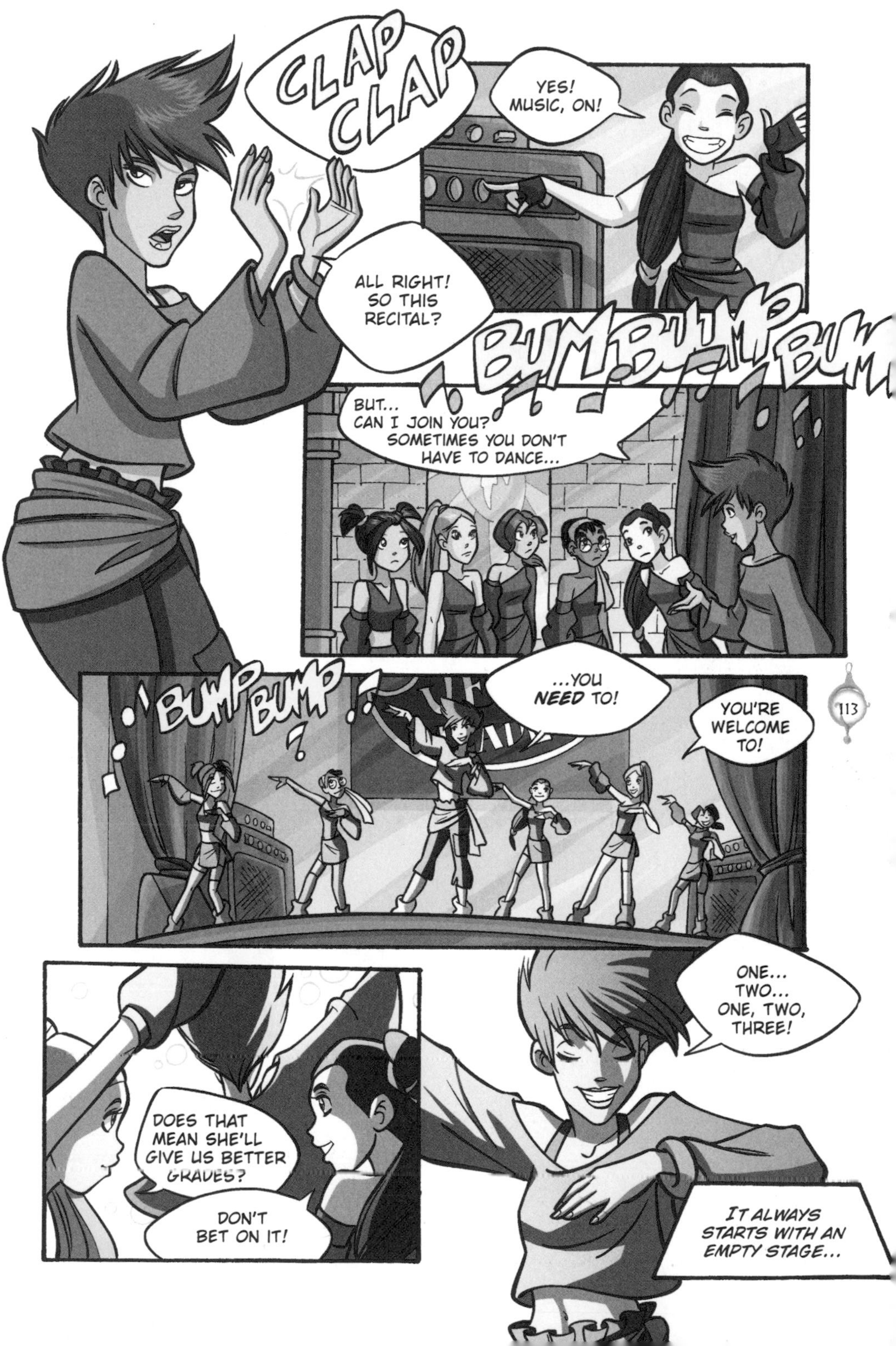
CLAP CLAP
YES! MUSIC, ON!
ALL RIGHT! SO THIS RECITAL?
BUM BUMP BUM
BUT... CAN I JOIN YOU? SOMETIMES YOU DON'T HAVE TO DANCE...
BUMP BUMP
...YOU NEED TO!
YOU'RE WELCOME TO!
ONE... TWO... ONE, TWO, THREE!
DOES THAT MEAN SHE'LL GIVE US BETTER GRADES?
DON'T BET ON IT!
IT ALWAYS STARTS WITH AN EMPTY STAGE...

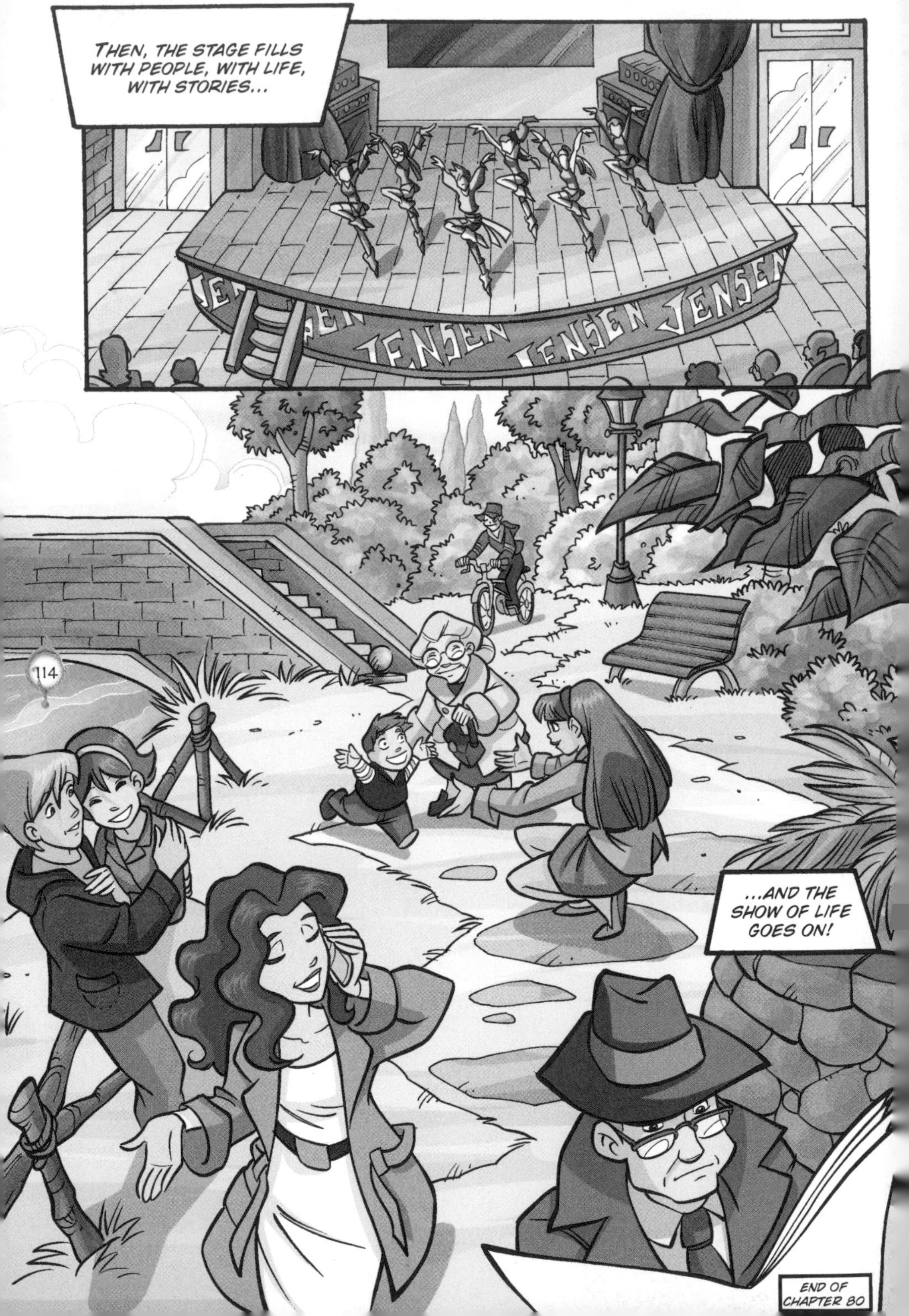
THEN, THE STAGE FILLS WITH PEOPLE, WITH LIFE, WITH STORIES...
JENSEN JENSEN JENSEN
...AND THE SHOW OF LIFE GOES ON!
END OF CHAPTER 80

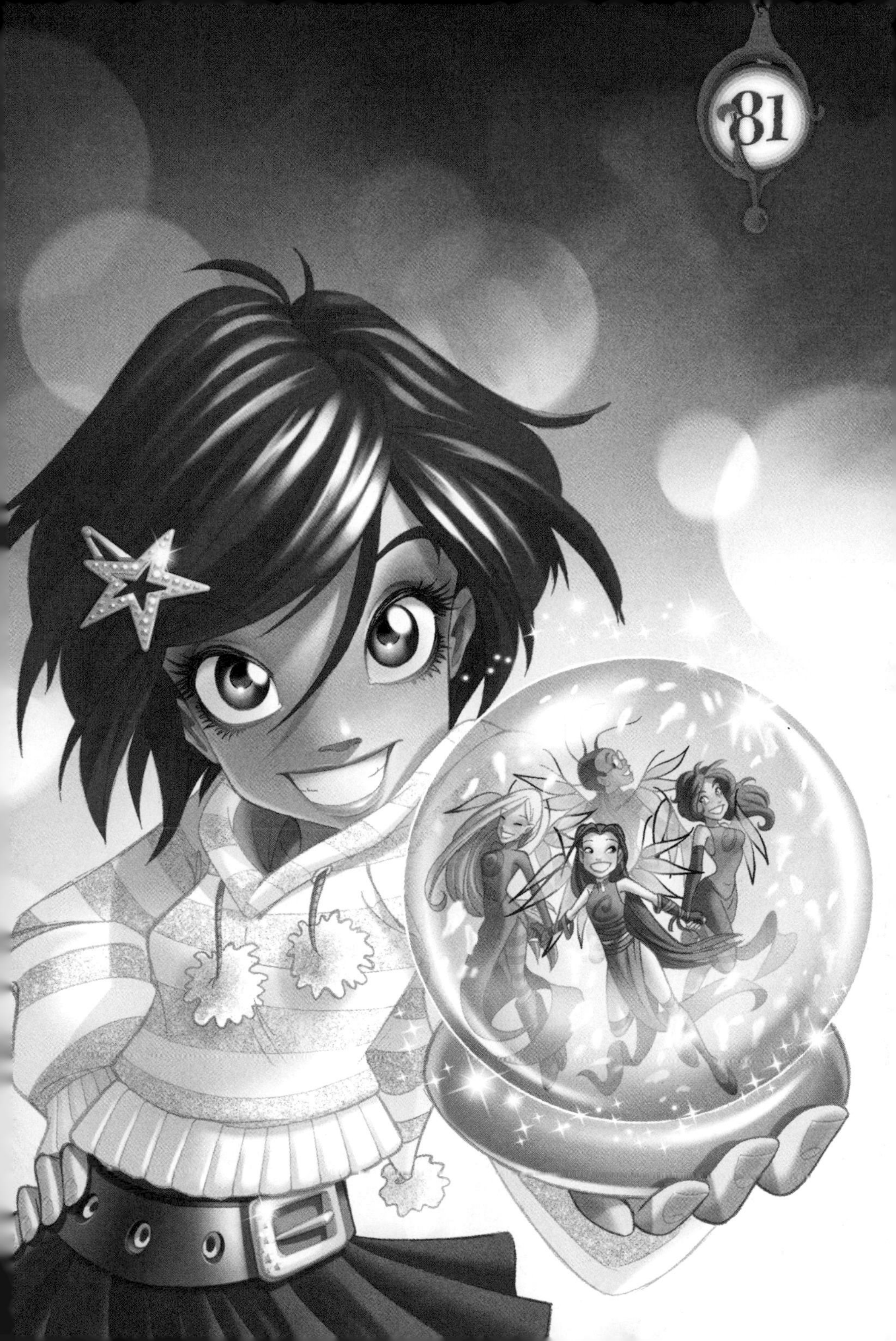
81

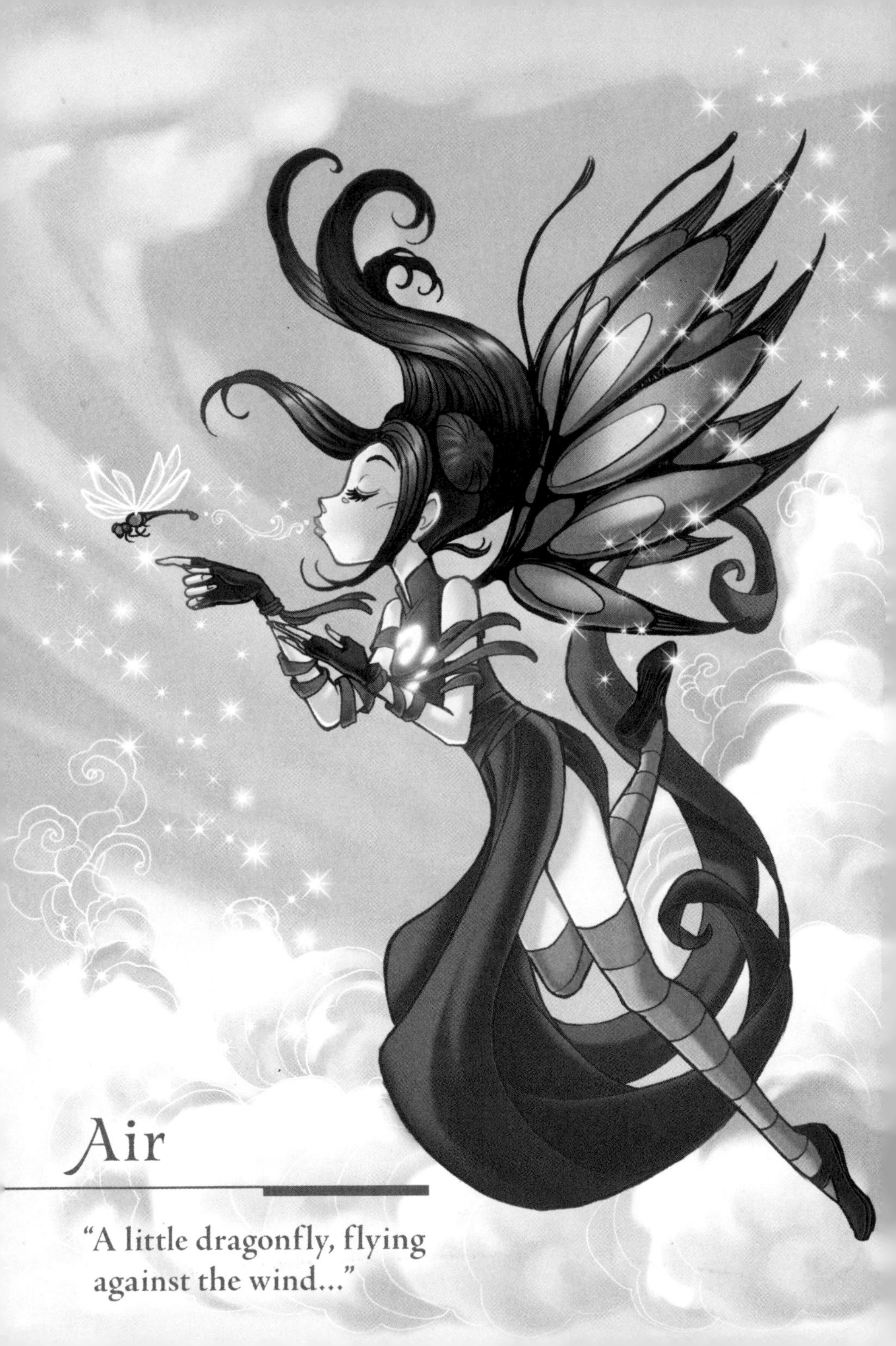

# Air

"A little dragonfly, flying against the wind..."

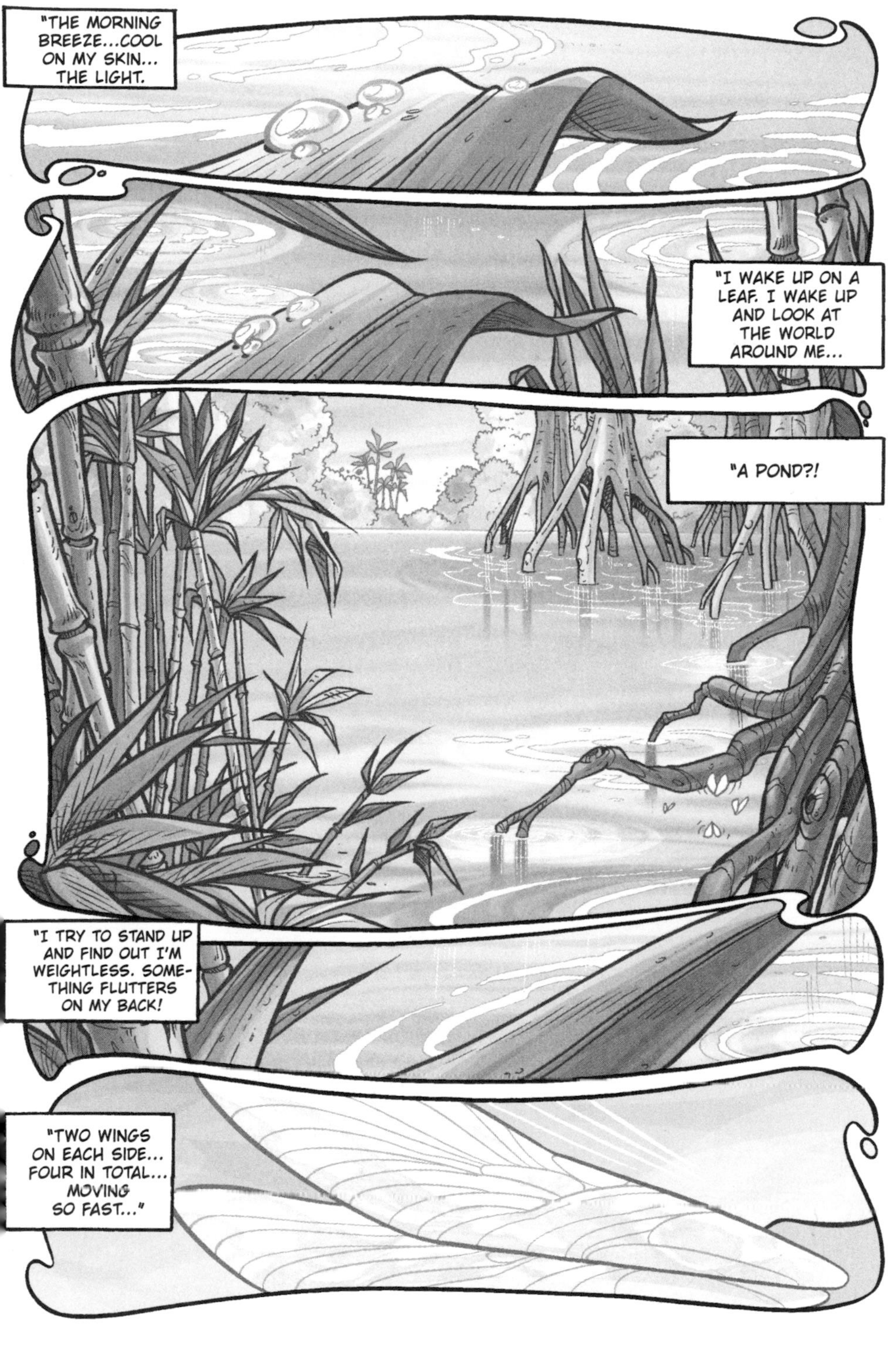
"THE MORNING BREEZE...COOL ON MY SKIN... THE LIGHT.
"I WAKE UP ON A LEAF. I WAKE UP AND LOOK AT THE WORLD AROUND ME...
"A POND?!
"I TRY TO STAND UP AND FIND OUT I'M WEIGHTLESS. SOMETHING FLUTTERS ON MY BACK!
"TWO WINGS ON EACH SIDE... FOUR IN TOTAL... MOVING SO FAST..."

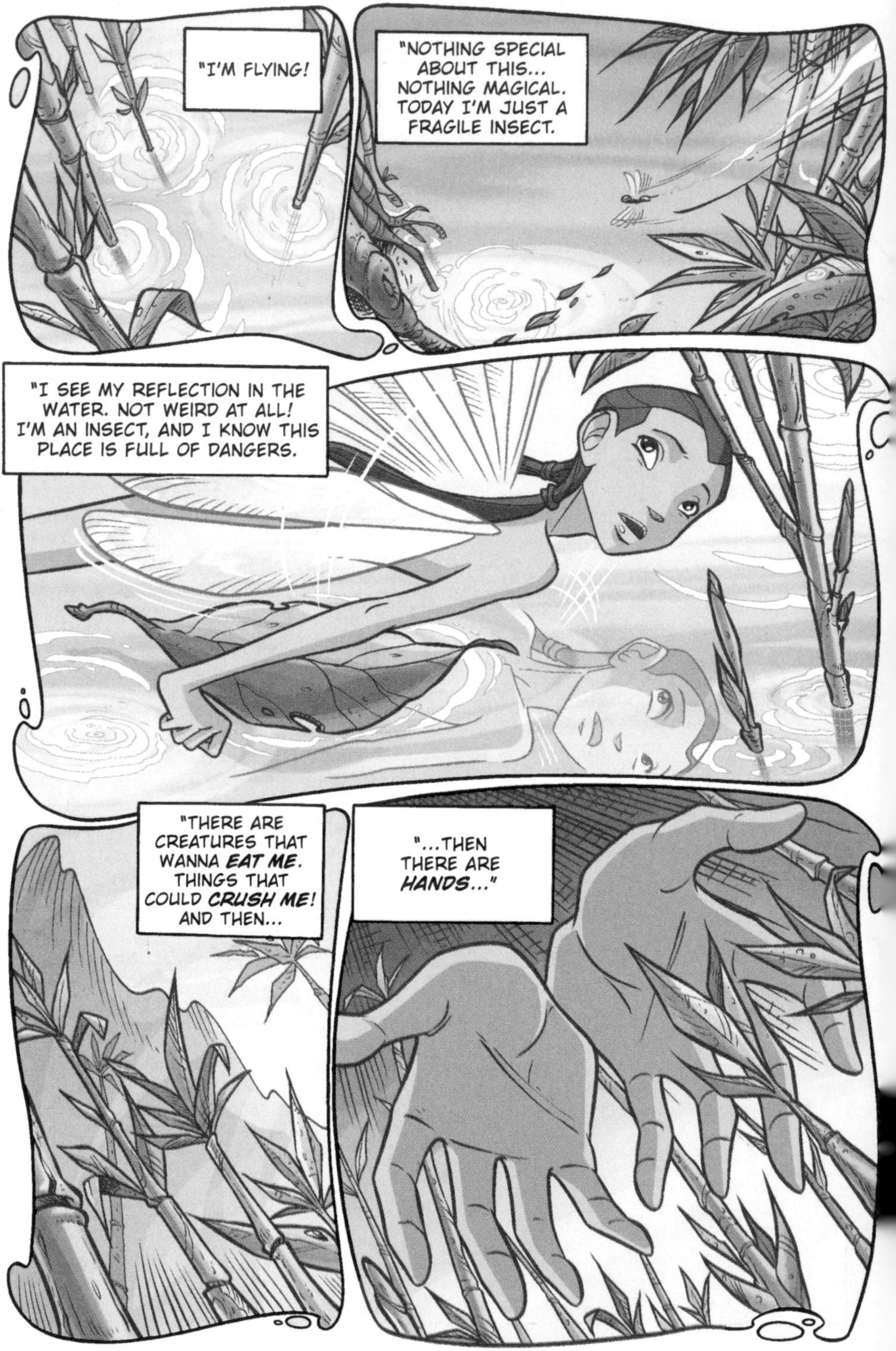
"I'M FLYING!
"NOTHING SPECIAL ABOUT THIS... NOTHING MAGICAL. TODAY I'M JUST A FRAGILE INSECT.
"I SEE MY REFLECTION IN THE WATER. NOT WEIRD AT ALL! I'M AN INSECT, AND I KNOW THIS PLACE IS FULL OF DANGERS.
"THERE ARE CREATURES THAT WANNA EAT ME. THINGS THAT COULD CRUSH ME! AND THEN...
"...THEN THERE ARE HANDS..."

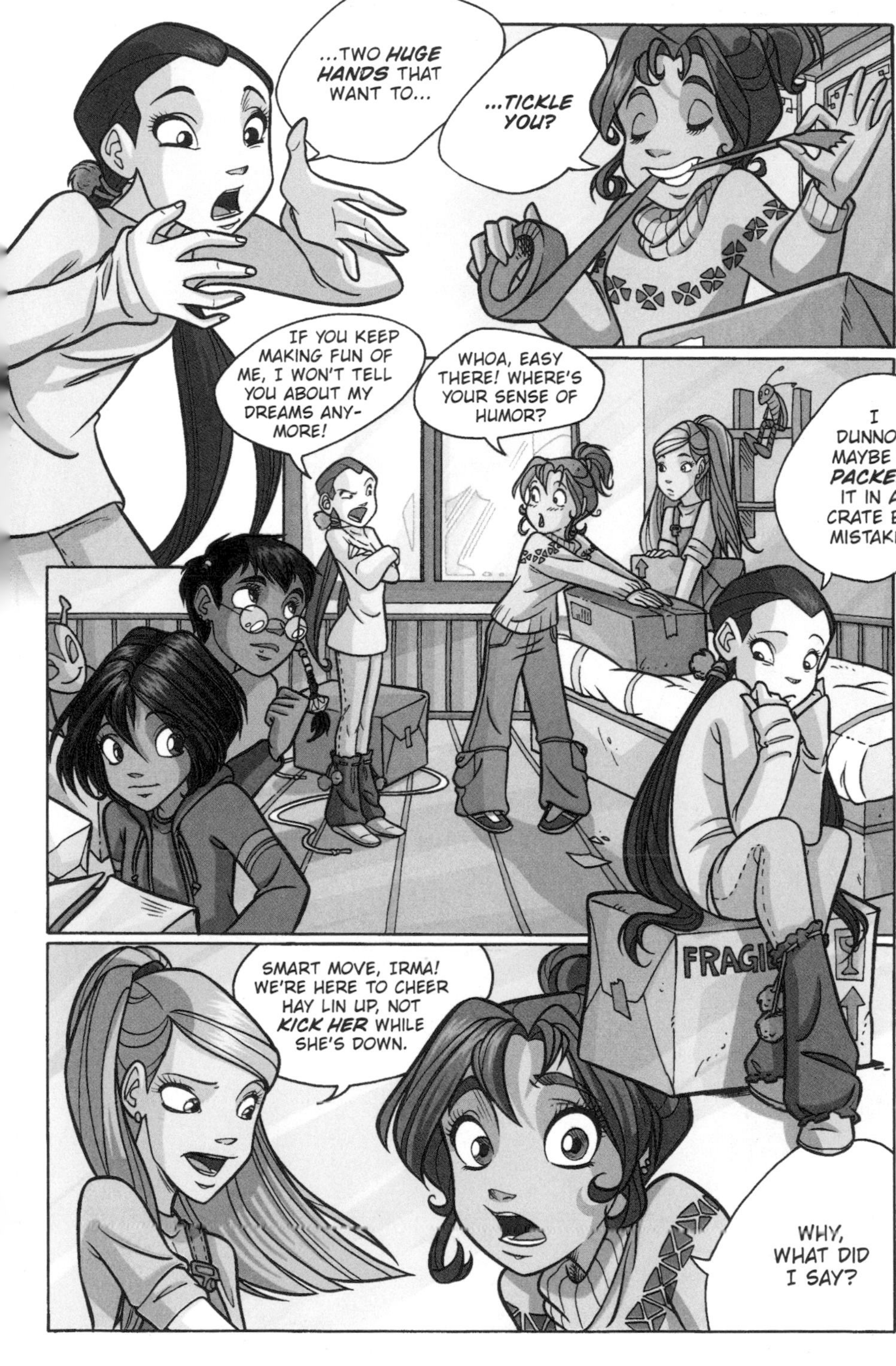
...TWO HUGE HANDS THAT WANT TO...
...TICKLE YOU?
IF YOU KEEP MAKING FUN OF ME, I WON'T TELL YOU ABOUT MY DREAMS ANY-MORE!
WHOA, EASY THERE! WHERE'S YOUR SENSE OF HUMOR?
I DUNNO! MAYBE I PACKED IT IN A CRATE BY MISTAKE.
FRAGI
SMART MOVE, IRMA! WE'RE HERE TO CHEER HAY LIN UP, NOT KICK HER WHILE SHE'S DOWN.
WHY, WHAT DID I SAY?

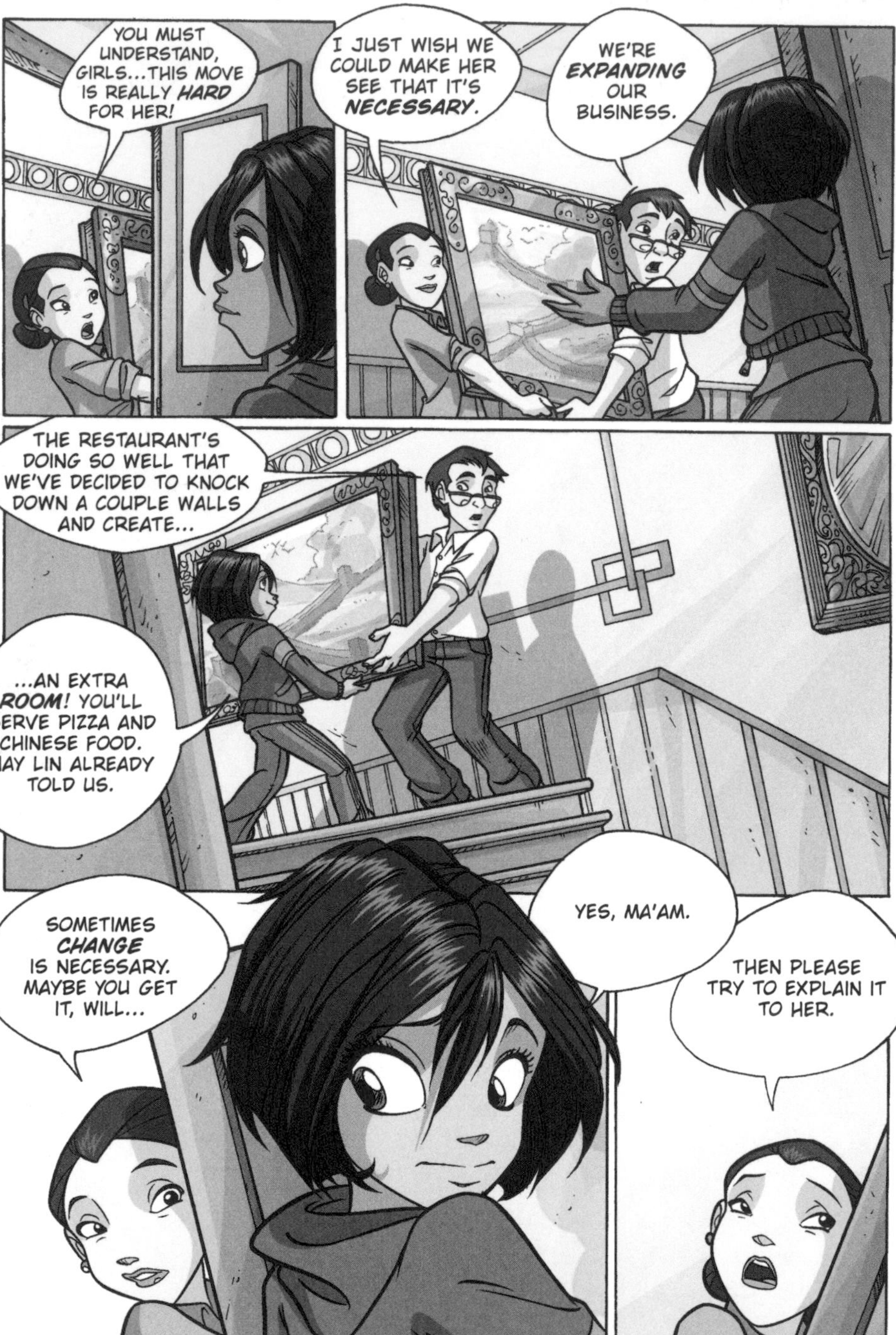
YOU MUST UNDERSTAND, GIRLS...THIS MOVE IS REALLY HARD FOR HER!
I JUST WISH WE COULD MAKE HER SEE THAT IT'S NECESSARY.
WE'RE EXPANDING OUR BUSINESS.
THE RESTAURANT'S DOING SO WELL THAT WE'VE DECIDED TO KNOCK DOWN A COUPLE WALLS AND CREATE...
...AN EXTRA ROOM! YOU'LL SERVE PIZZA AND CHINESE FOOD. HAY LIN ALREADY TOLD US.
SOMETIMES CHANGE IS NECESSARY. MAYBE YOU GET IT, WILL...
YES, MA'AM.
THEN PLEASE TRY TO EXPLAIN IT TO HER.

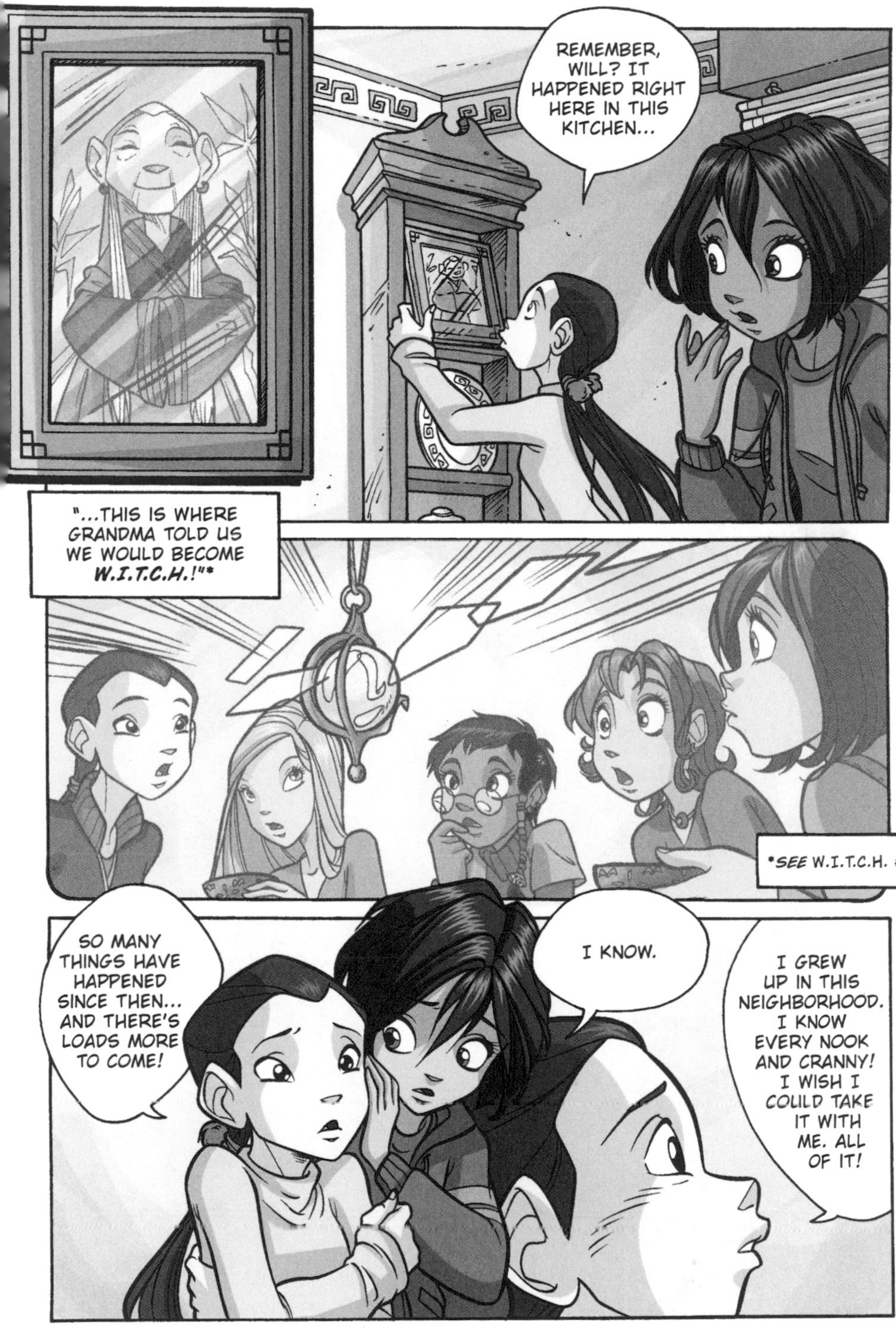
REMEMBER, WILL? IT HAPPENED RIGHT HERE IN THIS KITCHEN...
"...THIS IS WHERE GRANDMA TOLD US WE WOULD BECOME *W.I.T.C.H.*!"*
*SEE W.I.T.C.H. #1
SO MANY THINGS HAVE HAPPENED SINCE THEN... AND THERE'S LOADS MORE TO COME!
I KNOW.
I GREW UP IN THIS NEIGHBORHOOD. I KNOW EVERY NOOK AND CRANNY! I WISH I COULD TAKE IT WITH ME. ALL OF IT!

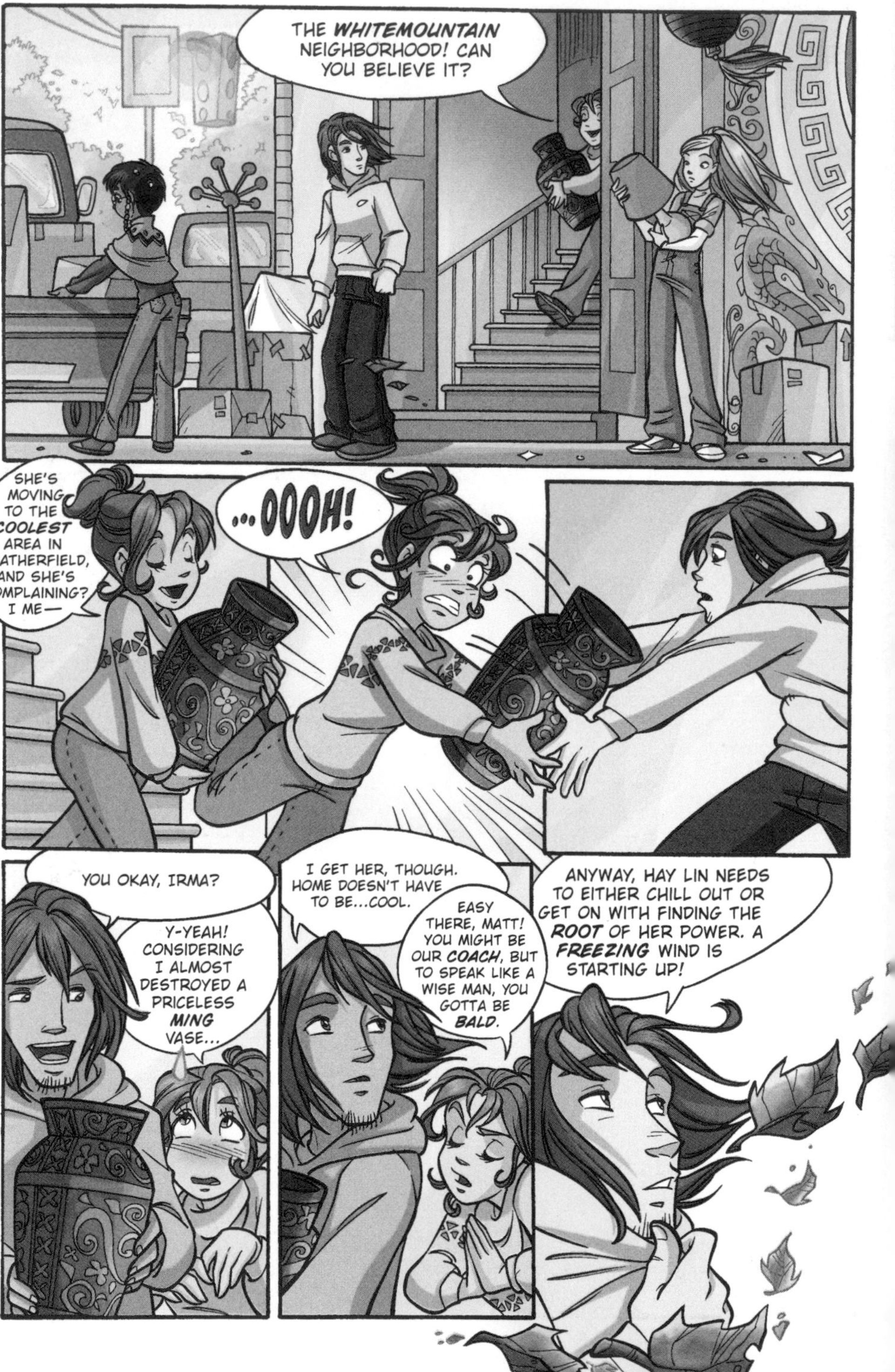
THE WHITEMOUNTAIN NEIGHBORHOOD! CAN YOU BELIEVE IT?
SHE'S MOVING TO THE COOLEST AREA IN HEATHERFIELD, AND SHE'S COMPLAINING? I ME—
...OOOH!
YOU OKAY, IRMA?
Y-YEAH! CONSIDERING I ALMOST DESTROYED A PRICELESS MING VASE...
I GET HER, THOUGH. HOME DOESN'T HAVE TO BE...COOL.
EASY THERE, MATT! YOU MIGHT BE OUR COACH, BUT TO SPEAK LIKE A WISE MAN, YOU GOTTA BE BALD.
ANYWAY, HAY LIN NEEDS TO EITHER CHILL OUT OR GET ON WITH FINDING THE ROOT OF HER POWER. A FREEZING WIND IS STARTING UP!

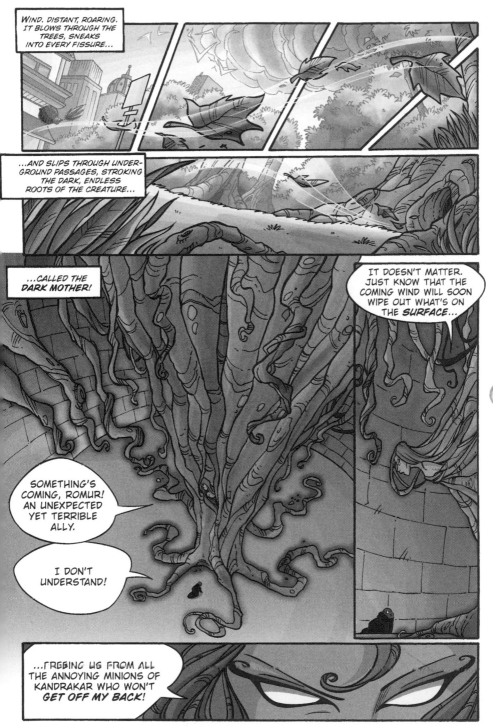

WIND. DISTANT, ROARING. IT BLOWS THROUGH THE TREES, SNEAKS INTO EVERY FISSURE...

...AND SLIPS THROUGH UNDER-GROUND PASSAGES, STROKING THE DARK, ENDLESS ROOTS OF THE CREATURE...

...CALLED THE *DARK MOTHER!*

IT DOESN'T MATTER. JUST KNOW THAT THE COMING WIND WILL SOON WIPE OUT WHAT'S ON THE *SURFACE...*

SOMETHING'S COMING, ROMUR! AN UNEXPECTED YET TERRIBLE ALLY.

I DON'T UNDERSTAND!

...FREEING US FROM ALL THE ANNOYING MINIONS OF KANDRAKAR WHO WON'T *GET OFF MY BACK!*

123

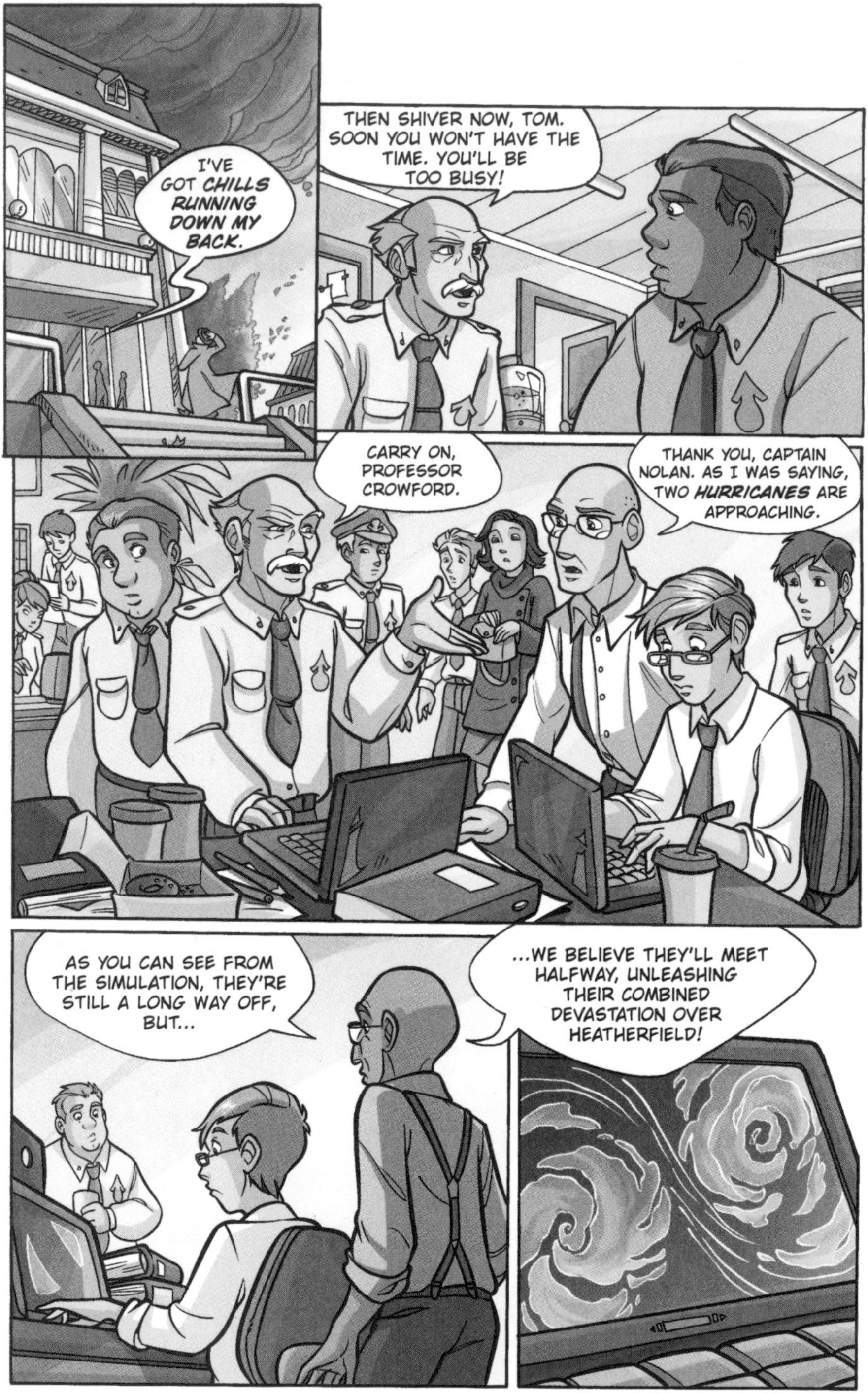
I'VE GOT CHILLS RUNNING DOWN MY BACK.
THEN SHIVER NOW, TOM. SOON YOU WON'T HAVE THE TIME. YOU'LL BE TOO BUSY!
CARRY ON, PROFESSOR CROWFORD.
THANK YOU, CAPTAIN NOLAN. AS I WAS SAYING, TWO HURRICANES ARE APPROACHING.
AS YOU CAN SEE FROM THE SIMULATION, THEY'RE STILL A LONG WAY OFF, BUT...
...WE BELIEVE THEY'LL MEET HALFWAY, UNLEASHING THEIR COMBINED DEVASTATION OVER HEATHERFIELD!

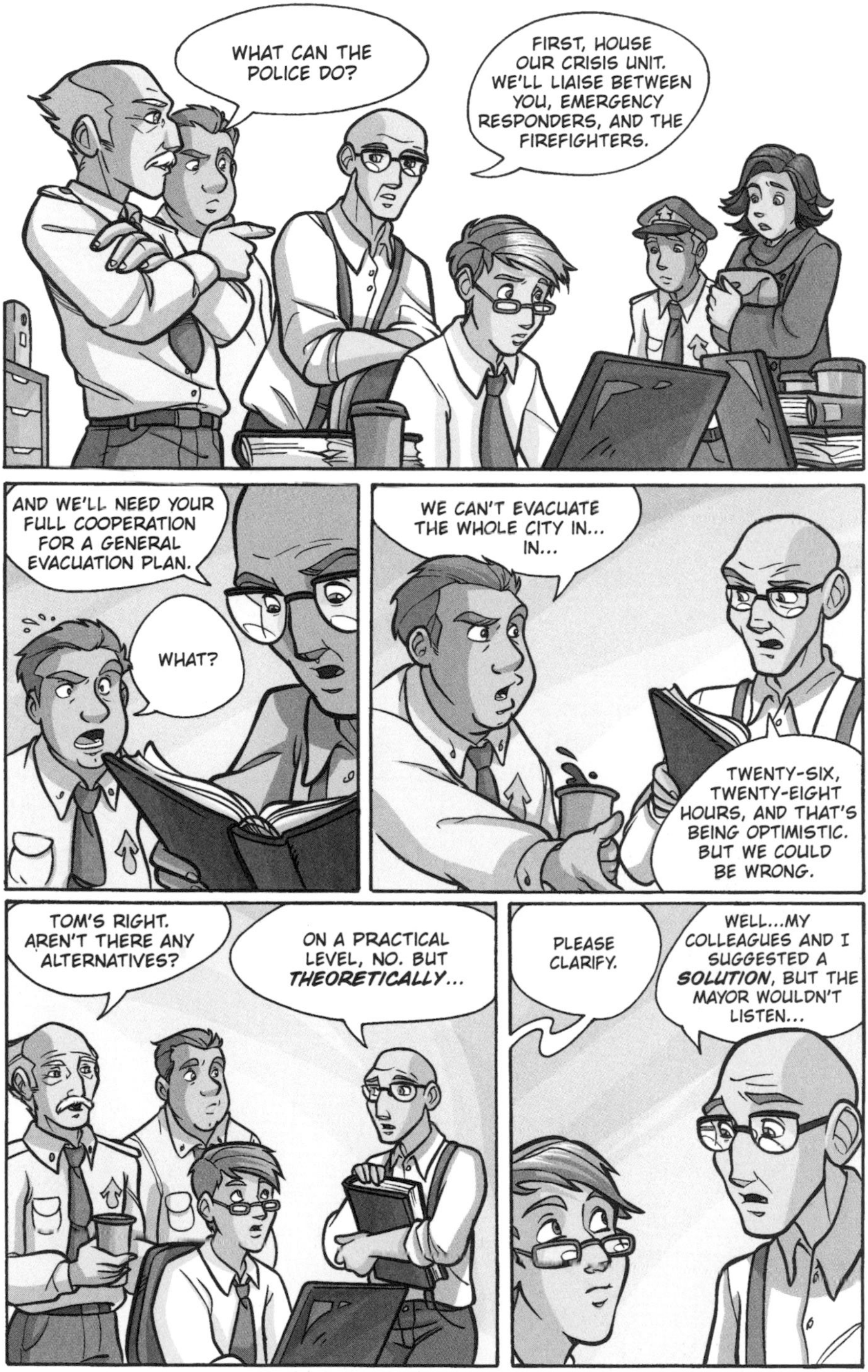
WHAT CAN THE POLICE DO?
FIRST, HOUSE OUR CRISIS UNIT. WE'LL LIAISE BETWEEN YOU, EMERGENCY RESPONDERS, AND THE FIREFIGHTERS.
AND WE'LL NEED YOUR FULL COOPERATION FOR A GENERAL EVACUATION PLAN.
WHAT?
WE CAN'T EVACUATE THE WHOLE CITY IN... IN...
TWENTY-SIX, TWENTY-EIGHT HOURS, AND THAT'S BEING OPTIMISTIC. BUT WE COULD BE WRONG.
TOM'S RIGHT. AREN'T THERE ANY ALTERNATIVES?
ON A PRACTICAL LEVEL, NO. BUT *THEORETICALLY*...
PLEASE CLARIFY.
WELL...MY COLLEAGUES AND I SUGGESTED A *SOLUTION*, BUT THE MAYOR WOULDN'T LISTEN...

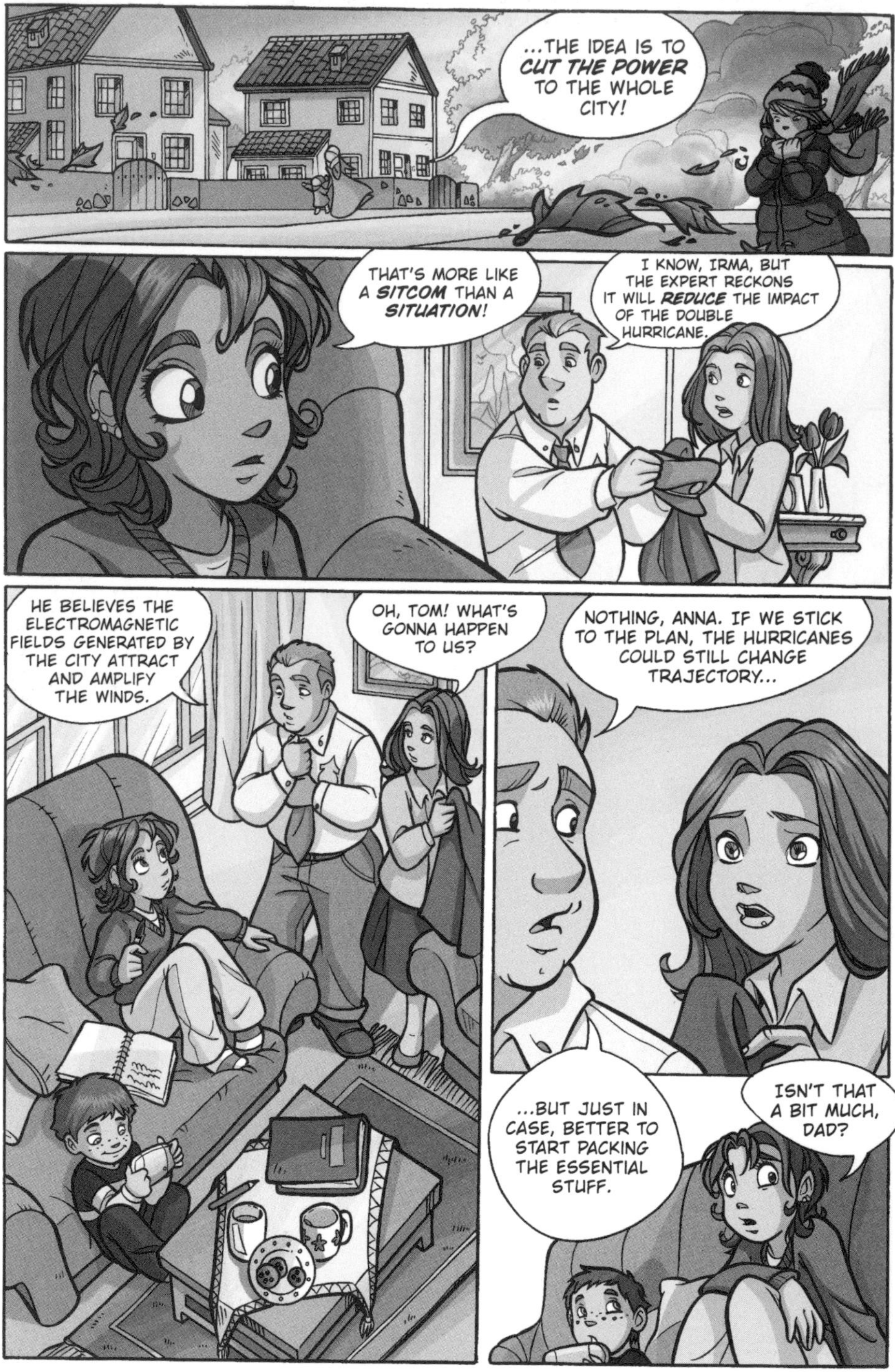
...THE IDEA IS TO CUT THE POWER TO THE WHOLE CITY!
THAT'S MORE LIKE A SITCOM THAN A SITUATION!
I KNOW, IRMA, BUT THE EXPERT RECKONS IT WILL REDUCE THE IMPACT OF THE DOUBLE HURRICANE.
HE BELIEVES THE ELECTROMAGNETIC FIELDS GENERATED BY THE CITY ATTRACT AND AMPLIFY THE WINDS.
OH, TOM! WHAT'S GONNA HAPPEN TO US?
NOTHING, ANNA. IF WE STICK TO THE PLAN, THE HURRICANES COULD STILL CHANGE TRAJECTORY...
...BUT JUST IN CASE, BETTER TO START PACKING THE ESSENTIAL STUFF.
ISN'T THAT A BIT MUCH, DAD?

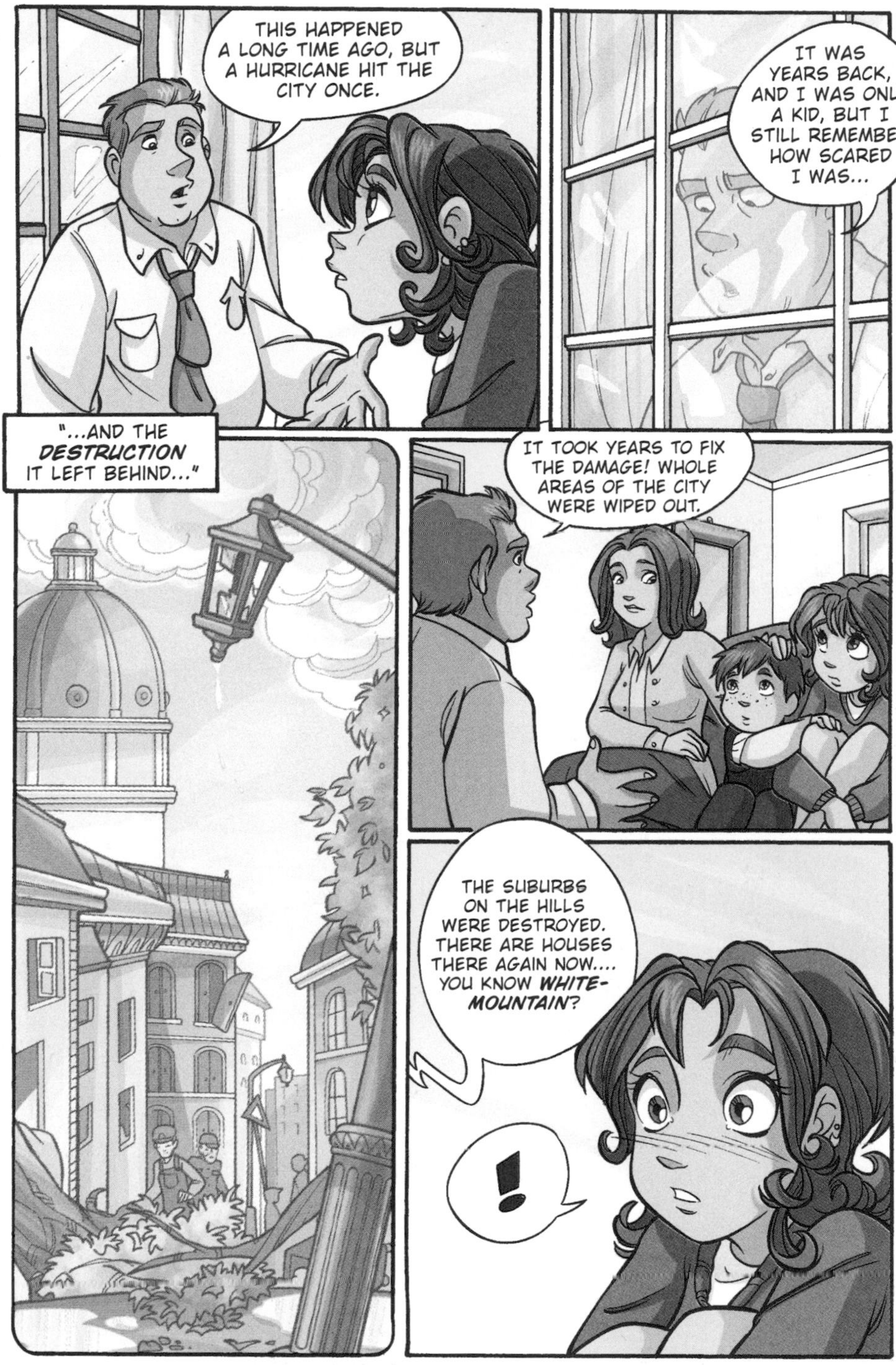
THIS HAPPENED A LONG TIME AGO, BUT A HURRICANE HIT THE CITY ONCE.
IT WAS YEARS BACK, AND I WAS ONLY A KID, BUT I STILL REMEMBER HOW SCARED I WAS...
"...AND THE *DESTRUCTION* IT LEFT BEHIND..."
IT TOOK YEARS TO FIX THE DAMAGE! WHOLE AREAS OF THE CITY WERE WIPED OUT.
THE SUBURBS ON THE HILLS WERE DESTROYED. THERE ARE HOUSES THERE AGAIN NOW.... YOU KNOW *WHITE-MOUNTAIN*?
!

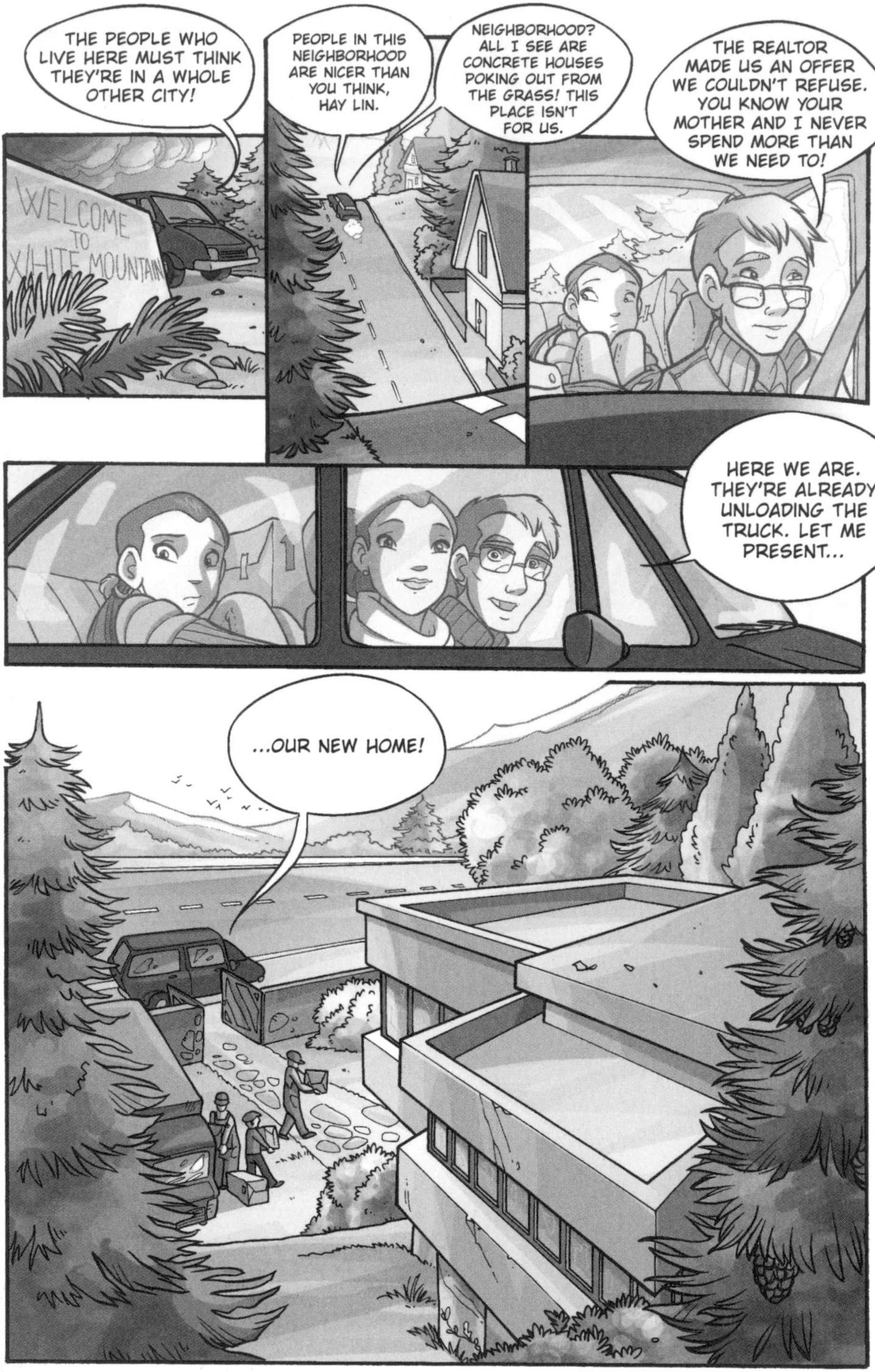
THE PEOPLE WHO LIVE HERE MUST THINK THEY'RE IN A WHOLE OTHER CITY!
WELCOME TO WHITE MOUNTAIN
PEOPLE IN THIS NEIGHBORHOOD ARE NICER THAN YOU THINK, HAY LIN.
NEIGHBORHOOD? ALL I SEE ARE CONCRETE HOUSES POKING OUT FROM THE GRASS! THIS PLACE ISN'T FOR US.
THE REALTOR MADE US AN OFFER WE COULDN'T REFUSE. YOU KNOW YOUR MOTHER AND I NEVER SPEND MORE THAN WE NEED TO!
HERE WE ARE. THEY'RE ALREADY UNLOADING THE TRUCK. LET ME PRESENT...
...OUR NEW HOME!

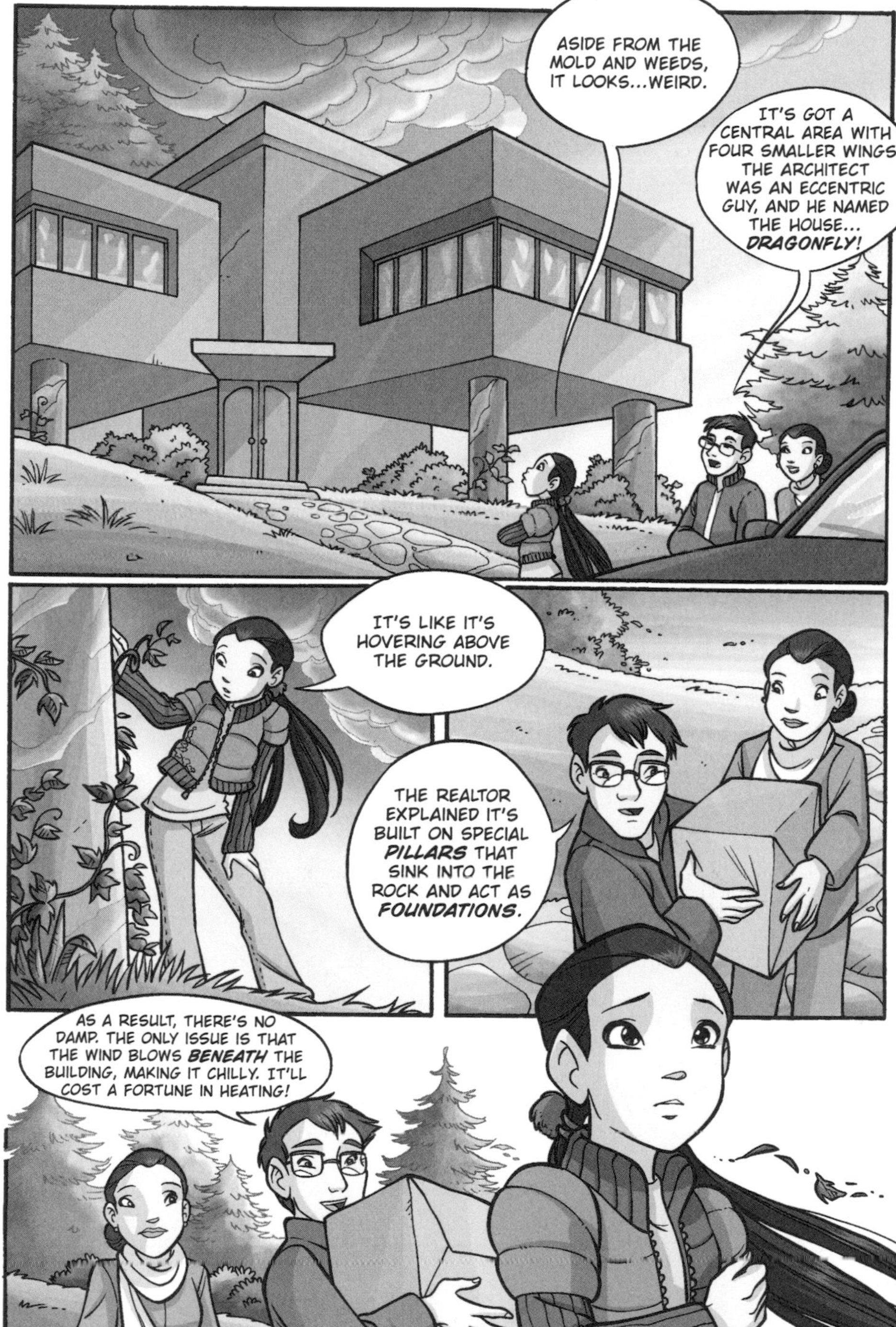
ASIDE FROM THE MOLD AND WEEDS, IT LOOKS...WEIRD.
IT'S GOT A CENTRAL AREA WITH FOUR SMALLER WINGS. THE ARCHITECT WAS AN ECCENTRIC GUY, AND HE NAMED THE HOUSE... DRAGONFLY!
IT'S LIKE IT'S HOVERING ABOVE THE GROUND.
THE REALTOR EXPLAINED IT'S BUILT ON SPECIAL PILLARS THAT SINK INTO THE ROCK AND ACT AS FOUNDATIONS.
AS A RESULT, THERE'S NO DAMP. THE ONLY ISSUE IS THAT THE WIND BLOWS BENEATH THE BUILDING, MAKING IT CHILLY. IT'LL COST A FORTUNE IN HEATING!

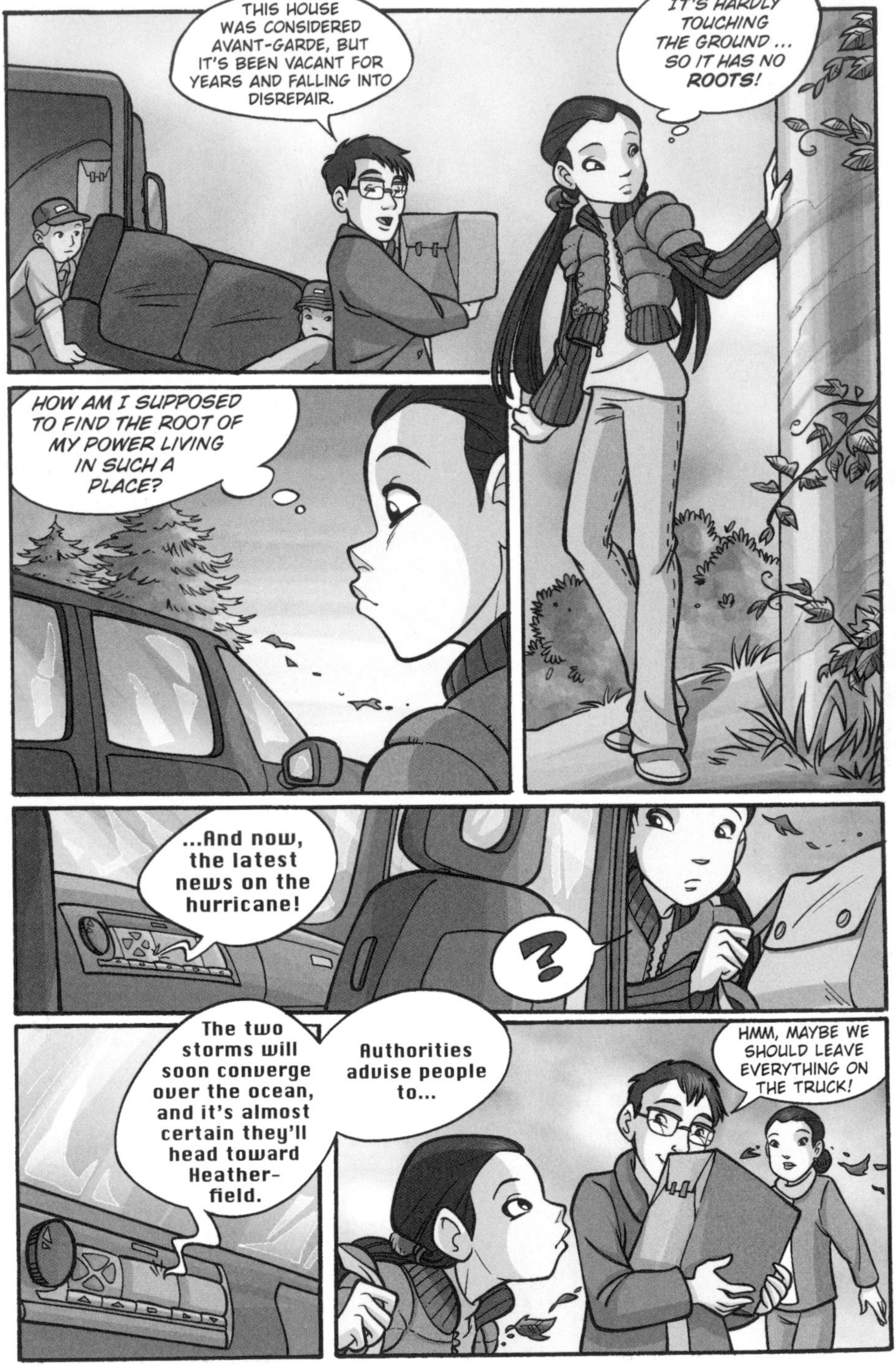
THIS HOUSE WAS CONSIDERED AVANT-GARDE, BUT IT'S BEEN VACANT FOR YEARS AND FALLING INTO DISREPAIR.
IT'S HARDLY TOUCHING THE GROUND ... SO IT HAS NO ROOTS!
HOW AM I SUPPOSED TO FIND THE ROOT OF MY POWER LIVING IN SUCH A PLACE?
...And now, the latest news on the hurricane!
?
The two storms will soon converge over the ocean, and it's almost certain they'll head toward Heather-field.
Authorities advise people to...
HMM, MAYBE WE SHOULD LEAVE EVERYTHING ON THE TRUCK!

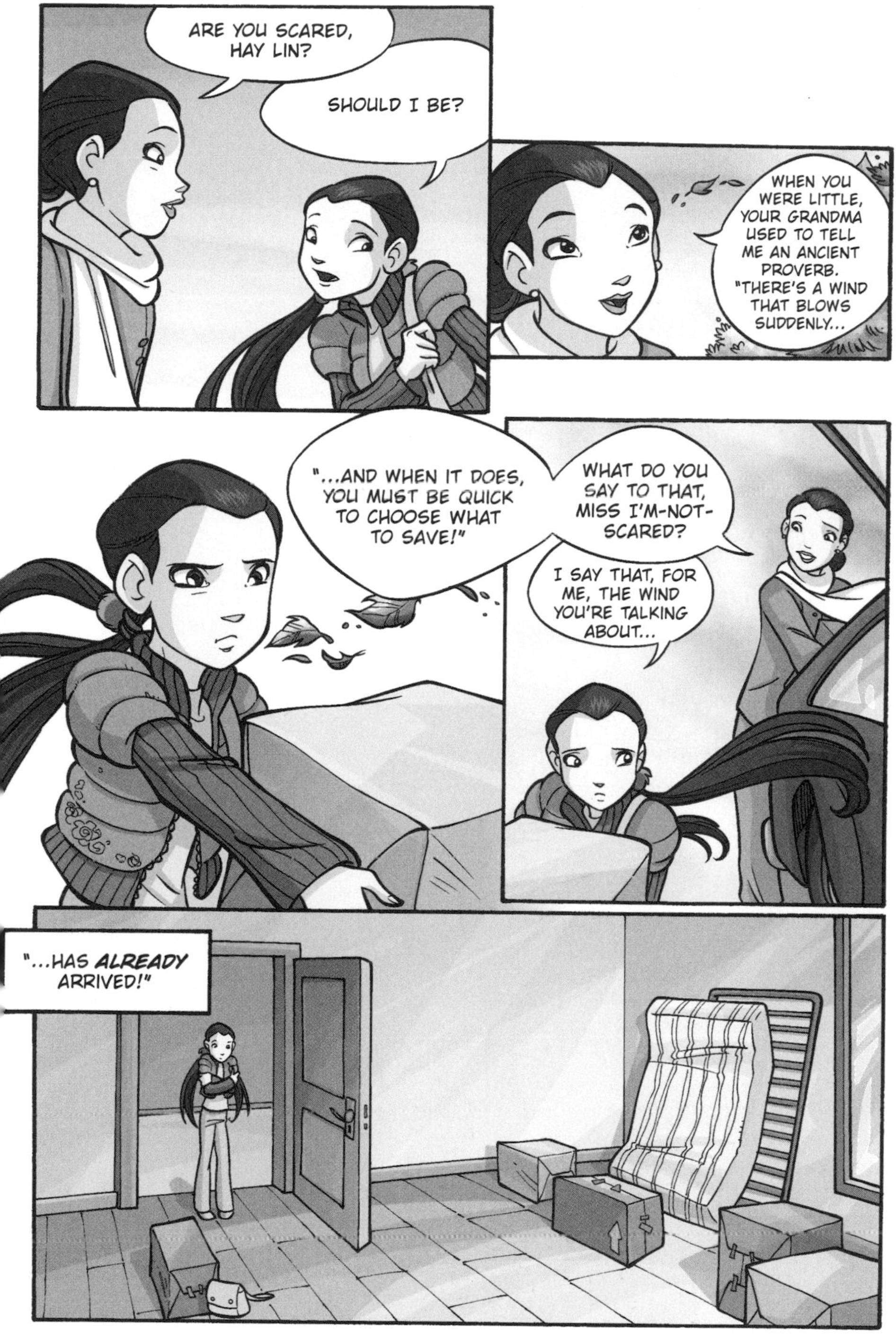
ARE YOU SCARED, HAY LIN?
SHOULD I BE?
WHEN YOU WERE LITTLE, YOUR GRANDMA USED TO TELL ME AN ANCIENT PROVERB. "THERE'S A WIND THAT BLOWS SUDDENLY...
"...AND WHEN IT DOES, YOU MUST BE QUICK TO CHOOSE WHAT TO SAVE!"
WHAT DO YOU SAY TO THAT, MISS I'M-NOT-SCARED?
I SAY THAT, FOR ME, THE WIND YOU'RE TALKING ABOUT...
"...HAS ALREADY ARRIVED!"

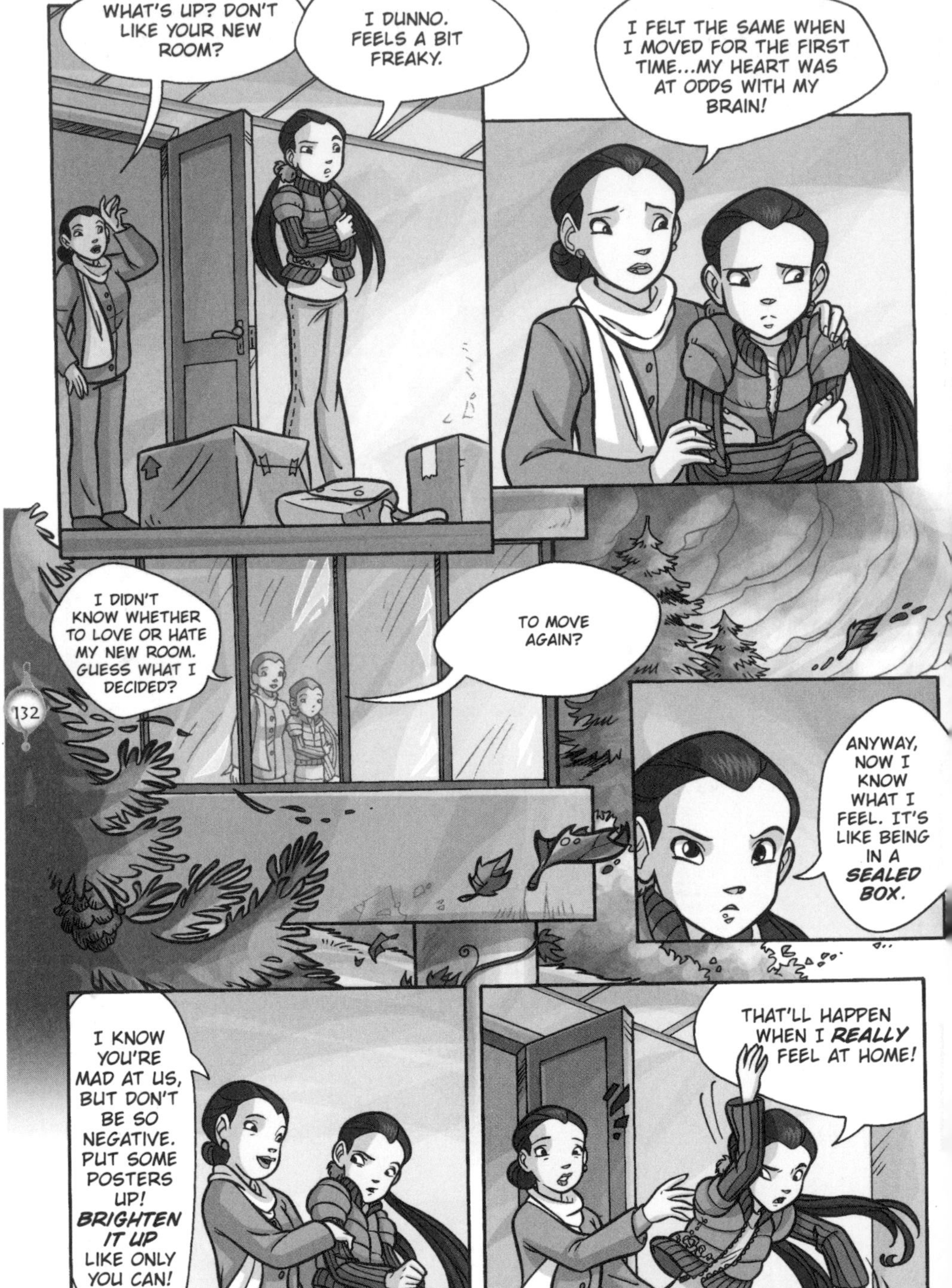

WHAT'S UP? DON'T LIKE YOUR NEW ROOM?
I DUNNO. FEELS A BIT FREAKY.
I FELT THE SAME WHEN I MOVED FOR THE FIRST TIME...MY HEART WAS AT ODDS WITH MY BRAIN!
I DIDN'T KNOW WHETHER TO LOVE OR HATE MY NEW ROOM. GUESS WHAT I DECIDED?
TO MOVE AGAIN?
ANYWAY, NOW I KNOW WHAT I FEEL. IT'S LIKE BEING IN A SEALED BOX.
I KNOW YOU'RE MAD AT US, BUT DON'T BE SO NEGATIVE. PUT SOME POSTERS UP! BRIGHTEN IT UP LIKE ONLY YOU CAN!
THAT'LL HAPPEN WHEN I REALLY FEEL AT HOME!

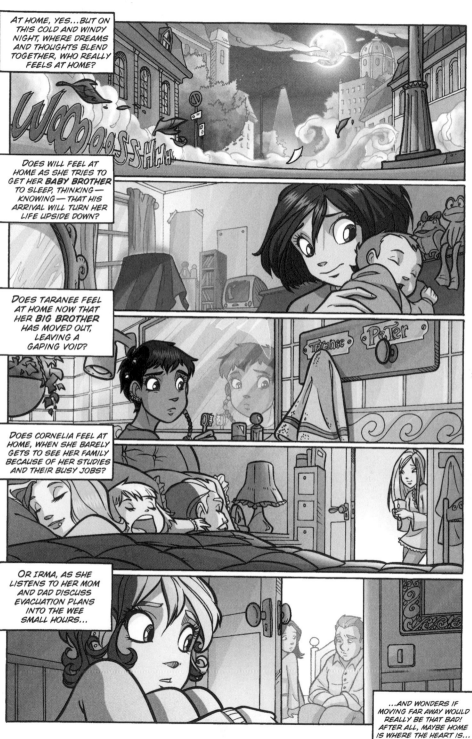

AT HOME, YES...BUT ON THIS COLD AND WINDY NIGHT, WHERE DREAMS AND THOUGHTS BLEND TOGETHER, WHO REALLY FEELS AT HOME?

WOOOOOSSHHH...

DOES WILL FEEL AT HOME AS SHE TRIES TO GET HER *BABY BROTHER* TO SLEEP, THINKING — KNOWING — THAT HIS ARRIVAL WILL TURN HER LIFE UPSIDE DOWN?

DOES TARANEE FEEL AT HOME NOW THAT HER *BIG BROTHER* HAS MOVED OUT, LEAVING A GAPING VOID?

DOES CORNELIA FEEL AT HOME, WHEN SHE BARELY GETS TO SEE HER FAMILY BECAUSE OF HER STUDIES AND THEIR BUSY JOBS?

OR IRMA, AS SHE LISTENS TO HER MOM AND DAD DISCUSS EVACUATION PLANS INTO THE WEE SMALL HOURS...

...AND WONDERS IF MOVING FAR AWAY WOULD REALLY BE THAT BAD! AFTER ALL, MAYBE HOME IS WHERE THE HEART IS...

133

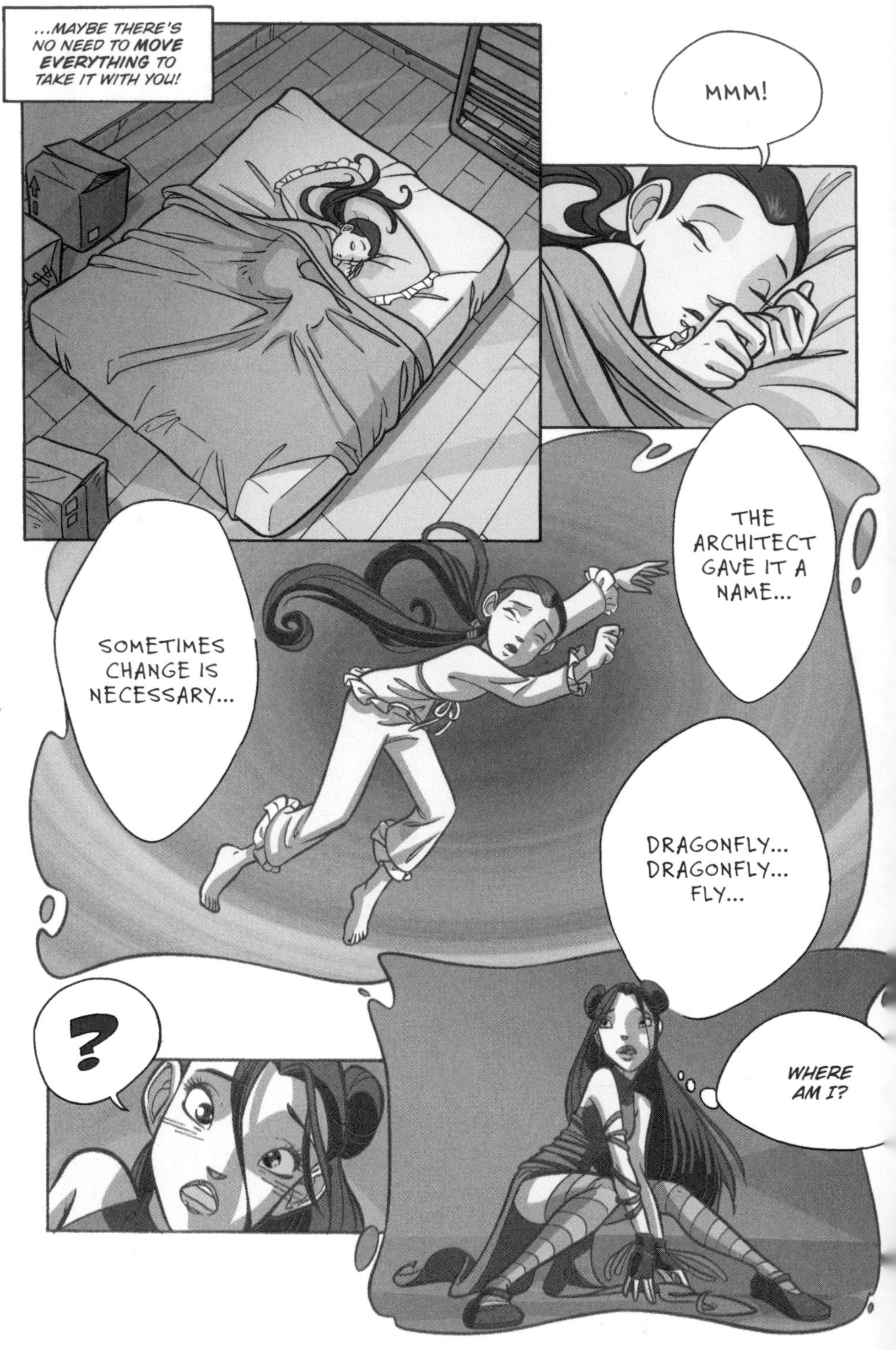

...MAYBE THERE'S NO NEED TO **MOVE EVERYTHING** TO TAKE IT WITH YOU!
MMM!
THE ARCHITECT GAVE IT A NAME...
SOMETIMES CHANGE IS NECESSARY...
DRAGONFLY... DRAGONFLY... FLY...
?
WHERE AM I?

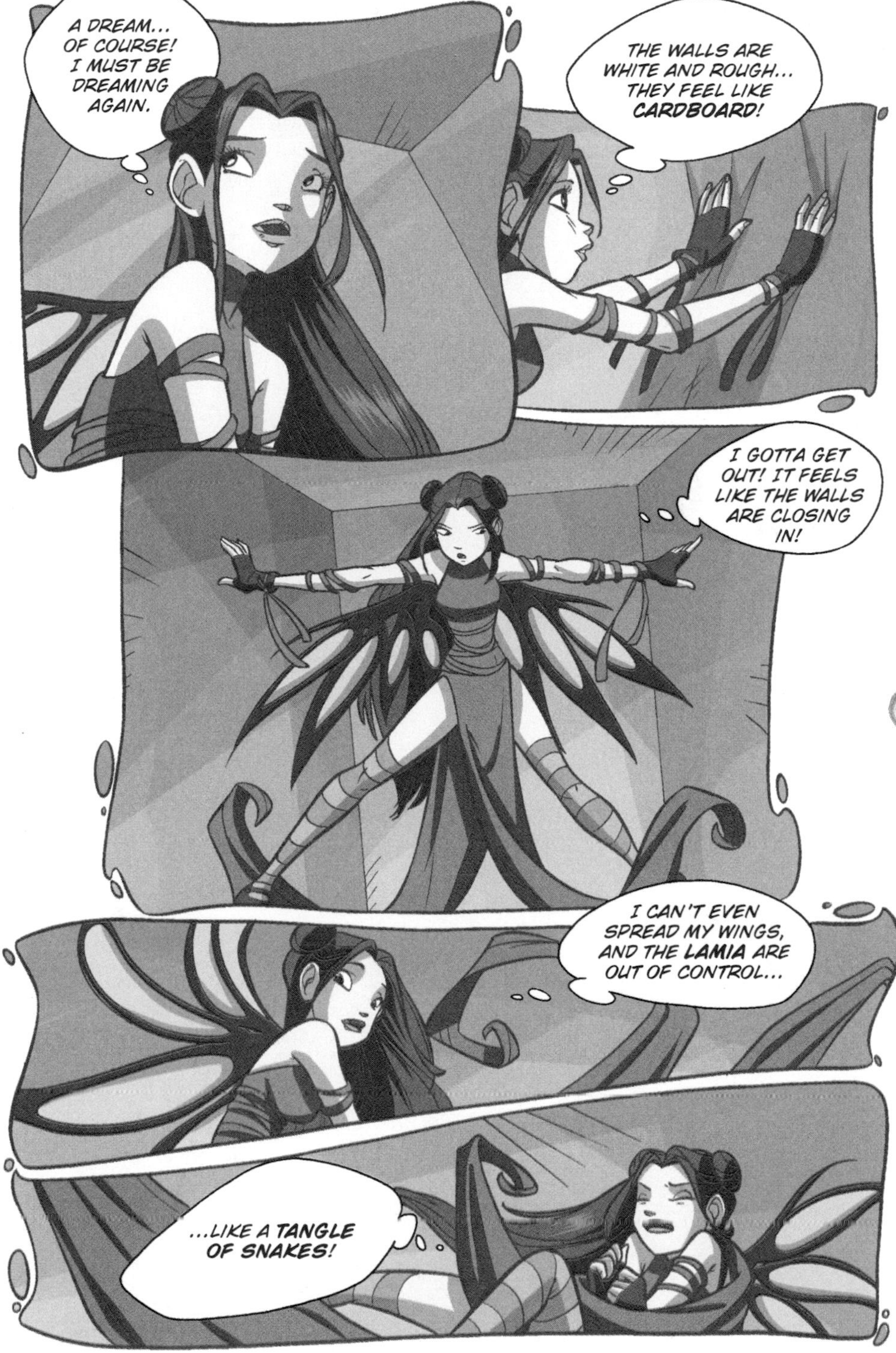
A DREAM... OF COURSE! I MUST BE DREAMING AGAIN.
THE WALLS ARE WHITE AND ROUGH... THEY FEEL LIKE CARDBOARD!
I GOTTA GET OUT! IT FEELS LIKE THE WALLS ARE CLOSING IN!
I CAN'T EVEN SPREAD MY WINGS, AND THE LAMIA ARE OUT OF CONTROL...
...LIKE A TANGLE OF SNAKES!

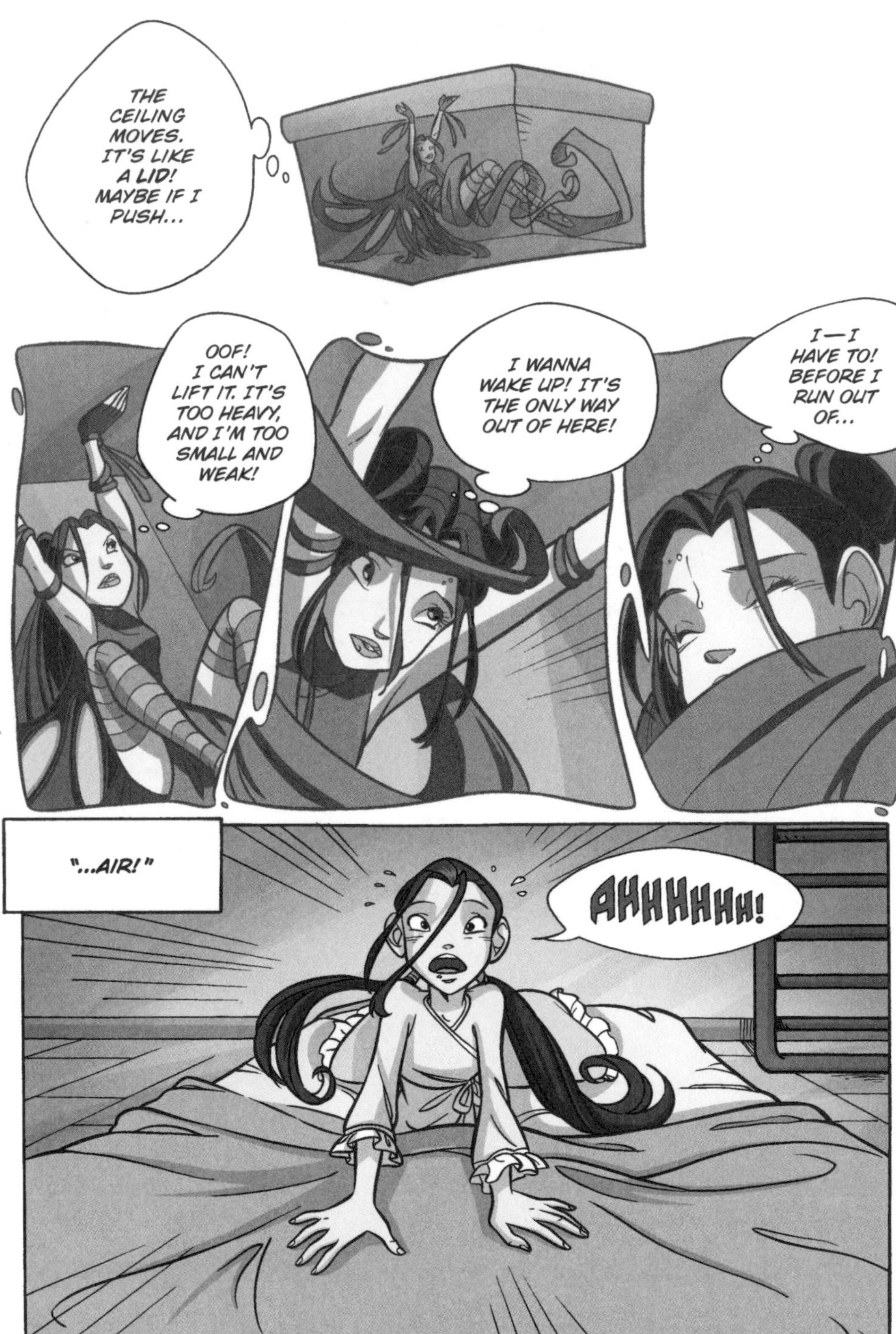
THE CEILING MOVES. IT'S LIKE A LID! MAYBE IF I PUSH...
OOF! I CAN'T LIFT IT. IT'S TOO HEAVY, AND I'M TOO SMALL AND WEAK!
I WANNA WAKE UP! IT'S THE ONLY WAY OUT OF HERE!
I—I HAVE TO! BEFORE I RUN OUT OF...
"...AIR!"
AHHHHHH!

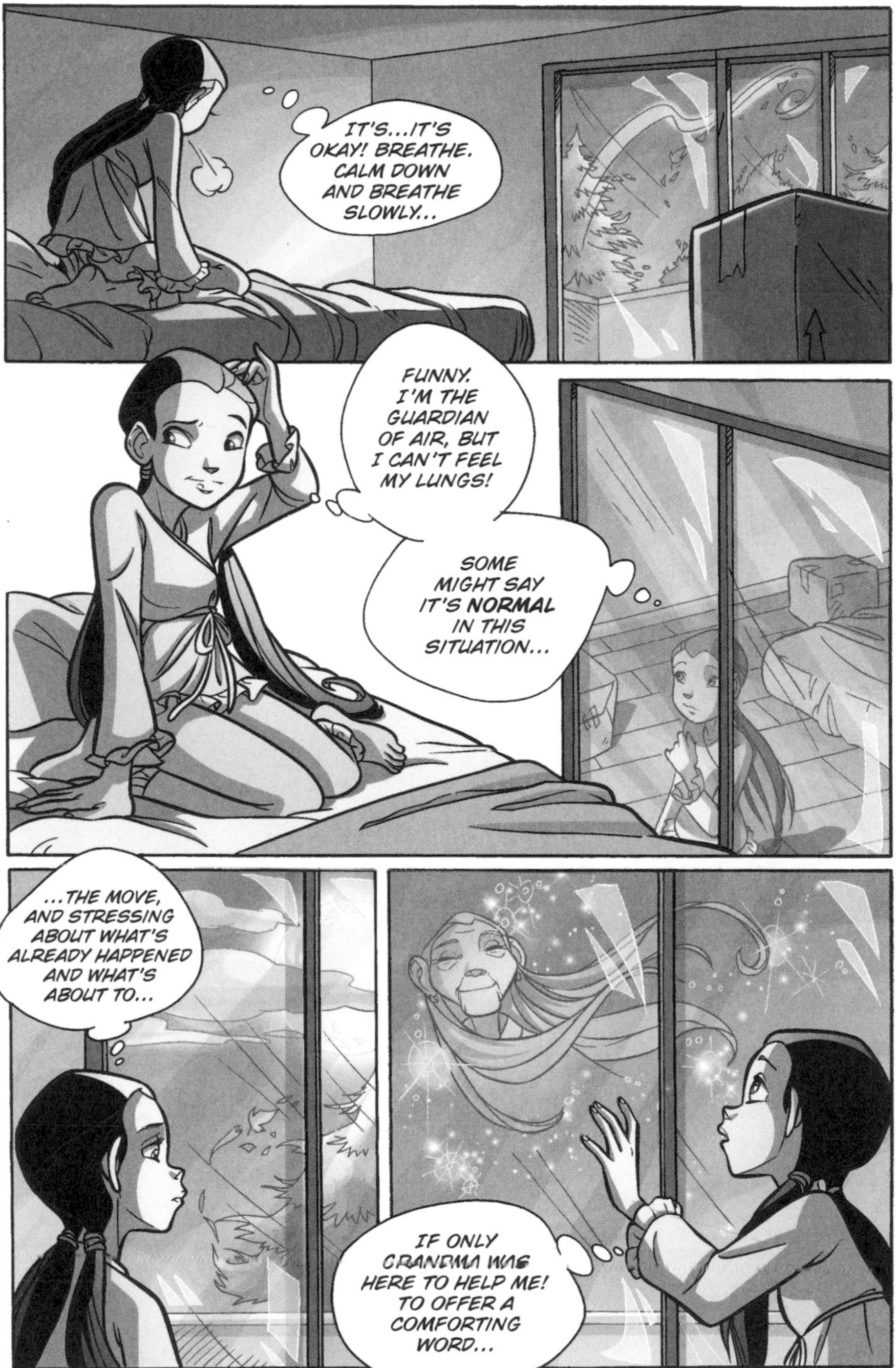
IT'S...IT'S OKAY! BREATHE. CALM DOWN AND BREATHE SLOWLY...
FUNNY. I'M THE GUARDIAN OF AIR, BUT I CAN'T FEEL MY LUNGS!
SOME MIGHT SAY IT'S **NORMAL** IN THIS SITUATION...
...THE MOVE, AND STRESSING ABOUT WHAT'S ALREADY HAPPENED AND WHAT'S ABOUT TO...
IF ONLY GRANDMA WAS HERE TO HELP ME! TO OFFER A COMFORTING WORD...

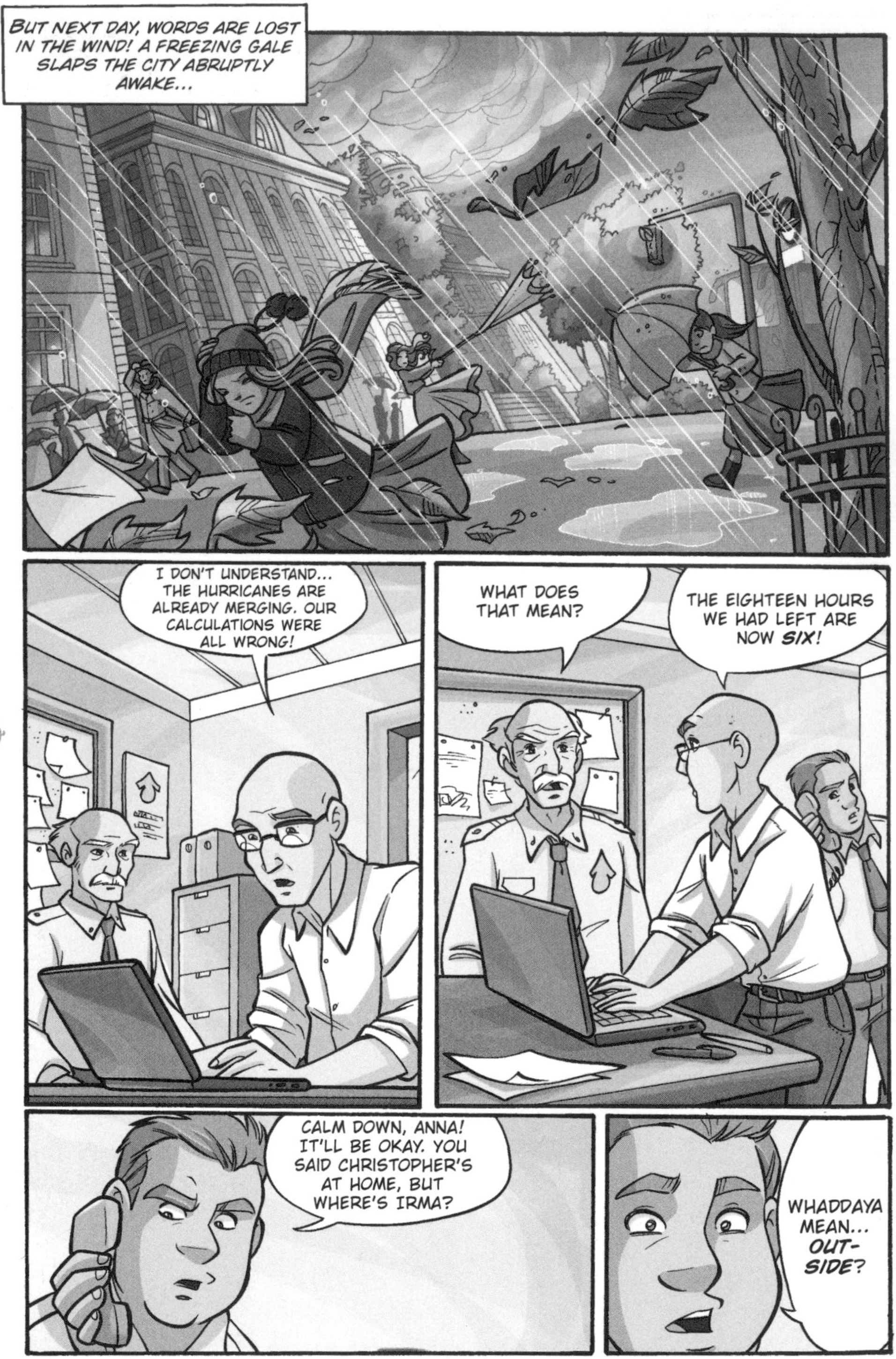
BUT NEXT DAY, WORDS ARE LOST IN THE WIND! A FREEZING GALE SLAPS THE CITY ABRUPTLY AWAKE...
I DON'T UNDERSTAND... THE HURRICANES ARE ALREADY MERGING. OUR CALCULATIONS WERE ALL WRONG!
WHAT DOES THAT MEAN?
THE EIGHTEEN HOURS WE HAD LEFT ARE NOW SIX!
CALM DOWN, ANNA! IT'LL BE OKAY. YOU SAID CHRISTOPHER'S AT HOME, BUT WHERE'S IRMA?
WHADDAYA MEAN... OUT-SIDE?

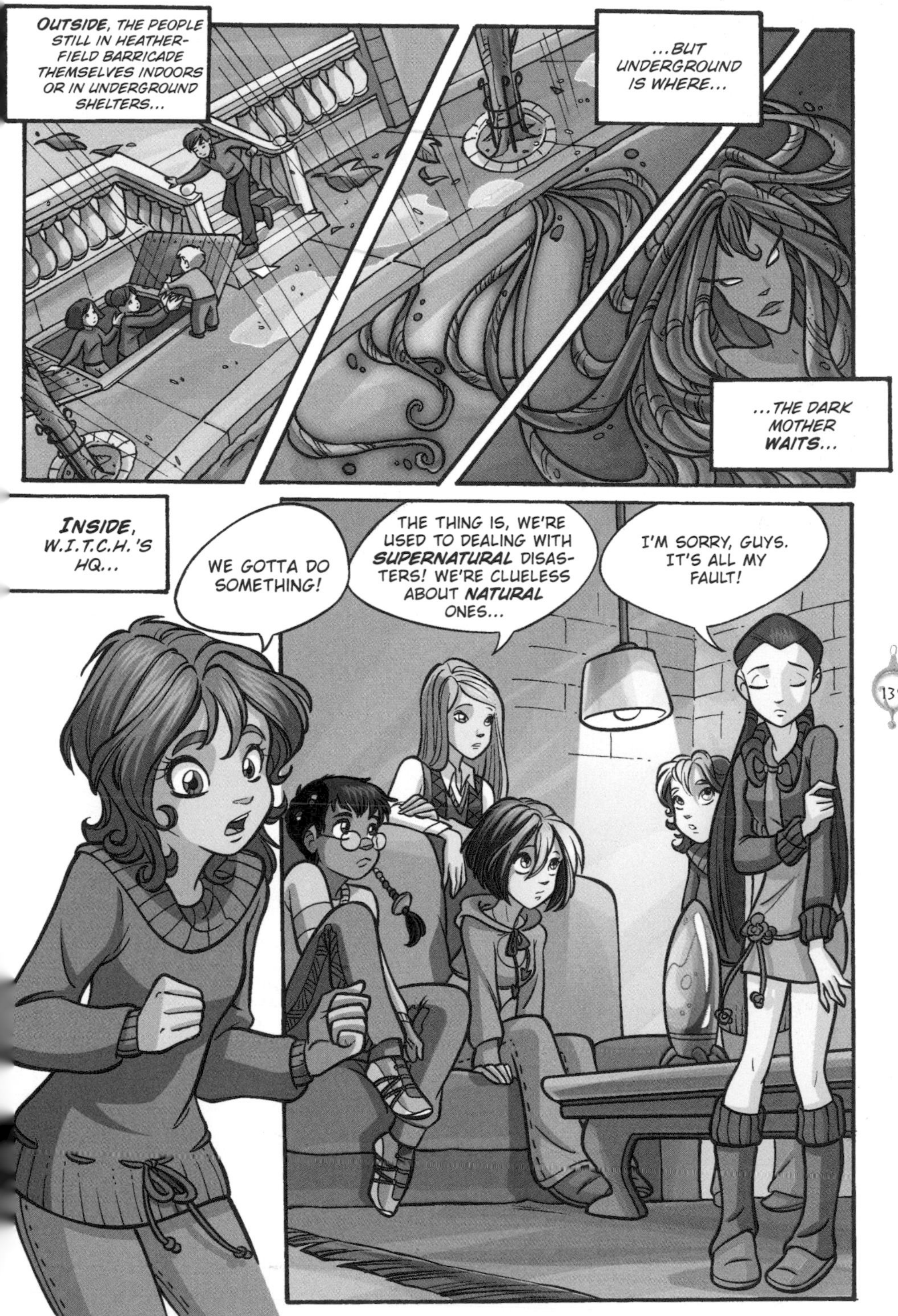

OUTSIDE, THE PEOPLE STILL IN HEATHER-FIELD BARRICADE THEMSELVES INDOORS OR IN UNDERGROUND SHELTERS...
...BUT UNDERGROUND IS WHERE...
...THE DARK MOTHER WAITS...
INSIDE, W.I.T.C.H.'S HQ...
WE GOTTA DO SOMETHING!
THE THING IS, WE'RE USED TO DEALING WITH SUPERNATURAL DISAS-TERS! WE'RE CLUELESS ABOUT NATURAL ONES...
I'M SORRY, GUYS. IT'S ALL MY FAULT!

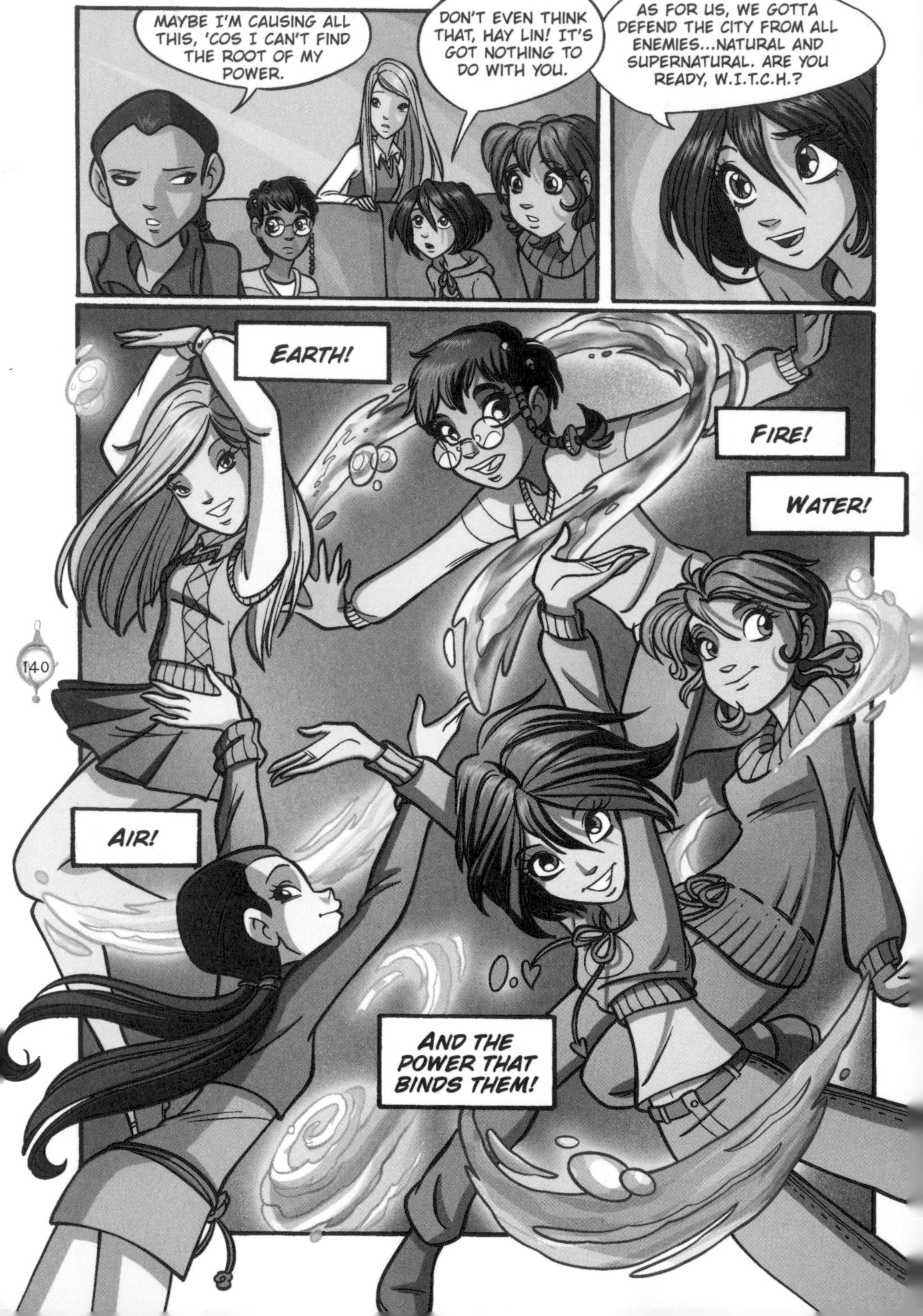
MAYBE I'M CAUSING ALL THIS, 'COS I CAN'T FIND THE ROOT OF MY POWER.
DON'T EVEN THINK THAT, HAY LIN! IT'S GOT NOTHING TO DO WITH YOU.
AS FOR US, WE GOTTA DEFEND THE CITY FROM ALL ENEMIES...NATURAL AND SUPERNATURAL. ARE YOU READY, W.I.T.C.H.?
EARTH!
FIRE!
WATER!
AIR!
AND THE POWER THAT BINDS THEM!

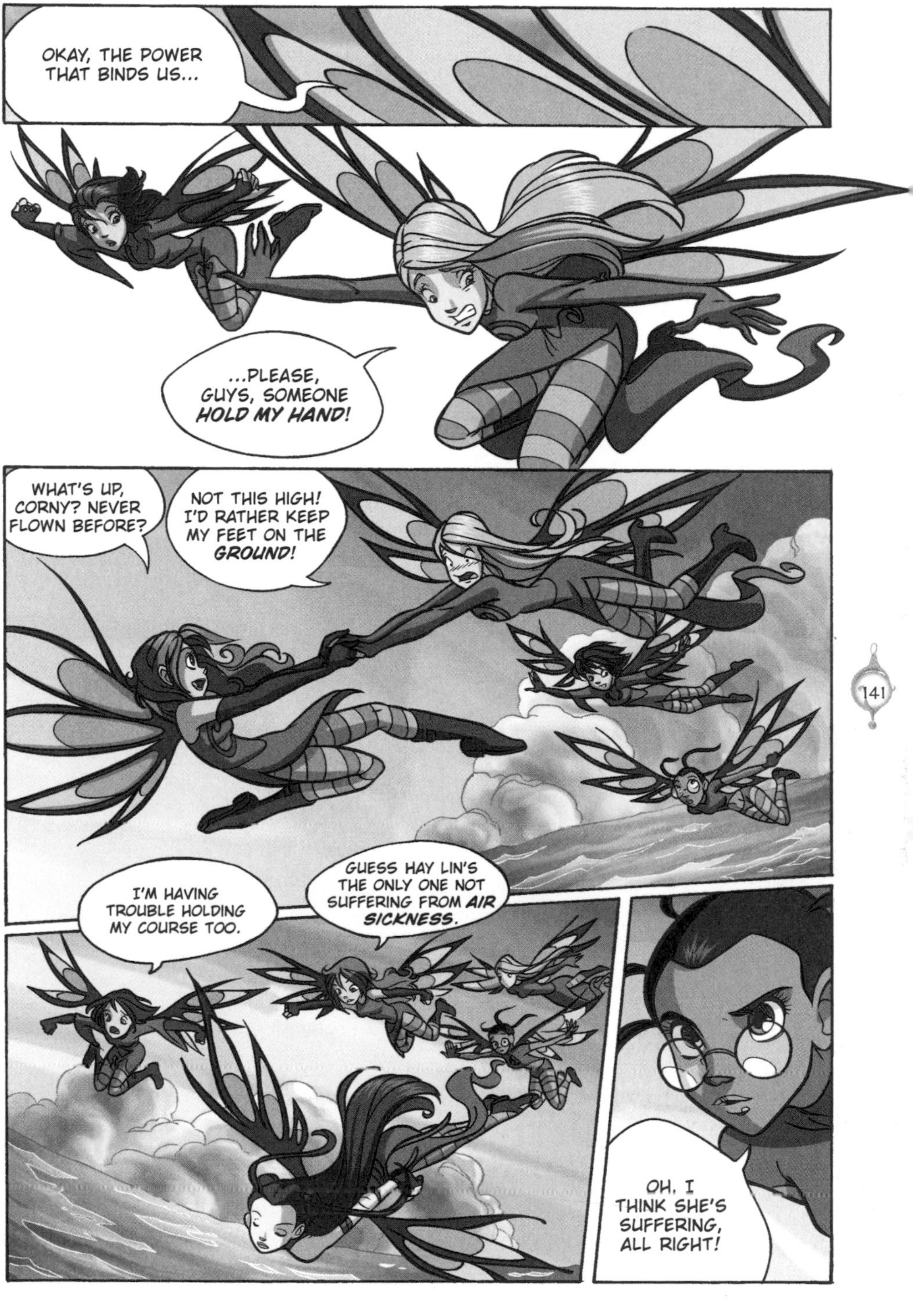

OKAY, THE POWER THAT BINDS US...
...PLEASE, GUYS, SOMEONE HOLD MY HAND!
WHAT'S UP, CORNY? NEVER FLOWN BEFORE?
NOT THIS HIGH! I'D RATHER KEEP MY FEET ON THE GROUND!
I'M HAVING TROUBLE HOLDING MY COURSE TOO.
GUESS HAY LIN'S THE ONLY ONE NOT SUFFERING FROM AIR SICKNESS.
OH, I THINK SHE'S SUFFERING, ALL RIGHT!

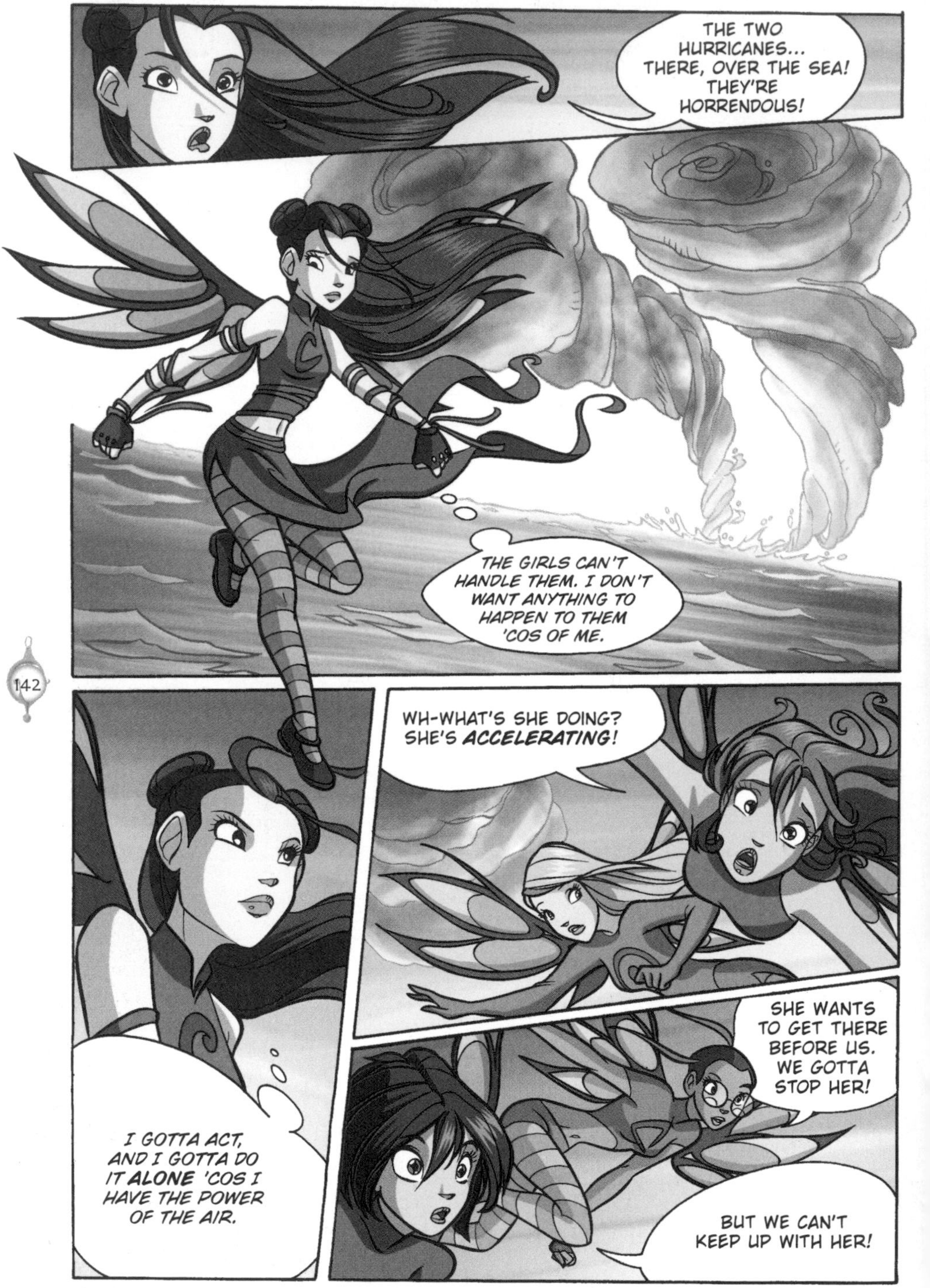
THE TWO HURRICANES... THERE, OVER THE SEA! THEY'RE HORRENDOUS!
THE GIRLS CAN'T HANDLE THEM. I DON'T WANT ANYTHING TO HAPPEN TO THEM 'COS OF ME.
I GOTTA ACT, AND I GOTTA DO IT ALONE 'COS I HAVE THE POWER OF THE AIR.
WH-WHAT'S SHE DOING? SHE'S ACCELERATING!
SHE WANTS TO GET THERE BEFORE US. WE GOTTA STOP HER!
BUT WE CAN'T KEEP UP WITH HER!

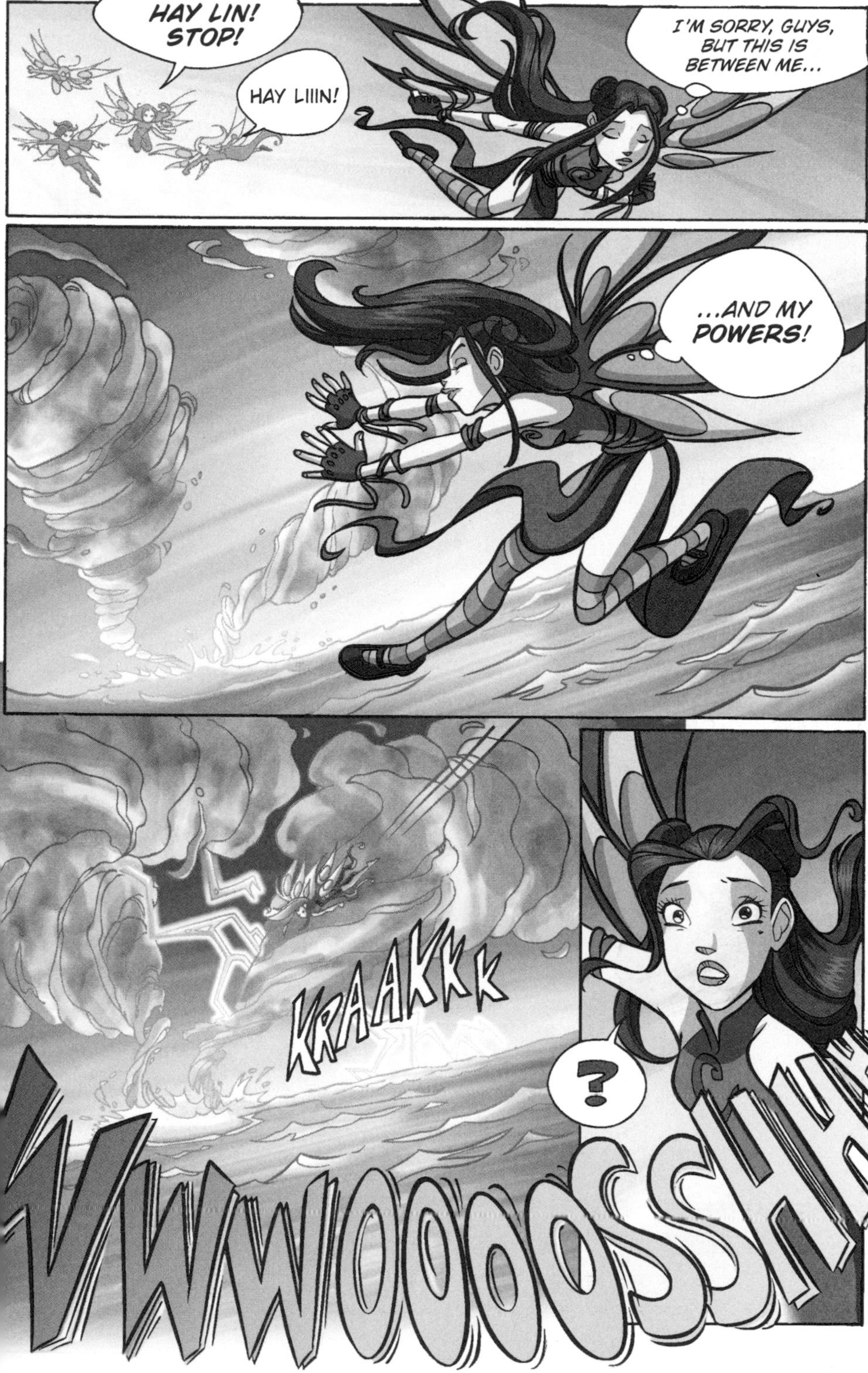
HAY LIN! STOP!
HAY LIIIN!
I'M SORRY, GUYS, BUT THIS IS BETWEEN ME...
...AND MY POWERS!
KRAAKKK
?
VWWOOOOSSHH

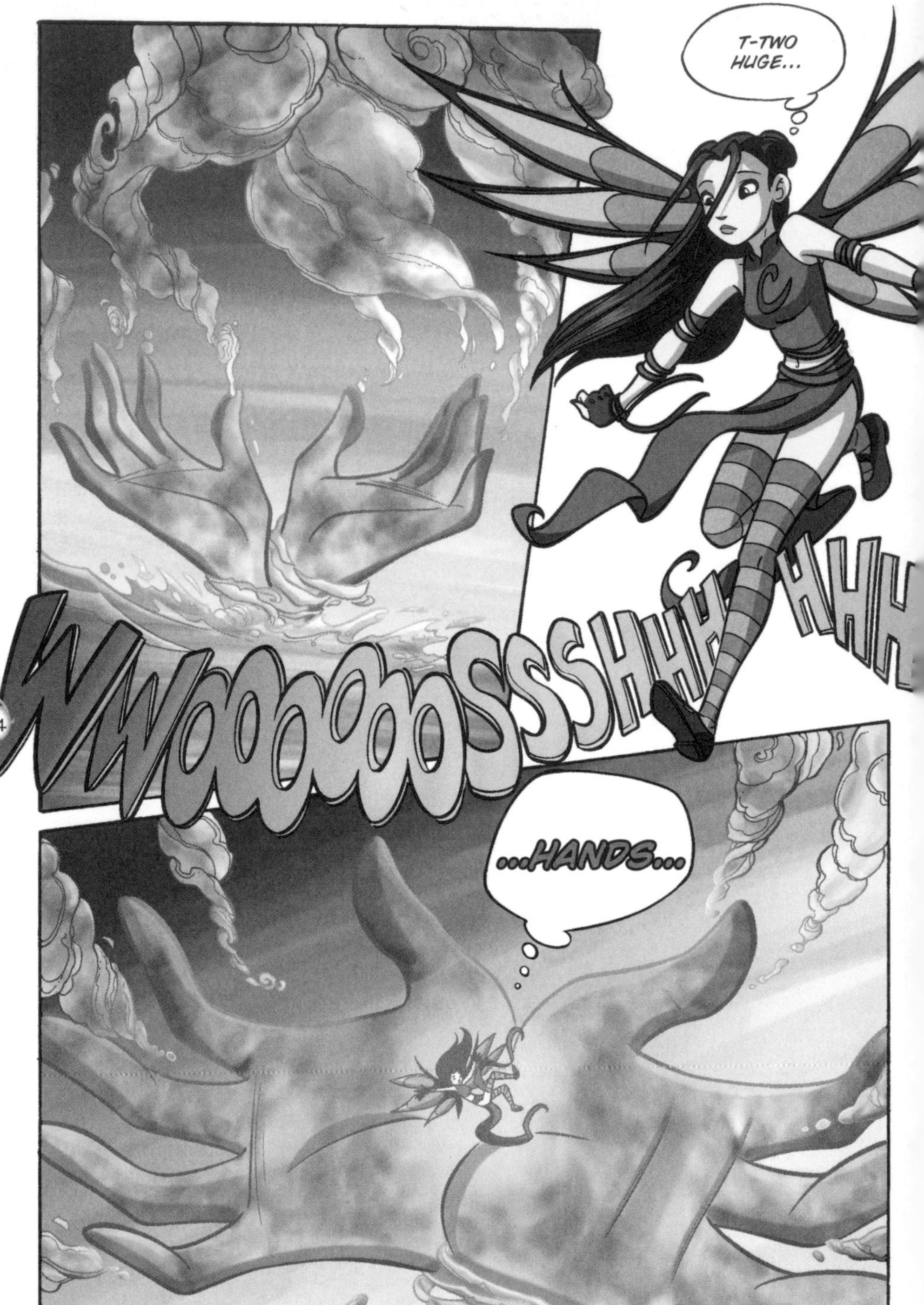
T-TWO HUGE...
WWOOOOOOSSSHHHHHHH
...HANDS...

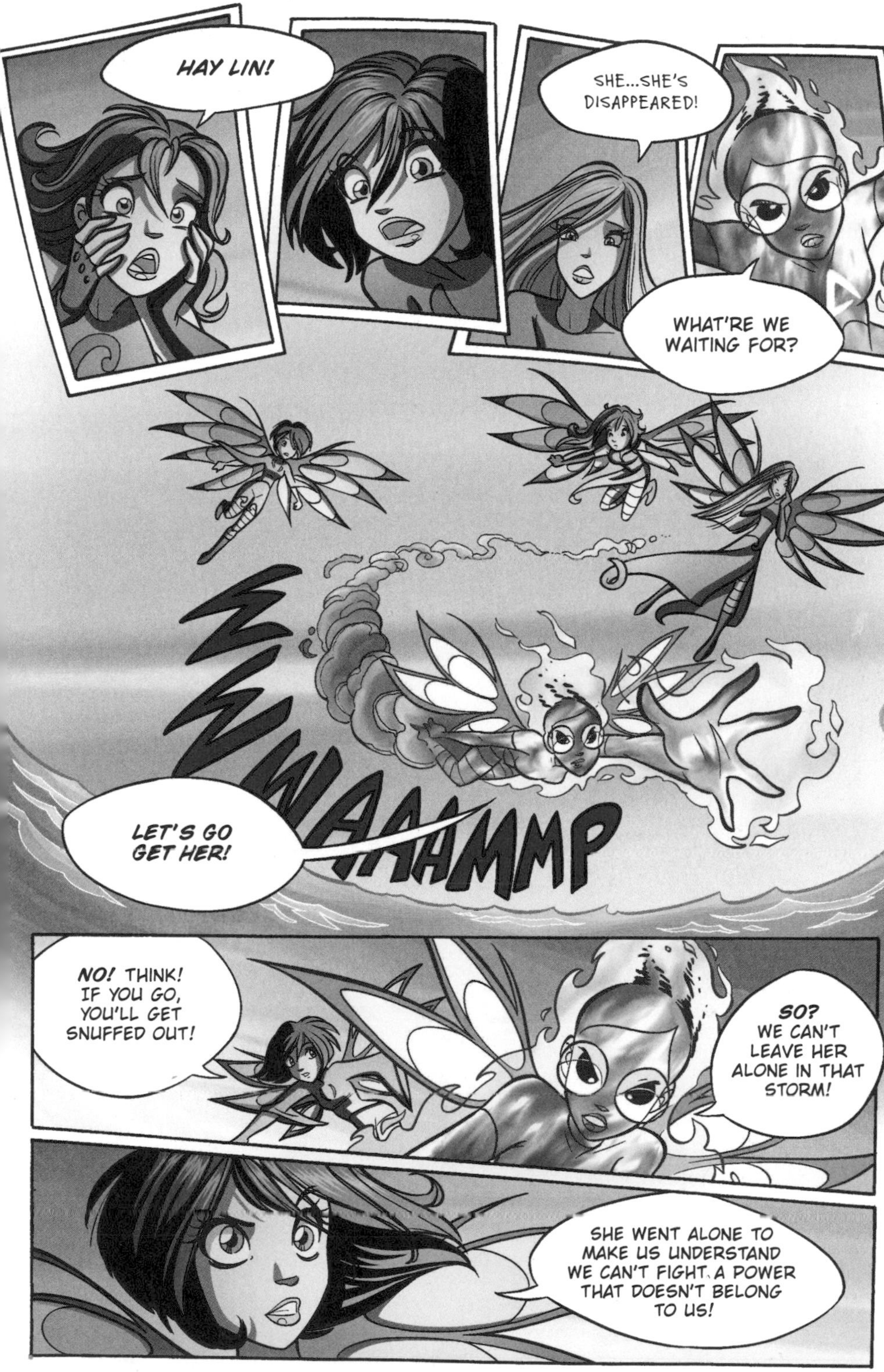
HAY LIN!
SHE...SHE'S DISAPPEARED!
WHAT'RE WE WAITING FOR?
WWAAAHMMP
LET'S GO GET HER!
NO! THINK! IF YOU GO, YOU'LL GET SNUFFED OUT!
SO? WE CAN'T LEAVE HER ALONE IN THAT STORM!
SHE WENT ALONE TO MAKE US UNDERSTAND WE CAN'T FIGHT A POWER THAT DOESN'T BELONG TO US!

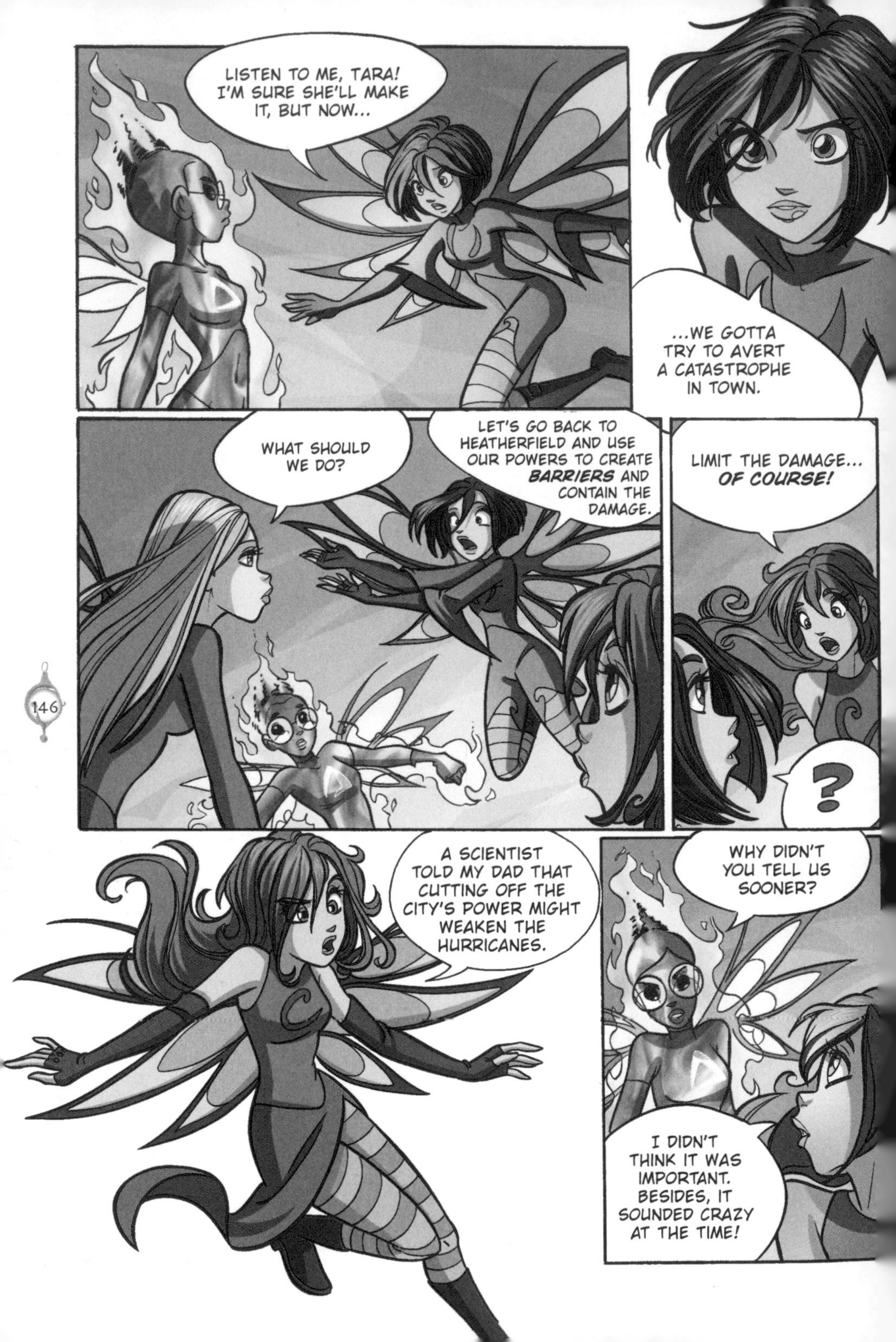
LISTEN TO ME, TARA! I'M SURE SHE'LL MAKE IT, BUT NOW...
...WE GOTTA TRY TO AVERT A CATASTROPHE IN TOWN.
WHAT SHOULD WE DO?
LET'S GO BACK TO HEATHERFIELD AND USE OUR POWERS TO CREATE BARRIERS AND CONTAIN THE DAMAGE.
LIMIT THE DAMAGE... OF COURSE!
?
A SCIENTIST TOLD MY DAD THAT CUTTING OFF THE CITY'S POWER MIGHT WEAKEN THE HURRICANES.
WHY DIDN'T YOU TELL US SOONER?
I DIDN'T THINK IT WAS IMPORTANT. BESIDES, IT SOUNDED CRAZY AT THE TIME!

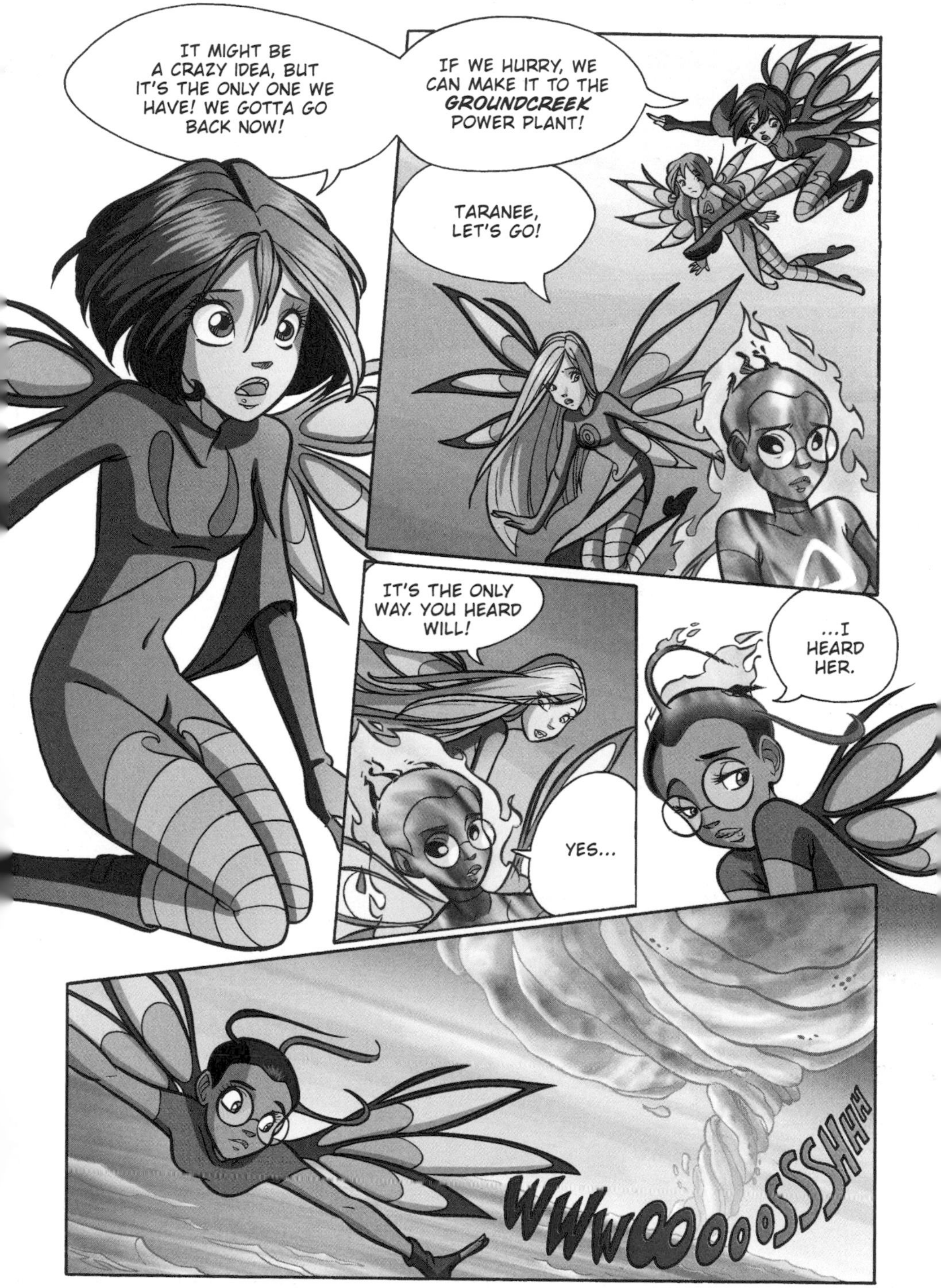
IT MIGHT BE A CRAZY IDEA, BUT IT'S THE ONLY ONE WE HAVE! WE GOTTA GO BACK NOW!
IF WE HURRY, WE CAN MAKE IT TO THE GROUNDCREEK POWER PLANT!
TARANEE, LET'S GO!
IT'S THE ONLY WAY. YOU HEARD WILL!
YES...
...I HEARD HER.
WWWOOOOOSSSHHH

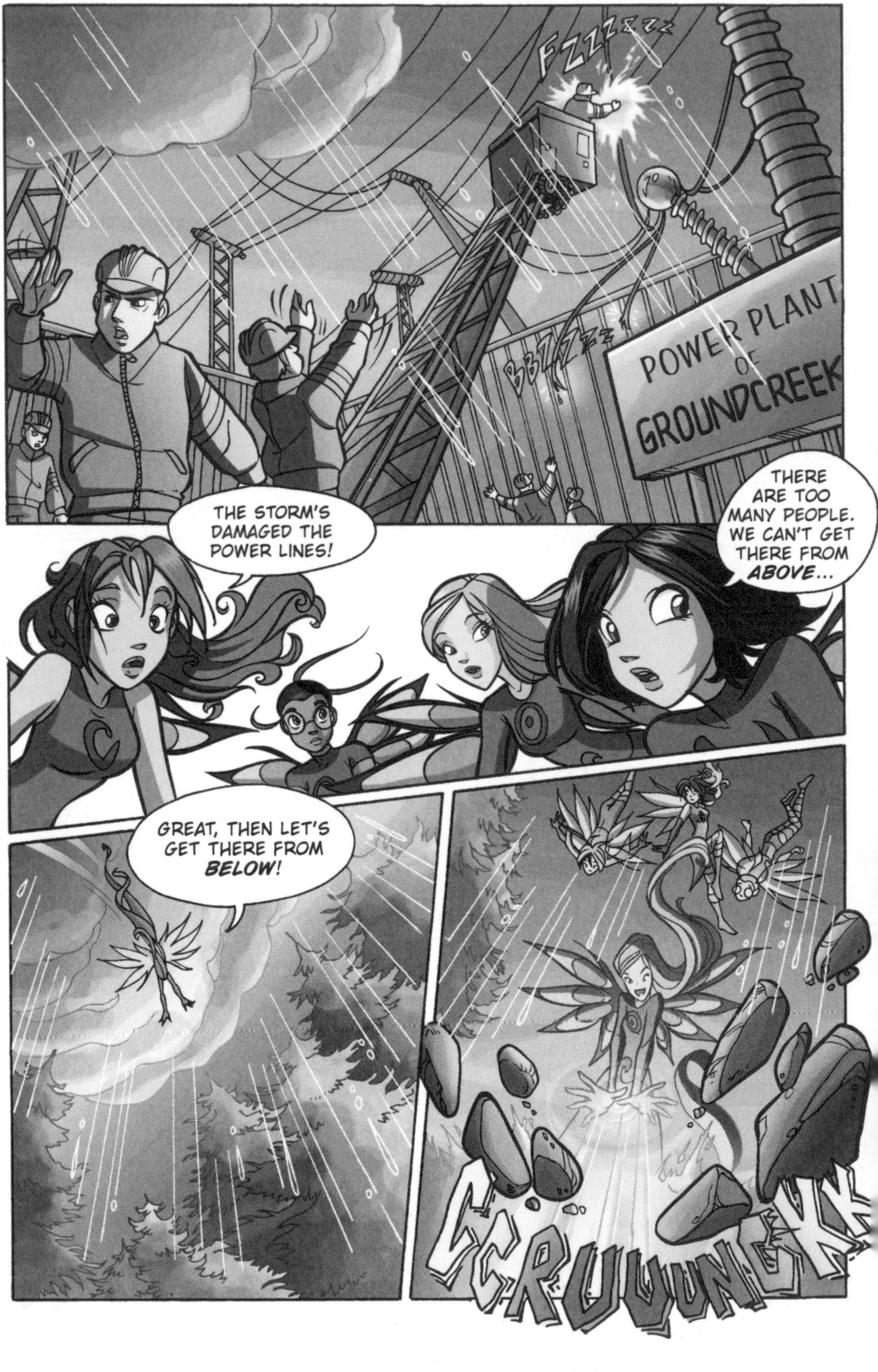
FZZZZZZZ
BBZZZZZ
POWER PLANT OF GROUNDCREEK
THE STORM'S DAMAGED THE POWER LINES!
THERE ARE TOO MANY PEOPLE. WE CAN'T GET THERE FROM ABOVE...
GREAT, THEN LET'S GET THERE FROM BELOW!
CCRUUUNCK

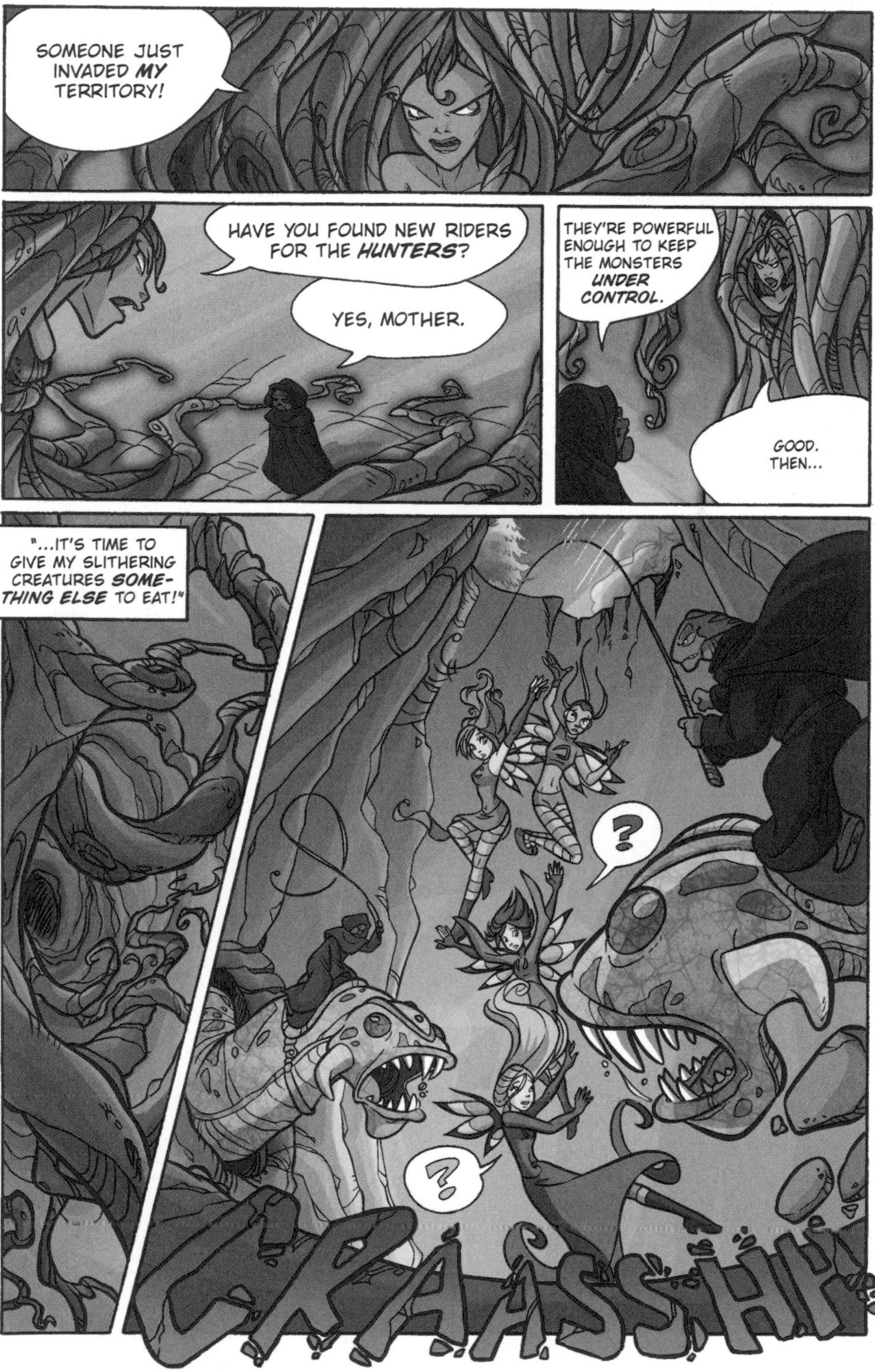

SOMEONE JUST INVADED MY TERRITORY!
HAVE YOU FOUND NEW RIDERS FOR THE HUNTERS?
YES, MOTHER.
THEY'RE POWERFUL ENOUGH TO KEEP THE MONSTERS UNDER CONTROL.
GOOD. THEN...
"...IT'S TIME TO GIVE MY SLITHERING CREATURES SOMETHING ELSE TO EAT!"
?
?
CRAASSHH

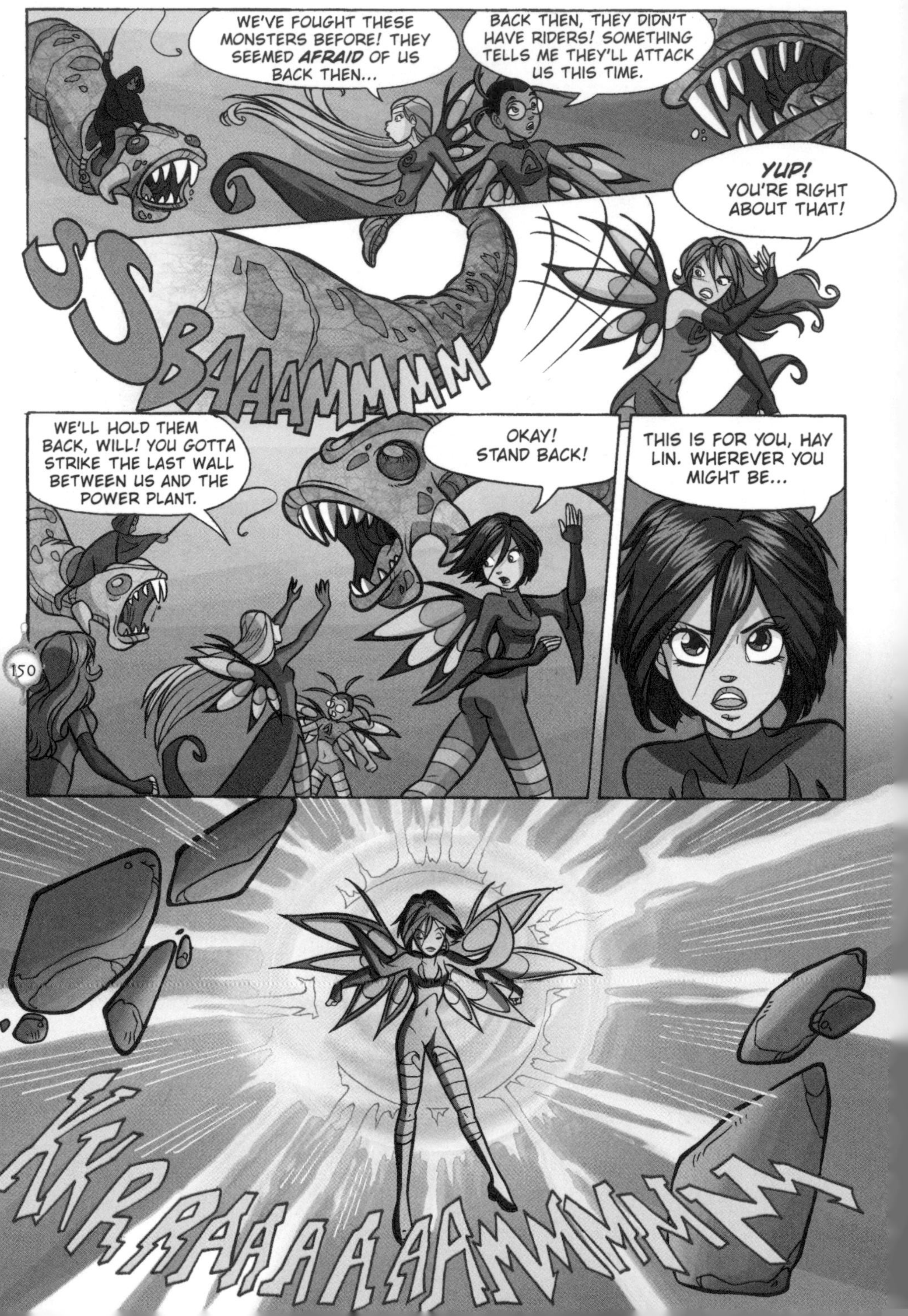
WE'VE FOUGHT THESE MONSTERS BEFORE! THEY SEEMED AFRAID OF US BACK THEN...
BACK THEN, THEY DIDN'T HAVE RIDERS! SOMETHING TELLS ME THEY'LL ATTACK US THIS TIME.
YUP! YOU'RE RIGHT ABOUT THAT!
SBAAAMMMM
WE'LL HOLD THEM BACK, WILL! YOU GOTTA STRIKE THE LAST WALL BETWEEN US AND THE POWER PLANT.
OKAY! STAND BACK!
THIS IS FOR YOU, HAY LIN. WHEREVER YOU MIGHT BE...
KRRAAAAAAMMMMMM

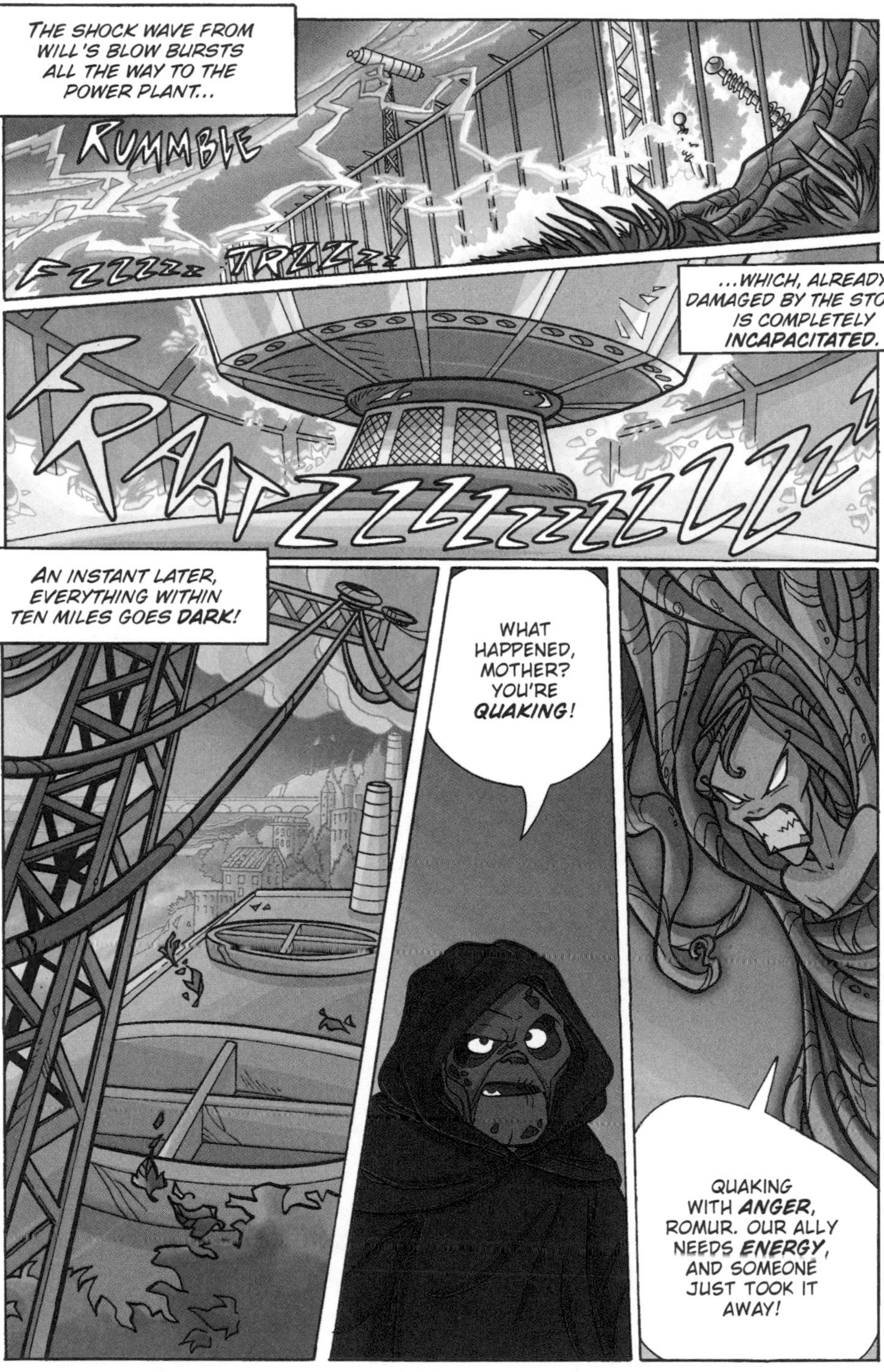
THE SHOCK WAVE FROM WILL'S BLOW BURSTS ALL THE WAY TO THE POWER PLANT...
RUMMBLE
FZZZZZ TRZZZzz
...WHICH, ALREADY DAMAGED BY THE STORM, IS COMPLETELY INCAPACITATED.
FRAATZZZZZZZZZZZZZ
AN INSTANT LATER, EVERYTHING WITHIN TEN MILES GOES DARK!
WHAT HAPPENED, MOTHER? YOU'RE QUAKING!
QUAKING WITH ANGER, ROMUR. OUR ALLY NEEDS ENERGY, AND SOMEONE JUST TOOK IT AWAY!

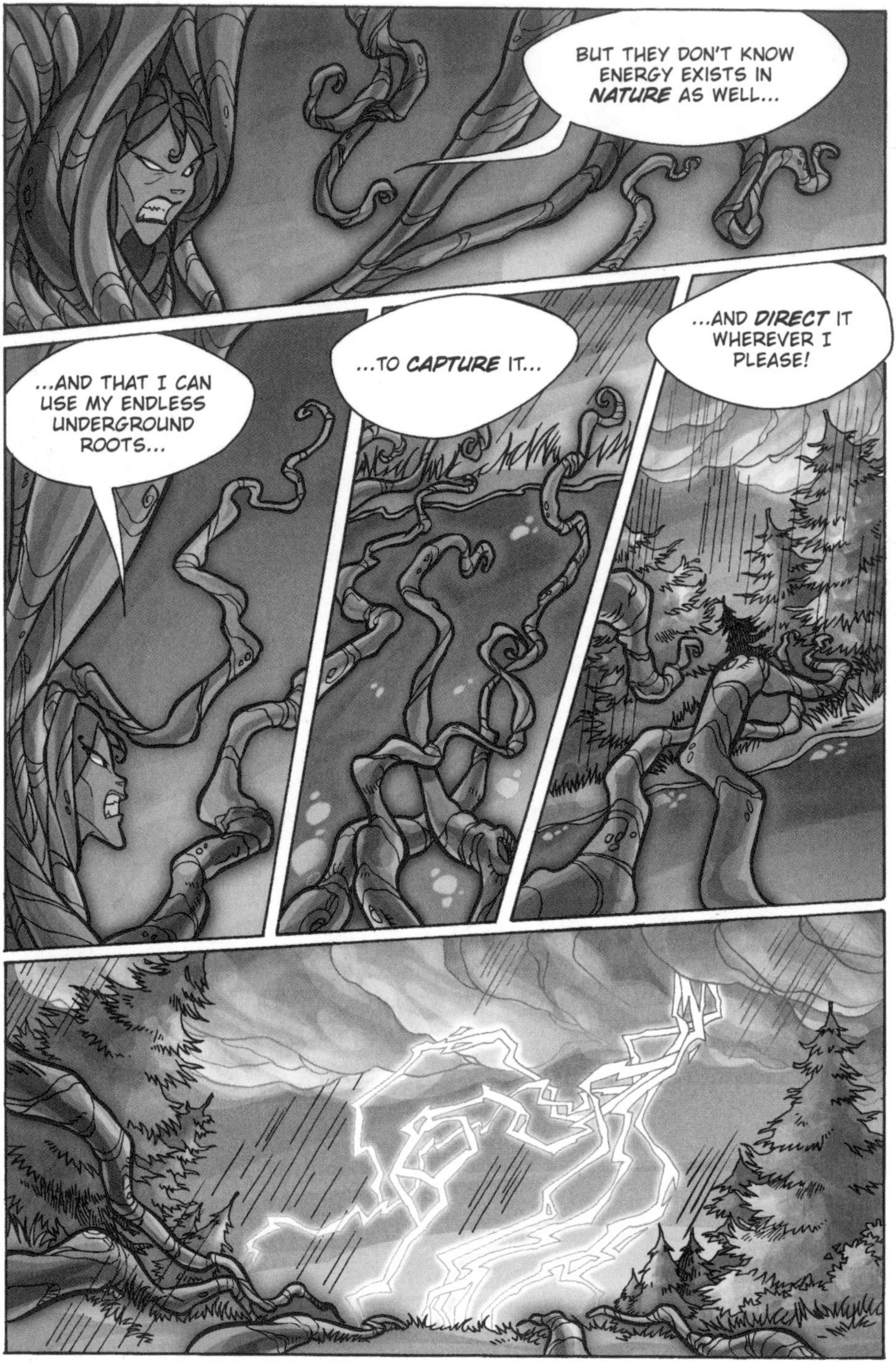
BUT THEY DON'T KNOW ENERGY EXISTS IN **NATURE** AS WELL...
...AND THAT I CAN USE MY ENDLESS UNDERGROUND ROOTS...
...TO **CAPTURE** IT...
...AND **DIRECT** IT WHEREVER I PLEASE!

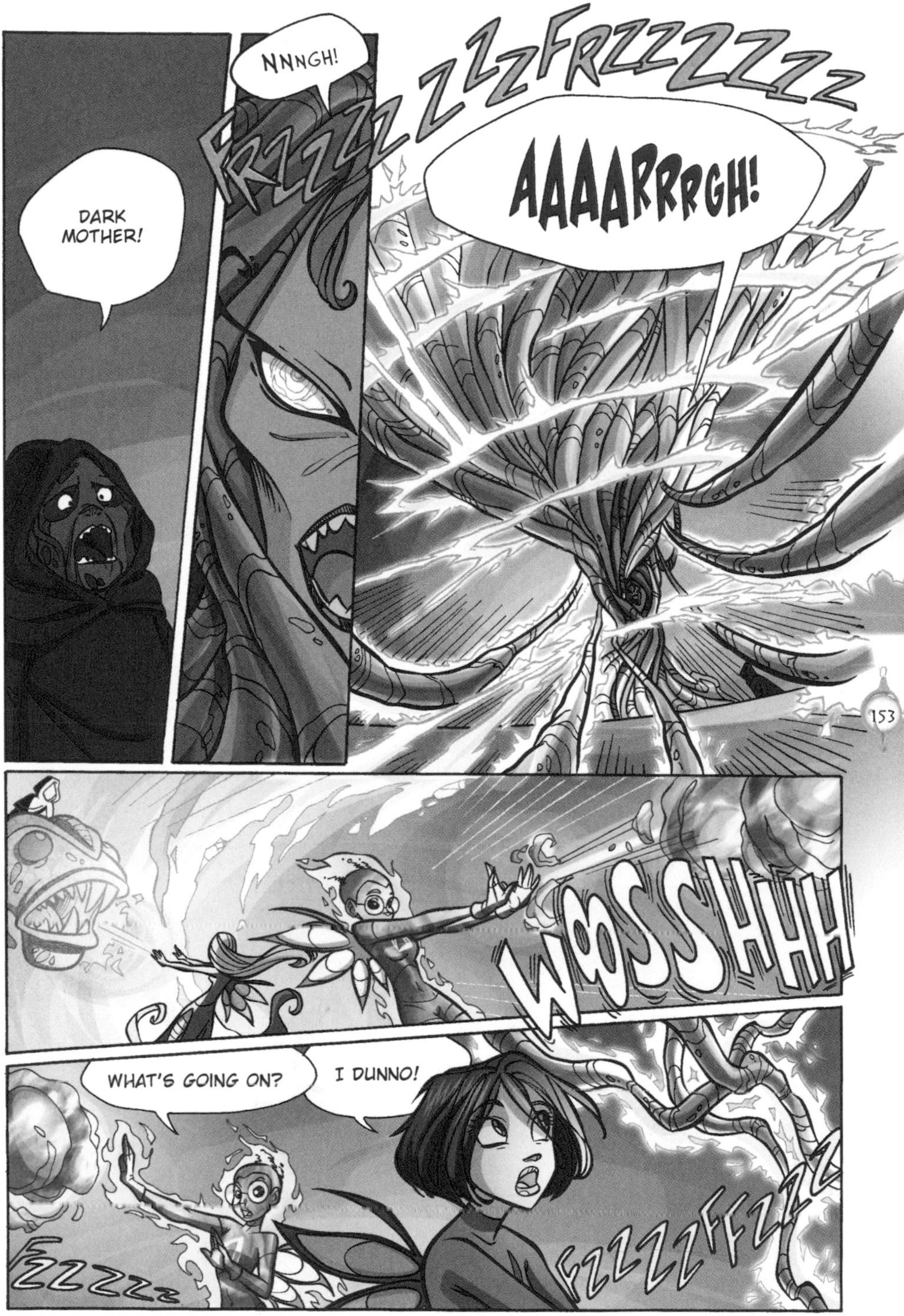
NNNGH!
FRZZZZZZZZFRZZZZZZZZ
AAAARRRGH!
DARK MOTHER!
WOOSSHHH
WHAT'S GOING ON?
I DUNNO!
FZZZZZ
FZZZZFFZZZ

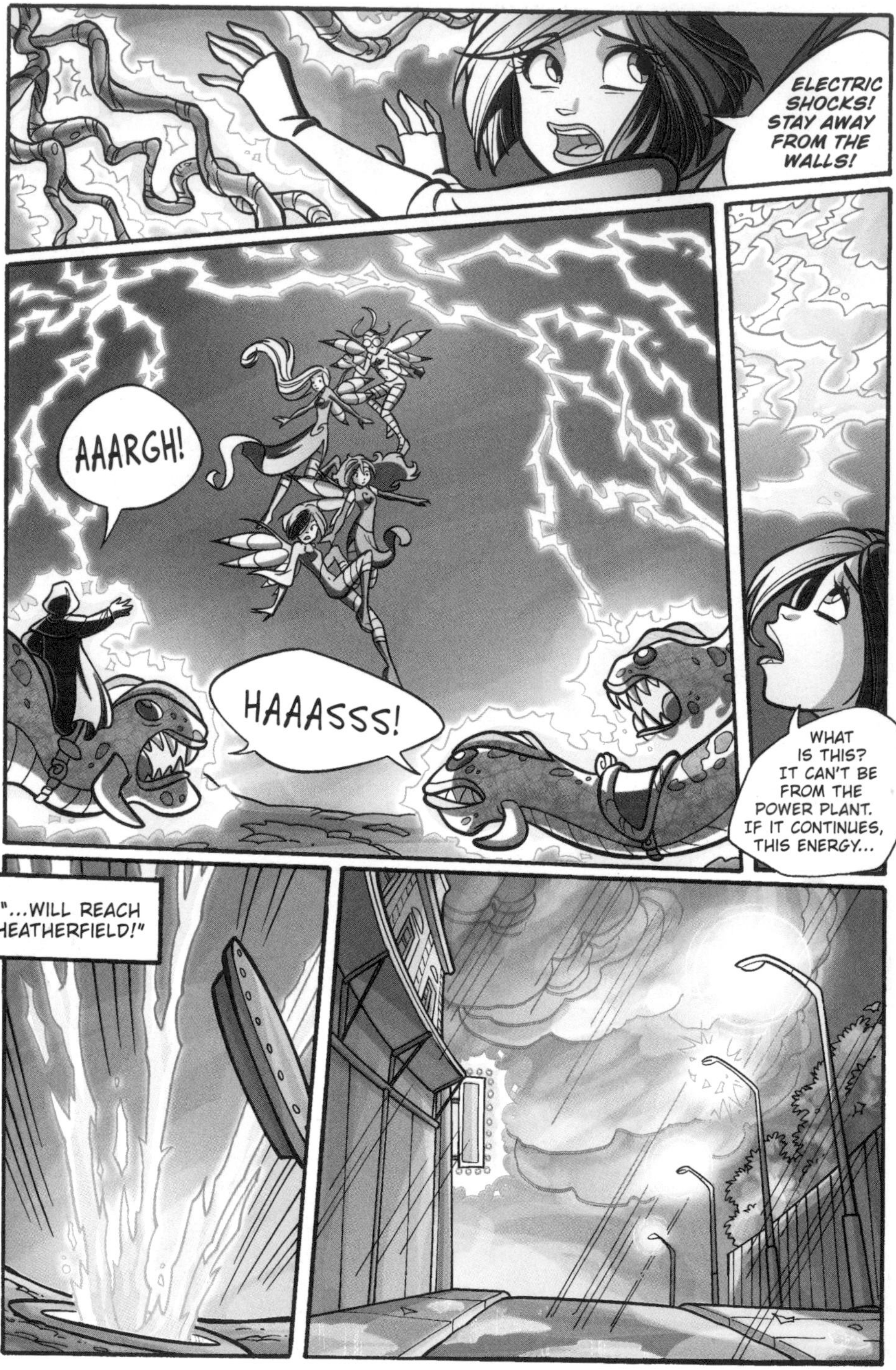
ELECTRIC SHOCKS! STAY AWAY FROM THE WALLS!
AAARGH!
HAAASSS!
WHAT IS THIS? IT CAN'T BE FROM THE POWER PLANT. IF IT CONTINUES, THIS ENERGY...
"...WILL REACH HEATHERFIELD!"

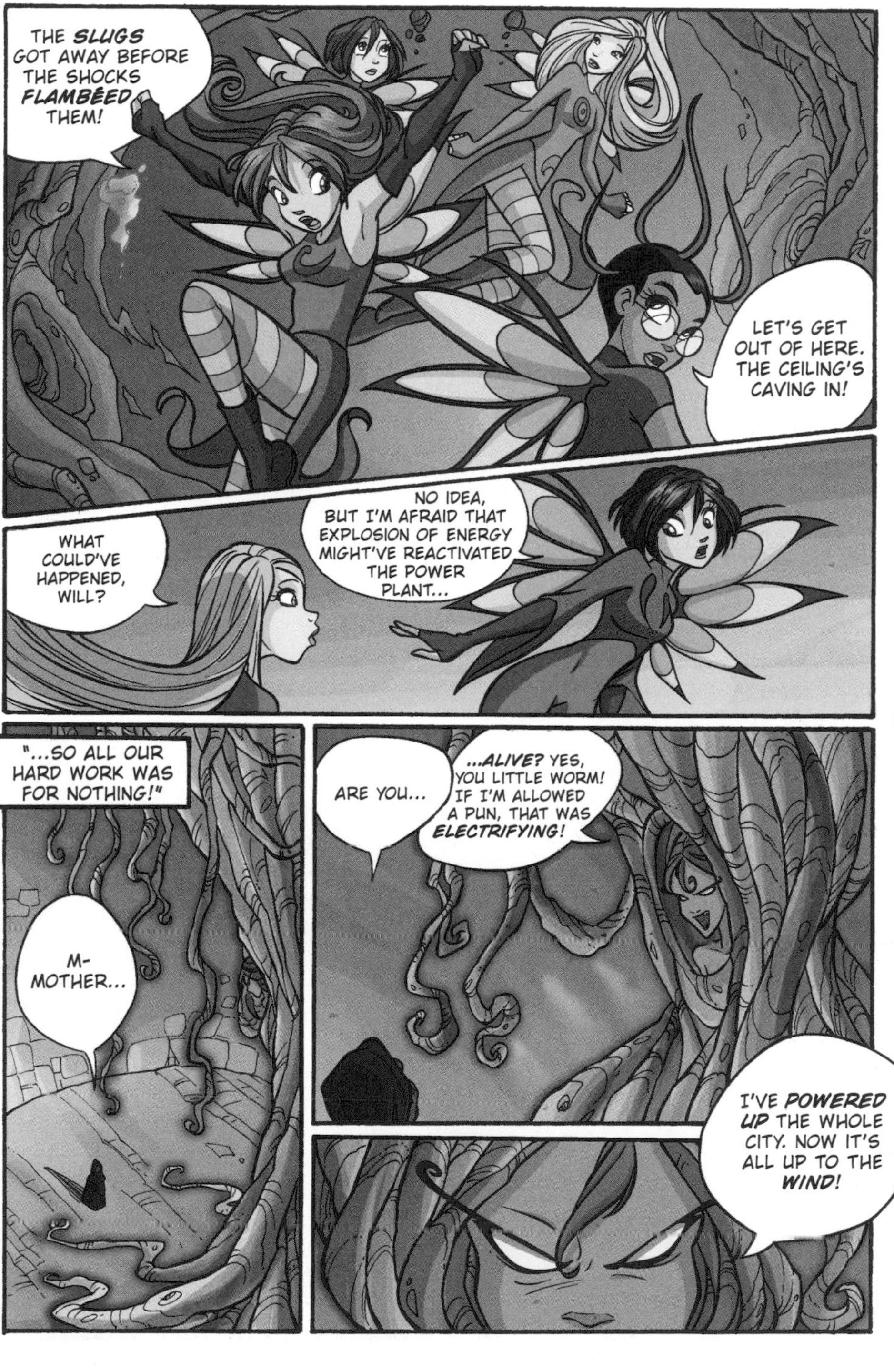
THE SLUGS GOT AWAY BEFORE THE SHOCKS FLAMBÉED THEM!
LET'S GET OUT OF HERE. THE CEILING'S CAVING IN!
WHAT COULD'VE HAPPENED, WILL?
NO IDEA, BUT I'M AFRAID THAT EXPLOSION OF ENERGY MIGHT'VE REACTIVATED THE POWER PLANT...
"...SO ALL OUR HARD WORK WAS FOR NOTHING!"
M-MOTHER...
ARE YOU...
...ALIVE? YES, YOU LITTLE WORM! IF I'M ALLOWED A PUN, THAT WAS ELECTRIFYING!
I'VE POWERED UP THE WHOLE CITY. NOW IT'S ALL UP TO THE WIND!

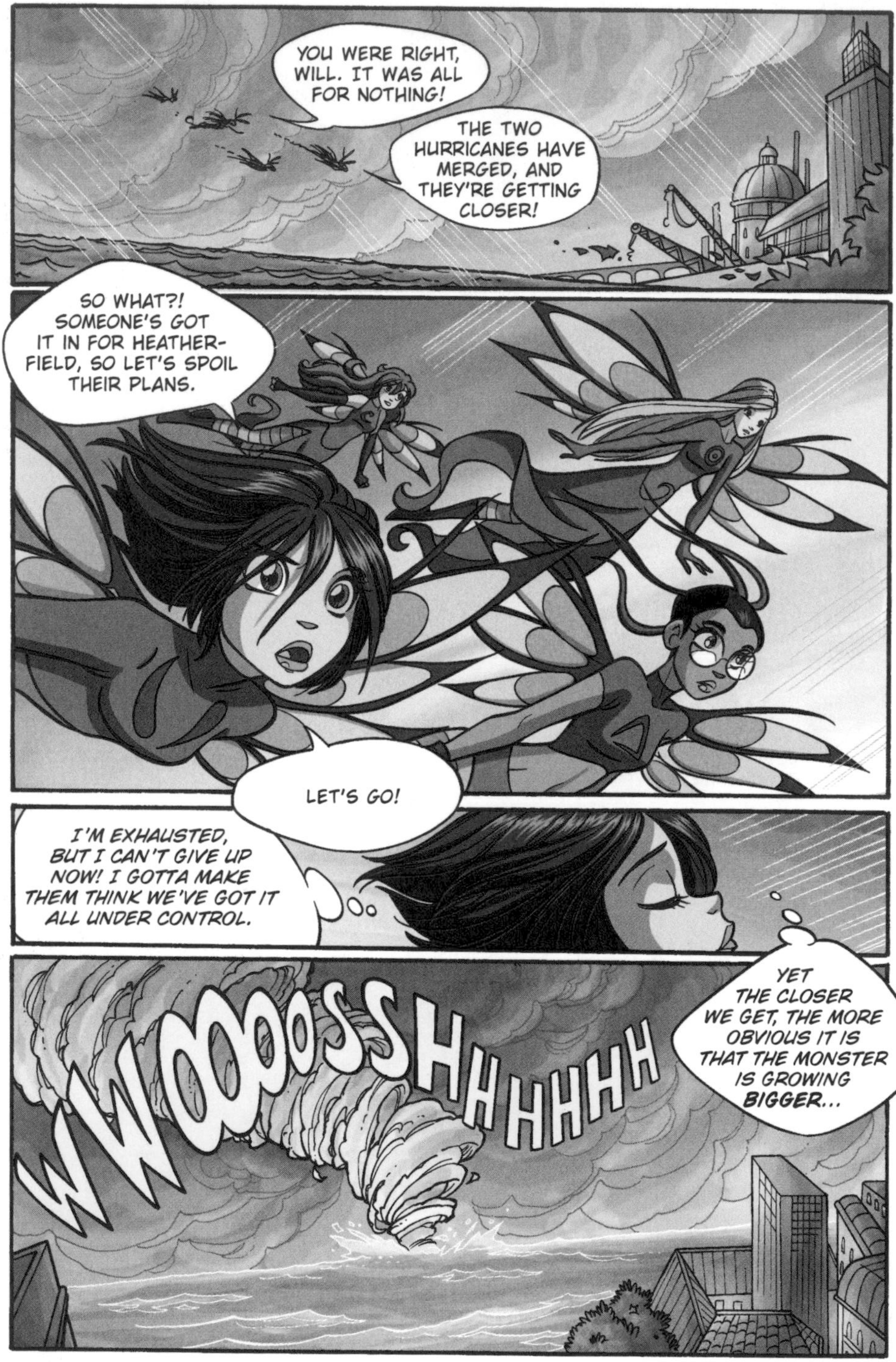
YOU WERE RIGHT, WILL. IT WAS ALL FOR NOTHING!
THE TWO HURRICANES HAVE MERGED, AND THEY'RE GETTING CLOSER!
SO WHAT?! SOMEONE'S GOT IT IN FOR HEATHER-FIELD, SO LET'S SPOIL THEIR PLANS.
LET'S GO!
I'M EXHAUSTED, BUT I CAN'T GIVE UP NOW! I GOTTA MAKE THEM THINK WE'VE GOT IT ALL UNDER CONTROL.
WWOOOOSSHHHHHH
YET THE CLOSER WE GET, THE MORE OBVIOUS IT IS THAT THE MONSTER IS GROWING BIGGER...

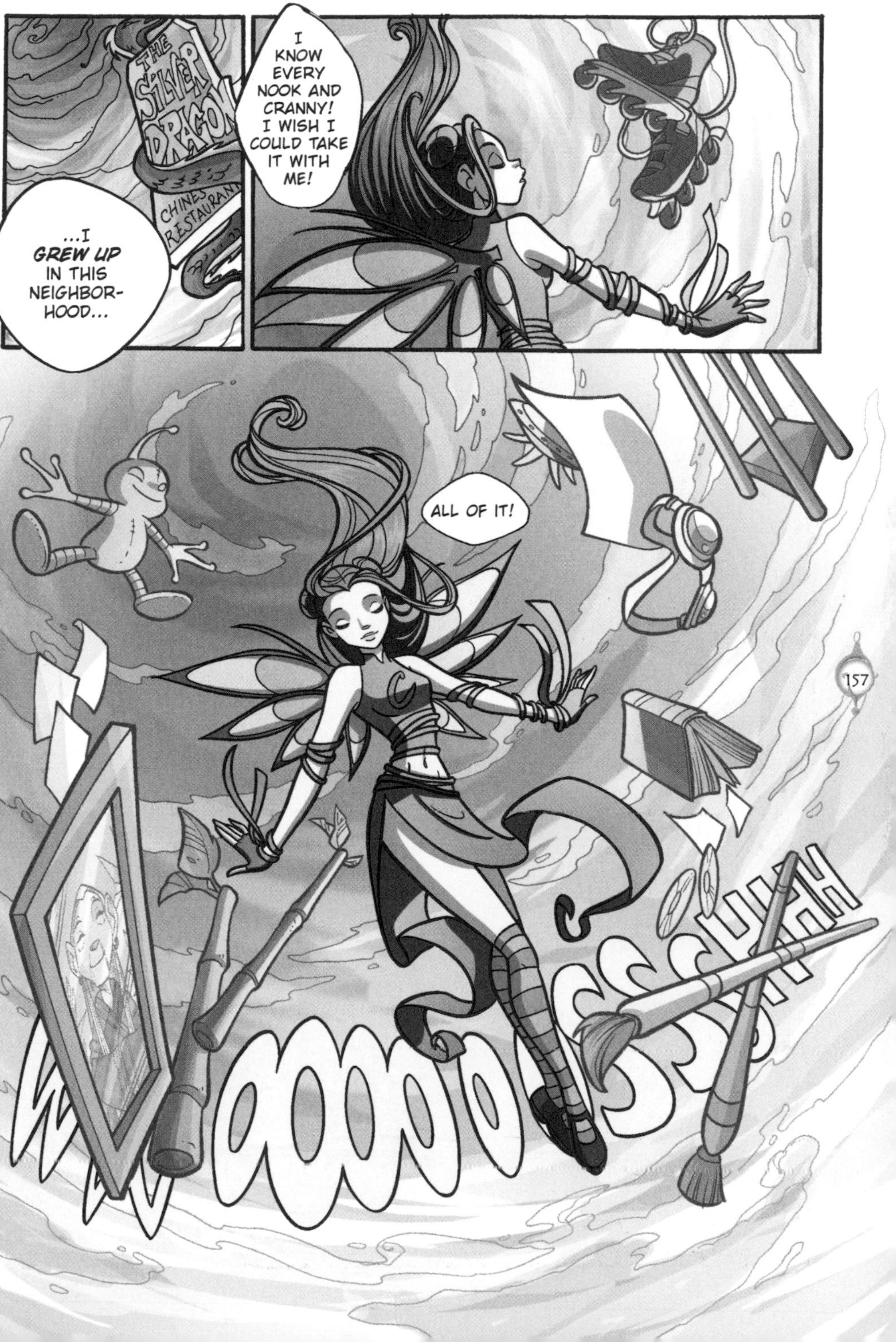
THE SILVER DRAGON
CHINES RESTAURANT
...I GREW UP IN THIS NEIGHBORHOOD...
I KNOW EVERY NOOK AND CRANNY! I WISH I COULD TAKE IT WITH ME!
ALL OF IT!
WOOOOOSSHHH

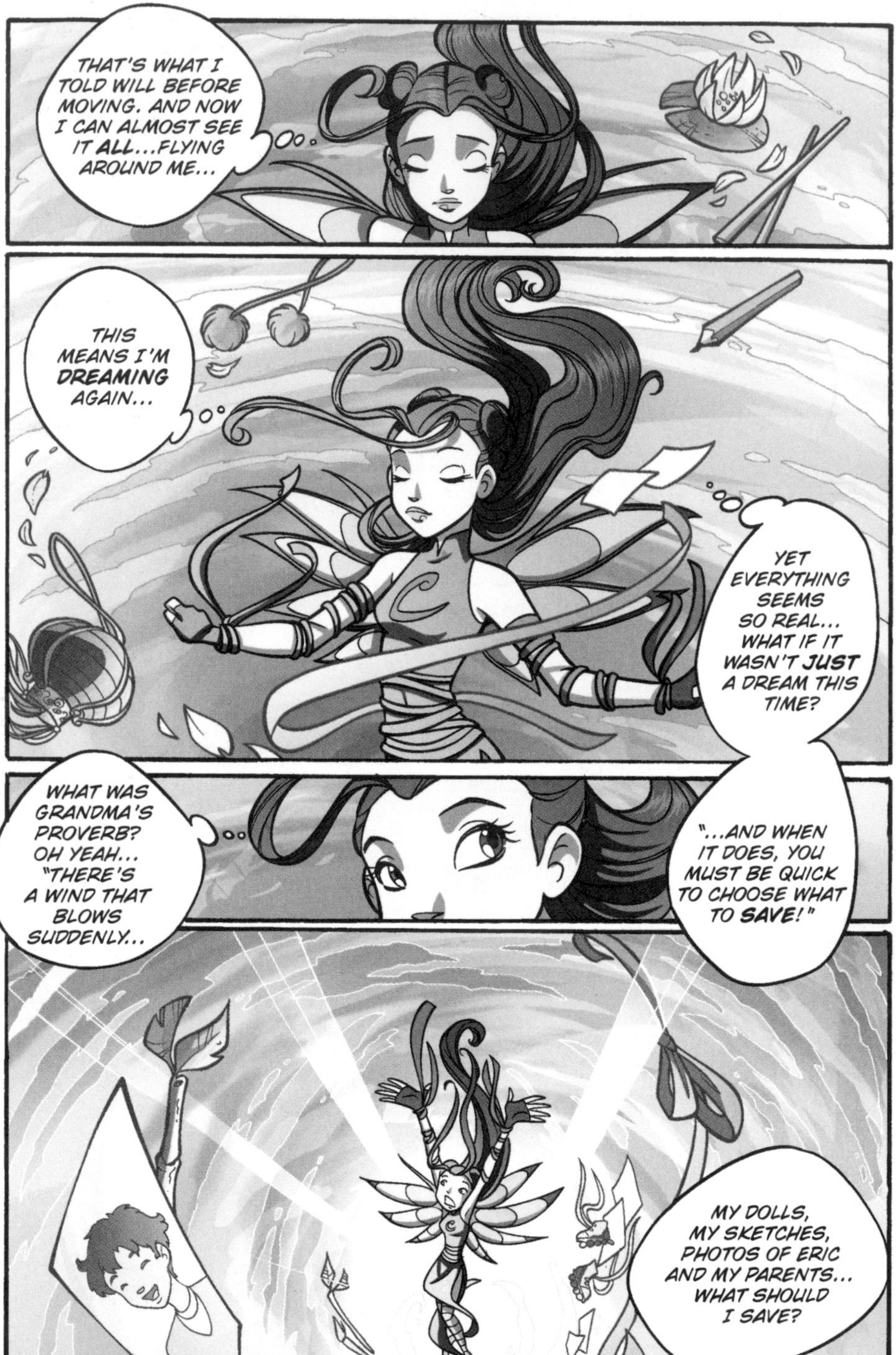
THAT'S WHAT I TOLD WILL BEFORE MOVING. AND NOW I CAN ALMOST SEE IT ALL...FLYING AROUND ME...
THIS MEANS I'M DREAMING AGAIN...
YET EVERYTHING SEEMS SO REAL... WHAT IF IT WASN'T JUST A DREAM THIS TIME?
WHAT WAS GRANDMA'S PROVERB? OH YEAH... "THERE'S A WIND THAT BLOWS SUDDENLY...
"...AND WHEN IT DOES, YOU MUST BE QUICK TO CHOOSE WHAT TO SAVE!"
MY DOLLS, MY SKETCHES, PHOTOS OF ERIC AND MY PARENTS... WHAT SHOULD I SAVE?

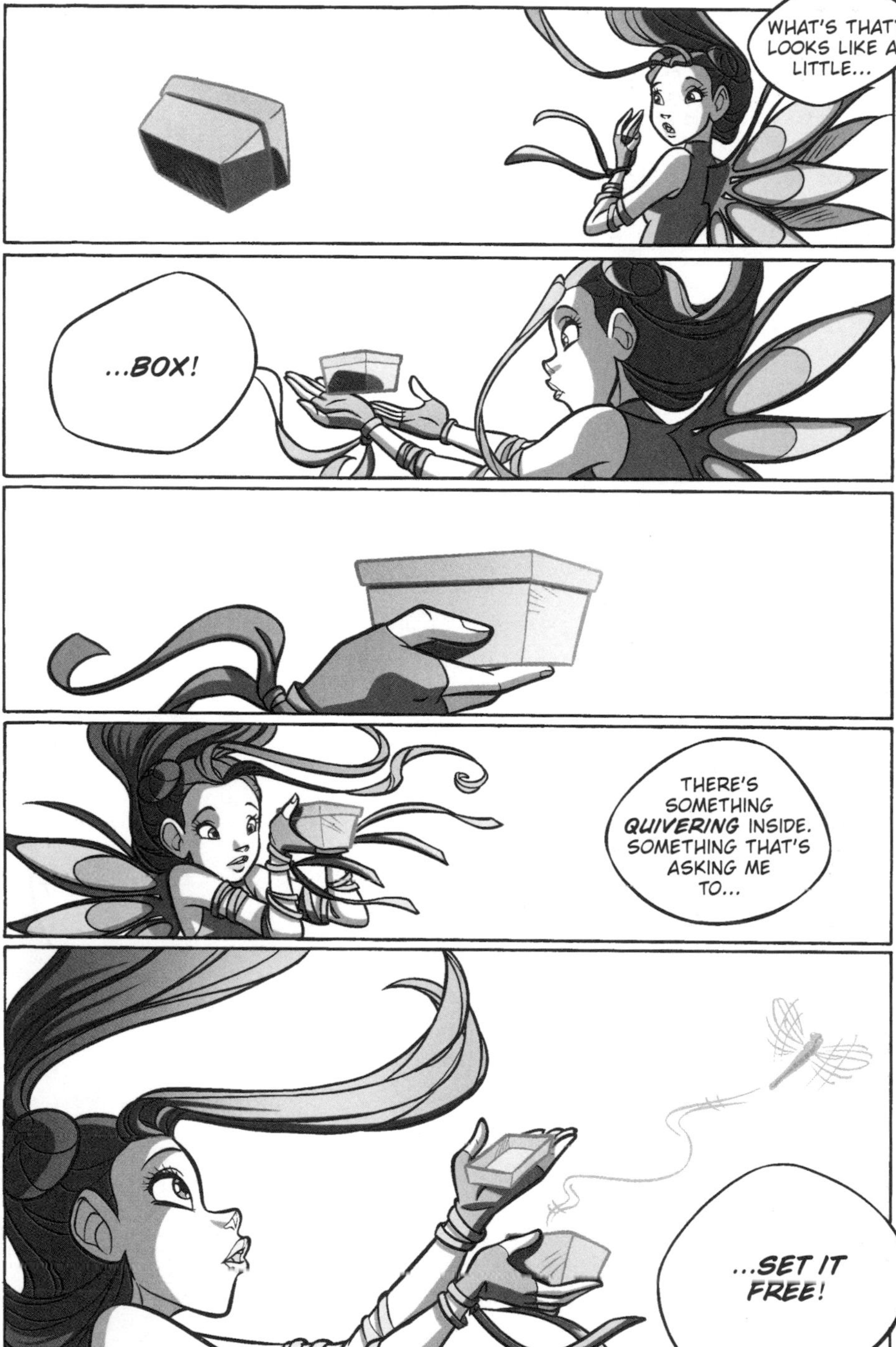
WHAT'S THAT? LOOKS LIKE A LITTLE...
...BOX!
THERE'S SOMETHING QUIVERING INSIDE. SOMETHING THAT'S ASKING ME TO...
...SET IT FREE!

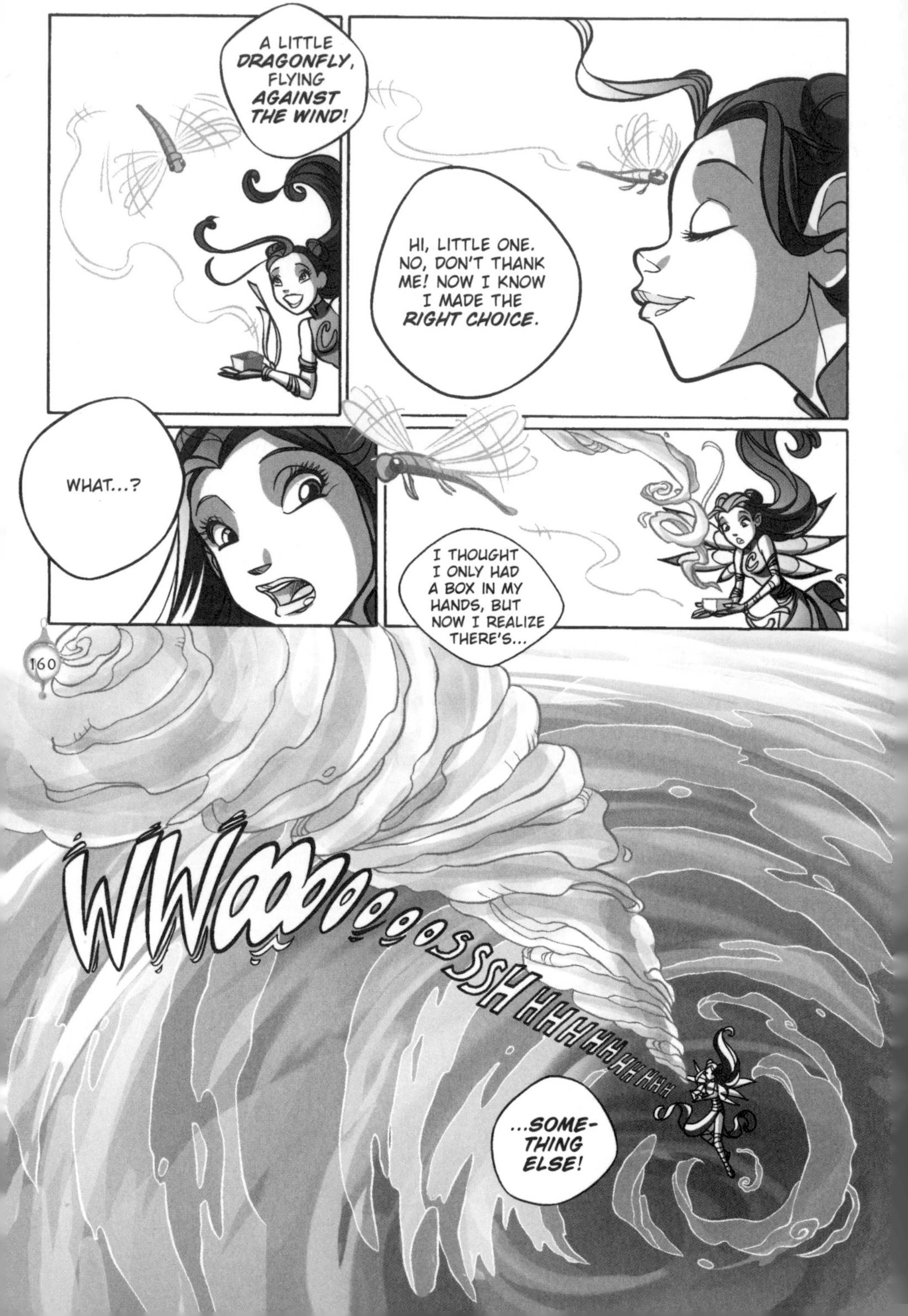
A LITTLE **DRAGONFLY**, FLYING **AGAINST THE WIND!**
HI, LITTLE ONE. NO, DON'T THANK ME! NOW I KNOW I MADE THE **RIGHT CHOICE**.
WHAT...?
I THOUGHT I ONLY HAD A BOX IN MY HANDS, BUT NOW I REALIZE THERE'S...
WWaaoooosssHHHHHHHHHHHH
...**SOME-THING ELSE!**

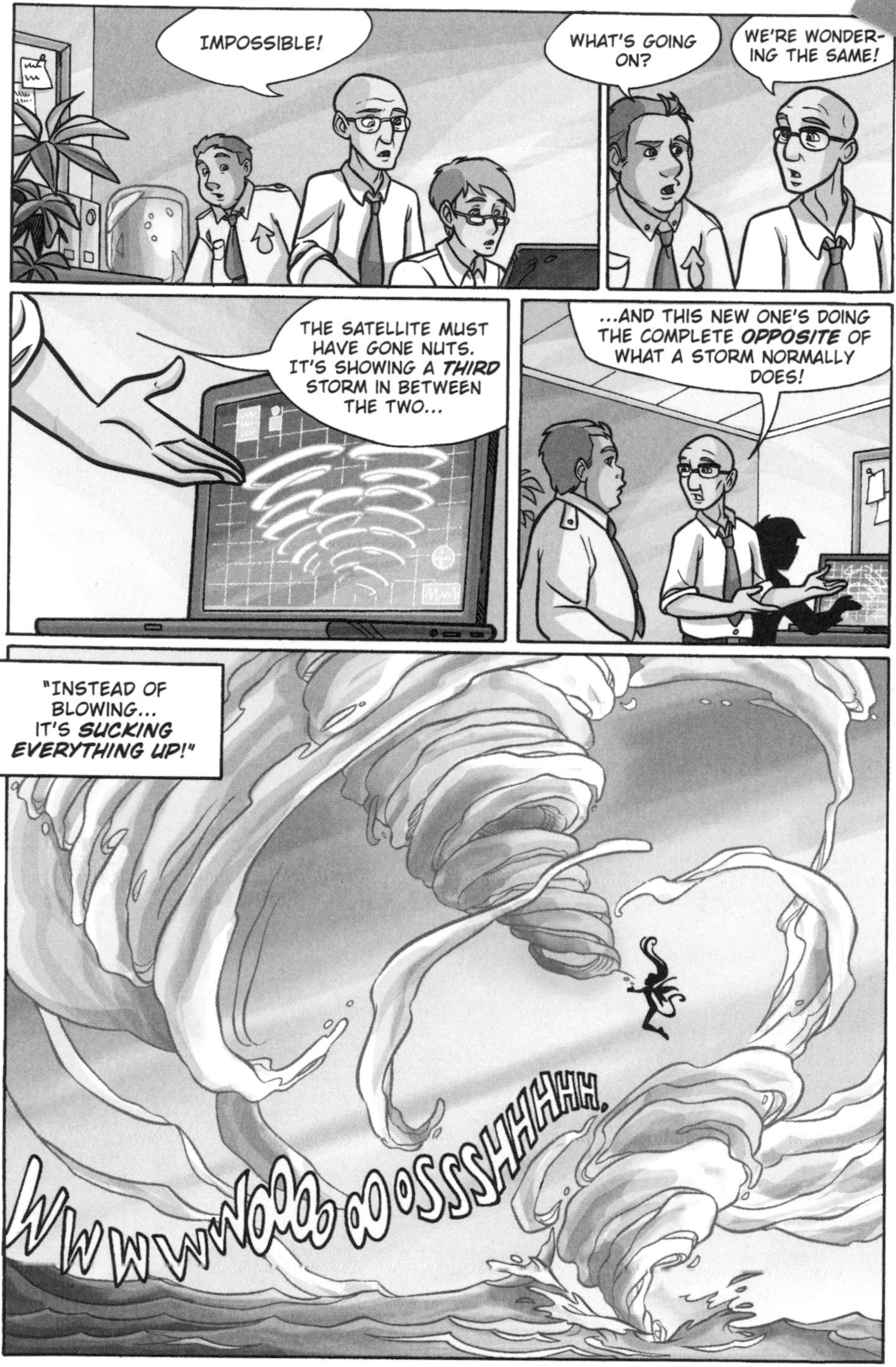
IMPOSSIBLE!
WHAT'S GOING ON?
WE'RE WONDERING THE SAME!
THE SATELLITE MUST HAVE GONE NUTS. IT'S SHOWING A *THIRD* STORM IN BETWEEN THE TWO...
...AND THIS NEW ONE'S DOING THE COMPLETE *OPPOSITE* OF WHAT A STORM NORMALLY DOES!
"INSTEAD OF BLOWING... IT'S *SUCKING EVERYTHING UP!*"
WWWWWOOOOOOOSSSSHHHHH

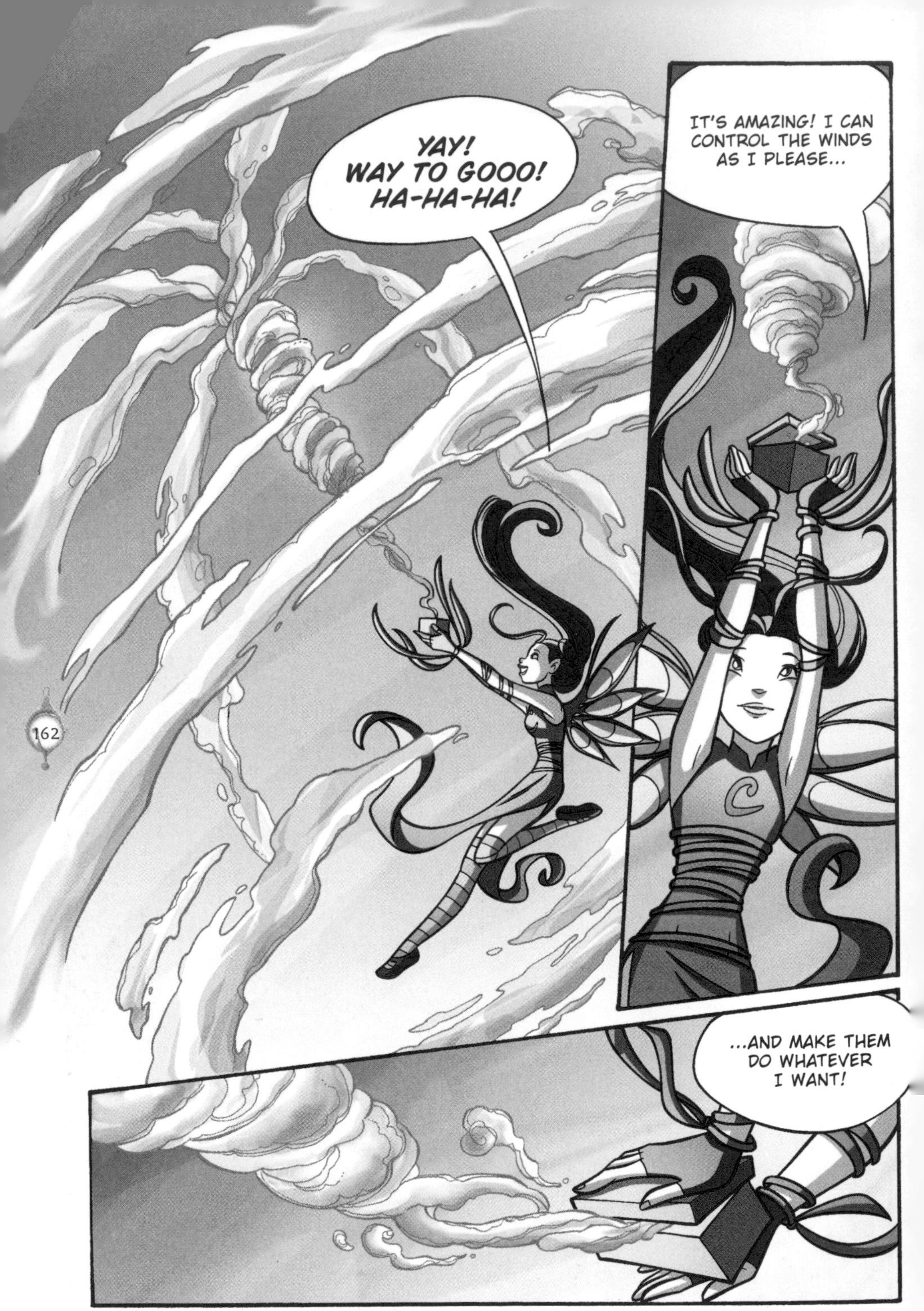
YAY! WAY TO GOOO! HA-HA-HA!
IT'S AMAZING! I CAN CONTROL THE WINDS AS I PLEASE...
...AND MAKE THEM DO WHATEVER I WANT!

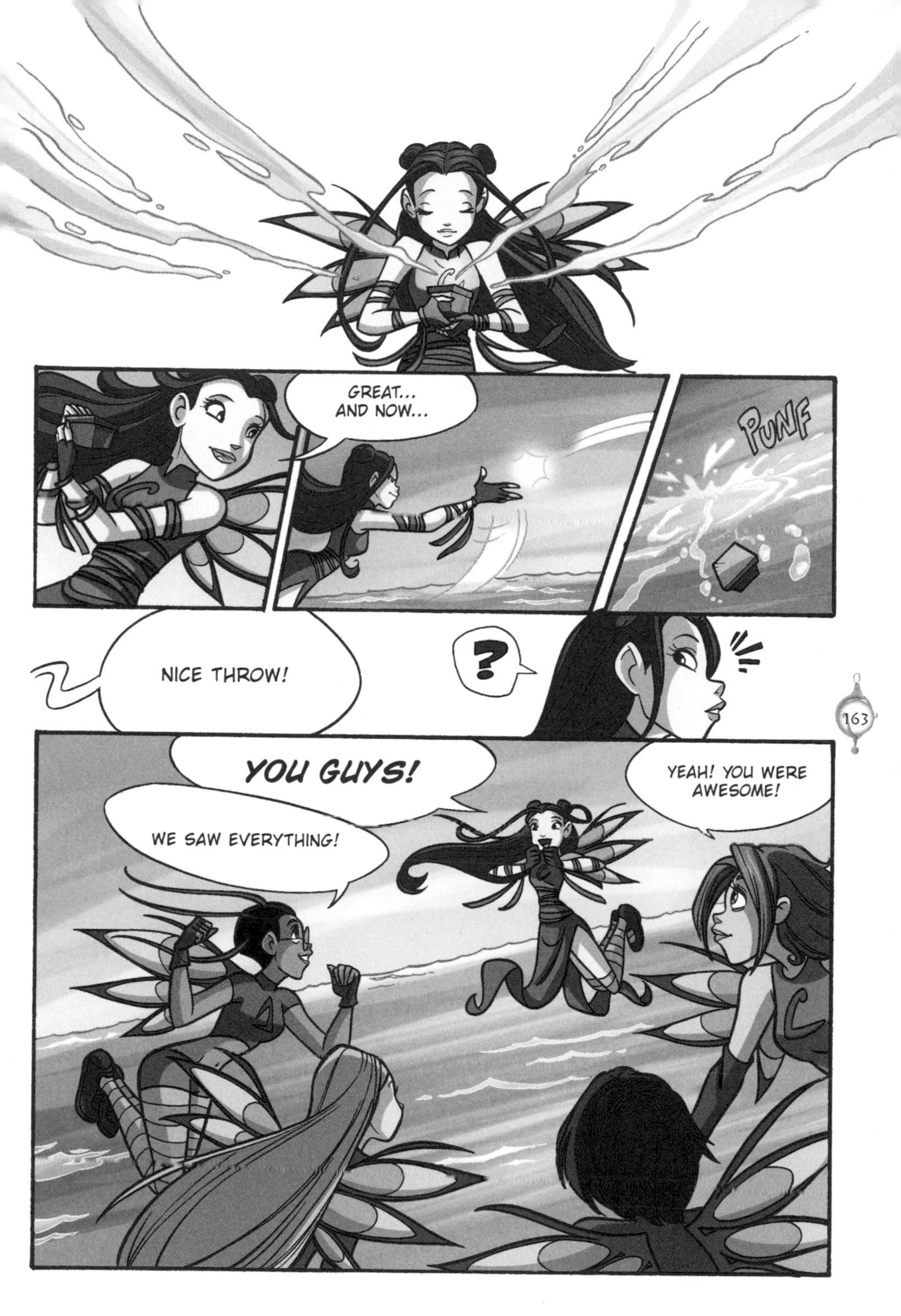
GREAT... AND NOW...
PUNF
NICE THROW!
?
YOU GUYS!
WE SAW EVERYTHING!
YEAH! YOU WERE AWESOME!

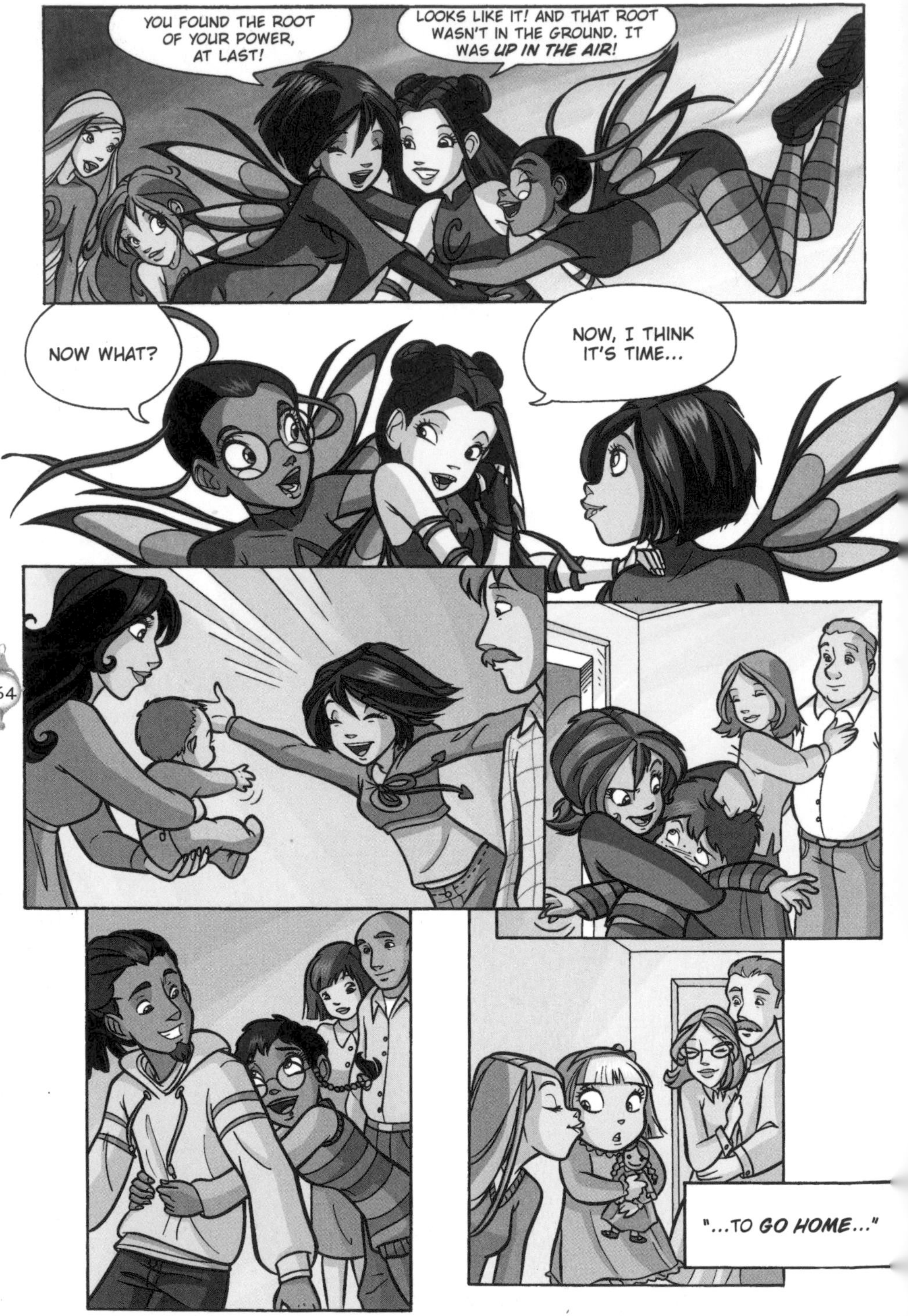
YOU FOUND THE ROOT OF YOUR POWER, AT LAST!
LOOKS LIKE IT! AND THAT ROOT WASN'T IN THE GROUND. IT WAS *UP IN THE AIR*!
NOW WHAT?
NOW, I THINK IT'S TIME...
"...TO *GO HOME*..."

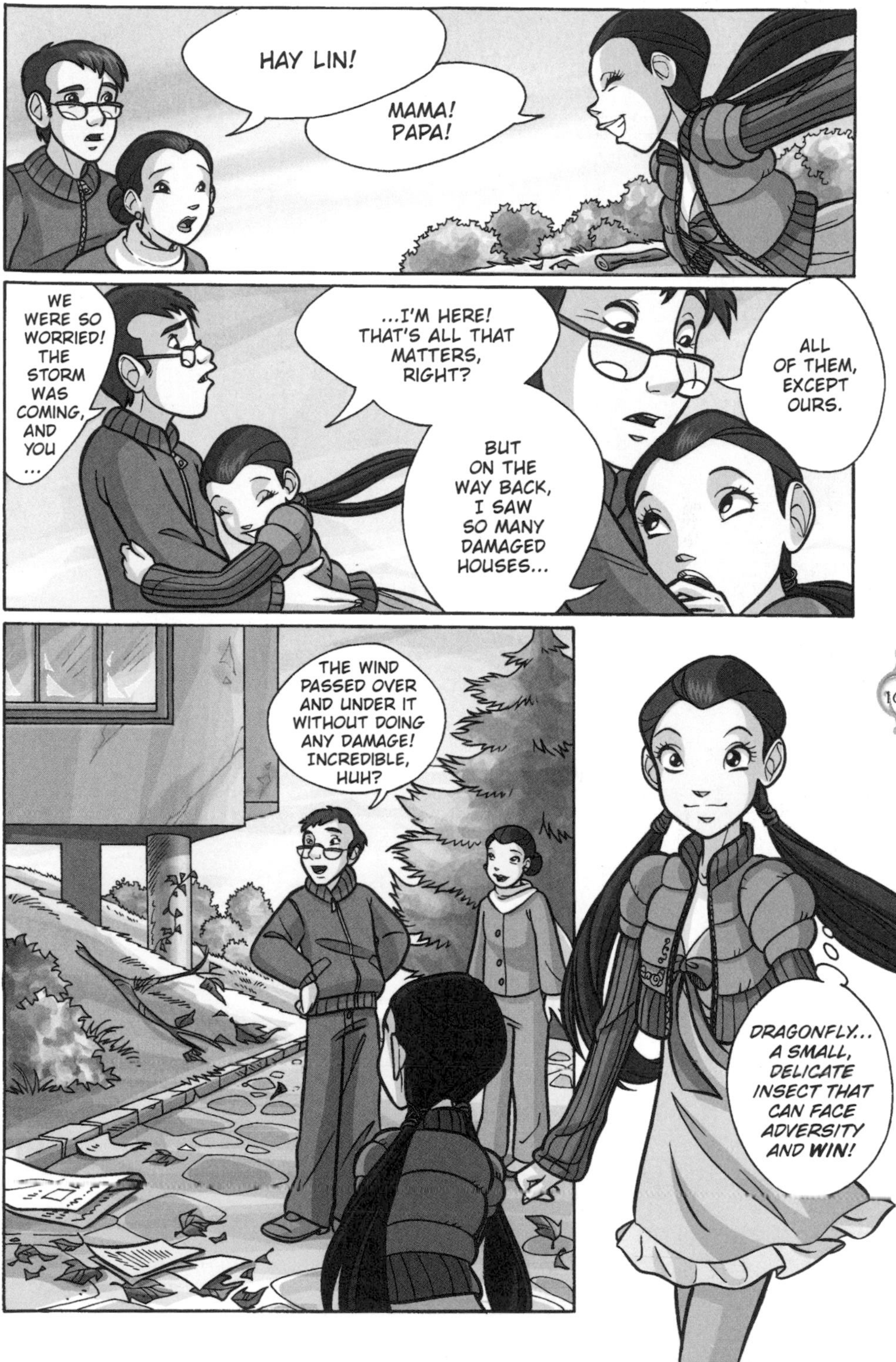
HAY LIN!
MAMA! PAPA!
WE WERE SO WORRIED! THE STORM WAS COMING, AND YOU ...
...I'M HERE! THAT'S ALL THAT MATTERS, RIGHT?
BUT ON THE WAY BACK, I SAW SO MANY DAMAGED HOUSES...
ALL OF THEM, EXCEPT OURS.
THE WIND PASSED OVER AND UNDER IT WITHOUT DOING ANY DAMAGE! INCREDIBLE, HUH?
DRAGONFLY... A SMALL, DELICATE INSECT THAT CAN FACE ADVERSITY AND WIN!

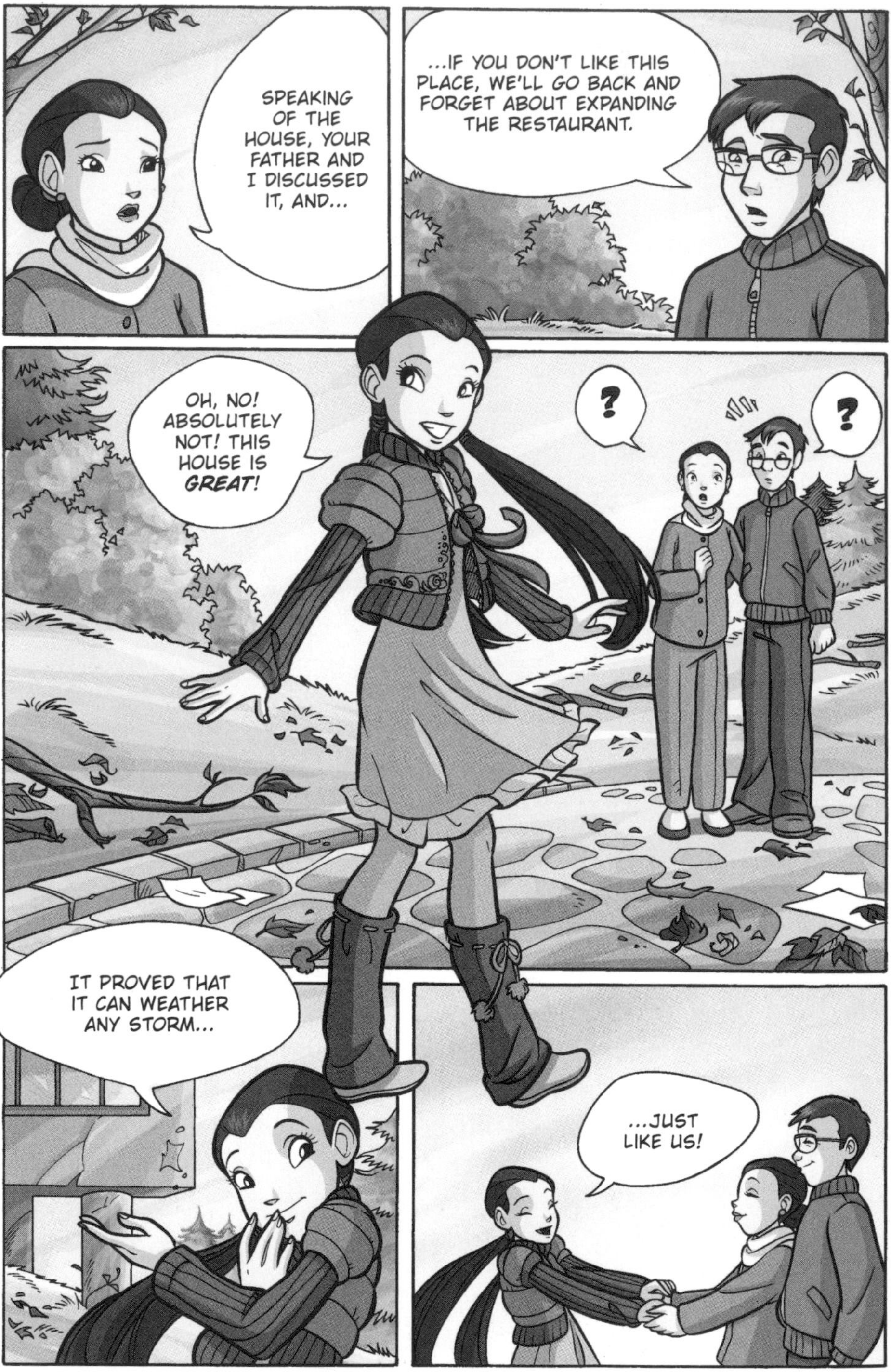
SPEAKING OF THE HOUSE, YOUR FATHER AND I DISCUSSED IT, AND...
...IF YOU DON'T LIKE THIS PLACE, WE'LL GO BACK AND FORGET ABOUT EXPANDING THE RESTAURANT.
OH, NO! ABSOLUTELY NOT! THIS HOUSE IS *GREAT*!
?
?
IT PROVED THAT IT CAN WEATHER ANY STORM...
...JUST LIKE US!

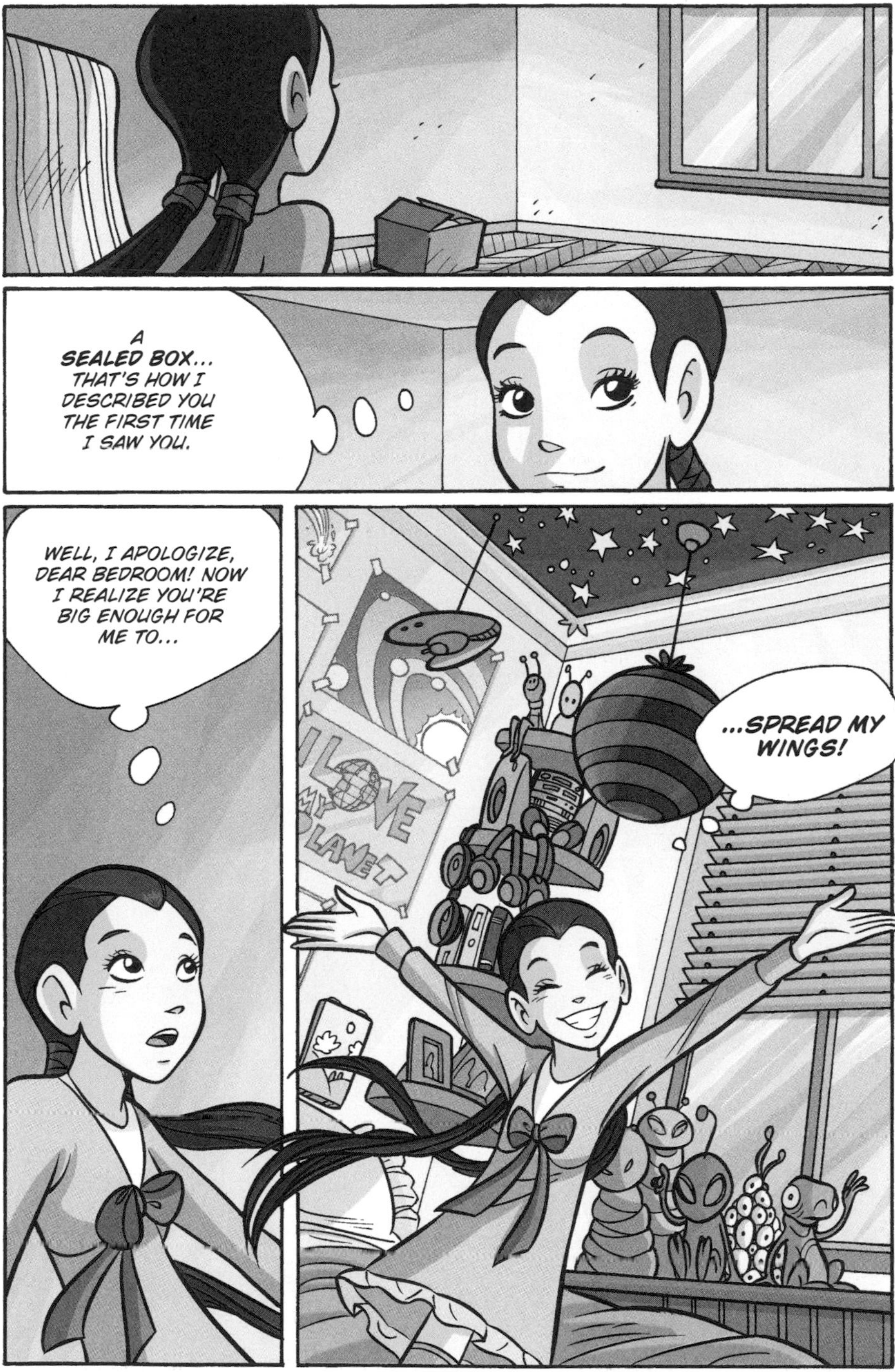
A SEALED BOX... THAT'S HOW I DESCRIBED YOU THE FIRST TIME I SAW YOU.
WELL, I APOLOGIZE, DEAR BEDROOM! NOW I REALIZE YOU'RE BIG ENOUGH FOR ME TO...
...SPREAD MY WINGS!
I LOVE MY PLANET

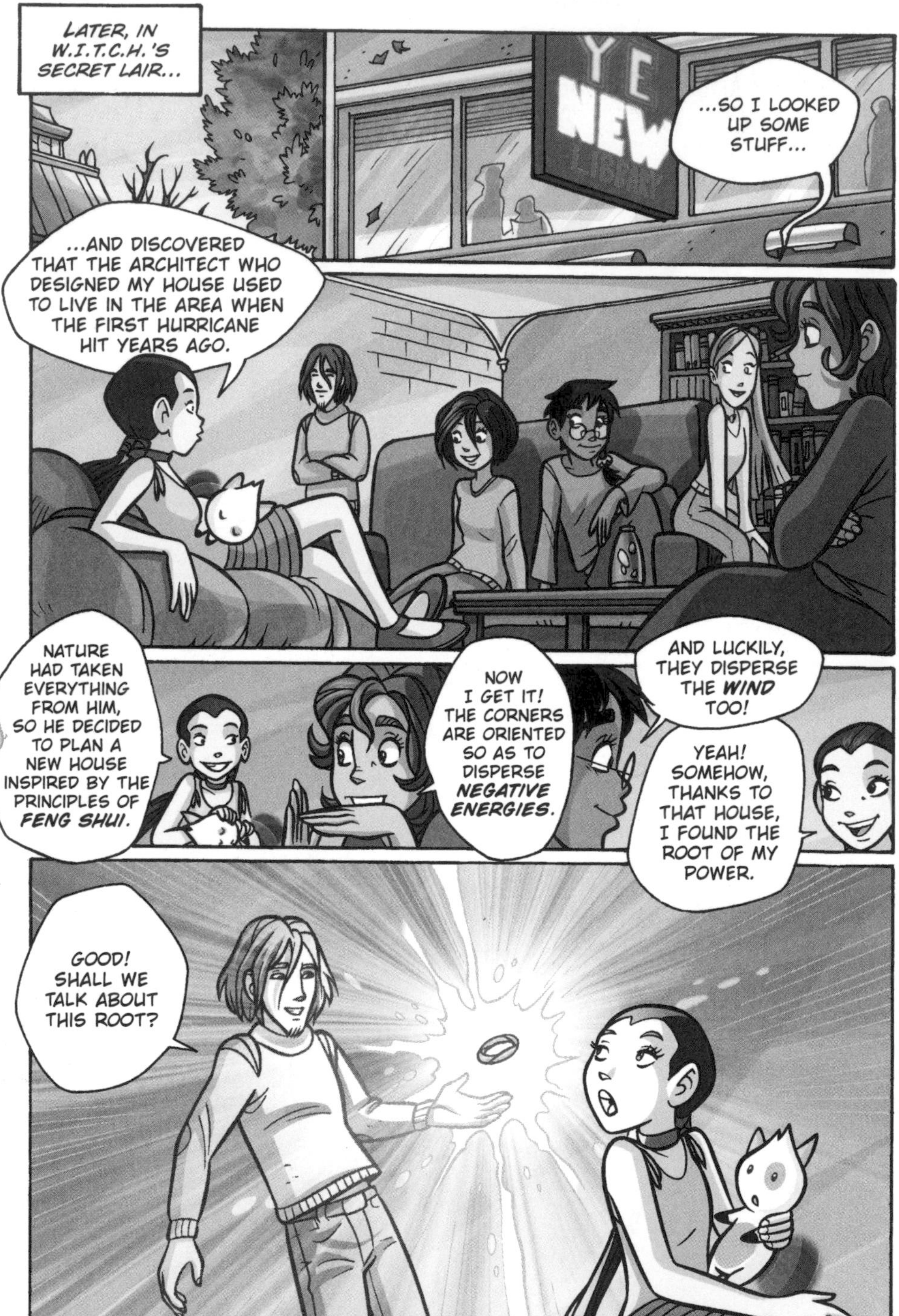
LATER, IN W.I.T.C.H.'S SECRET LAIR...
...SO I LOOKED UP SOME STUFF...
...AND DISCOVERED THAT THE ARCHITECT WHO DESIGNED MY HOUSE USED TO LIVE IN THE AREA WHEN THE FIRST HURRICANE HIT YEARS AGO.
NATURE HAD TAKEN EVERYTHING FROM HIM, SO HE DECIDED TO PLAN A NEW HOUSE INSPIRED BY THE PRINCIPLES OF FENG SHUI.
NOW I GET IT! THE CORNERS ARE ORIENTED SO AS TO DISPERSE NEGATIVE ENERGIES.
AND LUCKILY, THEY DISPERSE THE WIND TOO!
YEAH! SOMEHOW, THANKS TO THAT HOUSE, I FOUND THE ROOT OF MY POWER.
GOOD! SHALL WE TALK ABOUT THIS ROOT?

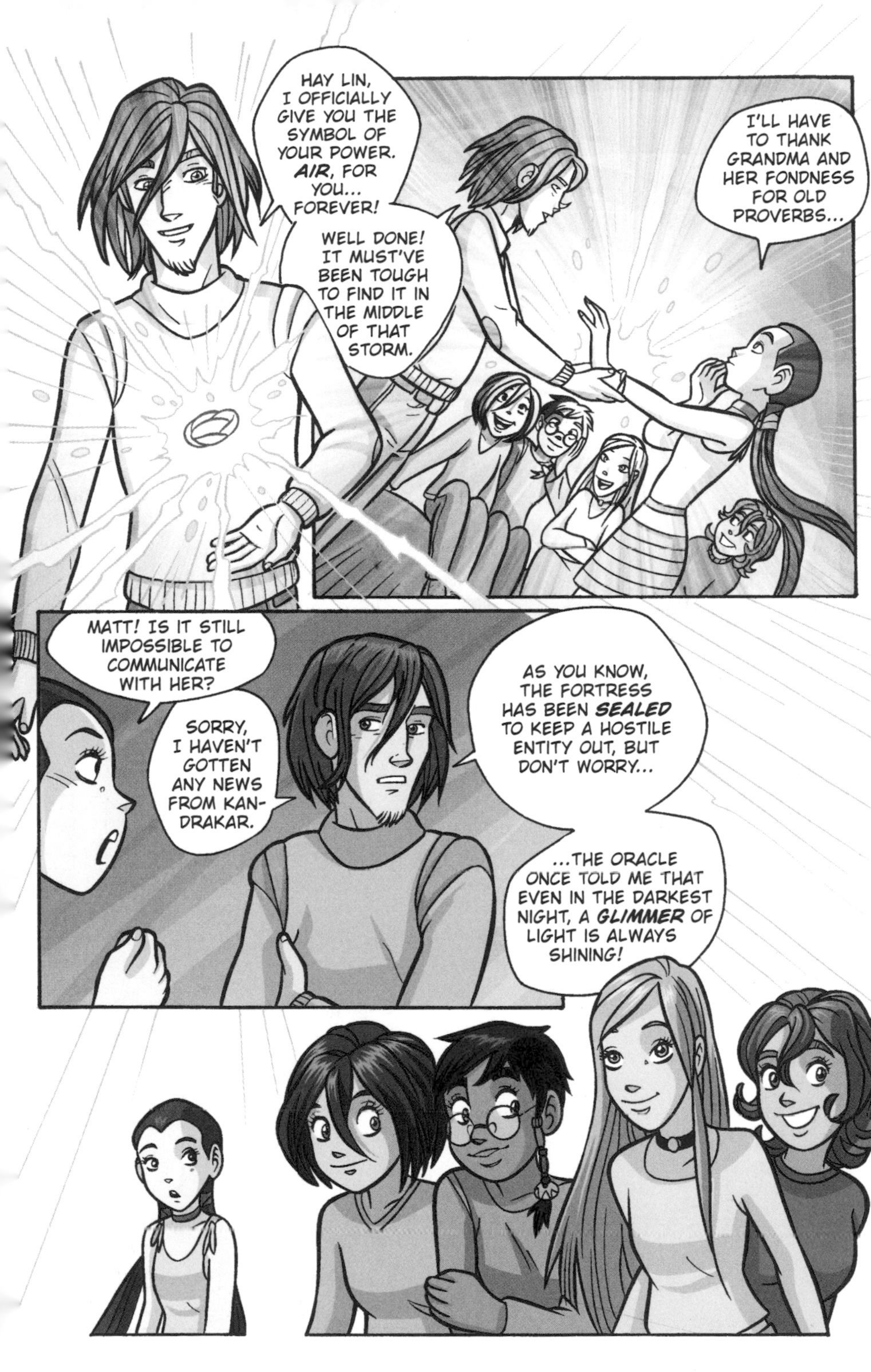
HAY LIN, I OFFICIALLY GIVE YOU THE SYMBOL OF YOUR POWER. AIR, FOR YOU... FOREVER!
WELL DONE! IT MUST'VE BEEN TOUGH TO FIND IT IN THE MIDDLE OF THAT STORM.
I'LL HAVE TO THANK GRANDMA AND HER FONDNESS FOR OLD PROVERBS...
MATT! IS IT STILL IMPOSSIBLE TO COMMUNICATE WITH HER?
SORRY, I HAVEN'T GOTTEN ANY NEWS FROM KAN-DRAKAR.
AS YOU KNOW, THE FORTRESS HAS BEEN SEALED TO KEEP A HOSTILE ENTITY OUT, BUT DON'T WORRY...
...THE ORACLE ONCE TOLD ME THAT EVEN IN THE DARKEST NIGHT, A GLIMMER OF LIGHT IS ALWAYS SHINING!

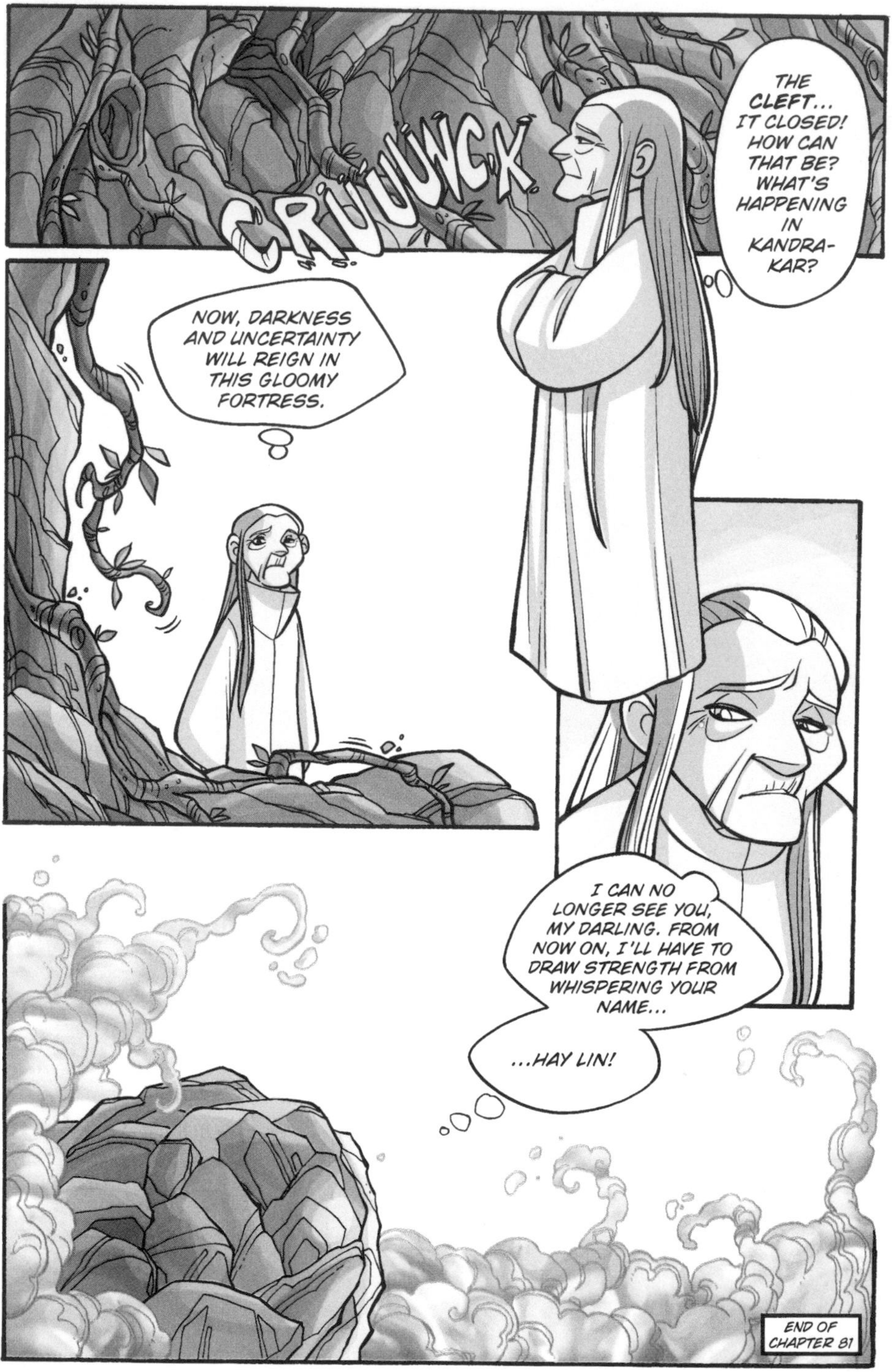
CRÜUUWCK
THE CLEFT... IT CLOSED! HOW CAN THAT BE? WHAT'S HAPPENING IN KANDRA-KAR?
NOW, DARKNESS AND UNCERTAINTY WILL REIGN IN THIS GLOOMY FORTRESS.
I CAN NO LONGER SEE YOU, MY DARLING. FROM NOW ON, I'LL HAVE TO DRAW STRENGTH FROM WHISPERING YOUR NAME...
...HAY LIN!
END OF CHAPTER 81

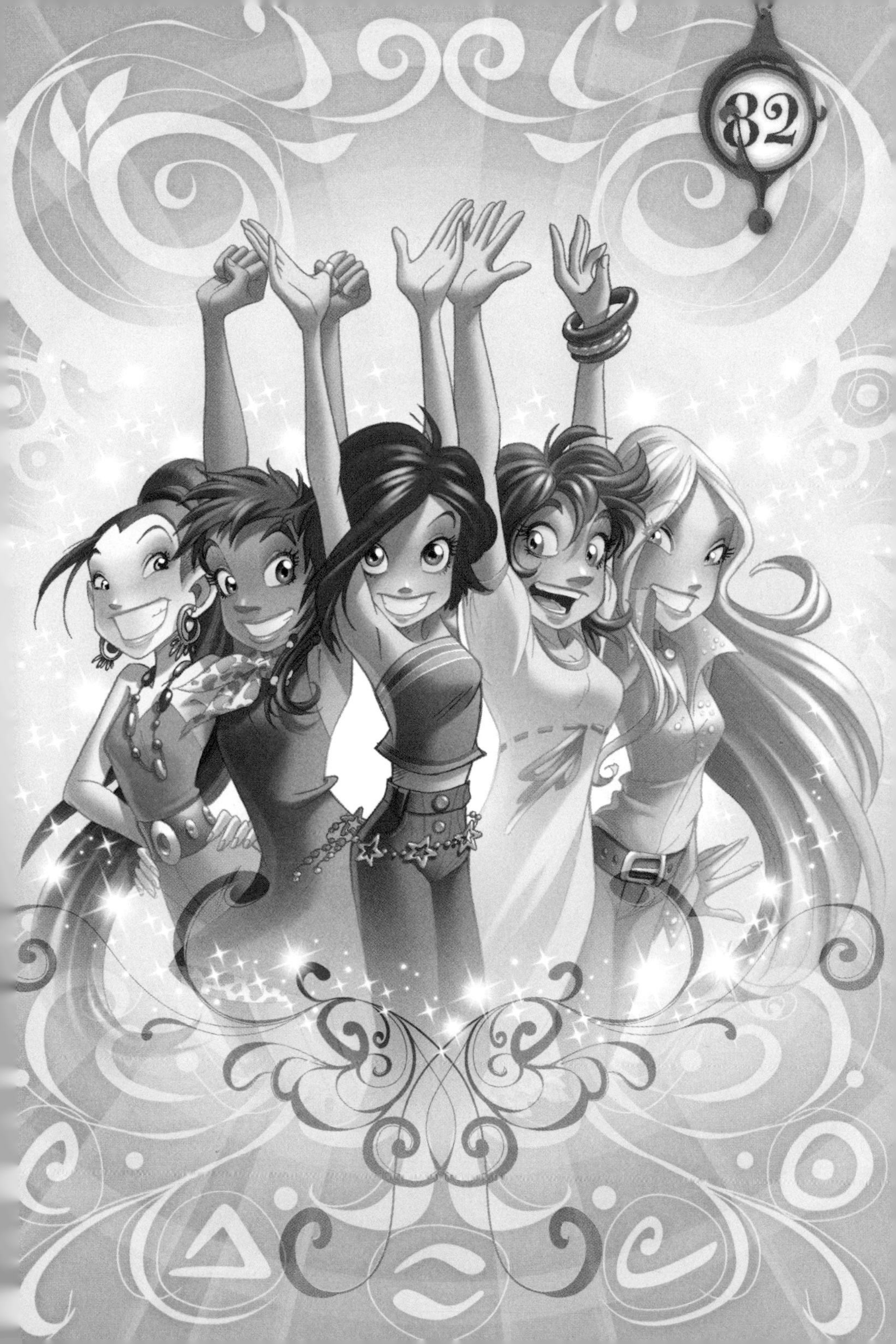
32

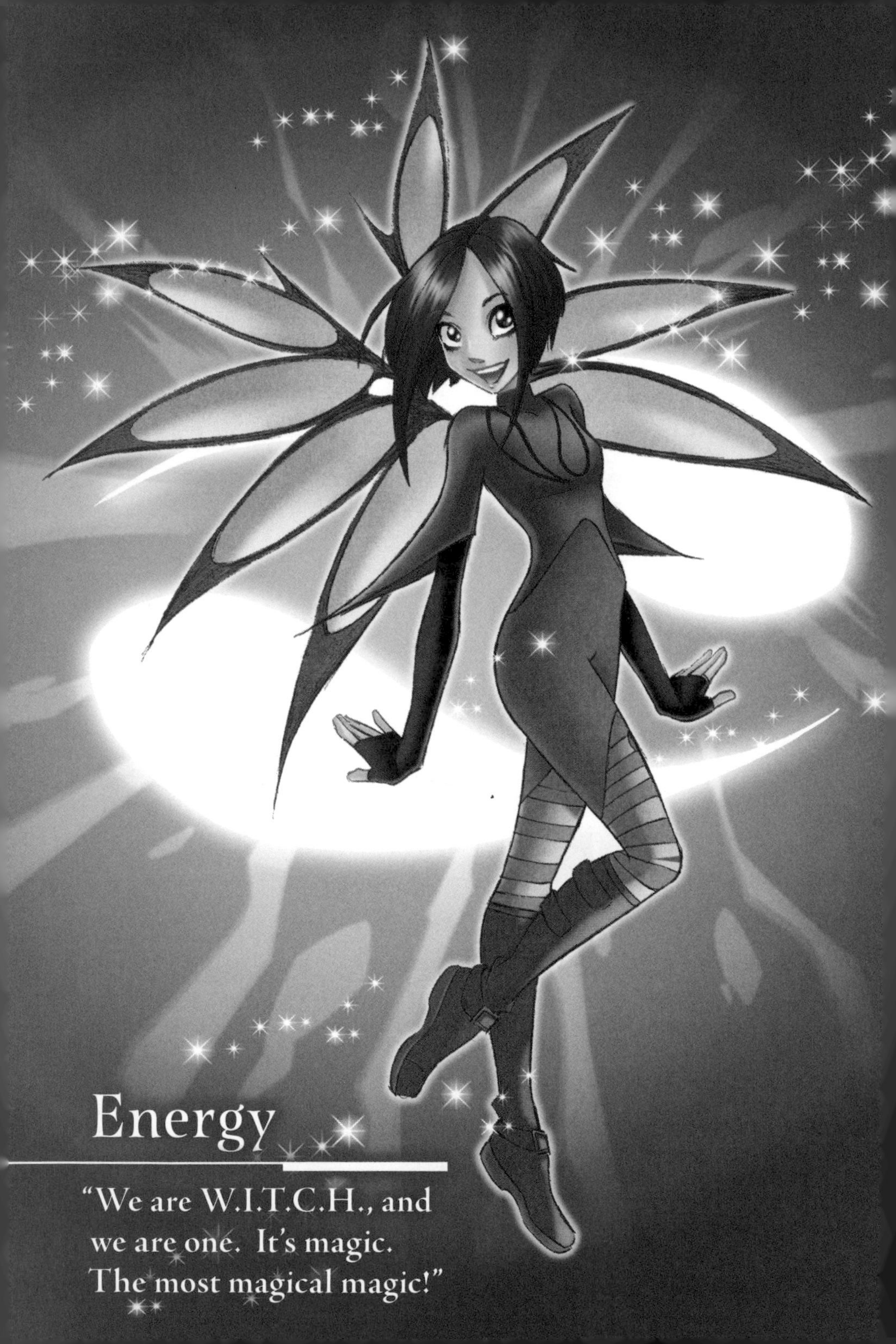
Energy
"We are W.I.T.C.H., and we are one. It's magic. The most magical magic!"

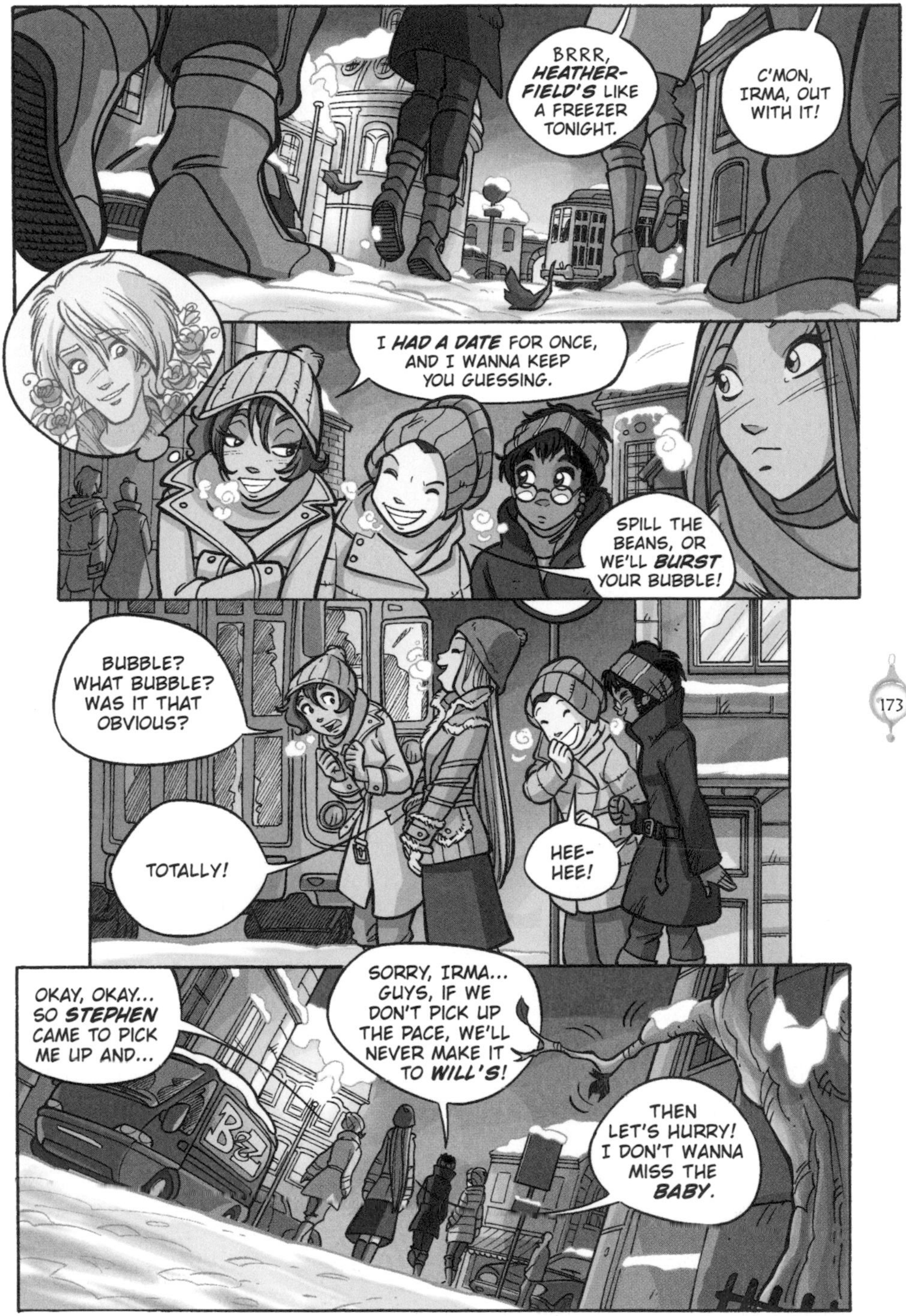
BRRR, HEATHER-FIELD'S LIKE A FREEZER TONIGHT.
C'MON, IRMA, OUT WITH IT!
I HAD A DATE FOR ONCE, AND I WANNA KEEP YOU GUESSING.
SPILL THE BEANS, OR WE'LL BURST YOUR BUBBLE!
BUBBLE? WHAT BUBBLE? WAS IT THAT OBVIOUS?
TOTALLY!
HEE-HEE!
OKAY, OKAY... SO STEPHEN CAME TO PICK ME UP AND...
SORRY, IRMA... GUYS, IF WE DON'T PICK UP THE PACE, WE'LL NEVER MAKE IT TO WILL'S!
THEN LET'S HURRY! I DON'T WANNA MISS THE BABY.

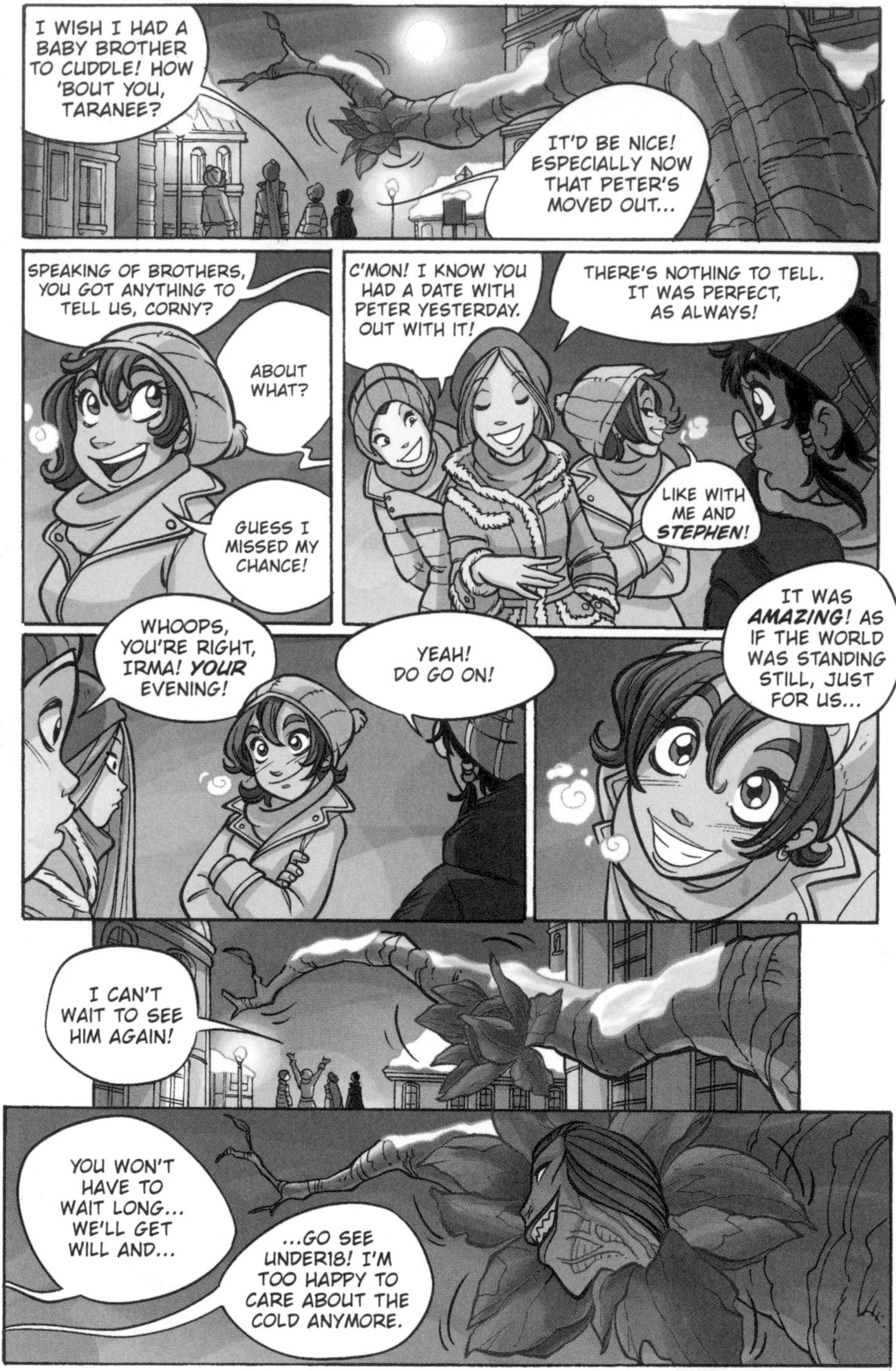

I WISH I HAD A BABY BROTHER TO CUDDLE! HOW 'BOUT YOU, TARANEE?
IT'D BE NICE! ESPECIALLY NOW THAT PETER'S MOVED OUT...
SPEAKING OF BROTHERS, YOU GOT ANYTHING TO TELL US, CORNY?
ABOUT WHAT?
GUESS I MISSED MY CHANCE!
C'MON! I KNOW YOU HAD A DATE WITH PETER YESTERDAY. OUT WITH IT!
THERE'S NOTHING TO TELL. IT WAS PERFECT, AS ALWAYS!
LIKE WITH ME AND *STEPHEN*!
WHOOPS, YOU'RE RIGHT, IRMA! ***YOUR*** EVENING!
YEAH! DO GO ON!
IT WAS ***AMAZING***! AS IF THE WORLD WAS STANDING STILL, JUST FOR US...
I CAN'T WAIT TO SEE HIM AGAIN!
YOU WON'T HAVE TO WAIT LONG... WE'LL GET WILL AND...
...GO SEE UNDER18! I'M TOO HAPPY TO CARE ABOUT THE COLD ANYMORE.

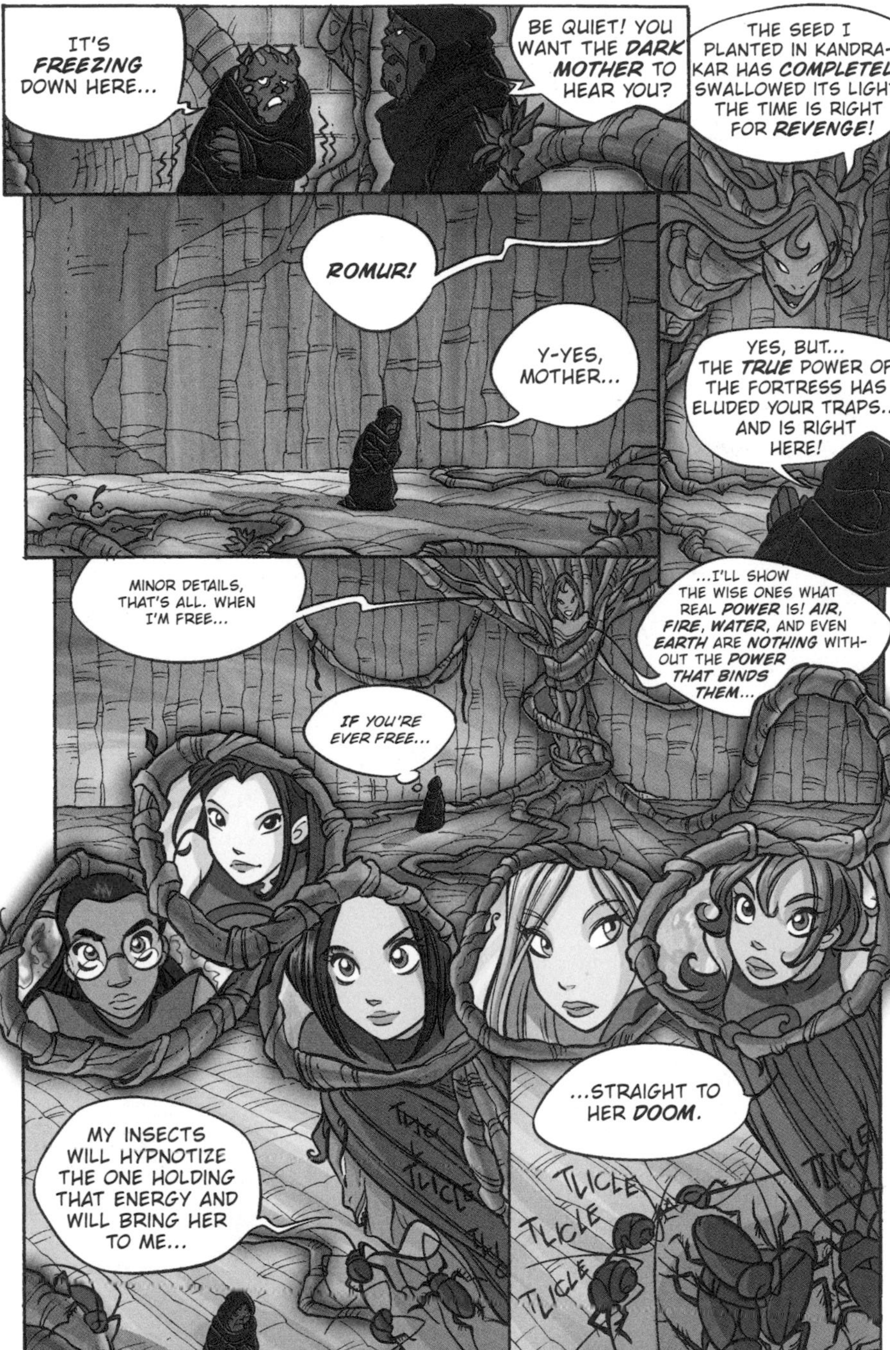
IT'S FREEZING DOWN HERE...
BE QUIET! YOU WANT THE DARK MOTHER TO HEAR YOU?
THE SEED I PLANTED IN KANDRAKAR HAS COMPLETELY SWALLOWED ITS LIGHT. THE TIME IS RIGHT FOR REVENGE!
ROMUR!
Y-YES, MOTHER...
YES, BUT... THE TRUE POWER OF THE FORTRESS HAS ELUDED YOUR TRAPS... AND IS RIGHT HERE!
MINOR DETAILS, THAT'S ALL. WHEN I'M FREE...
...I'LL SHOW THE WISE ONES WHAT REAL POWER IS! AIR, FIRE, WATER, AND EVEN EARTH ARE NOTHING WITHOUT THE POWER THAT BINDS THEM...
IF YOU'RE EVER FREE...
MY INSECTS WILL HYPNOTIZE THE ONE HOLDING THAT ENERGY AND WILL BRING HER TO ME...
...STRAIGHT TO HER DOOM.
TLICLE
TLICLE
TLICLE

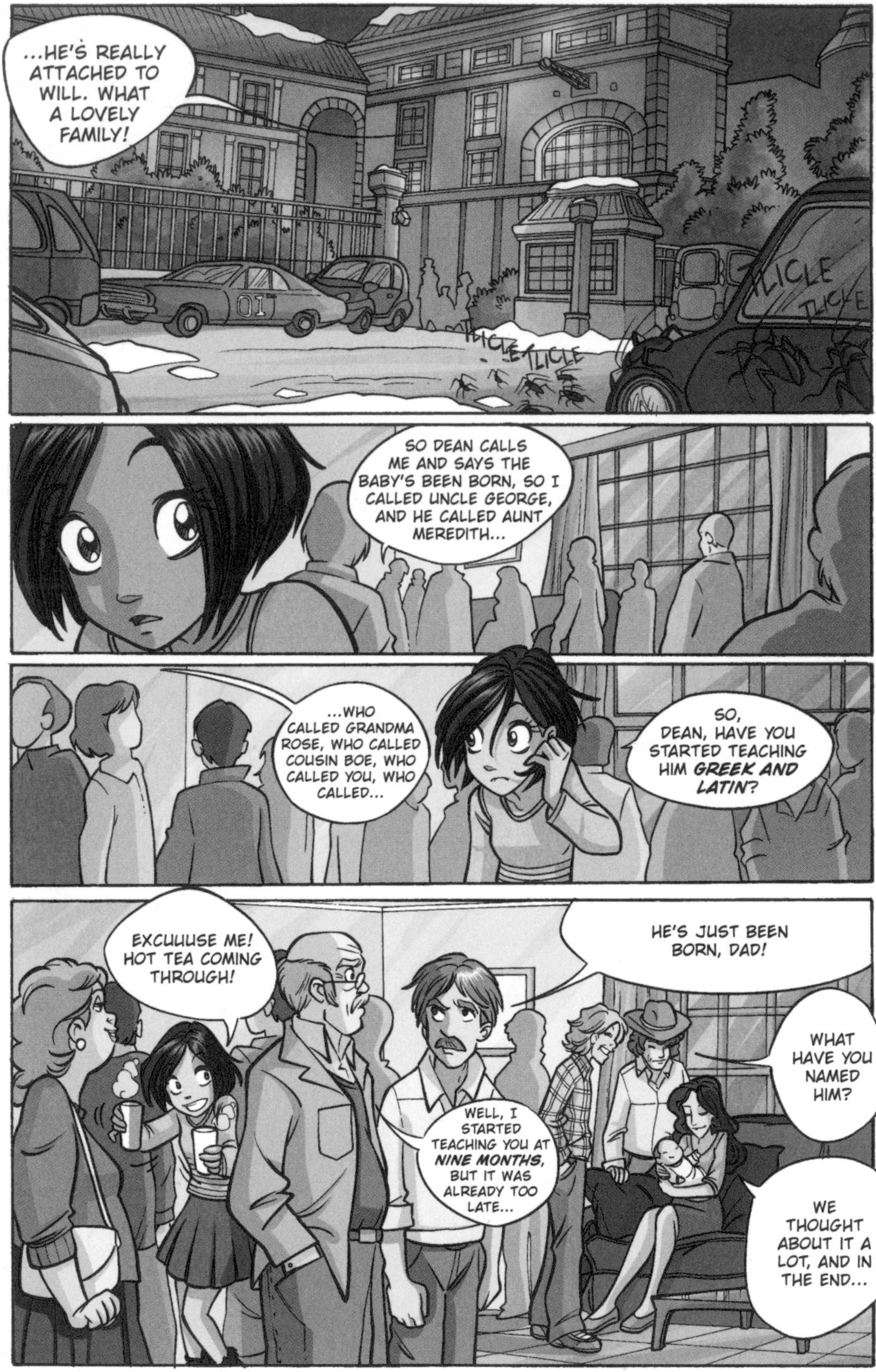
...HE'S REALLY ATTACHED TO WILL. WHAT A LOVELY FAMILY!
TLICLE TLICLE
TLICLE TLICLE
SO DEAN CALLS ME AND SAYS THE BABY'S BEEN BORN, SO I CALLED UNCLE GEORGE, AND HE CALLED AUNT MEREDITH...
...WHO CALLED GRANDMA ROSE, WHO CALLED COUSIN BOE, WHO CALLED YOU, WHO CALLED...
SO, DEAN, HAVE YOU STARTED TEACHING HIM **GREEK AND LATIN**?
EXCUUUSE ME! HOT TEA COMING THROUGH!
HE'S JUST BEEN BORN, DAD!
WELL, I STARTED TEACHING YOU AT **NINE MONTHS**, BUT IT WAS ALREADY TOO LATE...
WHAT HAVE YOU NAMED HIM?
WE THOUGHT ABOUT IT A LOT, AND IN THE END...

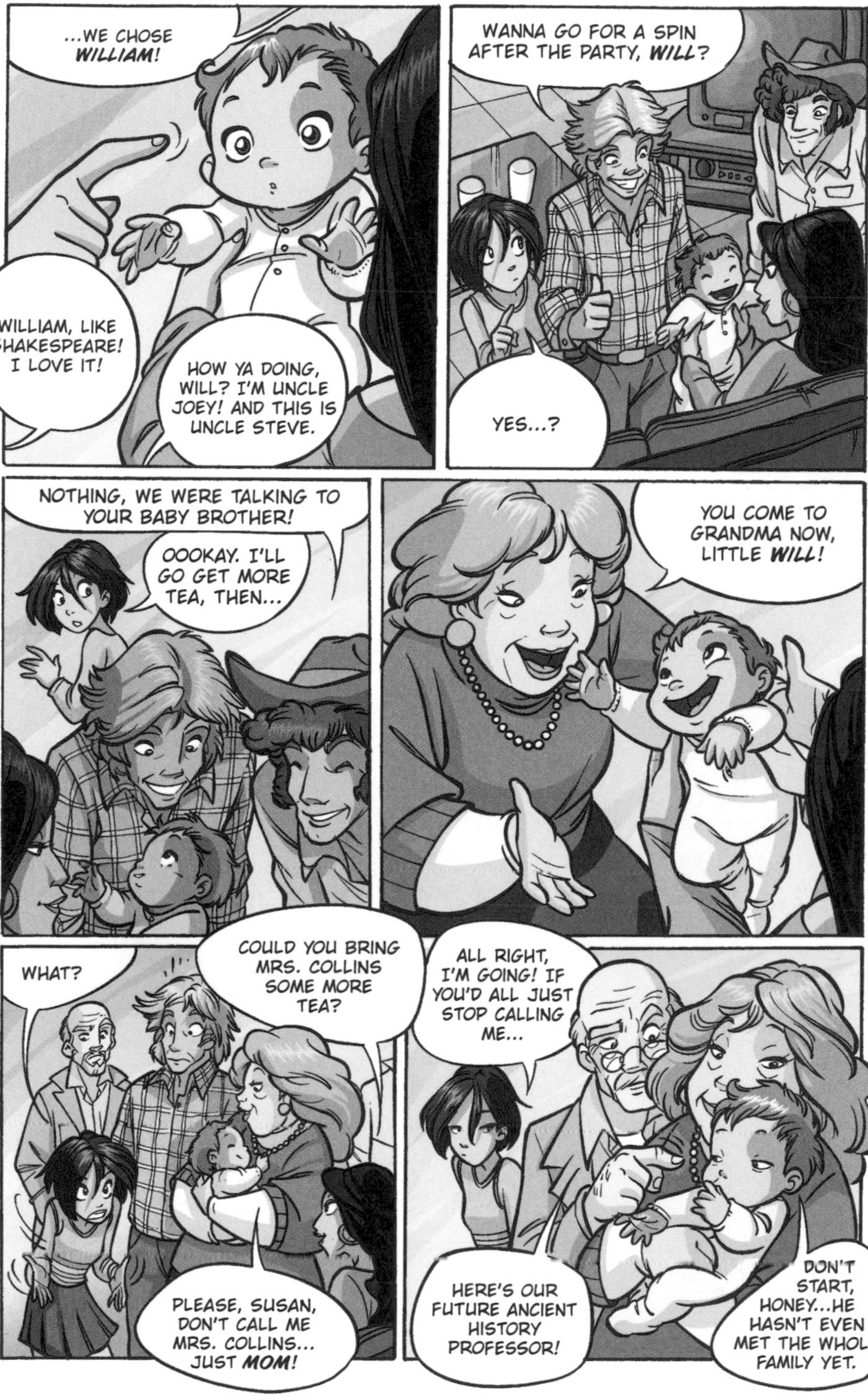
...WE CHOSE WILLIAM!
WILLIAM, LIKE SHAKESPEARE! I LOVE IT!
HOW YA DOING, WILL? I'M UNCLE JOEY! AND THIS IS UNCLE STEVE.
WANNA GO FOR A SPIN AFTER THE PARTY, WILL?
YES...?
NOTHING, WE WERE TALKING TO YOUR BABY BROTHER!
OOOKAY. I'LL GO GET MORE TEA, THEN...
YOU COME TO GRANDMA NOW, LITTLE WILL!
WHAT?
COULD YOU BRING MRS. COLLINS SOME MORE TEA?
PLEASE, SUSAN, DON'T CALL ME MRS. COLLINS... JUST MOM!
ALL RIGHT, I'M GOING! IF YOU'D ALL JUST STOP CALLING ME...
HERE'S OUR FUTURE ANCIENT HISTORY PROFESSOR!
DON'T START, HONEY...HE HASN'T EVEN MET THE WHOLE FAMILY YET.

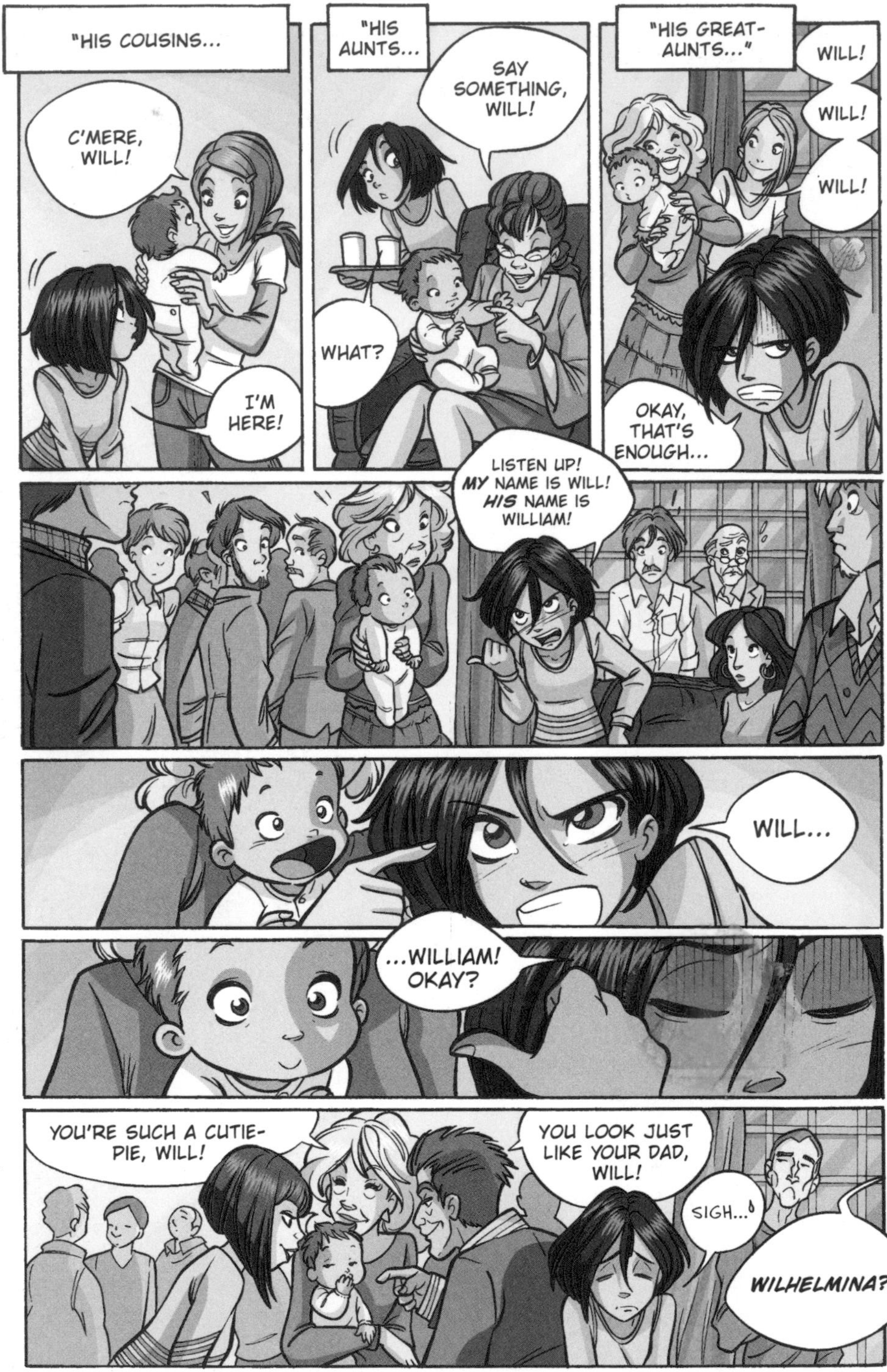
"HIS COUSINS...
C'MERE, WILL!
I'M HERE!
"HIS AUNTS...
SAY SOMETHING, WILL!
WHAT?
"HIS GREAT-AUNTS..."
WILL!
WILL!
WILL!
OKAY, THAT'S ENOUGH...
LISTEN UP! MY NAME IS WILL! HIS NAME IS WILLIAM!
WILL...
...WILLIAM! OKAY?
YOU'RE SUCH A CUTIE-PIE, WILL!
YOU LOOK JUST LIKE YOUR DAD, WILL!
SIGH...
WILHELMINA?

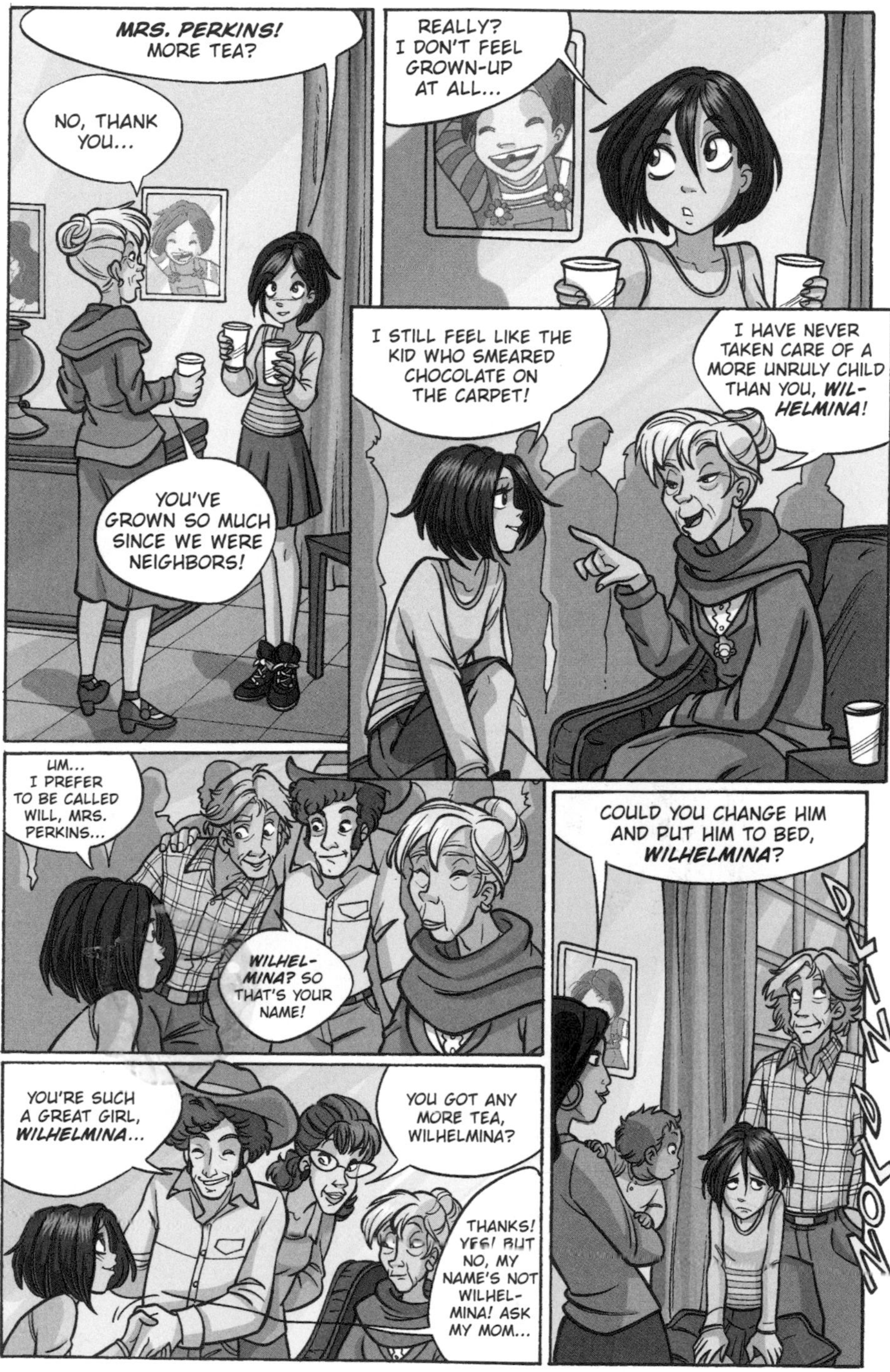
MRS. PERKINS! MORE TEA?
NO, THANK YOU...
YOU'VE GROWN SO MUCH SINCE WE WERE NEIGHBORS!
REALLY? I DON'T FEEL GROWN-UP AT ALL...
I STILL FEEL LIKE THE KID WHO SMEARED CHOCOLATE ON THE CARPET!
I HAVE NEVER TAKEN CARE OF A MORE UNRULY CHILD THAN YOU, WILHELMINA!
UM... I PREFER TO BE CALLED WILL, MRS. PERKINS...
WILHELMINA? SO THAT'S YOUR NAME!
COULD YOU CHANGE HIM AND PUT HIM TO BED, WILHELMINA?
YOU'RE SUCH A GREAT GIRL, WILHELMINA...
YOU GOT ANY MORE TEA, WILHELMINA?
THANKS! YES! BUT NO, MY NAME'S NOT WILHELMINA! ASK MY MOM...

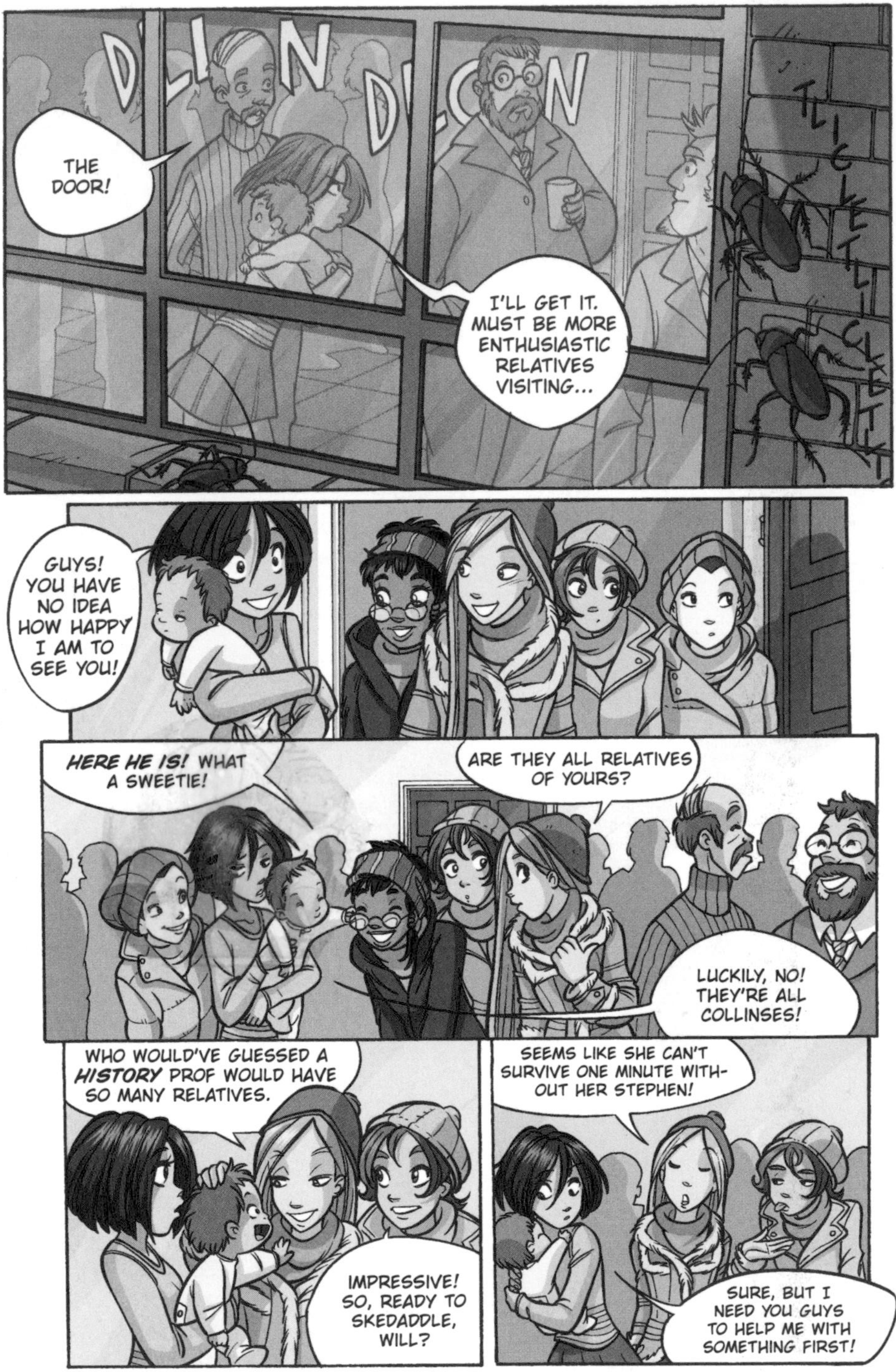
THE DOOR!
I'LL GET IT. MUST BE MORE ENTHUSIASTIC RELATIVES VISITING...
GUYS! YOU HAVE NO IDEA HOW HAPPY I AM TO SEE YOU!
HERE HE IS! WHAT A SWEETIE!
ARE THEY ALL RELATIVES OF YOURS?
LUCKILY, NO! THEY'RE ALL COLLINSES!
WHO WOULD'VE GUESSED A HISTORY PROF WOULD HAVE SO MANY RELATIVES.
IMPRESSIVE! SO, READY TO SKEDADDLE, WILL?
SEEMS LIKE SHE CAN'T SURVIVE ONE MINUTE WITH-OUT HER STEPHEN!
SURE, BUT I NEED YOU GUYS TO HELP ME WITH SOMETHING FIRST!

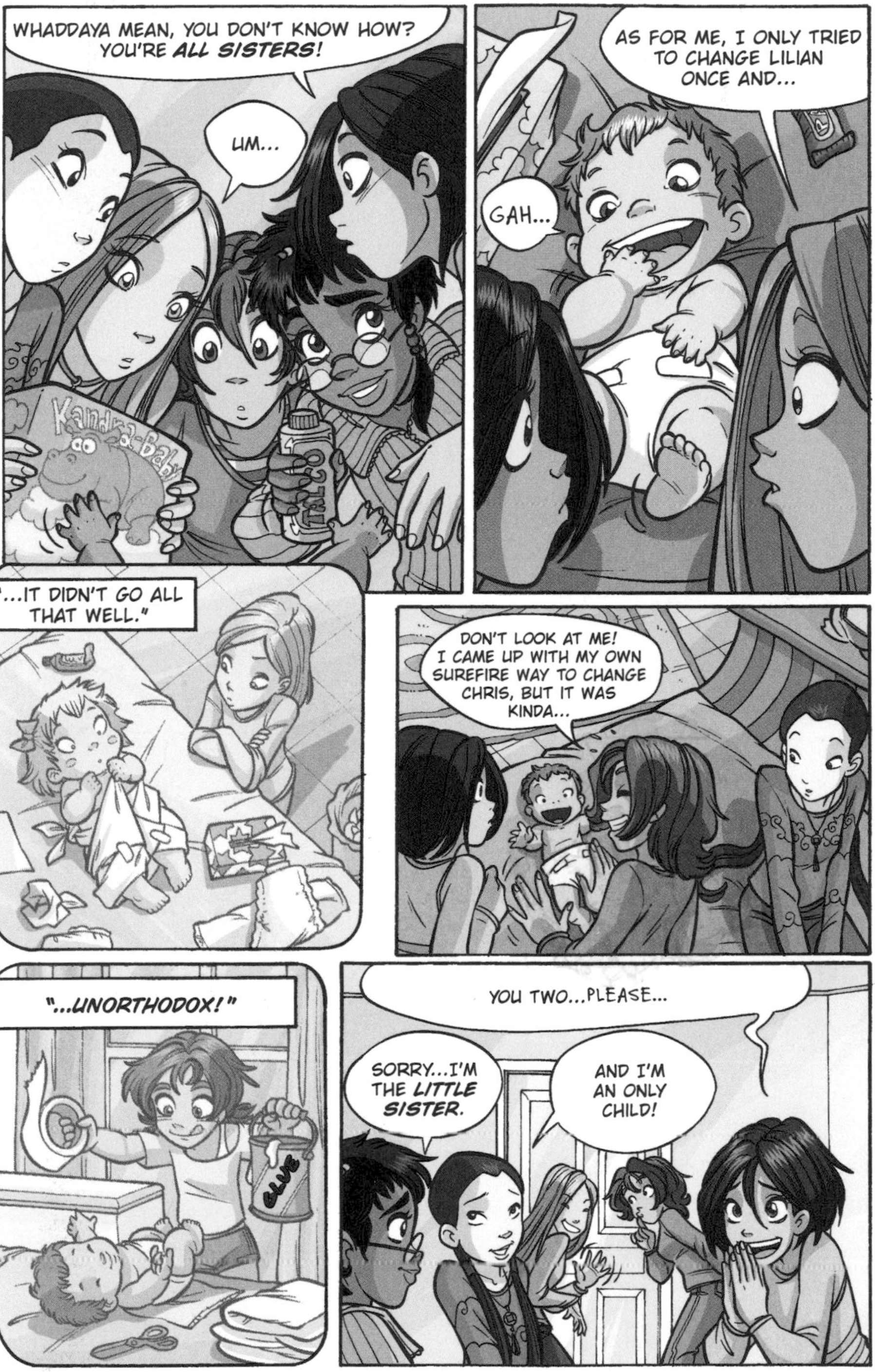
WHADDAYA MEAN, YOU DON'T KNOW HOW? YOU'RE **ALL SISTERS**!
UM...
Kandra-Baby
TALCO
AS FOR ME, I ONLY TRIED TO CHANGE LILIAN ONCE AND...
GAH...
"...IT DIDN'T GO ALL THAT WELL."
DON'T LOOK AT ME! I CAME UP WITH MY OWN SUREFIRE WAY TO CHANGE CHRIS, BUT IT WAS KINDA...
"...**UNORTHODOX!**"
GLUE
YOU TWO...PLEASE...
SORRY...I'M THE **LITTLE SISTER**.
AND I'M AN ONLY CHILD!

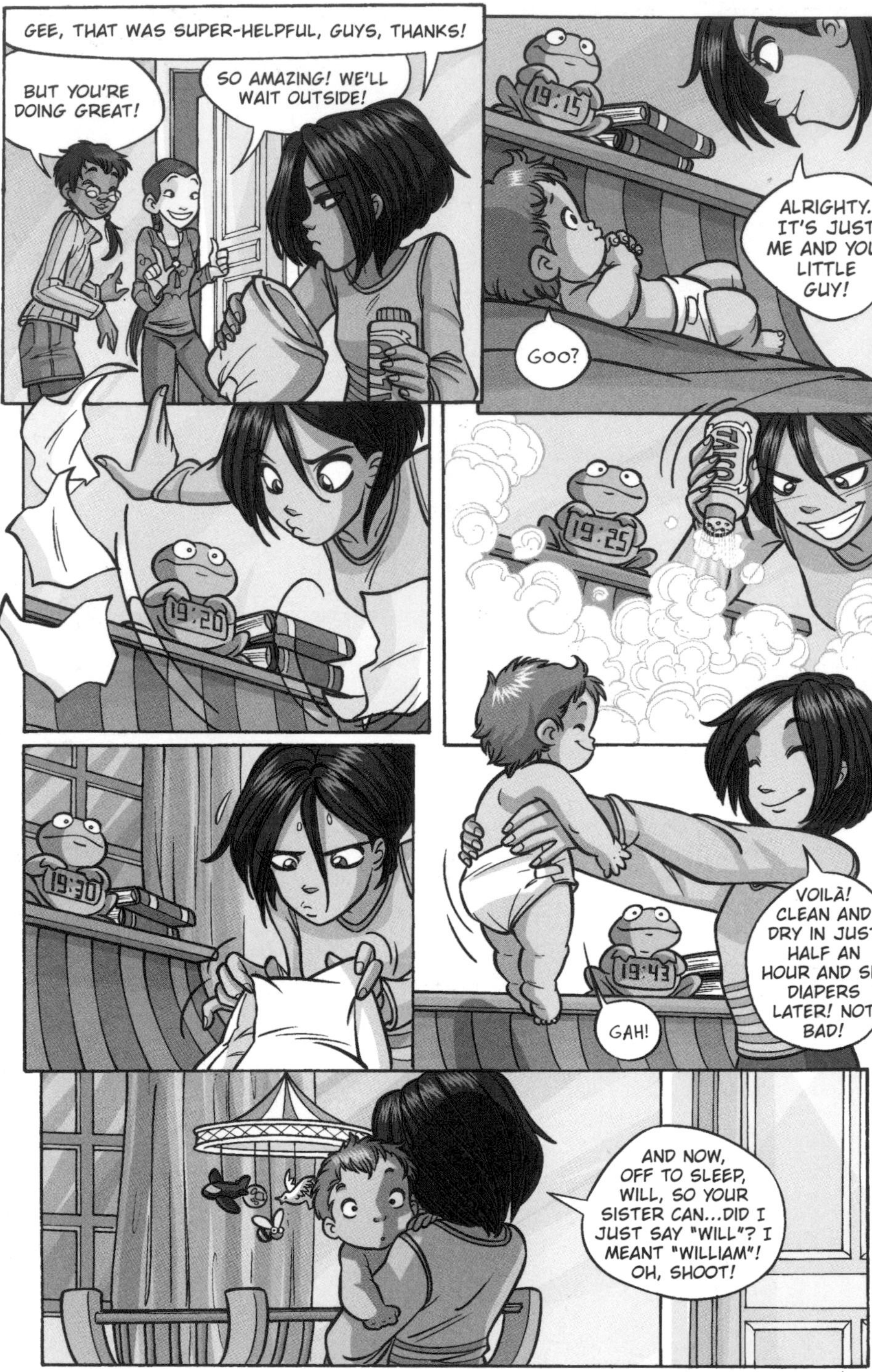
GEE, THAT WAS SUPER-HELPFUL, GUYS, THANKS!
BUT YOU'RE DOING GREAT!
SO AMAZING! WE'LL WAIT OUTSIDE!
19:15
ALRIGHTY. IT'S JUST ME AND YOU, LITTLE GUY!
GOO?
19:20
TALCO
19:25
19:30
19:43
VOILÀ! CLEAN AND DRY IN JUST HALF AN HOUR AND SIX DIAPERS LATER! NOT BAD!
GAH!
AND NOW, OFF TO SLEEP, WILL, SO YOUR SISTER CAN...DID I JUST SAY "WILL"? I MEANT "WILLIAM"! OH, SHOOT!

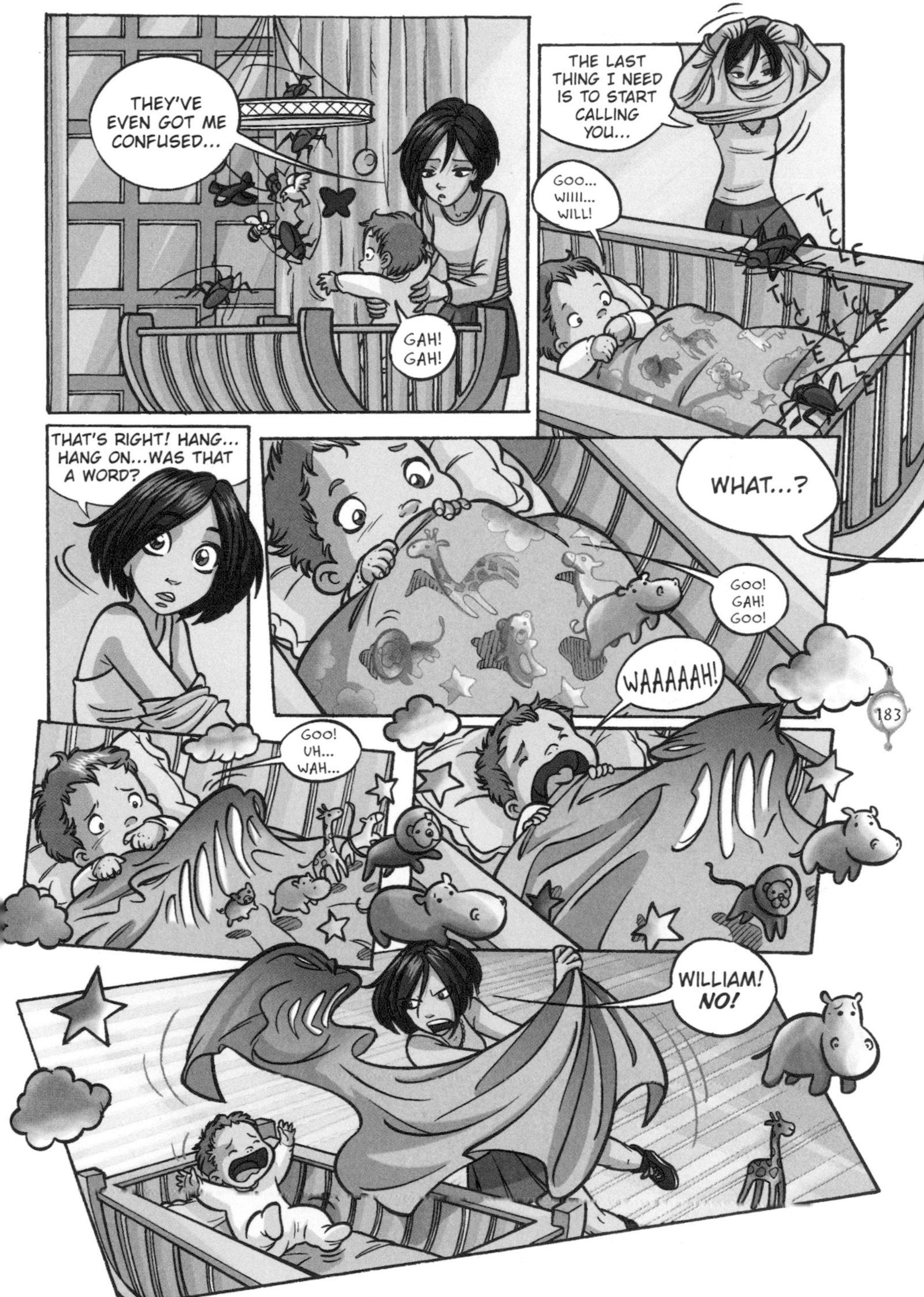
THEY'VE EVEN GOT ME CONFUSED...
GAH! GAH!
THE LAST THING I NEED IS TO START CALLING YOU...
GOO... WIIII... WILL!
THAT'S RIGHT! HANG... HANG ON...WAS THAT A WORD?
WHAT...?
GOO! GAH! GOO!
GOO! UH... WAH...
WAAAAAH!
WILLIAM! NO!

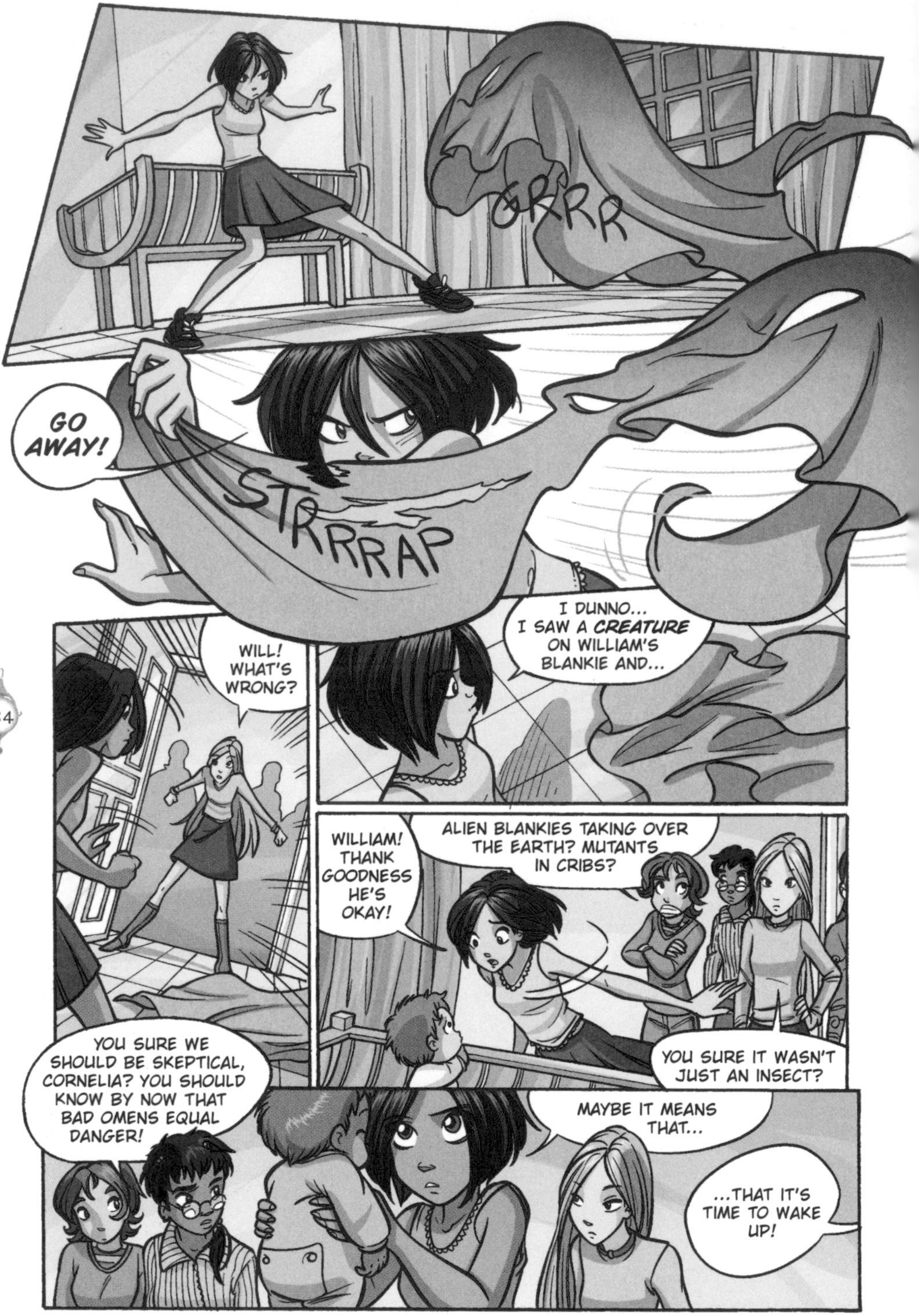
GRRR
GO AWAY!
STRRRRAP
WILL! WHAT'S WRONG?
I DUNNO... I SAW A CREATURE ON WILLIAM'S BLANKIE AND...
WILLIAM! THANK GOODNESS HE'S OKAY!
ALIEN BLANKIES TAKING OVER THE EARTH? MUTANTS IN CRIBS?
YOU SURE IT WASN'T JUST AN INSECT?
YOU SURE WE SHOULD BE SKEPTICAL, CORNELIA? YOU SHOULD KNOW BY NOW THAT BAD OMENS EQUAL DANGER!
MAYBE IT MEANS THAT...
...THAT IT'S TIME TO WAKE UP!

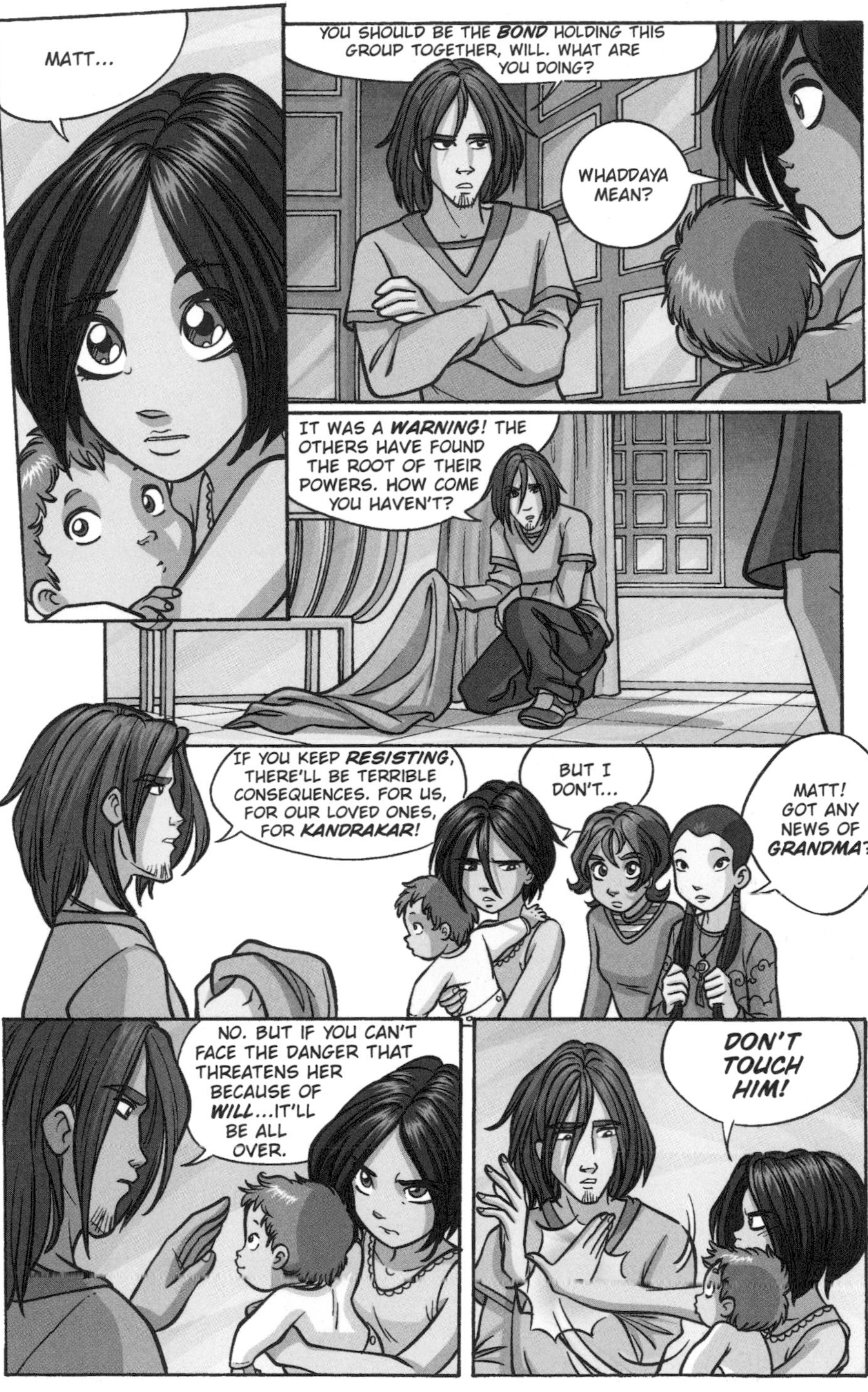
MATT...
YOU SHOULD BE THE BOND HOLDING THIS GROUP TOGETHER, WILL. WHAT ARE YOU DOING?
WHADDAYA MEAN?
IT WAS A WARNING! THE OTHERS HAVE FOUND THE ROOT OF THEIR POWERS. HOW COME YOU HAVEN'T?
IF YOU KEEP RESISTING, THERE'LL BE TERRIBLE CONSEQUENCES. FOR US, FOR OUR LOVED ONES, FOR KANDRAKAR!
BUT I DON'T...
MATT! GOT ANY NEWS OF GRANDMA?
NO. BUT IF YOU CAN'T FACE THE DANGER THAT THREATENS HER BECAUSE OF WILL...IT'LL BE ALL OVER.
DON'T TOUCH HIM!

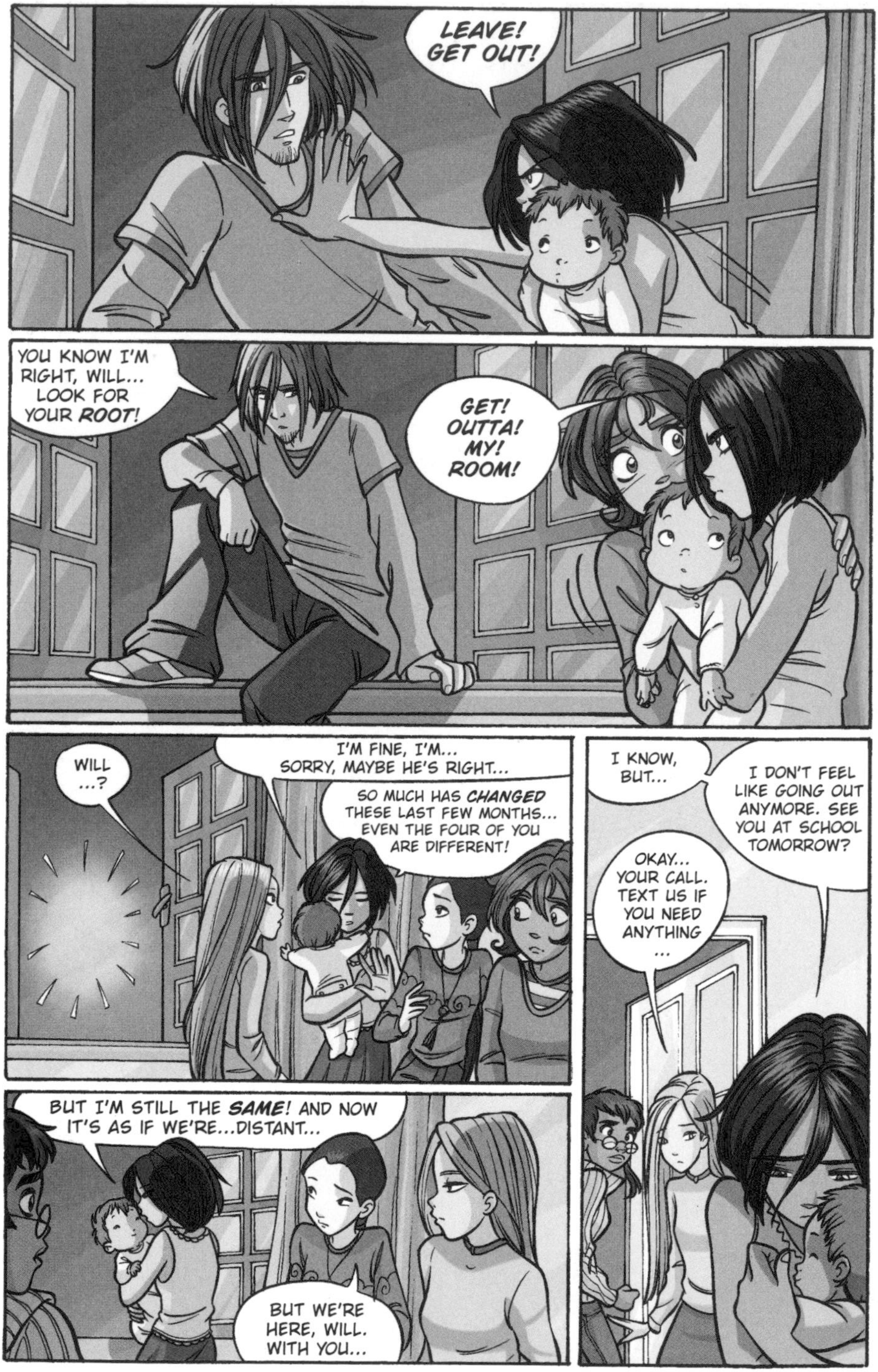

LEAVE! GET OUT!
YOU KNOW I'M RIGHT, WILL... LOOK FOR YOUR ROOT!
GET! OUTTA! MY! ROOM!
WILL ...?
I'M FINE, I'M... SORRY, MAYBE HE'S RIGHT...
SO MUCH HAS CHANGED THESE LAST FEW MONTHS... EVEN THE FOUR OF YOU ARE DIFFERENT!
BUT I'M STILL THE SAME! AND NOW IT'S AS IF WE'RE...DISTANT...
BUT WE'RE HERE, WILL. WITH YOU...
I KNOW, BUT...
I DON'T FEEL LIKE GOING OUT ANYMORE. SEE YOU AT SCHOOL TOMORROW?
OKAY... YOUR CALL. TEXT US IF YOU NEED ANYTHING ...

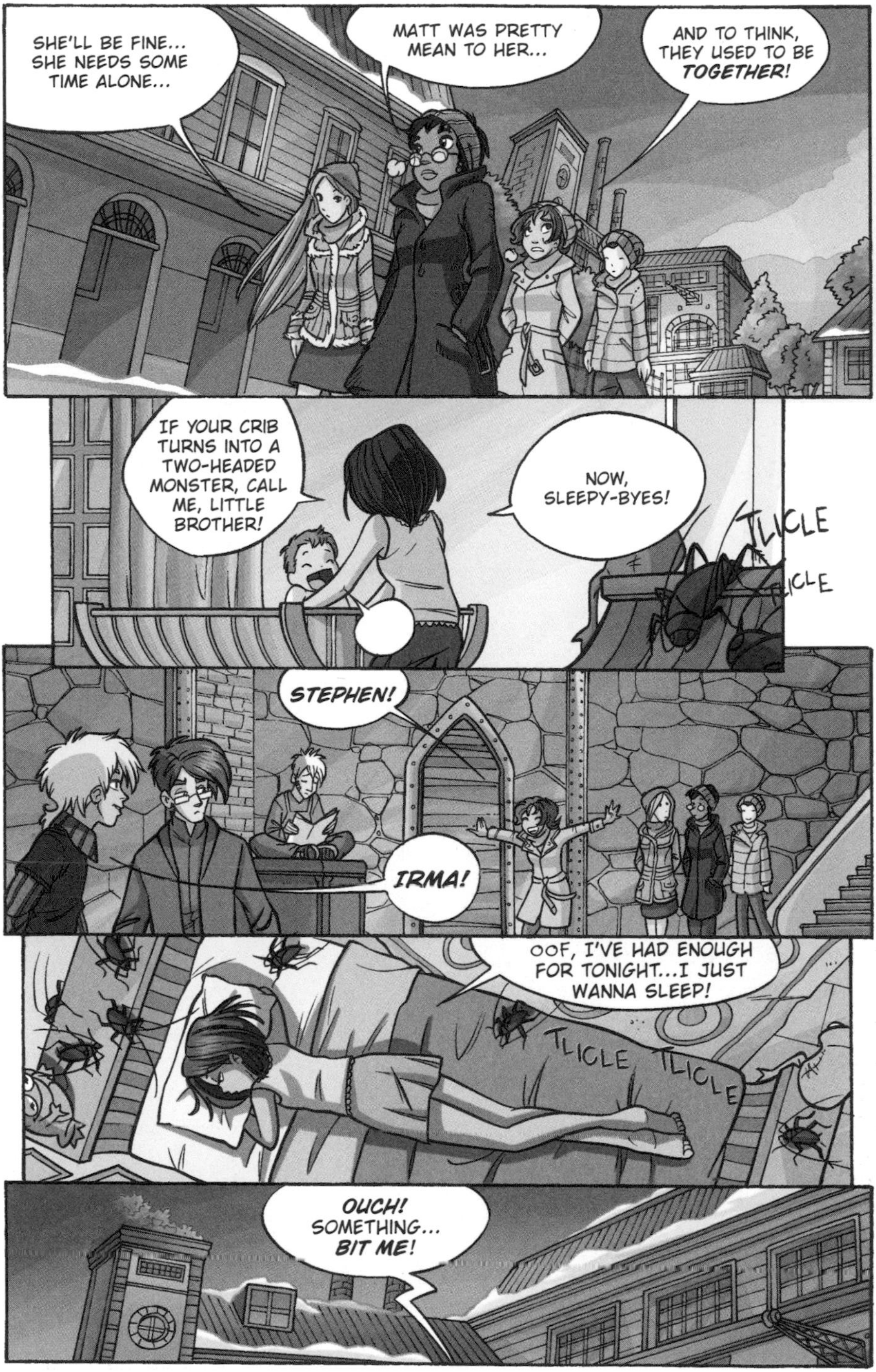
SHE'LL BE FINE... SHE NEEDS SOME TIME ALONE...
MATT WAS PRETTY MEAN TO HER...
AND TO THINK, THEY USED TO BE TOGETHER!
IF YOUR CRIB TURNS INTO A TWO-HEADED MONSTER, CALL ME, LITTLE BROTHER!
NOW, SLEEPY-BYES!
TLICLE
TLICLE
STEPHEN!
IRMA!
OOF, I'VE HAD ENOUGH FOR TONIGHT...I JUST WANNA SLEEP!
TLICLE TLICLE
OUCH! SOMETHING... BIT ME!

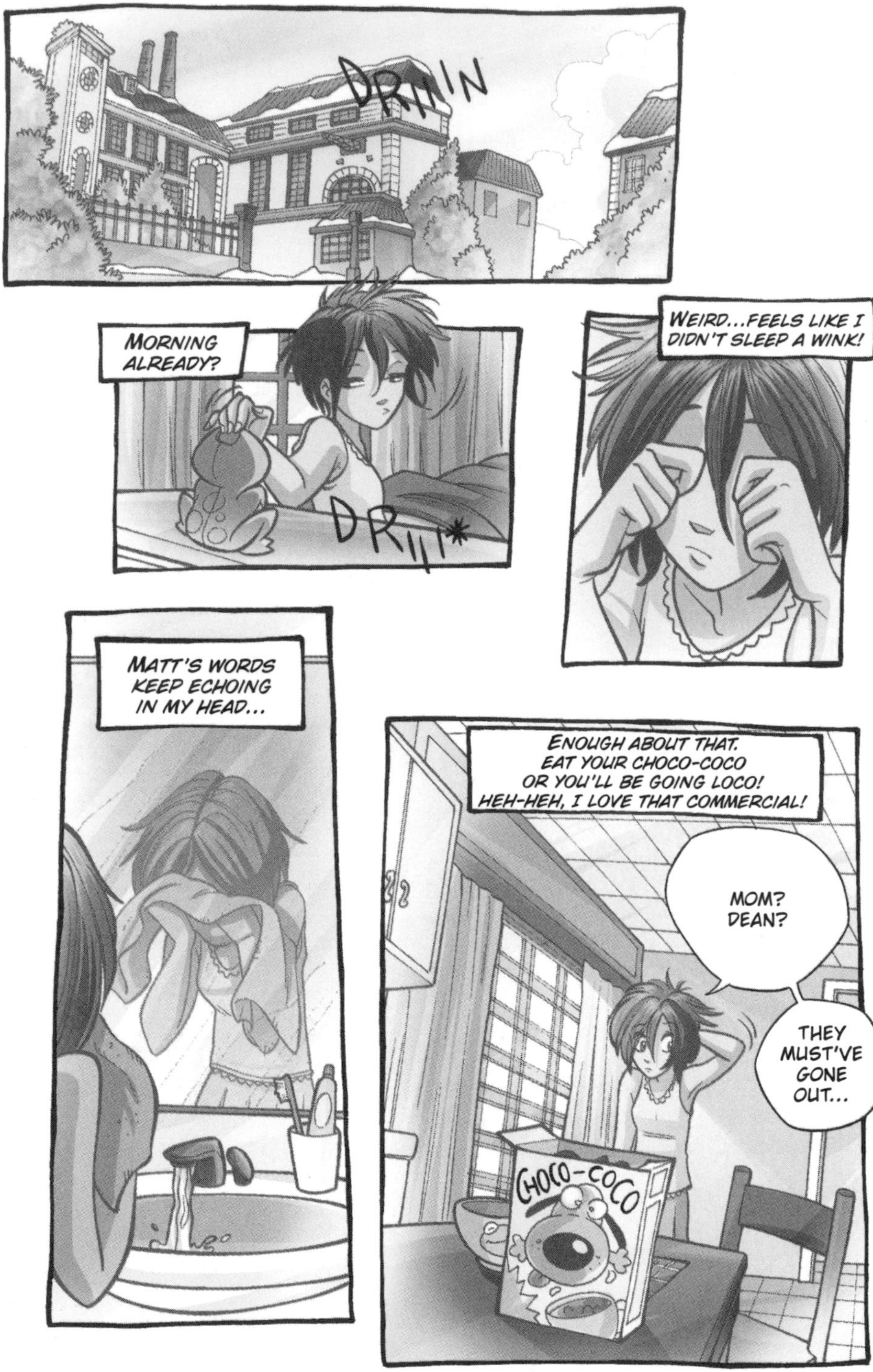
DRIIIN
MORNING ALREADY?
DRIII*
WEIRD...FEELS LIKE I DIDN'T SLEEP A WINK!
MATT'S WORDS KEEP ECHOING IN MY HEAD...
ENOUGH ABOUT THAT. EAT YOUR CHOCO-COCO OR YOU'LL BE GOING LOCO! HEH-HEH, I LOVE THAT COMMERCIAL!
MOM? DEAN?
THEY MUST'VE GONE OUT...
CHOCO-COCO

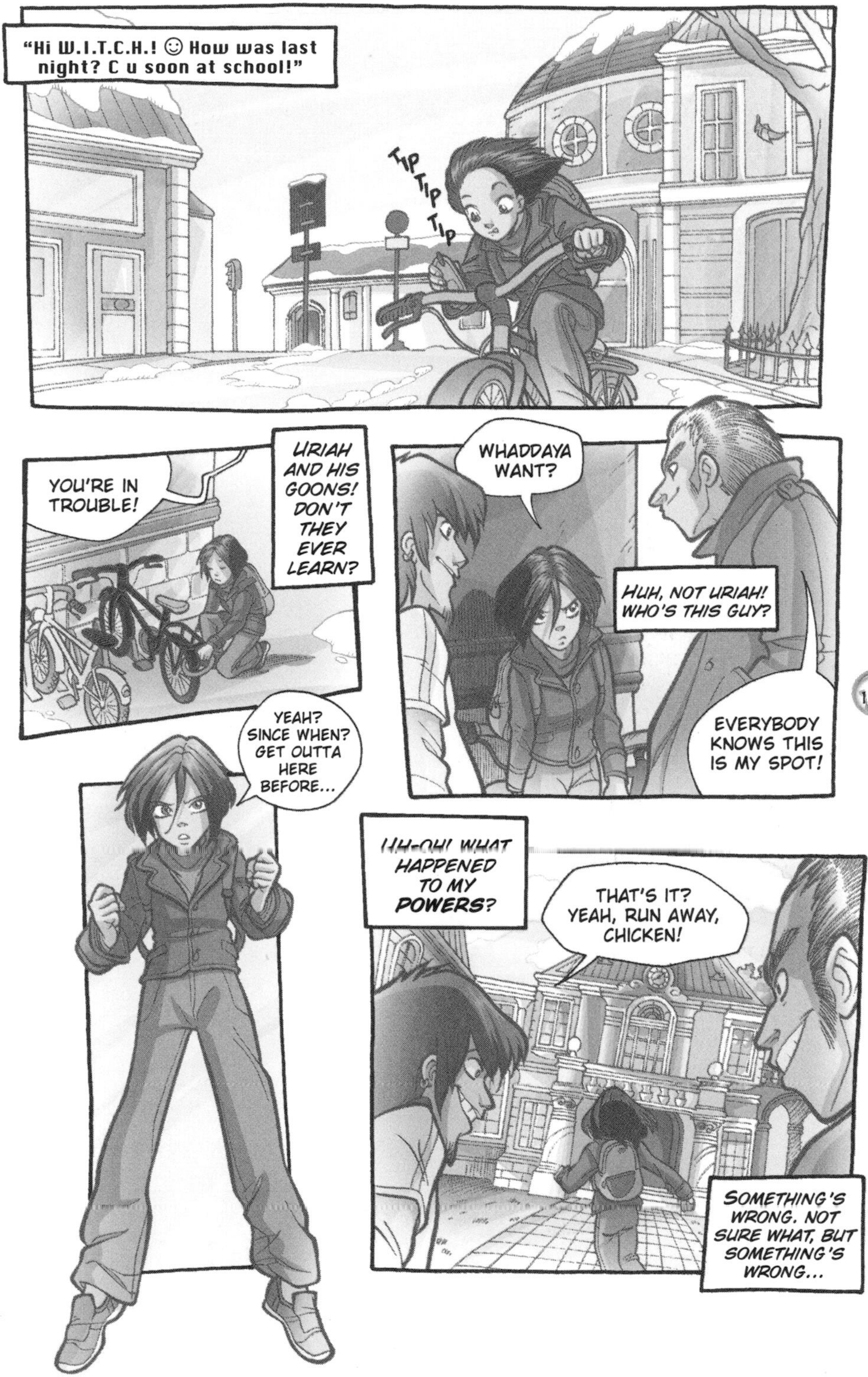
"Hi W.I.T.C.H.! ☺ How was last night? C u soon at school!"
TIP TIP TIP TIP
YOU'RE IN TROUBLE!
URIAH AND HIS GOONS! DON'T THEY EVER LEARN?
WHADDAYA WANT?
HUH, NOT URIAH! WHO'S THIS GUY?
EVERYBODY KNOWS THIS IS MY SPOT!
YEAH? SINCE WHEN? GET OUTTA HERE BEFORE...
UH-OH! WHAT HAPPENED TO MY POWERS?
THAT'S IT? YEAH, RUN AWAY, CHICKEN!
SOMETHING'S WRONG. NOT SURE WHAT, BUT SOMETHING'S WRONG...

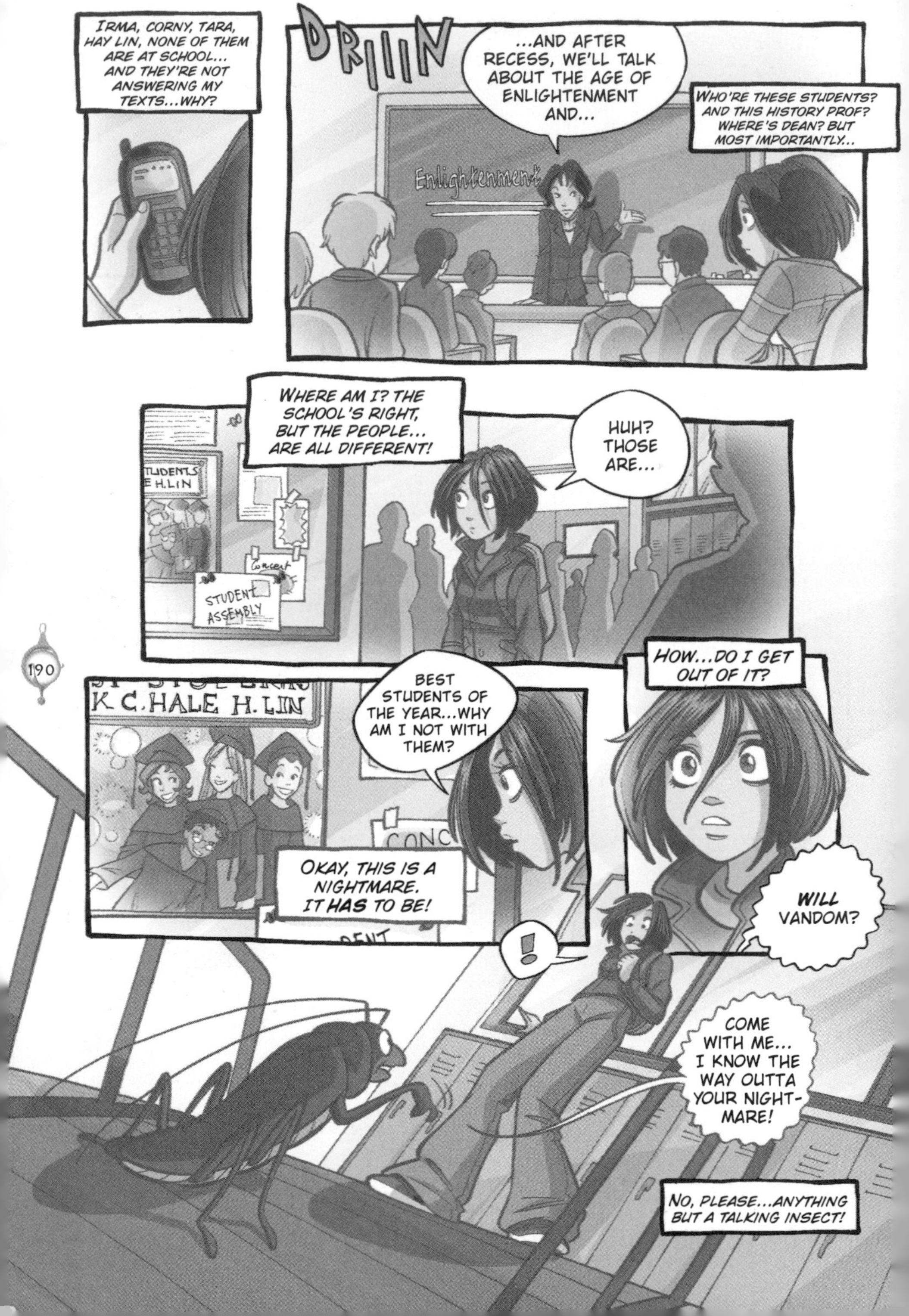
IRMA, CORNY, TARA, HAY LIN, NONE OF THEM ARE AT SCHOOL... AND THEY'RE NOT ANSWERING MY TEXTS...WHY?
DRIIIN
...AND AFTER RECESS, WE'LL TALK ABOUT THE AGE OF ENLIGHTENMENT AND...
WHO'RE THESE STUDENTS? AND THIS HISTORY PROF? WHERE'S DEAN? BUT MOST IMPORTANTLY...
Enlightenment
WHERE AM I? THE SCHOOL'S RIGHT, BUT THE PEOPLE... ARE ALL DIFFERENT!
HUH? THOSE ARE...
STUDENTS
E H.LIN
Concert
STUDENT ASSEMBLY
K.C.HALE H. LIN
BEST STUDENTS OF THE YEAR...WHY AM I NOT WITH THEM?
OKAY, THIS IS A NIGHTMARE. IT HAS TO BE!
HOW...DO I GET OUT OF IT?
WILL VANDOM?
!
COME WITH ME... I KNOW THE WAY OUTTA YOUR NIGHT-MARE!
NO, PLEASE...ANYTHING BUT A TALKING INSECT!

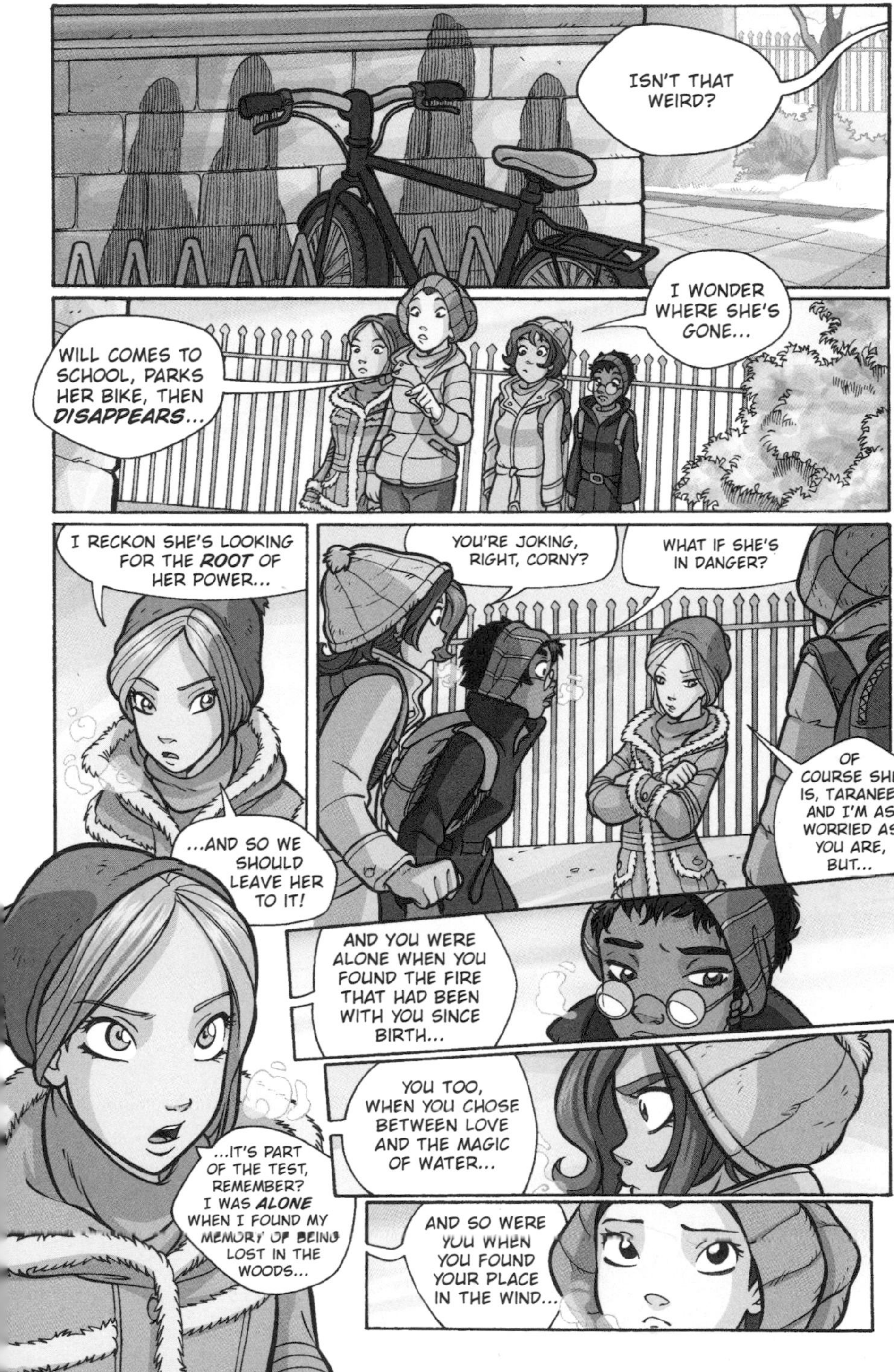
ISN'T THAT WEIRD?
WILL COMES TO SCHOOL, PARKS HER BIKE, THEN *DISAPPEARS*...
I WONDER WHERE SHE'S GONE...
I RECKON SHE'S LOOKING FOR THE *ROOT* OF HER POWER...
YOU'RE JOKING, RIGHT, CORNY?
WHAT IF SHE'S IN DANGER?
OF COURSE SHE IS, TARANEE. AND I'M AS WORRIED AS YOU ARE, BUT...
...AND SO WE SHOULD LEAVE HER TO IT!
...IT'S PART OF THE TEST, REMEMBER? I WAS *ALONE* WHEN I FOUND MY MEMORY OF BEING LOST IN THE WOODS...
AND YOU WERE ALONE WHEN YOU FOUND THE FIRE THAT HAD BEEN WITH YOU SINCE BIRTH...
YOU TOO, WHEN YOU CHOSE BETWEEN LOVE AND THE MAGIC OF WATER...
AND SO WERE YOU WHEN YOU FOUND YOUR PLACE IN THE WIND...

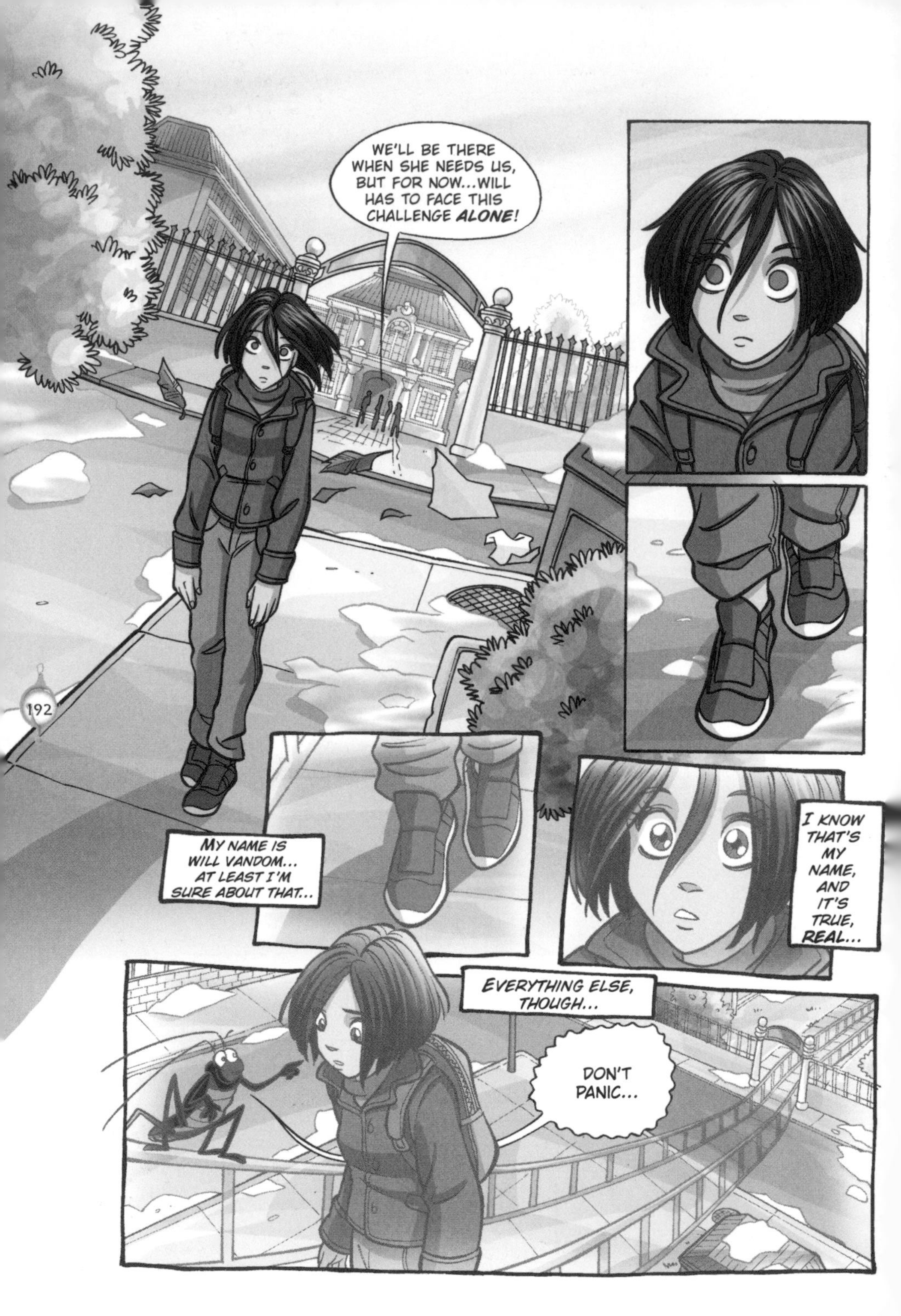

WE'LL BE THERE WHEN SHE NEEDS US, BUT FOR NOW...WILL HAS TO FACE THIS CHALLENGE ALONE!
MY NAME IS WILL VANDOM... AT LEAST I'M SURE ABOUT THAT...
I KNOW THAT'S MY NAME, AND IT'S TRUE, REAL...
EVERYTHING ELSE, THOUGH...
DON'T PANIC...

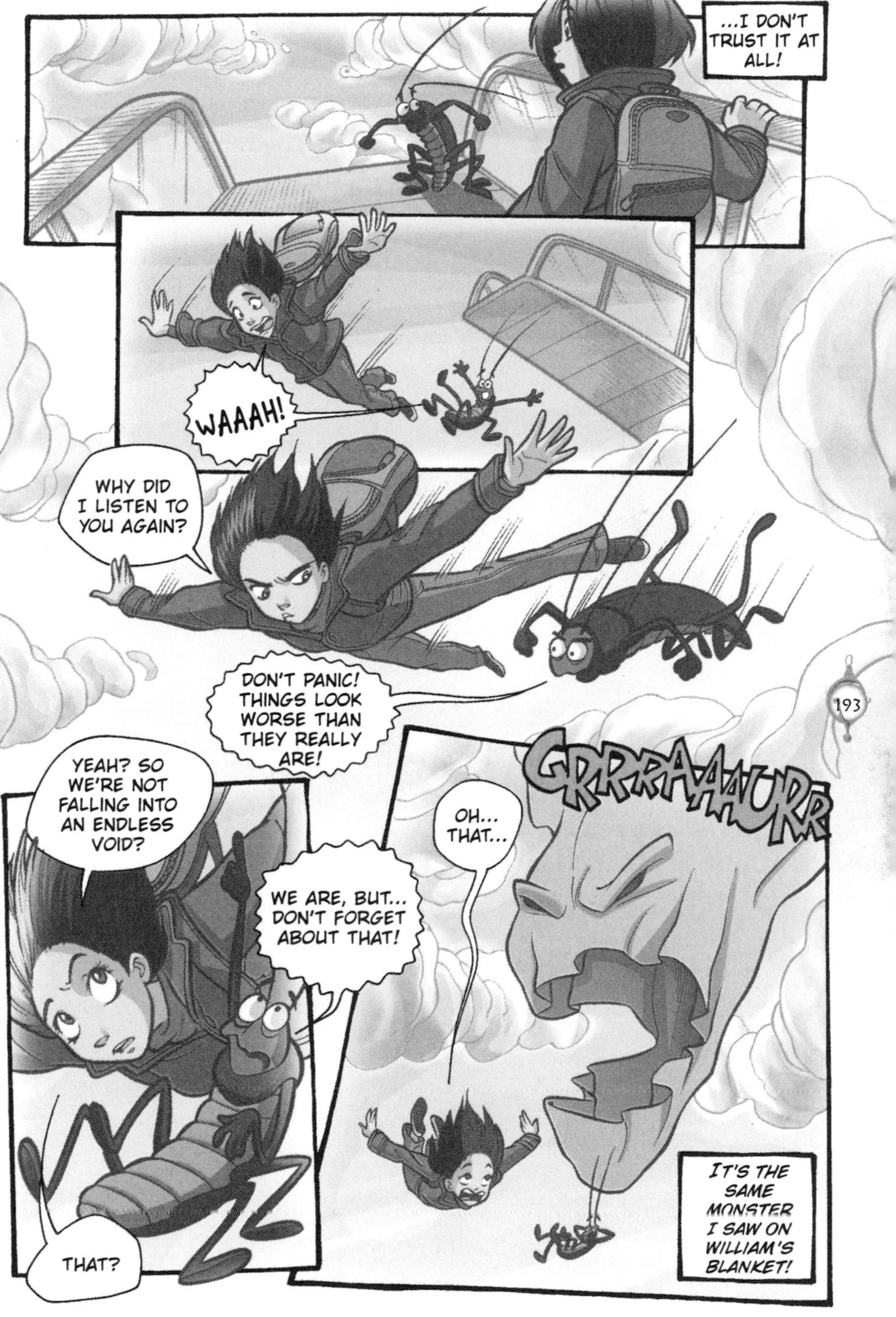
...I DON'T TRUST IT AT ALL!
WAAAH!
WHY DID I LISTEN TO YOU AGAIN?
DON'T PANIC! THINGS LOOK WORSE THAN THEY REALLY ARE!
YEAH? SO WE'RE NOT FALLING INTO AN ENDLESS VOID?
WE ARE, BUT... DON'T FORGET ABOUT THAT!
THAT?
GRRRAAAURR
OH... THAT...
IT'S THE SAME MONSTER I SAW ON WILLIAM'S BLANKET!

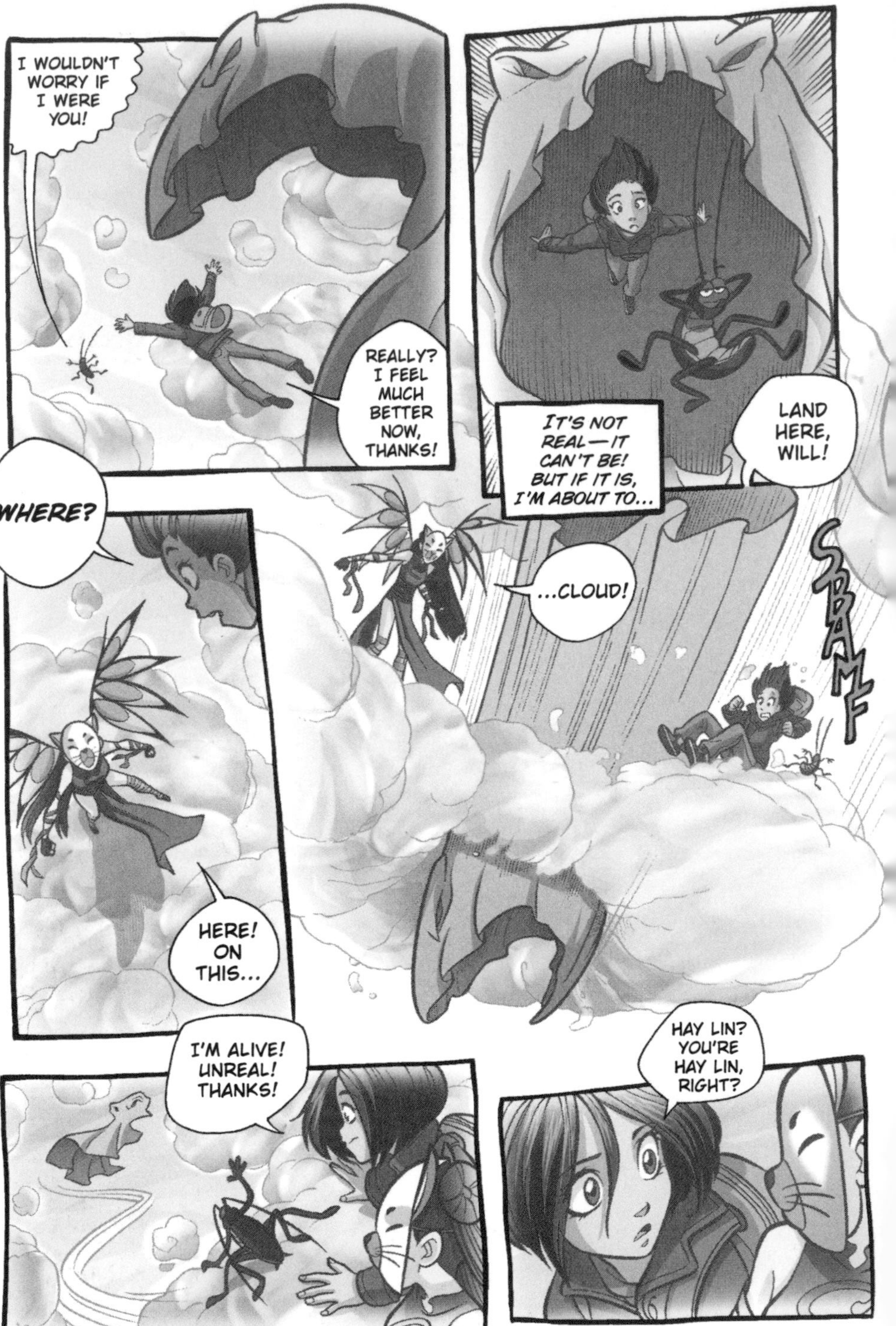

I WOULDN'T WORRY IF I WERE YOU!
REALLY? I FEEL MUCH BETTER NOW, THANKS!
IT'S NOT REAL—IT CAN'T BE! BUT IF IT IS, I'M ABOUT TO...
LAND HERE, WILL!
WHERE?
HERE! ON THIS...
...CLOUD!
SBAMF
I'M ALIVE! UNREAL! THANKS!
HAY LIN? YOU'RE HAY LIN, RIGHT?

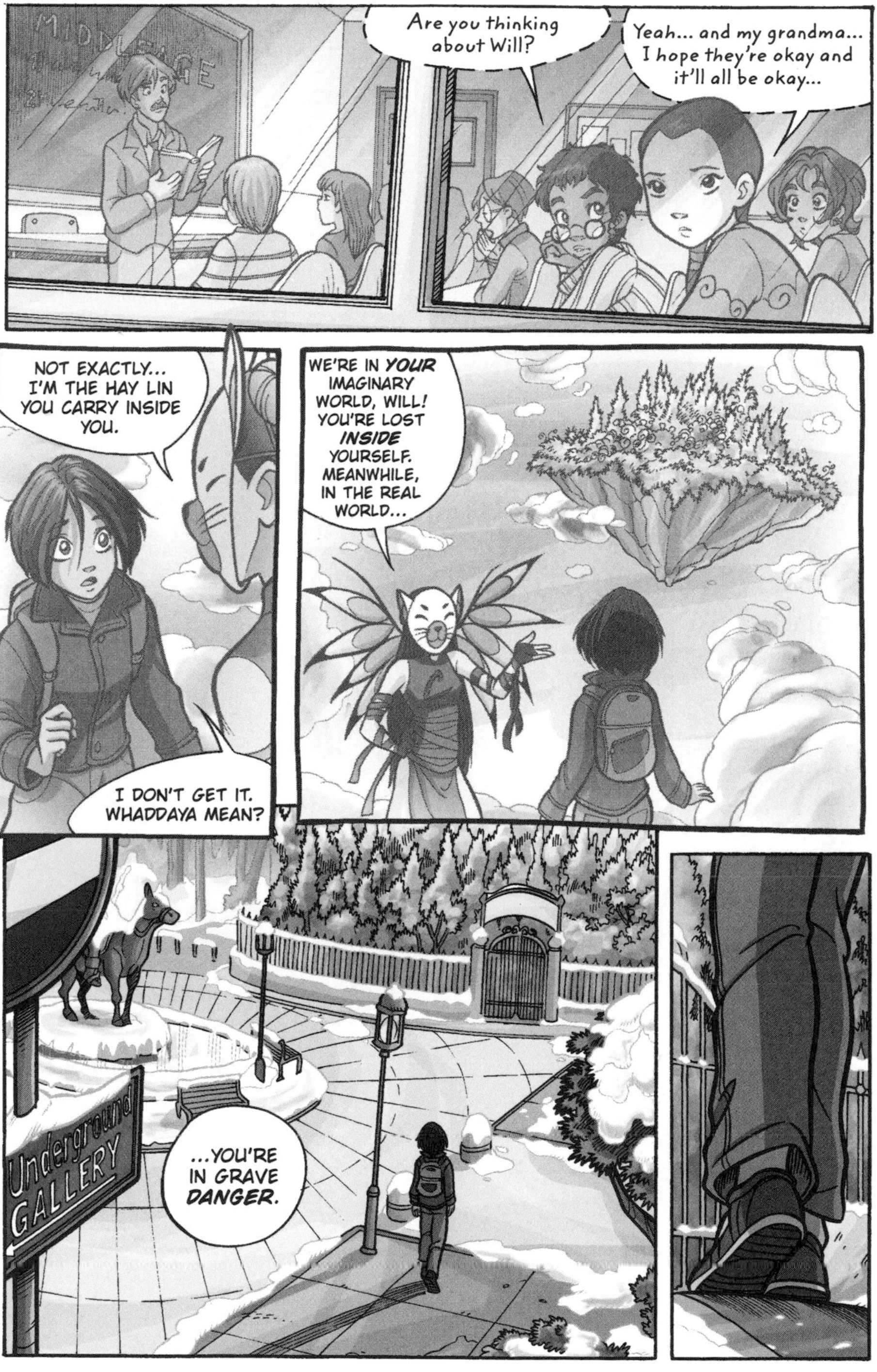
Are you thinking about Will?
Yeah... and my grandma... I hope they're okay and it'll all be okay...
NOT EXACTLY... I'M THE HAY LIN YOU CARRY INSIDE YOU.
I DON'T GET IT. WHADDAYA MEAN?
WE'RE IN *YOUR* IMAGINARY WORLD, WILL! YOU'RE LOST *INSIDE* YOURSELF. MEANWHILE, IN THE REAL WORLD...
Underground GALLERY
...YOU'RE IN GRAVE *DANGER*.

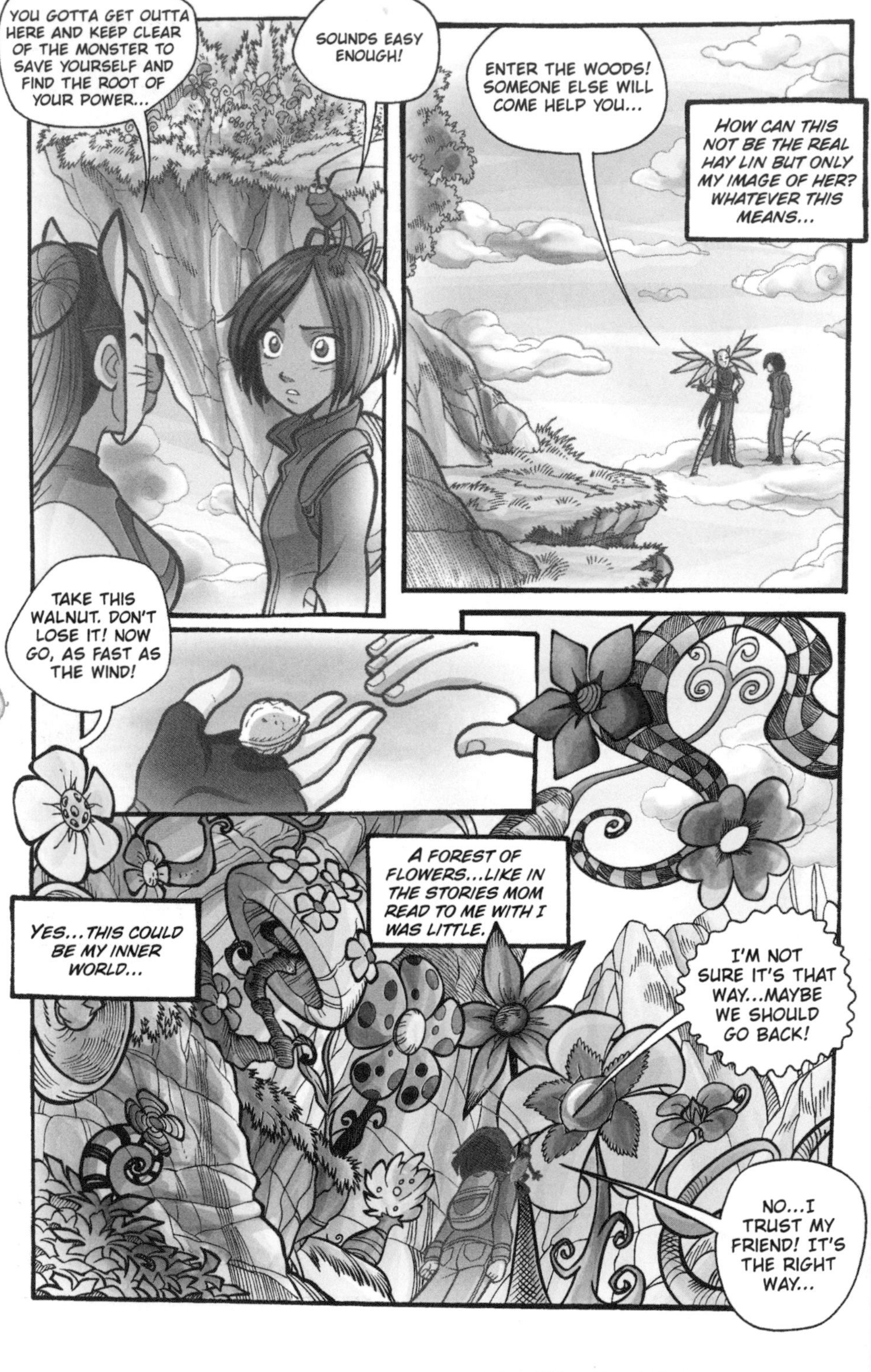

YOU GOTTA GET OUTTA HERE AND KEEP CLEAR OF THE MONSTER TO SAVE YOURSELF AND FIND THE ROOT OF YOUR POWER...
SOUNDS EASY ENOUGH!
ENTER THE WOODS! SOMEONE ELSE WILL COME HELP YOU...
HOW CAN THIS NOT BE THE REAL HAY LIN BUT ONLY MY IMAGE OF HER? WHATEVER THIS MEANS...
TAKE THIS WALNUT. DON'T LOSE IT! NOW GO, AS FAST AS THE WIND!
A FOREST OF FLOWERS...LIKE IN THE STORIES MOM READ TO ME WITH I WAS LITTLE.
YES...THIS COULD BE MY INNER WORLD...
I'M NOT SURE IT'S THAT WAY...MAYBE WE SHOULD GO BACK!
NO...I TRUST MY FRIEND! IT'S THE RIGHT WAY...


196

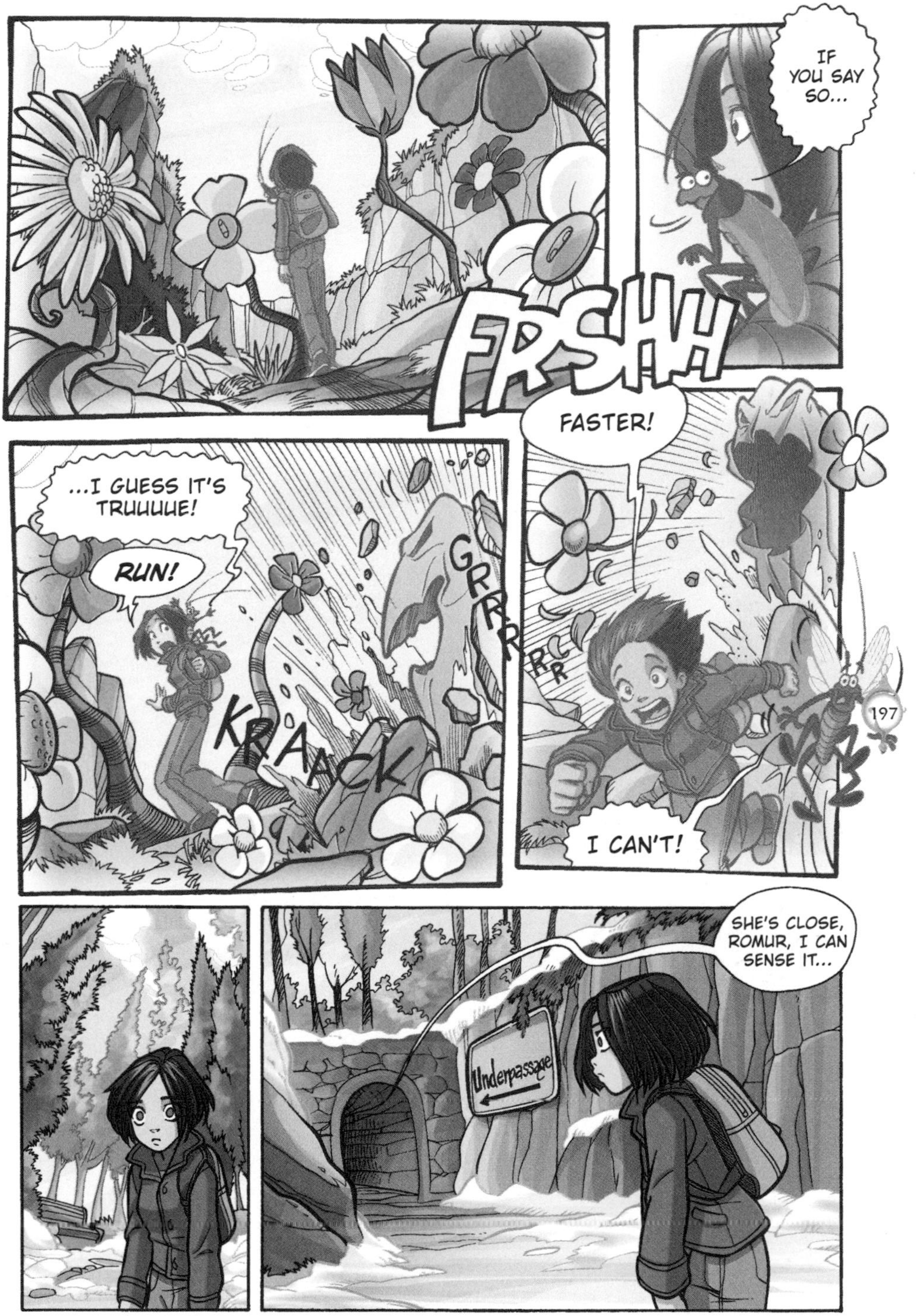
IF YOU SAY SO...
FRSHH
...I GUESS IT'S TRUUUUE!
RUN!
GRRRRRR
KRAACK
FASTER!
I CAN'T!
SHE'S CLOSE, ROMUR, I CAN SENSE IT...
Underpassage

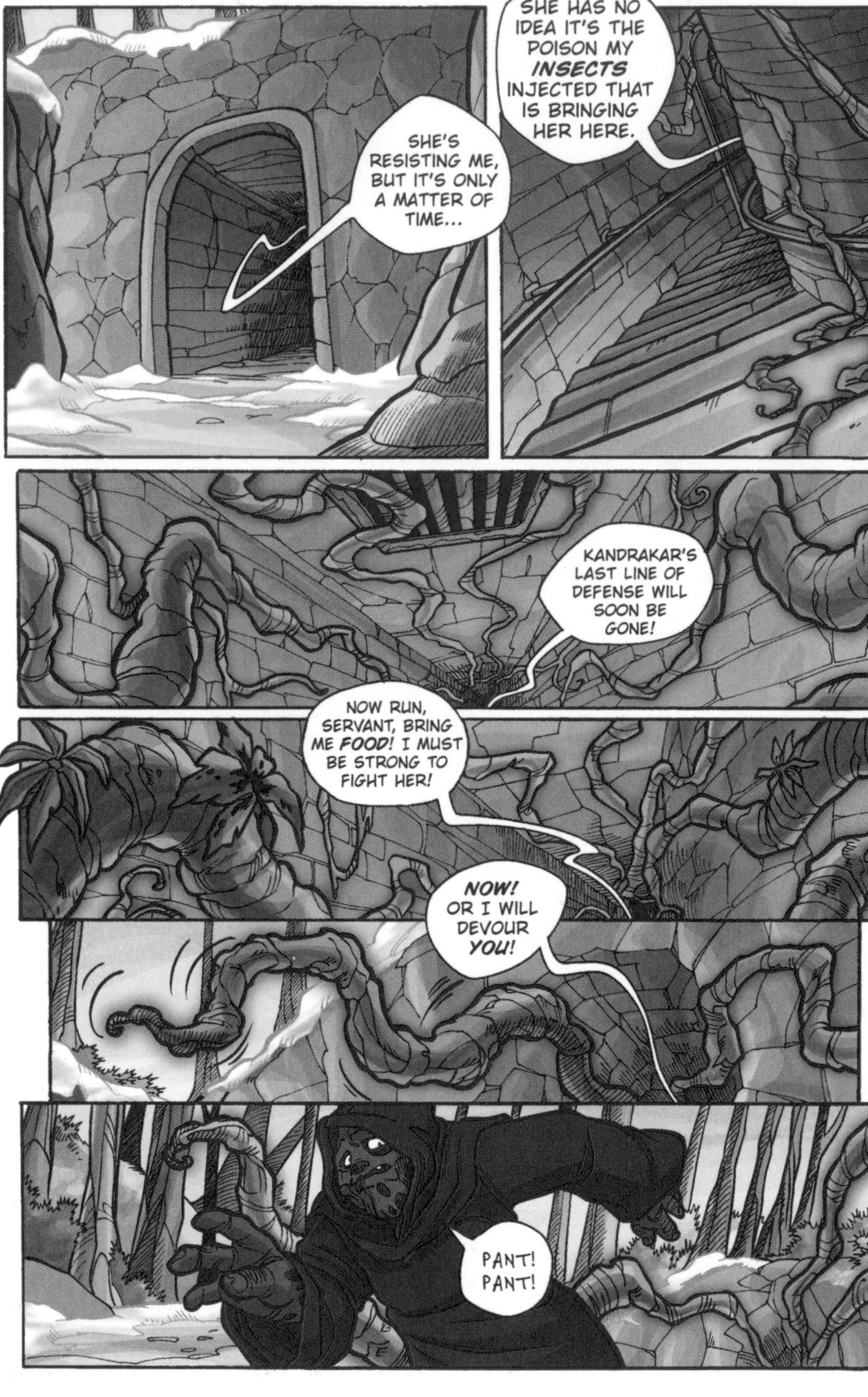
SHE'S RESISTING ME, BUT IT'S ONLY A MATTER OF TIME...
SHE HAS NO IDEA IT'S THE POISON MY INSECTS INJECTED THAT IS BRINGING HER HERE.
KANDRAKAR'S LAST LINE OF DEFENSE WILL SOON BE GONE!
NOW RUN, SERVANT, BRING ME FOOD! I MUST BE STRONG TO FIGHT HER!
NOW! OR I WILL DEVOUR YOU!
PANT! PANT!

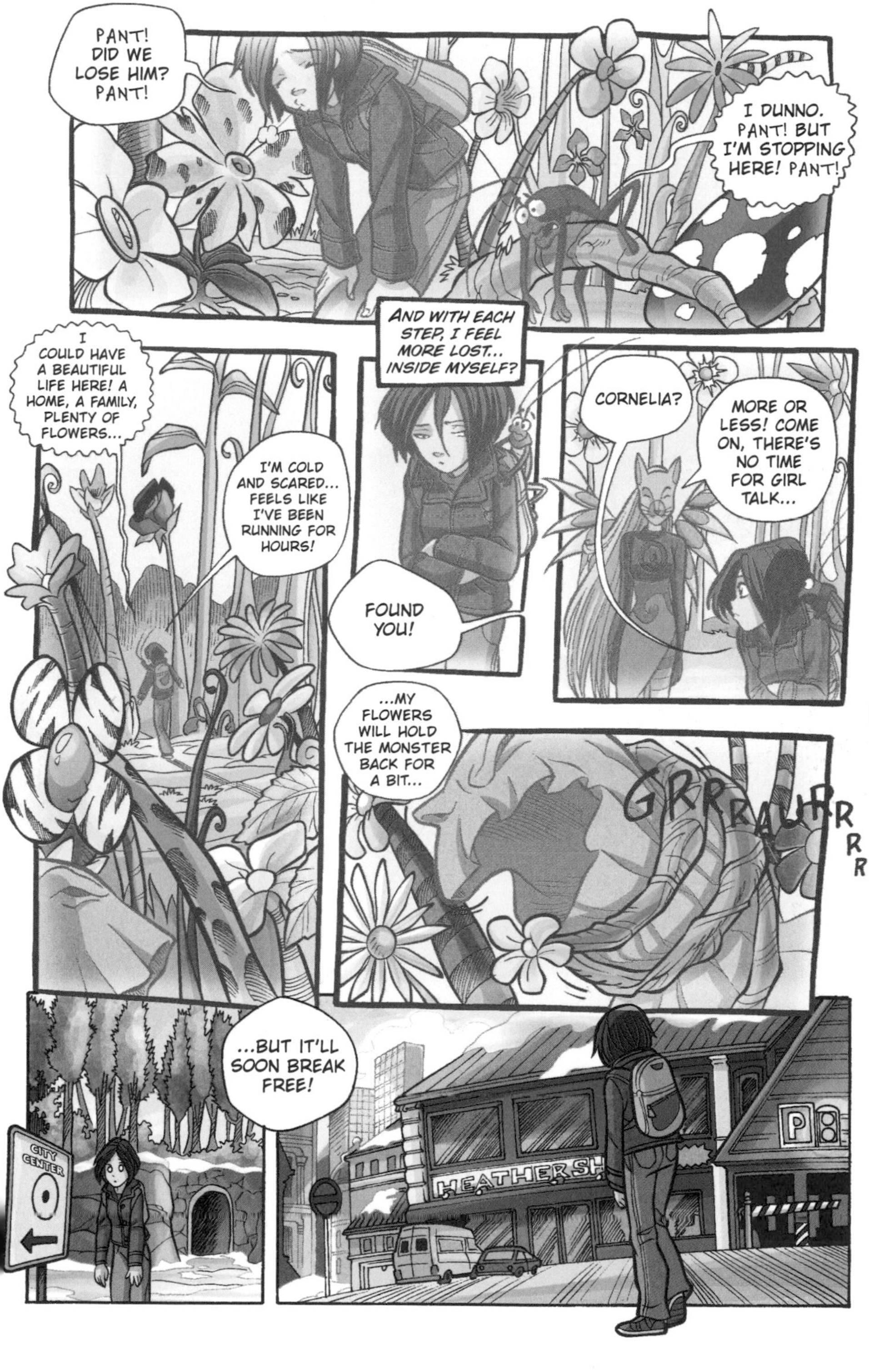
PANT! DID WE LOSE HIM? PANT!
I DUNNO. PANT! BUT I'M STOPPING HERE! PANT!
I COULD HAVE A BEAUTIFUL LIFE HERE! A HOME, A FAMILY, PLENTY OF FLOWERS...
I'M COLD AND SCARED... FEELS LIKE I'VE BEEN RUNNING FOR HOURS!
AND WITH EACH STEP, I FEEL MORE LOST... INSIDE MYSELF?
FOUND YOU!
CORNELIA?
MORE OR LESS! COME ON, THERE'S NO TIME FOR GIRL TALK...
...MY FLOWERS WILL HOLD THE MONSTER BACK FOR A BIT...
GRRRAURRRR
...BUT IT'LL SOON BREAK FREE!
CITY CENTER
HEATHERSH
P

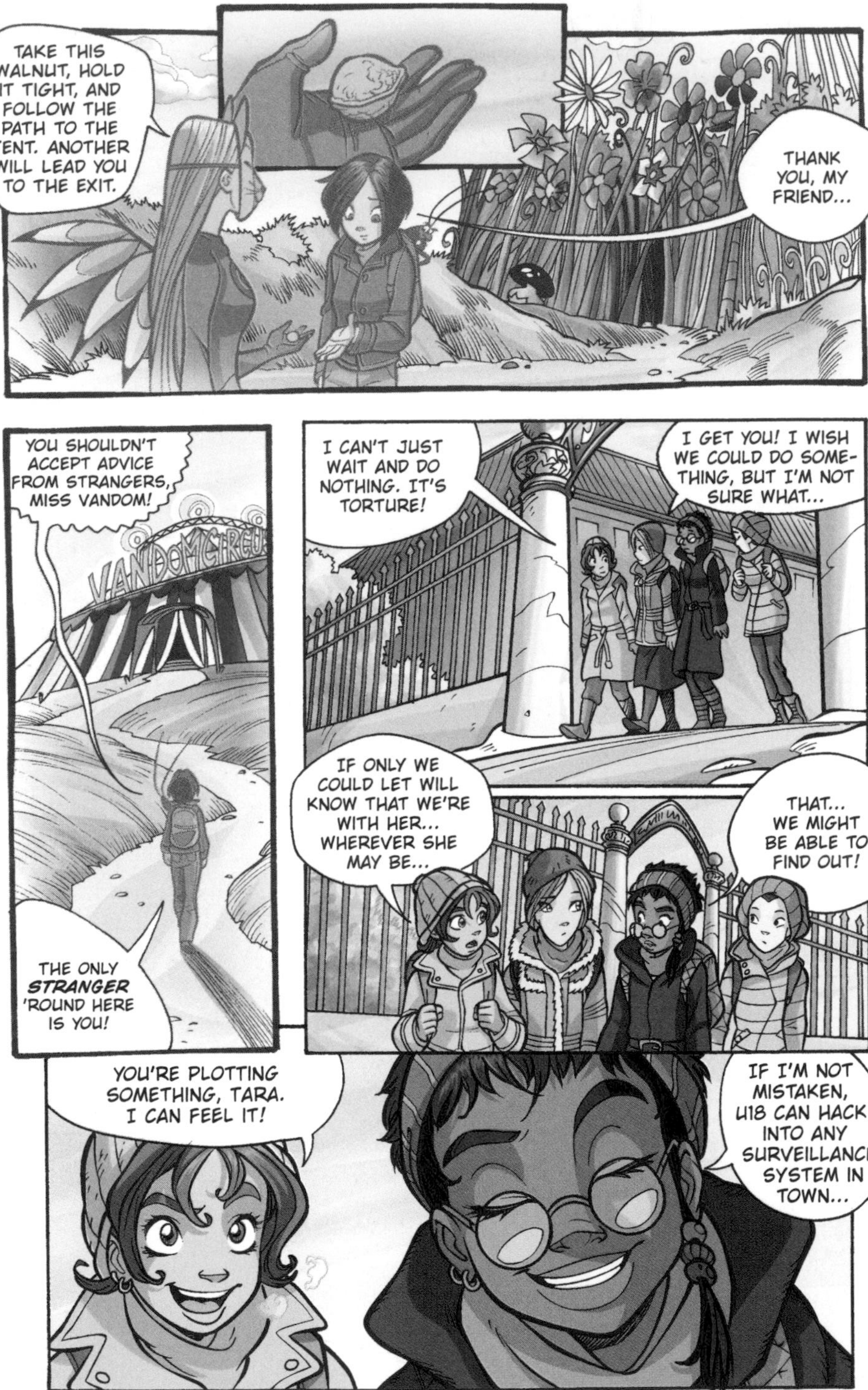
TAKE THIS WALNUT, HOLD IT TIGHT, AND FOLLOW THE PATH TO THE TENT. ANOTHER WILL LEAD YOU TO THE EXIT.
THANK YOU, MY FRIEND...
YOU SHOULDN'T ACCEPT ADVICE FROM STRANGERS, MISS VANDOM!
VANDOM CIRCUS
THE ONLY **STRANGER** 'ROUND HERE IS YOU!
I CAN'T JUST WAIT AND DO NOTHING. IT'S TORTURE!
I GET YOU! I WISH WE COULD DO SOMETHING, BUT I'M NOT SURE WHAT...
IF ONLY WE COULD LET WILL KNOW THAT WE'RE WITH HER... WHEREVER SHE MAY BE...
THAT... WE MIGHT BE ABLE TO FIND OUT!
YOU'RE PLOTTING SOMETHING, TARA. I CAN FEEL IT!
IF I'M NOT MISTAKEN, U18 CAN HACK INTO ANY SURVEILLANCE SYSTEM IN TOWN...

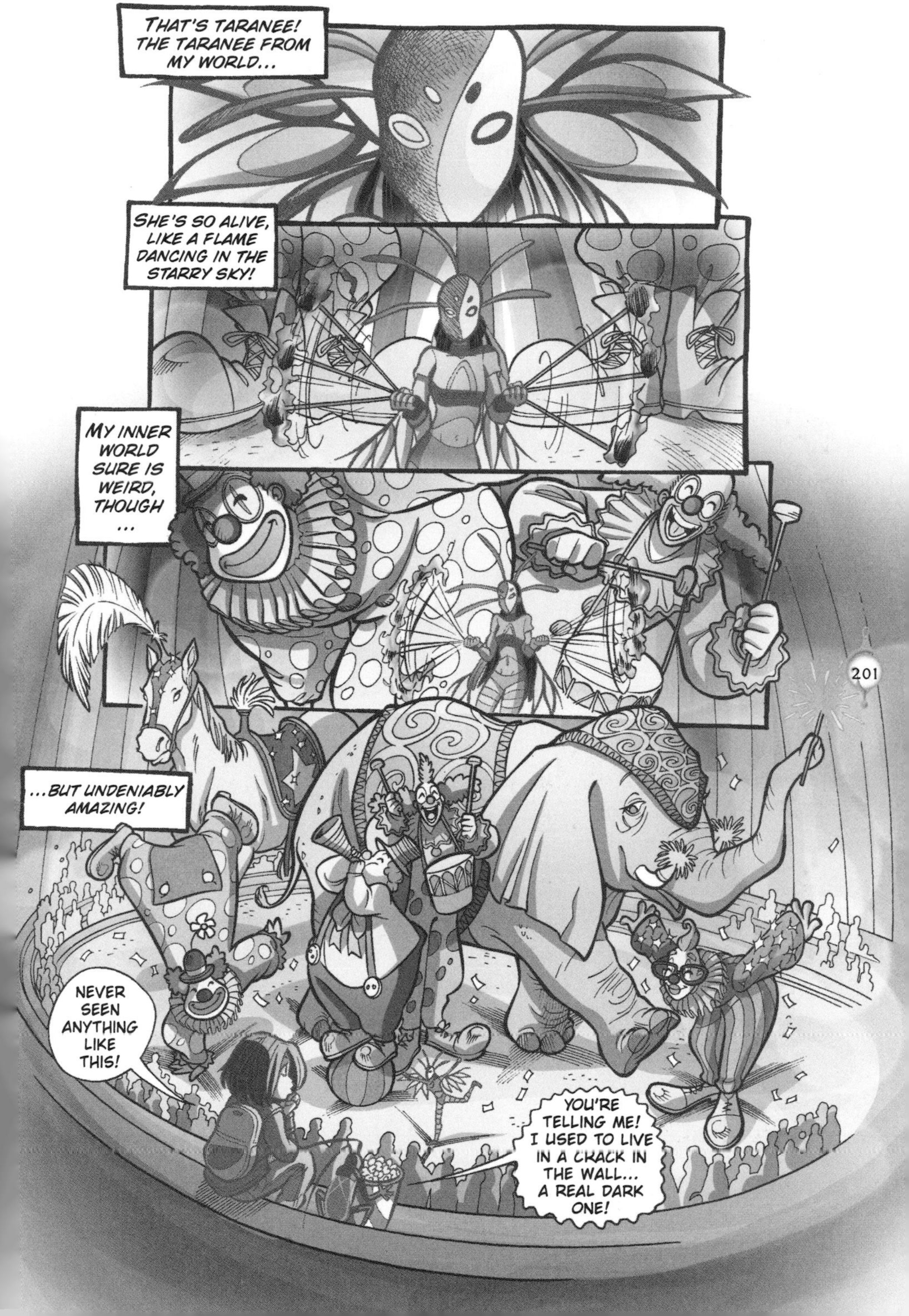
THAT'S TARANEE! THE TARANEE FROM MY WORLD...
SHE'S SO ALIVE, LIKE A FLAME DANCING IN THE STARRY SKY!
MY INNER WORLD SURE IS WEIRD, THOUGH ...
...BUT UNDENIABLY AMAZING!
NEVER SEEN ANYTHING LIKE THIS!
YOU'RE TELLING ME! I USED TO LIVE IN A CRACK IN THE WALL... A REAL DARK ONE!

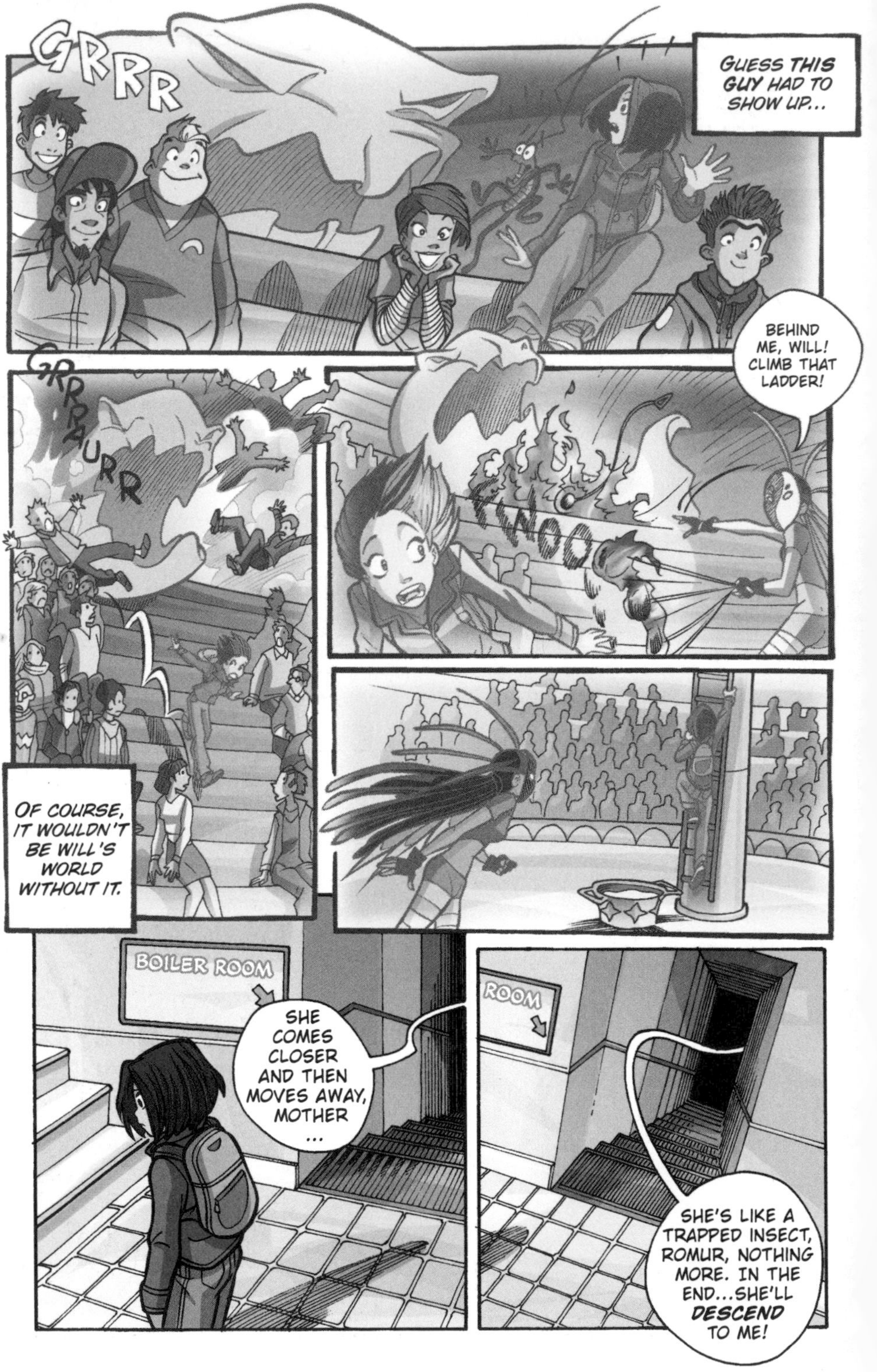
GRRR
GUESS THIS GUY HAD TO SHOW UP...
GRRRAURR
BEHIND ME, WILL! CLIMB THAT LADDER!
FWOOO
OF COURSE, IT WOULDN'T BE WILL'S WORLD WITHOUT IT.
BOILER ROOM
SHE COMES CLOSER AND THEN MOVES AWAY, MOTHER ...
ROOM
SHE'S LIKE A TRAPPED INSECT, ROMUR, NOTHING MORE. IN THE END...SHE'LL DESCEND TO ME!

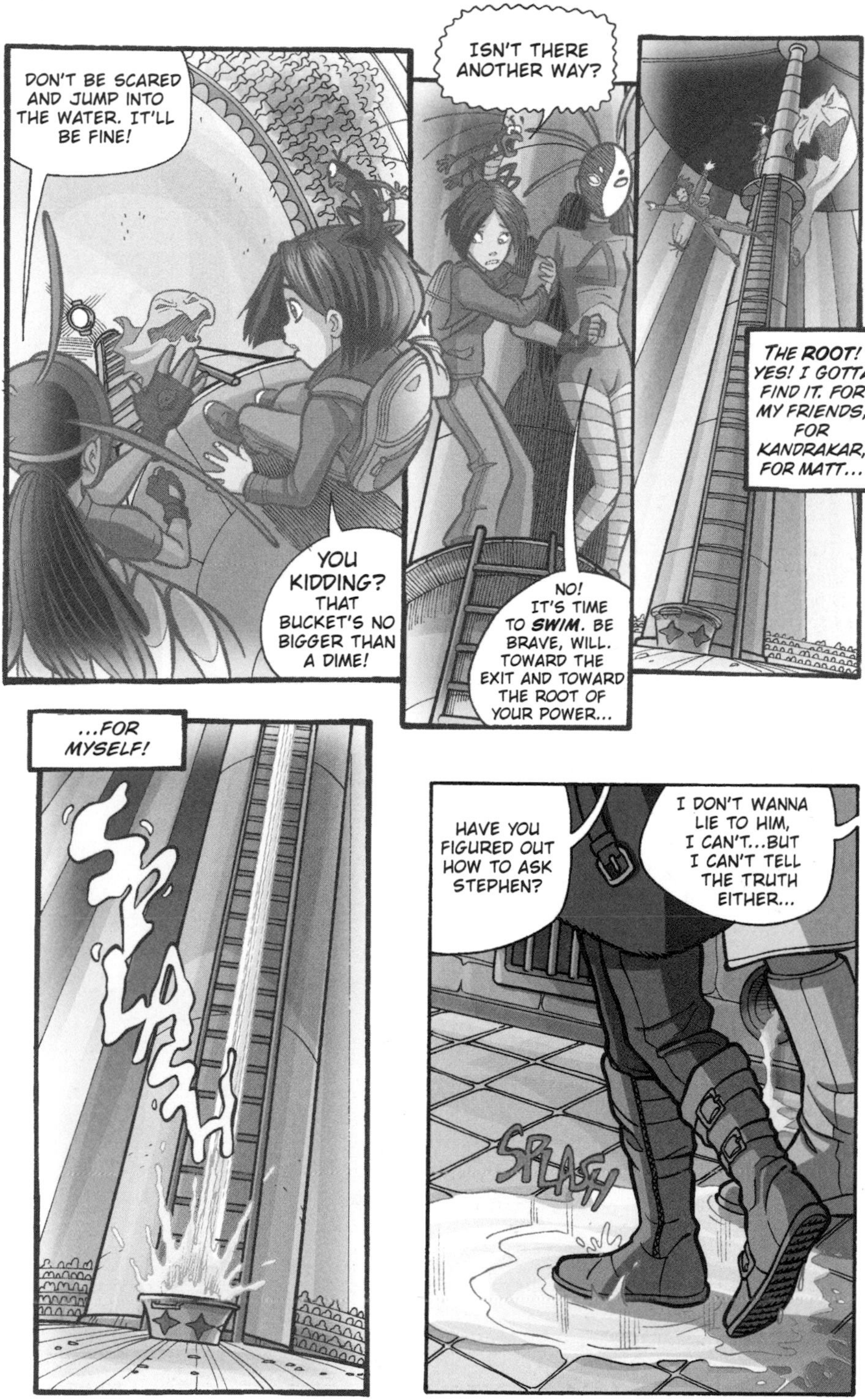

DON'T BE SCARED AND JUMP INTO THE WATER. IT'LL BE FINE!
YOU KIDDING? THAT BUCKET'S NO BIGGER THAN A DIME!
ISN'T THERE ANOTHER WAY?
NO! IT'S TIME TO SWIM. BE BRAVE, WILL. TOWARD THE EXIT AND TOWARD THE ROOT OF YOUR POWER...
THE ROOT! YES! I GOTTA FIND IT. FOR MY FRIENDS, FOR KANDRAKAR, FOR MATT...
...FOR MYSELF!
HAVE YOU FIGURED OUT HOW TO ASK STEPHEN?
I DON'T WANNA LIE TO HIM, I CAN'T...BUT I CAN'T TELL THE TRUTH EITHER...
SPLASH

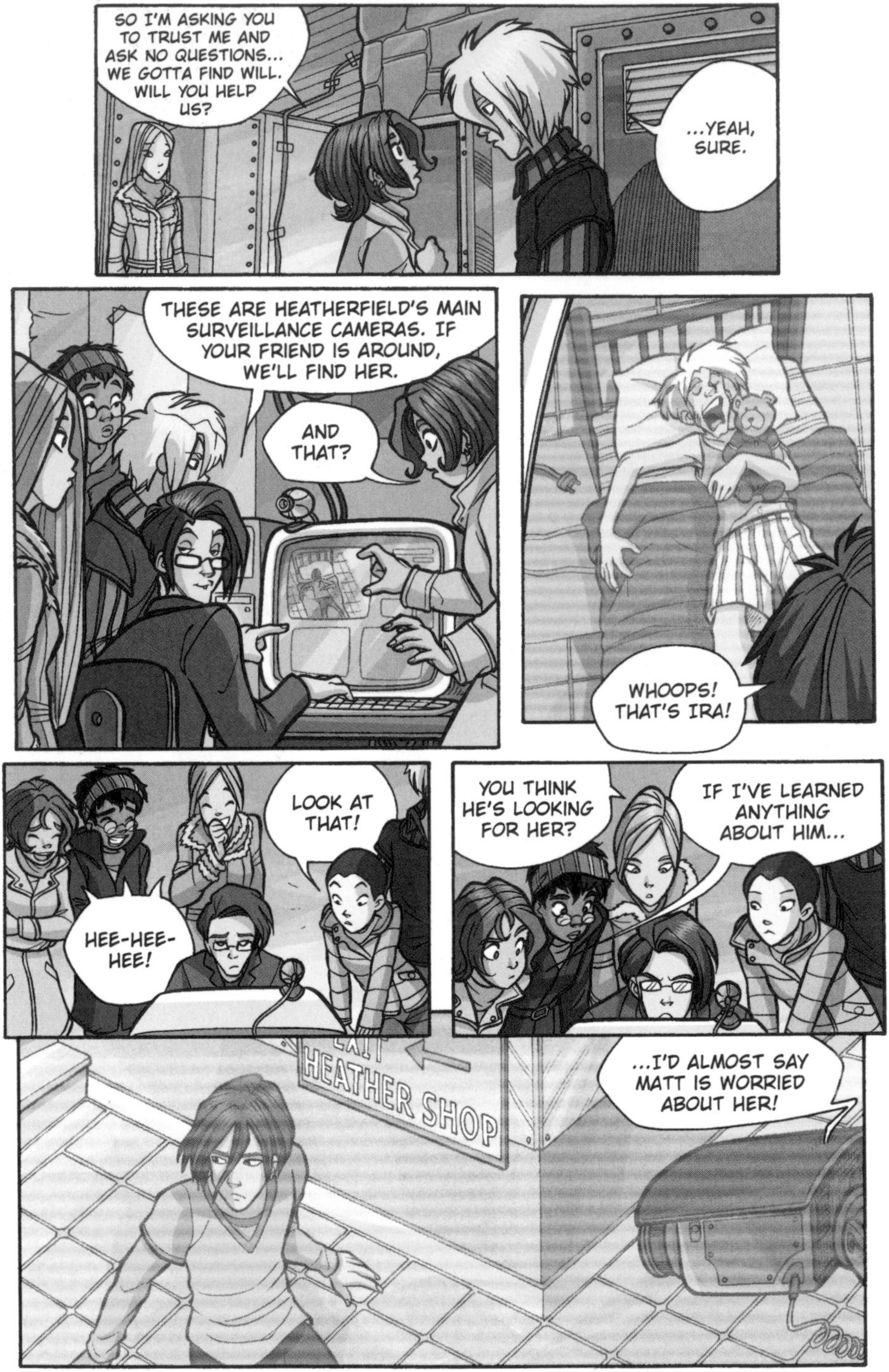
SO I'M ASKING YOU TO TRUST ME AND ASK NO QUESTIONS... WE GOTTA FIND WILL. WILL YOU HELP US?
...YEAH, SURE.
THESE ARE HEATHERFIELD'S MAIN SURVEILLANCE CAMERAS. IF YOUR FRIEND IS AROUND, WE'LL FIND HER.
AND THAT?
WHOOPS! THAT'S IRA!
LOOK AT THAT!
HEE-HEE-HEE!
YOU THINK HE'S LOOKING FOR HER?
IF I'VE LEARNED ANYTHING ABOUT HIM...
EXIT
HEATHER SHOP
...I'D ALMOST SAY MATT IS WORRIED ABOUT HER!

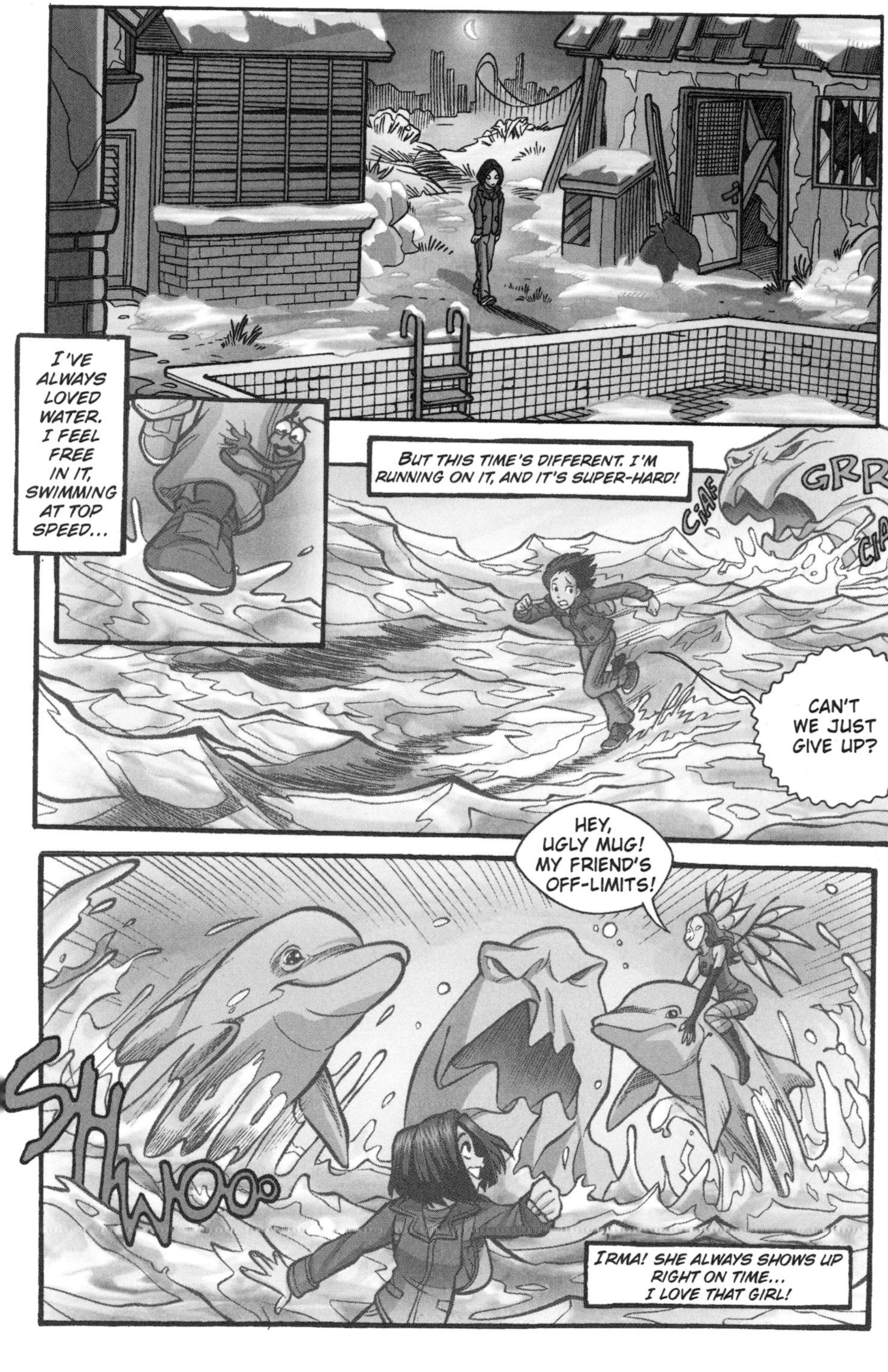

I'VE ALWAYS LOVED WATER. I FEEL FREE IN IT, SWIMMING AT TOP SPEED...
BUT THIS TIME'S DIFFERENT. I'M RUNNING ON IT, AND IT'S SUPER-HARD!
GRRR
CIAF
CIAF
CAN'T WE JUST GIVE UP?
HEY, UGLY MUG! MY FRIEND'S OFF-LIMITS!
SHWOOO
IRMA! SHE ALWAYS SHOWS UP RIGHT ON TIME... I LOVE THAT GIRL!

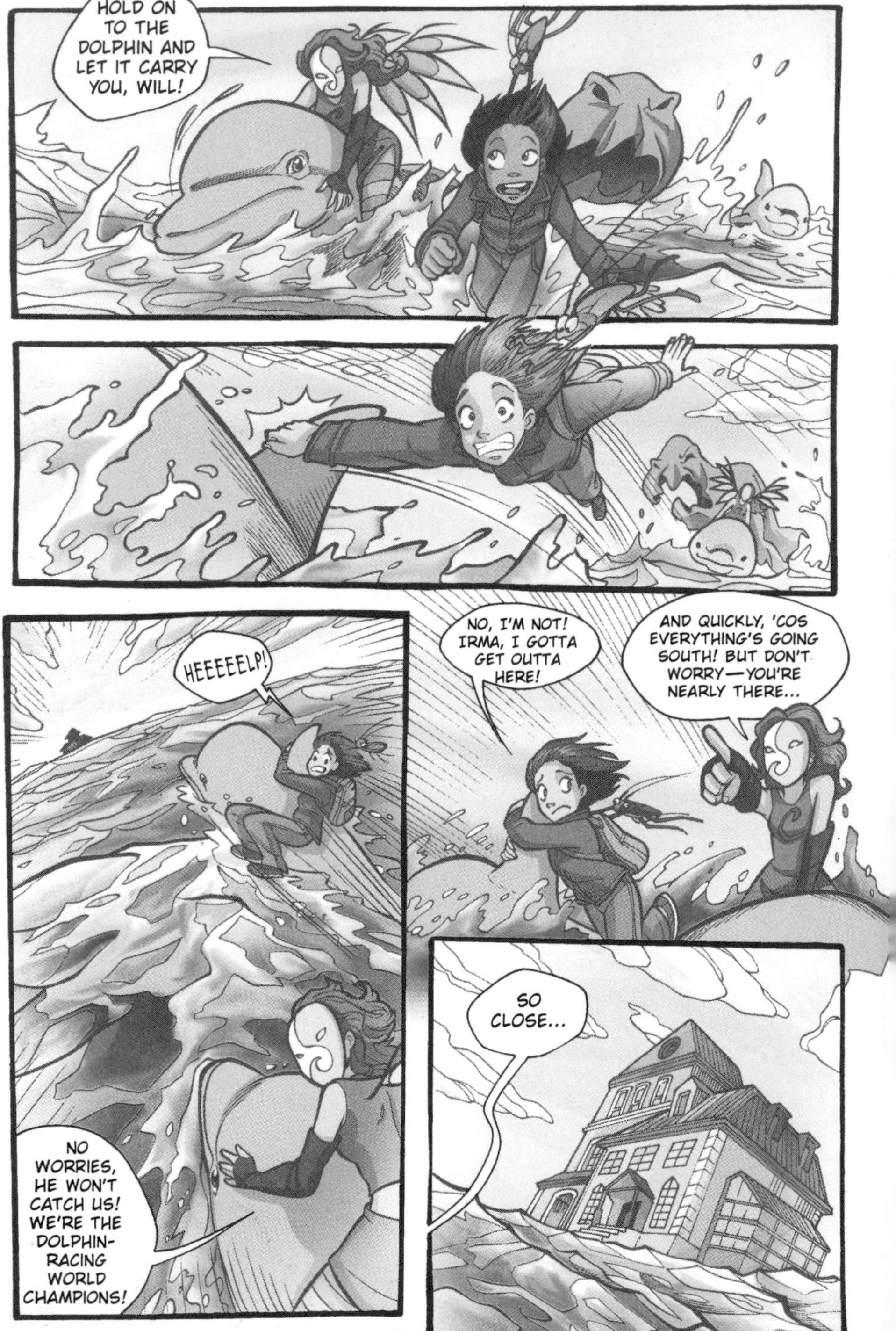
HOLD ON TO THE DOLPHIN AND LET IT CARRY YOU, WILL!
HEEEEELP!
NO, I'M NOT! IRMA, I GOTTA GET OUTTA HERE!
AND QUICKLY, 'COS EVERYTHING'S GOING SOUTH! BUT DON'T WORRY—YOU'RE NEARLY THERE...
NO WORRIES, HE WON'T CATCH US! WE'RE THE DOLPHIN-RACING WORLD CHAMPIONS!
SO CLOSE...

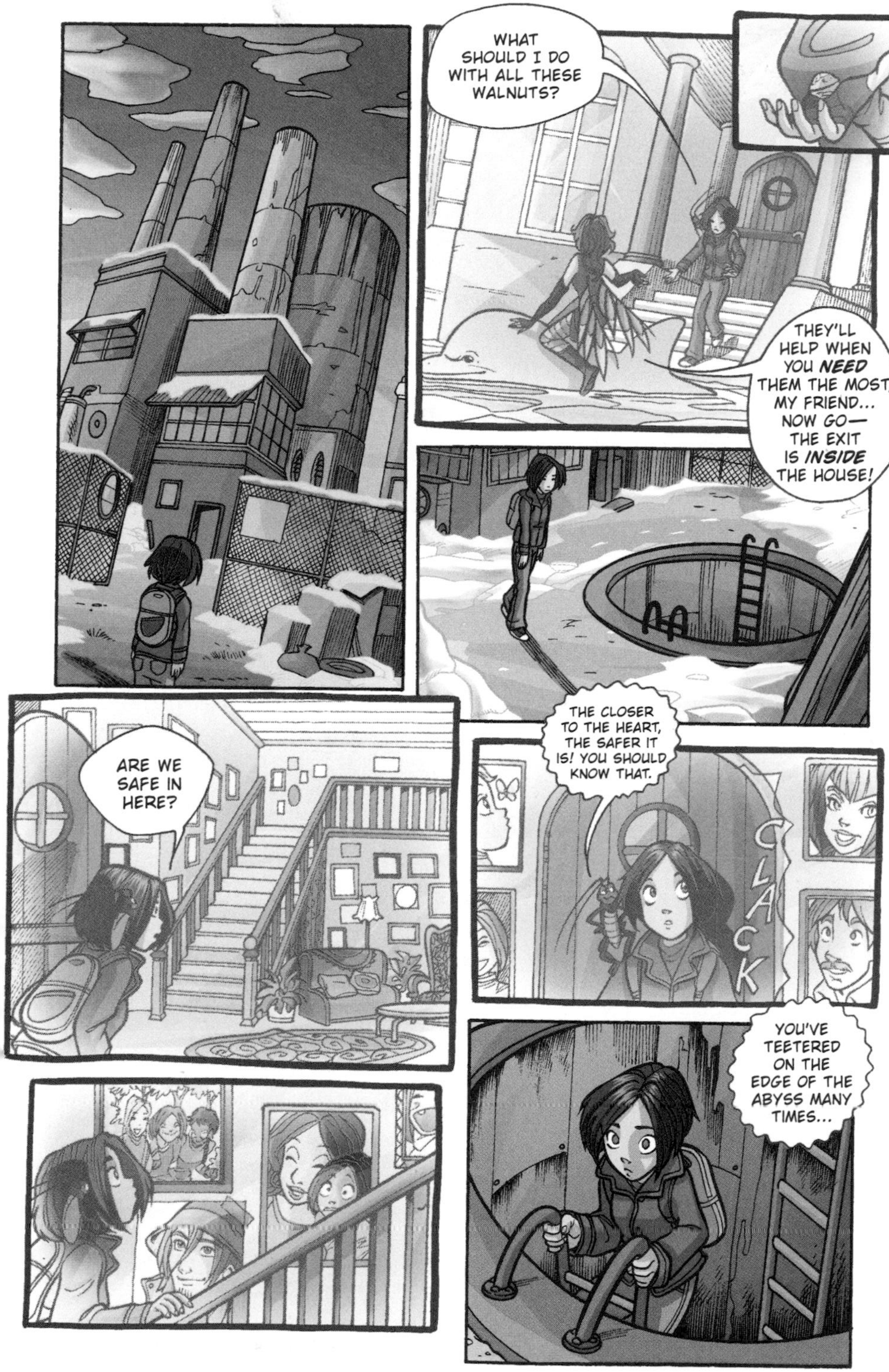
WHAT SHOULD I DO WITH ALL THESE WALNUTS?
THEY'LL HELP WHEN YOU **NEED** THEM THE MOST, MY FRIEND... NOW GO— THE EXIT IS ***INSIDE*** THE HOUSE!
ARE WE SAFE IN HERE?
THE CLOSER TO THE HEART, THE SAFER IT IS! YOU SHOULD KNOW THAT.
CLACK
YOU'VE TEETERED ON THE EDGE OF THE ABYSS MANY TIMES...

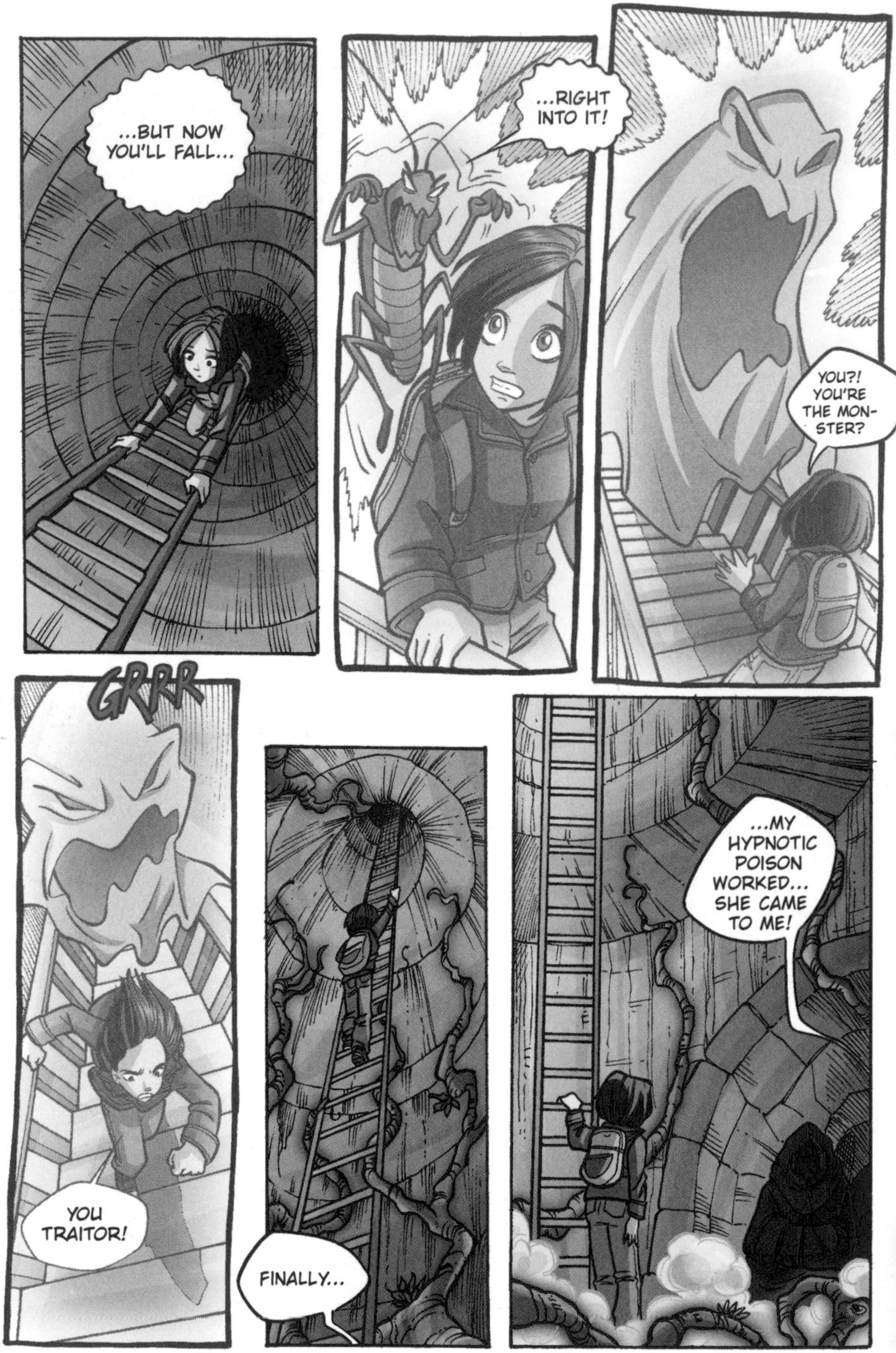
...BUT NOW YOU'LL FALL...
...RIGHT INTO IT!
YOU?! YOU'RE THE MON-STER?
GRRR
YOU TRAITOR!
FINALLY...
...MY HYPNOTIC POISON WORKED... SHE CAME TO ME!

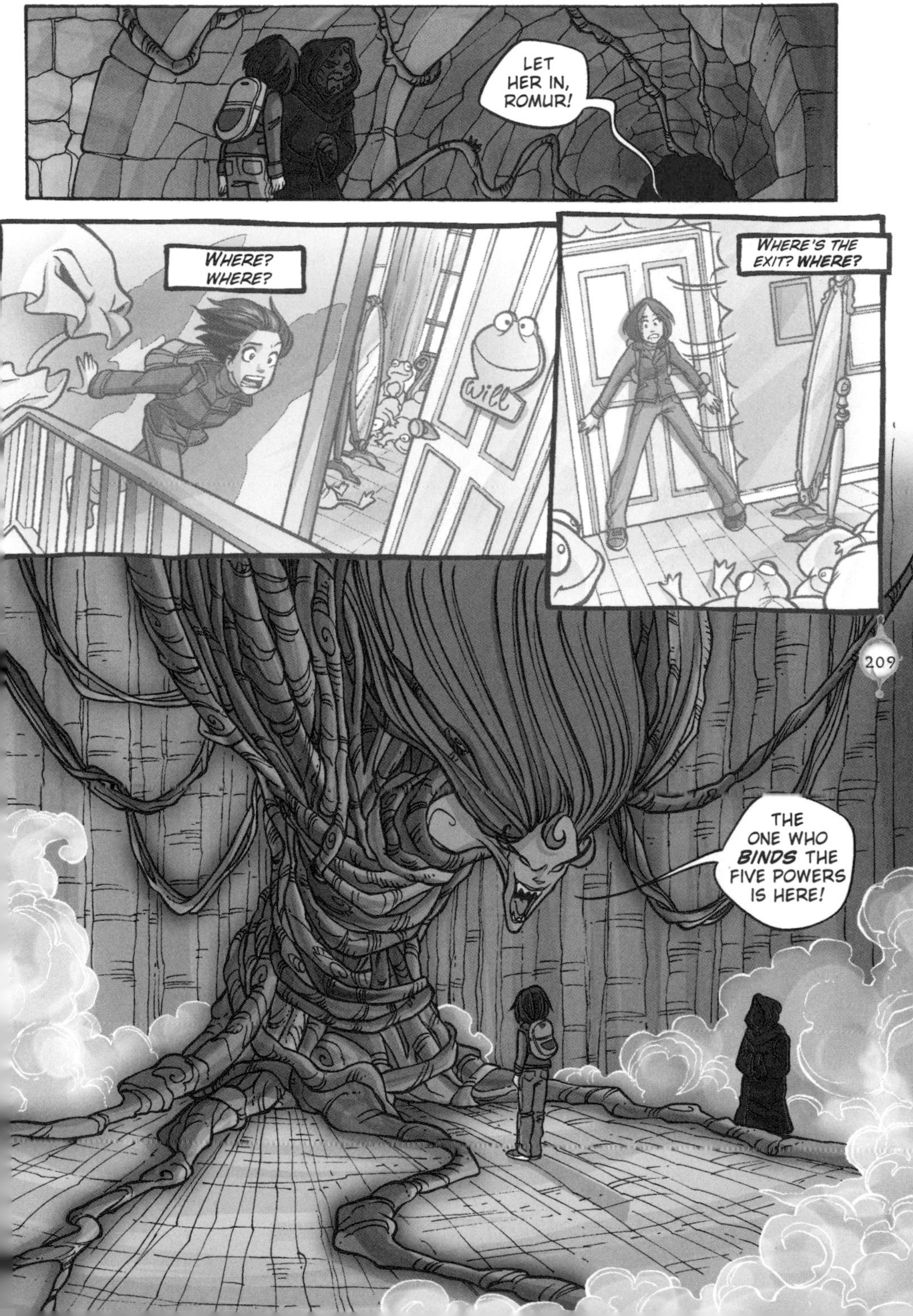
LET HER IN, ROMUR!
WHERE? WHERE?
WILL
WHERE'S THE EXIT? WHERE?
THE ONE WHO BINDS THE FIVE POWERS IS HERE!

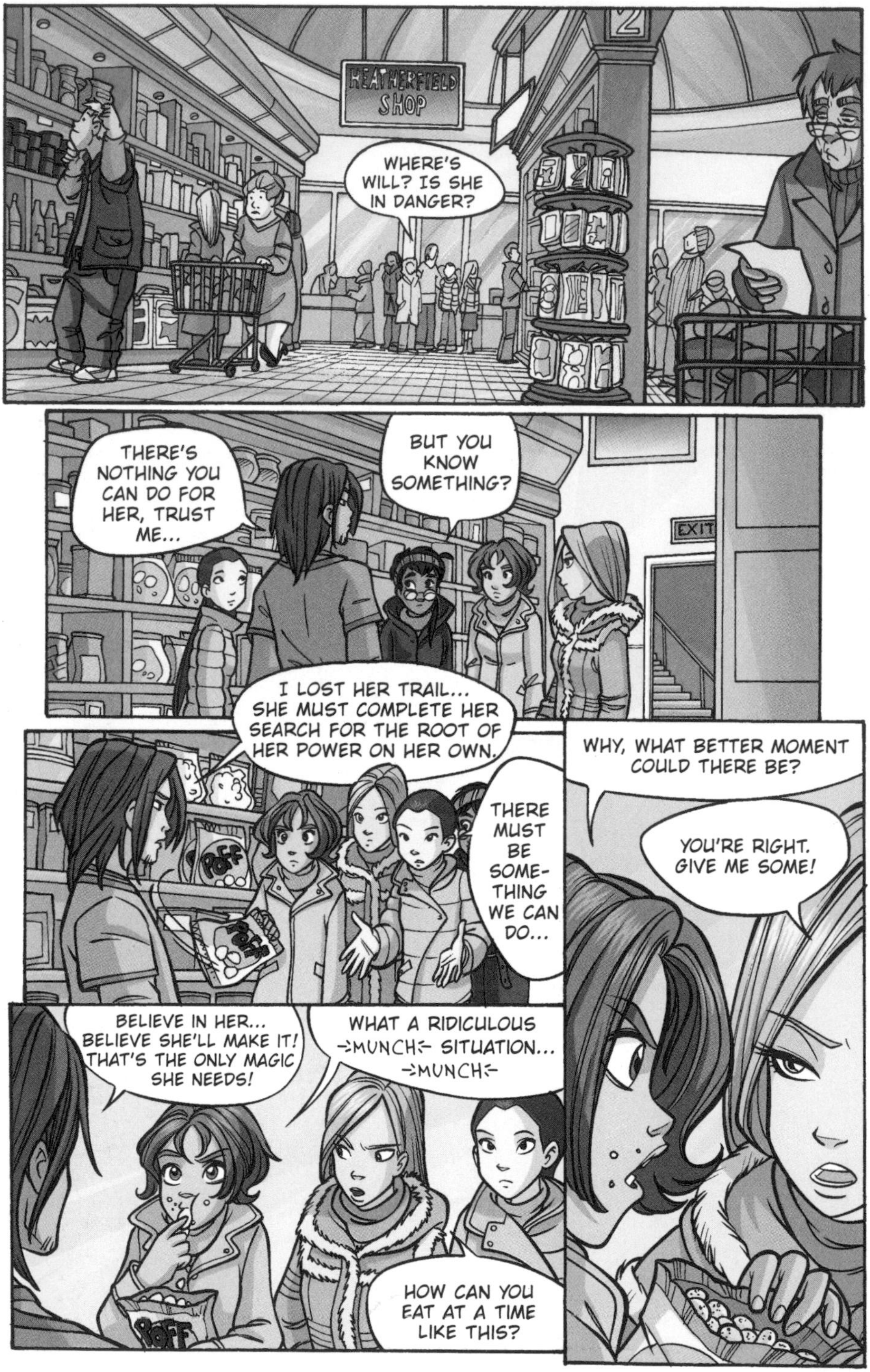
HEATHERFIELD SHOP
WHERE'S WILL? IS SHE IN DANGER?
THERE'S NOTHING YOU CAN DO FOR HER, TRUST ME...
BUT YOU KNOW SOMETHING?
EXIT
I LOST HER TRAIL... SHE MUST COMPLETE HER SEARCH FOR THE ROOT OF HER POWER ON HER OWN.
THERE MUST BE SOME-THING WE CAN DO...
POFF
BELIEVE IN HER... BELIEVE SHE'LL MAKE IT! THAT'S THE ONLY MAGIC SHE NEEDS!
WHAT A RIDICULOUS -MUNCH- SITUATION... -MUNCH-
HOW CAN YOU EAT AT A TIME LIKE THIS?
WHY, WHAT BETTER MOMENT COULD THERE BE?
YOU'RE RIGHT. GIVE ME SOME!

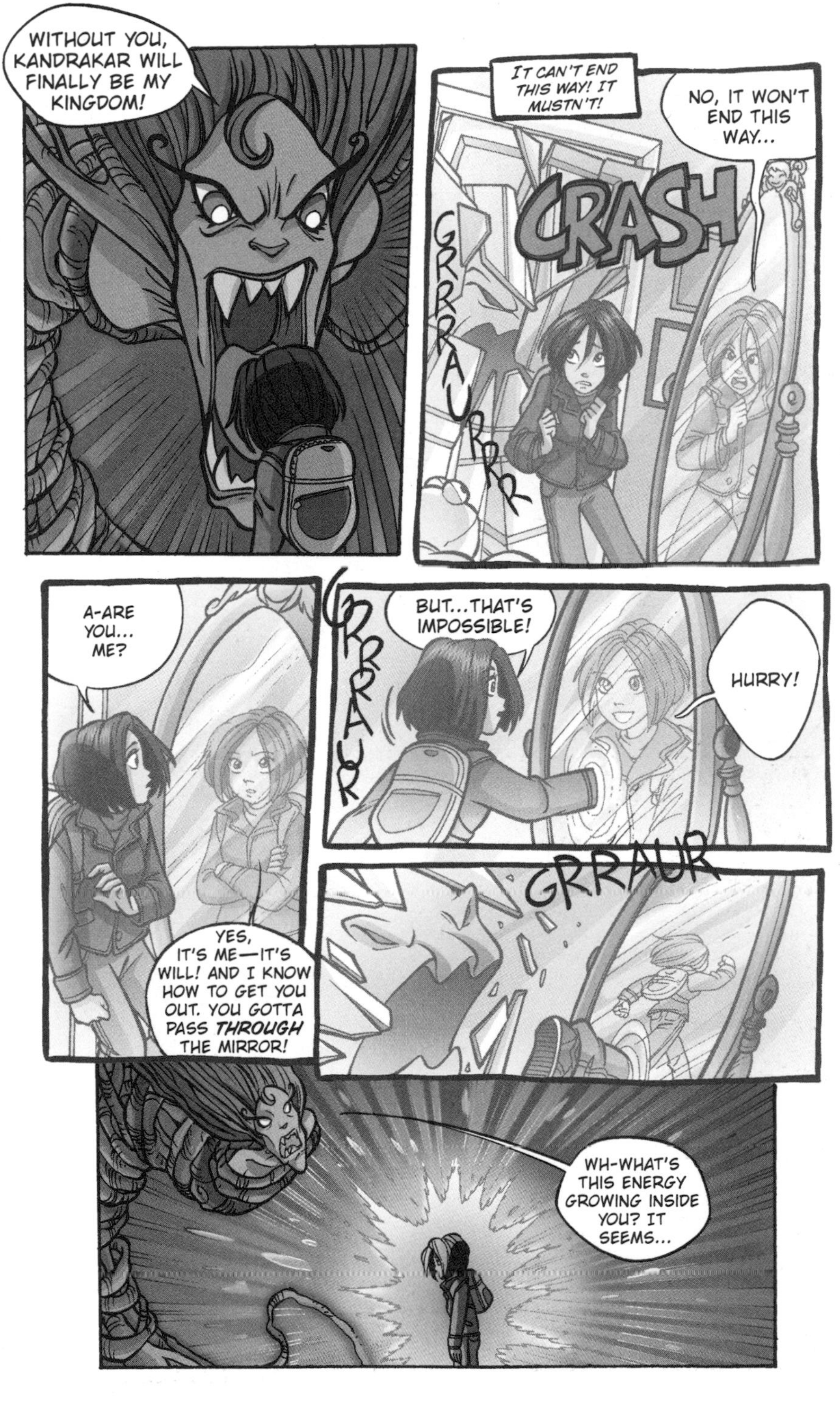
WITHOUT YOU, KANDRAKAR WILL FINALLY BE MY KINGDOM!
IT CAN'T END THIS WAY! IT MUSTN'T!
NO, IT WON'T END THIS WAY...
CRASH
GRRRAURRR
A-ARE YOU... ME?
GRRRAUR
BUT...THAT'S IMPOSSIBLE!
HURRY!
YES, IT'S ME—IT'S WILL! AND I KNOW HOW TO GET YOU OUT. YOU GOTTA PASS *THROUGH* THE MIRROR!
GRRAUR
WH-WHAT'S THIS ENERGY GROWING INSIDE YOU? IT SEEMS...

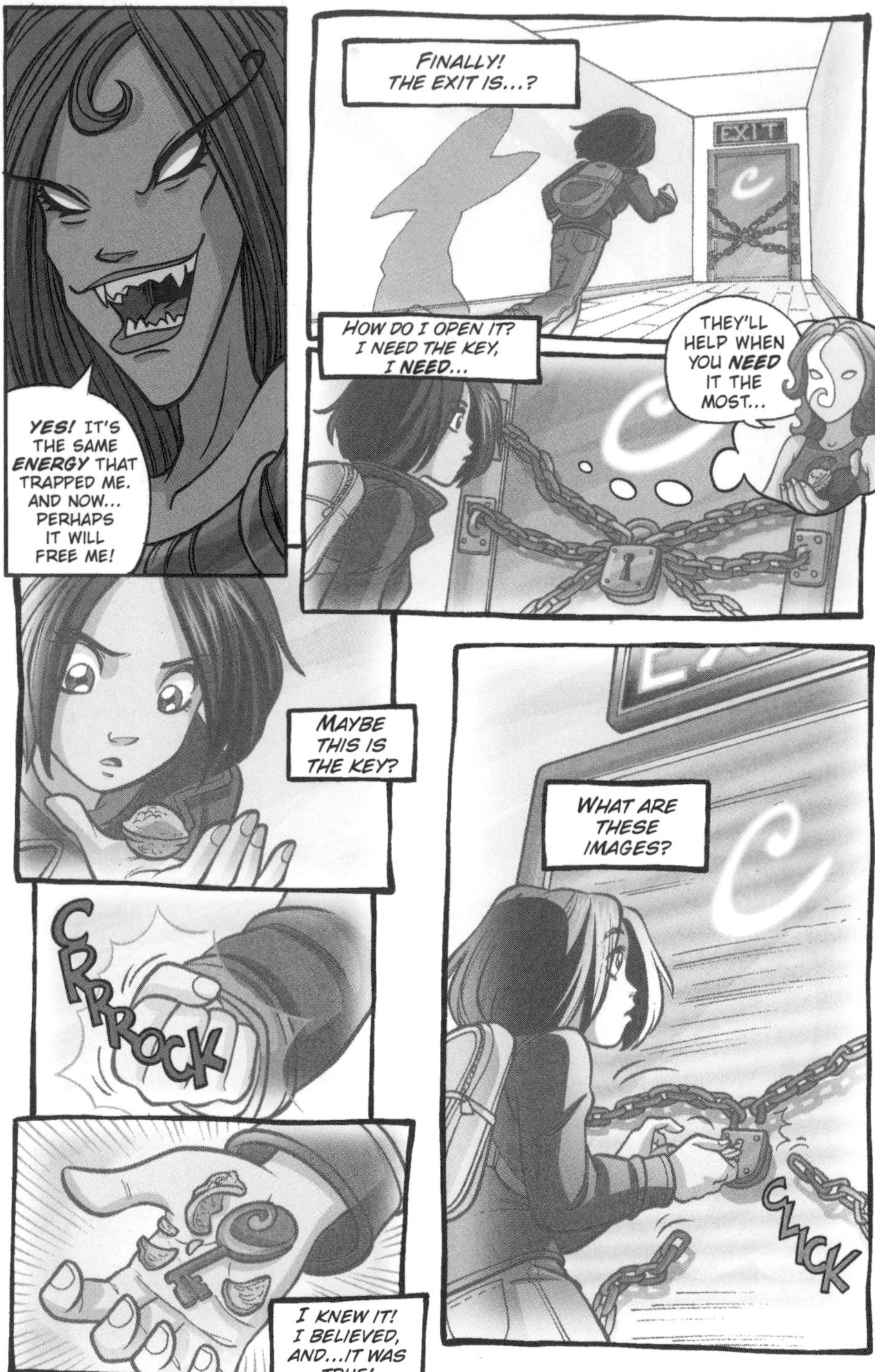

YES! IT'S THE SAME ENERGY THAT TRAPPED ME. AND NOW... PERHAPS IT WILL FREE ME!
FINALLY! THE EXIT IS...?
EXIT
HOW DO I OPEN IT? I NEED THE KEY, I NEED...
THEY'LL HELP WHEN YOU NEED IT THE MOST...
MAYBE THIS IS THE KEY?
CRRROCK
I KNEW IT! I BELIEVED, AND...IT WAS TRUE!
WHAT ARE THESE IMAGES?
CLICK

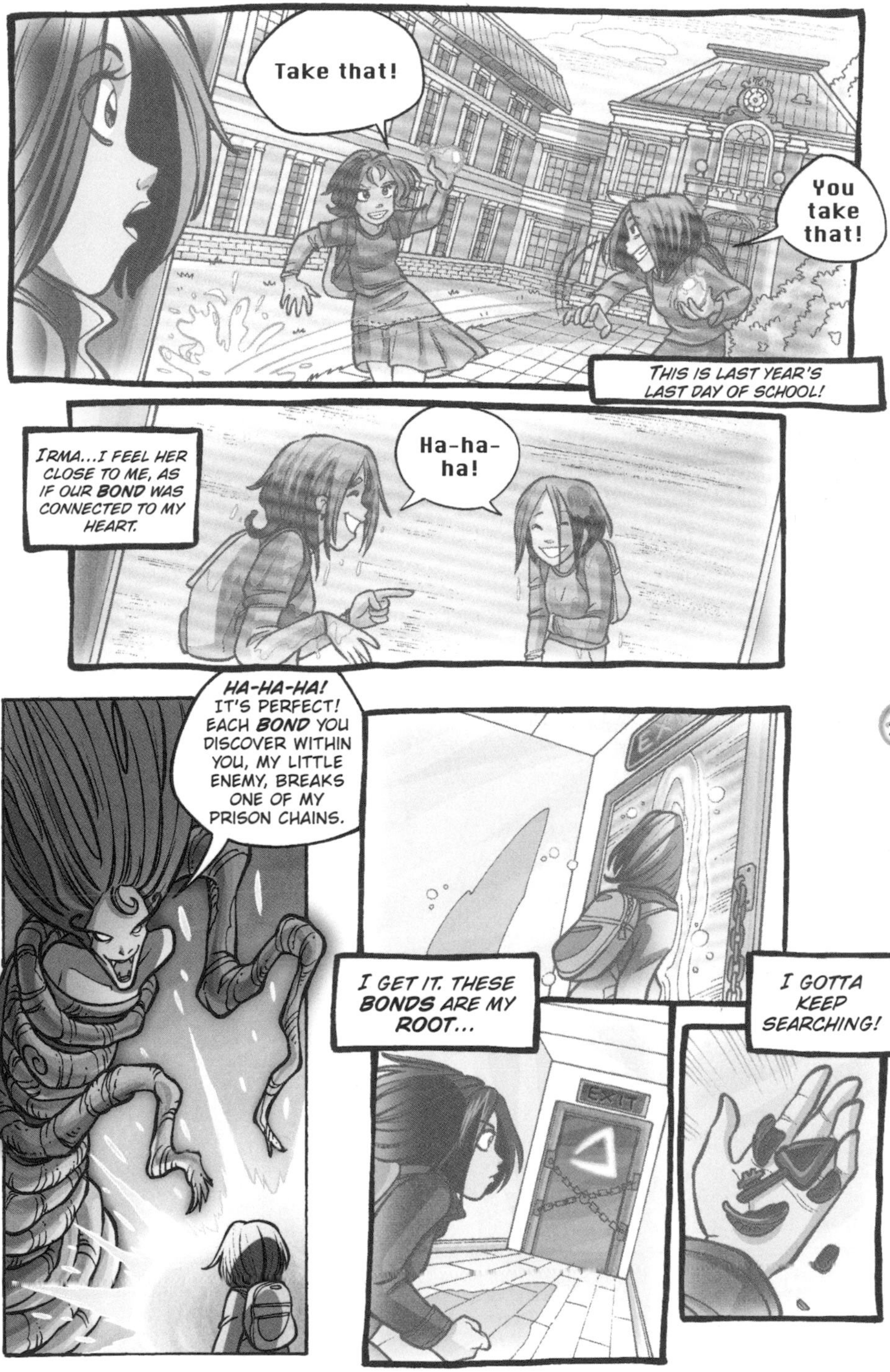
Take that!
You take that!
THIS IS LAST YEAR'S LAST DAY OF SCHOOL!
IRMA...I FEEL HER CLOSE TO ME, AS IF OUR BOND WAS CONNECTED TO MY HEART.
Ha-ha-ha!
HA-HA-HA! IT'S PERFECT! EACH BOND YOU DISCOVER WITHIN YOU, MY LITTLE ENEMY, BREAKS ONE OF MY PRISON CHAINS.
I GET IT. THESE BONDS ARE MY ROOT...
EXIT
I GOTTA KEEP SEARCHING!

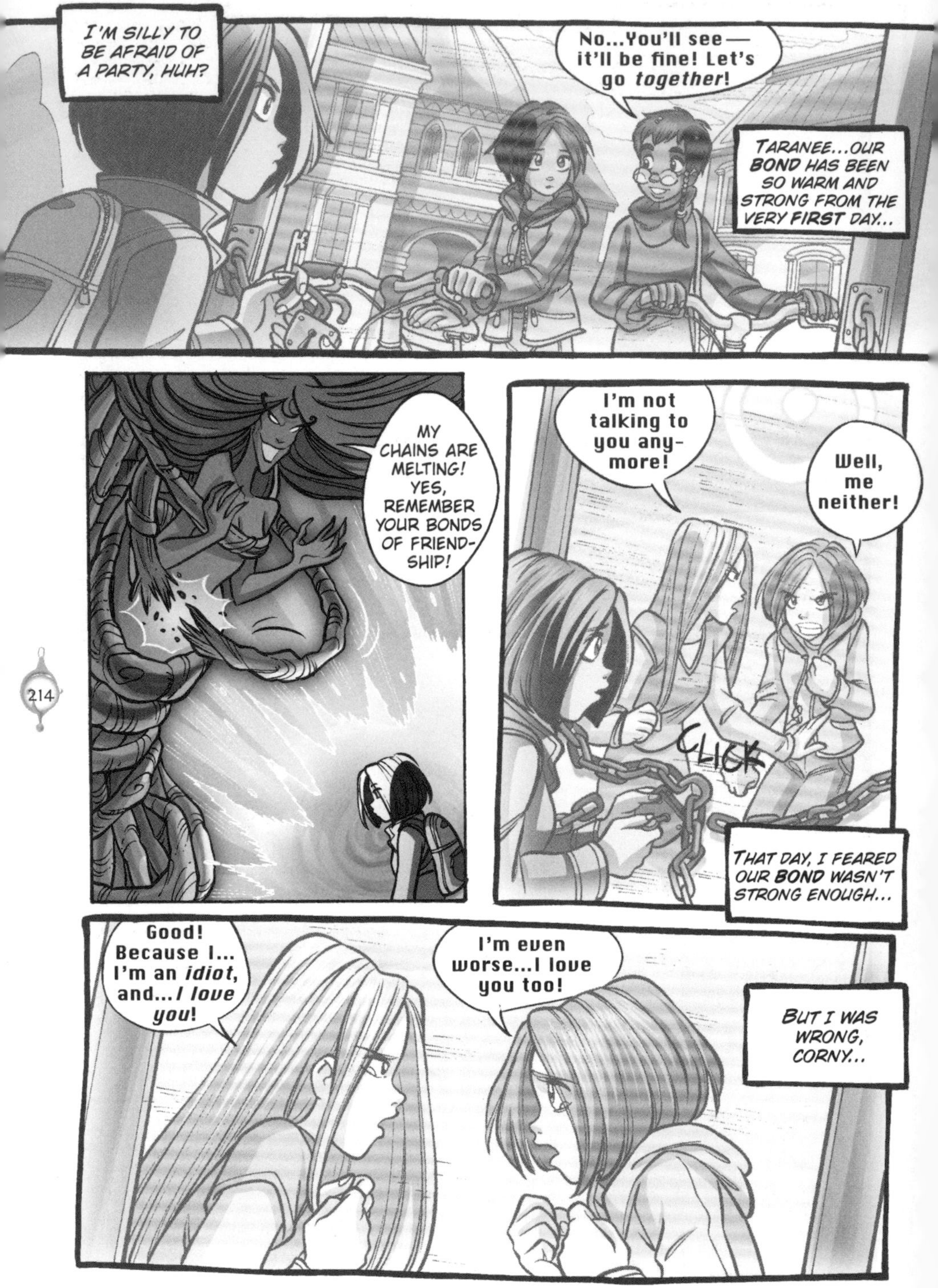
I'M SILLY TO BE AFRAID OF A PARTY, HUH?
No...You'll see— it'll be fine! Let's go *together*!
TARANEE...OUR **BOND** HAS BEEN SO WARM AND STRONG FROM THE VERY **FIRST** DAY...
MY CHAINS ARE MELTING! YES, REMEMBER YOUR BONDS OF FRIEND-SHIP!
I'm not talking to you any-more!
Well, me neither!
CLICK
THAT DAY, I FEARED OUR **BOND** WASN'T STRONG ENOUGH...
Good! Because I... I'm an *idiot*, and...*I love you*!
I'm even worse...I love you too!
BUT I WAS WRONG, CORNY...

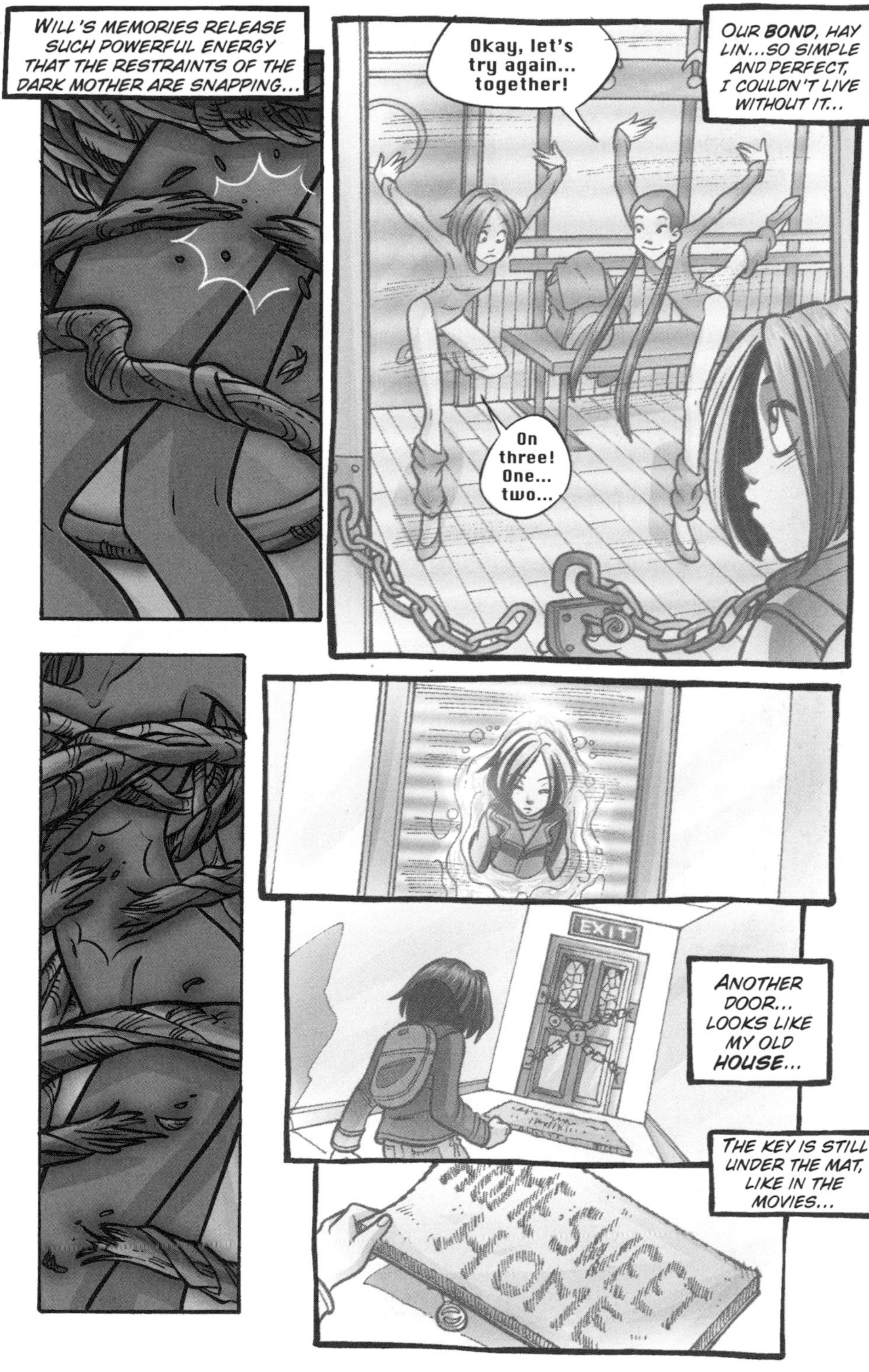
WILL'S MEMORIES RELEASE SUCH POWERFUL ENERGY THAT THE RESTRAINTS OF THE DARK MOTHER ARE SNAPPING...
Okay, let's try again... together!
OUR BOND, HAY LIN...SO SIMPLE AND PERFECT, I COULDN'T LIVE WITHOUT IT...
On three! One... two...
EXIT
ANOTHER DOOR... LOOKS LIKE MY OLD HOUSE...
THE KEY IS STILL UNDER THE MAT, LIKE IN THE MOVIES...

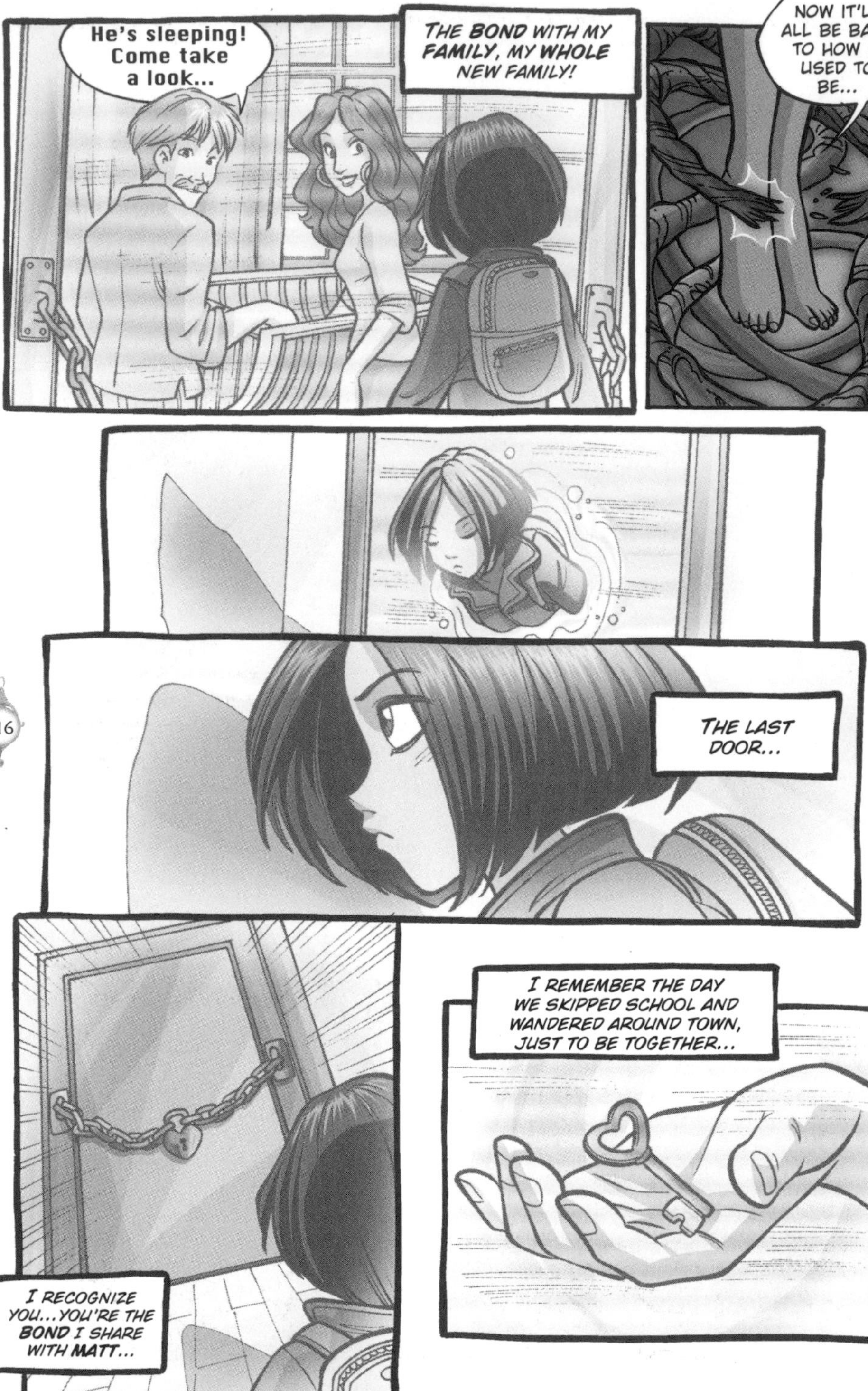
He's sleeping! Come take a look...
THE BOND WITH MY FAMILY, MY WHOLE NEW FAMILY!
NOW IT'LL ALL BE BACK TO HOW IT USED TO BE...
THE LAST DOOR...
I RECOGNIZE YOU...YOU'RE THE BOND I SHARE WITH MATT...
I REMEMBER THE DAY WE SKIPPED SCHOOL AND WANDERED AROUND TOWN, JUST TO BE TOGETHER...

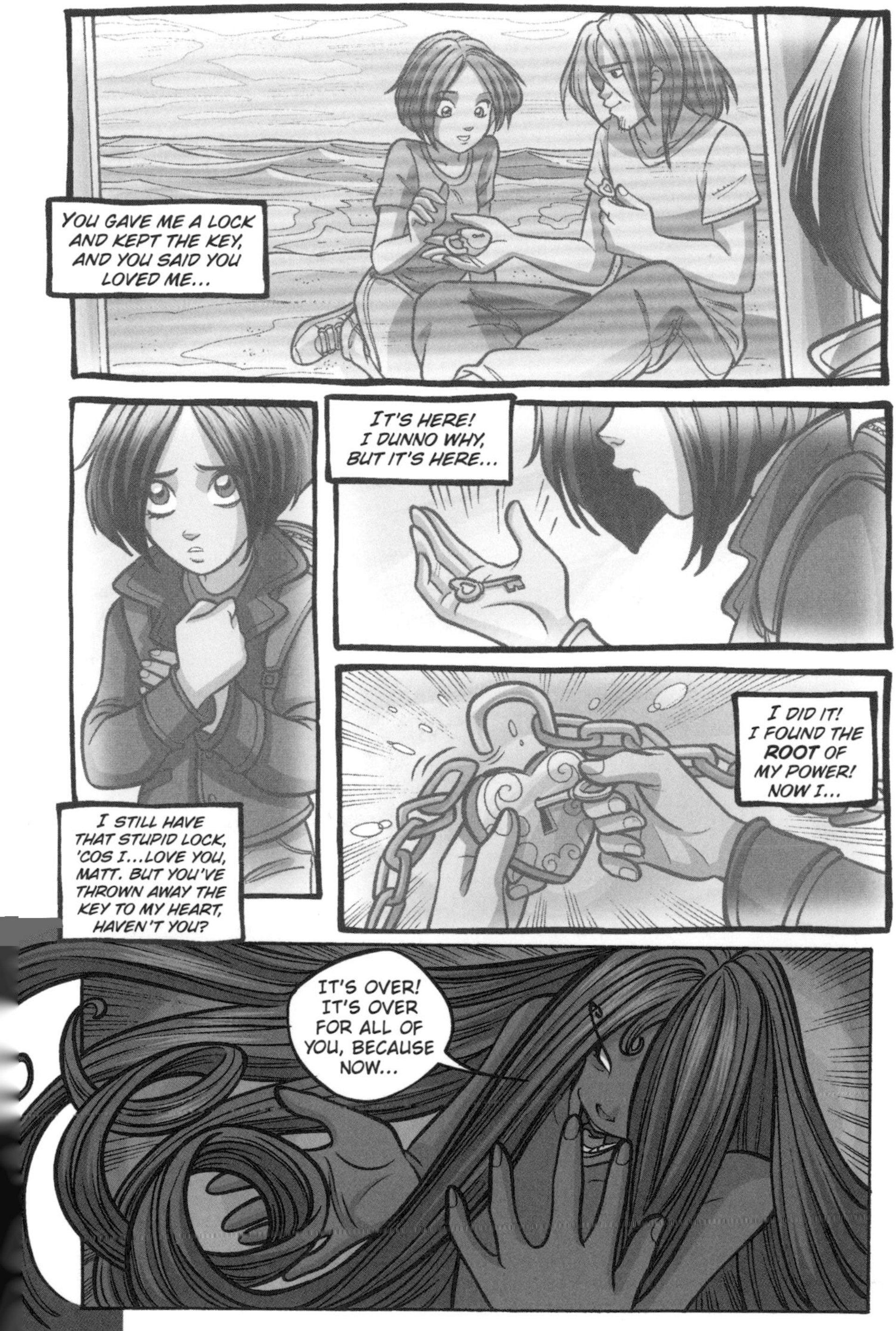
YOU GAVE ME A LOCK AND KEPT THE KEY, AND YOU SAID YOU LOVED ME...
IT'S HERE! I DUNNO WHY, BUT IT'S HERE...
I DID IT! I FOUND THE **ROOT** OF MY POWER! NOW I...
I STILL HAVE THAT STUPID LOCK, 'COS I...LOVE YOU, MATT. BUT YOU'VE THROWN AWAY THE KEY TO MY HEART, HAVEN'T YOU?
IT'S OVER! IT'S OVER FOR ALL OF YOU, BECAUSE NOW...

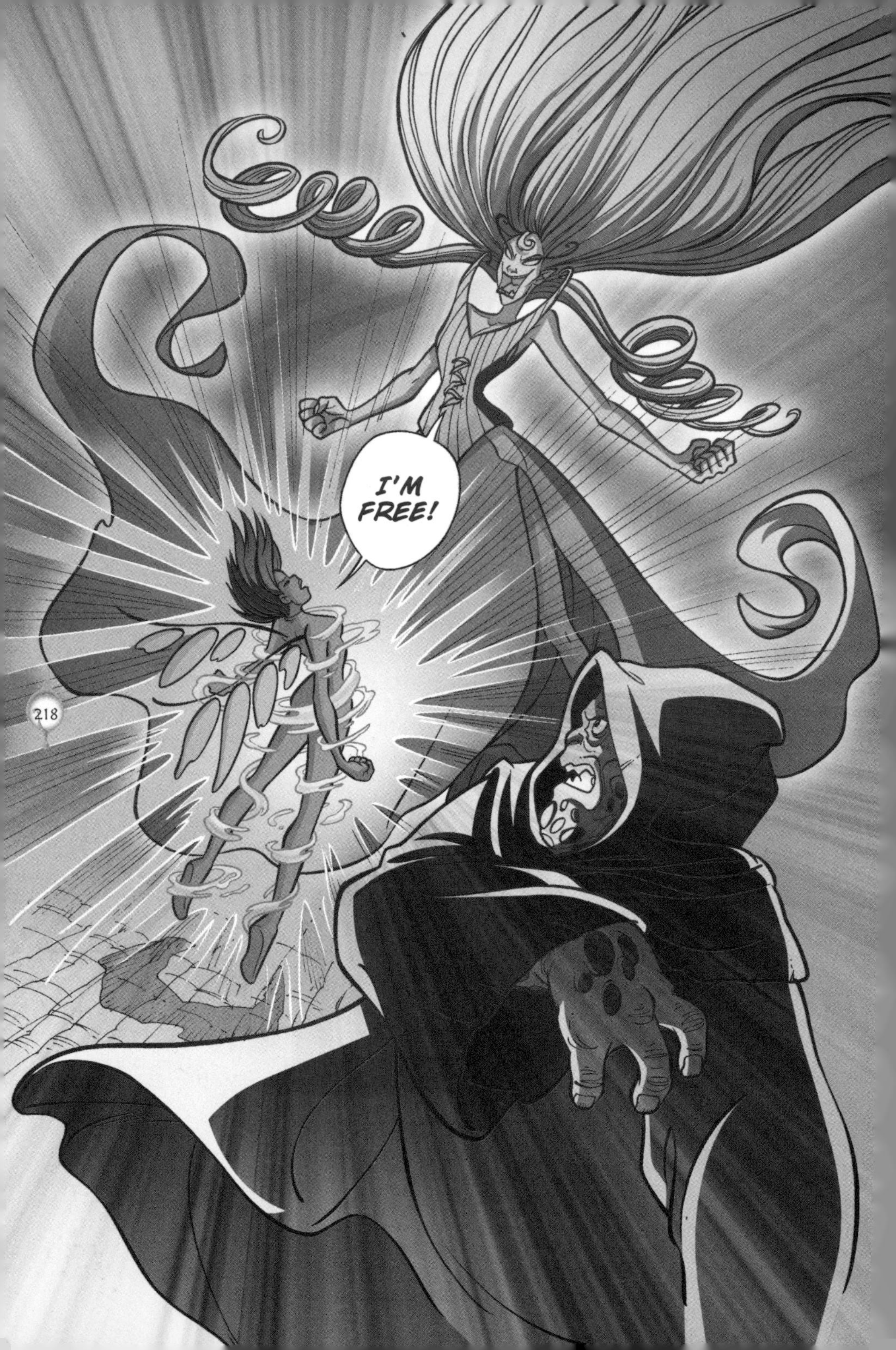
I'M FREE!

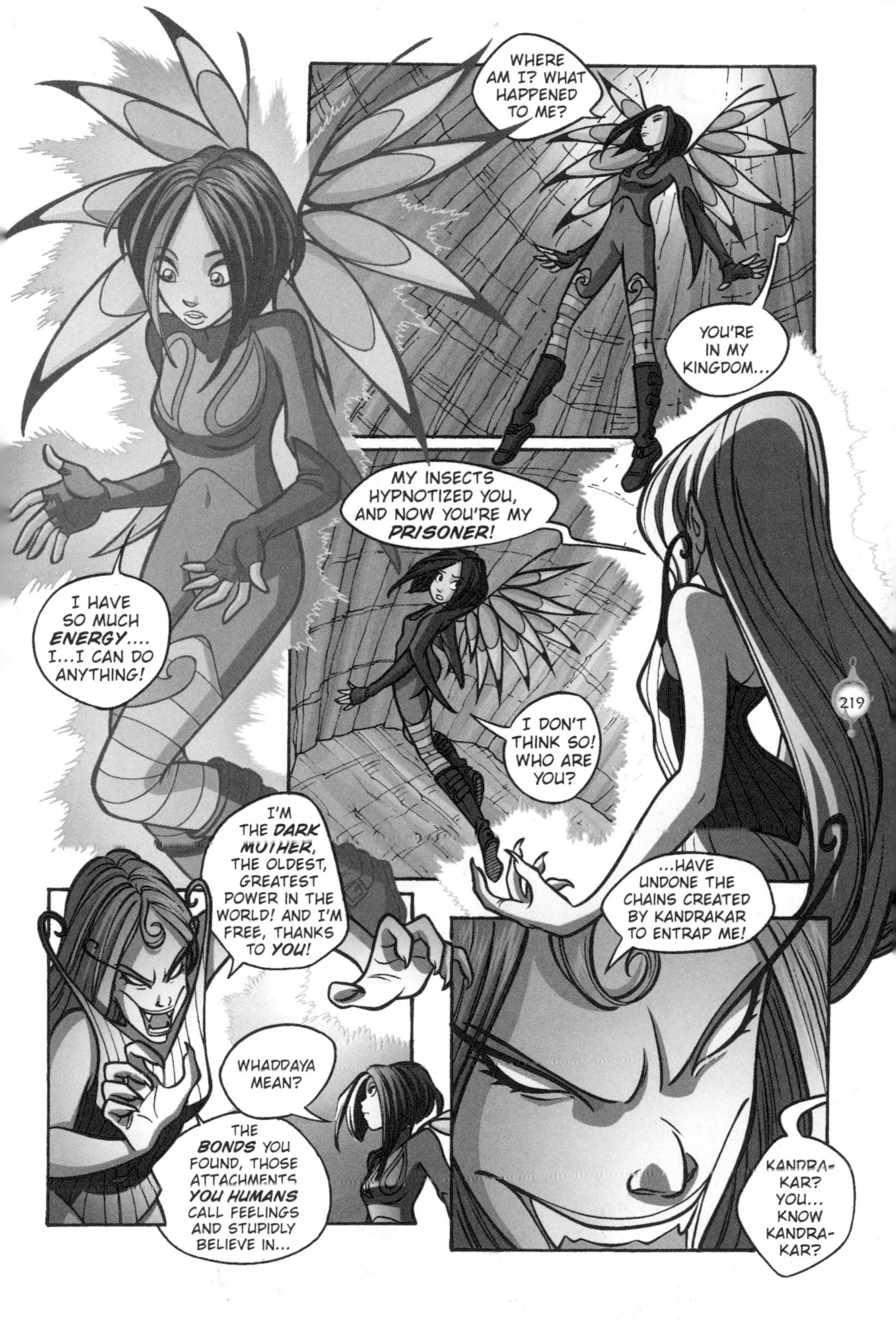
WHERE AM I? WHAT HAPPENED TO ME?
YOU'RE IN MY KINGDOM...
I HAVE SO MUCH ENERGY.... I...I CAN DO ANYTHING!
MY INSECTS HYPNOTIZED YOU, AND NOW YOU'RE MY PRISONER!
I DON'T THINK SO! WHO ARE YOU?
I'M THE DARK MUTHER, THE OLDEST, GREATEST POWER IN THE WORLD! AND I'M FREE, THANKS TO YOU!
WHADDAYA MEAN?
THE BONDS YOU FOUND, THOSE ATTACHMENTS YOU HUMANS CALL FEELINGS AND STUPIDLY BELIEVE IN...
...HAVE UNDONE THE CHAINS CREATED BY KANDRAKAR TO ENTRAP ME!
KANDRA-KAR? YOU... KNOW KANDRA-KAR?

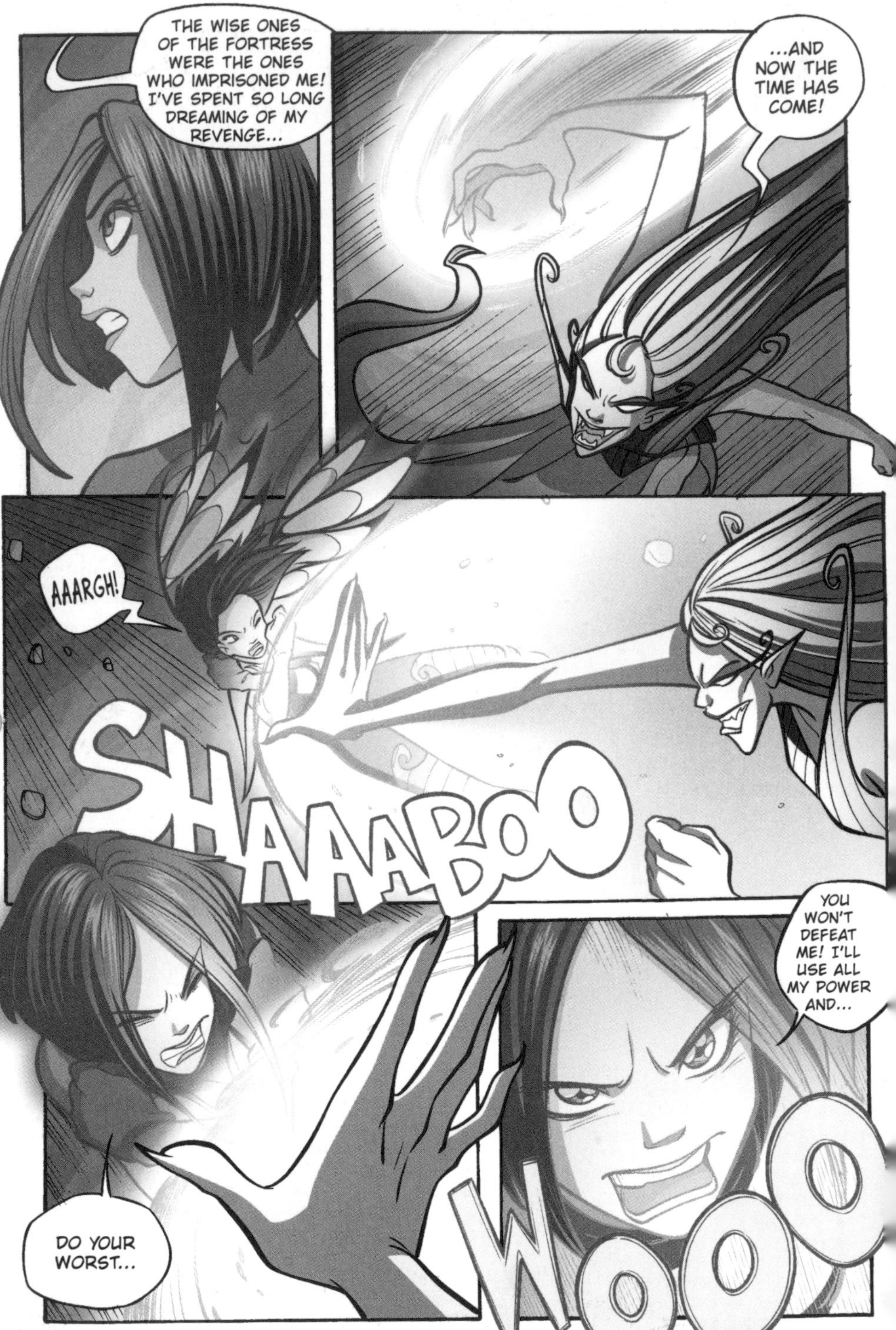

THE WISE ONES OF THE FORTRESS WERE THE ONES WHO IMPRISONED ME! I'VE SPENT SO LONG DREAMING OF MY REVENGE...
...AND NOW THE TIME HAS COME!
AAARGH!
SHAAABOO
YOU WON'T DEFEAT ME! I'LL USE ALL MY POWER AND...
DO YOUR WORST...
WOOOO

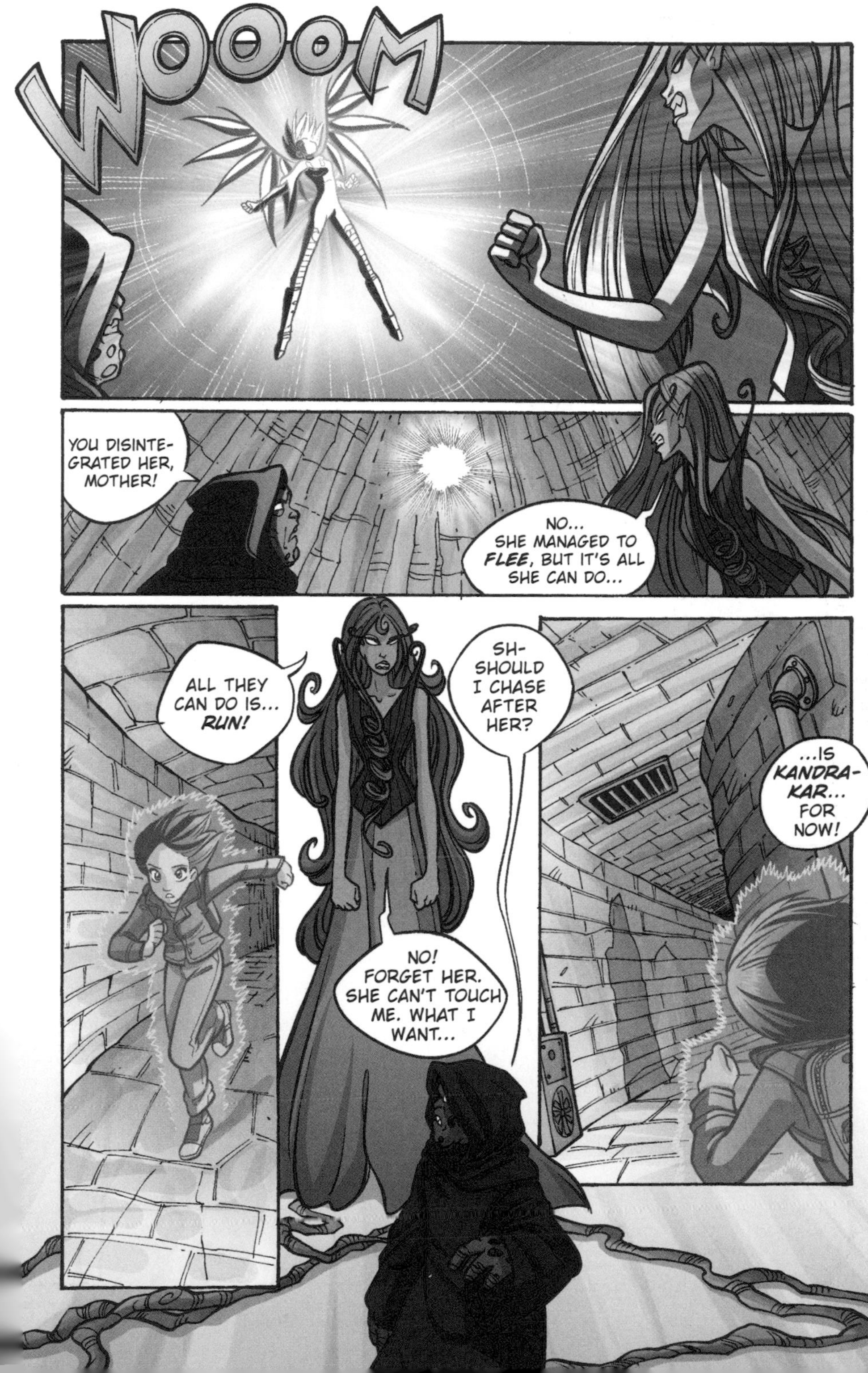
WOOOM
YOU DISINTE-GRATED HER, MOTHER!
NO... SHE MANAGED TO FLEE, BUT IT'S ALL SHE CAN DO...
ALL THEY CAN DO IS... RUN!
SH-SHOULD I CHASE AFTER HER?
NO! FORGET HER. SHE CAN'T TOUCH ME. WHAT I WANT...
...IS KANDRA-KAR... FOR NOW!

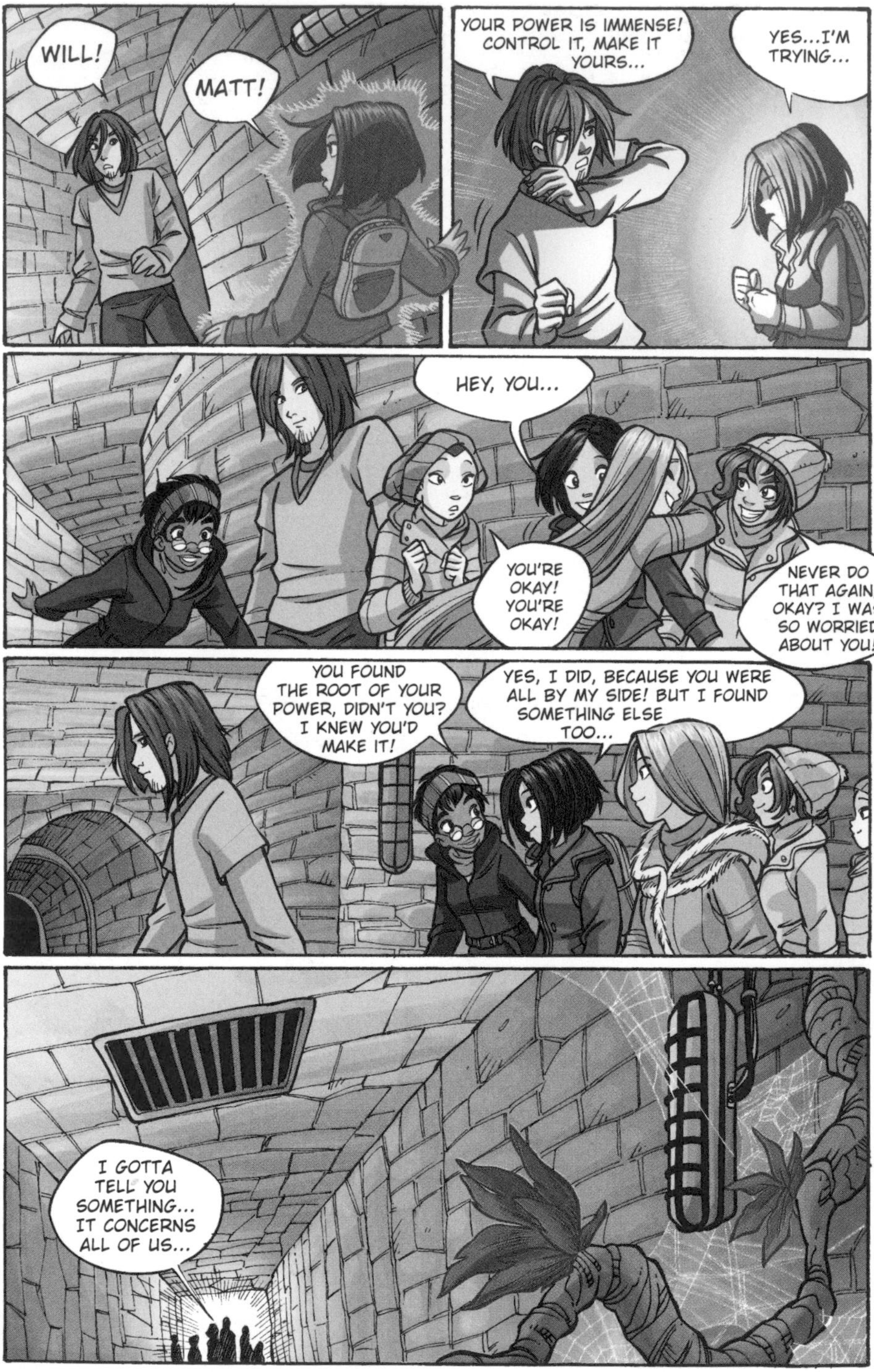
WILL!
MATT!
YOUR POWER IS IMMENSE! CONTROL IT, MAKE IT YOURS...
YES...I'M TRYING...
HEY, YOU...
YOU'RE OKAY! YOU'RE OKAY!
NEVER DO THAT AGAIN, OKAY? I WAS SO WORRIED ABOUT YOU!
YOU FOUND THE ROOT OF YOUR POWER, DIDN'T YOU? I KNEW YOU'D MAKE IT!
YES, I DID, BECAUSE YOU WERE ALL BY MY SIDE! BUT I FOUND SOMETHING ELSE TOO...
I GOTTA TELL YOU SOMETHING... IT CONCERNS ALL OF US...

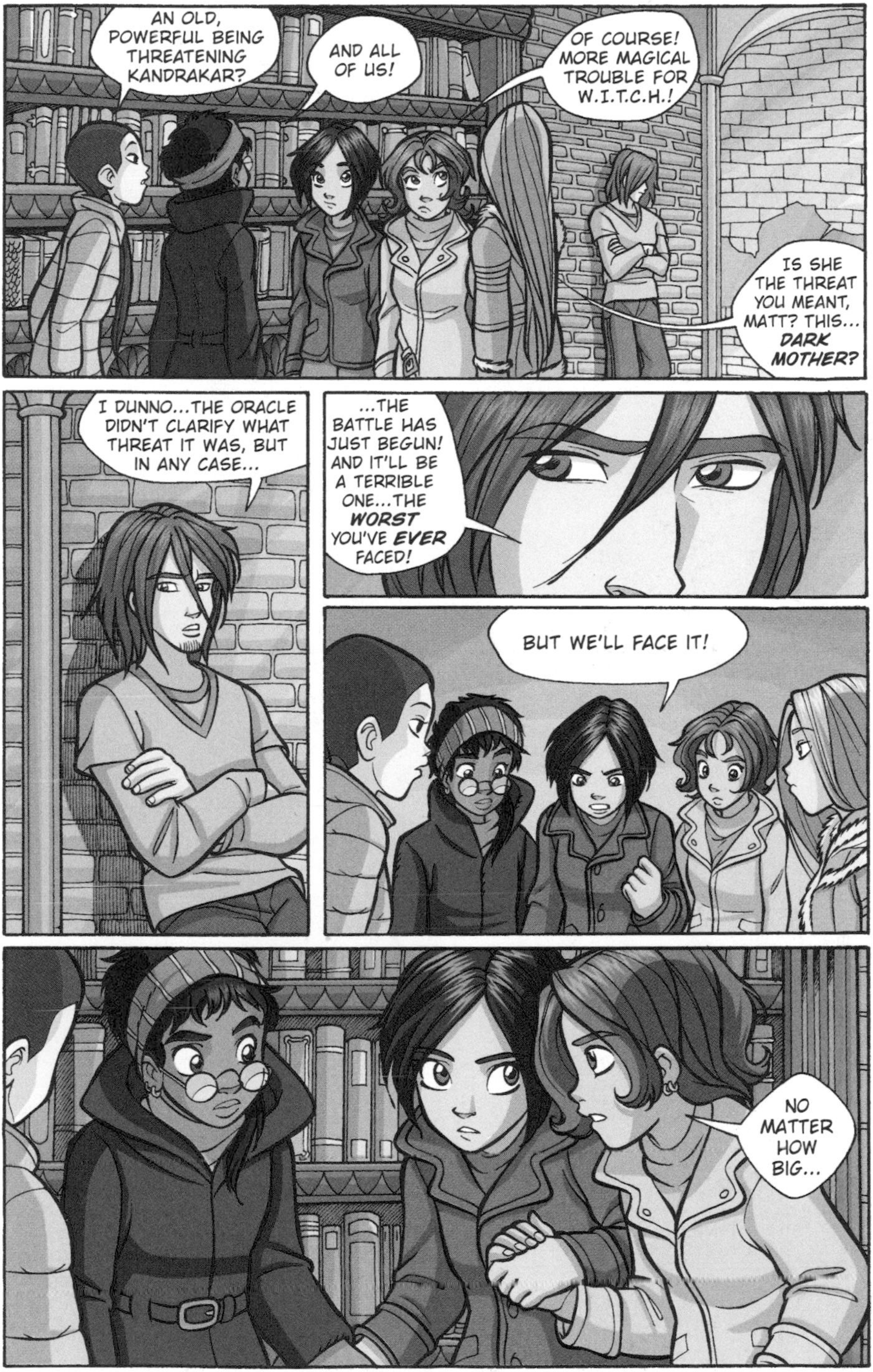
AN OLD, POWERFUL BEING THREATENING KANDRAKAR?
AND ALL OF US!
OF COURSE! MORE MAGICAL TROUBLE FOR W.I.T.C.H.!
IS SHE THE THREAT YOU MEANT, MATT? THIS... **DARK MOTHER?**
I DUNNO...THE ORACLE DIDN'T CLARIFY WHAT THREAT IT WAS, BUT IN ANY CASE...
...THE BATTLE HAS JUST BEGUN! AND IT'LL BE A TERRIBLE ONE...THE **WORST** YOU'VE **EVER** FACED!
BUT WE'LL FACE IT!
NO MATTER HOW BIG...

...HOW SCARY...

...HOW DANGER-OUS...

...WE WILL...

...FACE IT TOGETHER!

SPOKEN LIKE A TRUE LEADER! AS EXPECTED OF THE ONE WHO BRINGS YOUR POWERS TOGETHER...

YOUR SYMBOL, WILL...

BUT THAT'S...I DON'T BELIEVE IT. I DIDN'T THINK...

YOU...STILL HAVE THE KEY!

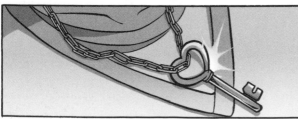

I DUNNO WHAT TO THINK... SHOULD I GET MAD, SCREAM, CRY, RUN AWAY...?

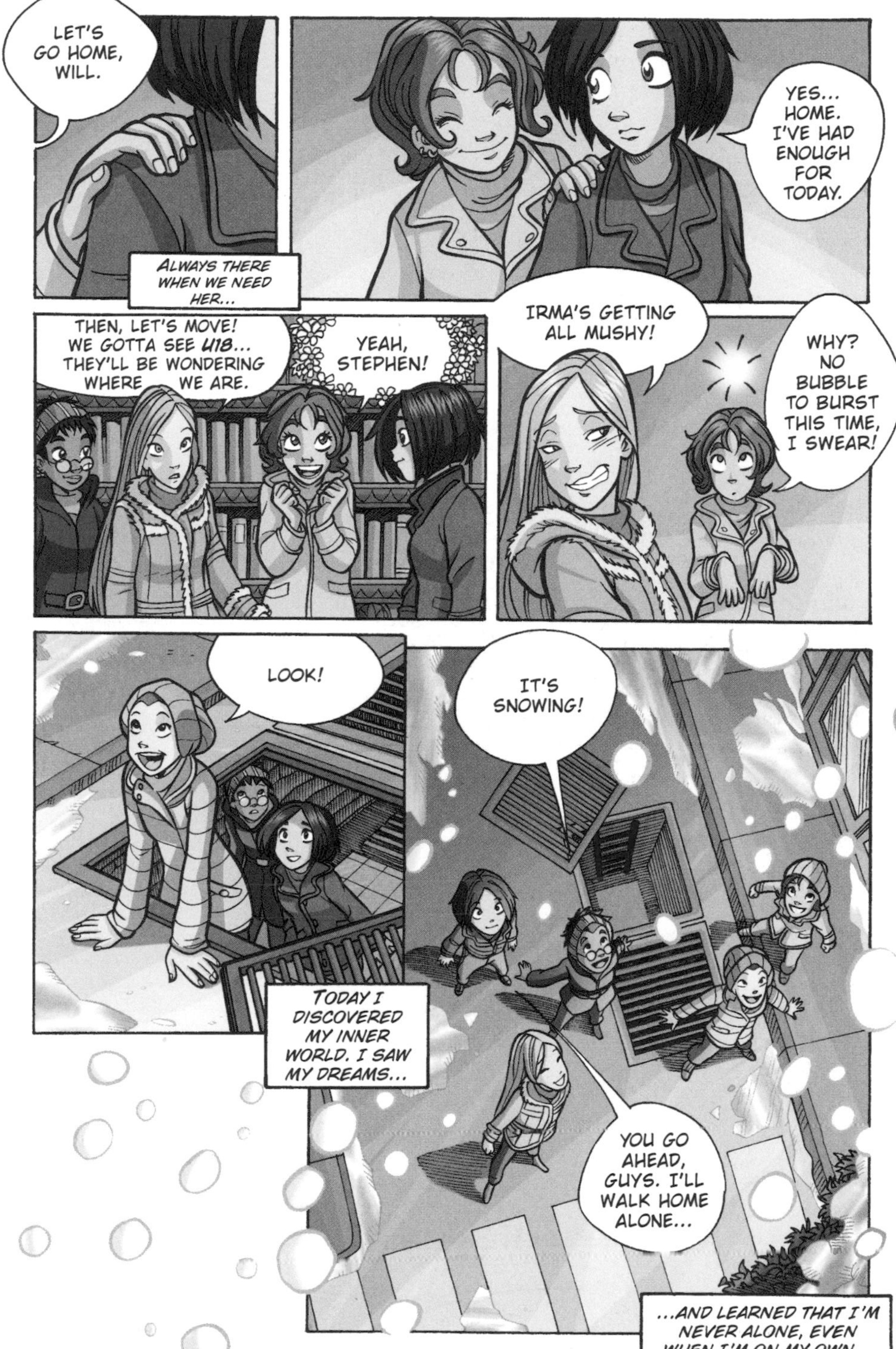
LET'S GO HOME, WILL.
YES... HOME. I'VE HAD ENOUGH FOR TODAY.
ALWAYS THERE WHEN WE NEED HER...
THEN, LET'S MOVE! WE GOTTA SEE U18... THEY'LL BE WONDERING WHERE WE ARE.
YEAH, STEPHEN!
IRMA'S GETTING ALL MUSHY!
WHY? NO BUBBLE TO BURST THIS TIME, I SWEAR!
LOOK!
IT'S SNOWING!
TODAY I DISCOVERED MY INNER WORLD. I SAW MY DREAMS...
YOU GO AHEAD, GUYS. I'LL WALK HOME ALONE...
...AND LEARNED THAT I'M NEVER ALONE, EVEN WHEN I'M ON MY OWN...

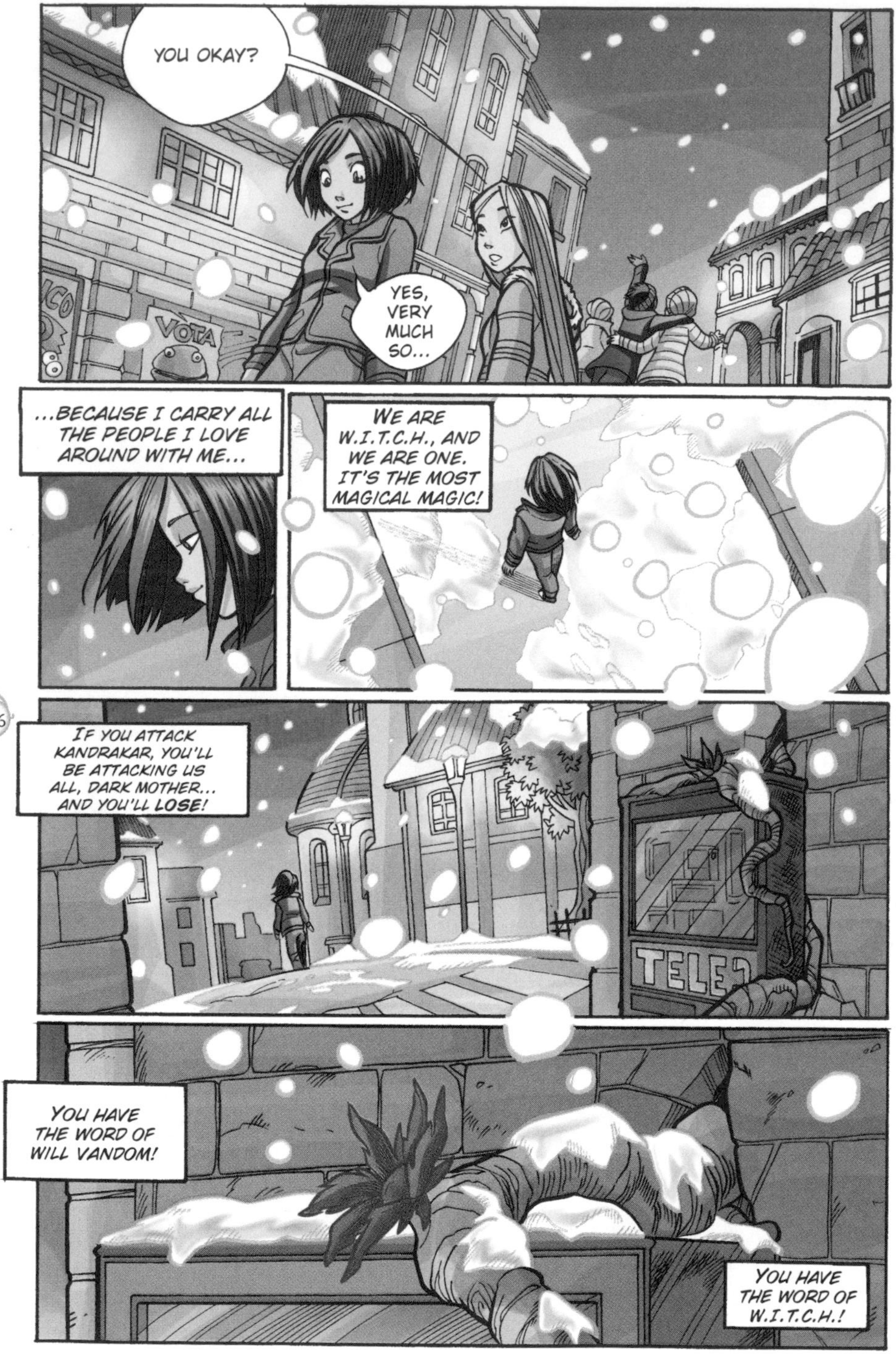
YOU OKAY?
YES, VERY MUCH SO...
...BECAUSE I CARRY ALL THE PEOPLE I LOVE AROUND WITH ME...
WE ARE W.I.T.C.H., AND WE ARE ONE. IT'S THE MOST MAGICAL MAGIC!
IF YOU ATTACK KANDRAKAR, YOU'LL BE ATTACKING US ALL, DARK MOTHER... AND YOU'LL LOSE!
YOU HAVE THE WORD OF WILL VANDOM!
YOU HAVE THE WORD OF W.I.T.C.H.!
VOTA
TELE

THE END

W.i.t.c.h.

Will Irma Taranee Cornelia Hay Lin

Read on in Volume 22!

Everything you need to know about Irma's family!

# Irma's family

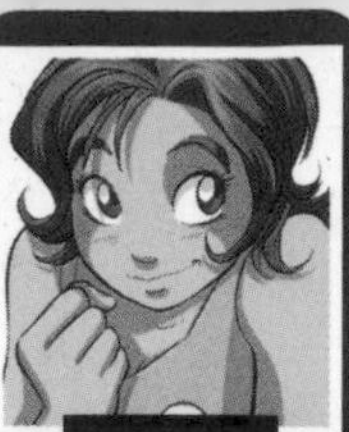

## Irma

Irma's gonna introduce you to her family… detective-style! She collected "evidence" of important events and profiled her family!

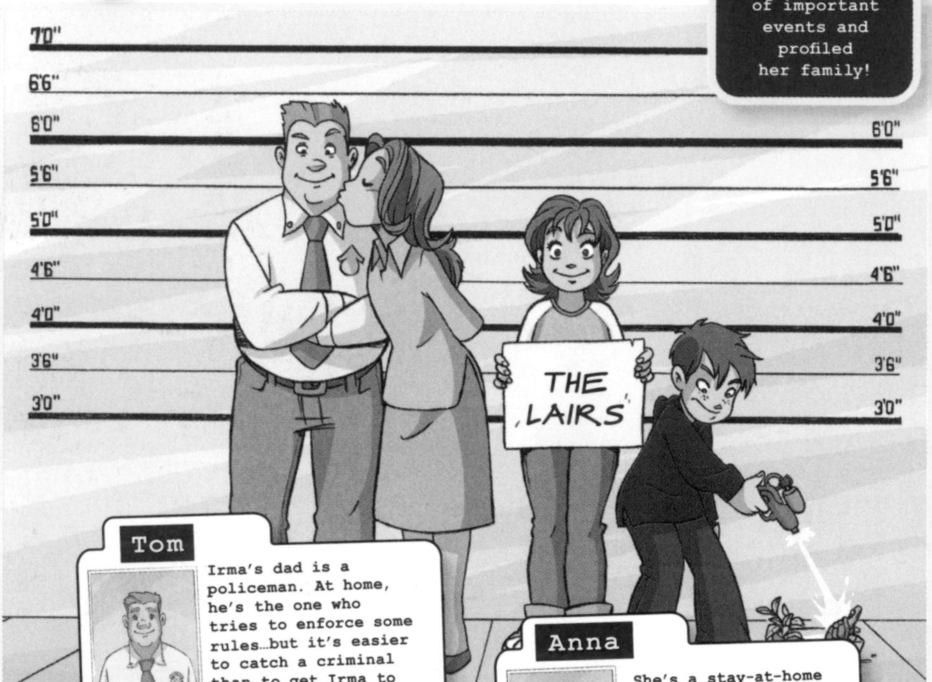

7'0"
6'6"
6'0"
5'6"
5'0"
4'6"
4'0"
3'6"
3'0"
THE LAIRS


## Tom

Irma's dad is a policeman. At home, he's the one who tries to enforce some rules…but it's easier to catch a criminal than to get Irma to turn down the music! Anyway, Tom is a sweet, caring, and fun dad!

Code name: Daddy, but he prefers Boss!

## Anna

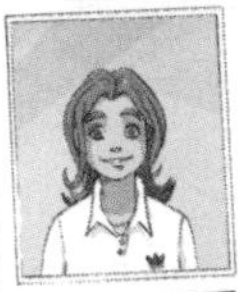

She's a stay-at-home mom, a great cook specializing in apple pies, and a super-patient woman always ready to listen to her beloved kids! In her free time, she likes reading crime novels.

Code name: Mom, a.k.a. "the good cop"!

## Christopher

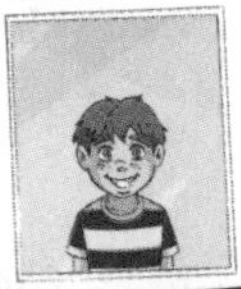

Quick and smart, Irma's little brother loves pranking his sister! Despite this, Irma often helps him with homework and cleaning up his room, full of toys and comic books!

Code name: Little Monster

## Lettuce

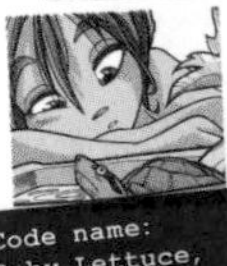

Irma's turtle might prefer to live in a quieter family! Once, looking for some peace, it hid under the washing machine, and the Lairs mobilized the whole police force looking for it!

Code name: Baby Lettuce, Little One

POLICE DEPARTMENT

The Lair family life may seem quiet and peaceful, but there are often funny moments and curious conversations! They laugh a lot, they help each other, and even if it looks chaotic, they have rules that everyone sticks to!

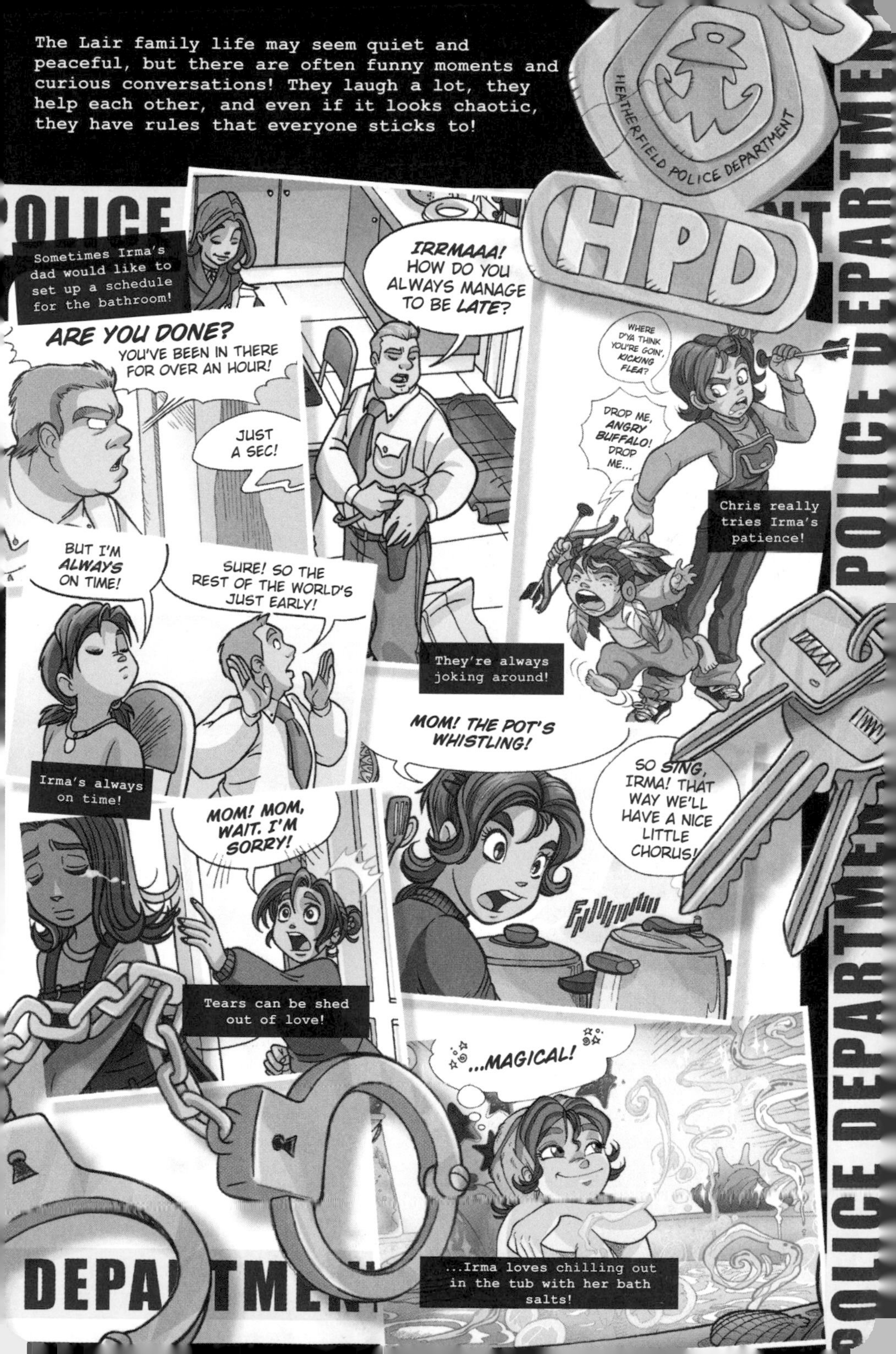
HEATHERFIELD POLICE DEPARTMENT
HPD
POLICE
DEPARTMENT
Sometimes Irma's dad would like to set up a schedule for the bathroom!
ARE YOU DONE? YOU'VE BEEN IN THERE FOR OVER AN HOUR!
JUST A SEC!
IRRMAAA! HOW DO YOU ALWAYS MANAGE TO BE LATE?
BUT I'M ALWAYS ON TIME!
SURE! SO THE REST OF THE WORLD'S JUST EARLY!
Irma's always on time!
They're always joking around!
WHERE D'YA THINK YOU'RE GOIN', KICKING FLEA?
DROP ME, ANGRY BUFFALO! DROP ME...
Chris really tries Irma's patience!
MOM! THE POT'S WHISTLING!
SO SING, IRMA! THAT WAY WE'LL HAVE A NICE LITTLE CHORUS!
MOM! MOM, WAIT. I'M SORRY!
Tears can be shed out of love!
...MAGICAL!
...Irma loves chilling out in the tub with her bath salts!

# Hay Lin's family

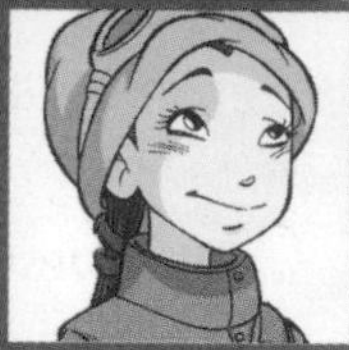

### Hay Lin

Hay Lin's gonna introduce you to her family with a bunch of photos snapped in their Chinese restaurant, the Silver Dragon, a beautiful, stylish place where the Lins spend most of their time.

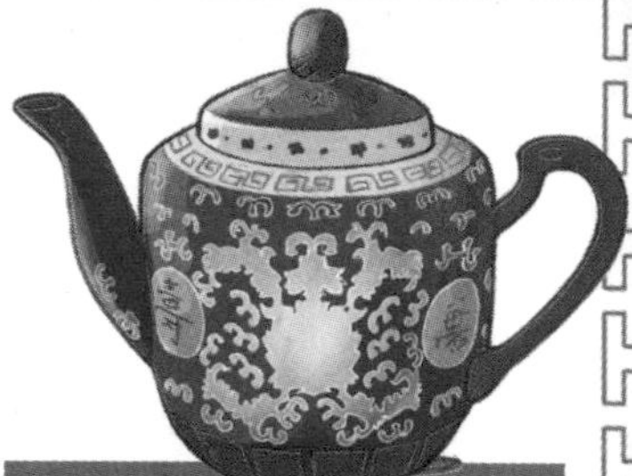

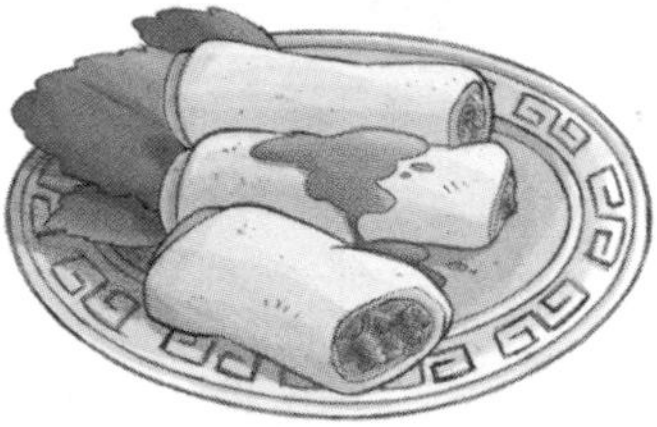

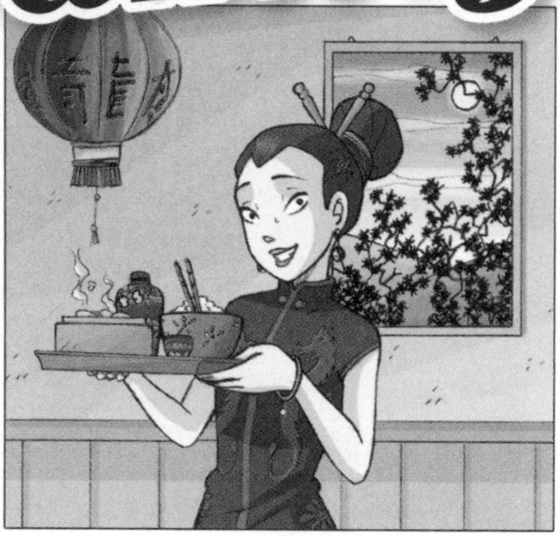

### Joan Lin

Hay Lin's mom is a practical woman, sweet and graceful. She works hard at the restaurant and at home, but she always finds the time to tell Hay Lin beautiful stories!

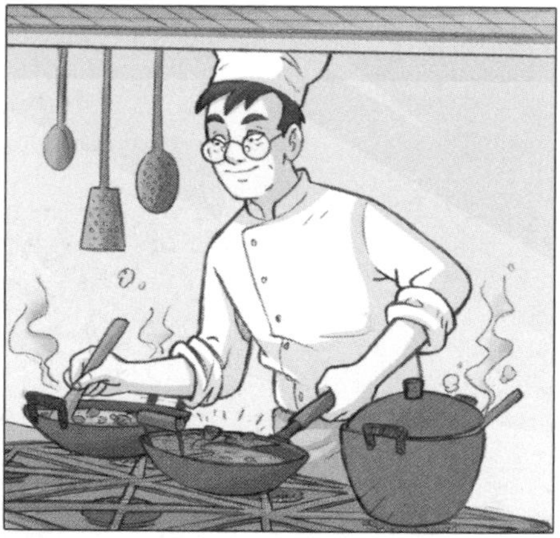

### Chen Lin

He's Yan Lin's son and the owner of the family restaurant. He's the chef, creating tons of delicious dishes!

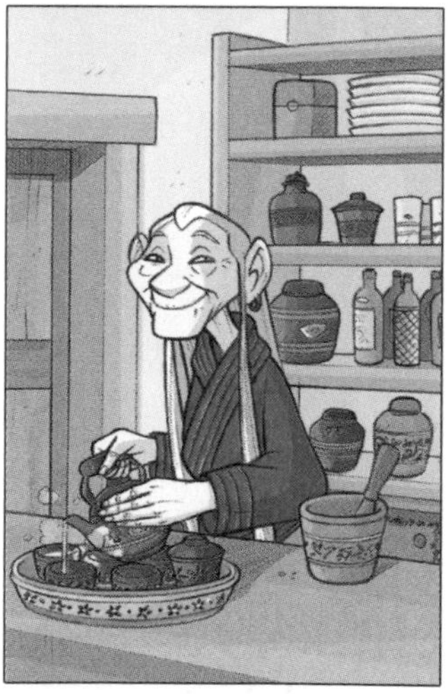

### Yan Lin

She's the wisest, most magical, and most understanding grandma in the world, and she adores her granddaughter! Yan Lin now lives in Kandrakar, where she is the Oracle's adviser.

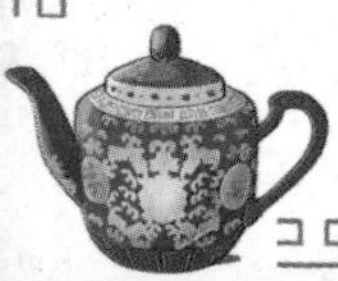

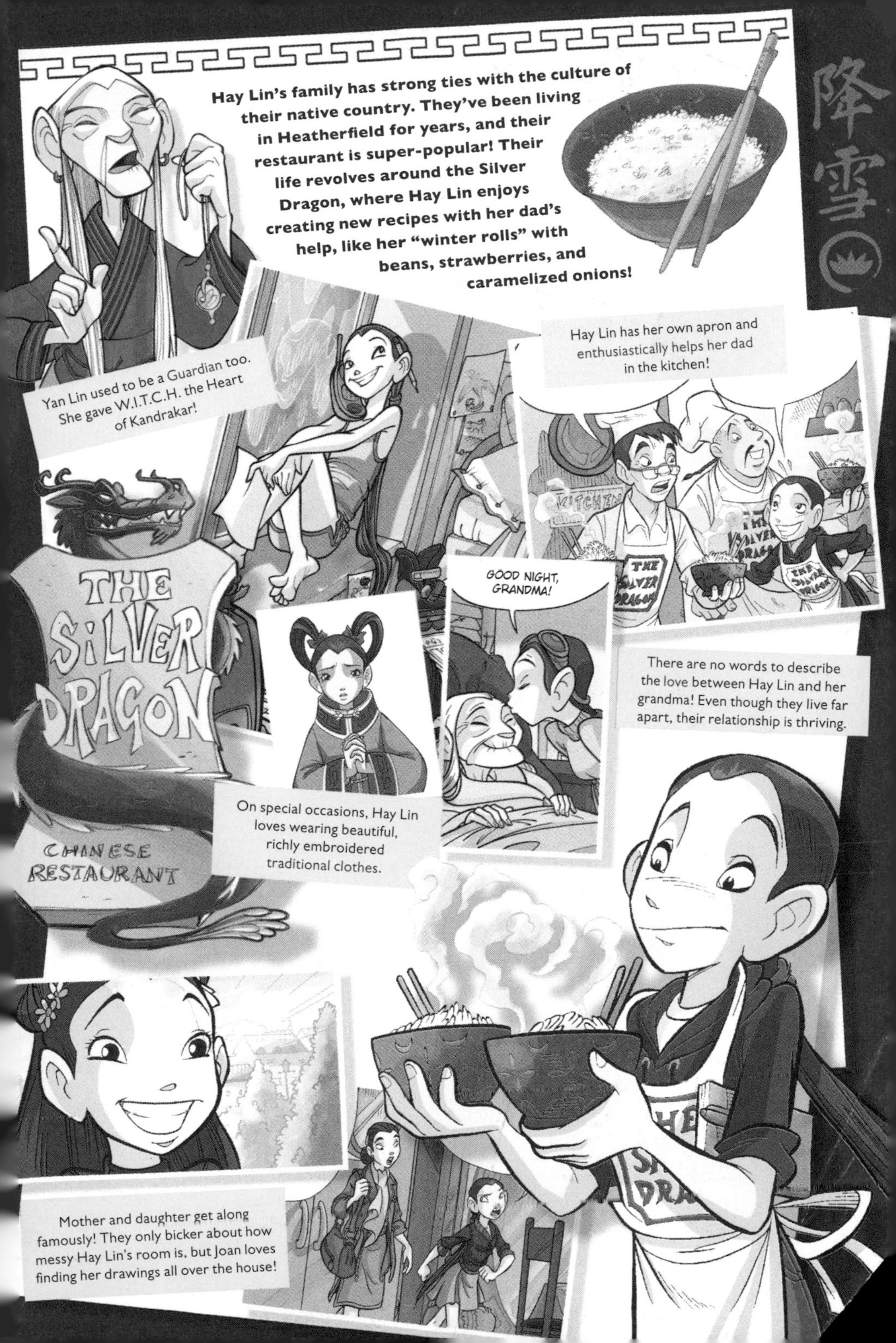
Hay Lin's family has strong ties with the culture of their native country. They've been living in Heatherfield for years, and their restaurant is super-popular! Their life revolves around the Silver Dragon, where Hay Lin enjoys creating new recipes with her dad's help, like her "winter rolls" with beans, strawberries, and caramelized onions!
降雪
Yan Lin used to be a Guardian too. She gave W.I.T.C.H. the Heart of Kandrakar!
Hay Lin has her own apron and enthusiastically helps her dad in the kitchen!
KITCHEN
THE SILVER DRAGON
THE SILVER DRAGON
THE SILVER DRAGON CHINESE RESTAURANT
GOOD NIGHT, GRANDMA!
There are no words to describe the love between Hay Lin and her grandma! Even though they live far apart, their relationship is thriving.
On special occasions, Hay Lin loves wearing beautiful, richly embroidered traditional clothes.
Mother and daughter get along famously! They only bicker about how messy Hay Lin's room is, but Joan loves finding her drawings all over the house!

## Part VII. New Power • Volume 2

# 21

Series Created by Elisabetta Gnone
Comic Art Direction: Alessandro Barbucci, Barbara Canepa

W.I.T.C.H.: The Graphic Novel, Part VII: New Power
© Disney Enterprises, Inc.

English translation © 2020 by Disney Enterprises, Inc.

JY
150 West 30th Street, 19th Floor
New York, NY 10001

Visit us at jyforkids.com
facebook.com/jyforkids
twitter.com/jyforkids
jyforkids.tumblr.com
instagram.com/jyforkids

First JY Edition: December 2020

JY is an imprint of Yen Press, LLC.
The JY name and logo are trademarks of Yen Press, LLC.

The publisher is not responsible for websites (or their content) that are not owned by the publisher.

Library of Congress Control Number: 2017950917

ISBNs:
978-1-9753-3299-0 (paperback)
978-1-9753-3315-7 (ebook)

10 9 8 7 6 5 4 3 2 1

LSC-C

Printed in the United States of America

Cover Art by Giada Perissinotto
Colors by Andrea Cagol

Translation by Linda Ghio and
Stephanie Dagg at Editing Zone
Lettering by Katie Blakeslee

### WATER

Concept and Script by Augusto Macchetto
Layout by Lucio Leoni
Pencils by Caterina Giorgetti
Inks by Marina Baggio and Roberta Zanotta
Color and Light Direction by Francesco Legramandi
Title Page Art by Lucio Leoni
with colors by Francesco Legramandi

### EMOTIONS

Concept and Script by Augusto Macchetto
Layout by Emilio Urbano
Pencils by Monica Catalano
Inks by Marina Baggio and Roberta Zanotta
Color and Light Direction by Francesco Legramandi
Title Page Art by Giada Perissinotto
with colors by Francesco Legramandi

### AIR

Concept and Script by Bruno Enna
Layout by Paolo Campinoti
Pencils by Federica Salfo
Inks by Marina Baggio, Cristina Giorgilli,
and Roberta Zanotta
Color and Light Direction by Francesco Legramandi
Title Page Art by Paolo Campinoti
with colors by Francesco Legramandi

### ENERGY

Concept and Script by Alessandro Ferrari
Layout by Alberto Zanon
Pencils by Davide Baldoni
Inks by Marina Baggio and Roberta Zanotta
Color and Light Direction by Francesco Legramandi
Title Page Art by Alberto Zanon
with colors by Francesco Legramandi